Joy Chambers was born in Ipswich, Queensland, Australia. The third child of an English father and an Australian mother. She began acting at an early age and went straight from school into a successful television career in Australia. She has appeared in numerous shows and has won awards over the years. She currently appears as Rosemary Daniels in the international television hit, 'Neighbours'. She views her writing as a natural extension of her self expression, and describes herself as a proud Australian Anglophile who loves America.

D0533285

Mayfield

Joy Chambers

HEADLINE

First published in 1992
by HEADLINE BOOK PUBLISHING PLC

First published in paperback in 1993
by HEADLINE BOOK PUBLISHING PLC

10 9 8 7 6 5 4 3 2 1

ISBN 0 7472 3863 4

Phototypeset by Intype, London

Printed and bound in Great Britain by
HarperCollins Manufacturing, Glasgow

HEADLINE BOOK PUBLISHING PLC
Headline House
79 Great Titchfield Street
London W1P 7FN

To my wonderful parents, my father Alan,
and my mother May.
Alan, who taught me love of the English word,
and May, who taught me love.

THANKS

To my darling husband, Reg Grundy OBE, who constantly encouraged me along the years of struggle and who loves Alan, Eve and John Stuart almost as much as I do.

To my brother, Dr Jack Chambers, for his lifetime support of me and my sister, Coral Chambers-Garner MA, for her continuing belief in me and in *Mayfield*.

To my dear friends, Commander John Ayres and his wife Di, who were never too busy to drive me into Mayfield Country, and to all Di's assistants over the years who helped me with Australian information when I was so far away.

To my dearest Aunt, Millicent Gedge, who read and loved *Mayfield* years ago.

And to all you others, my friends and family, who sustained me by your ongoing interest in *Mayfield* as it took shape and was born. You know who you are and I thank you.

CHAPTER ONE

'. . . till the future dares
Forget the past, his fate and fame shall be
An echo and a light unto eternity!'
'Adonais', Percy Bysshe Shelley, 1792–1822.

January 1849.
Bone-aching winter on the Southampton Docks in the south of England.

It was just after three o'clock in the afternoon and already it was almost dark. There was a fog in the harbour, and sleet interspersed with fine rain fell and drifted indifferently on the shoulders of the young naval lieutenant who stood on the Baltic Wharf looking up at the vessel berthed beside him. She was a sloop, a comparatively small though fleet ship of war carrying guns on her upper decks only. The man remained there a long time, his eyes roving back and forth from stem to stern. Silently he said her name, 'HMS *Coral Regis*.'

There was a movement at the bulwark above and he looked up into the face of his boatswain. 'Goodbye, Lieutenant Fletcher,' the sailor called down to him, and he lifted his hand in a farewell salute before he turned and resolutely walked away.

Reversing the collar of his overcoat up round his chin, he positioned his seaman's bag more comfortably on his square shoulders and set his body against the drizzling rain. He walked swiftly, unimpeded by his heavy greatcoat, listening to the familiar, languid sound of creaking timber as the ships of the line strained against their ropes.

The wharf labourers, moving lethargically in the icy air, looked involuntarily at him a second time as he strode along towards American Wharf, a grave expression on his face. There was an energy about him, not just the vitality that comes with youth, but a virile quality that somehow made him unforgettable. He wore no beard or moustache as was so characteristic of men of the sea, and his skin was smooth and sunbrowned, exuding health and strength. His nose was straight and the proportions of his face were in perfect harmony. His gait had barely any of the mariner's roll in it, which was surprising for a man who had spent over ten years at sea. His was an easy,

1

flowing movement more typical of one linked with open hills and valleys. His blue-grey eyes were the brightest thing on this dismal seafront, and they flickered now across the hawkers calling for his attention in the dark, cold alleys leading from the docks.

He stopped briefly in the encroaching dusk to watch some boys play a listless game of football in the biting wind before he made his way across the Chantrey meadows. Halting under the gloomy shapes of naked trees, rigid like twisted wire, on the edge of the public cricket ground, he stood reflectively before he turned into the deserted stand and sat down out of the wind, his bag at his feet. Below him on the pitch, two men moved doggedly back and forth finishing their day's work, but he hardly noticed them, his mind was elsewhere.

Today he had resigned his commission in the Royal Navy. He would miss it, for the ocean and its myriad moods over the years had gradually become his love. Yet he supposed in time he could come to like the land sufficiently. He must. And while he was not looking eagerly towards his new life, neither was he disinterested. Tomorrow, Squire Alan Fletcher would assume his new responsibilities in Somerset, beneath the Mendip Hills; the HMS *Coral Regis* and his crew replaced by 'Long Moss House', the tenant farmers and their families.

He had met the officer who would take over his ship. 'His' ship, he would always think of her that way. He would miss her decks beneath his feet even though he had only captained her for twenty months, his first command, and his last.

Eventually, he rose to his feet. It was totally dark now and, hoisting his bag to his right shoulder and adjusting his hat more firmly over his eyes, he proceeded to the railway terminus. There, he inquired about trains to take him home to Sedgemoor and his father's house, only to find he would have to stay the night in Southampton. The next train did not leave until the morning.

He left the footpath and crossed into Oxford Street, where the cosy lights of a tavern reminded him he had not eaten since breakfast. In the warmth and noise within, he ordered roast beef and Yorkshire pudding from a pink-cheeked girl, and sat in a corner with his reflections.

When he had heard of his father's death, he had been in Nelson's Dockyard in Antigua and his father had already been gone over two months. They had never been close, there had always been a distance between them; yet, it was sad for him to realise he would never see his parent again.

He had advanced rapidly in the Navy, from a seventeen-year-old midshipman to a full lieutenant with his own ship on discharge. His father had been against it from the start but after his mother's death in the spring, he had needed to get away. His mother . . . A soft expression passed across his face. He closed his eyes and he was a child again. He saw her coming across the lawn of Long Moss House, wide, lemon silk skirts enveloping him as she bent down to hug him. She had shone in his life like the morning star.

He remembered the morning of her funeral when all the tenant farmers' wives had come and bunched together at the front of the welcoming-arms stone steps. Beyond them had been a dray and, on the back of it, a blanket made entirely of flowers. The women had toiled through the night to weave it. They had interlaced lily of the valley with bluebells and marigolds, wild rose and daffodils, juniper and scarlet rhododendron. Woven in it were the words, 'Lady Fletcher of Long Moss House loved and missed'. His father had draped her coffin with it and when they had laid her to repose in the crypt below the family church, he had left it there, so bright and pretty against the insipid, grey coldness of her resting place.

Tomorrow Alan would take his father's place, become the squire and the country gentleman. 'You have finally made me quit the sea, Father,' he said softly to himself.

His cousin, Abel Crenshaw, his only male blood relative and his mother's sister's son, had been handling the estate's affairs since his father's death. No doubt Abel would help him understand the complexities of the place. He did not know his cousin well, for he was over ten years older, but he recalled him as a quiet, sober man, clever and conscientious.

Alan paid for his meal and ale and left the now crowded, smoky room. He joined those few outside who walked west towards High Street; the byways were more deserted now that the day's work was over. On the corner of Orchard Place, he stopped beneath the gas lamp to let a solitary cabriolet pass. Above his head tiny snowflakes were falling. In the light of the lamp, each one was illuminated intensely white for a second or two, and then, floating beyond the rim of brightness, joined forever the sombre grey of the footpath.

He hurried on towards the 'Dolphin Hotel' in High Street, the January chill biting through his thick greatcoat encouraging him to seek a night's lodging quickly.

He did not notice the two shadowy forms which had been trailing him from the moment he stepped ashore. They slithered from the doorway where they had been concealed, and continued to follow him.

The shortest distance to the hotel was through a long alleyway connecting Orchard Place to Canal Terrace and on to High Street.

3

In the narrow lane, he blinked in the darkness. The only semblance of light was the snow upon the ground. He strode vigorously to the centre of the alley where an old Tudor coach house, now a darkened butchery, projected out over the passage. Suddenly, he was aware of running footsteps behind him. In the blackness, he spun round and dropped his bag to the ground just as a figure leaped upon him.

His reflexes were perfect. He was powerfully strong, a veteran of hand-to-hand battles. He sidestepped the hurtling body and the man fell to the ground, only cuffing Alan with his arm and totally missing him with the long, razor-sharp dirk he had aimed at his throat.

As Alan wavered to keep his balance, a second form sprang from the side, stabbing at him with a thick dagger. He tensed to meet the new menace, throwing up his left arm to ward off the blade. There was a hot, searing pain as it entered his flesh. At the same time, he swung his body round and kicked, connecting with the ribs of the man. There was a loud howl and the figure fell moaning to the alley floor.

The first assailant rose from the ground lunging forward, crying obscenities. At this moment, another person entered the lane. He was a baker making his way home from his shop in Canal Walk, a stout, lumbering man. He was well into the passage before he realised what was before him. When he saw the scuffling shapes, he shouted, 'Hey, what happens here?'

'Some bastard comes,' warned the figure on the ground nursing his ribs, but Alan had the other attacker gripped by the throat and had seized his knife.

As the corpulent baker came up to them, the man with the injured ribs stood and, lifting his dagger, sank it deep into the newcomer's chest. There was a gurgling sound of death as the baker dropped to the ground.

Alan was peripherally aware of the murder, but could not turn his attention from the man he fought. Grappling with him, he managed to push the would-be assassin to arm's length and hit him a blow that knocked him senseless to the ground. Confidently, he turned sharply to face the killer, but his foot caught beneath the body at his feet and he twisted sideways into a fall. As he went down, the killer smashed the side of Alan's head with all the force he could muster. There was a sickening crunch as his head hit the cobblestones.

Alan was motionless, the wound in his forearm bleeding into the snow. The baker lay crumpled with a dagger in his heart. The first attacker lay unconscious, and the murderer leaned against the wall breathing heavily and holding his ribs.

For some moments all was still, except for the panting of the killer.

Then he collected himself and peering hurriedly up and down the dark passageway picked up his cohort's fallen dagger and moved quickly to his side. 'Come on, you. Ged up! We can't 'ang around 'ere. Ged up, I say!' And he began to slap the man to bring him back to consciousness. Before he was completely sensible, the murderer had lifted him to his feet and they hobbled out of the alley.

Alan was vaguely aware of the cold at his back and then hands roughly shaking him. The light from a firebrand shone in his eyes and he began to discern people above and around him.

'Coom on, it's off to prison with ye! Murder's a hangin' offence!'

Murder! Prison? Who were they talking about?

He was pulled into a standing position and then through the haze and pain he focused on a policeman. 'Coom on, young fella!' He was prodded in the ribs. 'It's off to gaol with ye!'

It was then Alan realised the constable's words were said to him. He looked in amazement at the plump face under the policeman's helmet. 'But I committed no murder. It was the other two. Did no one see them?' He looked to the faces encircling him. They looked back at him in silence. 'I was attacked. This poor man was an innocent witness.'

He kept down the nausea that rose in his throat as the policeman pushed him steadily along through the collection of people and the now heavily falling snow.

That night he lay awake, his senses invaded by the smell of bodies and straw. At least they had dressed the wound on his forearm and cleaned the blood from that part of his forehead which had hit the pavement, but still his arm ached and his brow ached. Over and over, he analysed the attack. It was obviously a mistake. He fell into a fitful sleep, thinking that tomorrow his name would be cleared. However, upon awakening the next morning, he discovered that overnight two witnesses had materialised who said they had seen Alan kill the baker in cold blood. They stated that the baker hit out with his dying breath and knocked the attacker down where his head struck the ground and he lost consciousness. Alan did not need to know more. He knew already who the 'witnesses' were. One of them would certainly carry a broken rib and the other a sore head!

Later that same morning, he was formally charged before the city magistrate with the murder of Byard Tennyson, baker of the City of Southampton.

For three weeks, he was detained in Southampton gaol where, daily, he asked to see Vice-Admiral St Nevis, his commanding officer, and to have his family solicitor and his cousin Abel notified. In due course, official and unhurried, contact was made.

Ten days after being charged, he was informed that he was to be tried at the coming February assizes, the periodic sessions held in each county to administer civil and criminal justice. This same day, he saw his family solicitor, Mr Bader. Entirely inadequate to the situation, the benign old man looked at Alan with sympathetic eyes. They conversed for about half an hour in a small, damp room in the confines of the prison and when the elderly man left, he promised to talk things over with Abel, who had been unable to leave Sedgemoor due to pressing business concerns.

After Mr Bader had gone, Alan lay on his bunk looking through the bars at that part of the outside stone wall he could see. It was cold and raining and he, too, felt bleak. He urged himself to optimism.

At nine o'clock in the morning of the following day he was taken from the cell he shared with eight others to meet the barrister retained to defend him. A warden led him along a dusty passageway, up a flight of steps to a door with a small metal grille in its centre and a gaoler lounging before it.

The room he entered was about ten feet square. A tired brocade curtain hung across a window to the left and a corpulent middle-aged man sat in front of it leafing through some pages. There was a small table to his side and an empty chair to which he motioned Alan with a courteous wave of his hand and a wide, friendly smile.

His eyes were large and he blinked continually as he spoke. 'Lieutenant Fletcher?'

'Yes,' said Alan as he sat.

'I'm Eams, Frederick Eams, your barrister-at-law.'

'How do you do.'

'Now then, I have the facts here, and I should like to hear what you have to say about them.' He placed his fat hands palm upwards on the table in a polite gesture to elicit information.

Alan met his eyes. 'And what facts are they?'

'Why, what I got from the prison records, indeed. About the happenings on the night of January tenth. I've read it all, Lieutenant Fletcher. Now then, tell me do, what have you to say?'

Alan told him what had occurred, and all the while Eams blinked and nodded sagely. When Alan completed his account, Eams leaned forward to pat his arm. 'I understand,' he gave another of his smiles, 'and I believe you, indeed. Unfortunately, you have no witnesses to give credence to your side of the story.'

'No.'

'Mmm, indeed, pity, pity.' He clutched his hands together and leaned forward. 'I have won many a case, Lieutenant, and would feel confident but for this new evidence showing your argument with the deceased. That's what's worrying me. The prosecution will see that as completely damning, I'm afraid, yes, indeed!'

Alan's face grew grave. He drew his right hand across the cut on his forehead. 'What new evidence? What argument?'

Eams's eyes seemed to become even larger and the blinking more disconcerted as he bent closer. 'Why? Haven't they told you? They should have. There's a local fellow, a Southampton man, who attests he saw you in the baker's shop the very afternoon of the murder, arguing fit to screaming with the dead man. You see, that is what troubles me, indeed. This new evidence.'

'But it's a lie,' Alan answered.

'I know, I know, Lieutenant Fletcher. But we have to convince others that it is.'

'And what time of day does this "new" witness say he saw the argument?' Alan's voice was cold.

'About thirty minutes past the hour of three in the afternoon.'

Alan nodded. 'That is what I expected.' Then to himself he added, 'While I sat alone in the cricket ground. Of course.'

'What is that you say?'

Alan looked directly at the large man. 'I wonder why they are doing this to me?'

'Who?'

'Whoever they are.'

The chair squeaked as Eams leaned back. He stretched his hand out and tapped his fingernails on the table. Alan noticed the skin on his knuckles was cracked.

The barrister drew in his breath noisily. 'Now, young man, unfortunately your defence is very weak. You see, in fact, there is only your word. Yes, indeed. But I have won many a case, as I say. Give me a night to think about it. To reflect. I shall return tomorrow.' And he lifted his bulk from the chair and, with another of his amiable smiles, departed.

During the next twenty-four hours, Alan went over the meeting many times in his mind, and when the hour arrived to confront Eams again, he was thoughtful as he entered the interview room.

'Sit down, Lieutenant Fletcher, indeed do,' Eams welcomed him with his customary friendliness, pointing to the empty chair.

They sat looking at each other for a few seconds, Eams blinking and Alan staring.

'Sooo,' the big man began. 'I have been pondering about what will be best for you . . . best in the long run. Indeed, we must do what is best.'

'And what is that?'

7

'Even with all my deliberations, I am still not entirely sure.' He shook his head and dropped his voice. 'Murder is a hanging offence, my friend.'

'But I murdered no one.'

'Indeed I know that. But you have . . . that is, *we* have no witnesses. The prosecution has witnesses, but we must not be despondent.'

'Do you think I have a chance?'

'Ah now,' Eams replied. 'There it is. We must believe so, indeed.'

'Will you be able to prove I am innocent?'

'Lieutenant, you are an intelligent man.' Eams smiled sadly. 'There is a witness who says he heard you argue and threaten the dead man. There are witnesses who say they saw you stab the dead man. It is to the prosecutor's advantage, indeed. But I am determined to do my best for you and that will not be inconsiderable.'

Alan nodded. 'My cousin is very concerned for my welfare?'

'Now that is true. Very concerned, I would say, yes.'

'And yet he has not been to see me.'

'Has he not? Ah well, indeed he is very busy no doubt . . . a very busy man. But he expressed great anxiety in respect to your welfare when he spoke to me. Of that you can be certain.'

It was then Alan smiled at Eams for the first time. Really smiled. Eams blinked, and as he blinked, Alan continued to smile.

Eams was most uncomfortable; he looked unhappy. 'Why are you amused?'

'Because now, Frederick Eams, I know what I did not know before. Now I realise the two men who attacked me were hired to kill me. They were not chance footpads. I was to have been found dead, the unlucky victim of a robbery, conveniently out of the way in a Southampton lane. But the ill-fated baker changed things and the attackers had to be set up as "witnesses" and I falsely charged as the murderer. I am still to be conveniently out of the way – hanged on a gibbet!'

Eams said nothing, but there was no smile on his face. Then he shook his head as he rose awkwardly. 'Now, Lieutenant,' he came closer, 'why do you say this? I'm sure you are wrong. I . . . I . . . am astounded.'

'And now,' Alan cut across him, 'a third "witness" to authenticate the story has been procured. An "impartial" man who "heard" me argue with the dead baker. Undeniably a secure trap now. It must be costing him a great deal of money.'

Eams's hand went out and took Alan by the shoulder. 'Young

man, come, sit down. Perhaps the prison is affecting your judgement, my friend.'

'Friend?' Alan shook off the man's hand. 'No, Mr barrister-at-law Eams, I think not. The entire Fletcher lands are to be his, are they not? And all of you very well paid to make sure I die on the gallows. How greatly my cousin Abel must desire my estate!'

'That is a terrible accusation to make, young man, especially against me. Indeed, I cannot believe you mean it!'

'But I do mean it. I would rather one of the thieves sharing my cell represent me than you, Frederick Eams.'

'You are mad, quite mad,' Eams retorted, head shaking, eyes blinking.

'Get out, Eams! You are but a cipher. Get out!' Alan brusquely swept the sheaf of papers to the floor and called for the guard.

The following day, he was returned to the same room.

Commodore James Trent of the Royal Navy awaited him there. Alan knew this man; he had served under him briefly as a midshipman some ten years before.

He saluted but the naval officer came forward and took his hand. 'Hello, Alan. Admiral St Nevis is at sea, but I hope I can help in his stead.' Trent was a fair-minded man and his good-humoured face was troubled. 'I've just spoken to the head gaoler. This all sounds wretched for you, I'm afraid. Yet I know you wouldn't be involved in a mess like this. What happened?'

At last someone had asked Alan unequivocally his version of the events.

Step by step, he related the incidents of 10 January from the moment of his departure from the *Coral Regis* to the assault in the alley and the baker's intervention.

When Alan finished, he stood looking at Commodore Trent who had listened without interrupting and now spoke at last. 'I believe every word you say, Alan. No one with your fine record would be involved in such a rum affair.'

Relief sounded in Alan's voice. 'Thank you, sir. It is good to hear you say that.'

'I have read what you've done since I last saw you and I am proud of you. I noted that a few months after you served with me, you were in Aden during the annexation. You were mentioned in dispatches – most unusual for one so young, and commendable.'

'Well, sir,' Alan smiled wearily, 'I had been there long enough to know a few Arabic words, and more than a few oaths. They came in handy when dealing with the tribesmen.'

9

The older man nodded. 'And your record shows you have been mentioned in dispatches at other times. The War Office clearly valued your achievements. They gave you your own ship. Perhaps the youngest captain in the Royal Navy.' He touched Alan affectionately on the shoulder. 'You are a fine sailor, and a brave man. I know.'

'Thank you for your belief in me, sir.'

'We will do what we can for you, Alan. Your record should stand you in good stead.' The commodore came forward and took his hand once more. 'Do you have somebody to defend you?'

'No, I do not.'

'Then I shall find you someone.'

The commodore's choice was Barrister-at-law Finnigan McGuire.

In the first days of his imprisonment, Alan had been angry and indignant at being accused of murder. These feelings had given way to frustration and sometimes almost desperation, but now that Finnigan was with him, his innate optimism rose again and he felt that with the barrister, the wrong that had been done to him had a chance of being righted. On the afternoon before the trial, Finnigan took Alan's hand; his tall brow crinkled as he explained, 'The case against you is strong, but I shall fight for you, Alan. I really shall.'

'Yes, I know you will.'

The next morning, the day of the assizes, a gaoler came for him before the hour of seven.

Ironically, Alan had been dubbed 'Squire' by the inmates of his crowded cell, and now as he said goodbye to his closest allies, two pickpockets, a poacher and a common thief, they wished him luck. He replied in kind and shook them all by the hand. The thief accompanied him to the door. 'I'll not be sharin' a cell with such excellence as ye again, Squire. Brought a bit o' tone to the place, ye did. Miss ye, we shall.'

He was given some lukewarm water to wash in, and clean clothes that Finnigan had arranged, and taken through the streets to the court building.

The judge presiding was the usual circuit judge, His Worship the Right Honourable Alexander Netterville, a man with a reputation for being objective although harsh on those found guilty.

The courtroom was filled to capacity. For the first time in over two years, Alan saw his cousin Abel and momentarily, all the disgust and fury he felt for the man exploded inside him. Then, he calmed himself while Abel sat there impassively, much as Alan remembered, solemn face, sandy hair, medium height and build.

And so the trial began.

The evidence mounted. The two witnesses claiming to have seen

10

the attack were from London, and when the first of them took the stand, he identified Alan as the man he and his companion had seen stab the baker. Finnigan took the attitude that he was a liar, and used strong words to press his charge. The judge reprimanded him, reminding the jury that the witness was not on trial. Then Finnigan tried another defence; he suggested that the alley was dark, so dark in fact that the two Londoners could not be sure whom they saw, if indeed they had seen anybody, and for a time there were jurors who looked at Alan more sympathetically.

The second London man, Christopher Scales, a tall, thin man with a high forehead, said he was positive of Alan's identity no matter whether the alley was dark or not. He and his friend had come within yards of the murderer while he struggled with the baker, and the uniform was easily identifiable. There was no doubt in his mind that the killer had worn the greatcoat of a naval lieutenant. 'Besides,' the liar said, 'it were him all right. 'Is eyes glinted there in the alley, they did. Fair give me the 'orrors! And who could ever forgit them eyes when turned upon ye?'

There was a whisper of agreement from some of the crowd.

Finnigan asked Scales why they had not attempted to help the baker and the man replied that Alan had dealt the death blow before they could reach him.

When his cousin Abel was called to the stand, he took the Bible in his hand and spoke so softly the judge made him repeat the oath.

'Speak more loudly, Abel Crenshaw. Louder!'

Finnigan tried to reveal Abel's real attitude to his cousin, but Abel only spoke of his 'love' for Alan.

'I was looking forward to dear Alan coming home,' he reiterated during the course of his cross examination.

Abel implied that Alan sometimes had a violent temper. 'While I do hate to say anything against my cousin, it is true he kicked my terrier once. So hard in the stomach it was,' he dropped his eyes to his agitated hands, 'my terrier died shortly afterwards.' He omitted to say that Alan's kick had been an automatic reaction when the animal attacked him.

Alan shook his head. It is you I should have kicked, Abel.

The man had been thorough, most thorough, in his forethought. There were even letters to Mr Bader saying he would be delighted to stay on and show his returning cousin the running of the estate, unless his cousin did not want him, in which case he was happy to leave Long Moss and return to his own thriving business in the wool trade.

For Alan, the whole proceeding was becoming like a bizarre dream.

He felt as if it must all disintegrate, the people, the room, the court, and once again he would be standing on the poop deck of the *Coral Regis* setting sail with the east wind blowing and the evening tide running him out of Southampton Water, down to the Solent.

When Mr Bader took the stand, the old man did his best for Alan. He told of Alan's sunny nature and praised his friendliness to all the tenant farmers. It was his belief that Alan would harm no creature or person. He spoke of Alan's kindness to animals and it was at this time that Finnigan showed there had in fact been a reason for Alan to treat the terrier as Abel had described.

The rector from the family church came down from Sedgemoor and he too gave evidence of Alan's good character.

Commodore Trent was better than his word. When he was called by Finnigan, he spoke glowingly of Alan and his service record. He told the court that in his opinion, ex-Lieutenant Fletcher was an honourable man of high moral principle, had been an exemplary, even a model officer in Her Majesty's Navy, and would never perform such a base act as murder. It was a peerless commendation and for a short time Alan thought he had a chance.

But it was followed by the testimony of the local Southampton man and his evidence proved disastrous.

'I call Benjamin Breely to the stand.'

The man who walked through the court was in his early twenties. He had golden hair and his candid face was round and smooth. His big blue eyes looked interestedly about as he took the stand. His dress was fashionable but there was no suggestion of the dandy about him. He was not a handsome man, but his aspect was innocently youthful and undefiled, and when he took the oath, his tones were sincere and distinct. There was an intangible quality about him somehow synonymous with truth and honesty.

Oh Abel! How you must have searched to find this one! He is perfect! You have found a corrupted man who looks sinless. This is a masterstroke! The jury will believe whatever he says.

Alan stood listening to the testimony of the cherub as the prosecutor examined him.

'I am going specifically to the baker, Mr Tennyson. He made the best cakes in Southampton don't you know!'

'And tell us what happened.'

'It was like this,' the cherub stated, looking virtuously at his questioner. 'I had just opened the door, mind you, and stepped inside. It was twilight and the lamps were lit. Mr Tennyson was out in the back, out where he cooks, and there was another man with him. The man with him was shouting. I do remember what he said.

12

"You'll give me what is mine, Tennyson. I'm not going to ask you any more. It's been long enough," and I sort of pushed Mr Tennyson roughly against the wall. "Leave me alone!" Mr Tennyson said, "I haven't got it!" And the man answered, "Blast your eyes! If you don't hand it over now, I swear I'll do for you!" '

The noise in the court rose.

'Quiet! Silence in the court!'

The Crown prosecutor continued, 'Mr Breely, what took place after that?'

The cherub looked serious. 'Well, you see, sir, that was when they turned and saw me.'

'Yes,' said the prosecutor, 'go on.'

'I remember they both came out to the front of the shop, and Mr Tennyson went behind the counter. The other man stood there for a few moments looking threatening-like. Then he said quietly, real cold-like, "I'm warning you, Tennyson," and he brushed past me and went out the door.'

'Is this man you speak of here today?' asked the prosecutor.

The young man's artless eyes looked around the room. He nodded his golden head. 'Yes, sir, he is, sir,' came the expected reply.

'Point to him, please.'

The cherub lifted his inoffensive right hand and with a definite motion pointed at Alan.

Alan stood silently shaking his head as Benjamin Breely left the stand and walked through the crowd.

The cherub and the two Londoners then went to wherever those who have sold their souls go, and Finnigan in his final speech admirably argued that it hardly seemed sensible for a young man who was returning home to inherited wealth to kill a humble baker. But Benjamin Breely's 'proof' still lived in all their memories. It took the better part of a day for the jury to deliberate. There were four men who tended to believe Alan but finally they succumbed to the evidence.

When they found him guilty, Alan was not surprised, although he had hoped for a miracle.

The judge coughed and moved uncomfortably on his chair. Twice more he coughed before, at last, he spoke. He had listened closely and concentrated earnestly for many days. 'Alan Fletcher, you have been found guilty of murder and with this finding goes the death sentence. But due to your impeccable record in Her Majesty's Navy and my own very complex feelings about this trial, I commute the death sentence to transportation for life to the colonies.'

This brought loud murmurs of opinion, and the voice that brought silence this time was the prisoner's. At the sound of Alan's voice, the room became still.

At the Southampton assizes in 1849 it was unheard of for a prisoner to speak after sentence and the whole congregation looked to Judge Netterville to silence him. It appeared for a moment as if he would, for he bent forward in his great oak chair and even lifted his hand palm upwards to the prisoner, but then he dropped it back on his bench, and for the only time in his life he allowed a sentenced man to speak.

Alan's eyes passed over the people.

They were fascinated by this turn of events, spellbound, and all those who heard him remembered his words. They told the story many times during their lives and could always recall the look and sound of him.

Slowly, and in a voice almost devoid of emotion, he spoke. 'That you have found me guilty does not make me so. I do not blame the jury or the judge for what has transpired. The liars did not flinch, and the evidence against me was powerful. You leave now to return to your homes. My cousin leaves now to return to mine! And I go . . . to a prison ship.' Here he stopped speaking and looked directly at Abel. His cousin stood on the far side of the court transfixed, his hands clenching and unclenching just as they had throughout the trial. For the space of a second or two it seemed as if Alan might smile, then he said, 'At least I need look on your face no more.'

People moved and whispered, but fell quiet when he spoke again.

'There are good men here,' and his eyes found Finnigan, and Commodore Trent and Mr Bader. 'There are good men here who have been duped,' and his eyes moved across the gathered people to the jury, to Judge Netterville. A hiatus followed as the crowd waited for his last words. 'The others are not men!' Then he turned his back on them, signalled to the guard, and left the dock.

Pandemonium broke out behind him.

It was said that Judge Netterville changed after the Fletcher trial. From that day at the Southampton assizes, it became apparent he had difficulty passing sentence on major crime. He no longer took satisfaction from his work; a year later, he retired from the Bench.

Alan was allowed to see his friends one final time.

It had been dark outside for hours when they met in a room lit by four wall candles in a wing of the courthouse. Finnigan took Alan's hand and promised he would continue to search for the proof to set him free.

14

Alan shook his head. 'Thank you, my true friend, but what is, is. I will be thousands of miles away in a few months and courts rarely change their minds.'

When he bade goodbye to Commodore Trent and Mr Bader, the old man's eyes were wet and the naval officer was weighed down by his disappointment. He could only shake his head and say, 'I'm sorry, Alan. It was a blasted, fraudulent sham, but they won.'

Even the policeman who came to take him away spoke sympathetically. 'Sorry, matey, don't seem right some'ow.'

Alan mustered a weary smile as he looked at the three faces he would never see again, then he shook their hands in turn and said a last goodbye.

CHAPTER TWO

'When she had passed, it seemed like the ceasing of exquisite music.'

'Evangeline', Henry Wadsworth Longfellow, 1807–1882.

January 1849.
Boston, New England.

In the failing light, a girl in matching blue bonnet and coat advanced along the snow-covered streets. She had remained on at school after classes to help make dolls to send with missionaries to the 'starving heathens of Africa', as her teacher, Miss Scrowcroft, called the eventual beneficiaries of their labour.

She hurried, hoping to arrive home before the darkness descended. The thought of the afternoon tea her sister Clare would have waiting for her brought a smile to her face. Once school was out, Clare had gone immediately home to take delivery of their two new dresses for the church concert on Sunday, and had promised to have a treat of fairy cakes and tea ready for her arrival.

She continued on her way by the South Congregational Church to Shawmut Avenue where the bitter wind brought her to a run. A hundred yards or so along the avenue she turned to cross an open lot which would bring her out close to her own home.

Her attention was taken by a small, soot-covered figure coming through the snow in the distance. She immediately recognised 'Grimy', as the little chimney sweep was known in the district. He was not an unusual sight, laden down with birch brooms and pail, for the tiny fellow cleaned most of the chimneys in and around this area. He worked with a team of boys all about eight or nine years old, for a man named Tartakoff who gave them room and lodging in return.

But today Grimy had other companions. He was scuttling along under his burden just ahead of a group of five or six warmly dressed boys. A few of the youths looked familiar; they were all around twelve, her own age, and one was definitely the son of their landlady, Mrs De Groot.

As she came closer, she realised that the boys were taunting Grimy. They often teased him and made jokes about him, it was part and parcel of being a chimney sweep, but this looked a lot more serious than that. Suddenly, she saw them push the little boy and he dropped his pail and some of his brooms. He turned bravely around to them and said something, at which they laughed and began to encircle him. The girl came to a halt, her face wrinkling with emotion for she knew Kenny De Groot was a bully, and it appeared his companions were no better.

There was jostling movement and then a cry of pain from Grimy. She saw him stumble and fall to the ground between them, letting go of the remainder of his brooms.

Forgotten were the fairy cakes and the tea; she was wholly occupied by this awful treatment of the little chimney sweep. She was unsure what to do; she looked around for an adult, but there was no one in sight. The tall trees on either side of the vacant ground gave it a lonely aspect.

Then Grimy cried out again and a determined expression came into her eyes. She hurried across the snow to the pack of boys. Their attention was on their sport; Grimy had been pulled to his feet and was being pushed around from one to the other. Then Kenny De Groot put out his foot and tripped him and immediately sat down on the tiny, protesting figure.

No one was aware of the girl's arrival until she shouted, 'Stop it! Stop it!'

The boys looked round in surprise, and Grimy, whose face was in the snow underneath Kenny De Groot, twisted his head to see who his benefactor was.

She dropped her satchel in the snow and pointed with her gloved hand at her landlady's son. 'Kenny De Groot, get off Grimy, immediately. How dare you!'

The other boys dropped away a little and Kenny, uncertain, shifted his weight, enabling the chimney sweep to extricate himself from underneath his bulk.

Kenny's aggressive face clouded. 'Eve Herman, mind your own business. Get away from here.'

'Yeah,' said one of the other boys, 'you're only a girl.'

There were rumbling sounds of animosity from one or two more but Eve did not waver although her heart was beating rapidly and she began to lose the confidence that had spurred her to help Grimy.

'Leave him alone, you bullies,' she answered, looking around their faces and meeting each of their eyes. She recognised one more boy and pointed at him. 'Eli Stephens, you should be ashamed.'

Grimy, blood running from his lip, was now on his feet and Eve moved over to stand beside him. 'Now, go away from here,' she said, face to face with Kenny De Groot, 'or else!'

'Or else what?' replied De Groot, running his eyes over her. 'What's he to you, anyway?' And he pushed Grimy once more, so that the boy staggered backwards. Then he brought his chin forward belligerently at Eve. 'What's the soot-covered chimney snake mean to you, eh?'

Without thinking, Eve stepped between Kenny and Grimy and with as fierce a look as she could bring to her spirited brown eyes said, 'Don't you dare touch him again.' She had no idea what she was going to do if Kenny did touch Grimy again, she was just trying desperately to bluff him. Her knees were shaking inside her long skirt as she shouted, 'If you, Kenny De Groot, or any of you, dare touch him again, I shall . . . I shall *report* you.' This was inspired. She had no conception of whom she would report them to, but the words served to baffle her listeners all the same. While they stood confused, she helped Grimy pick up his belongings and the two made their hurried departure across the snow together.

When they reached Shawmut Avenue and were out of sight of the boys, they halted in the waning light.

Grimy wiped his mouth. 'Thanks, miss. I reckon I was done for if youse hadn't come along.'

'Why were they doing that to you, Grimy?'

'Dunno. Guess they hates me.'

Eve stood staring at his small, pale face beneath the soot. 'I'm so sorry they did that. Perhaps you should try to avoid them.'

Grimy managed a smile. 'Won't have to; me mum's comin' for me.'

'Whatever do you mean?'

The child sniffed and gave her a long, penetrating look. Then, as if he decided she had passed his scrutiny, he explained in a voice incongruously adult coming from such a tiny soot-covered figure, 'I'm not stayin' with Mr Tartakoff. Me mum's comin' for me, Friday, noon-time, to take me to Noo York.'

Eve's face broke into a happy smile. 'Oh, I'm so pleased.'

'Me too.'

Eve bent forward to him. 'What's your real name?'

'Francis, me real name's Francis.'

'And mine's Eve.'

Eve held out her hand. Francis took it. It was darkening around them as they stood there in the now falling snow, regarding each other.

'Goodbye, then, Francis.'

The old, old child-eyes looked up into Eve's. 'Goodbye, then . . . Eve.'

A mile away from Shawmut Avenue, Ada Herman's beautiful brown eyes lifted skywards. Her lashes were so long they touched her eyebrows.

She shivered. There would be another heavy snowfall any minute. The wind was icy and even through all the heavy layers she wore she could feel the chill in her bones. This was the coldest winter she ever recalled.

There was a mist out in Boston Harbor and intermittent sleet fell across her path as she hurried along. She avoided the dirty water lying in a pool near the Customs House and crossed the open ground at the edge of Milk Street where a few youths lounged in the biting wind. She hurried on past the row of stark, leafless trees to the bank of steps leading up to India Street. Lifting her skirts, she mounted them slowly until she reached the top where she stopped for breath, putting her gloved hand out to rest on the worn stone wall. These days she felt tired after any exertion, and climbing steps was the worst.

She shivered again and drew her cape more tightly round her. Then she began to cough, she coughed so hard that it hurt her throat. Feeling quite dizzy, she stood still for a minute or so to regain her equanimity.

The coughing was more regular these days; she had suffered a most dreadful bout this morning. She would not tell Phillip of course, he would only worry, for he loved her so. And her gowns were a little loose on her now, whereas she had filled them quite firmly the previous summer.

'February is a bleak month, so very bleak,' she thought as she leaned against the wall, and then for a few minutes came the recollection of another February; the February she had married Phillip. She had met him in August and married him six months later. In fact, she had met him not far from where she stood this very minute.

She had been on an errand and had come this way along the wharves, for she so loved the ships and the smell of the sea, always had, as long as she could remember. It had been high summer and the sea birds were making great circles in the air. As she neared Central Wharf, she saw her friend Tessie Moore at the entrance, talking to a handsome young man with fair, wavy hair and an auburn moustache. Tessie had been quite proprietorial. 'Ada, this is my friend Phillip. Phillip Herman, meet Ada Farley.'

19

She recalled how poor Tessie's face had dropped when Phillip had shown his admiration by bowing low over her hand and kissing it. The instant attraction had been obvious. It had been a swift courtship.

She smiled now as she thought of her wedding day and the rain and wind whipping up Chambers Street to St Joseph's Church in the meadowlea, for she had not really seen the bleak weather that day. Even the grey waters of the Charles River had appeared blue to her. The sun had been shining in her heart, as it shone now when she thought of her husband.

Phillip was a trader, always had been, one way or another, and these days at last he was beginning to be successful. Boston was proving good to them, and for their two young daughters. For the first time they rented a real house instead of just rooms – well, half a house, anyway; the landlady, Mrs De Groot, lived at the back.

Phillip had grown up in Charleston, South Carolina, and they had gone there for a time after their marriage, and from there to Norfolk, Virginia, and from Norfolk to Baltimore and then New York, but nowhere had been kind to them and they had returned to Boston eighteen months ago. In her heart, Ada knew Phillip wanted to get away from Massachusetts again soon. He followed a dream. He believed in it, and she believed in him.

She wanted to stay strong for him and for her darling daughters, Evelyn May and Sarah Clare. She smiled as they came to her mind, their happy dark eyes like hers, their fair hair like Phillip's. At last they were going to a proper school. They learned English language, arithmetic, Latin verbs, etiquette and elocution.

Her daughters were different to herself, she knew that. Impetuous, they were, both of them, and determined, perhaps too much so at times, but not wilful, no, they were not wilful. They were so alike in so much, and yet so opposite too. Clare was always singing and dancing, while Eve was more thoughtful, but they were both talented. They played piano too, and very well, for it was the one thing she had always remained firm about; in all their moves, she had taken her piano along.

Ada traversed India Street as the light waned. Just as she was about to cross over to India Wharf, she noticed an old Irish woman signalling to her from the entrance of an alleyway beside the Mariners' Hotel. There were lots of Irish in Boston now; they were flooding in and had covered all of the old north end with workers' housing. Many of their aged folk idled hereabouts, waiting in and near the passages leading from the docks. They usually had something trivial to sell, and it was best to ignore them. The old woman beckoning her was certainly tenacious lingering in this awful weather.

A wrinkled hand lifted out from under the well-worn cape as Ada passed by. She was two or three yards on when she heard the words, 'Yeer lungs are bad, my pretty, aren't they? And the cough gets worse, does it not? Ah, Matthis can tell these things, and Matthis can tell much much more and all. Wouldn't ye like to know what Matthis can see, oh, so very clearly?'

Ada halted. She turned back. How could the woman know about her cough? She stood looking as the crone continued to wag her twisted fingers. 'Off to meet yeer husband, eh? On the wharf is it, my pretty? Visiting a ship, eh?'

Ada took a hesitant step towards her, the uncertainty she felt showing clearly in her face. 'Who are you?'

The ancient gaze lifted. The skin under the brows fell in so many layers the woman's eyes were half closed. But what Ada could see was astonishing. The irises were almost yellow they were so bright, and the eyeballs were clear and white like a child's might be. Ada's breath drew in sharply with surprise.

'Ha, ha, ha.' The laugh was a phantom sound. 'Who am I? I just told ye, Matthis. Matthis is who I am.'

'What . . . do you want?'

She made the laughing sound again. 'Only a few minutes of yeer time, my pretty. Not much to ask in this life.'

Ada felt very uncomfortable. She wanted to be away from this peculiar old woman, away to meet Phillip. But the ancient fascinated her.

'Cross my palm, sweet thing, not with a great deal, just with enough. And Matthis will tell ye past and future and what ye desire to know.'

Ada did not move. She did not turn away and hasten on as most of her mind was telling her to do.

Matthis sighed. 'Ah, my pretty, I must convince ye, eh? Then listen carefully. I am the seventh daughter of a seventh daughter. Do ye know what that signifies? Now, some say not so much as the seventh son of a seventh son, but I am living proof that they be wrong. I've had the unequalled gift since childhood, I have, and what Matthis sees is always true. Cross my palm with silver, pretty one, and I'll tell ye what ye dearly want to know.'

Ada still did not move. It all seemed quite unreal, standing here in the cold, wan light with this insistent old crone trying to inveigle her into handing over money for a fortune-telling.

Matthis stretched out her hand and, taking Ada by the arm, moved her down the alley a few paces. A part of Ada was astonished that she was allowing this to happen.

'In here, pretty one, come in out of the cold and learn things, just for a few coins.'

Ada found herself in a small, dingy room lit by five candles in chipped porcelain holders. They were arranged on a decrepit oak cabinet with highly polished hinges. It seemed strangely anomalous that the hinges should be brought to such a high shine on so feeble a piece of furniture. Above the cabinet hung a painting of a tiger and a bear in a black frame. The animals appeared to be fighting, but the more Ada looked, the more they seemed to be embracing. A fire burned in a grate behind a tiny occasional table covered with a many-coloured cloth. Two stools appeared to be the only seating. And there was an odd smell, not unpleasant, but odd.

'Ah, my very pretty, sit, sit.'

Ada sat.

'The money. Give Matthis the money.'

Suddenly, Ada felt it was all absurd. Or did she feel fear? She stood up and took out her small soft purse. She removed one cent and three half-cent coins, handed them to the Irishwoman, and turned to leave.

'Charity I will accept, dearie, but don't ye want to hear what will become of ye? And that husband ye have, yeer husband who moves ye from one place to another, regular-like, methinks.'

Ada turned back in amazement, her beautiful face pale. 'How can you possibly know this?'

The old woman beckoned her, her eyes gleaming with a singular brightness in the melancholy light from the fire and candles. 'I likes to air my gift. In fact, cannot help it, if the truth be spoken, but I have told ye all I can without help. I can only read so much from a body, my pretty. Now I needs help.'

Ada felt very peculiar. Slowly she came back and sat down.

The ancient shuffled a pack of worn cards. 'Take one.'

Ada did so.

'Take another.'

Ada took another.

'Turn them up, my pretty.'

There was an ace of hearts and a two of spades.

'Aah, now I see . . . yes, yes, quite clearly.' She stopped speaking and smiled a worn smile. 'Before I begin, I shall need another coin. Do ye have a silver one? I can see a lot more when I'm pleased, ye understand.'

Ada gave her the last coin in her purse, a silver half-dime. 'It's all I have.'

'It is more than sufficient.' The old face contorted into a genuinely happy smile showing wide gaps between long teeth. 'Now, take three more cards.'

They were the nine of hearts, the three of clubs, and the king of clubs.

Matthis took up Ada's soft, white, left hand in her gaunt and bony ones, and traced the lines with a long yellow fingernail. 'You will travel far. You have travelled already, I can see. Take another card.'

Ada was absorbed in this mystery now; there was no thought of leaving. When she turned it up it was an eight of diamonds.

The bright yellow eyes concentrated. Then they left the card and met Ada's young apprehensive ones.

'As was clear to me when ye came towards me in the street, yeer health is not good. It is the coughing and the pain in the chest. Ye have good days and bad days. Yeer husband has been to see yeer doctor. There has been talk of a warmer climate between them.'

'Really?'

'I see two letters big and bright in yeer life, a P and I think an M . . . No! No, wait a bit. It's an H.'

'Yes, yes,' replied Ada, 'they are his initials, P.H., Phillip Herman, my husband.'

'Certainly they are. Now, as ye came down India Street I was trying to concentrate on yeer own name but it was escaping me.' There was a deep frown lodged among the confusion of creases in Matthis's brow. She gave a grunt of concentration and shook her head. Then, looking up at Ada, abruptly asked, 'What the devil is yeer name?'

'Ada, Ada is my name.'

Matthis tapped with her misshapen middle finger on the eight of diamonds. 'Then who is this Eve?'

'Eve is my daughter.'

Matthis slapped her hands together. 'Of course, of course, yeer daughter, and she be the eight of diamonds, ye see, my pretty. No, I don't aspose ye do, but be that as it may, there she is on the table large as life, yeer daughter Eve.' Matthis tapped again on the card. 'And this Eve is a fiery young filly with a kind heart, I see. There'll come a time when she's a fine lady in silks and pearls. Diamonds too.' She lifted the eight and rubbed it between her palms, caressing it, repeating, 'There'll come a time.'

She took a deep breath and the sound of the crackling, ghostly mirth came from her again. 'Why, never since I've been using the

23

gift have I seen so much money. Quite tickles my fancy, it do.'

'Really? Money? Where? For us?' Ada was excited now, completely involved in the ancient's reading.

Matthis shook her head. 'No, my pretty, I'm afraid not for ye, though don't fret, for ye will have enough, enough. After ye have left Boston and gone away.'

'And when will that be?'

Matthis took up the six cards that Ada had chosen from the pack. 'Sooner than ye think. Take another.'

Ada was automatically following the commands. It was as if she were not in the real world. It was all fantastic, but she was convinced; she believed every word the old woman said, every word.

This time, Matthis took the card, a ten of clubs, added it to the other six she already held, shuffled them, and put them down face up in a line in front of her. She looked at them without speaking for some seconds.

'What else can you see?'

'Give Matthis yeer right hand.'

Ada did so and now could not restrain from asking the question that concerned her most: 'How long do I have? Can you see that? How long have I yet to live?'

'It is best ye do not know.'

'Why?' The young woman closed her eyes. 'Is it so short a time?'

'Listen, my pretty.' Matthis raised her long scrawny hand close to Ada's lovely face. Ada's eyes opened and widened but she did not draw away. Matthis shook her forefinger to emphasise her words. 'It is hard to see the length of one life exactly, even for those as gifted as Matthis, even for the seventh daughter of a seventh daughter, and what if I could see? Should I tell ye?' She touched Ada's dark curls in a brief, tender movement, then placed her hand back on the cards. 'But I can tell ye this. Ye will leave Boston, and ye will live elsewhere, long enough to see a fine house built, of yeer own, and to sleep in a bed of fashioned mahogany when all about ye live in shacks and tents.'

'Where . . . where is this place?'

'Across the wide continent, though ye shall travel on the sea to get there. It be filled with hopeful men, hopeful of finding gold!'

'Oh!'

Matthis was nodding to herself. She handed Ada back all the cards she had taken. 'Now, return them to my well-used pack – it's told many a heart what it desired to know – and for one last time I shall look into the future which surrounds yeer soul.'

Ada did as she was requested. Matthis mixed the cards once more. Ada's heart was racing and a high colour had come to her neck and cheeks.

'Take another.'

This time Ada reached into the pack and took out, for the second time, the eight of diamonds.

Matthis started slightly and her wrinkled mouth tightened. She shook her head and muttered, 'Confusing me . . . confusing me . . .'

'Why? What does it mean?'

'Don't like to be confused,' Matthis whispered, the skin puckering into infinite furrows in her forehead. 'Show me yeer palms, again.'

Ada did so and now she asked, 'My little girls, can you see them? Do I live long enough to see my little daughters become adults?'

Matthis's yellow eyes came up sharply to Ada's face, her voice high-pitched and shrill. 'Daughters! So that's it. Plural. There is not one alone. Matthis was seeing only one, but there be two!'

'Yes, I have—'

'Quiet, quiet, let the gift work.'

Ada fell silent.

Matthis closed her eyes. 'Ah, finally, I see. Yes, yes, there they are . . . behind ye, my pretty, clear as daylight now.' She shook her head and grinned with real satisfaction. 'Yeer daughters will travel much further than ye. Across the wide ocean, and one will travel oceans in multiple, though which girl I cannot say.' She nodded her head again, eyes closed, and raised her bony fingers to her temple. 'One will be loved by many, the other will be loved by few. In the few will be noble men and in the many will be ignoble.'

She fell silent. Ada dared not speak. She sat entranced, watching the flickering light make strange shadows on the time-worn face opposite.

The old woman did not open her eyes and now the words came slowly and were hardly above a whisper. 'The one called Eve is overpowering. I do wonder why. I see the word "Father", funny that. There is a marriage. But there are two men. Remarkable, outstanding men. Both powerful? No, I cannot clutch it. It passes, but there is a word, an important word. It starts with . . . M. It is of life importance to the one called Eve. It is difficult to decipher in the everlasting mists. Can I see it? Try, Matthis, try. M . . . A . . . Y . . . F . . . ? Yes, that is right. It begins Mayf. But it fades, I am losing it. It's gone.'

Matthis shook her head. 'Finished.' The movement was final, the reading had obviously ended. She opened her eyes and now to Ada's amazement they were not bright at all. The irises seemed hazel and the eyeballs were no longer white, but like all very old eyes, dull and bloodshot.

'Goodbye, Ada Herman.' Once more Matthis reached out and touched Ada's hair in the same, almost affectionate, movement of earlier. Then she rose in a jerky manner, inducing Ada to stand. Matthis propelled her expertly to the door, and Ada was highly conscious of the bony hand on her back. At the door, she thanked the old woman and there was the sound of the ghostly eccentric laughter again; then Ada was alone in the deserted alleyway.

It was night and the rain and sleet had given way to snowflakes. She hurried as fast as she could across the road to the wharf, her mind a blur of confused thoughts. The things Matthis had said about her daughters were fantastic. And the word, what was the word she had begun to spell? M A Y F. Whatever could it be? It appeared someday Eve and Clare would be going to a faraway land. And what of now? They were all going away again to a warmer climate.

She was not feeling the fierce cold as she hastened by the large well-lit central arch which graced the warehouses and she was oblivious of the six or seven Irish immigrant labourers who stopped their work to watch her pass, with her perfect skin and long dark hair trailing in curls over her shoulders underneath her headscarf.

Matthis had not told her how long she had left with her darling Phillip and her little girls, but she knew it was not a very long time.

When she came to the brig *Ipswich*, a two-masted square-rigged ship built in Baltimore twenty years before, it sat low in the water for it was almost fully loaded with the stores for its coming long voyage round the Horn. Slowly, she mounted the gangplank. At the top, before she stepped on deck, she halted for a minute in the bitter cold. She was breathing heavily.

'There you are at last, my precious darlin'!'

She turned and her husband came striding towards her from a hatchway. Beside him came a good-looking gent in dark uniform, great mutton-chop whiskers framing his strong jaw.

'Sweetheart, if I had realised it would turn so cold this afternoon, I would never have suggested that you meet me here,' Phillip Herman said as he kissed her forehead in greeting and put his arm round her. 'This is Captain Bernard Yorke, my wife Ada Herman.'

'How d'you do, ma'rm. Pleased indeed to make your acquaintance. Terrible weather it is. It will be better, I hope, in forty-eight hours when we set sail.'

'Yes, I hope so,' Ada replied.

There was silence for a few moments, before the Captain asked,

'Would you like to see over the ship, Mrs Herman? She's a fine, seaworthy vessel, she is.'

Ada looked to Phillip. He nodded.

Ten minutes later, they were in the passengers' accommodation.

'And so you see, ma'rm, the cabins are quite roomy really, bein' as we only have seven in all. We keep passengers to a minimum, you understand.'

Ada nodded. 'Yes, they are quite nice, clean and painted colourfully.'

'That they are,' agreed the captain flicking his hand across the side of the bunk and checking for dust. 'A body needs nice sleeping arrangements on a long journey, I always say.'

'Well, thank you for showing my wife your ship, Captain Yorke.'

They ascended to the deck. Phillip nodded goodnight to the boatswain who stood further along the deck in the lantern light and moved his wife to the top of the gangplank.

'Goodbye, Captain Yorke. I shall see you tomorrow.'

'Aye, indeed, Mr Herman, we shall be here.' The seaman took Ada's hand. ''Bye for now then, Mrs Herman.'

Ada smiled goodbye and they descended to the wharf.

Phillip looked at his wife with concern. 'Come, my darlin', we must get a cabriolet, it is far too cold for you to be walking. You can wait inside Laskey's corn store at the end of the wharf while I go and find a vehicle.'

While Ada sat on the tall stool inside Laskey's she was deep in thought. Captain Yorke had told her the *Ipswich* sailed in forty-eight hours and both men had seemed very keen for her to see the passenger cabins. What had Matthis said? She would be leaving Boston sooner than she thought. Her heart began to beat a little more swiftly. Was this goodbye to Boston? Had Phillip organised a passage on the *Ipswich* without telling her?

When her husband returned, he bustled her across the footpath in the falling snow and into the cabriolet.

'So, you liked the ship then, Ada, my love?'

'Yes, Phillip, and I am aware it is important that I did so.'

He looked a little surprised. 'What do you mean, love?'

'We are going on it, aren't we? No doubt everything is arranged. And you've done it without consulting me, haven't you? Oh, Phillip, how could you?'

Phillip was disconcerted. He moved from where he sat opposite her and put his arm round her. She shook it off. He took up her hand. She removed it.

'I see I am correct,' she said abruptly.

'Oh, Adee, I am sorry. I never wish to hurt you. Never. But, yes it is true, I am thinking of taking us on her.'

She looked accusingly. 'Thinking of it? More like you've booked passage. Be honest, you have, haven't you?'

His mouth drew down with guilt. 'Oh, Adee, there I was supplying them with stores for the voyage and when I found out the destination, I was tempted. I began considering, and then planning, and before I knew it I was committed. And I'd not said a word to you.'

'It's California and the gold, isn't it?' his wife continued.

Now Phillip really was surprised. 'Yes, love, that's so. But don't you see, my darlin', it's all for you. California is warm and the sun shines all the time. In truth, I believe your cough will disappear over there and you'll be well again, and they say it will be a state by year's end.'

Tears rose to her eyes and she looked away from him out the cabriolet's window into the darkness and falling snowflakes.

'Darlin' Adee, don't cry. I hate to see you cry. But I swear by all that is dear to me, I want to get you to the sunshine. I went to see Dr St James about you last week, love, and he said—'

'Oh, I know all that,' Ada answered as a tear welled over her lid.

'You do?' A puzzled frown creased his brow for a moment, and then he went on, 'Sweetheart, I love you so. Please forgive me.'

She remained facing away from him, gazing out the window.

'Well, the upshot is, darlin', we're supposed to leave on her when she sails.' He took up her hand again and kissed it. She removed it quickly.

'Adee, California is the place for us. Listen, dearest. It's not for the gold we go, no. A trader can make a fortune supplying the diggers with necessities. We will have our own home at last. I shall be successful.'

'It's a fine speech you make, Phillip Herman, and I've heard it one way and another many times in the last fifteen years.'

'Darlin', I'm doing it for you, and the future of the girls, and I'm truly sorry I didn't tell you.' He took up her hand again, and this time she did not remove it.

Ada was thinking about all the things that Matthis had said. She was visualising the wrinkled face and the odd little room with its peculiar smell. Was there any point in resisting?

She turned to face her husband. He looked so remorseful. She loved him so much. 'Phillip Herman, it all seems to be predestined anyway, settled long before you made the arrangements. So, I shall make no more fuss. I shall come with you.'

He had no idea what his beautiful wife meant, but he had heard

28

her say she would come. He whooped with joy and hugged her to him.

She felt happy, happy because she had made him so.

When Ada and Phillip arrived at their home, Mrs De Groot was waiting in the front hall, large arms folded across her breast, looking down her nose at them. There had been some trouble between her son Kenny and Eve, she informed them. She had not 'got to the bottom of it yet', but it appeared Eve had meddled in the boy's affairs. Perhaps they could 'have a word with Eve', for Kenny had said she had acted in 'a bossy and unladylike manner'. She paused briefly giving Phillip an opportunity to respond.

'Mrs De Groot, we will speak to Eve. And as for any trouble with Kenny, don't concern yourself over it for we are leaving this house, for ever, the day after tomorrow.' Holding Ada's arm, he moved her quickly past the landlady to the staircase. 'And as I'm sure you will appreciate, we must begin packing immediately.'

Mrs De Groot was so surprised she actually allowed them to climb the stairs without answering.

Ada and Phillip found their daughters in the music room and when they asked Eve for an explanation of the events with Kenny De Groot, she told them what had happened. 'Kenny and the boys were so cruel, and there was no one but me there to do anything about it.'

Phillip drew Eve into his embrace. 'All right, darlin', it seems Mrs De Groot has been given a different version of the events. You acted properly and did right to defend the child. We are very, very proud of you.' Then Phillip held out his arm and brought his other daughter to his side as he smiled first at Ada and then back to the sisters. 'And you can forget Kenny and Mrs De Groot, for we're going on a ship south round the Horn. We shall see the exotic West Indies and South America and people of different races, and life will be bright and new and meaningful. Our destination is California where the gold is!'

As her father spoke a shiver of excitement tingled through Eve. How wonderful it would be to sail south round the 'Horn', as her father had called it; to see unusual people and places. They were going to the goldfields. Her eyes brightened with enthusiasm and an eager smile broke across her mouth.

In contrast, Clare's mouth drew down unhappily, and when her father finished she spoke her thoughts. 'Oh no, that means we won't go to the concert on Sunday. There'll be no singing and dancing and we won't be able to wear our beautiful new dresses.'

Eve turned to her with an expression of delight in her eyes. 'But we shall be on a ship, out at sea, having a wonderful adventure. That will be much better than a concert, don't you see?'

Phillip took Clare's hand. 'Yes, my little darlin', our Eve is right. You'll like it. There will be lots of things, so much fun, so different and new.' His eyes found Ada's. 'In fact, I think we'll all enjoy it.'

Clare, capricious and quickly convinced, brightened visibly. 'I suppose you're right, Daddy.' Her pretty round eyes left her father and looked pleadingly at her mother. 'But what about our new dresses? Can we wear them on the ship, Mother? Can we?'

'I'm sure you can,' Ada smiled.

For a moment Clare hesitated, then abruptly she laughed and pulled her sister over beside her to dance round the room. 'We're going to sea, we're going to sea,' they sang excitedly, their golden curls flying.

CHAPTER THREE

'Have mercy upon us, miserable offenders.'
The Book of Common Prayer, General Confession.

Alan awoke to the sound of creaking timbers. He could hear the familiar lapping of water against the ship's side and for some seconds he felt content. Then he remembered where he was. Aboard the convict ship *Mount Stewart Elphinstone* at anchor in Cork Harbour, Ireland.

Immediately his senses were assailed by the stench of bodies.

Besides the foul odours of closely packed humanity came a whole series of other smells. The smell of the bilge – he was used to that; eleven years at sea had hardened his nose to that one, there it was, insidiously pervading; but there were others that left him uncertain. Was that the stink of rats? Once, years ago, the rats had become so bad on HMS *Falcon* that he had been able to smell them. In these insanitary conditions, it probably was rats.

He opened his eyes and then immediately wished he had not.

The rows of tiny wooden bunks that reached from floor to ceiling were filled with all manner of dishevelled, disreputable-looking men. A game of pitch and toss was in progress a few feet away and more sat in rings on the decking, playing cards. The only paper they had been issued with were religious books. Every eight prisoners had been given two Books of Common Prayer, two Books of Psalms and a copy of the New Testament, while a single Bible had been supplied for every sixteen men. Yet cards had appeared even before they had reached Cork.

The night they had boarded, they were given a lecture on the 'evils of idleness' by the surgeon-superintendent, Mr George Mocksey, the man responsible for the convicts. He had waved his arm across the prisoners gathered in the stern of the ship below him, his large, heavy face settling in severe lines.

'Now, all of you listen and listen carefully. This is not my maiden voyage so I have the advantage on all of you, in every way. There are a few things you should know and heed. You are accountable to me until I land you at our destination, and you will follow my rules.

There will be no trafficking of spirits or food. I will not tolerate movement between cots after lights out. There will be no buggery on my ship! And let it be here understood that there will be no compromise. It's fifty lashes apiece for any who attempt the like.'

He turned slightly to look sidelong at his assistant, a young, handsome man in his twenties standing at attention beside him, then his eyes came back to the prisoners and he leaned forward, his pale hands gripping the railing of the deck above them. 'We head for New South Wales, though I cannot tell you what part of that colony you will disembark. Reform is possible on the long journey ahead. I hope there are those who will see the voyage as an opportunity. Read your Bible, attend the classes that are made available, foster no evil thoughts and remember that every one of you, to a man, is here to pay his debt to the society he wronged.'

Alan recalled Mr Mocksey's words as he moved on his bunk and watched those about him. There were all manner of thieves and robbers – poachers, burglars, pickpockets, smugglers – as well as vagrants, kidnappers, rapists. The surgeon was an optimist! These were the scruffiest, filthiest men he had ever encountered. All his years in the Navy had not prepared him for them. As they set sail that first night, the hold had echoed with lewd songs, and from Spithead to Cork, he hardly spoke. When he did, those of his companions who were not ill were quick to notice his educated accent and rough jokes were made about him.

Most of them had been brought on board on 30 May, the day before they sailed from Spithead. Many of the prisoners had never been to sea. Some, from places like Stepney, Poplar and Soho in London, had never 'seen' the sea. Sea-sickness was rife.

The ship, a vessel built in Bombay in 1826, though large and heavy working was as speedy and seaworthy as many in Her Majesty's Navy. Nevertheless, the winds were high and she rolled a little when she crossed St George's Channel. To Alan, it was relatively smooth but most of those about him ailed loudly. When they anchored in Cork Harbour and their ranks grew by seventy Irish convicts, it was obvious to Alan the ventilation would be inadequate if ever any of the hatches had to be closed.

The prison complement on this ship was made up of 'exiles' and transported convicts. Of the two hundred and thirty-two men, one hundred and twenty were exiles – prisoners who had served part of their sentences in Great Britain and, on condition of deportation, would work as free men for a master after arrival in the colony. Yet, there was not a man here, exile or not, who looked forward to the future. The great majority left family of some kind behind with no hope of ever seeing them again. The faces that Alan looked into were those of despair.

Thank God they were not ironed. One of the prisoners had shouted to the entire 'between decks' that when his father had been shipped out twenty years before, they had been ironed for the whole voyage! How did they live through it?

They had been in Cork three days and now, once more, they were to set sail. How he wished he were above – where he belonged. He prayed for numbness, repressing a desire to scream. He did not belong here. These men were hostile, barbarous. He was a 'lifer' and it was wrong, all wrong. For the first time since the appalling events in the Southampton lane, Alan Fletcher was feeling sorry for himself.

Each day, they were sent on deck for recreation in three divisions. When the weather was fair, they were allowed fresh air for two hours, twice a day. Sometimes they were put to work, scrubbing and holy-stoning the decks or scraping and swabbing, but much of their time was free. They were encouraged to sing and dance and to take classes, but convicts have no mind to learn and this last suggestion died a natural death.

Each morning, water in buckets was thrown over them and twice weekly they carried the bottom boards of their berths on deck and washed them with salt water. Fortnightly, the convict contingent in its entirety was brought above and the prison fumigated. Still, it was impossible to keep between decks clean and even with the methodical efforts of the surgeon-superintendent and his assistant, the prison hold stank with the multitude of smells made by two hundred and thirty-two imprisoned men. Thus, the hours of the day most longed for were the intervals spent on deck.

As the days rolled into steady, dull repetition, Alan drew himself back to reality and made himself adapt.

It was during the respite above decks that he noticed himself being watched by a small, middle-aged, Irish convict. He was easily the oldest prisoner on board, the average age being twenty-six. Daniel Dwyer did not interfere with Alan's solitude until a week after they departed Tenerife.

The ship was entering the tropics and the sea air was glorious above, while below it was stifling, for the air lay heavy and lifeless in the hold where even the pitch in the seams of the ship was softening in the heat. Every man lived even more now for the relief of the few hours above. The early company had come up from the hold at six o'clock in the morning, immediately after breakfast, which was cooked on deck and then brought below by those convicts designated

33

as cooks. It was a gleaming morning and the line of prisoners stretched in a circle round the deck were having a shave and a haircut. The shave was a weekly event, the haircut fortnightly. As each man's turn was completed, he was released to wander freely. Alan found a spot as remote from his comrades as possible and sat staring to windward. He was interested in the course the ship was taking. Daily it was becoming more evident to him that the *Mount Stewart Elphinstone* was not set for Rio, the Falklands and the Horn, but was headed south-south-east towards Cape Town.

He breathed deeply, picturing himself on the *Coral Regis*. He was staring at the horizon when a shadow fell across him. He looked up to see two of the prisoners about to sit down. There was no restriction on conversation as long as the numbers did not become too large, and many of the men stayed in clan-like groups. Usually, if a man sat near Alan, he would turn away, and reply monosyllabically if spoken to, but this morning as these two men bent to sit beside him, he stood to leave. He found them particularly obnoxious. One was Thadius Boucher, a London thug being transported for kidnapping, and the other, Paul Cratten, a one-eyed, illiterate thief from the streets of Manchester. Both had made their presence felt and several men were already in fear of them. The London ruffian, though not tall, was powerfully built, a massive man. He barred the way as Alan stood.

'And why would ye be movin' away, Fletcher?'

Alan looked steadily in his eyes. 'I don't like the air up here when it becomes infested with the stench from below.'

'What does that mean, ye bastard? Are ye insultin' us?' He looked to Cratten, whose mean face was blank though he moved intimidatingly closer.

The Londoner took Alan's wrist in his right hand. His eyes were full of menace as he brought his flat, ugly face closer. 'Listen, Mr 'Igh an' Mighty, I've bin noticin' 'ow none of us are good enough for ye. Well, I'll be changin' yer uppity face for ye. Yeah, I'll do for ye, I will, one night when ye be asleep!' He made a sinister sound between missing teeth and began to twist Alan's arm.

Suddenly, there was a lilting Irish voice from behind. 'Be much more likely he'll do for you, Thadius Boucher. I wouldn't be meddling with a lifer now. He's probably murdered the likes of you!'

It was the middle-aged Irishman speaking. How did he know Alan was a lifer? No mention of their crimes had ever been made, unless it was by themselves, and Alan had never spoken about himself to anyone.

The big villain's eyes narrowed with interest, perhaps even with

34

admiration. He did not move out of Alan's way but he released his wrist. 'Well now, we might just be preferrin' it 'ere without the likes of ye anyway, Mr bloody 'Igh an' Mighty.'

Alan moved round him and the Irishman fell immediately in step with him.

'How the devil did you know that?' Alan questioned, once they were out of earshot.

'Know what?'

'That I was a lifer?'

The small man looked up at Alan. 'Ah, I must confess that a few days out of Cork Harbour I overheard the sergeant of the guard say as ye were one, and by our Lord Jesus I didn't think you had the appearance for it at all. Still don't. But it needed to be told to those two bullies, for lifers get respect in this company, and they'll not rush to intimidate you again. And they'll leave me be as well, for now they'll regard me as your friend.' Then he smiled a huge smile; his mouth was wide and generous and the proportions of it seemed to reach his ears. 'You see, I've watched you a bit. I notice how you remain aloof and I'm thinking you have a story to tell!'

'And I'll be certain you have too,' countered Alan.

'Yes, well, there you are, and if you like, I'll tell you mine first.'

'All right, if you must, though I would rather not hear it.'

The Irishman stopped walking suddenly and Alan turned to him. There was a serious expression pulling the corners of the older man's mouth down.

'Now look, young man. There are precious few aboard as I'd want to be knowing well. But you are different. I remarked it as soon as I looked into these eyes of yours. A man's going to need friends before this voyage is over. It's time you faced whatever it is you cannot face.' He took a deep breath. 'So, you had best be coming down to earth from wherever it is you've been since you boarded this ship.'

For some seconds, Alan stood gazing down at the man. He had said what was true, of course, although Alan had been loath to admit it. He had been resisting the fact that he was here on this prison transport somewhere off the coast of West Africa. He was resisting being a convict among all these convicts on the way to New South Wales. He was fighting reality, he who had taken the injustice of a life sentence and had said to Finnigan, 'What is, is.'

The eyes looking up at his were concerned, even friendly.

Abruptly, he held out his hand. 'I am Alan Fletcher,' he said. 'And yes, I will tell you my story although I do not think you will believe me.'

35

The Irishman took Alan's hand in both of his. 'I'm Daniel Dwyer and I'll believe you, lad, for I know you'll be telling me the truth.'

They sat at the bottom of the mainbrace on the recently holystoned deck and Daniel began. Instinctively he told Alan the whole truth and instinctively Alan knew he spoke from his soul.

Daniel Sean Dwyer had been brought up the eldest son of a master builder in Killorglin, County Kerry. He had gone to Dublin College and when he was twenty-one had entered a firm of architects. He learned quickly and his main field of work had been the restoration of churches. He was over thirty when he married pretty Audrey McAllister whom he worshipped, and shortly afterwards, with the money left him on his father's death, had begun his own business. He returned to County Kerry, to Tralee, where he employed his brothers who had followed in his father's footsteps, and for many years he had prospered as an architect-builder.

He and Audrey had been married for twelve years before she fell with child at the advanced age of thirty-six. She died in childbirth. 'She was me darlin' colleen, Audrey was, and life was never the same without her.'

Daniel began to drink and the business began to suffer. There were lean years and when the great famine saw the people of Ireland starving and dying, his business collapsed. When his last brother left him to go back to the family in Killorglin, Daniel in desperation did what so many have been tempted to do. He forged some cheques. They were not for enormous sums, just for enough to have him transported for seven years.

'So, there you see, Alan Fletcher, I'm fifty-five years of age and not smart enough but to be doing something unlawful.'

At that moment, the sergeant of the guard's voice sounded. 'All right, time's up! Step lively! All muster here!'

'Shall we continue our conversation below, lad?'

Alan nodded. 'I'll come to you.'

On Daniel's bunk they passed the hours. It was the first of many such days on the voyage. Alan told Daniel all that had happened to him and at times throughout his narrative the older man would shake his head sympathetically. When Alan recounted the trial and the false evidence of the cherub, Daniel simply closed his eyes and sighed. And when he came at last to where he had spoken out to the courtroom after being sentenced, Daniel exclaimed, 'You did right, Alan, you did right!'

When he completed his tale, Alan sat looking at his new friend. It had been a strain, but now he felt lightened by the telling, and was glad he had done so.

Then Daniel moved closer and took his hand and patted it slowly as he spoke. It was a fatherly gesture and Alan did not remove it for he was somewhat comforted by the older man's touch.

'Well, Alan, I don't doubt a single word. The minute I laid eyes on you, I could see there was something terribly awry for such as you to be on this ship. Don't know why the damn fool judge and jury couldn't see it. Nevertheless, it's fact. You are here and I am here and nobody else!'

'Yes,' answered Alan, 'and it is a miracle to have found you aboard.'

Daniel smiled widely and his face seemed to disappear beneath it. Later, he grew serious. 'So, you are the son of an English landowner? Well, there are many of my countrymen as would say I should not be speaking to the likes of you, let alone befriend you. But they are not here and I am. Circumstances change perspective, eh?'

Alan, too, looked grave. 'Yes, Daniel. There are problems in Ireland right enough and the absentee landlords don't help. I believe Home Rule is the answer, though that, no doubt, is a condition Irishmen themselves will not agree upon. Your values, religious and other, differ mightily all over the Emerald Isle.'

'Aye, that is the truth,' the older man agreed. Then he shook his head sadly. 'My poor, dear country! The inconclusive warfare between Catholic and Protestant and landlord and tenant, and tenant and sub-tenant has been going on, never ending, for hundreds of years. Feuds continue in my land where those fighting have forgotten why it started!' He sighed. 'So I am Catholic Irish and you are Protestant English, but those are mere words. And perhaps all the more reason that we be friends?'

Alan looked into Daniel's eyes and the two truly saw each other. 'Yes, Daniel, and we will be.'

As the days passed, the deep and abiding caring that was to endure for the rest of Daniel's life was cemented.

The *Mount Stewart Elphinstone* arrived in Table Bay nine weeks after departing Spithead. She had made swift passage and in the ninth week had logged three splendid daily distances, all close to two hundred miles.

As the sun set and night fell, the lights of Cape Town and its twenty thousand souls shimmered in the distance across the black water; and at dawn, the watch could see the glow on the rooftops nestling at the feet of the flat-topped mountain that gave the bay its name. It was August and the ship had sailed from summer into the winter of the southern hemisphere. There was a stale chill and damp below decks now, where before there had been heat and perspiration.

After sojourning briefly in this outpost of the Empire, they weighed anchor with the evening tide on the third day while the weather was equable. They rounded the Cape of Good Hope and twenty miles later passed to the south of Cape Agulhas. In front of them lay the Southern Ocean and their straight course for New South Wales. For two weeks they sailed with the wind.

Alan first noticed the change in the weather after the evening meal. He was on Daniel's bunk talking, as was their habit until 'lights out'. Two youths had the berths opposite and above and they also were in the conversation. These young men had begun their days in the 'Rookery' of St Giles, one of the labyrinthian confusions of sordidness north of the Strand in London, a home for thieves, prostitutes and worse. Nicknamed Swiftie and Lawless, their real names, Jonathan Lochran and Arnold Drake, were used only at roll call. They both had been professional pickpockets. 'I used to be a cadger before I turned professional,' was how Swiftie put it when introducing himself. He was seventeen and Lawless had recently turned twenty-three. Lawless had been one of five children brought up by his mother to steal. His earliest memories were of being taught to pilfer from coat pockets and handbags. Both young men had taken a strong liking to Alan. They called him 'guv'nor' and would linger in his company. The way he spoke enchanted them.

It was always stuffy below decks even in the winter temperatures, but earlier Alan had noticed an intangible change in the air, and he could feel the gradual reduction in the humidity.

'I think the glass will be dropping,' he said softly to Daniel.

'What does that mean, guv'nor?' asked Swiftie leaning across towards him. 'What's the "glass droppin"?'

Alan turned to face him. The boy's cheeky, too thin, grey face peered across the space between the bunks.

'Swiftie, the glass is a term for the barometer. It is an instrument, a long glass filled with mercury, which measures the atmosphere. When the mercury drops it indicates a change in the weather.'

'Cor,' replied Swiftie. 'What does "in . . . indicet" mean?'

'Indicate,' corrected Daniel from where he lay. 'It means "shows".'

'Ah!' observed the youth.

'So ye think there's to be a change in the weather, do ye, guv'nor?' questioned Lawless, not to be left out of the exchange.

'Yes, Lawless.'

'How is it ye know such things? How can ye tell?'

'If you had been to sea as many times as I have, lad, you would be able to tell too. And I'm afraid the change is not a pleasant one.'

'Bloody hell!' commented the youth.

For the next hour or so, nothing altered greatly. Then the batch of prisoners who had been exercising above came below complaining loudly at the curtailment of their recreation.

On the deck above, there was the scurry and hustle of movement that Alan recognised as preparation for a storm. He could imagine the sailors working to bring in the canvas. He could picture them reefing the maintopsail, shortening sail and dropping rope to the deck as the ship began to bow before the increasing wind. Vibrations reached the prison hold as the hands moved heavily across the planking. Things began to slide and bump as the ocean swelled in the wind.

'Now, lads,' Alan said to those about him, 'when the storm hits, it may last a long time, even days. During the worst of it, the ship will be thrown about, but do not be tempted to leave your bunks. Take a good firm hold with your hands and feet, and brace yourselves – and stay there.'

The rain started to fall heavily, blown on the rising wind. As the spray and rain increased, it came into the hold. The hatches were not battened down immediately and so much water was taken in that the bedding was drenched on the bunks near the opening and water ran freely. Finally, orders were given to close the hatches. The hold, though cold and damp, now became unbearably fetid. The night was ghastly. The force of the wind rose and the ship began to pitch and toss. The waves ran higher than the yardarms as the vessel laboured ponderously against them. Men screamed and retched, cursed and vomited and the pessimists hurled their certainty of destruction back and forth. Everything movable rushed around and even lifted from the floor.

When there was a brief lull in the din, Swiftie's frightened voice sounded across the darkness. 'Have ye ever been in a gale as bad as this, guv'nor?'

'Yes,' shouted Alan, 'and I'm sorry to say, lad, it is far from over.'

'Oh Gawd!'

'Take no notice of the others,' Alan continued above the clamour, 'for as you see, I am still here, just as you will be when it's over.'

The wailing was long and intense, and though this night was to prove the worst, Alan's prediction was right; the gale lasted. The ship, fighting the wind, continued to pitch viciously and somewhere a man kept calling that his arm was broken.

Why don't they let her run before it? Furl the foretopsail and yield to it! All hands must be at the pumps. The wind is so violent it must be pushing the white tops of the waves to many feet above the ship's side. She shuddered under the impact as she continued to take the relentless blows. Soon she must lose spars and sail, if she had not already.

Up above, the helm was lashed and all available hands worked the pumps. The *Mount Stewart Elphinstone* was a sturdy vessel, six hundred and eleven tons, making her third trip from England to New South Wales and had indeed hit turbulent seas before, but this was a powerful wind and now her frailties appeared. She began to lean and stay down for interminable periods.

The noise above decks from the sea and the wind was ear-splitting. The noise below decks from the convicts' cries was worse.

Alan, conscious of the fight the ship was having, knew she was spending too much time over on her side. *With this battering, her seams must be opening and closing like the mouth of a chattering monkey. Why is the master fighting it? She cannot take much more.*

When it seemed she would lean and stay down for ever, Alan felt her turn. *Good man! At last! At last!*

Now, finally, the ship began to have rhythm in her dives. The vicious plunging up and down became an unsteady rising and falling. They had brought her to, and she was running before it. No doubt she would be many a league off course when the storm abated, but she would not be at the bottom of the ocean as Alan had been beginning to fear.

The *Mount Stewart Elphinstone* ran before the gale for six long, hellish days, while the prisoners locked in foul blackness existed as best they could. Food was brought along the gangways and dumped inside the hold by the soldiers, and the convicts fended for themselves. When at last the wind moderated and a modicum of comfort returned to the motion of the ship, she was many miles off her course. Ultimately, the guard came to open the hatches. Up rose the stench from the vomit and excreta below like a solid wall in the faces of those who released the openings. To a man, they turned away and retched in the scuppers.

All the convicts looked haggard and ill, their eyes enlarged in their gaunt and wasted faces. After the surgeon and his assistant examined the two hundred and thirty-two men in the hold, fifty were declared too ill to move from their bunks. Seven had concussion, three had fractured wrists, two had broken fingers, two had broken arms, one a broken ankle, and one a dislocated hip. Seventeen had swollen joints from various sprains. Two hundred and thirty-one had bruises, black eyes, cuts and lumps. And one was dead.

Alan was the least injured of them all. With his expertise, he had braced himself properly during the worst of the storm, and though he had felt fiercely ill during most of it, had only a few bruises and cuts to show.

Of the little band of Alan, Daniel, Swiftie and Lawless, the youths were the worst. Both had been violently seasick and Swiftie had cut his head badly on the side of his bunk. Lawless had been thrown from his and it was he who had dislocated his hip. Daniel was ministering to them as best he could, and although in time Lawless's hip would mend, ever afterwards he was to be slightly lame.

The hold was cleaned in cursory fashion by the convicts who could walk and then they were all mustered on deck. They were deep in the Southern Ocean now, and the light wind carried sleet in it. Wrapped in blankets, the felons crowded aft, while amidships stood the soldiers and their wives and children who were accompanying them to New South Wales. Further forward gathered the sailors. They all listened while prayers were held giving thanks for survival.

As prayers ended and the sailors, soldiers and their families dispersed, the commander of the guard gestured to the sergeant who called the convicts to order. 'Silence for the first mate, Mr Connah.'

He stood on the quarterdeck looking down at the motley gathering crowded in the stern. 'We have all come through a bad gale. Thanks be to the Lord for our deliverance. The result? We are many leagues off course. The master is presently calculating the distance. Until this is rectified, provisions and water will be restricted. From tomorrow, each prisoner will go on to half rations.'

Groans and grumbles met the news.

'Quiet now, no complaints! Sergeant, take them below!'

Since the beginning of the voyage they had been divided into 'messes' of six men. Each mess was apportioned weekly, receiving measures of bread, flour, beef, pork, rice, boiled peas, butter, suet, raisins, oatmeal, sugar, vinegar and lime juice. Alan had found the rationing fair and as good as that in many a ship in Her Majesty's Navy. But half rations were another matter.

When they were all once more in the hold, they were set to work cleaning it thoroughly and for the next few hours there was too much to do for any of them to vent their anger, but when night fell, the unhappy rumblings of the day gave way to the rise of temper and discontent. As the night passed, the more obstructive prisoners vented their spleen on those about them and a number of fist fights broke out. Next morning, even though there was still grumbling and discord, all seemed calmer. It was late that afternoon when Alan sensed that something more was awry.

He and Daniel had been taking turns to nurse Swiftie and Lawless. The worst of the cases had been taken to the ship's hospital, but it was so full, the less injured had to remain in their bunks.

Once, while Alan was dabbing Swiftie's hot head with a wet rag,

41

the boy had looked up, his eyes glassy in his pale, exhausted face, and said, 'Thanks for lookin' after us, guv. Just like a real mum, ye be.' A weak grin covered his features.

Daniel, who sat leaning on one end of his bunk across from the boy, asked quietly, 'Tell us, Swiftie lad, where is your mum and all? Does she know her son is a prisoner of Her Majesty?'

Swiftie shook his head. 'Never had one. Not as I recall.' Then his tone took on faint derision as if Daniel should know better. 'Lots of us in the Rookery never had a mum.'

'Too right,' commented Lawless from where he lay, 'and those of us what did could've done without her.'

At that moment, Alan lifted his eyes and noted a group of men in a huddle. Although they appeared to be playing cards, it was the particular individuals that drew his attention. Thadius Boucher's arm was round a Surrey poacher, Samuel Cooper. On the far side of Cooper was Paul Cratten and next to him was another thief and troublemaker, 'Gaffer' Gordon. The other two were Davey Keating from Dublin and Luke Talbot, the only other lifer, who enjoyed telling how he had bashed two policemen so badly in a riot that later they had died. These were the most feared men between decks and it augured ill that they had their heads together. After ten minutes or so, the villainous group broke up. Over the next twenty-four hours, Alan observed the same six men together again. And during the burial of the poor devil who had died, he noticed them in company once more.

Alan had now guessed what these men were planning. Therefore it was no real surprise, as he lay on his bunk that night, to feel a tap on his foot and to open his eyes to find Boucher and Talbot looking at him. Boucher put his heavy hand to his mouth and in conspiratorial fashion said, 'We'd like a word with ye, Fletcher, private like!'

'And where do you propose we go for privacy?'

Talbot beckoned 'Over 'ere.'

The eternal card games were taking place in the corridors between the beds, which left a number of cots unoccupied. Boucher and Talbot led Alan to an empty spot against the bulwark.

Alan spoke first. 'Well, what's so important?'

'We've 'ad enough. We're gonna do sommat about it,' began Boucher.

Talbot nodded. 'Those bastards! Half rations!' He spat on the floor. 'Didn't hear nothin' about them goin' on half rations, did we?' Then he lowered his voice. 'We reckon we can take it – the ship.'

Alan kept silent, and Talbot continued, 'There be twenty of us in it definite. We'll recruit more just 'afore we mutiny. Most o' the real cons will join wiv us. Cratten and Keating 'ave talked to a few of the exiles and they be for it as well. But ye . . . well, we'd like ye in wiv us. Ye be real popular with them young uns, they'll com' easy if ye be wiv us. Besides, ye've nothin' to lose, ye bein' a lifer like mesel'.'

'And how do you intend to seize her?'

'In the wee hours when the guards be less and the ship's asleep,' answered Boucher. 'And we be bound on takin' 'er the night after tomorrow. That be Friday. Them soldiers gets drunker Friday night than any other, eh?'

Talbot grinned. He put his big paw confidentially on Alan's shoulder. 'We'll get rid o' the master an' Mocksey an' them officers. Then we puts the rest of 'em ashore at the first point o' land. After that we'll be free!'

'Free to be pirates, if you get away with it,' Alan answered softly. 'And what do you mean by "get rid of the officers"?'

'Get rid of 'em, see,' said Boucher, drawing his finger across his throat.

'It's not a simple thing to take a ship. Not without guns and weapons.'

'We'll soon 'ave those,' answered Boucher.

Alan looked sceptical. 'Perhaps you should think on this a little longer. So we're on half rations, but we haven't been ironed, and they've been light on the lash. But if you mutiny and it fails . . .'

Talbot shook his head. 'By Christ, we won't bloody fail.'

Alan's expression did not change. 'And the women and children?'

A lascivious grin widened Boucher's mouth, and Talbot pursed his lips. 'Well, some of us be for takin' the women along wie us.'

Alan looked from one to the other. 'But they're the soldiers' wives.'

Talbot smiled. 'So?'

Alan thought for a second or two before he spoke again. 'I ask you to take this into account. There have been only a few successful mutinies in the entire history of the Navy. There has been only one successful mutiny on board a convict ship. That was fifty years ago and it was carried off by the blasted guard, not the convicts. Tell me, what separates your mutiny from all the failures of the past?'

Boucher spat on the back of his hand. 'Look, ye bastard, we're goin' ta do it! Ye'll not be frightenin' us wie all that stuff. Now are ye wie us?'

Alan shook his head. 'The soldiers are armed, you fools. Whether they're drunk or not, they're military men, used to fighting. Water surrounds us. You cannot get away. They will have you trapped and—'

'Christ sake,' interrupted Boucher angrily, 'are ye wie us or agin us?'

'I don't think you have a chance. Ask me again when we're on dry land.'

Talbot's face clouded. 'Are ye sayin' ye'll not join wiv us?'

'I'm saying I will not join you.'

'Bloody coward!' said Boucher, his voice rising.

'Shaddup, Boucher!' snapped Talbot. He tapped Alan on the chest. 'It's wrong of ye not to throw in with us. Ye'll be sorry. Just keep out of the way an' don't interfere. An' don't say nothin'.'

'Certainly.' Alan turned from them and went back to his bunk. He desired to be free as much as any man on board. He had been given a life sentence, from which there was no release. Lifers did not get their sentences reduced. But mutiny was not the way. He would have to wait until the voyage was over, then he would watch for his time to escape. He could not, would not, live his life in subjection when he had committed no crime.

The next day during recreation on deck the mutineers made one last approach to Alan. This time it was Cratten and Samuel Cooper. The thief stood silently watching him with his single bloodshot eye, while Cooper asked if Alan would not reconsider. When he verified that he would not, the poacher paid what was as close to a compliment as he could come. 'I'm sorry ye won't come along with us, man. I reckon ye'd be good in a scuffle.'

'Thanks, Cooper,' replied Alan.

The next forty-eight hours passed quietly and on Friday night, just before the official bedtime at ten o'clock, one of the youths, a lad about seventeen called Kerry Tyson, came to join Alan and Daniel by Swiftie's bunk. Swiftie was regaining health and was much brighter than previously, but Lawless had deteriorated and had been removed to the hospital.

Kerry had a strange look in his eyes and he seemed unnaturally stimulated. He leaned in towards them and spoke in an excited whisper. 'We're goin' to be takin' the ship tonight, Swiftie. I've been in a meetin' with Talbot.'

Swiftie looked astonished. 'What do you mean, Kerry?'

'Now listen, lad,' Alan said taking Kerry by the arm and sitting him on the bunk. 'Do not get involved. This is a convict transport. My guess is that already there has been an informer. That means the guard will be in wait. It's the way of most mutinies, and even if there has not been a warning, the chances of taking over are minimal.'

Daniel nodded in agreement as Alan went on, 'I do not want you involved, Kerry. You or any of the other lads. Men might be killed.

If it is a failure, it will mean severe punishment, irons, even flogging. They will deal brutally with those they catch.'

Kerry did not look quite so inflamed with excitement at the thought of irons and flogging. He rested his head against the upright of the bunk. 'What'll I do?'

Alan took his arm. 'Go back to Talbot and tell him you've decided to stay out of it. Say I talked you into it if you like, but do not be a part of it. Tell the others I said to stay in their bunks tonight.'

'Yeah, Kerry,' whispered Swiftie. 'The guv wouldn't lead ye astray.'

The youth nodded solemnly and left to find Talbot as the shout from the guard ordered them to retire.

After what seemed a long time, Alan fell to sleep.

At three o'clock in the morning he was wakened by an uproar. Shots were fired and men screamed, there was thudding and shouting, and from the direction of the fore hatchway a brief rousing cry urged, 'Forward, boys! Attack! Attack!'

Alan raised himself on his elbow and peered through the gloom in the direction of the sounds. In the burning night light he saw the hatch was open and prisoners were climbing up to the deck. Later, he was to learn that all of the stanchions on the fore hatch had been loosened by a guard apparently bribed to help the mutineers.

Suddenly there was another volley of shots and more shouting. A man fell back grotesquely from the hatchway, screaming in agony. This was followed by screeches of terror and more gunfire from above. Men scrambled back from the opening as others tumbled from their bunks, bumping each other and yelling in the confusion to avoid being hit.

Alan's bunk was away from the gunfire and he leaped down and called, 'Daniel! Daniel! Where are you? Swiftie, where are you?'

'We be here, Alan,' the cadence of the Irish voice sounded at his elbow. 'Aye, in truth, the guard were waiting for them, as you foresaw.'

Swiftie's white face was peering from behind Daniel's shoulder and in the rear were Kerry and some other youths. Good!

Shortly the convicts returned to their cots, and the hold fell into an uneasy peace, except for four who remained at the bottom of the hatchway groaning. Within a few minutes, the prison door opened and in the light of firebrands held by sailors, a dozen soldiers entered with rifles levelled. The sergeant and the assistant surgeon followed.

The assistant surgeon, Anthony Miller, was on his first voyage in a transport. He was young and innocent of the ways of the sea. He had been warned that there were often attempts of mutiny and cautioned to be wary of a rising, for all convict ships were hellholes of trouble. He was an earnest young man from farm stock in Essex and though he had been shocked at the attempted takeover of the ship, he had rallied quickly. Followed by armed soldiers, he walked through the gangway looking left and right, saying, 'Listen, you lot, stay exactly where you are. We have the ringleaders, all bar one.'

Alan felt a presentiment at the young man's statement.

When the assistant surgeon reached the injured, he knelt down. 'Now steady. We shall soon have you mended, though damn fools you are!'

The wounded men were removed to the already crowded hospital and then the sergeant turned to the prisoners, his features ruddy in the glow from the firebrands. 'Where's Fletcher? Alan Fletcher?' he shouted.

'Here,' replied Alan from the mass of dark shapes and shadows.

'Come with me.'

Alan left his bunk and as he passed the row where Daniel lay, the older man called, 'What the devil is going on, sonny?'

Alan shrugged his shoulders, 'Don't know, Dan.' But he had a theory about it.

He followed the sergeant out the prison door to a part of the ship the prisoners never saw: the cabin of the joint captain of the *Mount Stewart Elphinstone*, Surgeon-superintendent George Mocksey.

Convict transports had two men in charge: the master who captained the ship and took care of navigation and the crew; and the surgeon-superintendent who was solely responsible for the welfare of the prisoners. The third dominant individual was the commander of the guard. He was requested by the War Office to co-operate with the joint heads in supervising the ship. Their united exertions were on some ships, equable, on others, disagreeable, but on the majority each man kept to his designated duties.

On the *Mount Stewart Elphinstone* Master Henry Loney left the scurrilous riffraff below decks entirely to George Mocksey. Master Loney was on his first and only voyage to New South Wales. He saw himself as the principal director, engaged with the trust of sailing the ship safely from England to New South Wales. Surgeon-superintendent George Mocksey was on his fourth trip to New South Wales. The pay until recently had been poor and the trips were exacting. There was no luxury on a transport. His responsibilities were vast. He rationed the food and handled its distribution. Every cask of provisions was opened in his presence. He inspected the convicts and visited the hospital daily. The prisoners' cleanliness and the cleaning of their quarters were his specific responsibilities. He locked the prison at night and tended all sick on board, including the crew and soldiers and their wives and children. His list of duties seemed endless. At least on this voyage he had an assistant.

George Mocksey fulfilled his obligations adequately, but he was an embittered and disillusioned man who had drifted permanently into the convict service. His wife and daughter had accompanied him on his first voyage to New South Wales and the child had died of cholera in Rio de Janeiro. It was exactly ten years since the tragedy and he still had not forgiven the world. He was now in his forty-eighth year. His marriage had gone sour, his wife could bear no more children, and on his recent stay in England he had not bothered to journey to Sheffield to see her. His hair receded and what was left was streaked with grey. A decade ago he had been good-looking, but now his face had dropped to form jowls on either side of his mouth, giving him an unhappy appearance. And his appearance reflected himself.

As the sergeant of the guard stood in front of Alan and knocked on Mr Mocksey's door, the surgeon-superintendent was studying the crimes list. Now that he had experienced a mutiny, he thought it pertinent to know the calibre of the leaders. He put down the book at the sound of the tapping. 'Come in.'

The sergeant entered, followed by Alan.

'Wait outside, Sergeant, I will call if I need you. And send for the others. I will have them all here together.'

Alan looked around him. The cabin was small like they all were, but how well it reminded him of his past – the lamp swinging moodily to and fro from the familiar deck beams overhead, a map or two on the walls, the cot against the bulkhead. He gave the suggestion of a sigh as he brought his eyes round to the surgeon-superintendent.

While Alan surveyed the cabin, surgeon-superintendent Mocksey studied him. So this was Fletcher. Strange he had not noticed the man. He should have read the crimes list before. In Fletcher's case it made puzzling reading. He had once captained his own ship in the Royal Navy and now it seemed he was keen to get another. It was odd he was not caught with the other ringleaders on deck. Still, the convict who had informed on the mutiny said he was one. He had seen him whispering with a number of the ringleaders more than once.

Now he remembered he had heard the guards occasionally talking about a man named Fletcher. For a convict he must be unique. He was to have been the squire of a large estate in Somerset!

'Well, Fletcher, do you know why you are here?' Mocksey's voice was of the north countryman.

'I can only guess that I have somehow been implicated in the mutiny.'

'Somehow been implicated, is it? A little stronger than that,

47

prisoner. You have been named as one of the ringleaders, my man.'

Alan's eyes met his, indignation apparent. 'Really? By whom?'

There was something disconcerting about this Fletcher. Surgeon-superintendent Mocksey felt he was losing charge. 'Now listen, Fletcher,' he said, rising to his feet, 'I'll do the interrogating here.'

'All right,' Alan answered.

The surgeon coughed, and pointed to the pages he had been reading. 'To my astonishment I see you were captain of your own ship.'

'Yes, for eighteen months, the *Coral Regis*.'

'You were very young to be a commander in the Navy.'

'Yes,' replied Alan. 'My cabin bore a close resemblance to this – perhaps a mite larger.'

'Really?' The surgeon-superintendent was watching his aristocratic killer-convict closely. He came around his desk a little nearer and his voice was almost conciliatory. 'Why did you get involved in this uprising? Surely as a former naval officer you knew better?'

'Yes, I did,' answered Alan, glancing over the surgeon's head to the map on the wall.

Once again Mocksey felt disconcerted and his voice rose impatiently. 'What the devil does that mean?'

'I was not involved in the uprising.'

'My information is to the contrary.'

'Then your information is incorrect.'

Mocksey turned away. 'Silence!' He stood with his back to Alan as the seconds passed, then he turned and demanded, 'All right, Fletcher, let me have your story. Who do you say were the ringleaders?'

'I do not say.' Alan was looking directly at the commander. 'What I do say is I am not one of them.'

The surgeon felt himself becoming angry, affronted. This man was a convict. A criminal should be more accommodating. It was all his easy years in affluence that made him this disagreeable.

For some time the noises of the creaking timber and the grating of the hanging lantern were intensified by the silence between the two men. Their shadows grew and diminished alternately as the lamp swung above them.

A sharp knocking on the door interrupted the stillness.

Mocksey moved to his desk. When he was seated, he called loudly, 'Enter!'

Through the cabin door were pushed four men. Talbot limped badly from a deep cutlass slash in his right leg. Boucher's thick frame was stooped. There was a gash on his cheek and he nursed a bullet wound in his right shoulder. Keating's head was covered with a bloody bandage, a shot had ripped off his ear, and Cooper's left hand was bandaged where a bullet had passed cleanly through. The two thieves, Cratten and Gordon, were not with them.

In the rear of the four prisoners came Mr Miller, the first mate, the sergeant of the guard, and two soldiers with rifles at the ready. The four rebels registered Alan's presence. Obvious surprise appeared on the faces of Cooper and Keating but Boucher and Talbot showed no emotion.

'This is what's left of the ringleaders, sir,' said the sergeant, motioning towards the newcomers with his head.

'Thank you, Sergeant. The others are dead, I gather.'

'Yes, sir,' answered Mr Miller, 'dead on arrival at the hospital.'

The surgeon-superintendent stood again. His mouth had set in a hard straight line and he presented himself truly in charge. He turned briefly to face the mate. 'Mr Connah, you will note sentence and pass it on to Master Loney to be recorded in the log.'

'Aye, aye, sir.'

The joint commander of the ship looked at the prisoners and rapped his fist on the desk in emphasis. 'This vessel has suffered enough at your hands. You have proved to be the brutes I suspected. Mutiny is the most serious crime on the sea. You are all guilty of it, of inciting the other prisoners to rise and of attempting a bloody takeover of the *Mount Stewart Elphinstone*. My decision is to separate you from the others for the rest of the voyage. You will be ironed and will take but two hours exercise a day. When your wounds are sufficiently healed, you will take your punishment. Each of you will be confined in the box for a total of six hours a day for seven consecutive days.'

There was a groan from Cooper while Keating mouthed the words, 'Oh God!'

This was a ghastly punishment, even more feared than flogging. The 'box' was infamous. It was described in the log as 'a strictly confining wooden structure, something like a sentry box, only much smaller, somewhat over six feet high with only enough room for a man to stand. Six auger holes enable a man to see and breathe as he stands inside. Half a dozen hours in the box is all a strong man can endure. After a week of six hours in the box each day, his spirit is broken.'

The commander finished passing judgment. 'Sergeant! Mr Connah!'

'Yes, sir!'

'As Fletcher has no injury he can begin the box this coming

afternoon. The remainder of the prisoners will be ironed at night until we complete our journey. I will crush any repetition of rebellion before it begins.' Then he turned his back on them, saying as he did so, 'Take them away!'

As the sergeant began to hustle the sentenced men towards the door, Samuel Cooper turned back into the cabin and, to the surprise of all, spoke. His voice was subdued but what he said was unmistakably plain. 'Excuse me, Mr Mocksey, sir, but if ye include Fletcher along with us, it's a proper disgraceful act and no mistake. For he's not guilty of nothin'.'

'Shaddup, you!' said Boucher putting out his left hand to silence him.

Alan stopped walking and faced Cooper. He looked intently at the man. There was more in the character of the Surrey poacher than he had suspected.

'What is that you say?' asked the surgeon-superintendent, turning back towards them.

'You bloody fool!' growled Talbot.

'I said that Fletcher was not one of us, sir. He would have nothin' to do with the mutiny.'

The commander's brows drew closer as he regarded the little man. 'Really now?'

'Yes, sir. We wanted him to join with us, but he would be havin' none of it. Twice we asked him and twice he refused.'

The surgeon looked across at Alan and their eyes met once more. 'It seems you have a champion, Fletcher.' He turned back to Cooper who spoke again.

'T'aint fair for ye to suffer for somethin' ye had naught to do with, Fletcher.'

'Thank you, Cooper.'

'So,' declared Mr Mocksey reflectively, 'we have one who is at variance with the proceedings. Well, what about you other three? Was Fletcher with you or against you?'

Boucher's eyes narrowed to slits. 'I dunno what goes on 'ere but 'e were wie us right enough, right from the start. It was 'is idea ye might say. But once the firin' started 'e disappeared! Where did ye run to, Mr 'Igh and Mighty? Back to yer bunk, yer coward?' He stared at Alan with obvious hatred.

Alan simply looked away. He found the man contemptible.

The surgeon-superintendent pursed his lips. 'And you other two, come, what do you say? Was he with you or not?'

As Talbot's and Keating's eyes met, Alan knew it was useless to defend himself. Talbot answered. 'Yeah, that's right, we were all in together. I suppose it's true it were 'is idea.'

'But it's not true, they—' began Cooper.

'Silence! I'll have no more of this,' interrupted Mr Mocksey, bringing his hand down heavily on his desk. He took a deep breath and looked round the five felons in front of him. Four signalled their circumstances and social inferiority in every nuance of their beings, whereas Fletcher had the bearing of the privileged. Yes, he looked like the heir to a large estate. Yes, he looked like a captain of a ship of the line.

Surgeon-superintendent Mocksey was irritated, his irritation influenced by many emotions. He felt inferiority, envy, even enmity and hostility. He did not wish to examine his feelings too closely. All he knew was that he had just heard three of the mutineers agree that Fletcher had been the ringleader and, too, there was the evidence of the informer. This salved his conscience. 'I am in charge here,' he said, 'and while I'm not Solomon, I have heard three out of four say you were a mutineer, Fletcher, and the leader. You will begin your days in the box as sentenced. How many will remain at my discretion. Take them away, Sergeant!'

'Oh no!' whispered Cooper, his face wrinkling with dismay.

'You heard,' came the sergeant's loud voice. 'Come on, you lot. Move!'

As they departed, Alan looked down at Cooper. The poacher shook his head sadly at him and shrugged his shoulders. When they were outside in the gangway, Alan placed his hand on the little man's bony shoulder and said softly, 'Thank you, Samuel Cooper. It took a brave man to speak the truth back there.'

'Didn't do no good but,' came Samuel's defeated reply. 'Fact is, made it ten times worse.'

'Yes, but the deed was commendable. There was honour in it.'

Anthony Miller had not spoken during the proceedings. He returned to the hospital to inspect the wounded in a thoughtful mood.

After the cabin door had closed, the joint commander of the *Mount Stewart Elphinstone* stood some minutes, face flushed, staring at his desk. Served him right. Anyway, wasn't he here to pay his debt to society? After all, he was a proven bloody murderer.

Soon the first rays of dawn broke over the horizon. The *Mount Stewart Elphinstone* glistened, catching the wind on the rolling ocean. Her unfurled sails were a spotless white against the blue of the sea as she continued majestically running the easting down.

As a medieval castle was magnificence and grandeur on the outside, hiding offensive dungeons within, so too did this splendid sight carry rancorous, dark holes. To one of these, beneath the forecastle, the prisoners were taken.

On the way, Keating fainted from his head wound and was transferred to the hospital. Alan and the other three were double-ironed in the dank chill space. Boucher and Talbot lapsed into sullen silence, but Alan and Samuel talked.

'I'm real sorry, Fletcher,' the little man said.

'It's not your fault, Cooper.' Alan turned his head, attempting to look squarely at him in the murky darkness. 'What made you try to help me?'

Samuel lifted his good hand, rattling his chains as he pointed at the others. They were out of reach, attached to the far wall. 'Well, after we were captured, methinks I heard them say to the sergeant somethin' about the leader of the mutiny not bein' with us, but I weren't sure, ye see. Then, when we were taken in to Mocksey and ye be there, it still never hit me straight off. Then I realised them had dobbed ye. Well, it just didn't seem right somehow.'

'Shaddup, Cooper, ya little bastard!' Boucher growled from the far side of the space.

Samuel Cooper answered almost to himself, 'Well, I done it and I be glad.' Then turning his puny face to Alan he said, 'I feel different now, somehow.'

'Good,' Alan answered softly.

The poacher was silent for a few seconds, then he said, 'And to think ye will be in that bloody box in the freezin' winds and that lot won't be doin' it until we be in warmer waters. God, where's the justice?'

Alan peered at the face turned towards him. 'Don't think on it, Cooper, for I would rather not until the time comes. Tell me about yourself. What part of Surrey are you from?'

Then Samuel Cooper smiled a small smile for he could not remember the last time a person had asked him about himself. He whispered many things there under the forecastle until finally the guards came to take Alan away.

As he stood to leave, Samuel said, 'Courage, my . . . my friend!' and put out his good right hand. Alan took it and held it a second or two.

'I'll see you in six hours, Samuel.'

When he came up on deck, he looked aft and saw the convicts in a mass watching him. Each man was wrapped in a blanket against the biting wind. He made out Daniel, white-faced with alarm, but he gave no sign of having seen them. Some of the wives of the soldiers and their children in expectation of the spectacle had gathered to watch.

Alan stood in front of the grim wooden box that had been erected amidships that morning. He had heard of the use of this form of punishment on some vessels, but never had he been on a ship where such measures had been taken. One of the soldiers unlocked the door, a thick, solid plank hinged at the side. It seemed to beckon him like an open coffin.

God! These things were barbaric! Even from here the narrow restrictions were frightening. Locked in, the oppression within the compartment would be like being smothered! Above his head he would have only about an inch or so to spare. It was made of solid wood, with small air holes in the door. Six hours in here? What fiend had conjured up this?

'Turn round, Fletcher, ye'll have to back in, matey.'

With his double irons this was achieved with difficulty. He stood in the rectangle looking out at the guards, the closeness of the wood bearing down upon him already, and the door still open. One of the soldiers shook his head in sympathy. Then the door was closed and their faces were gone.

Blackness. Nothing but startling blackness.

'Click' went the lock on the door.

Why was it he could not see? There were perforations in the door. Surely he was not going mad already? The door had been pierced in five or six places. He had seen them. He moved his head to left and right, but there was no light. Why? What was wrong?

Then he realised. The tiny auger holes were below the level of his eyes and he could not see out. Panic rose in his chest as if to stifle him. He pushed it down by remembering what he had said to his father about going to sea: 'I will accept responsibility for my decision.' And so he must accept responsibility for being in this Godless black hole. If he had not joined the Navy, he would have been at home all those years and Abel would not have had the opportunity to thwart him, and so lead him to this.

The feeling of panic built as he heard the wind rattle the door.

He must lift his arms, but of course he could not.

There was a dryness in his throat and his mind clouded over with hysteria. If only he could lift his arms, the phobia might go. God, he must not scream! They had only just closed the door on him. There were six hours of this to endure day after day until that relentless Mocksey chose to stop it. How many days would there be? No, don't think of how long, simply think of now. Courage! As Samuel Cooper had said, he must concentrate on other things. That was it. Believe he was simply standing with his eyes closed, thinking. Spend the time meditating and recall days gone by when there were no prisons, no hate or horrors in his life.

What of the days at Long Moss House when his mother had been alive? Yes, he would remember them one by one. From his first memories. He would see again the house and the stream that came down from the Mendip Hills to run by the stables, where the delicate fronds of the weeping willows brushed the water. He would picture his mother coming to him through the spring flowers, her pale skirt brushing the daffodils of the meadow, her arms full of red and pink tulips. She would call and wave and hold her hat to stop it flying away in the breeze. He was four and the sun was shining brightly.

He would look up at Sophie, pretty Sophie his nurse, with her cupid's bow mouth and happy eyes and fair curls, smiling down at him indulgently. His mother would turn to her and load her arms with the flowers and laugh. Sophie would laugh too, a carefree sound from behind the blooms, and then his mother would bend forward, and the rose would fall from her hatband as she leaned down to lift him in her arms. Then he too would laugh and Sophie would pick up the fallen flower in her fine fingers and run, looking back and calling to them joyfully, and the sweet aroma of his mother would envelop him, clean and warm.

Warm? But it was not warm. It was bitterly cold and his feet had gone to sleep. There was a stiffness throughout him. He ached. Every muscle ached. And what was that noise? It sounded like hammering on the wood around him. What was going on? Oh yes, it was rain. Of course. Everything was disoriented. He had not recognised the sound on the wood so close to his ears. It sounded like lead dropping.

Pain seared through him. If only he could lift his arms . . . He felt as if he were suffocating.

How long had he been in here? It must be many hours.

He did not know how much later it was that the water started dripping on his shoulder.

Between decks, some of the convicts, villainous and deceitful though they might be, had voiced their feelings about Alan's ill treatment. They had supported Daniel when he asked repeatedly to see the surgeon-superintendent or his assistant. Hours passed before the prison door finally opened and Daniel's name was called. He followed the guard, who cursed the heavily falling rain, to the assistant surgeon's cabin, aft of the hospital.

The voice within called them to enter as soon as the guard knocked.

Anthony Miller looked up immediately Daniel entered. The cabin was tiny and he sat winding bandages behind a wooden desk that dominated the space. He was overworked and tired and had consented to see this man only out of duty.

'Yes, Dwyer,' he began, 'what is it you have been clamouring about?'

'Alan, sir. Alan Fletcher.'

'Yes?'

Daniel took a deep breath and began speaking. The words tumbled out of him so fast the young man had to make a concentrated effort to follow him.

'Well, sir, at this very moment he's above on deck in the . . . the damnable box. It's been a terrible mistake, a most dreadful miscarriage of justice, it is. He was not in the mutiny. In fact he told them not to be such fools, that it was madness, and now something's gone terrible wrong and he's being punished for something he did not do. It's dishonourable. I'm not the only one saying so, all the prisoners are against it, sir.' His eyes closed in emphasis.

The assistant surgeon was young. He did his job to the best of his ability. He was not used to convict ships and lived in fear of Mr Mocksey. His superior had instilled into him that all convicts were liars, malingerers, toadies, parasites, sycophants and worse. Certainly they would go to any lengths to avoid their own punishment and they would never care about another's. So it surprised Anthony Miller to hear this prisoner speaking in defence of another. This was the second time today, Samuel Cooper having done the same thing for the same man. He had listened to his superior pass judgment on Alan Fletcher and he had flinched at the time, for it had appeared obvious to him that Boucher and Talbot lied.

'He was not in the mutiny in any way, you say?'

'He was not, sir.'

'And there are others in the hold that agree with this?'

Daniel nodded his head vehemently. 'Yes. You can ask them.'

The assistant surgeon looked grave and scratched his chin. He stood up. 'I'll see what I can do.'

'Why, thank you, sir. Thank you so very much.'

When Anthony Miller came to the surgeon-superintendent, he was cursorily dealt with.

'I am surgeon-superintendent of this ship, Mr assistant surgeon, and I do not value your opinion in this matter. I am satisfied that Fletcher was one of them. There was evidence enough. Methinks you have been fooled by the scum in the hold. That is my last word on it.'

Anthony Miller returned to his duties. In his mind lurked the uneasy feeling that Fletcher's manner had not pleased Mr Mocksey and that the man was allowing himself to be vindictive. He thought about going to Master Loney, but he knew it was useless. He was genuinely sorry when he sent for Daniel and told him the matter was out of his hands. His face was troubled.

'I'm sorry, Dwyer, I truly am.'

That night, when the soldiers came to the confinement box amidships at seven o'clock, it had been raining on and off for over three hours.

At first the drips on Alan's shoulder had been bearable, but after the prolonged heavy rain, they became a trickle. Later, there were two running streams, one on his shoulder and another running across his forehead into his eye and down his face. When he moved his head it ran into his ear. Finally, he found that by leaning his head forward on the door, one stream hit the back of his head and ran down his neck and the other fell on his shoulderblade. He continued in this position until his whole body screamed with tension and he was forced to return to his first position.

It was bitterly cold in these latitudes and with the added torture of the rain, he was shivering so much that it racked his entire frame. He shook involuntarily; he had no control. Pain scorched through every limb. For what had seemed like an eternity he had wanted desperately to stretch his arms above his head. But now he could no longer feel his arms. He did not know whether he could feel his legs or not.

This was only the first day. He would not be able to face it for a protracted period. No one could.

Courage! Nothing lasts forever! If only the mind could leave the body. But it could not and the cold and wet forced itself into every corner of his brain.

They had forgotten him . . . God . . . they were going to leave him here. He felt himself slipping . . . slipping into unconsciousness. His body crumpled, as much as the restricted space allowed. There was more agony coming from somewhere. He thought it must be from his knees.

The horror continued relentlessly.

At first Alan thought he was hallucinating when the blackness in front of his eyes turned red. Then, slowly, he focused and his mind recognised the red coats of the soldiers in the lantern light. What was that behind them? Something white. Yes, a white face, with concerned eyes. Who was that? The numbness that was his mind finally identified the assistant surgeon.

'Come on, lad,' said the same corporal who had put him in six hours before, 'Mr Miller 'ere wants you taken straight to the 'orspital.'

He tried to step forward but instead he fell out of the box towards them. They caught him before he hit the deck.

An hour later, Alan lay sleeping on a cot in the hospital. Anthony Miller had admitted him. His soaking clothing had been removed and replaced with dry ones. He had been put to bed and fed warm broth.

When they brought Alan in, Lawless was being removed from the hospital back to the hold. Shocked at the sight of Alan, he cried, 'Guv'nor! What have they done to ye?'

'Don't worry,' Anthony Miller replied. 'I'll take care of him.' And he had done so. He spent much of the night beside Alan.

At eight o'clock the next morning, two guards came to the hospital. The assistant surgeon was about to go off duty and was ministering to one of the prisoners who had been badly wounded in the uprising. As the soldiers entered the door, he turned towards them questioningly.

'We've come for Fletcher, sir. He's to be returned to the fo'c'sle and to be placed in the box again this afternoon at one o'clock sharp.'

'But I object most strongly, the man is in my care. Has this order come from Mr Mocksey?'

'Yes, sir, none other.'

Miller looked across at Alan who lay with his eyes closed. Then he shook his head. He was worried and unsure. 'This . . . this is not right. It is inhuman. The temperatures are falling all the time. I will go to Mr Mocksey. You soldiers do nothing until I return. Leave Fletcher where he is.'

When he found Mr Mocksey, he was on deck measuring out lemon juice from a large cask. His solid back was bent forward to three crew members. It was not raining but there was a cold wind blowing again and the rain clouds were still in evidence, hanging threateningly above the ship.

Fear rose in the young man and his heart raced as he came up behind the man booming instructions. He took a deep breath and spoke quietly. 'Excuse me, Mr Mocksey, but I need a word with you, now please. Urgently.'

The man stood up and turned in a slow and measured movement. He did not like to be interrupted in the middle of any of his procedures and his voice became heavy with sarcasm. 'Oh, so it's a word you need, is it? And urgent at that! Well, well.'

'Yes, sir, it's important.'

'It can wait until I finish here,' he snapped, turning back to the cask.

Then the young man amazed himself as he heard his voice saying, 'No, sir, Mr Mocksey, it cannot wait. I . . . I demand to speak with you now!'

The surgeon looked up quickly. This was not like Miller. He handed the nearest crew member the measuring spoon and beckoning his assistant, walked to the starboard side of the deck where he stood feet apart and hand on hip in indignation. 'What the hell do you mean by "demanding" to speak with me?'

The earnest eyes looked back at him. 'I need to speak with you about Alan Fletcher.'

'What about him?'

'Two guards came to the hospital not five minutes ago to return him to the forecastle. They say that at one o'clock he is to be placed again in the confinement box. They say it's on your orders.'

'So?'

Anthony Miller's hands were sweating even in the chill wind. He put them behind his back and held them together tightly as he went on, 'The man was in that thing in freezing temperatures and heavy rain hour after hour. He was totally drenched, the damn thing leaks. His legs and arms were numb, he could not walk. His knees were bruised. It's a wonder he's not delirious or dreadfully ill with pneumonia. I must formally object to his being placed in it again . . . at least until we are in warmer waters.'

Mocksey stiffened. 'Is Fletcher ill?'

'Yes. He's not well enough to g . . . go back in that thing.' He pointed towards midships where the stark construction stood.

The superior's eyes grew hard. 'Does he have pneumonia?'

'I . . . I don't know. I don't think so. But he is sick.'

'There's many a sick man has taken his punishment before today.'

The young man took another deep breath and summoned up all his courage. 'But you are supposed to be on board this ship to help keep the prisoners well, not to inflict them with punitive measures that could jeopardise their lives!'

For a second or two, the commander looked as if he were going to lash out and strike the face in front of him. His lips twitched and the veins in his neck swelled. With obvious control he answered, 'Are you daring to suggest I am not carrying out my duty in a responsible manner?'

Once more Anthony Miller found himself saying words that astonished him. Later, in the privacy of his cabin, he would find difficulty believing he had actually said them. 'No, Mr Mocksey, I'm not. I think that in the majority of your work you are, at the least, capable. It is only where this one man is concerned that you have lost your sense of proportion. I think . . . You seem to have a vendetta with him.'

The surgeon-superintendent pulled himself up to his full height, which was a little taller than his young assistant's. 'The punishment of convicts on board this vessel is my responsibility. *My* responsibility, do you hear? Fletcher was found guilty. There was enough evidence for me. He will continue in the box for six hours each day no matter whether this blasted ship freezes over or sinks from rain water. Do you understand, boy?'

The young man braced himself. There was rage now, too, in Anthony Miller as he countered, 'The maximum time in the box is supposed to be four hours!'

'That is in the tropics, Miller, don't try to teach me the rules!'

'But this freezing cold and damp is just as bad as heat – worse! He may die, and . . . and you will be responsible!' rose the young man's voice.

The older man was livid. His face had turned a purplish colour.

For some seconds they stared at each other, while the surgeon reached a decision. If Fletcher did die in the box, there could be an inquiry. Perhaps he should be careful. Especially as this young idiot had decided to fight his cause.

'All right,' he said. 'If you want to mollycoddle the prisoner and take him to the hospital each night after his punishment, then that is your affair. I will not hinder you. But he will do his days in the box as I see fit. I am in authority here and will not speak about this again. Return to your duties.' He turned his back on Anthony Miller and walked away.

For longer than a minute the assistant surgeon remained rigidly at the bulwark. His hands shook nervously and he was damp with perspiration but he felt a strength he had never known before. He had fought as well as he knew how. He had not stopped the vile torture, but what he had gained was the chance to keep Alan Fletcher alive. He would do his utmost for that.

For twelve days Mr Mocksey continued the horror of the box for Alan. Some days there was only the freezing wind; on others there was sleet and rain. And always, relentlessly, there was the wood bearing down on him, confining him in the horrible phobia-making darkness where the searing pain continued. Yet after this hell, always came the respite when Anthony Miller would tend him caringly, like a brother. Night after night Miller would dry him, put him to bed, comb his hair, speak softly to him, and feed him when Alan's hands were deadened by the cold. The young man even made him a leather cape which Alan wore in the box as a defence against the icy, wet, interminable days.

On the eleventh and twelfth days, Alan was delirious. He remembered nothing of the box or of the interval in the assistant surgeon's care. It was not until he opened his eyes in the hospital cot on the fifteenth day after the ordeal had begun that he grasped the fact he had indeed done twelve days in the box. On the twenty-third day from when his days of torture began, he was returned to the forecastle where he remained ironed for the rest of the journey.

Anthony Miller put out his hand to Alan as he left the hospital. 'You have a magnificent constitution. I don't know how you survived, but thank God you did.'

Alan took the younger man's hand and smiled. 'I survived because of you. You alone are the reason. You are an honourable and benevolent man, Mr Miller, and I thank you.'

The ship was already in warmer waters and the weather more equable. Soon the temperatures climbed from the forties to the fifties and the sixties. The ship's carpenter erected three more boxes, and as their wounds were now healed, Samuel Cooper, Boucher, Talbot and Keating did their time. They spent seven days in the boxes, six hours a day.

On the fifth day, Boucher screamed so loudly the whole ship could hear, and Keating took up his call. On the sixth day Boucher raged again, seeming to have taken leave of his senses. After his confinement, Anthony Miller took him to the hospital where he had convulsions.

On the seventh day, as the guards went to back him into the box, he became quite deranged. He smashed one guard in the face in frenzy and pushed the other to the deck. While the stunned onlookers watched, he pulled himself up over the bulwark and leapt overboard. The astounded soldiers rushed to the side only to see his white face upturned in supplication, the eyes wide at last in death as he sank beneath the waves.

When the ship reached Sydney, the capital of New South Wales, one hundred and fifty-four days after departing Spithead, it was late October 1849. The *Mount Stewart Elphinstone* was not allowed to land its prisoners. For the previous decade, there had been open discontent in the colony over the sending of any more felons out from the United Kingdom. Petitions against the system had been repeatedly sent to Earl Henry Grey, the secretary for the Colonies in England. While much of the local born population had one and often two convict parents, they did not wish to be reminded of their beginnings and wanted to rid themselves of the stigma associated with the convict ethos.

Hence, no one was allowed ashore from the *Mount Stewart Elphinstone* except for two prisoners bound for Hobart. The ship rode at anchor for a week while the politicians argued. Finally, it was decided to send it on to the settlement at Moreton Bay, five hundred miles to the north, where labour was in short supply.

Of the two hundred and thirty-two men embarked in the United Kingdom, two hundred and twenty-six disembarked at Moreton Bay. Only six were missing: the two sent to Hobart, the two shot in the mutiny, the one who had died during the hurricane, and Boucher who had committed suicide.

Mr Loney and Mr Mocksey were commended for bringing so many prisoners through alive.

CHAPTER FOUR

'What are the wild waves saying,
Sister, the whole day long?'
'What Are the Wild Waves Saying',
Joseph Edwards Carpenter, 1813–1885.

Over three years later. February 1853.
Sydney town.

Sydney Harbour's two hundred and sixty miles of shoreline basked
in the glaring sunlight, the headlands, reaches, coves, bays and creeks
illuminated by that stark bright iridescence found only in the great
south lands.

On the decks of the two ships sailing between the north and south
headlands, the eager eyes of those on board looked left and right.
The harbour they had entered could only be called magnificent – the
combined fleets of the world, naval and mercantile, could anchor
here – and when they caught their first glimpse of Sydney town
across spits of sandstone and scrubby trees, seemingly surrounded by
windmills, it brought a smile to their faces.

Closer still, halfway up the waters of Port Jackson, the town was
the illusion of elegance and fine buildings. But as they drew nearer
and began to define what the eye before had run together, they were
not so convinced of its beauty; and by the time they had arrived at
Circular Wharf, the encrustation of swiftly built dwellings along the
sea front, the narrow unpaved streets, and the blight of the rookeries
of the Rocks were all too apparent.

The settlement was a haphazard affair, but it was not without
grand edifices of durable red and grey sandstone, a prophecy of the
future, rising from the tumbledown buildings around them. Government House was a substantial monument for Her Majesty's representative, and there were others imposing enough: the Customs' House,
the Supreme Court, the Legislative Council building and the Australian Library in Macquarie Street. Further west, the best hotel, the
Royal, with its portico supported by wide Doric columns, invited
the affluent traveller to enter. Yet the most impressive buildings were

the churches: St Andrew's and St Mary's Cathedrals and the Churches of St James and St Phillip, all indicative of the conscientious and pious esteem in which the colonists held their God. Neither were the outer districts without occasional grandeur. The colony's wealthy had resided there for decades. The hoi polloi for miles around knew the mansions of the Wentworths at Vaucluse, the Macleays at Elizabeth Bay and the Macarthurs out at Camden.

Sydney town itself was vastly overcrowded. The gold that had been discovered at Summerfield Creek exactly two years before had been responsible for the now extending conglomerate of men of all races and creeds who had descended from ships, sanguine in the belief that they were the chosen of the gold rush. Some had come directly from San Francisco after they had been disappointed on the California goldfields.

One man had started from San Francisco the previous June of 1852, not because he had not done well in California, but he needed to move on after his darlin' wife died in April. They had been in California for just three years. He had been inconsolable at her loss, for she had been the keystone of his life.

For forty consecutive days, Phillip Herman had sat alone beside Ada's burial place, often four and five hours at a time. He pictured her beautiful eyes with the curling lashes, and her long dark hair moulded round her curving shoulders. He heard her voice and remembered the thrill of her touch. He ached with a terrible grief.

On the forty-first day he had come to the grave site on the hill overlooking San Francisco's wide harbour as the seagulls made their final sweep overhead in the summer evening. 'Adee, darlin',' he said softly, holding his hands prayer-like in front of him. 'I've made another big decision without consulting you.' He gave a wan smile and knelt down. 'This morning I went to the shipping agents, you know, Haddy and Row, near the claims office. Well, darlin', the upshot is, I have booked passage for Eve and Clare and myself down to the British colony of New South Wales in the South Pacific Ocean. You know, where the gold was discovered last year.'

He bent forward to touch the earth as he continued speaking. 'Ada, I know what you're thinking, and yes, I have a thriving business, but San Francisco is desolate without you, darlin'. Down there, I'll supply those off to the diggings again. We know that works, don't we, love? They say Sydney town is quite sophisticated, not like this place, and now that the girls are teenage . . . Ah, Adee, truth is, I cannot abide it here without you and this way I can try to start anew. I must, for Eve and Clare. You do understand, don't you, Adee love?'

And so, forty-nine days after Ada's death, Phillip and his daughters had caught the clipper *Fair Wind* and sailed past the very promontory where she lay in her resting place on the hillside.

Two days out of Honolulu, Phillip had fallen ill. With the aid of the ship's doctor, his daughters nursed him. But he steadily worsened, and in the grey light of a cold wet morning, at latitude fifteen degrees and longitude one hundred and sixty-three, he joined his darlin' Ada. His illness had not been diagnosed.

The *Fair Wind* sailed on and carried the two sisters across the wide Pacific Ocean to deposit them upon the dock at Sydney Cove on the bleak, southern winter day of 31 July.

The few friends they had made on the voyage soon dispersed, and the woebegone sisters found that the cold weather echoed their reception in the unfamiliar colony. Within a week, they had been duped out of their father's savings by a local swindler and were alone and friendless. But they had each other, and the will to survive is paramount, especially in the young.

The miserable and destitute of Sydney town gravitated to the Rocks, the oldest area, not only of the colony but of the country. Here many houses and cottages from early in the century still stood in partially formed lines along the terraces of stone. It was a jumble of lanes, byways and steep passages, home to vagrants, maritime deserters, the disillusioned of the gold rush, and all forms of criminals, both petty and major. The despairing sisters soon found their way to this part of the town.

Wandering the alleyways they had been noticed by Mrs Maggs, a long-time inhabitant of the area who ran the Ship Inn, a tavern of more than dubious reputation which backed onto the harbour near Dawes Point round from the battery. The old woman had been quick to see that the two pretty teenage girls would enhance business for very little outlay. Thus, in return for lodgings and sixpence between them a week, they had been 'taken in' by Mrs Maggs and her husband. Assigned servants were paid more, but Eve's and Clare's position was such they did not have even the bargaining power of an ex-convict.

The girls lived in a room at the back of the tavern, their single window opening out onto the waters of the harbour. They were called 'serving girls', although a better description would have been 'cleaners-cooks-barmaids-servants'. Each day they worked from the hour of ten in the morning until the inn closed, which was often two o'clock the next morning.

They had been half a year under the subjection of the Maggses when February 1853 discharged its heat and humidity upon the population. In that time they had experienced enough to change them from the simple and artless teenagers who had disembarked from the *Fair Wind* and quickly lost their money to the first cheat who came along. They had not deteriorated into the scheming, insincere, and artful, whom they were forced daily to wait upon, but had they been landing on the Circular Quay today, they would have been more shrewd.

Every Monday, Eve was sent by Mrs Maggs to pick up her weekly parcel of tobacco, while Clare took a delivery of rum in another direction.

'And don't take all day in gettin' there and back. Methinks you regard it as a flamin' bloody holiday, dawdling along.'

'I don't dawdle,' Eve answered, dodging a badly aimed cuff at her head as she scurried past the old woman.

'And don't back-answer me,' the old woman shouted after her as she left the tavern. 'Flamin' bloody cheek!'

Eve smiled as she gained the street. It was such a pleasure to be out in the open air. She had removed her apron and donned a calico bonnet to protect her face from the sun. How she looked forward to this respite away from the chores of the tavern and the demands of the 'Maggots', as she and Clare had soon dubbed the tavern owners. She had to traverse the entire length of George Street, for Mrs Maggs was not one to forego a bargain, and the cheapest tobacco in the town was to be had from a Chinese store in a lane at the side of the Hay Market, about a mile and a half from the Ship Inn.

Eve's was a swift walk, and already at only sixteen it was a smooth, almost stately movement. She held her head high, her blonde curls peeping from under her bonnet, and even though her dress was worn in places, her natural vivacity and youthful charm gave her a dignity that overcame her poor appearance. She drew second glances from many of the habitués of the Sydney streets.

As she turned into George Street, she halted. Her way was barred by a tall ex-sailor called Grayson, a deserter from an American clipper ship and a frequent customer at the Ship Inn. He often joked how he was cousin to Eve and Clare because of his Boston origins. He was the lover of Lucy, the barmaid, but recently had turned his attentions to Eve and Clare. Eve had deflected his advances, having become quite adept at this skill, but Clare was attracted to him and had responded. She and Grayson had left the tavern together on more than one occasion and Clare had not returned until the following morning. It had caused more than one row between the two sisters.

Now Grayson bent into Eve's face, smiling broadly. 'Hey, is that you, Eve, under there?'

'Yes. Hello, Grayson.'

'Wasn't sure for a moment,' he replied. 'How are you?'

'Well, thank you,' she responded as she went to pass by.

'What's the hurry?'

'I'm going for Mrs Maggs' tobacco. You know what she's like. I can't stand here talking.'

'Now wait a bit,' he answered, taking her arm. 'Come in here to Stanley's and have a quick drink.' His hand went skilfully from her arm to her waist and he moved her sideways into the darkened entry of Stanley's Pub.

'Grayson, I can't.'

'A few minutes won't hurt,' he said pushing her gently up against the stone wall of the passage and putting his arms to either side of her body, effectively pinioning her against the wall. He bent down to her. He was a handsome man in his mid-twenties. His face was smooth, a healthy brown from the sun, his eyes were the colour of the sky, and his mouth could have been chiselled by Michaelangelo. He was looking into her eyes and smiling.

For a moment, her alert, brown eyes returned his look. Then she startled him. 'Where the devil did you take my sister again on Saturday night?' She pushed him sharply so that his head jerked back abruptly. 'I know what you're up to, Grayson. You stay away from her, damn it! Poor Lucy knows nothing of it for a start! Men like you think you can treat girls like rubbish, like playthings, then discard them. Well, there'll be a change one day and the likes of you won't get away with it. So leave Clare alone. And leave me alone!' she finished, throwing off his arms and moving out of the stone entry.

Grayson watched her go, a dubious look on his agreeable face, then he burst out laughing, shook his head and turned back into Stanley's Pub.

Eve's walk became quite spirited as she crossed the street to continue along past the three-foot-high stone wall surrounding the cove and the ships berthed on her left. She was unaware of the urchins playing around the piles of cannon balls stacked at intervals along the sea front, and totally ignored the fish seller who lifted a whiting from his cart to dangle it for her inspection.

She was thinking about Grayson, handsome dog that he was. Lord above, did he want all the girls in Sydney town? That was the trouble, poor girls were at the mercy of men like Grayson. How very angry she had been with Clare when she had finally returned home on Sunday morning. Why couldn't she see the sort of man he was? And it wasn't the first time. Eve knew her sister had done it before, with other men. No proper man would ever look at her if she continued this way. How could Clare, who was so like her in so many ways, be this different?

And poor Lucy, she was in love with Grayson. She already had a child by some cove who had run out on her. What sort of life was that? Eve knew Clare had no intention of hurting Lucy. Clare never really wanted to hurt anyone; she just didn't think at times. These days her way of enjoying life was to love and be loved by handsome men and Grayson certainly fell into that category.

Eve's perfect brow puckered determinedly. That was one thing that was not going to happen to Evelyn May Herman. She did not know how she was going to achieve it, but she would lift herself up out of this mess no matter what! She felt sure she was capable of getting somewhere in this life if she could make the chance. She was not afraid of work. Her chin lifted determinedly as she walked along. She was never going to debase herself into a life like that of the Maggots and their kind; it was the one thing she promised herself.

If only she could get some money. If only.

She had heard this very morning that Sully Tomkins in Hunter Street was looking for someone to lease his shed. It had small living quarters at the back and he wanted four shillings a week for it. The news had sent a thrill down Eve's spine. If only she could get some money, oh how much she would like to rent that shed.

She had something that she doubted anyone else in the whole of New South Wales had. Something that could earn her a lot of money, enable her and Clare to live properly, respectably. It had been left at the Ship Inn by an American man off to the goldfields. 'You keep this,' he had said to Eve, 'it's too damn cumbersome. Don't know why I brought it with me.' When Mrs Maggs had taken no interest, simply calling it a 'new-fangled thing', Eve had removed the object and put it by her bed. She had been studying it in the privacy of their little room, studying and using it and learning all about it.

The 'new-fangled thing' was a machine. There was a needle with an eye near the point which contained a thread. You placed a piece of cloth in it and there was a sort of shuttle which carried another thread below the cloth on a small reel. The needle was fastened to an arm that vibrated on a pivot. Movement of the arm by a wheel forced the needle through the cloth. The shuttle carried the under thread through the loop of the upper thread, thus making a locked stitch. The machine had come with a tin full of various fitting parts and numerous special needles. On the tin was the name Elias Howe and a New York address. With it Eve could sew very much faster than the most skilful seamstress ever could.

She had enterprising ideas. There were so many folk in Sydney who needed things mended and sewn. If only she could find money to rent Sully Tomkins' shed, she and Clare would be able to free themselves from the Maggots and make a good life together, not one where you were fearful a drunken sailor would knock down your door.

The dream was running through her mind as she hurried on between the lofty houses decorating either side of this part of George Street. Eve had become accustomed to Sydney; it wasn't such a bad place. She had seen many worse, like the ramshackle, awful villages in the West Indies and South America where the *Ipswich* had anchored on its way to California. Yet in her heart she longed to be away from Sydney, out in the country somewhere. Perhaps one day they would be, if only they could make some money of their own. She was still deep in her meditations when she passed the old barrack square and the banking houses and merchants' offices. It was not until she reached Hastey's, one of the many auction rooms in George Street, that she came out of her reverie. It was open to the street and she could hear old Hastey. 'Going . . . going . . . gone!'

She did not stop now, for this was her 'return treat' as she called it. She would stop on the way back and listen for a few minutes to the odd and often remarkable things that Hastey auctioned.

Soon she came to the Post Office with its line of billboards across the footpath announcing the WANTED of the colony. Some of their crimes were truly awful and some appeared so trivial it seemed ridiculous to her that they were all listed side by side.

The next landmark was the formidable Royal Hotel with its solid Doric columns. Eve stopped to let two people enter by the many-coloured glass door. She looked in after them. She had never been inside, though sometimes she dreamed of doing so. She sighed and moved on to the large covered-in marketplace a few paces away. It was abounding with salesmen and their wares, a meeting spot for Sydney-siders from dawn until midnight, full of carts and cabs and omnibuses and private vehicles, both splendid and simple.

After passing the market, she invariably quickened her pace, for next came the police office and there was always at least one poor devil manacled in the stocks outside. Today there were two. A shiver ran through her, for while she tried not to look at them, she could not help it. They were covered in flies and looked half dead. She ran by.

By the time she reached St Andrew's Cathedral which sat sedately in its sward of green, her pace had slowed in the debilitating heat. Then it was downhill for a quarter of a mile past rows of two- and three-storeyed houses until she came at last to the Hay Market at the

foot of Brickfield Hill. She made her way through the centre of the
business area past the turret clock and then into the back lane at the
side of the market.

'Hello, Mr Ling.'

'Herro, Eve.'

'I've come for the tobacco.'

He took the pouch Eve had brought and moved to the back of his
shop in the short trotting steps of the Oriental.

Eve waited, passing among the large cubical tea chests lined with
sheet lead and full of tea leaves. Some of them had quaint Chinese
characters written on them. Here she lingered, dipping in her hands
and lifting fistfuls of the wonderfully aromatic tea leaves to smell.

On her return journey she walked swiftly until she came back to
Hastey's Auction Room. There was an auction in progress and old
Hastey was still shouting to those gathered around him. He stood
behind a high horseshoe desk, his gavel in his hand. His beard was
so long it almost reached his waist. Eve often wondered why he
bothered to wear the neat bow tied at his throat, for it could only be
seen from the side.

The people spilled out onto the street for the room was quite full.
Eve edged her way through those standing to get a better view. At
the front were four rows of wooden forms filled with potential buyers.
Today, Hastey's wife was here. She only helped when they had a
large auction with numerous lots. Her name was Doreen. Everyone
knew her name because he would always turn to her and ask, 'And
what is next for these lucky folk, Doreen, my sweet?' She was a fine-
looking woman, long and slender, with straight golden hair pulled
into a topknot, and she was presently holding a gilded cage with two
yellow canaries inside.

'I have heard one and tuppence for this fine cage and grand specimens of bird life, do I hear more?' Hastey was saying. 'My fellow
travellers, these birds are direct descendants of a pair owned by the
Queen of Tonga herself! Why, the cage alone is worth one and
tuppence!'

There were no more bids. Hastey looked disappointed as he
knocked down the canaries to a lady in the front row.

The next lot was a hundred and fifty dozen kangaroo skins.

'Now, my friends, my fellow travellers, here is a sample of the
superb kangaroo skins on offer today. Hold it up, Doreen, my sweet.'

Eve had gradually forced her way forward until she was now at
the front of those people who were standing, and right next to the
table where Hastey's assistant stood with the items yet to come up
for bids. This was what fascinated her most, the divers things for

sale. She took delight in wondering from what faraway place they had come and how they had arrived here, who had owned or made them. She conjured up stories about the ones that appealed to her and her eyes sparkled with the fantasies that filled her mind. It lifted her up out of the grime and poverty of Sydney town and for a few minutes she was simply a teenage girl in reverie.

The auction had been on for some time, but there were a number of lots remaining. A large, ornate harpsichord was set near two bales of calico. There were four ivory-handled hammers, a box of cutlery, an anchor and a chain, six down pillows, a leatherbound dictionary, some baby linen, a water colour of a horse, a sign which said 'Lansdown Station, in the district of Moreton Bay, 8,000 sheep', and closest to her was the thing that brought a wistful smile to her face – a string of pearls with a diamond clasp, and a matching brooch. They lay in a red velvet box gleaming up at her. Her mother used to have a set of pearls. They were so lovely. Whatever had become of them? How she missed her mother and father, and often felt lonely, especially now that Clare spent so much time with men.

Hastey was calling loudly to his audience about the next item and Eve heard him say, 'I start the bidding at ten sovereigns! Do I hear ten?'

Someone began the bidding.

Ten sovereigns Eve thought. Fancy having ten whole sovereigns. A fortune. If only she had ten sovereigns she could rent Sully Tomkins' shed, begin her sewing business and transform her and her sister's life. Well, eight sovereigns, even five would do.

The bidding continued.

She looked down at the jewels, so clean, pure, lustrous.

The bidding ended. The item was sold.

The pearls were so beautiful. She put out her hand and with the tip of a finger touched them.

Suddenly her wrist was in a vice-like grip, and Hastey's assistant was shouting. 'So we have a would-be thief in our midst, do we?'

Eve looked up to him in surprise. 'But I wasn't—'

'Wasn't my eye! You thought no one was looking.'

Doreen and Hastey turned to the noise, as did everyone in the room.

Eve threw off the man's hand. 'I was only touching them. My mother used to have some.'

This brought gales of laughter. A thin girl in a cheap, calico bonnet and threadbare dress, wearing shoes that had seen better times and carrying a tobacco pouch had a mother who wore pearls and diamonds!

Hastey's assistant grabbed her again and dragged her roughly forward. 'Tell it to the police. Come on.'

'No, damn it, leave me alone! I was only looking at them.' Eve was pulling away but the man held her fast.

'You thieves are all alike. You can explain it to the police.'

Just then, someone spoke. He was a clergyman, in reverse collar and black frock coat. He held his hat in his hand and his thick dark hair was only faintly streaked with grey at his temples, although he was in his sixtieth year. He had been standing beside Eve.

'Stop it! This child is with me.'

Hastey's assistant raised his eyebrows. 'Oh, I see, Reverend, really? With you, is she? Then all I can say is you should spend a touch more money on outfitting your daughter.'

More tittering and laughter sounded.

The cleric had the intense eyes of a zealot, yet he was in fact a moderate and temperate priest; they rested now with all their force on Hastey's assistant. 'You merely show your stupidity. I did not say she was my daughter, what I did say is that she is with me. She wished only to touch the pearls. I saw many women handling them before the auction began. If you do not want your goods touched during the auction, there should be a sign to say so.' He took Eve's arm. 'Come away from here.'

The assistant reluctantly released her, and they made their way through the crowd to the street.

Eve could not believe what had happened. This minister had saved her from being taken to that awful police office; the touch of his hand made her feel suddenly quite happy, somehow warmed, with a sense of well-being.

He smiled down at her, and to Eve's surprise his eyes seemed to soften. She responded with a smile of her own. 'I don't know how to thank you, sir. They would not have believed me.'

'Perhaps not, young lady, but for my part I think your honesty shows in your face.'

Eve was very moved by his words. 'Oh, sir, thank you. I was brought up to be truthful and never to covet things, sir. I do truly thank you for recognising it.'

The Reverend could not help smiling to himself. She was certainly forthright. He felt quite drawn to her. 'I should stay away from this auction room for a time,' he suggested.

She nodded.

'Do you live near here?'

This reminded her. She must leave. She had been gone long enough. Mrs Maggot would be waiting.

'Yes, I do. Not far away. But I must go, I am very late, sir. I have been on an errand and am very late.'

'What accent is that?'

'I am from America, sir.'

'America? How is it, child, that you are here in Sydney?'

'We came last year. Oh sir, I really am truly grateful for what you did just now, but I must go. Thank you again. Goodbye, sir.'

The minister's eyes were still upon her as she turned and moved quickly away through the people in the street. He shook his head. There were dozens of waifs like her in Sydney town, but this child had appealed to him, and now he realised why. She reminded him of his darling Josephine. Yes, the shape of her brow and the earnest round, brown eyes beneath, even her smile of gratitude reminded him of his sweet sister. Josephine had been a similar age to this girl when she died. He took a deep breath, shaking his head sadly in remembrance, and walked away.

Eve was so concerned with the hour, she really hurried now, breaking into a run by the time she reached the deserted barrack square. It was well after four o'clock when she passed the battery of cannon facing out across the water at Dawes Point, and she accelerated for the final hundred yards. Mrs Maggs was sitting on her stool beside the swing doors of the tavern, holding her empty pipe in her hand and tapping impatiently with her wooden clogs on the worn stone doorstep.

'Where the bloody hell have you been, gel? Me tongue's hangin' out for me pipe and ye dawdlin' along as if it were a month of Sundays.'

'You saw me running, damn it,' Eve replied.

'Ah ha! I wasn't born yesterday, me. Sure, ye run the last few bloody yards when I can see ye.'

Eve handed her the pouch of tobacco and the woman called 'Sly wench!' to her retreating back, then abruptly forgot her annoyance in the prospect of a puff on her pipe.

That night, Grayson came to the tavern around eleven o'clock. Eve watched him; when he was not making eyes at Lucy he was making eyes at Clare, and for fifteen minutes around midnight he and Clare were both missing. Lucy did not notice and Eve did not mention it. When the tavern closed just before two in the morning, he left in company with Lucy.

'Why are you friendly with Grayson?' Eve asked her sister when they were at last in bed.

'Why not?' answered Clare.

'You know why not. It's not proper.'

'Don't be such a prig, Eve. He's so handsome, and quite a gentle-man, really when you get to know him.'

'But what about Lucy? She's in love with him.'

Clare's voice dropped with guilt. 'Yes, I suppose she is, but I think I am too.'

Eve half rose and leaned on her elbow to face Clare. She could make out her sister's dark form in the cot opposite, below the barrels of rum that were stacked against the wall. Eve was not at all sure Clare was in love. She seemed to be in love every few months. It disconcerted her that her sister was so changed since they had arrived in Sydney. 'I know he's handsome but I think you're a damn fool to be involved with him at all. I don't think he loves anyone but himself.'

Her sister's voice took on an exasperated note. 'Oh, for heaven's sake, Eve, I can't explain it to you. If you haven't experienced what it's like being with a man, then it's like talking to a child.'

Eve knew she was not worldly like Clare, but she did not want to be. When she spoke now her voice held an edge of exasperation. 'Why do you do that thing with him? He's only taking advantage of you, can't you see that?'

Clare sprang to his defence. 'No, he's not. You just don't under-stand.' Then her voice dropped to a confidential tone. 'Evelyn, he makes me feel wonderful all over. I've never felt as good as I do with him, and do you know what?'

'What?'

'He's going to buy me that dress in Penny's Store up by the Quay.' Her voice lifted with excitement. 'You know, that lovely one, all red satin with lace and pearl buttons. How I do yearn for it. I haven't had a new dress for so long, and it's so beautiful, isn't it?'

'Yes, it is. But I still think it's wrong.'

'Why?'

'Oh hell, Clare, Lucy thinks Grayson is serious about her. She'll be heartbroken.' Her sister was silent for such an extended time that Eve spoke again. 'Well?'

Clare sighed sadly. 'I do feel awful about Lucy. I don't want to hurt her, honestly, but Grayson swears it's never been serious with her, that Lucy's known all along he didn't intend to stay with her; so, it's not my fault.' Then her voice became intimate. 'Eve, he says he's never been with a girl who has a body as beautiful as mine.'

'Do you really believe that?'

'Yes, of course. He wouldn't lie to me.'

Eve could feel her eyes filling with tears of frustration. She was angry with Clare, angry with Grayson, angry with the way their lives were. 'What would Mummy and Daddy think?' she demanded. 'They would be ashamed of you.'

Her sister fell quiet again. The only sound was the constant lapping of the water below their window. Then she whispered, 'Don't be angry, darling. It's pointless to wonder what they would think.'

Eve turned to face the wall. She was at a loss to continue this conversation. More and more she did not understand Clare. She was trying not to feel lonely and frightened. 'How I wish we could get away from this place,' she said, 'build ourselves a proper, respectable life. Be like we used to be, happy and free of worry. Oh, how I do wish that.'

The next morning dawned ever bright and hot.

Eve and Clare were sweeping the stone corridor that led to a grassy yard at the side of the inn where horses were tethered when Mr Maggs came out of the taproom. He was a big man and almost filled the corridor as he came by. He squeezed Clare's bottom in an intimate manner as he moved past.

'Men,' she laughed, stopping work to lean on her broom. 'They all think about one thing.'

'Because you let them, for Heaven's sake,' Eve retorted.

'Well, in this very mess of a world, we might as well have fun with them.'

Eve shook her head. 'Oh Clare, don't say that. What about Daddy? He wasn't like these men. And Grandpa? Can't you remember?'

Clare shook her head sadly. 'They're dead. Dead men don't count.'

Now Eve stopped sweeping and placed her broom against the wall. 'I hate the way you're so changed.'

Clare moved to her and took up her hands. 'No, darling, I've grown up, that's all.' Then she hugged Eve tightly. 'And you will too one day.'

Eve sighed. She did love her sister, even though she could not accept what she was doing. She tilted her chin. 'No, Clare, I don't want to be like you. You place no value on yourself and that's an awful mistake.'

Clare turned sharply away and Eve realised she had hurt her. She moved closer and smoothed Clare's hair affectionately. 'I'm sorry, but I wish you would listen to me.'

Suddenly, shouts sounded from the street and were answered in the taproom. 'Hey, come and look, ye all! Old Sam Wright's boat has been hit by a ferry and there's someone swimming for his life in the harbour!'

Sam Wright was an ex-convict who had died a few months before and the rumour was that he had been worth a million guineas sterling, but he had left only the house he lived in to his wife and his old fishing boat to his son. The speculation as to where the rest of his money had gone was still rife in Sydney Town.

The sounds of shouting intensified and people were running into the street. The two sisters ran through the yard to the gathering crowd. People were coming out of houses and lanes and heading west to Walsh Bay at the entrance to Darling Harbour, a short distance away. Even Mrs Maggot had left the tavern and was clopping along around the hill, pipe in hand.

When the sisters reached the bay, men and women were pressing forward over the sea wall to catch a glimpse of a figure swimming a few strokes and then floating, obviously obstructed by his clothing.

'There goes Knobby Jones to save him!'

A boat had pushed out from one of the small docks along the bay and was heading towards the swimmer. The crowd watched, until Knobby Jones picked up the water-logged individual and brought him ashore. 'It's Charlie Wright!'

It wasn't until later that the full story came out. Apparently the boat had not been hit by a ferry but had sprung a leak and sunk swiftly. Charlie Wright was not alone, but had two companions with him. One saved himself by getting to Goat Island which lay a few hundred yards west. The other man could not swim and had drowned.

The crowd began to disperse and Eve looked around for Clare who had been beside her only a few moments earlier. There she was, leaning on a hitching rail, chatting to Grayson. Eve went over. Grayson smiled roguishly at her. She nodded stiffly.

'We had better get back, Clare. The Maggots will be on us otherwise.'

'You go ahead, Eve love. I'll be by in just a minute.'

Eve started back towards Dawes Point, and Grayson took a swift glance after her. Some of the crowd were still milling about in the narrow street where a hot breeze was blowing, lifting a little dust on the unpaved thoroughfare. They had been joined by a few well-dressed people, for this part of Sydney was over the hill from the Rocks and had an occasional better house and a sprinkling of enticing shops. Eve did not get to this section of town very often, even though it was close by. Her errands and her work took her the other way into Sydney proper. She stopped, intrigued by a brightly coloured sign which hung on two chains from an ornamental metal arm. It had an open book painted on it and the words, 'Welcome, All Lovers of the Written Word, William Pell, The Wandering Poet, Seller of Fine Poetry and Books'.

How she missed her own books. How she missed her piano. How she missed the afternoons with her mother when they would read and play piano and sing. She and Clare had begun to learn to play when they were only four. She remembered entering a city contest in Boston when she was ten years old. She had won the pianoforte for children under fourteen and Clare had won the singing. She made a soft, wistful sound and began to peruse the titles of the books stacked in the wooden stands along the front of the shop. Her hand went out to a leather-covered volume of William Wordsworth's works and then she paused as she noticed a man coming out of the shop next door.

It was the clergyman from yesterday's auction. He was taking leave of a gentleman who appeared to be the shop owner. They said their goodbyes, the clergyman tipped his hat and walked towards a cabriolet waiting in the narrow roadway. As he stepped up into the cab, his hand went into the pocket of his frock coat and he took out his handkerchief. As the handkerchief came out, so too did a gold watch and it fell to the ground while he continued into the cab, oblivious.

The vehicle moved.

'Sir! Sir!' Eve called. 'You've dropped your watch.' She ran forward, picked up the timepiece and shouted again. The cab driver heard her and halted.

The minister looked down and a joyful smile spread across his face as he recognised Eve. 'My goodness, it's the young American lady of yesterday!' He opened the door and stepped back down to Eve who handed him his property.

'You dropped it from your pocket, sir.'

'Really? God bless you, thank you, child.'

Eve smiled.

'We didn't get time to introduce ourselves yesterday.' He bowed ever so slightly from the shoulders. 'I am Leslie Billings, of All Saints' Church in Bathurst town, across the Blue Mountains.' He held out his hand and she placed hers in his.

She was experiencing the same happy glow that she had in his company the day before. 'How do you do. I am Eve Herman of the Ship Inn and, as I mentioned yesterday, lately of America, sir.'

'I am truly happy to meet you, child.'

'And I you, though I fear I must go again. I really shouldn't be

76

here, there'll be the devil to pay when I get back. We all came to see poor Charlie Wright swimming from his sunken boat. I . . . must get back to work now.'

'Yes, I too saw the fellow,' the reverend said. 'Lucky to be alive.' Then he took her right hand and placed his watch in her palm. 'You must have it.' He had almost said, 'You must have it, Josephine.' The style of the girl was so like his dead sister, it was disconcerting. 'I insist you have it. Do just as you please with it. It is yours.'

'Oh, I couldn't, sir. It's gold, sir.' She had never held anything more beautiful. It was intricately worked with design and was very heavy. She went to return it to him but he shook his head.

'Yes, it is solid gold, and child it is yours now. You must allow me the pleasure of giving it to you.'

She didn't know what to say. It was like a miracle. 'Oh . . . I . . . it is so beautiful. And after what you did for me yesterday. You are too generous. Thank you so much, sir.'

He simply smiled. It was such a poignant feeling he had about this thin girl with fair curls and brown eyes and smudge of dirt on her cheek. He was quite certain she had that same valiant strength of spirit that his dear sister had possessed.

'This Ship Inn you mentioned. Is it near here?'

'Yes, sir, at Dawes Point. I live there.'

'Do your parents own it?'

She shook her head. 'My parents are dead, sir.'

'I see.'

Leslie Billings was studying her. He suspected she was unhappy at this inn for she had seemed alarmed both times she had mentioned it. He wanted to help her, if he could.

If only he had known her thoughts. How she was longing that this moment could be extended.

'Well, thank you, sir. You are so kind, generous. Thank you again. Goodbye.'

'Goodbye, Miss Herman.' She was reluctant to leave and as she backed away from him he added, 'I leave Sydney tomorrow. If you ever find yourself in Bathurst, do please come and see me and my wife.'

She nodded and turned quickly from him now, for her eyes had filled with tears. She started off at a run along the street. He watched her until she disappeared out of sight.

The tears ran from Eve's eyes as she hurried along. What a kind, lovely, old man . . .

She was put immediately to work on her return, for the tavern was full of seamen, four ships having berthed on the morning tide. She had to wait some hours before she found a minute to take Clare aside into their little room.

'Clare, darling, a miracle has happened.'

Her sister's eyes widened. 'What?'

Eve took the gold watch from her pocket.

'Oh, Evelyn, where did you get it? It looks like solid gold.'

'It is.' She turned it in her hands and opened it and the face had a diamond where the XII, the IX, the VI, and the III would normally be.

'A kind man gave it to me. A minister, from Bathurst, across the Blue Mountains.'

'Oh Lord, Eve, it must be worth ten or fifteen sovereigns at least.'

'Yes.' Eve's face was flushed. Her eyes shone with the light of her dream. Everything was possible now. 'He said for me to do anything I liked with it, and the first chance I have, I shall slip round to Hunter Street to Sully Tomkins.'

'Why?'

'Because we are going to rent his premises and start a business with this.' She turned to pat the sewing machine affectionately. 'We're getting out of this blasted hole. The Maggots can go to flamin' blazes. We're going to have a good, respectable life of our own.'

Within forty-eight hours the sisters were instated in Hunter Street. The following Tuesday a letter came addressed to: 'Miss E. Herman, c/o "The Ship Inn", Dawes Point, Sydney.'

Mrs Maggs took it and opened it. It read:

All Saints' Parsonage
Bathurst.
Fri. 4th February, 1853.

Dear Miss Herman,

Since our two chance meetings in the streets of Sydney this week, I have thought often about you. And in retrospect I am come to the conclusion you are not happy in your present circumstances at 'The Ship Inn'.

Please ignore the rest of this letter if I have misjudged your sentiments.

I do not wish to appear presumptuous, but my wife has encouraged me to write and tell you of a house the church owns here in Bathurst. It is a rambling old building with a number of bedrooms. We have a gentle, motherly, elderly lady, Miss Hopkins, who is in residence here, with five orphan girls, three

78

of whom I would calculate are similar in age to your own.

I have spoken to the church fathers and we would like to offer you and your sister lodgings here with Miss Hopkins. The older girls all have work in the town and do odd jobs for the church and generally take care of the house itself. The younger ones attend our church school. It is a happy and healthy outdoor life they lead.

Once again, I do hope I have not misread your feelings in our two brief meetings.

My wife and I have enclosed a bank note for two pounds which should well cover the cost of transferring yourselves by coach to our small town here on the plain across the mountains.

Yours sincerely,
Leslie Billings.
Rector, All Saints' C of E.

Mrs Maggs' face contorted into a delighted, toothless grin. She shook her pipe gleefully in the air.

'Ah, Lordy me! Easiest two bloody quid I've ever made.'

She tucked the bank note into her voluminous pocket, turned and walked out of the side door of the tavern into the yard, crossed to the water's edge, squashed up the letter into a small ball, and threw it as far as she could into the water of the harbour.

'That'll bloody teach ye to walk out on me, gel!'

Each Christmas a letter addressed to Eve arrived at the Ship Inn. It was from the Reverend and Mrs Billings in Bathurst.

Each year, Mrs Maggs read it and disposed of it in the harbour.

CHAPTER FIVE

'Come, my friends,
'Tis not too late to seek a newer world.'
      'Ulysses', Alfred, Lord Tennyson, 1809–1892.

February, 1853. Moreton Bay.
The same day that Eve met Reverend Billings at Hastey's Auction Rooms.

'All right, you lags! Ten minutes' rest. Bring in the water. Move!'

Alan and Daniel, who had been working side by side, put down their shovels and moved towards the water cart. Daniel's face was very red from the intense heat, and although he was now fifty-eight he worked side by side with the youngest of the convicts. The summer heat took its toll upon him and often after the luncheon or water breaks he was the last to rise to his feet.

This year, the entire Moreton Bay district was stifling, made worse by the bushfires that ringed the settlement. The horizon was lost in smoke clouds and the temperature rose daily to over one hundred degrees. So many of the labourers had fainted that the sergeant in charge begrudgingly agreed to more water breaks and to halt work entirely between noon and two o'clock each day.

The convicts jostled each other in their eagerness for the water.

Alan's hand went round Daniel's shoulder as they joined the line. 'Are you all right, Danny?'

'Yes, son. The summers never seem to improve, do they?'

It had been the same since they had arrived here exactly three years and three months ago. Had they undergone this hell for years? Alan remembered the day they had landed at Moreton Bay. The first of November 1849. They had been greeted in true Australian fashion that day too: searing ninety-four-degree heat, sticky humidity, and flies.

They were led single file down the gangplank to the wooden wharf on the shore of the Brisbane River, named after Sir Thomas Brisbane, the Governor of New South Wales from 1821 to 1826. There they waited for over two hours, each man carrying his worldly possessions in a cloth bag: two blankets and his regulation dress comprising two jackets and waistcoats of kersey cloth, two pairs of duck trousers, two coarse linen shirts, yarn stockings and one woollen cap. During the worst of the voyage's cold, most convicts had worn their entire wardrobe day and night, but now as the sun beat down on them from a cloudless sky, many wore nothing on their upper bodies and some tucked their waistcoats up under their caps, Arab style, to get relief. Yet it was so much more preferable to the confines of *Mount Stewart Elphinstone*'s hold that they were positively cheerful.

In the enervating heat, the prisoners soon broke ranks, and the guards, tired and lethargic themselves, allowed them to find shade. Daniel picked up a dirty piece of newspaper as it drifted by in the hot breeze. It was the first newspaper he had seen since before he was sentenced and it cheered him just to hold one.

'Lads, listen to this! They don't want the likes of us here in their precious little colony!'

'What's that you say, Dan?' asked Samuel Cooper, who was now an accepted member of the little band.

'This,' he held up the paper and shook it, 'holds an article which concerns all you dear delightful companions of our happy voyage!'

Soon there were thirty or forty men gathered round him.

'It's the *Moreton Bay Courier* and is dated October the twenty-fifth, eighteen forty-nine, which was last Thursday.' His musical Irish voice emphasised the more expressive words. "This continued influx of convicts to our *beautiful* colony may in some cases give an impetus to the progress of certain districts; but there will be consequences which generations to come may have *grave* cause to regret. It is our *children* we must remember. There are numerous objections to the presence of these *unseemly* arrivals, not the least of which are the apprehension of *danger* and the strong sense of *indignity*."

'Bleedin' cheek!' commented Swiftie.

Daniel nodded and went on. 'This is the choice part. "These criminals are from the *dregs of society*. We must refuse to accept *vice* for the economic advantage of cheap labour. There is at last a growing interest in organised societies against this insult. The Anti-Transportation Leagues must be supported. These ships arrive, not with luxuries for our women or commodities for a *civilised* community, but with the *lowest immoral insult* to any settlement, the chosen criminals of Great Britain!"'

'Gawd, who do they think they are?' remarked Samuel. 'They was all bloody convicts theirselves. And now they be manifestin' all holy!'

'Yes,' agreed Peter Biggs, an embezzler from Birmingham, 'the worst bastards are the reformed bastards!'

At this, there was much laughter and loud agreement.

'Well, I've been pardoned,' called one of the exiles. 'I'm as good as the pompous berk who wrote that.'

Although they did not realise it theirs was the second last prison transport ever to land its human cargo in the colony of New South Wales. The last, the *Bangalore*, would come exactly six months later. These two ships were the only ones to come directly to Moreton Bay at any time, and solely accepted because of the lack of manpower in this quickly expanding area. Since the First Fleet had landed in 1788, over seventy thousand men and women convicts had been brought to New South Wales, as well as many tens of thousands to the other colonies and Norfolk Island, the 'horror island', earning its ghastly reputation from the constant ill-treatment of its prisoners isolated in the Pacific, a thousand miles to the east of Moreton Bay. In 1868, when the last transport to Australia arrived in the colony of Western Australia, the number sent to the entire country would be in excess of one hundred and sixty thousand.

Daniel handed the paper to Alan. 'Some of it seems to have been quoted by a cove called Henry Parkes.'

Alan's eyes ran over the article while Swiftie looked over his shoulder although he could not read. 'What do you think, guv?'

'No doubt he believes he has a cause.' Then he smiled to himself thinking how five months ago he had thought precisely the same of his companions as this journalist.

'He sounds just like a flamin' politician to me,' decided Evan Evans, a burglar from Wales.

Lawless waved his hand in disgust. 'This all looks like a bleedin' dung heap anyway. What sane man would possibly choose to come 'ere?'

This gave rise to immediate agreement.

'Yeah, "beautiful" that arse called it! Why, the river looks like shit!'

'The bleeders can 'ave their stinkin' hot Moreton Bay.'

'Friggin' hole should be called Mangrove Bay, I reckon.'

In the distance a group of adults and their children milled around. A number of the convicts turned towards them and, hailing them, gestured with rude and obscene signs.

Abruptly across the babble the sergeant's voice broke, sonorous, in parade fashion. 'All right! Attention! Jump to it! We be movin' out!'

They spent the night in rough wooden barracks on the outskirts of Brisbane town. The buildings had been unused for years. Dust was inches thick under the bunks and along the skirting boards. Big black cockroaches ran up the wooden walls and across the floor in the candlelight, and small brown spiders with long thin legs shook in their webs in the corners of the unused bunks.

It was still eighty degrees at ten o'clock, over three hours after sunset.

It took the authorities in Brisbane a week to decide what to do with them. On the seventh morning after their arrival, they were divided. The exiles went to be assigned to settler masters and the convicts were separated into two chain gangs to clear the bush and build roads. There were forty-eight men in Alan's gang – all those having names beginning with the letters A to L; those beginning with M to Z made up the other.

'It's a miracle,' Daniel exclaimed. 'God saw fit to give the five of us names that come early in the alphabet so we all stay together. I tell you, it's the Divine working.'

Lawless lifted his eyes skywards as he patted Daniel on the back. 'And I tell ye, Daniel, my dear, it were yer ma and pa working. That's where ye got "Dwyer" from. There was naught Divine in it!'

Daniel smiled pityingly. 'Lawless, it's a poor ignorant heathen you are.'

They were herded into carts and travelled much of the day in a south-westerly direction and in the late afternoon made camp in tents on the banks of the Bremer, a tributary of the Brisbane River. They cooked over open fires in the short summer evening. It was totally dark by seven o'clock, so different from the long twilights of the old country.

Many of the chain gangs in the past had been left in the care of exile and convict overseers and abuses had been rife. This was not the case with Alan's gang where soldiers had been made available to keep order, though the Crown surveyor who accompanied them was in charge.

After the evening meal the convicts were allowed to sit in recreation on the river bank, in view of their guards. The inevitable card games began in the dusk and it was apparent that those who had gambled away their rations at sea would be the same to lose them on land.

It was a cooler evening than the previous ones, made so by an appeasing breeze coming from the river. Alan sat in thought while those around him talked. Now and then his hand would wave in front of his eyes to chase an insistent fly. The intense heat in this land fostered flies and snakes and other vermin and for a moment he was sick at heart for England. He looked across the narrow river to where some olive-green weeping willows, planted by a settler, drooped to the dark water. Sharply, a picture of the dignified willows at Long Moss House came to him, vivid, bright green fronds trailing to the clear stream that ran from the graceful hills. He wondered for a moment if he would ever see Long Moss House again. Then quite surely he knew he would not. He had crossed the Rubicon and inherited this sun-smothered land, the antipodes of England. His heart was heavy with yearning for the past; then, philosophically, he told himself that unfavourably comparing this land with the one he had left would serve no purpose but to promote more discontent, and there was enough of that emotion already in his life. So, with a deep breath, he assessed the view in front of him, adopting an unjaundiced eye.

It was a simple terrain. It reminded him of the country near Port Nolloth in South Africa where he had been with the Navy. The hills were a blue-purple in the twilight, and nearby stately, slate-grey gums threw long shadows across the tethered horses below. In the distance, severe granite rocks reflected a metal glossiness in the last rays of the sun. Yes, one could find a type of beauty here; different, stark, unEuropean, but beauty nevertheless. He breathed a sigh. Perhaps a man could grow to love this country in time – if his days were not blighted by being a convict!

For the next three years they lived nomadic lives, working south-west of the small district of Ipswich which lay twenty-three miles from the settlement of Brisbane and had been opened to free settlers in 1843.

Because of the close daily contact, there were always some guards who would become friendly with the prisoners. To discourage association, the soldiers and the surveyor were recalled and replaced every six months. But there was mateship born of shared experience and the new arrivals followed the same pattern as their predecessors. There were few attempts at escape; even though the guards were often sociable, they were still soldiers. The prisoners were well watched and, every sundown, ironed for the night. Alan was constantly alert for he had always known that the only hope for him was to escape. 'No one's soul could withstand a lifetime of this, Daniel,' he confided, and the older man nodded.

'Simply tell me the moment, son, and I'll be ready.'

Samuel, Lawless and Swiftie had long since agreed that if ever the opportunity arose, they were all of the same mind.

There were a number of occasions when Alan had viable escape plans, but each time they were thwarted. In 1852, his schemes had come nearest to fruition. The first time, several of the soldiers had fallen ill with fever, and because of their diminished numbers, escape appeared possible. Then Swiftie and Lawless came down with the same fever. They trembled and shook, complaining of being cold. Alan had seen malaria in the ports of South America and this was similar. He would not go without the two young men and by the time they were better, so too were the soldiers. On another occasion, after months of bribery with their rum rations, Alan had convinced the exile overseer to 'forget' to lock their shackles and to escape with them. The lives of the exile overseers on the chain gangs were almost as bad as the convicts'. The escape was to take place on a Friday night when the soldiers received their rum ration and the overseer locked the prisoners' shackles by himself. Two days before the plan was to go into action, the man fell and broke his leg; he was taken to the nearest settlement and they never saw him again.

It was virtually impossible to escape during the day, for while they worked, mounted soldiers patrolled around them. Three times in the first eighteen months men had been tempted to make a break for it into the scrub, only to be shot dead. Theirs was hard, monotonous, back-breaking labour. They built roads and cleared bushland. In the summer, the mind-deadening heat from the fierce Australian sun hammered into them. The only variations from this perpetual condition were rain storms exploding lightning and thunder, or short dust storms forcing them to retreat inside the tents. In the winter they shivered from the overnight frosts and the westerly winds, but the winters were brief. It was the summers that were protracted and almost unbearable.

Occasionally, a kindly farmer would augment their rations with fresh milk or fruit, and there was the bright spot, the weekly tots of rum. Their muscles hardened and their hands grew calloused. The puny youths of the *Mount Stewart Elphinstone* developed into strong, powerful men. Fights broke out now and then and there were unpleasant repercussions, but for the most part their custodians those first years were fair-minded men, as reasonable as the system allowed.

And so the days turned into weeks, into months, into years, and through it all . . . the felons endured.

The pattern of the six-monthly change in their guard and surveyor altered just before Christmas 1852. The guard had been waiting for their replacements for over three weeks. On the sultry hot Sunday evening of 12 December a stranger rode into camp just on sunset. Behind him came the ration cart and five other horse-drawn carriers, all empty. His loud voice called across the encampment, 'Where the devil are Surveyor Clarke and Corporal Raleigh?' He was a thin man in a sergeant's uniform and he looked weary from his long ride. There was two days' growth of whiskers on his ruddy face, and his hair hung lankly across a furrowed brow. His uniform was open at

the neck and his lean fingers pulled at the opening in habitual movement. 'Hey! Who's in charge of this rum lot? You, man!' he shouted
to a soldier. 'Where's the corporal?'

'Why, he be with the lags, sir, it's wash-up time over yonder.' The
redcoat gestured with his hand towards the southern end of the camp.

Corporal Raleigh's face broke into a smile when he saw the newcomer, then seeing no accompanying soldiers he frowned. 'Where's
the replacement troop? Ye have come to replace us, haven't ye?'

'Aye, in a way. But my orders are for you to accompany me, along
with this lot,' he waved his hand over the convicts, 'across south of
the Beau Desert property. Seems someone important wants the land
cleared and a road and bridges built, and your beauties are to do the
job, eh? Special orders. When you've delivered the prisoners, you
return to Moreton Bay. I stay on in command with a new troop until
the job's done. There will be two years' work in it.' He wiped the
back of his hand across his perspiring brow. 'We leave at sunrise.'

When, many days later, they reached their destination, they found
a disused shed which they adapted to house eighteen men while the
others lived as before, in tents. Each tent held seven men and was
made semi-permanent by being fortified on the inside with wooden
planking and floorboards, leaving only the front flap free for entry
and exit.

Surveyor Clarke and Corporal Raleigh and his men left a few days
before Christmas, and Sergeant Eric Dobbs with twelve recently
arrived horse soldiers took charge. The new surveyor did not join
them until January and the convicts meanwhile cleared the bush,
chopping down trees and removing the scraggy shrubs and plants of
the scrub.

Christmas Day was a Saturday and in honour of the birth of Christ
the convicts rested. They spent the hours lying in the shade of the
eucalyptus trees on the banks of a stony creek running west from the
feeble Albert River. The day passed, as the others before it had,
heat, flies, cockroaches and sweat being the yuletide gifts to the
convicts.

Within a week, it was obvious that Dobbs was not simply strict;
he resorted to the lash for even petty offences. Standing trance-like,
he would watch the punishment, while his hand pulled mechanically
at his shirt collar.

Eric Dobbs had joined the army as a ten-year-old drummer boy.
His character had been fashioned by hardship, discipline and orders.
He had risen to the rank of sergeant by being a sycophant and a
bully. He saw weakness as a thing to be exploited, yet in the army's
normal chain of command, his cruelty was not apparent. It was only

now, when in sole charge, that it emerged. He made sport of all in his care, especially of the weak and the sick. His sadism was general, applied to all, and he occasionally vented his spleen on his own soldiers as well. While the magistrate rode from the Brisbane settlement regularly and the prisoners were encouraged to bring grievances to him, there was rarely a complaint for fear of retaliation when he left.

When Mr Stonebridge the engineer-surveyor arrived, nothing changed. He was a kindly man, whose name was a source of amusement to the prisoners and they called him 'Stony' affectionately behind his back. He was a big man but his size did not mirror his courage. His was a genteel nature, opposed to violence and conflict, preferring appeasement and conciliation. He simply did his job. He built his roads and his bridges with care, but each evening he left to billet in relative comfort at a nearby farm, leaving Dobbs in charge.

The sergeant had examined closely the forty-six men in his chain gang. Bloody lags, all they understood was strength. They would not get the better of him. He soon realised the calibre of the prisoner called Fletcher. His incongruity among his ill-educated comrades was apparent whether he bent double in a field or waited half-naked to be doused with a bucket of water at wash-up time. There was a charisma about the man. Some idolised him, and it was plain, all respected him. But Eric Dobbs was not impressed. He would spare no one. He would break Fletcher just as he would break them all. Yet it was difficult to find a reason to discipline the man and when Dobbs goaded him, he had never received anything more for his efforts than a brief, penetrating look.

With Dobbs in charge Alan knew he had to escape. He had spent over three years in an existence that passed for a life and he was determined not to spend any more under a sadist. He had been shaping a plan, and by now, the first week in February, he had the details clear. He had chosen the following Friday night as the time. Each Friday fortnight, the sergeant allowed his soldiers double rum rations and though they did not get hopelessly drunk, they were not as clear-headed as usual.

Alan reviewed the plan as they rested during the water break. Too soon the peace was broken as an overseer called them back to work. 'Time's up!'

They stood from under the tree where they had been sitting, and suddenly Daniel's face turned dark red. He leaned back against the tree trunk and his breath came in short gasps.

'Daniel, what's wrong?'

'Don't know, sonny. Feel a bit tight in the chest, bit dizzy.'

87

Alan looked to Swiftie. 'Get some more water, lad.' The young man quickly complied and held a cup to Daniel's lips. He sipped a little.

At that moment the overseer shouted again. Alan motioned Swiftie and the others who had gathered round to leave, while he remained on the ground beside Daniel, lifting his arm to feel his pulse.

Sergeant Dobbs, sitting in the shade of a gum some thirty yards away, noticed the two men still on the ground. 'Hey!' he shouted. 'You two, get up, move off! Rest time's finished. I'm tired of all this bloody fainting and malingering. Flamin' tired of it, I say!'

Daniel's eyes were glazed. He tried to rise but he fell back, an expression of pain crossing his face. 'Go, son, go, I'll not have Dobbs screaming at you too.'

'Where does it hurt, Dan?'

'It'll pass, Alan. Don't be worrying. I'll be all right. Go. Please go . . .'

By now Dobbs had realised who the two men were. Fletcher and Dwyer! They were too brotherly by half. Pulling at his shirt collar, he rose and hastened across. 'What the devil goes on here? You two have been called back to work, don't you know?'

Alan did not look up as he said, 'Can't you see he cannot rise? He must rest. He needs a doctor.'

'A doctor!' Dobbs's voice rose. 'More like he's feignin'. Doesn't want to work in the heat. I've got a bridge to build, Fletcher, and you and Dwyer sitting here in the shade won't get it done. Come on, Dwyer, move!'

Alan's voice held steady as he looked up into the face above him. 'Leave him alone. The others are half his age. He's sick I tell you!'

Dobbs was all agitation. There was an excited sound now in his voice. 'Shut up, Fletcher! I'm tired of this. Sick nothin'! Get up this instant, Dwyer, if you know what's good for you.' He moved his foot to Daniel's side and dug at him, but Daniel did not move. Then he grabbed Alan's shirt collar pulling him away so that he overbalanced. 'I told you to get back to work, Fletcher! I'll deal with you for insubordination later.' He turned his back on Alan and stood towering above the older man.

Alan regained his feet but did not move away.

Then Dobbs bent down and grabbed Daniel under the armpits to lift him bodily to his feet. Daniel was shaking; he could not rise. Dobbs let go and Daniel fell heavily back to the ground.

'Look, you bastard, you're not the only one who's hot. We're all bloody hot. Get up!'

Daniel's hand went to his forehead. His eyes blinked. He tried once more to rise, but he could not.

Dobbs's shouting could be heard a hundred yards away. 'Blast your eyes! You're nothin' but useless, bloody well useless! I give you lags hours off work in the best part of the day and still you play these games on me!' He shook his fist at the convicts who stood watching. Again he tugged at his shirt collar. He seemed to lose all rationality as he looked down at Daniel, lifted his foot and kicked him in the side.

It was too much for Alan. With a movement so swift that the onlookers hardly grasped what they saw, Alan's left hand went out and pulled Dobbs round to him. Amazement covered the vicious man's features as he saw the fist bursting into his face.

With all the force of Alan's might, it exploded into Dobbs's mouth. Up through his whole body from the soles of his feet rose the blow. Up out of his life came the outrage . . . the injury . . . the fury . . . the affront, that he had carried for years. He hit his cousin Abel, he hit the liars at his trial, he hit Mocksey, he hit all the injustice he had seen and suffered; and too, he hit Dobbs. The violence of the blow actually lifted the sergeant from the ground before he fell heavily backwards with a loud cry.

Two soldiers came running over. They brought Dobbs groaning to his feet. There was a large swelling appearing at the side of his face. Blood covered his broken teeth.

'Strewth, Sergeant, I think 'e's gone and broke your friggin' jaw!'

There was seething hatred in the sergeant's face now as he held his chin and moaned. He was livid and in agony. He screamed through broken teeth, 'Lock him up! Iron him! Iron him! Get me to a doctor. Quickly!'

Two more soldiers hurried over and took Alan roughly by the shoulders.

The sergeant's eyes bulged. He was shaking. Blood ran down his ashen jaw. He needed support to stand and all the while groaned in pain.

Horses were hastily brought.

Before he mounted, Dobbs turned back. His hand shook as he lifted it towards Alan. It was difficult for him to speak but the evil menace in his words was not lost on those who heard him. 'I'll do for you, Fletcher. You wait. You'll suffer. You'll wish you were a bloody dead man.'

From the second Alan had hit him, he did not look in Dobbs's direction again. He had disassociated himself from the man. His eyes and thoughts were only for Daniel. As Dobbs departed and the soldiers took Alan away, he shouted, 'For God's sake, do something for Daniel Dwyer. It's he who should see a doctor!'

At last Daniel was carried to his tent and Swiftie sent to tend him. Mr Stonebridge was over a mile away from the camp at the quarry where they dug out the stone. By the time a soldier had been dispatched to him and he had returned, Alan had been chained to a tree trunk and left waiting outside the barracks.

The engineer rode up to where Alan stood and dismounted. He shook his head ruefully a number of times. 'Ah, Fletcher,' he began and then stopped and shook his head again. He was baffled by the situation and unsure of what action he should take. He liked Fletcher. The man was a fine worker and an intelligent help to him often. There were even times he sought his opinion. Why had he caused this trouble and hit Dobbs? Dobbs would retaliate in an ugly fashion, there was no doubt about that. It discouraged him to think about it. Once more he shook his head. 'Fletcher, you have brought this on yourself. Why in Heaven's name did you hit the sergeant?'

'Because the man is an animal. He kicked Dan Dwyer. I have done no more than he deserved, Mr Stonebridge, you know that.'

Mr Stonebridge agreed with Fletcher, but he could not say so. Instead he stood awkwardly tapping his large chin with his fingers. 'I will send for the magistrate. It is more his affair, but as it is five o'clock in the afternoon, I fear he'll not be here until tomorrow or even the next day. I'm sorry, Fletcher, but there is little I can do. Sergeant Dobbs will no doubt stay with Dr Chester on the Beau Desert property tonight if his jaw is broken as they say, but I'm afraid you'll have to take whatever he metes out to you in the morning. After all, man, I mean to say, you are a convict.'

Alan made no reply and the engineer coughed, an embarrassed sound, before he turned and walked away. Alan was taken to his tent where he was chained to the centre pole. A yard away Daniel lay on his bunk; a damp towel rested on his forehead and Swiftie was beside him.

When the soldiers left, Alan turned as best he could to his friends. 'How is he, Swiftie?'

For answer Daniel opened his eyes. He raised himself on his elbow, drank some water and replied, 'I'm feeling much better now, laddie, have done so ever since you smashed Dobbs.'

Alan smiled.

'It were beautiful, guv'nor,' Swiftie approved. 'Best thing I've ever seen. Broke his bloody jaw straight off.' Then he frowned and looked unhappy. 'Though Gawd knows what will happen now.'

Daniel sat up again. 'Well, I know what has to happen now. I don't think we have any alternative.'

Alan and Swiftie both looked questioningly.

The older man took a deep breath and shook his head decisively. He wagged his finger in the air for emphasis as he spoke. 'Now is the time to be putting your plan of escape into action, Alan. Tonight must be the night. We cannot wait until next Friday.'

Alan opened his mouth to reply but Daniel went on before he could speak. 'Dobbs will stay the night with the doctor for certain. Stony will go to the farm as usual. It will be the first night ever the soldiers won't have a commander here and we know what they'll be doing.'

'They'll drink their heads off with Dobbs out of the way and no mistake,' interjected Swiftie.

'Yes,' agreed Alan, 'but Danny, my friend, you cannot run for it. And I'll not leave you here.'

Daniel looked across at Alan and, putting his hand on his chest, patted his heart. He looked determined and spoke severely. 'Now you listen, Alan Fletcher. This old heart's still beating, and I'm feeling pounds better, that's the truth. It was more the blasted heat than anything. This is the finest opportunity we've ever had. The soldiers will begin drinking early, as Swiftie suggests, and I'll be a darn sight better away from here. I want no more talk of me, for there's too much at stake. Far too much. So be it.'

For some seconds Alan looked sceptically at his friend who sat on the bunk smiling benignly at him. Then he nodded gently. When at last he spoke, it was decisively. He outlined the plan again.

It was six o'clock when the men returned from the fields to the camp and Mr Stonebridge left as usual for the farm. As Swiftie had predicted, the soldiers began drinking immediately, positive they would not see Dobbs that night.

Within an hour, the convicts had eaten their evening meal and the soldiers, eager for the night ahead, decided to put the men in their leg irons. This normally did not happen until lights out at ten o'clock and the prisoners spent the hours after sunset in a recreation compound near the guard house. Tonight, as they were sent to their tents and ironed, there were loud and angry complaints. To keep them quiet, the soldiers brought rum in a bucket to distribute to each man.

The guards slept in a large wooden hut next to the main barracks in the centre of the camp. As the sun went down, five of them congregated there with the rum barrel. Two had gone with Dobbs, two patrolled the camp, one minded the horses and the other two were putting the prisoners in irons.

In Alan's tent, the last in a line of four from the barracks, Lawless, Swiftie, Daniel, Sam and the two others, Peter Biggs and Evan

Evans, were tense with excitement.

'Goodo!' Lawless said when told the escape had been brought forward. 'At last. We shall be free men, Swiftie, my dear.'

Swiftie grinned. 'I'm game, matey.'

They tried the board they had been loosening for weeks at the tent side and it lifted up and out of its position easily. It exposed the canvas which later they would rip open and use as exit.

For an hour, Alan had timed the two patrolling soldiers. With the relaxed discipline and no supervision they walked side by side and passed the back of the tent approximately every four minutes. The drinking soldiers were doubtless set for a night of gaiety, and a general echo of noisiness reverberated through the camp from the convicts who had already received their rum.

When the overseer and two guards arrived outside Alan's tent, it was perhaps twenty minutes after sunset. An early moon had risen, spreading a weak radiance across the camp.

'Outside 'ere, you lot!' called the overseer, the chains clinking in his hands.

'But what will we do with Dan Dwyer? He can't get off his bunk,' came Swiftie's worried voice, 'and Alan Fletcher still be chained to the tent post.'

The overseer put down his lantern and poked his head in through the tent flap. 'The rest o' you then, get out here. I'll handle them later.'

Alan had hoped the overseer and the soldiers would enter the tent without encouragement. He needed them inside to disarm them. Any attack outside risked being seen.

Sam, Lawless, Evans and Biggs issued from the tent.

'Where's Lochran?' asked the overseer. 'You, Lochran, get out here with the rest like I told you!'

Once more, Swiftie's plaintive voice came from inside the tent. 'I really don't like the looks of Dwyer. Someone should do somethin'. And quick. Methinks he's dyin'!'

The overseer just wanted the prisoners chained so he could join in the festivities. 'Oh damn, that's all we need, Dwyer dyin',' he grumbled impatiently as he entered the tent. He walked forward to where Daniel lay moaning on his bunk.

At that moment the heavy tread of the two patrolling soldiers passed by the back of the tent. Alan's and Swiftie's eyes met across the head of the overseer as he bent down to Daniel. They had four minutes!

Daniel rolled his eyes back and at the same time groaned loudly.

That was the signal for Biggs outside. He was a large man and he moved himself across the tent opening, blocking the view inside from the soldiers. At that precise moment Swiftie acted. He was now a powerful young man with wide shoulders and muscular arms. He brought a rabbit killer punch to the back of the overseer's neck as he bent over Daniel. The man crumpled.

Swiftie moved rapidly to the right of the tent opening. Then Alan's voice sounded in alarm, 'Quick, guards, the overseer's collapsed!'

The two soldiers outside acted on impulse. One pushed past Biggs to enter the tent and the other automatically followed. With an anxious look towards the guards' quarters, Biggs thrust as hard as he could on the back of the second man, called Parker, who still held the bucket of rum in one hand and his weapon in the other. He fell forward into the tent, followed immediately by Biggs, Lawless, Evans and Sam.

As the first soldier came through the tent flap, Swiftie ripped the gun from his hands and pushed it hard in the shocked man's stomach, while Evans jumped past the others and grabbed him from behind and took his bayonet.

Parker, who had lost his balance from the smash in his back, was leaped upon by Biggs. There was a half-smothered cry from him as Sam grabbed his rifle, looking regretfully as the bucket of rum dropped and spilled all over the floor. Biggs pinioned the soldier beneath his body, saying, 'If you call out, you be a dead man!'

Swiftie handed the rifle he held to Alan.

The overseer had risen with the idea of dashing out, but when he saw the guns had changed hands he held still while Lawless relieved him of his keys and unlocked Alan's manacles.

The noise of the roisterers floated to them across the camp.

'Nice of your mates to be busy enough to ignore us,' Alan said as he bent to relieve Parker of his belt and bayonet.

The man looked up defiantly from beneath Biggs. 'You're mad, Fletcher. Where can you go? You'll hang for this!'

Alan's voice grew menacing. 'Silence now, or you won't live to know what happens next. Bind them fast!'

The overseer and the other soldier, Gatling, were pushed to the floor beside Parker. With the bonds made earlier from their blankets, they began to tie the three men.

'Quickly, lads,' urged Alan. Then getting down on one knee he asked the captives, 'How many guards are down with the horses?'

'Damn you,' answered Parker, 'I'll not tell.'

Evans brought the bayonet close to Parker's face. 'Then ye shall just have to die with this bayonet in yer gizzard.'

Alan leaned forward. 'We are desperate men and though I admire your courage, I don't see why you would both want to die here on this tent floor tonight.'

Gatling, in fear, answered for his comrade, 'One, there's only Bates down at the corral.'

'Thank you. You're a sensible man. Now gag them.'

Parker, still hostile, spoke quickly before Evans stuffed a gag in his mouth. 'You'll hang, Fletcher. They'll hang you for sure in the end.'

Alan, in the act of rising and buckling the soldier's belt round his waist, knelt back on his knee and looked down into Parker's eyes. The expression the soldier read there was sinister; whether it was or not, only Alan knew, but as the seconds passed it served to make Parker cold with fear behind his gag. Then, to Parker's eternal surprise, Alan smiled broadly. 'I have avoided that consequence once already, soldier. And you should avoid dabbling in prophecy, for I will continue. I will *never* hang!' He lifted his eyes from Parker's and stood, just as they heard the approach of the two patrolling soldiers.

Four minutes exactly!

As the sound of their boots drew close, the odour of the spilled bucket of rum rose to Alan's nostrils. For ever afterwards, the smell of rum would bring back the memory of this – the inside of the boarded tent, the heavy breathing of those about him and the redcoats on the floor below, their buttons glinting in the mellow lamplight.

The footsteps halted. The soldiers were talking. 'Now where the devil are Parker and Gatling? Said they'd bring us a measure after chaining the lags.'

'Yeah, well, they were doing Fletcher's tent before. They'll not be far. Somewhere 'ereabouts, no doubt.'

Alan looked down to where Gatling and Parker lay at his feet. Swiftie stifled a nervous laugh.

The voice outside continued, 'We'll find them if they don't find us. Hey, I wonder how bloody old Dobbs is?'

The ground crunched beneath their feet as the soldiers walked away and the other's answer drifted back. 'Who cares? I reckon the bastard deserved it.'

As soon as their voices faded, Lawless moved to the front of the tent and looked cautiously through. 'Two guards on the verandah. Can see no others, guv'nor.'

'Good,' answered Alan, turning to where Swiftie and Biggs were already prising the plank from the side of the tent. 'Then it's out we go.'

The planking was lifted away and Evans began to cut through the canvas of the tent with the bayonet he had taken from Gatling. As soon as the hole was cut, they crawled through: Lawless, Daniel, Evans, Swiftie, Biggs, followed by Sam and Alan carrying the rifles.

Just before Sam stepped through the hole he turned back into the tent; the spilled bucket of rum was on the floor and the dispensing cup lay beside it with rum left in the bottom. He picked it up, gulped it down, winked at Alan and disappeared through the opening.

Twelve yards from the side of the tent, the tall grass and scrub began and ran down close to the horses. There were no trees, so the escapees could not walk upright. They doubled over, moving swiftly. They would get as close as possible to Bates, the guard with the horses, and then Alan and Sam would take him by surprise, while the others freed the animals. As they edged through the bush, the laughter of the merry soldiers sounded in the distance.

It was a hot, humid, still night, though the escapees perspired as much from the tension as from the temperature. Daniel, breathing in a laboured fashion, was the slowest of the seven and now, half supported by Alan, brought up the rear. By the time they all came together about ten yards from the man with the horses, minutes had passed. Alan looked round the ring of strained faces in the moonlight.

Suddenly the alarm was raised! Shouting and yelling sounded loudly behind them. 'Escape! Escape!'

The two patrolling guards had gone in search of Gatling and Parker and the promised rum, leaving their beat to walk between the tents. The rent in the canvas, though not obvious at a distance, was clearly visible up close. They had realised something was amiss and inside the tent found their mates and the overseer.

At the sound of the shouts, Alan saw Bates at the corral leap to his feet and grab his rifle. He turned, uneasy and alert, in the direction of the yelling. He faced slightly away from the seven men in the undergrowth.

With a violent leap, Alan came up and over the intervening space. It was a magnificent move, but the soldier was young and had drunk no rum. At the sound from the bush he turned, firing even before he sighted the convict uniform flying at him.

Alan charged, arms extended. The cartridge hit him in the left forearm but the momentum of his spring carried him forward onto Bates. They both fell heavily to the ground, Alan on top. Bates began to struggle but Sam was now beside them pushing his rifle in the soldier's face. 'Lie still, matey, or I promise I'll blow your head off!' The man stiffened and lay still.

Alan stood.

'Are you all right, guv'nor?' Sam asked, grabbing the soldier's fallen rifle and throwing it to Lawless.

'Yes,' replied Alan who was so stimulated that he felt nothing although the blood ran freely from his wound.

Swiftie and Lawless were already at the horse railings, removing the bar which held the gate.

The rifle shot had warned the camp of the direction of the escapees. Just what they had wanted to avoid. Soldiers were tumbling out of their quarters, guns in hand, looking dazedly around.

Speed, they needed speed. The bar was thrown aside and the gate opened.

Some of the horses had reared at the sound of the gunshot and now jostled each other as the convicts tried to put makeshift bridles over their heads. They managed to restrain four of the animals while most of the others escaped from the yard.

A redcoat was running down the hill shouting and the other soldiers were calling and yelling to each other. Even in their disarray they were well trained enough to assess the situation. Five ran towards the corral and fired at the convict uniforms. The bullets whistled past and thudded into the open gate beside Alan and Sam.

'Hey, stop! I'm down here!' shouted Bates as he crawled quickly away.

While the soldiers reloaded, Alan turned to those with him. There was an excited light in his eyes, giving him a wild, ferocious look; the bayonet lodged in the scabbard at his waist, the blood running down over the back of his hand and dripping from his fingers. There, like an untamed Delacroix mountain brigand, he stood in the moonlight, the rifle raised high in his good hand.

'All right, boys, mount quickly! Sam and I shall hold them.'

Onto the rails of the fence yard they climbed and from there to the bare backs of the animals. Daniel, Evans and Biggs could ride but Swiftie and Lawless had spent their days in the byways of London and had never been on a horse. They were willing but awkward. They mounted behind the more skilful.

Alan had already turned back to the soldiers. They would soon be upon them. 'Aim low,' he said to Sam.

He fired. Sam too fired beside him. One soldier fell with a wound in his leg and the others pulled up sharply and dropped to their knees in battle fashion. Most had not realised that the escapees had the rifles of their bound comrades. They had believed they were firing on unarmed men.

While the guards on their knees rallied and took aim, Alan and Sam turned in the darkness and ran back to the others. They mounted the free horse and charged away just as the soldiers fired again. Swiftie uttered a cry and thudded forward hard onto Daniel's back.

'Oh no!' said Daniel still pressing the horse onwards. 'Are you hit, laddie? Are you hit?' He threw his left arm backwards round his young friend to steady him as more gunshots echoed after them.

Onward they sped, taking the horses down a steep incline. They were making for the Albert River. It was not a wide or deep river and, once over, they would head south and up through the rain forest and the mountains. They knew the countryside around the camp for miles and were not disoriented in the darkness.

'Are you all right, Swiftie? Laddie, answer me, please!' Daniel cried.

For reply, the young man groaned.

Daniel felt his throat constrict with fear for the boy. They rode on another minute or so, then he sensed the young man beginning to slide. In an anguished voice he called, 'Alan! Alan! They hit Swiftie!'

'Halt!' Alan shouted as he brought his large, pale grey stallion to a standstill.

Swiftie made a strange strangled sound and began to slip sideways.

Alan dismounted and ran back in time to catch him as he slid off the horse. With his good arm he tried to steady the young man but Swiftie buckled at the knees. Alan eased him to the bush floor. 'Easy, lad, easy.'

Lawless, his face blanched, jumped down and came to his friend. The others, too, dismounted and gathered round.

Swiftie's face was contorted with pain. Blood gushed from the middle of his back down over Alan's good arm, staining the earth in the darkness.

Biggs looked back towards the camp. 'We'll not have long before they catch some of the horses and mount a chase.'

Daniel dug him in the ribs to silence him.

Lawless's eyes filled with tears. 'Oh Gawd, matey! Oh Gawd!' He touched Swiftie's face tenderly and took his hand.

In the moonglow Swiftie looked at Lawless and then up to Alan who held him. He sighed deeply, and they saw his face change as the pain left him. There was almost a saintly peace in his drawn young face.

'Lawless . . . guv'nor . . . I . . . there be no more hurt . . .' He closed his eyes then opened them again. They were glassy as he tried to concentrate on Alan's face above. 'I'm dyin' . . . aren't I, guv'nor?'

Alan looked at the young face upturned to his. He would have been twenty-one in a few weeks' time. Spasms of sorrow ran through him. Swiftie had become like a cherished young brother. Alan fought back the anguish that rose in his throat as he searched for an answer. 'Ah lad, you've been so brave, so courageous . . . dear Swiftie . . .'

The tears were now streaming down Lawless's face; he kept repeating, 'No, matey, no,' as Daniel gripped his shoulders, murmuring a prayer.

With effort Swiftie spoke again. 'But . . . I'm dyin' a free man . . . aren't I, guv'nor?'

'Yes, Swiftie, my dear dear lad, you are.'

The death rattle was a gentle thing.

The others rose while Lawless remained kneeling, sobbing quietly and holding his friend's hand.

'What'll we do, Alan?' Daniel asked. 'We can't leave the boy here.'

'No, we won't leave him here. We shall take him with us.'

'But how can we ride with a dead man?' demanded Biggs.

Sam turned savagely. 'If the guv'nor says we do, we damn well do!'

Alan motioned to his horse. 'I will ride with him.'

At that moment there was the noise of men and animals not far behind and a loud shout sounded clearly through the bush. They lifted and lay Swiftie's body across the horse in front of Alan, and remounted speedily.

Even bareback, Alan was a masterful rider and though it was nigh on five years since he had sat a horse, he was as comfortable as if it had been five hours. While his arm was painful now and continued to seep blood, it was not flowing freely as it had been some minutes before. Luck had indeed been with him, for the cartridge had hit no nerves, instead lodging between the radius and the ulna, leaving him use of his hand and fingers.

After a five-minute ride over rough ground and through trees and scrub, they came to the river. They had made good time and the camp was nearly a mile behind. They reined in at the river's edge and listened. Their mounts snorted and their own heavy breathing was loud in their ears. The sounds of horses and men were not far behind.

Alan looked round the anxious eyes in the darkness. 'They're coming this way, and are aware of the general direction we rode. We must cross the river. So too will they, but they'll be unsure after that. How much of the country can they search? There cannot be many of them, and I think they'll not have the sense of direction I can deliver.'

'Nevertheless,' spoke up Biggs, 'maybe we should be separatin', Alan. Might 'ave more of a chance in two groups.'

'If you wish, Peter,' Alan replied pressing his horse on into the river.

As they reached the other bank, the noise of pursuit was closer. Another gunshot sounded.

'Listen, Alan,' Peter Biggs shouted. 'Evans here and I are of a mind to go our own way!'

'All right,' replied Alan. 'You already have one of the bayonets. Give them a rifle, Sam.'

Sam reluctantly handed over one of the guns.

'Good luck,' Alan added as he turned his horse away. 'Come on then, lads! Let's go.'

Without saddles, it was the hardest ride they would ever make. Alan's knowledge of direction was the single distinction which ensured them their freedom. As a navigator at sea, he had studied the stars of both the northern and southern hemispheres and now he took them unerringly south even without a compass.

Those that gave chase had guessed accurately at first and followed across the river. There they divided into two parties and after an hour were hopelessly lost in the bush. When the following morning dawned, only one of the groups of searchers was back in camp. They arrived tired and defeated shortly before midnight. The others rode in three hours after the sun was up. They had been lost in the hills all night.

In contrast, when morning dawned over the escapees, they were on a rise close to nineteen miles due south of the camp. They had made slow but steady progress, resting briefly every half-hour or so. At one point, they had been forced to retrace their steps when the bush was too dense for penetration; nevertheless, they had averaged almost two and a half miles an hour and had ridden for eight hours.

As the sun came up, Sam dug the cartridge from Alan's arm with a bayonet. Amazingly, it had entered in the same spot where he carried a scar from the stabbing years before, in Southampton.

'Don't worry, guv,' the little man kept saying as Alan grimaced throughout the operation. 'I've removed a thousand cartridges from pheasant and the like. There'll hardly be a mark when I finish.' This was more appeasement than truth and Alan remained carrying an L-shaped scar on his left arm ever afterward.

It was there on the hilltop they buried Swiftie. They left him beneath a grove of tall eucalypts, their trunks a soft dappled pink, looking down to a bush valley of mottled yellows and greens. To mark the spot, Lawless and Daniel made a cross from saplings and Lawless carved, 'Swiftie Lochran, matey, 1832–1853'.

Daniel said a prayer and Lawless picked a bunch of tiny white wild flowers and laid them on the grave.

Before they continued on their way, Sam looked to Alan and asked the question they all wanted answered. 'What will we do now, guv'nor? I mean, we'll always be hunted men. How can we be stayin' free? And how will we live?'

Alan stood with his good arm round Lawless's shoulders looking across Swiftie's grave down to the bush below. As he listened to Sam's question, he turned round to face the morning sun.

There was resolve in the very way he stood. His handsome mouth was set in a grim line and the expression in his eyes was suddenly hard and uncompromising. They had never seen him like this before. He appeared almost callous and it surprised them. He was thinking of Swiftie, left here on the hillside. His death was the price they had paid for their freedom. All that lay ahead of them was danger. There was no sanctuary for escaped convicts.

He looked slowly over the three faces turned towards him. 'We *will* stay free, as long as we are careful and keep ourselves to ourselves. And how will we live, Samuel? There is only one thing we can do, only one thing escaped convicts are qualified for: we are about to become bushrangers!'

Sergeant Eric Dobbs was court-martialled at Brisbane barracks on 5 March 1853. Three officers and one judge advocate presided.

He was charged with neglect of duty and with accountability for being away from his office of responsibility while an escape took place. After an hour's deliberation, he was found not guilty of the charge of neglect, but guilty of accountability. It was ascertained that his attitude towards his prisoners and his men had been responsible for the attack upon himself which removed him overnight from his place of duty.

He was stripped of his rank and sentenced to one year's hard labour in the military prison at Brisbane barracks.

Fifteen days after the escape, Evan Evans and Peter Biggs stole a boat from the Brisbane River and were shipwrecked on Stradbroke Island. They were found four months later and re-sentenced.

CHAPTER SIX

'She was a phantom of delight
When first she gleamed upon my sight;
A lovely apparition.'
'She Was a Phantom of Delight', William Wordsworth,
1770–1850.

A decade later, 1863.

The mail coach swung across the almost treeless plain on the flat, dusty road that led into Bathurst, a sturdy little settlement of wide, unpaved streets and mostly wooden houses, named in 1815 after Henry, third Earl Bathurst and Principal Secretary of State for the Colonies.

The vehicle was now on the verge of the township, and after a long, wearying, hot ride, the passengers inside were looking forward to a cooling bath at the Royal Hotel where they would spend the night.

A light, evening wind had risen, and as the coach trundled by, it lifted leaves from a lonely silver-gum tree. They hung in the air as if for a moment they could determine their next movements, then, in swirling, spiralling pattern, descended to the fields below. Some skimmed across the top of the passing coach to find their resting places in a tangle of morning glory. Three farmers' children played among the pretty vine, threading the soft, blue-purple, cone-shaped flowers through the buttonholes in their pinafores, and running trailing azure streaks of blossom in the wind.

Inside the coach an angular-faced man turned from the cheerful view of the children and continued speaking. 'So, as I have said, I'm here to do something about them. Ah yes, to help Sir Frederick Pottinger, though he's made a few asinine moves at times in my opinion.' The speaker liked to talk and he had been loquacious all the long way from Sydney town. Newly appointed by the Government of New South Wales, Sir Rutherford Blake was a famous criminalist from London. He was what had recently been termed a 'detective policeman', and had brought to justice many who had evaded capture

101

for years. Sir Rutherford had been invited by a troubled colonial government to advise and guide on their ever compounding problem, the western outlaws, the 'bushrangers'.

Although Sir Frederick Pottinger was the Police Inspector of the Western District, Sir Rutherford Blake was autonomous, liaising directly with the Chief Secretary of the Colony and the Inspector General of Police in Sydney. He was presently directing his extensive knowledge at John Stuart Wakeman who shared the coach.

John Stuart Wakeman. His very name was a byword for wealth and grandeur. He was of the new breed, the landed gentry of Australia. His father, though originally but a surveyor from a country family in Sussex, England, had founded the fabulous property of Mayfield on the banks of the Lachlan River in 1826, where John Stuart now lived in splendour.

He had listened carefully to Sir Rutherford's opinions for over one hundred miles, listened, and in the main agreed. He liked the tenacity and the vigilance that he recognised in the other. He knew Frederick Pottinger, and it was his opinion that the man would have trouble keeping up with the subtle sharp mind that was Sir Rutherford.

A serious expression appeared now on John Stuart's handsome, sunbrowned face as he clasped his hands round his knee and lifted his black burnished boot from the floor. 'Yes, Sir Rutherford,' he replied. 'Unfortunately here in the west the bushrangers have grown into a menace these last few years. There seem to be more and more of them all the time.'

The other passengers, Timothy, John Stuart's valet, and David Elrington, a young Crown prosecutor and Sir Rutherford Blake's assistant, nodded vigorously in agreement.

Sir Rutherford's eyelids almost closed as he leaned forward to John Stuart in friendly fashion. He had been in New South Wales only two months but he spoke with knowledge and authority. 'It's a sign of the times, people are loose. Ah yes. We had only the odd bushranger until the start of the sixties and they were all escaped convicts, bolters the lot. But now these "wild colonial boys", just uncaught criminals is all they are. Ah yes, I've spent every waking moment since I landed engaged in learning about them. You could say I already "know" many of them intimately, and I'm ready for a few field trips.'

John Stuart smiled.

Sir Rutherford returned the smile, his face contorting to show an expanse of gum above his top teeth. 'Ah yes, since the infamous gold robbery near Eugowra last June, the records show that the number of travellers stopped on the roads has burgeoned to where it is clearly

102

a state of emergency to my way of thinking.'

'But there seems some sympathy for them. The bushrangers, I mean,' spoke up David Elrington, his freckled face attentive, 'though I cannot understand it myself.'

Sir Rutherford now turned his attention to his assistant. 'Ah yes and that is because you are law-abiding and brought up as such, Mr Elrington. It is the middle-aged who are former convicts themselves that sympathise. They carry an innate resentment for law and the police.'

'True,' agreed John Stuart, 'and the city-bred often exacerbate the problem with their attitude. They do not always understand and they associate the bushrangers with the gallantry of the highwaymen myth. We country-born know better and recognise them to be but illiterate malcontents in the main.'

'Ah yes, definitely,' nodded the expert grimly, 'and my motto has always been, break those who break the law, and I shall continue to live by it.'

Local children ran and shouted alongside the vehicle as it neared its journey's end. The arrival of the coach always excited great interest and the youngsters accompanied it the last hundred yards or so and waited, wide-eyed, to see the passengers, people who came from far-off romantic places like the Blue Mountains and Sydney town, places the children had never seen.

It was the Tuesday before Easter, 31 March. At five minutes past the hour of four in the afternoon, John Stuart Wakeman stepped down outside the Royal Hotel in William Street followed by Sir Rutherford Blake. As his foot touched the street, there was a welcome freshness in the evening brought by the same wind of the fields that had entered Bathurst in tandem with the carriage. To the local folk, it was consolation after the solid heat of the day.

'Why, it be Mr Wakeman of Mayfield!' one of the children cried, an intelligent lad who knew many of the landed gentry by sight. There were yelps of delight at this news for, to them, his name was synonymous with bright threepenny pieces.

At this announcement, a few tradesmen came out into the street to look. It was not often they got to see the master of Mayfield, although everyone had known he was coming soon, for his own coach had been sitting in the coaching house being polished for the best part of three days, waiting to carry him the nigh on eighty miles to Mayfield House.

John Stuart was returning from a cattle drive and business in Sydney. Thirty miles west of that capital was the railhead township of Penrith where he had driven a herd of fattened Herefords and sold them at market. He had travelled on from Penrith to Sydney for a few days' business. It was the first time he had ever led a drive without Joe Larmer, Mayfield's manager and John Stuart's confidant and trusted adviser. A week before the drive was to begin, Joe had broken a bone in his foot and his place had been taken by Jack Hennessy, Joe's second-in-command.

In Sydney, John Stuart had stayed at Government House with Sir John Young, the Governor. He had remained only four days and declined to stay for a masked ball that was to be given in his honour by the Premier, James Martin, feeling not quite comfortable without Joe Larmer at this side. It was in the capital that he had been introduced to Sir Rutherford Blake and circumstances had led them to make the long journey into the west together. They took leave of each other in the hall of the Royal, and agreed to meet later for a meal.

Alone in his room, the best the hotel offered, John Stuart bathed off the dust of travel in the large hip-bath carried up for him on the shoulders of two burly youths. The late afternoon sun streamed through his window and reflected in the long mirror as he put on the fresh clothing laid out by Timothy.

He descended the stairway into the front hall where he received obsequious attention from the publican and his wife, a rotund pair who thrilled to the importance of their guest. Seemingly oblivious of their care, he passed out into the street where he found Timothy and a growing group of children who waited, hoping to see the 'fairy tale' person.

He did not disappoint them. John Stuart was tall and wonderfully handsome. Thick dark hair, serious brown eyes, faultless features and an expression that verged on brooding but which merely added to the sum of his attractiveness. Even the children who clustered round him recognised this man as distinctly out of the ordinary.

Good-naturedly he chatted with them briefly. Then, as was his pattern, Timothy took the youngsters' attention with four shining threepenny pieces temptingly held between his thumb and forefinger. 'Now, leave the master be. These are for the winners in a game of marbles.' And with the toe of his shoe, he drew a ring in the dirt and the children, their eyes wide with expectation, left John Stuart and came to Timothy.

John Stuart proceeded along William Street, the main street of the township, named after King William IV, predecessor of Victoria now on the throne. The town's business had ceased for the day and the street was quiet except for a happy buzz issuing from the bar of the Empire Hotel. When he came to George Street, he turned left round the corner, slowing down to watch the too bright sun descend in a cloudless evening sky, before he crossed to the parkland, a square of trees and gardens that few towns in the colony, let alone this side of the Blue Mountains, could boast.

As he entered through the orderly hedge, part of his mind was contemplating the onward journey. Today was Tuesday. He would start early and be in the township of Blayney by nine o'clock in the morning. There they would change horses and a brisk ride would see him in the small community of Cowra by mid-afternoon and home in his beloved Mayfield before dinner time. He breathed deeply, wishing he were home already.

He walked towards the setting sun, watching the glint of its dying rays and enjoying the strong breeze that caressed his face and caught at his coat tails. Around him were dozens of great, deep-green pines, so dark and European here in this southern land of grey-green and brown. Planted by the townsfolk to remind them of 'home', they stood in neat rows silhouetted against the rooftops of the sprawling settlement.

He made an intriguing figure in the waning light. He had changed his elegant travelling suit for a mixture of city and country wear. His fashionable, impeccably cut jacket and shirt were from David Jones' store in Sydney and his knee-high, shining boots were imported from London. But his trousers were serviceable country wear from Thelma's needle and thread, with a reinforced seat for sitting a horse days at a time. Thelma, Joe Larmer's wife, still did much of his sewing after all these years. She had always been there, ever since his mother had gone away when he was three years old.

John Stuart almost never thought of his mother, and it was odd that she momentarily came to his mind now as he strode beneath the pines in the anonymity of their deep purple shadows. A wistful look appeared for a second on his features before his mouth turned down disconsolately.

He paused in the twilight gloom, his outline barely visible against the dark mass of the tree trunks. As he moved to face the north he frowned. A woman was coming towards him. She had appeared suddenly like some ethereal creature rising out of the hedge at twilight, moving quickly, gracefully, swinging in her right hand a small crocheted bag on pink strings.

It was obvious she took pleasure from the evening breeze on her face, for she stopped as she gained the inside of the hedge and took off her bonnet. Then she continued, her curls blowing away from her face, revealing the high colour in her cheeks. Her lips were slightly apart as she breathed deeply, radiating vitality. She wore a light gown of floral cotton open at the neck and it seemed to him that the skin of her throat shone faintly golden in the setting sun.

John Stuart stood and watched her move forward, draw near, come level, and pass by. There was a quick swell of feeling within him. He thought he had never seen anyone to equal her. She made her way through the park unconscious of the attention even though she had come to within seven feet of where he halted. As she gained the far side of the park, she stopped; she had dropped her bonnet and she bent to retrieve it. Then she turned and looked back the way she had come. To him it seemed as if she looked straight at him there in the shadows of the trees and he interpreted it almost as a sign. When, in a few seconds, she continued on her way, to his surprise, he followed her.

She was some distance ahead and his eyes held to the pale dress and the moving bonnet, softly illuminated in the closing darkness. She continued until she turned into Russell Street, a thoroughfare of small stone cottages and wooden houses. When she reached number twenty-two, she passed through a fence covered with the dead blooms of a wisteria vine, and entered the house. In spring and summer, wisteria hung in masses of colour from fences, sills and eaves, staining the dusty community with a pastel loveliness.

Long after the lamps glowed into life through the windows of the town on this last day of March, John Stuart stood on the roadway some yards away from the small house. He could hardly believe he had followed the woman home. He knew many women: daughters of politicians vied for his attention on his visits to the capital and many an affluent grazier's daughter had tried to catch him. There was no bachelor more desirable in the entire country, for not only was he immensely wealthy, he was exceptionally good-looking. Until now, he had avoided any serious romantic attachment. He disliked women who threw themselves at him. If he had thought at all about a wife, it had been in terms of someone he had not yet met, a woman who was beautiful, virtuous, dignified, pure. In short, he sought perfection. As he stood in the darkness of Russell Street, he was confused by his reaction to the woman he had followed. But one thing he could not deny: she had captivated him. The moon was up and the stars had appeared before he finally left and returned the short distance to the Royal Hotel.

An hour later, he dined with Sir Rutherford in a private room. He did not mention the woman, and the two new friends parted after a hearty meal and another discourse on Sir Rutherford's passion, the bushrangers.

John Stuart slept fitfully and woke early. During the night, a light rain had fallen and the day had been ushered in under a cloudy sky. When he came downstairs, Deke Edwards, his coach driver, and Leeroy Barton, the guard, were ready and waiting in the front hall. Deke's sun-weary face of creases and lines smiled at him. 'We be waitin' for ye, sir. The coach be shinin' ready to go, as soon as ye be wantin' to leave.'

The master of Mayfield frowned. 'I'll not leave until after luncheon, Deke. We can travel into the night. We've done it before.'

'That's right then, sir, just as ye say.'

John Stuart left the hotel and walked down to the livery stables, drawing respectful and admiring gazes on every side.

An hour later he tethered his horse to a tree at the bottom of a solitary hill on the plain that surrounded the Bathurst settlement. He climbed to the crest, swinging his riding crop at the flies that thought him new and agreeable game. At the top, he breathed deeply. He loved the clean smell of this sunny land, even more distilled today after the slight rain of the night. He bent and picked up some dirt; it seeped through his fingers onto his polished boot.

A crow cawed in the sky above. He watched as it came to land some twenty feet distant from him. Its mournful cry filled the air, black beak open to the sky, its feathers the lustre of polished ebony.

He felt the loneliness of the mighty country around him. It was possible he was the first man ever to stand in this particular spot. The enormity of that held him for many minutes. John Stuart was a highly literate, deep thinker, who, while hidebound by the morality of the times, mistrusted religious dogma, searched for rationale in reaching conclusions about life, and consequently was sympathetic with the free thinkers of the time. His peers were strictly religious, making him unique for a squatter and Australian country gentleman.

He looked up at the dispassionate sky where his companion, the crow, had now risen. He thought of Mayfield and smiled. As always, when he reflected on his home contentment and joy enveloped him.

Abruptly, a picture of the woman he had followed the evening before disturbed his tranquillity. He admitted she was the reason he was still here. Who the devil was she? How could she have affected him this way? He had not even spoken to her. He wished Joe were here.

The expanse of country beneath him which had filled him with such composure and happiness a mere minute before had lost its power. He returned down the hill in great strides, mounted his horse, and was soon riding swiftly back to Bathurst. It was no coincidence that once in the settlement his direction took him along Russell Street. Bringing his horse to a walk, he passed by number twenty-two. There, attached to the front wall, was a brass sign which had been concealed in the dark of the night before. It read: 'Miss Evelyn May Herman, Piano Lessons, Apply Within.'

John Stuart registered 'Miss'. He made a decision. He would not leave this afternoon. He must learn whether she was the 'Miss' designated in the sign. He had to know more of her. Must ask someone about her, but whom?

Just then a little girl carrying a satchel ran into the street from a house a few doors down. She was not exactly what he had in mind, but he thought she would be able to answer his questions and have less curiosity about them than any grown-up he knew. He called the child to him.

'Yes, sir?'

He smiled, and it was immediately duplicated on the little face gazing up.

'The lady who lives at number twenty-two, there with the mullioned windows.' He pointed with his riding crop. 'Does she live alone?'

The little girl was happy to supply the information. 'Why, surely, sir. She's the piano teacher.'

'You say alone, no one at all lives with her then?'

'No, sir, I . . . I don't think so. She's the piano teacher.' The child had repeated the last statement as if it supplied all reasons for the lady's solitary existence.

A bright sixpence soon gleamed in the small hand and she ran off with a smile of positive bliss on her freckled face.

John Stuart returned to the Royal. He called Timothy and gave instructions to cancel their onward journey, and he refused lunch. Timothy took these two changes with equanimity; a good valet never questioned his master's motives.

By mid-afternoon, John Stuart was on his roan mare again riding down Bentwick Street towards the Macquarie River. He must meet this woman. But there was a part of him that delayed his next move; intermingled with his desire to see her again was the fear that in the darkness of the previous dusk, he may have imagined grace where there had been only ease of movement, and beauty where there was but a pleasing look.

In the midst of his thoughts a woman turned the corner and came towards him. A hot feeling rose inside his throat and he felt as if his neck expanded; his shirt collar was choking him. As he watched her, she stopped and touched a climbing rose on a tressle above one of the fences. There she was again, another beautiful picture encapsulated like the vision of the evening before.

He pulled his horse back to a walk as she advanced. It was by now after three o'clock, and the sun was behind him. The bonnet she wore had practically no brim and he could see her face clearly as the light fell upon it. Relieved, he saw he had imagined nothing. There was a freshness about her that he could not remember any woman having before. She looked virtuous and dignified. It was obvious she was young, but not in her teens. This pleased him too; he disliked very young women, found them awkward and trivial. Her features were regular, almost refined, except for a little fullness of her mouth, and he liked that too. No, he had imagined nothing.

When she passed he could not help but speak. 'Good afternoon, Miss Herman.' His voice sounded loud to his ears.

'And good afternoon to you too, sir,' she replied and the sound of the 'a' vowel and rounded 'rs' was most unusual. He fancied the accent to be similar to Irish but he was not sure. 'Herman' was hardly Irish.

She looked up and raised her hand to protect her eyes and to see who it was that greeted her, but the sun was too strong and he appeared only as a silhouette on a horse. He rode on by and did not look back. If he had, he would have seen her turn to watch him.

Three hours after the meeting in Bentwick Street, he stood opposite 22 Russell Street, just as he had done the night before. As he watched, the front door opened and a small boy carrying sheets of music came running at high speed from the house as if released from captivity. He swung his body over the broken fence and went racing down the street.

John Stuart felt the breeze on his back and at the same time the lace curtains in the bay window of number twenty-two lifted, ballooned and danced a little. They glided forward through the opening and were blown about, flickering back and forth, pointing like white lace fingers at the neatly lettered brass sign attached to the wall. Moments later she came to the window and leaned forward to retrieve the offending curtain. She looked in his direction. He smiled, nodded his head and tipped his broad-brimmed hat to her. She returned a slight nod, but quickly and firmly drew in the curtain, closed the window, and pulled down the blind.

He stood another few minutes there in the twilight before he walked slowly back to his hotel.

Eve turned from the window paying little heed to the gentleman who had taken her eye for a moment. She had hardly registered him.

She sat on the piano stool and closed her eyes. She was pleased to see little David Dean leave. The child hated learning to play. Some lessons were so different, really enjoyable, especially with the girls at 'All Saints' School' where she taught. With them, instructing was a pleasure.

She felt tired. Thank goodness it was Maundy Thursday tomorrow when the Easter holidays would begin. She stood and, catching her reflection in the mirror over the mantel, sighed as she pushed back a fallen curl from her forehead.

There was a poise in Eve now. It was not merely the fulfilment of that promise seen in the sixteen-year-old girl of Sydney town. It was a combination of things. She was at peace. She did not need to apply the solitary strength that she had so relied upon in her teen years. Too, she had learned to check herself, and her tongue. She had dropped 'blazes' and 'devil' and 'damnation' from her vocabulary under Reverend Billings' tutelage, although the undaunted spirit that inspired those words still remained. She smiled gently at the thought of him; she could trust and depend upon him; with him there was security, the single most important thing missing from her life after her parents died.

She moved through her parlour by the picture of Queen Victoria, the Parian bust of Lord Melbourne, the antimacassars and the ruby glass, all representative of the niche she had found for herself here, and she thanked the Lord every day for finally having brought her here in February 1858, five years ago.

It had been like a miracle to rediscover Reverend Billings and to settle into a new life with him and Mrs Billings. The rector was her mentor, her friend and her surrogate father. She even called him 'Father', a tradition rarely used in the Church of England and having the other connotation for Eve. It felt right for both of them. A natural progression had occurred over the years, and his wife, Lillian, had encouraged Eve to call her 'Mother'.

From the first day she had ever seen Reverend Billings at Hastey's Auction Rooms there had been an affinity between them and, as always with attractions, it was a myriad intangibles that over the years had made them close.

The money from the sale of the watch he had given her had enabled her to rent Sully Tompkins' shed and start her sewing business. At first, it had been very difficult to get clients, and she had spent many weeks trudging the streets of Sydney door to door. The first year had been one of hardship, long hours and parsimony, but she had forced herself to be strong and remain determined. She had constantly encouraged Clare who sometimes had wished to give in, until finally the orders had come regularly, and they had been able at all times to make ends meet and to be independent.

There had been one young man in Eve's life: Sully Tompkins' son, William. Sully had become an alderman of Sydney and had two successful haberdashery shops. William was learning the business. He was well educated, temperate and considerate, and very deeply in love with Eve, and while Eve was very cautious, in time she came to have a real affection for him.

Clare had been involved with a succession of men and at age eighteen and unmarried, she had given birth to a stillborn son. William's parents had been mortified and forbidden him to see Eve because of her sister, but Billy, as Eve called him, had stood up to them and continued to call on Eve.

Clare was beautiful, addicted to pleasure, sceptical and yet at the same time gullible. She always believed every handsome man who said he loved her. So, while it hurt Eve, it did not really surprise her when she found Clare's note on their little mantelshelf one October morning in 1856.

Darling,

Forgive me, but I have gone with Harry to Adelaide. He has acquired a most commendable position with the newspaper there. Do be happy for me as I am for myself. He has promised to marry me, Evelyn. I know you have never really cared for him, but he is good to me. I believe it is all very auspicious and that everything is for the best.

I have taken most of the money we had saved, but you will understand, I know. And it won't take long for you to earn some more, you are so very capable and clever.

I am truly happy and I shall write to you the minute we have lodgings.

Your loving sister,
Clare

Within two weeks of Clare's departure, Billy asked Eve to marry him.

Eve thought about it. Clare was gone. She was alone. Billy gave her compassion and care and love. In her solitary moments, she admitted she did not return his love, but he was such a dear man and she liked him immensely. He had the ability to make her laugh and to lift her spirits. He was proper and reputable and, at his side, she would be accepted and respectable.

She agreed to his proposal and six weeks later they became engaged, much to the chagrin of Mr and Mrs Tompkins. They had

111

been engaged for ten months and were to be married at the year's end when Billy went with a group of young men on a day's outing. It was unseasonably hot that September of 1857 and they all swam in a creek outside Sydney. Within a week, Billy was dead. He and two other young men had caught diphtheria.

Eve was distraught. She had to see her sister. She closed the shop temporarily and went to Adelaide, only to find things had not worked out between Clare and Harry. Clare had been living with another man since the previous January. Eve spent ten days in Adelaide trying to convince her sister to come back to Sydney. Clare was living in tiny rented rooms with her new man, but Eve did not meet him, for he had gone briefly north-east to the Barossa Valley. In truth, Clare was pleased, for she feared that Eve's desire to have her return to Sydney might lead her sister to say something that would spoil things with him. 'It is better that you don't meet him, darling. You never like the men I like anyway.'

The last time Eve saw her sister, they met at the small tavern in Rundle Street where Clare worked and walked together down South Terrace to the path along the Torrens River. It was a grey afternoon. Eve held Clare's hands and looked into the eyes so very like her own. 'Why cannot you come back to Sydney with me?'

'Evelyn, darling, please understand. I truly love Nathaniel. I want to stay here.'

Eve shook her head. 'Oh, Clare. When in Hades are you going to learn? He hasn't married you, has he? Just like the others: Grayson, Larry Hutchins, Donald Blainey, Harry, and now this . . . Nathaniel whoever he is. You've had as many men in as many years; more if I know the truth. Damnation, Clare, I want you to come home.'

Clare's eyes filled with tears. 'I can't.'

Eve turned away in frustration. There were leaves drifting by on the river current; she thought how like her sister they were, without direction or will of their own. Yet she loved Clare. She sighed. 'I miss you, Clare.'

'And I you, darling. Stay here. Now there's an idea. You stay here.'

Eve turned back to face her sister. 'What? And work in a blasted tavern again like you do?' Springing to Eve's eyes was the old anger with Clare for not placing worth on herself. 'That is the one thing I've promised myself I'll never do again. Never! I have a business in Sydney, which even now I'm neglecting. I'm returning tomorrow and I beg you to come with me. Give yourself a chance, Clare.'

Her sister did not reply.

'I'm leaving from Victoria Wharf at eleven o'clock in the morning. Please be there.'

'Evelyn, you just don't understand.'

'No, and I never have. And, my dear sister, I never will. The next man who holds me, holds me in the marriage bed.' Eve looked in despair at the lovely face opposite, then she hugged Clare tightly and left her standing there.

The following morning, Eve departed from Adelaide alone.

Back in Sydney, she spent many hours walking in the Domain encircling Government House and down the gentle slope of the Botanical Gardens to the shore of peaceful Farm Cove by Fort Macquarie. She wandered and sat looking across the water, missing Billy and his laugh, and missing Clare. She thought how distant she and her sister had become. How different their needs were. She felt sad for Clare, the way her life was, and yet she knew Clare did not want pity. She had made her choice knowingly. Eve wished she could get away to somewhere fresh and new, start again, but that seemed impossible.

Then on Christmas Day she read the advertisement which altered her life.

She had just come home from St James's Church in Macquarie Street. She was an Episcopalian, which translated to Church of England here in the British colony. In her small living quarters, she made tea and perused two recent copies of the *Sydney Morning Herald*. Her eyes ran down the 'Situations Vacant' columns and she drew in her breath in sharp surprise as she read:

SITUATION VACANT

There is a vacancy for a Pianoforte Teacher at All Saints' Church of England School, Bathurst, New South Wales. Students are girls between the ages of seven and fourteen, all from paying families in and around the Bathurst district.

The applicants must be prepared to play the church organ (gratis) for services on Mondays, Thursdays and Sundays and take sewing classes with children of most tender years, all under the age of nine.

The successful applicant should be a genteel, unmarried lady with an earnest attitude and a sedate, willing, and pious nature who enjoys the country life.

Church housing can be arranged. And wages will be explained by return post to those ladies making serious application. Apply to: Mrs Hazel Wiggers, Head Mistress, All Saints' Church of

England School, William St, Bathurst.

The advertisement was for the very church that she remembered her clergyman belonging to! How often in the past years she had thought of him, the wonderful man who had given her the gold watch that day in the street in Walsh Bay.

She had written to him after she had taken lease of Sully Tomkins' shed thanking him for helping her. She had been painfully disappointed when he had not replied, for she had really felt a kindred spirit with him in their two brief meetings. Little did she know that her letter had never reached its destination. Instead, it had been thrown in the bracken by the Sydney roadside having been on a coach that was robbed near Katoomba in the Blue Mountains.

She wondered if the cleric was still at the church in Bathurst.

The situation advertised was one she could fill quite ably, even down to the sewing. Why, she could take her sewing machine with her! She was not exactly sure about the 'sedate, willing and pious' part. She had a little laugh at that. It was the thought of a country life that appealed greatly to her. And to be able to play piano again would be heaven.

She stood and walked out her back door. She looked out on the rear of Ma Whirley's Hotel and the two-storeyed building that was the office of the *Shipping Gazette*. Between the two she had a narrow view of the waters of the harbour. Everyone she cared for had left her, and while she still believed in herself, her strength and resilience, there was nothing holding her in Sydney now. What was a business without someone to share it? She brought her hands together. 'I'll do it!' she said aloud. She went back inside and wrote two letters. One was to Mrs Wiggers as the advertisement suggested, enclosing a letter of introduction from Canon Robert Allwood of St James's Church; the other was to Reverend Billings.

This time, to her delight and surprise, she received a letter back from the parson within a week. It assured her that he remembered her and urged her to come to Bathurst anyway. She closed down her business and moved her life. It was not until she finally met Reverend Billings that they both found out that their earlier letters had gone so fatefully astray; and in their hearts, they both thought it a miracle that they had discovered each other again.

All the years, she had continued to correspond with Clare. But these days her sister's address was a post office box at the General Post Office in Adelaide and she did not hear from her very often. Clare was not a good correspondent, and while Eve wrote many times a year, her sister replied perhaps only once or twice. A letter had come from Clare only a few days ago, and Eve read it again before she went to sleep on this first day of April. It was short and cheerful. Clare's notes were always optimistic. She was still in Adelaide, still working in a tavern and still living with some fellow. Eve could always be sure that Clare would have a man. 'Tall and handsome' was Clare's description. 'Naturally,' Eve said aloud.

It was not until later, when she was in that semi-world between yielding to sleep and actually sleeping, that she recalled the man who had stood across the street from her house in the dusk. Odd that he had been standing looking at her home. Who was he? What had he been doing there? Her thoughts floated over the scene. He had been well-dressed, far too refined for the Bathurst streets, and dark under his wide-brimmed hat.

When she did sleep she dreamed. Of strange men, tastefully dressed and wearing hats that hid their faces. John Stuart, on the other hand, hardly slept at all. He spent much of the night thinking of her.

His position in the colony was of unmistakable importance. Mayfield was enormous, hundreds of square miles, the largest property in the colony and in the country. He was powerful and earnest about his power. Born into the upper echelon of the community, consequently his pattern of behaviour must contain the highest, socially acceptable standards of morality. In this reign of Victoria, it was accepted for a young man of Bathurst town to introduce himself to a lady he admired. Townsmen and countrymen alike could speak freely to a lady after seeing her only once in the street or the field. But for John Stuart Wakeman, such was not the case. He pursued the 'proper' social code which neither encouraged, nor allowed him, to introduce himself to a female. This made it all the more remarkable that he had actually spoken to Eve in Bentwick Street. For all his scientific free thinking, his personal behaviour was formal.

If he had been less taken by Eve, he might have judged a Bathurst music teacher unworthy of his attentions. But as he lay sleepless that night, he had no interest in her station, but thought of her in the most physical of senses. She was different to other women, he was sure of it. He had convinced himself she was chaste and pure in her heart and mind, but physically she aroused and attracted him. He wanted his hands on her silken skin and his face in her hair. He wanted to breathe in the scent of her, to taste the wetness of her mouth. He had to know this woman, know her and have her, but at the same time he knew he desired to protect and comfort her. When finally he slept, it was just before dawn broke over Maundy Thursday with a brilliant sun.

115

Eve woke not long after John Stuart at last slipped into sleep. She was to spend the day with Father and Mother Billings at the parsonage. As she left her house in Russell Street it was with the happy expectation of a carefree day in their company. In truth, they would have liked Eve to live with them, but they were wise enough to realise her need for independence and so had not pursued the matter even though some folk deemed it odd that an unmarried young woman lived alone. She did not know, but she was often referred to as the 'pretty piano teacher' by those of the population not given to envy, and as 'that American woman' by those who were.

Eve walked the short distance from her home to the parsonage. She wore a light-blue cotton dress and a straw hat. As she crossed the street to enter the whitewashed wooden gate of the rectory, the vendors in the fruit, vegetable and poultry market opposite turned to watch her.

In the last five years, a number of suitors had courted Eve, but she had not responded to any, and each in time had dropped off and married others. She could not help it, she wanted someone of distinction whom she could love and admire; someone like Father, intelligent and well bred and a gentleman, and all that tiny Bathurst had to offer were local tradesmen or clerks or farmers. All her friends were married, except for one other teacher at All Saints', but still she did not care. She had the stability of Father and Mother now; she could wait.

Mother opened the front door to greet Eve and as she drew her into the hall, she wrapped her arms round her visitor. 'He's expecting you, my love, and as usual he is being particular about what I feed you for luncheon.'

The two women laughed affectionately and passed arm in arm down the long hall to the study.

Father Billings rose as they entered, his face lighting up in a broad smile as he took Eve's hands in his. 'Good morning, how bright you make the day, Eve.' She returned his greeting and kissed him.

His earnest eyes softened now as they rested on the two women. These were the flowers of his flock. The one he had been married to for forty years he loved quietly, a balanced and harmonious love; the other, who had come into his life five short years before, he loved with exquisite intensity. She was the precious daughter bestowed when all hope of such a one had long been abandoned. At times she still reminded him of his beloved sister, Josephine, but now he loved her for herself, as Eve.

'My dears, I am looking for some misplaced church funds at the moment, but no doubt will find them eventually. Now you are here, Eve, you can help me.'

Mother smiled at them. 'You two are to be in the back garden at one o'clock sharp for luncheon.' And she left them to themselves.

They worked the morning, happy in each other's company, comfortable and familiar. Once or twice he called her 'Evvy', his pet name for her, and she smiled up at him from the pile of papers around her.

Before luncheon, the two of them took their customary walk, arm in arm, through the grounds of All Saints', but they were in the back garden under the big jacaranda tree on the dot of one o'clock. During the meal Father was brought a note by Mistress Lottie Thatcher, the housekeeper at the parsonage. She was a comely, country woman of a similar height and colouring to Eve, though older and with the unequivocal direct gaze of the bush folk. She was unmarried and had been devoted to the Billingses for seventeen years. She stood watching Father dispassionately as he read the message.

He handed the paper back to her as he stood from the table. 'Thank you, Lottie. Excuse me, my loves, but a gentleman wishes to see me. I hope the intrusion is not long.' He strode across the lawn and into the house followed closely by Lottie in her swirling brown skirt.

In the front hall stood John Stuart Wakeman.

Reverend Billings had not seen John Stuart since his father, Sir Arthur Wakeman, had died over seven years before, though he read about him regularly in the Sydney and country newspapers. The cleric had been a friend of Sir Arthur and had visited Mayfield on occasions in the past. He knew the son did not inherit the father's good opinion of the Church and had noticed the generous yearly donation had ended after his friend's death.

John Stuart had changed little since the cleric had last seen him. The only difference the elapsed years had brought were more maturity and a dark moustache. He would be over thirty now, had always been a good-looking man, similar to his father, except his eyes were brown where his father's had been light blue. His bearing was the same, unmistakably that of a Wakeman. There was the particular presence his father had owned, but more so in John Stuart, for he was taller than his father had been by two or three inches. The clergyman held out his hand. 'John Stuart, what brings you here after so long a time?'

For a second or two an expression of irritation appeared on his visitor's face. Was it that he little liked to be reminded of his inadequacies? He had not seen Leslie Billings, one of his father's dearest friends, for many years. Then the look submerged in an affable nod of the head and an open smile. 'Good to see you, sir, good to see you.'

'Thank you, son. Are you here in Bathurst for long? Do come into my study, we can talk more freely there.'

When John Stuart had bent his long frame into a rosewood chair and Father had done the same, the clergyman looked inquiringly at him.

He coughed. 'Sir, I've come to approach you on a delicate matter, and to ask you for your . . .' He paused as if resisting the next word, then added, 'help.'

'If I can, my boy, I will.'

He paused again and Father said nothing. In the hiatus the ticking of the large ormolu clock on the mantelshelf seemed loud. John Stuart appeared unsure of how to proceed. He was wishing Joe Larmer were with him. He took a breath and his mouth turned up into a half smile. 'You see, there is a lady in this town. I saw her first the day before yesterday, in the park. She . . . well . . . she exemplifies everything I regard as desirable in womankind.'

For some incalculable reason, the Reverend had an uncanny feeling that he knew exactly who she was.

'The matter which I wish you to attend to, sir, is that of an introduction. Now she may not be one of your parish, but I hope you will accommodate me.'

Father passed his hand across his eyes. It was an uncomfortable gesture. 'This lady . . . you wish to meet her with a view to spending time in her company when you pass this way?'

John Stuart did not reply for fully half a minute. His dark eyes closed. When he opened them and focused them on the preacher they held a resolve that echoed the determination in his voice. 'Sir, my desire is to marry her.'

The older man suddenly looked very weary. At that moment, the future with all its absurd contingencies seemed revealed to him. He felt as if he were in a flooded river, inextricably washed along. He knew the answer to his question even as the words came from his lips. 'And who is this lady? Do you know her name?'

'Yes. Her name is Evelyn Herman, she lives in Russell Street. Do you know her?'

At this very moment the heavy study door opened and Eve breezed in, saying, 'Father dear, I have been sent to find . . .' Her words trailed off as she caught sight of John Stuart in the chair.

Both men stood in unison.

John Stuart looked in amazement at Eve. 'But this is the very lady . . . How is it she is here and calls you Father?'

The clergyman did not reply. It was as if he could not speak. He was a capable man, chance events normally did not disconcert him and he could understand any man wanting to marry his Evvy, she was a beautiful prize in his eyes, but the declaration by John Stuart had taken him quite unprepared.

Eve advanced to his side, swiftly answering for him. 'Father is what I call the Reverend. We both prefer it.' Then she looked questioningly up to the pastor.

He put a protective arm round her shoulders and with an almost visible effort said, 'Eve, my love, this is John Stuart Wakeman of Mayfield. He has wished to meet you after seeing you in the park on Tuesday.'

John Stuart, evidently entranced by her arrival, bowed. 'How do you do, Miss Herman.'

Eve had heard of John Stuart Wakeman, who in the colony had not? She was fascinated to meet him. She stretched out her hand which he took and held. She felt a tingle of pleasure as he continued to hold it until she extricated it. Then suddenly a look of recognition came into her face. 'My goodness!' she said. 'I know who you are! You're the man who stood across from my house last night, aren't you? Of course, and the man on the horse in Bentwick Street yesterday, I . . .' She turned to Father with a baffled smile.

Father looked questioningly. 'You stood outside her house last night?'

John Stuart's eyes were intent on every small detail of her, and as he answered the Reverend, he remained looking at Eve. 'I'm afraid it is true. And I confess I stood there the night before as well, only that time she was unaware of me.' He continued looking in her eyes. 'My admission extends. You see, I followed you home from the park on Tuesday night.'

She laughed a small surprised laugh. 'Oh,' she said. 'I did not realise it.' She could not help being flattered by John Stuart's obvious attraction to her. She thought him quite the best-looking man she had ever seen. A pleasant lunch with Father and Mother had turned into something much more exciting. She looked up at Father, taking the initiative and saying, 'Mother sent me to find you. She will wonder what the delay is. Why don't we invite Mr Wakeman to lunch? We've only just begun and there's so much food.'

The lunch was an exceptional success for John Stuart. He was openly captivated by Eve and she was unmistakably interested in him.

119

She compared him with the men she knew. This was no plain Bathurst man, he was a man of authority and station. He spoke lucidly on the colony, its inadequacies, its achievements and its future. When she mentioned her homeland, he expressed his wide knowledge of her own country and the civil war that now gripped it. He even enlightened her on the series of recent victories for the southern army in Virginia, in particular the northern defeat at Fredericksburg on 13 December, and how it appeared otherwise on the Mississippi where the northern army had badly damaged the southerners. She listened to him gravely and marvelled at the range of his information.

The look of confusion that lingered in Father's eyes that afternoon did not disturb Eve, for she did not notice it. Her attention was on the eminent guest.

His distinguished air attracted her.

His assertiveness attracted her.

His physical appearance attracted her.

After his departure, she remained in the back garden alone for a time, an expectant expression in her lively eyes.

CHAPTER SEVEN

'Twice or thrice had I loved thee,
Before I knew thy face or name.'
'Air and Angels', John Donne, 1572–1631.

On the Saturday after Easter, a horse and chaise stood to the side of a dirt track two miles from Bathurst. Near the vehicle grazed two saddled horses, and a hundred yards away on the bank of the Macquarie River, under the shade of a large wattle tree, four people sat on a blanket eating sandwiches.

Eve's eyes twinkled as she swallowed a mouthful. 'I really do enjoy picnics.'

Father smiled and Mother waved a teacloth at a party of insistent flies. 'I would, except for these little wretches.'

John Stuart lifted his handkerchief and joined Mother's attempts to swat the flies. He had remained in Bathurst since meeting Eve at the parsonage on Maundy Thursday. He had set up residence at the Royal Hotel and his obvious attention to Eve Herman was the constant talk of the entire four thousand souls of the borough. On Good Friday he had come to the parsonage after church service and he and Eve had sat for a long time talking in the garden. On Easter Saturday he arrived for tea and again after church on Easter Day. On the Monday, which was a holiday, he invited Eve and Mother to dine with him at the Royal. During the work days that followed, he met Eve after school and they took tea in the garden of the rectory under the poinciana tree.

Eve was doing a lot of thinking. Although she was clear-headed, discerning and watchful where men were concerned, to find herself in the position of having John Stuart in attendance was something out of a dream. She had never been with anyone so scholarly, so worldly, so sophisticated and so handsome. Nor had most of the population of Australia, for there were few John Stuart Wakemans available. He was articulate, and could speak fluently on almost any subject. She marvelled at his knowledge of the world, at his understanding of science and poetry and literature. She could not help being flattered that he was interested in her opinions and how

121

she reacted to things. They talked a lot about music and she played the piano for him.

He had a certain way of watching her that at times made her feel a little embarrassed, but in the most exciting, womanly way. She thought he represented everything that was strong and manly.

As the days went by, and John Stuart remained in Bathurst, Father had confided to his wife what had passed between himself and John Stuart in his study. Mother had been delighted. 'Really? But that is wonderful, Leslie dear. What a perfect couple they will make.'

He took her hands in his. 'Ah, my love, I suppose you are right, but I have the feeling that John Stuart is so captivated by our darling that he will take her from us very soon if she agrees.' Then he added quickly, 'Not that I want to keep her when she can have a home of her own like Mayfield, and a husband of John Stuart's position. It's just that I think all this goes too swiftly.'

'It doesn't matter if they are right for each other,' his wife answered, and Father had nodded and looked pensively into the distance. His expression was the same now as Eve and John Stuart stood up to go for a walk along the river bank.

Eve smiled down at him. 'We shan't be long.'

'Don't worry about us,' Mother replied, 'enjoy yourselves.'

John Stuart held out his arm and Eve slipped her hand round it as they moved away.

For a little time they walked in silence. It was a warm afternoon and they kept in the shade of the numerous casuarina trees, commonly known as she-oaks, that grew along the water's edge. When they rounded a bend, ahead of them was a clump of eucalyptus trees and Eve stood for a long time watching a koala bear, while John Stuart spent most of the time watching her. Finally he asked, 'What is that you would like more than anything else in the world?'

Eve turned to him and laughed. 'Oh, my goodness, that's hard to answer.'

'Well, try.'

'More than anything in the world?'

'Yes.'

A grave look rose in her face and she pursed her lips in reflection. 'It's an awfully difficult question, John Stuart, but as you ask me, I think that I would like people to be kinder to each other, and to know that there was no more cruelty, and that poor girls could be delivered from being deceived by the lies of certain men. Yes, and that the world did not judge as harshly as it does or that horrible disease did not kill people before their time, and that poor little children did not have—' She stopped short for John Stuart had begun to laugh. A deep frown of disapproval lodged between her eyes. 'Why are you so amused?'

He took up her hand and kissed it. 'Evelyn, I fear you have been too long with the parson. All these wishes for mankind are wonderful and lofty, no doubt, but I was meaning what do *you* want more than anything in the world.'

There was a stubbornness now in Eve's brown eyes. Her mouth tightened just a little as she turned from him and walked on, saying, 'I have just told you.'

The amused look remained on John Stuart's face for a second or two before it faded and he followed her. 'Please wait,' he called, hurrying after her. 'Evelyn, I'm sorry I laughed.'

She did not look at him but continued on in silence.

'Eve, please, believe me, I'm sorry, truly.'

'You do not take me seriously. I meant the things I said. The world needs changes.'

He took her hand and stopped her from walking on. He turned her solemn face to his. 'All right, I admit I was frivolous. I apologise. You have told me and I accept what you say. I am in awe of you and your altruism, Miss Herman.' He lifted her hand to his mouth and kissed her fingertips. 'So, please, will you indulge me in my disgrace and allow me to tell you what I want more than anything?'

She sighed. 'All right, tell me.'

'You.'

She drew her breath in sharply.

There was no mirth in his eyes now, only sincerity. 'Eve, you must realise why I have remained in Bathurst. To see you. To be with you. I am in love with you, Evelyn May Herman, and I want to take you home to Mayfield.' His expression was soft, loving. 'I want you to know Mayfield as I do. Eve, I am asking you to be my wife. Now, soon.'

'I have only known you nine days.'

'What does that matter? I love you, have loved from the moment I saw you in the park. Say yes, my darling. Please.'

She was looking up at him, doubt and uncertainty clearly in her eyes. He stepped closer and slipped his arms round her back and drew her to him. He was looking into her eyes as he brought his lips down upon hers and slowly kissed her. At the contact, Eve felt a thrill of excitement run through her, sharp and tantalising. His mouth was delightfully wet and warm as he enclosed her lips inside his. She was conscious of his hands through the material of her dress as they moved over her back, and down her spine. The pressure of his firm body against her breasts aroused her. Gently, he forced open her lips and she felt the shiver of excitement extend through her body as she tasted his mouth for the first time.

She felt warm and womanly and wonderful.

When he drew away, his hands lingered on her bare arms. A hot breeze lifted her skirt and blew it forward to wind round his leg. They stood there in silence, both aware of the response in the other.

'What do you say, my darling?' he asked at last. 'Will you be my wife?'

She moved away to look across the river. Her emotions were in confusion. She did not know what to think, and what to say completely evaded her.

As she stood there she felt his hand on her shoulder. It moved slowly across to the naked skin of her throat in caressing, gentle movements. She felt another sensual thrill at the touch of his fingers. His face came close behind her, his lips in her hair. 'Eve, say yes. Then we can be married soon, and go home to Mayfield. You will love it there.' He sighed. 'You and Mayfield, both beautiful; how I do love you both.'

Eve's heart was racing. She turned round to face him. He looked so solemn now, so earnest and imploring.

'Please, Eve, answer me.'

She took a deep breath. 'Just give me some time to think, a little time.'

He leaned forward and kissed her again, stirring up the jumble of emotions within her.

'All right,' he said, 'I'll wait until tomorrow. Promise me you will tell me tomorrow.'

She stood looking up at him. A cockatoo somewhere in the scrub screeched loudly. He smiled. She loved his smile. It sat now a touch crooked on his face as it sometimes did, and for a second or two she thought she saw the boy in the man, making him seem vulnerable. That surprised her, she had thought there were no insecurities in John Stuart's personality. She lifted her hand to the collar of his shirt and touched it in an affectionate manner. 'All right, I'll tell you tomorrow, but now we should get back to Mother and Father, don't you think?'

He nodded, he could wait until tomorrow. Taking up her hand he tucked it inside his arm and slowly they made their way back along the river, but he could not help continuing his attempts to convince her. 'Eve, listen to me, we can have a great life, a perfect life, together. You'll love Mayfield. It's unique. You can ride all day across rolling hills and valleys. The sunlight on the house in the mornings is a golden splendour and the way the dusk inches up through the green trees of the park in the evening brings a peace I cannot explain.' He sighed, imbued with his love for his home. 'You'll see, you'll be so happy there.'

That night Eve stayed at the rectory as she often did on weekends. She hardly slept at all. She tossed and turned and by the dawn light she rose and was washed and dressed and in the garden sitting under the poinciana tree before six o'clock. She was completely absorbed by John Stuart's marriage proposal. She knew she felt comfortable and happy in his company. She admired him and trusted him. She felt somewhat overwhelmed by his ardent vows of love for she had always been independent; even here with Father and Mother, she had a life of her own, she lived alone and made her own decisions. But this was marriage; this was permanent. This was what men never offered Clare. Did she want to marry John Stuart? Did she love him? Well, perhaps not the way he said he loved her, but she knew that her response to his affection and his kiss was strong and passionate and valid.

She leaned down from where she sat and brushed the dew on the grass with her fingertips. Through her mind ran the words that she had been recalling all night long. The words her mother had said to her when she was dying. How clearly she recalled her beautiful mother, wasted and gaunt, in the big mahogany bed in San Francisco.

Ada had asked to see each of her daughters separately, and when it had been her turn, her mother had taken her hand. She had smiled wanly and drawn Eve down to her. She kissed her and then whispered, 'Do not tell your sister, for I do not know that it is so with her, but you will be a fine lady, Eve . . . in silk and pearls . . . diamonds too . . . always remember that.'

'But how do you know, Mother?'

Ada had replied in the oddest manner. 'Matthis told me . . . Matthis . . . and thus there is . . . no doubt of it . . .'

'But who is Matthis?'

Ada had not seemed to hear. 'Remember these letters. M . . . A . . . Y . . . F. They will mean something of great importance . . . to you . . . and only you . . . There were others, but Matthis could not see them all . . . yes . . . great importance . . . remember them always.' Then Ada had tried to lift herself a little and put out her hand to touch Eve's face. 'And you will be loved, greatly loved . . .' She had begun to cough then, and her father had come in with the nurse.

Eve had thought her mother was delirious and she had never told anyone about it, but from the hour in the back garden of the parsonage when she had met John Stuart, it had been on her mind. For

125

the letters spelt the beginning of 'Mayfield'.

'Darling, you're up early.'

She turned on the seat to see Father coming down the steps from the kitchen. 'Yes. I want to come to early Communion this morning.'

He smiled. 'Good.'

The Communion service ended at a quarter to nine and when Eve and Father returned across the back garden from church, Lottie met them near the kitchen door. She pointed back through the house. 'Mr Wakeman is on the front verandah. He waits for you, Miss Eve.'

Father looked inquiringly at Eve. 'He's here early.'

'Yes.' She dropped his arm. 'Lottie, please tell Mr Wakeman I am coming.' When Lottie had gone, Eve turned to the cleric. 'John Stuart wants to marry me.'

Slowly Father nodded. 'Yes, my darling, I know.'

'I had better go and see him.'

He smiled. It was a reassuring smile, full of love and tenderness and understanding. 'Evvy, I want you always to be happy. You know that, don't you?'

'Yes, I know that.'

She walked away from him to the steps and turned at the top to look down at him standing in the morning sun, watching her.

'I'll always love you,' she said.

'I'll always love you, too,' he answered.

Eve woke with a start. For a few seconds she lay there gathering her thoughts and examining the green canopy of the bed above her. She was in her usual bedroom at the rectory. It was five weeks from the day she had met John Stuart and it was her wedding day.

She smiled a slow smile and snuggled more deeply into the bed-clothes. Then into the warm glow of her mind came thoughts of Clare. She sat up, a frown on her face. She had written to her sister the day after she had agreed to marry John Stuart. Of course letters took weeks to get from Sydney to Adelaide and she knew she would not hear from Clare before the wedding. She truly wished she could have shared her happiness with her sister. It would have been wonderful if Clare could have been here today. A guilty little shiver ran through her for she had never mentioned Clare to John Stuart. From the moment of meeting him, things had happened so quickly that there had never seemed an appropriate time to apprise him. They had talked much about the future and their lives together, and while Eve had told John Stuart about coming out from America and the deaths of her mother and father and about the sewing business in Sydney, she had always held back the existence of Clare. She had felt embarrassed and was not sure how to broach the subject, nor was she sure how John Stuart would react.

The only people in Bathurst who knew about Clare were Father and Mother. A few days ago, Father had counselled Eve to tell her future husband everything, but she had been adamant that it was the wrong time, that when they were married she would find a quiet moment and explain. She felt it would be easier then. Father Billings had acceded to his darling's point of view against his better judgement and let the subject lapse.

Eve took a deep breath and sighed just as Mother bustled in saying, 'Eve, my love, time to get up. Our Lottie's here with the water hot for your bath.'

Behind her came Lottie struggling with a large jug. 'And Jennie's got another as well, Miss Eve, coming right away.'

Later, left alone to bathe, she did something she had not done since girlhood. Standing in front of the large cedar wardrobe she untied her nightdress and let it fall to the floor. Her naked reflection stared out of the mirror.

Slowly, she lifted her right hand and, studying each part of herself, traced an imaginary line down her nose, across her mouth, under her chin over the little hollow at the base of her neck to her breasts. She traced round her nipples with her forefinger. They hardened to her touch. She flattened her palms down across her belly into the curly pubic hair below. A tremulous movement lifted the tight spirals out from her body and they sprang back from her fingers. Small erotic shivers of expectation trembled through her at the thought of intimacy with John Stuart. Eve was not a person given to great vanity, but she enjoyed the look of the woman reflected. Her body was slender and free of imperfections. She smiled at the woman in the mirror and turned away to her toilet.

Mother and Lottie spent the next hour helping her to dress.

The ceremony was at half past nine, and it appeared the whole borough of Bathurst had gathered outside All Saints'. Children had climbed the four casuarina trees that grew on the footpath and some hung precariously from the branches, shouting excitedly to each other.

Eve looked through the window at the crowd. Everything had happened quickly, perhaps a little too quickly for Father. Nevertheless, once she had agreed to marry John Stuart, he had convinced her that waiting was futile. 'I want to take you home, to our home, Mayfield.' The wedding banns had been hastily read and John Stuart's power and influence lent respectability to this unconventional behaviour.

She was going to be Mrs Wakeman. To be mistress of so much and married to John Stuart as well was like a blessing bestowed by her guardian angel. She knew she was the envy of every young woman in the colony and she wanted so much to be worthy of him, to be a good wife. This was not merely respectability; this was prestige, honour, prominence. In her heart she believed in herself, just as she always had. While he brought wealth and rank and station to her and the fulfilment of many of her dreams, she brought things to him. She knew she was loyal and caring and competent. She looked forward to learning about the property and believed she could help him with the people who lived and worked there. She wanted to learn, and be involved with his life; to be his partner, his lover and his friend.

When she finally passed from the rectory to the church door on Father's arm, she was exhilarated. A long, white veil hid her face, and her white silk dress and train were covered in hearts decorated with seed pearls. They had come by special courier from Sydney. On her finger was the ring encrusted with diamonds and rubies that her husband-to-be had placed on her finger a week ago. Highly aware of the throng, she held tightly to Father's arm. It was hard for her to believe that they were here to see her. As they neared the church porch, the crowd pushed forward and clearly she heard the voice of Miss Macdonald, the old washerwoman. 'Good on ye, Eve gel, ye be gettin' the pick of the whole ruddy colony.'

All Saints' was brimming with dignitaries. The Governor of the colony, Sir John Young, shared the front row with Thelma Larmer, Joe's wife, and Daydee, his seventeen-year-old daughter. The Premier, Mr Charles Cowper, sat with the Colonial Secretary, the Speaker of the Legislative Assembly and a number of the elected from parliament. The Mayor of Bathurst, Mr Richard Young Cousins, bestowed his broad smile to right and left. Some rows back was Sir Rutherford Blake, arms folded in front of him, with his assistant Mr Elrington at his right hand.

John Stuart's side of the church far overbalanced the left, for while Eve's friends numbered Lottie and Jennie and Mrs Wiggers, the headmistress of All Saints' School, and the other teachers and some married friends, John Stuart had scores of guests.

Joe Larmer and Mother were standing for the celebrators and they waited at the altar rail with John Stuart.

Soon after Eve had agreed to marry him, John Stuart had gone home to Mayfield. He explained to Eve that he was concerned about being away from Mayfield for so long, and this she understood. He was a businessman after all, and the property was his life. He was away thirteen days and returned to her ten days before the wedding, bringing Joe Larmer with him. Eve quickly realised that Joe was not only proud of John Stuart but loved him deeply. It was evident the feeling was mutual. Theirs was a father and son relationship and she recognised that there was no one on earth closer to the master of Mayfield than his manager.

When Thelma and Daydee arrived three days before the wedding, Eve responded warmly to Joe's wife, a motherly person of about fifty-five who wore her long hair tied severely back in a bun, a style that accentuated her wide forehead and large, sincere, hazel eyes. It was apparent to Eve from the start that Thelma was a simple, unaffected soul. She had taken Eve in her arms and hugged her affectionately. Her daughter, Daydee, a slight, dark-haired girl of seventeen, dressed in cream silk, was less enthusiastic to Eve, although her greeting to John Stuart was almost excessive. She threw herself into his arms saying, 'Uncle John Stuart, I've missed you terribly. Why, what with the cattle drive and everything, you've only been home thirteen days in the last fifty, for I have counted them!' And John Stuart had laughed indulgently, half lifting her off the floor as she embraced him. Eve had watched the display, not sure what to make of it.

The inside of the church was resplendent, the work of Mother and Thelma who knew each other from the days of Arthur Wakeman. There were beautiful flowers on every available flat surface, and decorated horseshoes, the old Irish tradition for luck in marriage, hanging at the end of the pews.

Outside, the noise grew even above the organ, and as John Stuart turned and watched his bride come towards him, Martin Carlyle, the church warden, could be heard at the door shouting, 'Please, be quiet! In the name of God!'

Eve relinquished Father's arm to take the hand John Stuart extended.

Father was not in essence a selfish man, in fact he was as charitable as men of his calling are supposed to be, but where Eve was concerned he was cautious and protective. In the whole country he could not have chosen a better partner for his dearest Evvy. But the Reverend was not interested in looks and material success. He was concerned only with real happiness for his 'daughter' and, in the beginning, he had thought the marriage too hasty and the celebrators too unfamiliar. He had asked himself if he were being prejudiced because he was losing Eve, and he answered that he wanted only the best for her, and so had come to terms with the speed of the union. Still, his heart was beating rapidly as he looked from one to the other and said, 'I now pronounce you man and wife.'

When the ceremony was complete and the papers signed, the couple walked back down the aisle to the strains of one of Mozart's motets lifting from the organ and the musicians that John Stuart had hired to play. The minister turned back to the altar and offered up a prayer to God. The prayer was short and passionate and full of benefits for Eve. Later, there were times when the good man thought his God had not been listening.

A peal of bells began as the bride and groom issued from the church. Father was proud of the bells. The tower had been completed in 1852 and the bells rung for the very first time during the Crimean War, when they heard the good news of the Battle of Inkerman. John Stuart and Eve passed through the well-wishers and the curious into the morning sun where the Mayfield coach waited for them.

The journey would take them at least twelve hours, probably more, so they had decided to forego a formal wedding breakfast in the interests of making a good start. Their guests were to be entertained at a most elaborate feast where they would eat and drink for much of the remainder of the day. Even the ordinary townsfolk were to enjoy the celebration; Joe had seen to it that pies, cakes and drinks were to be made available to them in the park.

The population cheered and John Stuart made a short speech. He stood on the church steps, his hand holding his wife's arm. Eve thought him a regal figure in his formal morning dress, and his voice rang happily over the crowd. 'Thank you one and all for being here to celebrate this occasion with my wife and myself. We leave shortly for our life together on Mayfield, but the interest and concern you have shown towards us this day, consistent with the nature of country folk, will for ever be remembered. Bathurst will always have a special meaning to us.' He looked down at Eve as he said the last words and she smiled up at him as the crowd cheered again.

They retired for twenty minutes to the rectory. There were tears in Eve's eyes and in those of her surrogate parents as she held onto them in the entry hall of the parsonage to say her final farewells. Father took John Stuart's hand and said, 'Take care of our daughter.' Eve hugged them all in turn and Mother whispered, 'God bless you, darling, God bless you.' Lottie fussed about making sure Eve's travelling dress was straight, and everyone wiped wet eyes. Yet it was Daydee who cried the most. She and her mother were staying on in Bathurst for a week with Thelma's cousin and the girl clung to both her father and John Stuart as if she were to be separated from them for a decade.

And so Mr and Mrs Wakeman departed in the shining coach with the Wakeman blazon upon the door, and Bathurst, in one voice, cheered the fairytale couple.

Father thought later he had seen nothing in his long life to equal the beauty of Eve's face that morning. He spent much of the day in the chapel, his favourite place to meditate. His wife left him alone and when he returned home after evening prayers, they sat silently, close together on the old sofa in their big, homely kitchen, comfortable and secure in their own abiding love.

It had been a wrench for Eve to leave her adopted parents and her secure life with them, but once she had, she looked forward to her future. She glowed, her skin shone and when she looked into her new husband's eyes her heartbeat quickened. 'You are beautiful, Mrs Wakeman,' he repeated many times, turning to her in the bumping carriage and kissing her lightly on the lips or lifting her hand to his mouth. Eve laughed, a lover's laugh, in anticipation of what was to come.

The road ran through virgin bush where now and then sparrows in flocks flew overhead. To left and right was a land of olive-greens, greys and soft browns, the colours of the iron-bark and stringy-bark gums. Much of the country consisted of long, undulating hills and a few miles before their arrival in Blayney a big buck kangaroo left its herd and kept pace with the coach, impressively leaping gullies and scrub, its massive hindquarters lifting it seemingly effortlessly into the air. Her husband explained this was not uncommon, there seemed to be something about a moving vehicle that fascinated the big kangaroos and Eve leaned out the window, entranced.

John Stuart smiled at his wife's delight. When he did so he exposed two rows of even white teeth beneath his dark moustache. He looked boyish and Eve felt a sharp and sudden sympathy for him, she knew not why. She bent towards him and took his hand. He squeezed hers in return and with his left hand he took out the fine, gold timepiece he carried in the fob pocket of his waistband. Looking at it he said proudly, 'Well, my darling, we've made splendid time, even though the road is bad, like all the damned roads in the colony. My six Mayfield beauties are averaging a good seven miles an hour. I think we'll be at the Albion Hotel in Blayney by three o'clock.'

They were, and there they rested briefly while the horses were changed to a new team brought north from Mayfield. As they were leaving the hotel to rejoin the vehicle an odd thing occurred.

Joe was already mounted and sitting beside Deke Edwards, the driver, when Eve and John Stuart came out across the wide dirt footpath towards Timothy who held open the coach door. Eve was a few paces ahead of her husband and as she neared the coach a woman came towards her. She was poorly dressed and bonnetless, her slight frame burdened with an infant and some awkward parcels. She halted to let Eve, dressed so elegantly, pass by. As she paused, the woman dropped one of the items she was carrying and Eve turned to her saying, 'Just a moment, I'll get it for you.' A brief smile of gratitude broke across the woman's thin face but before Eve could bend to retrieve it, John Stuart had leaped forward and almost bodily lifted Eve away towards the coach.

'I'll do it, Eve, you get in the carriage!' His voice was so agitated and his action so extreme that Eve unhesitatingly complied. He turned back to where the woman was now bending to the article herself. She was awkward and unsteady under the weight of the child and her other packages. With his face deliberately averted from her, John Stuart steadied her with his right hand until she stood up again. There was unmistakable distaste on his face and when she moved away, he unconsciously wiped his hand in a cleansing motion on the skirt of his jacket. The movement was so automatic that he did not know he had done it, but his bride, who watched from the coach, did.

As the vehicle gathered speed, Eve looked questioningly at her husband. 'Who was that woman?'

He turned towards her and took her hand. 'Eve,' he spoke almost condescendingly, 'you are my wife. There are some people . . . people with whom you should never have contact. She is one of these, and—'

'But John Stuart,' Eve interrupted, 'she looked quite harmless to me, the poor thing.'

A note of exasperation crept into her husband's voice. 'She should not walk the same street as you. She's a damned whore! Everyone knows! Let it be enough for me to tell you she has been in two *de facto* relationships and is now on to her third. The waif she carried is the offspring of God knows who!' He took a deep breath. 'She's disgusting!'

With his words rose the thought of Clare and a chill began creeping all over Eve. It began at the back of her neck and prickled down her arms and spine, a feeling that was destined to become familiar to her as time passed. She made a half-hearted defence of the poor woman in Blayney. 'But, John Stuart, dearest, we don't know the circumstances which have brought her to this end. She may not be to blame.'

'She's to blame all right. That's unquestionable,' came his obdurate reply. 'She's like my mother was. They make the choice, these women. They are detestable.'

132

Eve was aware that her husband's mother had returned to Scotland when he was only three years old. Father had told her there had been an affair, a scandal in which an army officer was involved. It appeared she had been sent away. That John Stuart held a grudge against his mother Eve learned early, for when she had mentioned her in the first week of their acquaintance, he had silenced her by saying, 'Eve, my mother has not been in my life since I was a baby. Please do not speak of her ever again. She is nothing to me, less than nothing.'

Now he had referred to her again, in direct comparison to the woman in Blayney. Eve began to see that he was disgusted by any female he judged unworthy. It was a disconcerting revelation for her and the more she thought of Clare, the more she wished she had told him about her.

It did not take John Stuart long to forget the incident. Within a minute or two, his good spirits had returned. To him, what had happened was just an unfortunate occurrence. It was not so easy for his bride to dismiss and it took her a little longer before she pushed the disquiet from her mind, promising to find a way of telling him when the time was right.

He had relinquished her hand and now he took it again from where it lay in her lap and kissed it. They turned to each other, forgetting the recent disturbance in the newness of their passion and their love. Eve ran her fingers through his hair and smiled up into his eyes, a playful, mischievous smile, beckoning her handsome husband-lover. He took her in his arms and she lay across his body, her legs up on the seat. She touched his lips with her fingers, and he took a fingertip into his mouth. The wetness on her skin was deliciously inviting and the thought of soon being loved by him sent sensual shivers trembling through her limbs. She welcomed it. He pulled her close and she felt his muscular chest beneath the softness of his shirt pressing into her breasts. His mouth came down to hers, his arms enfolding her and caressing her. The taste of him was heady, thrilling, exciting.

He thought he held a piece of heaven, so soft and wonderful did she feel. He had seen her, wanted her, attained her and as each minute passed, this bumpy swaying vehicle was bringing him closer to the consummation of his ultimate desire. He drew his mouth from hers. 'You tempt me to love you right here, my darling, but I fear we would be covered in bruises. Perhaps we should watch the bush for a while.'

She smiled, moving gently away from him. 'Yes, dearest, I think we should, this carriage lurches quite dangerously at times.'

So for the next two hours the newly-weds were lighthearted. They

133

chatted, laughed, touched each other and were happy.

The day was closing. The glow of evening radiated from the orange ball on the horizon and the long shadows heralding twilight reached across in front of the coach. As they turned a sharp bend in the road, suddenly there was a shout from Joe above and abruptly the coach pitched to the left, skidding on its wheels. Loudly straining in all its joints, it slewed sideways into the bank at the roadside, sending dirt and dust high into the air.

There was a scream from Timothy as he toppled from his seat dragging Deke with him, who still clutched the reins tightly in his hands. They fell off the coach onto the earthen bank and Joe was tossed face down onto the footboard. The horses reared and whinnied plaintively as they were brought to a sudden, jarring halt. Inside, Eve was thrown against the carriage door and John Stuart fell on top of her. His chin came down sharply on her head and for some moments they were dazed.

The vehicle righted itself, shaking and groaning, and John Stuart, disentangling himself from Eve's skirt, called, 'What the devil is going on?'

The answer came in Joe's deep, controlled voice, as he lifted himself up on his knees. 'Road's blocked, m'boy. Gum trees across it!'

And there in the middle of the road not twenty yards from the coach was a barricade of solid gum branches.

John Stuart hurriedly helped Eve to the seat and, seeing she was unhurt, jumped down from the coach. Eve, in the act of following him, halted at the next words she heard.

'Bail up! Stand and deliver! Don't move or we'll shoot!' The words came from behind the foliage that lay across the road.

'What in damnation—' began John Stuart.

''Fraid we've been held up, m'boy,' interrupted the calm tones of Joe.

'Bloody bushrangers!' spat out Deke, who only now was rising, covered in dirt with blood on his lip.

'Oh no!' exclaimed Timothy who brushed the dust and grime from his previously immaculate outfit.

'That's right,' called the disembodied voice, 'so don't ye be givin' us trouble or ye'll be sorry. And drop the gun, mister! I can nail ye from here, quicker'n a flash!'

The last statement was aimed at Joe who, holding his rifle, had jumped down from the carriage and moved protectively in front of John Stuart who said, 'Drop it, Joe. It's not worth it. Don't be a hero.'

134

From the branches the mocking tones of the same voice called, 'That's right, Joe, be a good boy and drop it. Don't be a dead hero, Joe!'

Joe looked at John Stuart and then realising the hopelessness dropped the weapon in disgust. As the rifle hit the ground, three men emerged from behind the debris. All carried guns and had coverings over their faces. At the same time, two others rode in behind the coach, leading three riderless horses. They too had their faces hidden behind handkerchiefs.

Eve's heartbeat had quickened a little and she was concerned for John Stuart, but somehow she did not really feel frightened. She watched from within the coach as one of the men on the ground left his two companions and walked forward.

He was strikingly different, dressed in grey with black knee-high boots. The covering on his face was black, and light brown hair was touching his collar under his dark hat. He moved with a fluid action and his sunbrowned hand motioned to Joe's rifle on the ground.

One of the men behind him, a small, ferret-like individual, retrieved it, saying in the same voice that had spoken previously, 'Yeah, guv'nor, we could do with this.' He patted the barrel lovingly. 'Why, it's a Whitworth! My Lord, didn't think there were any here. It's a beauty!'

One of the horsemen dismounted and came to meet the three men on foot. He was slim but well-built with solid shoulders and walked with a slight limp. He carried a Colt pocket pistol in his right hand which he waved in the direction of John Stuart, Joe, Deke and Timothy. His eyes on the man in the grey clothing, obviously the leader, he asked, 'What do ye make of this lot, guv'nor? They look a rum team to me. Wouldn't be givin' ye much for the big one, overdressed for the back country.' He pointed with the firearm at John Stuart. The other bushrangers, who now stood covering the captives, burst into laughter.

John Stuart, who had been silently bristling with anger, spoke. 'This is outrageous! Don't you know what coach this is?'

The man with the limp stopped chuckling. 'We don't stop coaches without knowin' what they are! It's the monthly payroll inside we be interested in, not the Mayfield crest on the door.'

John Stuart took a step forward. 'Yes, this is a Mayfield coach, you fool! But it carries no payroll. I'm John Stuart Wakeman. You'll be sorry for this.'

There was silence for some seconds while the disguised men looked at each other. Then the man who wore grey spoke for the first time. Unlike the speech of the two before him, his was refined, the voice of an educated man, and pleasant to hear. It came as a great surprise to his captives.

'Wakeman, you say? And this is not the payroll coach? Can we have made a mistake, lads?' He gave a short cynical laugh. 'But then on the other hand perhaps Mr Wakeman does not remember the ninth commandment which deals with the telling of lies. We will have to see for ourselves.' And he moved swiftly towards the door of the coach.

John Stuart lunged forward, raising his fist in a futile gesture. 'Stay away from there, damn you!'

A rifle was pushed quickly and keenly into his rib cage with such force that he staggered backwards. 'Stay where you are, Wakeman, unless you're sick of bloody livin',' accompanied the blow. This was the fourth man on foot speaking. He was larger than any of the others, being broader and taller even than John Stuart.

John Stuart groaned slightly and recovered his balance. 'Stay away from that coach, I tell you! There is no payroll. It contains nothing but my wife!'

The leader, who was now at the coach door, turned back at this statement. He stood there, his spare frame covered in grey, his black boots polished to gleaming. He was not as tall as John Stuart who stood six feet one but he was perfectly proportioned with a physical harmony about him; rarely, if ever, had John Stuart or Joe seen anyone more charismatic. A figure not belonging to the tales told of the unkempt robber of the bush roads. His eyes looked sceptically above his mask at the property owner.

'Your wife, Wakeman?' He laughed the same short laugh as before. It was a disconcerting sound, as if it came from him but not of him. 'I shall just make sure of that.' He reached for the handle to open the door.

John Stuart, anger, pain, exasperation and embarrassment welling within him, cried, 'Damn your eyes! I'll see you all hang for this.'

'Shaddup you or I'll blast you right now, I will!' retorted the big man who held the gun in his ribs.

'Calm, m'boy,' came the steady voice of Joe as he laid a restraining hand on John Stuart's arm. 'Stay quiet, she'll come to no harm.'

By this time the leader had opened the coach door.

Eve sat motionless as his eyes lit on a brown, soft leather shoe and moved up over a dark green skirt to a white bow and the face above.

As his hard blue-grey eyes encountered her soft, light brown, Eve felt the oddest sensation. It was almost as if he had touched her, as if there had been physical contact. Her eyes did not leave his as he continued to look at her silently.

She felt very peculiar, uncomfortable and yet not uncomfortable, both at the same time. She was conscious only of the steely, blue-grey eyes, sitting mesmerised, staring into them. She thought she saw suffering, and then she felt she recognised tranquillity and the suffering was illusion.

'Don't touch her, you scum!' shouted John Stuart.

'Shaddup, Wakeman!' and once more he was jabbed in the ribs with the rifle barrel.

The man at the coach door looked away from Eve and, casting a glance round the empty interior, turned abruptly and moved from the coach. Eve experienced a most disturbing feeling, a kind of ebbing of herself after him. It left her confused and dismayed.

The man with the limp broke from the group and came towards the leader. 'Well, guv'nor, what is it? What's there?'

'No payroll, lad. It seems he speaks the truth.'

The man moved past the leader to the open door. 'Well, blast me!' He looked Eve up and down. 'Only his woman after all. No payroll! No wonder there was but one guard!'

A general groan of frustration sounded. Then the large man who held the gun on John Stuart shouted, 'Well, I'll be buggered if we leave with nothin'. This bastard must have somethin' on him!' With that he pulled on the gold chain hanging from John Stuart's fob pocket and abruptly tugged out the watch. 'And this'll do for a start!' He handed his gun to the little man beside him and began to go through the prisoners' pockets while John Stuart's and Joe's eyes met. Joe's silent look told his companion to do nothing.

There was a slight lifting of spirits when the bushrangers found ten guineas, four gold sovereigns and some silver in John Stuart's wallet. After emptying all four of their captives' pockets, there were seventeen pounds two shillings and sixpence on the ground before them.

Then the man who was still mounted spoke. It was an Irish voice. 'While it's not a payroll, it'll help us poor unfortunates of the bush to pay the rent!'

Sounds of mirth broke from the outlaws.

The big man who had just counted the money turned and, lifting his bounty in the air, called, 'Well, we've got this, but what about her in the coach, boys? Married to this bastard, she'll have a diamond or two. Bring her out here and let's take a look!'

The leader held out his arm, checking the man's move towards the coach. 'We're not down to robbing women, lad. Let her be!'

'Oh, boss! Why not? She's fair game.'

'Do like the guv'nor says!' called the one with the limp as he walked to the horses.

The big man looked round sharply, but he did not continue with his complaint and, falling silent, turned moodily back to his prisoners.

Eve, fascinated, had moved to the open coach door. The man in grey had not once looked back towards her and now he came to a halt in front of her husband. Together, they were somehow overwhelming. Eve's every sense was intensified. They were both imposing, both sunbrowned, both faultless physically, both seemingly inflexible; the one dark-eyed, dark-haired, in brown velvet and silk, the other lighter-eyed, lighter-haired, in grey and black. There was more than their material actuality for Eve. There was an inconceivable 'oneness' about them, an immense significance in their being side by side. For the fleeting moments these two men stood together, she was unnaturally alert. It was uncanny – or was it ridiculous? Had she truly experienced those fantastic sensations when the bushranger looked at her? For the second time on her wedding day, a cold chill crept up across her body until she shivered almost uncontrollably.

This would be the only time in her life she would see them side by side. In the years to come, often she would picture them in her mind's eye, standing here in the dusk together. But always in the future she would imagine them both with their faces uncovered, unlike this day.

Beneath the mask, the intervening years had made scant change to Alan's face. He was as memorable as ever. The passing of time had drawn his cheeks a little, but there was no marked difference in him. His clean-shaven face was remarkably clear of lines for his years and inherent in his expression was the same disturbing mixture of the noble and the simple that had been there in the Southampton courtroom so long ago.

But it was only her husband's face Eve could see now, and his appealing features thinly veiled the rage that filled him.

John Stuart examined the man who now stood in front of him. To his surprise the eyes held no malice. Instead, there was a candour and integrity that he had not expected. He had seen hate in the eyes of the big man who had smashed him in the ribs and he was not prepared for this contrast. Disconcerted, his own anger subsided a little.

Alan spoke to him. 'Mr Wakeman, I am sorry to have put you to this inconvenience. I assure you I would have much preferred your payroll coach to yourself.' He began to move away, then suddenly he turned back. 'Nevertheless, methinks your priorities need a little readjustment – four heavily armed guards for your usual pay coach and one for your wife!'

John Stuart endeavoured to control himself but the anger tumbled out. 'The damned roads could be traversed without any guards if it weren't for the likes of you and your rabble.'

Joe stepped forward and broke in quickly, 'Now you have our money, will you not leave us in peace?'

Alan glanced at Joe and gave a curt nod of acquiescence before he faced back to John Stuart. His attitude suggested he wished to say more and he stood this way for some seconds while their eyes met again. John Stuart felt his annoyance subside during the moments their eyes were locked, for while he knew it was ludicrous, he could not help almost liking the expression he observed. Then, without speaking, as if he changed his mind, Alan turned sharply on his heel and walked to his horse. 'Let's go, boys.'

The day was dying as the bushrangers climbed into their saddles.

'Yeah, we'd best be goin', I promised me mum I wouldn't stay out after dark,' the big man shouted, having regained his humour. The others all laughed.

Alan mounted his horse, a fine grey stallion sired by the one he had escaped from Moreton Bay upon; and, Goya-like, the animal rose up on its hind legs in relief against the shadowy bush. 'Be careful on the rest of your journey, the country's full of bushrangers,' he said, and he and his band faded into the rapidly descending night.

Eve moved to the carriage step, watching them depart. John Stuart ran to her. 'Are you all right, my love?'

'Yes, perfectly, thank you.' She stepped to the ground beside him.

He took her in his arms and kissed her forehead. 'What a thing to happen! Where the devil is Sir Rutherford when one wants him?'

'Second time I been held up, it is,' Deke announced. 'Gettin' used to this, I am. First time Old Joe Daily, this time I'm for thinkin' it must have been the Hall gang. They be cheeky beggars, right enough.'

John Stuart shook his head. 'No, that was not Ben Hall, of that I'm positive. The leader spoke like an aristocrat. Sir Rutherford mentioned them all, and I'm sure he said one was born into wealth and position but I'm damned if I recall his name.'

Joe took John Stuart's arm. 'Yes, m'boy, I have heard tell of a gang led by a man they call the Governor and I think we just now had an introduction to the fellow.'

'That's right, they called him the Governor right enough, I know that, yes,' muttered Deke, nodding his head in agreement with himself.

Then Timothy spoke up for the first time. 'Mr Wakeman, sir, I remember what Sir Rutherford said. He said the bushranger from the rich family was called Alan Fletcher.'

139

Eve shivered and John Stuart's arm went protectively round her shoulder as he replied, 'Yes, Tim, you're correct. Alan Fletcher. I too remember now. Well, the roads should be free of them. Damn thieves! I'd like to see them all launched into eternity.'

Joe and Deke grunted approval but Eve found herself startled at the suggestion. 'John Stuart, that's a harsh judgment of them.'

John Stuart squeezed her closer, 'No, my darling, not harsh, just. You are innocent of the ways of the world. One must meet fire with fire.' As he said these words, he remembered the look of benevolence he had recognised in the leader's eyes, the expression he had actually liked, and he added softly, 'I truly wonder what brings them to a life of crime.'

'Yes, I do too,' his wife agreed with a far-away look on her face.

It took only minutes for them to move the felled trees from the road. Deke cleaned up the carriage and lit the one remaining, unbroken, interior oil lamp. Even so, it was completely dark and the moon had risen before the coach was once more on its way.

Joe rode inside now, John Stuart had insisted on it. Timothy, who was good with horses, had relieved Deke in the driver's seat and Deke rested beside him, eyes closed, as the animals made a slow pace in the moonlight on the bumpy, pot-holed road.

Inside, the married couple and Joe propped themselves up on cushions and contemplated the day's events from their own particular points of view.

CHAPTER EIGHT

'A land of sombre, silent hills, where mountain cattle go
By twisted tracks on sidelings steep, where giant gum trees
grow
And the wind replies, in the river oaks, to the song of the
stream below.'

'Australian Scenery,' Andrew Barton (Banjo) Paterson,
1864–1941.

Eve had been sleeping fitfully for some hours lying along the length
of one of the carriage seats, her head on John Stuart's lap, when he
gently woke her. 'Darling, wake up, you can see Mayfield House in
the distance.' His voice was filled with excitement and the strains of
the day had disappeared from his face.

Eve sat up and followed the direction of his hand. They were on
high ground and she noticed the coach was not bumping as it had
been before she went to sleep. They had been inside the Mayfield
boundary for over two hours, where the roads were known to be the
smoothest in the colony, some being macadam.

John Stuart pointed through the window. There, far in the distance
on the left, she made out a building, palely illuminated in the night
light. 'That's it, do you see it?' The pride sounded in his voice.

'Yes, I see it. It shines. It's beautiful.'

'That's exactly what it is,' Joe agreed quietly, turning to smile at
John Stuart.

He nodded. 'I estimate it's well after midnight, though I can't be
sure.' The oblique reference to his stolen watch caused him to think
again of the robbery, but he was soon distracted by the significance
of being home and the enjoyment in pointing things out to Eve.

Soon, they passed through two large stone pillars with glowing
lamps set in alcoves, and along an avenue between huge trees. Eve
thought she saw hedges and lawns to right and left.

'Is it a park?' she asked.

John Stuart, smiling, replied, 'Yes, it is. It's almost half a mile in
diameter and Mayfield House sits in the middle.'

Eve drew in her breath with surprise. The carriageway was smooth and as they rolled along she watched enchantedly for there were lanterns hanging in the trees and people lining the drive. 'All these people, who are they?' Her voice lifted with excitement.

'They have come to welcome you,' he answered waving through the window to a group of people who called congratulations loudly as the coach crept by. 'It appears a great many have stayed up. Good show!'

And then the house loomed in front of them. She was amazed at its size, even in the moonlight it looked enormous. It reminded her of the Boston mansions of her childhood, only larger, and the whole place seemed to be lit inside and out. She was startled. Everything was so grand, the people, the lanterns, the gardens, the house. She was not prepared for this display. Suddenly came the awareness that she had married a man whose wealth and position she had estimated quite inadequately. Of course she had heard of Mayfield before meeting John Stuart, everybody had, and she knew it was large, but nothing had prepared her for this magnificence.

As the coach came to a halt, she calculated there must be close to two hundred people gathered to meet them and it was the middle of the night! The door was opened from outside. John Stuart jumped to the ground and helped her down. As Eve descended, a cheer went up and a small sleepy-eyed boy handed her a beautiful bouquet of flowers.

'Why I . . . thank you.'

Her husband took her hand and they ascended to the verandah. There they turned back to face those collected. John Stuart motioned to Joe and the older man mounted the steps to stand closely behind him.

Eve watched her new husband, happy and composed, showing none of the vexation of earlier, as he made his speech. All the faces were turned towards him and there was an expectancy in the air.

'My wife,' he touched Eve's arm with a proprietorial movement, 'and I have travelled this day from Bathurst, a long journey as you all realise.' There were murmurs of agreement. 'We appreciate your patience in waiting until this late hour. That you have done so has made us both proud and grateful, especially as some of you no doubt are on the early watch, as I will be.' He alluded here to the Mayfield colloquialism for those due to make an early start and laughter greeted it. 'We are tired but nothing can spoil the joy of being back home.' A cheer greeted these words. Then a change came over his face. Those gathered seemed to notice it, for the cheer was followed by total hush. .

'This land of mine, of yours also,' he said more quietly, lifting his arm in a sweeping movement to gesture over their heads, 'is where my heart lies. I quote my father, Sir Arthur, who used to say, "Whenever I am away from Mayfield, I am not quite whole".' For a second or two after this he did not speak. Then, as if gathering himself together, as if he had shown too much, he finished in the strong voice of the John Stuart they knew so well. 'So to one and all I say sleep well and content knowing that Mayfield at last has a mistress worthy of it. Tomorrow evening we shall finish our work early,' he half turned to Joe, 'for Mr Larmer tells me there is to be a general celebration on the lawns and you are all invited. Good night to you all.'

His concluding remark was drowned in the deafening sound of cheers and calls. Then he took up his wife's hand and ushered her through the huge white cedar doors.

Once inside, Eve met Mrs Smith, the housekeeper, a small woman with a straight back and a severe expression, except when her eyes rested on her master, for then they softened noticeably. She and Mr Baines, the butler, had seen to it that a marvellous supper was laid in the small dining room, although none of the travellers ate their share.

Joe soon bade them goodnight and left for his own home, a substantial brick house standing at the edge of the park, north of the west gate and built for him in Sir Arthur Wakeman's day.

John Stuart wished to move his new wife as swiftly as possible to the marital bed, before the stress and exertion of the day at last assailed them. By the time they finally found themselves between the soft luxurious sheets of their massive bed, desire had revived them.

John Stuart was conscious of the sensibilities of refined women, and his wife represented his conception of what was pure and delicate and good, and while he was a careful lover, his desire for her was ardent and demanding. As she came to him at the bedside in her white lace gown, he smiled his half smile, and Eve's heartbeat quickened, for he looked like a faultless statue by David come to life in the lamp glow. She thought him beautifully made with his perfect features, his wide shoulders, hard muscles of his chest and stomach, and the firm, long body with bronze skin and patches of dark hair. He held out his hands and took hers, bringing her to him and holding her close to press kisses on her forehead, her eyelids, her lips, her neck. She tingled with sensual pleasure as he pushed the lace gown from her shoulders and it slipped co-operatively down. His voice was thick with urgent emotion as he looked at her breasts, her belly, her thighs, slender and naked, in the flickering light. 'You are beautiful, Eve.'

He drew her down upon the bed beside him and his wet mouth passed from her lips down the side of her neck to suckle her hardened nipples. As his hands moved over her skin, fondling, exploring, wanting, needing, she murmured gentle, willing sounds. She was ready and prepared to give herself in their union. When he opened her legs, he whispered, 'I want you, I love you,' and she replied, 'Yes, darling, yes.' And as he penetrated her, a tiny murmur escaped her lips and she kissed his mouth, his neck, his wide, smooth shoulders as he moved within her.

He moaned with sweet passion at her surrender, and his pleasure soared as he held her, tasted her, his vision and his wife. There was no orgasm for Eve that first night but her body had responded fervidly, passionately, to his. She was falling deeply in love with this wonderful, noble man. Yet for a long time afterwards she lay sleepless and disturbed, for once during their lovemaking the memory of the bushranger flashed through her mind. It had been only a second or two but, guilt-stricken, she felt that in some way she had violated their union.

When John Stuart slept it was deeply, peacefully, the events of his wedding day lost in the closeness of his new wife's body. When Eve finally slept, it was peacefully at first, but later she was troubled by an uncomfortable dream. It came from the uneasy memory of the day's encounter now lodged in the penetralia of her mind. She was lost and there was a masked man somewhere at hand whose steely eyes kept finding hers in swirling mist.

While the new mistress of Mayfield lay dreaming, the night was surrendering to the strength of the waking day. Mayfield was still asleep but shortly would be stirring. Fires would be lit in the cottages south across the Lachlan River and the married workers would breakfast with their wives before riding out to their work. In large quarters to the west, the single men, too, would wake and begin their day's labour.

Even though it was cattle that had made Mayfield famous, many square miles were used for farming and the property sustained many lives and was, in the majority of needs, self-sufficient. There were wheat and corn fields and orchards running along the river banks. A large dairy sat on the northern bank and all manner of vegetable crops grew to the south irrigated by a series of small aqueducts built especially for the purpose by John Stuart, who was constantly reading scientific journals and from them introducing new methods and tools to employ on Mayfield. To sow he had stump jump ploughs, and to harvest the latest reapers with a mechanical rake that swept the cut stalks from a platform to the waiting workers to stack.

Mayfield's northern border was some twenty-five miles long. No other land owned by a single family was within one-tenth of the size. The country was good for raising cattle and sheep and John Stuart, akin to the cattle barons of the Americas, scorned sheep, though his father had not. He ran many head of cattle, numbering at any one time in the thousands. His meat fed most of the colony of New South Wales and his salt beef was sold in all the colonies and exported to New Zealand. His plans for growth and expansion were constantly in development. His was a single-minded desire for Mayfield to thrive and, in that, John Stuart was indeed the son of Sir Arthur Francis Wakeman.

Arthur Wakeman had been born in 1798 in England, in the serenity of the Sussex countryside. The graceful village of his birth, Mayfield, sat on the high weald and from almost any part of it there were sweeping views down across the serene green woods and farmland. Arthur loved this place of his boyhood, the tranquillity and beauty of his surroundings. He played in the grassy banks and hedgerows and lay on his back in the meadows, watching skylarks high in the heavens on the long evenings of midsummer.

His father was a small freehold farmer, his mother the daughter of the village tailor. Arthur, the youngest of three, was a thoughtful boy who liked his own company. He would often wander alone through the yard of the village church, St Dunstan's, after a day spent in the church school. He read aloud from the tombstones in a deep and sombre voice and sat musing for an hour at a time under the dark old yew tree in the corner of the yard. It was here on his fifteenth birthday, 15 May 1813, that his second cousin, Millicent Baker, found him. His serious young face lit up, for he liked his cousin. During their conversation, he read the nearest tombstone to her. 'Here lyeth the body of Thomas Sands who was buried May the 15, 1713 aged 72 years.' The two 7s had been carved backwards and Millicent, finding it amusing, began to laugh. Soon Arthur's face lightened and he smiled at her. 'You know, Millicent, that is exactly one hundred years ago. I'm taking it as an omen.'

His cousin looked at him in wonder. 'An omen?'

He became grave again. 'I love this village and the peace of it and this churchyard. But there is more out there, even beyond London, far away.' He waved his arm in a wide arc. 'There is something in me telling me not to live out seventy-two years here as old Thomas Sands did a hundred years ago.'

Her happy eyes clouded over, for what he said frightened her. No one she had ever known had gone further than London. 'But where will you go, Arthur?'

'I don't know yet. But I know I'm going to leave Mayfield. My brothers seem content to stay here, but not I. All I know is I am going across the seas. It is 1813, Millicent, and the world is large.'

At the very moment he spoke, in a land thirteen thousand miles to the south, three men and their company were trudging across tall, wooded 'Blue Mountains', finding the pass to the plains beyond; finding the pass over which he, Arthur Wakeman, would journey in less than ten years from this day, to his Mayfield of the southland and his future.

But as he spoke he was yet a boy and the ensuing years saw him at school in Tunbridge Wells and London. He qualified as a surveyor when he was twenty-two and in the late summer of 1820 he came home to spend a few brief weeks with his family. Soon, he would sail to the colony of New South Wales in the position of one of the Crown surveyors, under the new Governor, Brigadier-General Sir Thomas Brisbane.

He walked through the High Street for what was to be the last time. He looked on the stone and timbered buildings of his youth, the cottages with hollyhock and bluebells and wallflowers climbing to the window sills. He listened again as he had when a boy to the tales of Mr Firman, the ancient, jolly, weatherbeaten driver of the village carrier cart. He sat alone under the yew in the corner of the churchyard and took leave of all his friends, the dead souls there. He patted Thomas Sands' headstone and said a silent farewell.

In the evening, he stood and looked across the green valley behind his cousin Millicent's home, Middle House, and he was moved to tears. She stood beside him and they cried softly together, for she understood him and knew his passionate love for this village, this county, this island, this country. And yet she knew he wanted more, and she recognised there was a joy in him too, imperative, moving him inexorably on, taking him away.

His parting with his mother was the worst. He, her youngest and her dearest, was leaving for ever. She knew it, although he said it was not so and promised to return. It hurt to leave her, but he did, as all sons of mothers for all time are wont to do.

In October of that year he sailed to Sydney town, in the convict colony of New South Wales. In the following January, he crossed the pass in the Blue Mountains and for the next three and a half years he surveyed much of the land south-west of the tiny settlement of Bathurst, the muster of 1820 having shown there to be one hundred and fourteen in the district, including seventy-five convicts. His field trips were mostly made from a small convict settlement north of the Lachlan River.

He was a thorough and competent young man and his ability was obvious. His work soon drew the attention of his superiors and for his services the outgoing Governor granted him two thousand acres of the land he had surveyed. Arthur Wakeman called it Mayfield after that other part of the earth he felt was his. This Mayfield was a piece of ground on the banks of the Lachlan River. There, with a few assigned convicts and ticket-of-leave men, as convicts granted partial freedom were called, he successfully ran some sheep and grew crops. But it was during the office of the following Governor, Lieutenant-General Ralph Darling, that he expanded his claim. He bought another two thousand acres of Crown land on the southern bank of the Lachlan opposite the land he now owned, at five shillings an acre, and he was so successful as a grazier and farmer that he was equalled only by his well-known rival, John Macarthur Junior.

His enterprises flourished, and by 1826 he had been granted another larger tract of land to the south. Subsequently, he ventured into cattle. It seemed that Arthur Wakeman had the golden touch. In 1827, with a few other squatters he opened a bank; and in that same year he married Caroline Burnett, the youngest daughter of a Scottish nobleman. The marriage had been arranged between the two parties with the help of the Governor who saw the prosperous young Wakeman as his protégé. In March 1828 John Stuart was born and his father continued expanding his claim to the south and the east. By 1830, Mayfield was the largest single-owned property in the land and still developing.

Arthur Wakeman had grown to cherish this Mayfield, where a man could ride all day and still be unconfined, just as he did the memory of those emerald meadows and dales so far away. There was a tenderness in his heart as he watched the sun set behind the grand white house he was building on a hillside a mile north of the river.

By the end of Governor Darling's term, Arthur Francis Wakeman, at the age of thirty-two, was a man to be reckoned with, a force in the colony. Wealthy and influential men fostered friendships with him. But fate has a way of disregarding achievement, and it was in this year that the two great catastrophes of his life occurred.

He had planned to bring his mother and father from the sleepy English village to reside with him in the grand style he now could offer them. The ship which was to bring them arrived at Sydney Quay in August without them. Instead of his parents, there was a letter from his father informing him that his darling mother had died in the winter and that he, at his advancing age, could not envisage the long sea journey without her. To sublimate his grief in the months that followed, he toiled alongside his men, branding, farming, building, fencing and putting roads across the miles of Mayfield.

Then, the second blow. His marriage failed. Perhaps Caroline had been left too much on her own; whatever the reason, she had an affair with an Army officer. The result was her departure. In August 1831, she returned to her family in Scotland, leaving her three-year-old son behind with his father. She had no choice in the matter, Arthur Wakeman was the powerful one and he wanted his son.

Thus it was an even more single-minded Arthur Wakeman who looked on New Year's Day 1832. From then on, it seemed he was endowed with second sight in matters material. With his influence, he expanded Mayfield even more and was able to buy land to the south and west in enormous tracts. At this time he began exporting red cedar to England and the Cape Colony, which proved exceedingly successful, and by the late 1840s his ability and efficiency had made Mayfield fabled. He and his growing son could afford to live in the style of European noblemen.

He never communicated with his wife again. He lived out his life without ever returning to England, although in his quiet times he toyed with the idea of seeing again that other land he loved. And he thought it necessary to send John Stuart, in the keeping of Joe Larmer, on a visit 'home', as he called it, when the boy was twenty-one.

Arthur Francis Wakeman was knighted when he was forty-five years old and died of pneumonia at fifty-seven, after insisting that he participate in a cattle drive which drove into wind and rain for four days on end.

Of all the many and varied interests he left his son, his greatest legacy was Mayfield, the most flourishing and profitable property in the colonies. The patriarch had gone and his son was determined to follow in his footsteps.

CHAPTER NINE

'She has done with the world's anger and world's mirth
Sunshine and rain showers.'
'Rest her soul, she's dead!' John Masefield, 1878–1967.

The first months of Eve and John Stuart's marriage passed peacefully. They were days of discovery for Eve about her new home and those who inhabited it. She was enthusiastic and earnest, finding her new role as mistress of Mayfield stimulating and exciting, and also daunting at times when she realised the extent of her responsibilities. But she was determined to accomplish all she could and she spent weeks learning how the huge property functioned. At first, when she would arrive back from a ride of many miles having watched the herding of cattle, or men fencing, or the harvesting of crops, or visiting the stockmen's wives, John Stuart would smile indulgently. But he finally saw that the days she passed in these ways and the time spent in studying the inventories or assisting Mr Oldfield, his secretary, were not a passing whim, that Eve was serious about being mistress of so much and so many, and serious, too, in her role as his wife and his active partner.

In their intimate moments, she was passionate and loving to him, giving herself freely and responding to him with a vibrancy and ardour he took delight in sharing. He was proud of her, certain in his view that she was unequalled by others; unadulterated, good, charitable and tender.

If ever a stray thought of Clare or the disconcerting memory of the bushranger found their way to Eve's mind, she would adroitly block them, so determined was she to hold the peace of these days. She had this power over her waking hours, but unfortunately when she slept her subconscious had its way, and too often her dreams were frequented by her sister and the outlaw. She was disturbed by this and when she actually tried examining her feelings about the bushranger, she dismissed the exceptional sensations she had felt that day of the hold-up as some sort of superficial fascination with an outlaw.

Thelma was becoming her good friend. The older woman had

149

responded to Eve the first minute she had seen her in Bathurst. She had recognised something innately strong and courageous about John Stuart's bride, and since coming to Mayfield Thelma thought Eve had proved those characteristics. A different woman to Thelma would not have welcomed a young, beautiful mistress to Mayfield, would have seen Eve as usurping her role. But Thelma Larmer was not of the same ilk as her daughter Daydee; there was not a jealous bone in Thelma. She had welcomed the younger woman's enthusiasm and spirit and their relationship had flourished to the point where she felt a real affection for Eve and real happiness for John Stuart to think he had found someone so capable and so very worthy of being the mistress of Mayfield. Through Thelma, Eve met the wives of the married workers and, as time passed, she visited them, listened to them, shared their troubles and gradually gained the respect and trust of these fine pioneer women.

One Monday morning in winter, Eve was taking her usual walk. She had always liked to walk, and now, with so large a property at her disposal, she did so almost daily. Sometimes, Thelma joined her but Eve enjoyed walking swiftly and usually preferred to take her exercise alone, covering two or three miles, occasionally even further. One of her favourite walks was along the Lachlan to the east from Larmer's Crossing, as the bridge over the Lachlan was known. Years before, in Sir Arthur Wakeman's time, Joe had seen to the laying and securing of a chain of tree trunks across the natural shallows to form an effective bridge. It had been improved since then, but the trunks remained the basis of the construction.

Today the weather was cold but pleasant, for the sun was mounted in a cloudless sky and there was no wind. Eve looked across the river to where the married workers' cottages stood, the first of them about a hundred yards or so away from the bank beyond clumps of vine and scrub and tall grass. Lots of wild flowers grew along the river bank and flocks of unusual birds nested in sight of it.

A spot of blue was moving in Eve's direction, about thirty yards across the Lachlan. It was a little girl, no more than about two years old, wobbling happily through the grass. Eve's eyes scanned the bush but there was no one about, the child was alone. What was she doing down here on her own? A chill ran through Eve as onwards the infant came towards the opposite bank, heading straight for the river. The Lachlan here was not deep but there was a current and it was about four feet to the bottom.

Eve had learned all the children's names and she knew each one. It was little Laura Dale who ran so merrily towards danger.

'Laura, stop!'

The child saw Eve and, laughing more, accelerated.

'Go back, Laura. Stop! No! No!'

But the baby was oblivious to what lay ahead and so she came, unsteadily but unerringly, to the water's edge.

Eve could see clearly what was about to happen. She continued to cry out even as she threw off her shoes and ripped off her jacket and skirt. Laura, heedless of her peril, plunged over the side of the bank into the Lachlan. As Laura's cry sounded, Eve jumped into the bitterly cold water.

Reeds caught at her arms and pantaloons as she fought through the river towards the child. Her clothes were slowing her down but her whole being was focused on getting to Laura who was struggling beneath the water. Eve was using every ounce of strength she had to wade, push, strive towards the little battling body. She felt her foot hit something sharp and pain seared up through her leg but she urged herself forward.

The icy water was taking her breath away and Eve realised with horror that the current was now beginning to move Laura downstream. She attempted to throw herself to the baby even as Laura's body turned in a swirling movement away from her. With a last, violent effort Eve forced herself, arms outstretched, towards the child. She felt her fingers contact the material of Laura's dress and she grabbed with every ounce of strength and took hold. She was gasping, choking, but her grip was fast on the dress. Then her other arm came round and she took the girl in her arms, lifting her head up above the water. Staggering to the bank with Laura raised in front of her, Eve pulled herself and the water-logged infant up onto the bank.

Eve was shivering, her teeth chattering, her foot hurting, but all her attention was on Laura. The child was inert, did not seem to be breathing. Oh Lord! What to do? She stopped herself from panicking and tried to think. John Stuart had told her about a method of reviving people. She looked in Laura's mouth and it was empty. She turned the baby over on her tummy, putting her tiny head to the side. Then, gently, she began to push in constant rhythm on the child's back, praying fiercely all the time.

Push . . . push . . . Come on, Laura, please. Oh Lord, please let her live, please let her live. Push . . . push . . .

Then a tremor of delighted relief ran throughout Eve for the little one gave a gurgle and a cough and began breathing again.

Mrs Dale's eyes widened in astonishment when she answered the insistent knocking on her back door. There stood the mistress in her pantaloons with blood on her foot, holding Laura in her arms, both soaking wet and looking bedraggled and half-drowned.

'Good grief! M'lady!' the woman exclaimed.

That very afternoon Eve went to see Jack Hennessy, Joe Larmer's able second-in-command, who had his offices close by the stables. Her foot was bandaged where she had cut it on the rock in the river, and as she limped into his office, he stood quickly from behind his desk.

She came swiftly to the reason for her visit.

'Mr Hennessy, this morning a baby almost drowned in the Lachlan. I want to make sure that such a thing cannot happen to our children again. If a fence were to be built along the southern bank of the Lachlan near where the married workers' cottages are, the children would be safe. I would like to know how long it would take and how much it would cost.'

Jack Hennessy looked thoughtful. 'It would depend on the length of it, and what sort of a fence it was.'

Eve unfolded a map she had drawn. 'Mrs Larmer and I have measured the distance and I think it should go from here,' she pointed to Larmer's Crossing, 'and run for, say, three hundred and fifty to four hundred yards to where the ground rises.'

Jack Hennessy nodded. 'Are we speaking of a wooden fence or a stone wall, Mrs Wakeman?'

Eve thought for a minute. 'Whatever is most effective, I suppose.'

He stood. 'I'll just get Stephen Watson in, Mrs Wakeman. He is the one who knows exact costs of this sort of thing.'

That night, when John Stuart came home, he was surprised and upset to hear of his wife's adventure. 'Darling, you were wonderful. But it concerns me to think that you were all alone when such a thing occurred. Not only was the child in danger, but so too were you.'

'No, my love, I was not really, for the Lachlan is not deep there. It's only that there is a current.' Then she took him by the arm. 'Now please come and sit down for I have something I wish to discuss with you.'

She guided him to a sofa and began. 'I want to make certain that no other of our Mayfield children can wander into such life-threatening peril again. So, with your permission, I would like to have a fence built along the southern side of the river.' She brought out her map and traced along it for him as she had done for Jack Hennessy.

John Stuart smiled tolerantly at her. 'Eve, a fence down there might be unsightly. We've deliberately not built anything there to keep the look of the bushland near the cottages. And in any case, this is something for Jack Hennessy or Stephen Watson. I don't know if we've got the men or the time to do it and we would have to know the cost.'

She nodded and unfolded another piece of paper, starting to read. 'If the wall were stone, it would have to be quarried and that is time-consuming and expensive. So a wooden fence seems the best idea, along which we could plant creepers and vines. With regular watering and care, within two summers the fence should be covered and look like part of the bushland. A fencing team of twelve men could put up a wooden fence four feet high and three hundred and fifty yards long in seven to ten days. Mr Hennessy has assured me he can spare the men.' She handed her husband the paper. 'I have detailed costs of everything here.'

John Stuart was looking at her with a strange expression on his face. 'You have been to Jack Hennessy with all this already?'

'Yes, this afternoon.'

He did not know what to make of his vivacious, vital, determined wife. Each day she surprised him in some way or other. She was conscientious and caring and so very dear to him. He shook his head in admiration. 'It seems you move with great speed when you have an idea in your head, Mrs Wakeman.'

She smiled with satisfaction. 'So, Mr Wakeman, do we have the master's agreement to put up the fence?'

He laughed and drew her to him, kissing her. 'How could I refuse?'

The fence was up by the time Eve's birthday approached, and one Sunday afternoon John Stuart and Eve went over to inspect it. As they returned towards Larmer's Crossing, they passed some of the married workers coming back from church in Cowra. The settlement was close to eighteen miles from Mayfield House; fortunately, however, ten of those miles were within the boundary of Mayfield where the roads were sealed. Even so, it took the faithful the better part of the day to make the pilgrimage to and from church.

That religion was indispensable to most people was a fact that John Stuart tolerated and he did not try to change them. He employed Protestant and Catholic alike, and would have employed Jews had there been any, but there were few in this Christian land. He was different, out of step with common belief. His money and influence allowed him to hold and act on his unconventional views without penalty. Nevertheless, his statement that 'priests are parasites whatever their colour', shocked his wife and she answered him quite sternly with an energetic defence of Father and all those like him of all religions, to which he nodded wearing his beguiling half-smile and she finished by begging him never to say it in front of other people. 'I have said it to Joe,' he replied, and she answered, 'Yes, but Joe would let you blaspheme at the Lord himself, so much does he care about you. Please promise me you will say it to no one else.'

The people Eve had known in her life were all of some religious faith or other, she had never really thought about rejecting Jesus or debating belief in God, so it greatly interested her that her handsome, intelligent, articulate husband was deeply philosophical and that he came to his own conclusions about life and the universe.

As Eve rode with him now along the path towards the river, they came within fifty yards of the churchgoers and waved. Eve looked to him. 'I miss each Sunday at All Saints'; it was such a part of my life with Father and Mother.'

Her husband turned in the saddle to face her. 'I know. But you do go to service in Cowra every other week with Thelma.'

'Yes, and I appreciate that you realise how important it is to me, for I know you are a heathen.' She sighed and gave him a slightly disapproving shake of her head though she smiled openly at him. Then she teased, 'And I know now why you were over thirty before you married.'

He looked quizzically. 'Oh, and why is that?'

'Simple, my dear. It was the fear of having to go inside a church!'

John Stuart burst into laughter. Then, leaning across, he took her hand. 'My father was a Godly man but I fear he lacked discipline with my religious training. All my tutors were men of science, thinkers; in fact some were quite the reverse of religious. I was taught to be rational.' He smiled in recollection. 'And there was not a religious establishment between here and yours at Bathurst when I was growing, I'm glad to say. So there you are. You are lucky I let you drag me just the once to an altar.'

She laughed. 'John Stuart, you are incorrigible!'

They rode on in silence for a few minutes, John Stuart on Diomed, his chestnut stallion, Eve on Moonlight, one of her wedding gifts. He still held her hand and, squeezing it, asked, 'What is it you would like most for your birthday? It will be upon us in three weeks. How would you like to spend the day? Shall we grant a holiday like the Queen does on the twenty-fourth of May?'

Eve smiled. 'No, my dear, I do not consider myself in quite the same class as Victoria. A holiday will not be necessary.' A small frown appeared on her brow. 'But there is one thing I would enjoy more than anything else.'

'And what is that?'

'I would like you to invite Father and Mother here to celebrate it.'

John Stuart let go her hand and rubbed his chin. 'Damn it, Eve, you have the better of me. Now I must agree. It seems I must have religion under my very roof to sup with me now that you are my wife.'

'It will do you good. And thank you for consenting to my request in such an enthusiastic and gracious manner.'

He gave his hearty laugh again, then leaning back in the saddle said, 'I'll race you back to the stables for a—' Before he could finish, she had sped Moonlight forward over the long grass towards the river and he shouted, 'Cheat! Cheat! You did not wait to hear my wager.'

Nineteen days later, Father and Mother Billings arrived in the Mayfield coach which had been sent for them. John Stuart was a man who did not overmuch like house guests whoever they were. They threw off his routine and robbed him of precious hours on his land. Once a year, at Christmas, he grudgingly asked some of his friends, including the Governor, down for a week and invariably they accepted, for not even at Government House was the food as good or the accommodation as luxurious.

The day before her birthday, at the expected arrival time, Eve waited on the verandah. She had been there for the previous hour and, bright with anticipation, she imagined that every distant sound was made by the wheels of the carriage.

Stephanie, her personal maid, waiting with her, became infected by the excitement and when at last it was actually the sound of the coach wheels crunching on the gravel of the drive, she clapped her hands. Soon Deke brought the carriage expertly to the front of the house.

Eve was ecstatic. She flew down the steps into the strong, secure embrace of Father.

That afternoon and night Eve bubbled with joy and rejoiced to have the people she loved all together. If she had not been quite so exuberant she would have noticed that there was something disturbing her beloved Father. He chatted affably enough to John Stuart about Mayfield and cattle and crops, and he smiled on his darling Eve with pride, but there was something in his mood, something that checked his spirit. But Eve and John Stuart were both impervious; Eve because of her delight, John Stuart because of his unfamiliarity with the cleric and his natural preoccupation with other matters.

Because the parson and his wife were staying, John Stuart had arranged a dinner party in celebration of Eve's day. A string and woodwind octette would play and a singer would entertain. John Stuart had asked twelve in all: Thelma, Joe and Daydee would be there of course, and an ebullient middle-aged couple, Stanley and Myrtle Ford, graziers on a property the western side of Cowra, were coming with their 25-year-old son, Roy, a gentle young man who was extremely fond of Daydee. John Stuart's friend Sir Rutherfold Blake was in Cowra at present with his assistant, five police troopers and Sir Frederick Pottinger. They were interviewing victims of Old Joe Daily, a bushranger who had been carrying out hold-ups on the Sydney road north of the township, so Sir Rutherford and David Elrington would make up the company of twelve. The latter five would stay overnight.

Eve's birthday was, in the main, a happy day for her. The only moments that marred it were when thoughts of Clare came to her mind and the old dissatisfaction with herself for not having told John Stuart about her sister rose within her. But she quashed these reflections as she always had before, and she and Mother spent the morning with Thelma, arranging the dozens of magnificent flowers that had appeared overnight, while Father, trying to read the latest London *Times*, looked up at them indulgently every now and then from behind his spectacles.

Later, he and Eve rode for two hours along the Lachlan together. They had missed each other and spoke those inmost private things that they had been unable to say for many months. Eve told him how she was settling into life on Mayfield. 'This place is so easy to love, Father, and I feel such an integral part of it already. John Stuart jokes that Mayfield is written on his heart.' They both laughed. 'He is so kind and generous and what do you think? He knows every single man who works here by name, and there are hundreds. He quite amazes me. I'm so lucky and each day I fall more in love with him.'

When they returned, John Stuart met them as they walked up from the stables. 'Oh, John Stuart,' Eve called, 'what brings you home so early?'

'It is your birthday, darling,' he replied with a smile as he stepped between her and Father and, kissing the top of her head, linked her arm to his.

The sunset that afternoon was particularly brilliant. There was a luminous, rosy pink over all the western sky. 'That means it will be a cold day tomorrow,' predicted Thelma.

That evening, a little after half past seven, John Stuart, in black evening trousers and white silk evening shirt, was tying a bow at his throat when his wife entered. She had donned her gown, a pale, shimmering, pink silk that was cut wide at the neck and embroidered with masses of deep pink beads down across the tightly fitting bodice. Her curls hung loosely over her shoulders. 'Do you want some help with your bow, my love?' she asked.

For answer he stopped what he was doing and smiled.

She came to him and began to tie the bow. In the lamplight, the rounded tops of her breasts showed a creamy gold and the perfume of her drifted up seductively. 'You are so beautiful, my lovely Eve.'

She looked up. 'And so are you.'

His half smile played on his mouth. 'Men are not beautiful.'

'You are,' she answered standing on tiptoe and kissing him lightly on his mouth as his arms slid round her.

'Now I have you,' he laughed. 'You cannot slip away.'

She smiled. 'Perhaps I don't wish to.'

Their lips reached for each other. The kiss lasted a long time. John Stuart whispered into her curls, 'We have to meet our guests downstairs in less than thirty minutes.'

She kissed the side of his neck and whispered in reply, 'I know.'

His tongue touched the lobe of her ear. 'This is silly,' he murmured.

Again she whispered, 'I know,' playfully running her fingers through his hair.

'We should stop,' he replied, kissing the side of her neck.

'I know we should,' she answered.

In one movement they snaked slowly down to the thick Axminster carpet, the bow tie so recently tied now untied, and the silk shirt cast on top of it, while the series of hooks at the back of Eve's dress co-operated with John Stuart's fingers to deliver her breasts enticingly to him.

They rolled together in that delicious hunger called desire, until Eve parted her legs to feel the exquisite strength of her husband push in and drive down inside her and the two beautiful, naked bodies fulfilled their need.

'I'm wrong,' he said when at last the final vibration of pleasure rippled through them, and he came to rest upon her. 'This is not silly at all.'

She laughed up at him. 'I'm glad I hadn't done my hair.'

The host and hostess did in fact keep their guests waiting, but only briefly, some fourteen minutes in total. They made their entry hand in hand, Eve radiant, John Stuart debonair, an elegant Victorian couple.

He sat at the head of the mahogany table which could seat twenty-six when fully extended; behind him hung a portrait of Sir Arthur and himself at sixteen, painted by Conrad Martens, one of the very few portraits this early leader of the Australian school had ever done. Martens had been parliamentary librarian and painting in his spare time when Arthur Wakeman had met him in Sydney and been impressed with his work.

Sir Arthur had fostered colonial art and had remained a patron of the country's painters all his life. Here in the dining room a number of contemporary artists were represented: convict artist Thomas Griffiths Wainewright; John Glover, and George French Angus who had lived a short time in South Australia. Highlighted over the magnificently carved sideboard of mahogany and plate glass were a series of six paintings of the Lachlan Valley by a man called John Skinner Prout, whom Sir Arthur had found working as one of his stockmen. The Europeans hung in the other reception areas; Eve's favourite was by George Romney and showed three children on stepping stones crossing a brook.

The dining room was reminiscent of the regal rooms in the royal houses of Europe and tonight's guests were lit by four magnificent chandeliers hanging from the sixteen-feet-high ceiling. It was only the second time the room had been used in almost five months of their marriage and Eve found it awesome.

On Eve's right was Father. On John Stuart's right was Joe. The meal progressed. The food was splendid. The wine flowed. The conversation sparkled. The musicians played softly on a raised dais in one corner of the room and around the table radiated the strong personalities there.

At the beginning of the meal, Daydee spoke little. Roy, who was obviously keen to talk to her, worked hard to get any acknowledgement. She sat rather sedately until John Stuart directed some questions specifically to her and she replied eagerly with an animated smile. From then on she brightened visibly and began bestowing a sweet smile on Roy who glowed with appreciation. Only once after that did her eyes lose their merriment, when John Stuart stood to propose the toast to his wife. As everyone turned to John Stuart, she looked back down the table at Eve and her eyes narrowed with hate. The expression spanned scarcely a second and Eve was oblivious.

John Stuart stood at the head of his table. Eve sat admiring him at the other end. 'You are all here to celebrate the birthday of my dearest wife, Evelyn.' He turned and raised his glass to the painting of his father. 'Sir Arthur would be proud and pleased if he could see this night. September is an important month for me, as it was for him. It was the month he founded Mayfield.' This received polite applause. 'And, too, it was the month my father departed this life.' He looked back to those present. 'It was the month I went on my first cattle drive.'

'Too right it was,' Joe murmured.

'And now it is the month in which my wife has her birthday.' His eyes glinted in the candlelight as he bent slightly forward and raised his glass to her. 'My dear, I wish you many happy returns of this day and may we repeat today's pleasurable moments often again in the future.' His dark eyes were meaningful above the roguish half smile on his mouth. She understood the implication immediately, and her eyes sparkled provocatively at him over the rim of her wine glass.

The guests rose and drank her health and when she in turn stood to reply, there was a flush of pink in her cheeks. Her speech was brief. 'Thank you for being here. Thank you all for my beautiful gifts, and thank you, my darling husband, for your kind words.'

As she sat down, Clare rose uncomfortably in her mind. Clare, Clare, beautiful, loquacious, enchanting. Who are you wasting yourself upon tonight? If only you were here. I wonder where you are? Her head had dropped slightly and her face had become grave. Suddenly she was aware of Father holding her forearm and saying in a quiet voice, 'Evvy, what is wrong?'

She looked up into his eyes. 'Oh, nothing, Father, dear, nothing.'

He smiled gently. With his empathy for her, he had guessed what was in her mind. 'Come, my Evvy, no painful thoughts tonight,' he whispered as the birthday cake arrived, a grand three-tiered arrangement with an exquisite white marchpane house representing Mayfield on top, and iced yellow roses trailing down the sides, with the words 'Happy Birthday Dear Evelyn' written round each of the tiers. The candles burned brightly as Mr Baines, the butler, carefully placed this work of art in front of Eve.

She had never seen a cake like it. It was exquisite. She closed her eyes and made her wish. Clare, I am so happy, and thus my wish is for you. I want you to have peace and happiness wherever you are.

At the end of the meal, John Stuart called for Mr Free who, in the European manner, liked to be known as the 'chef', and everyone applauded his expertise. Then the ladies retired to the drawing room to await the men who continued to sit some twenty minutes or so, as Victorians did, and discussed those subjects which in delusion they believed women should not hear.

When they rejoined the ladies, the singer, a large-bosomed woman brought from Bathurst, rendered a number of songs. In a break, John Stuart turned to Eve and asked her to entertain them at the piano. She played 'Land That We Love' and the musicians accompanied her.

Then John Stuart nodded to Daydee and asked her to recite. She smiled to him, a gratified smile, and rose to her feet with a toss of her head. She chose 'Ode to the West Wind'. Confident and pleasing, her high young voice rang through the room. 'The trumpet of a prophecy! O wind, if winter comes, can spring be far behind?'

After the final song, 'The Last Rose of Summer', everyone was offered tea or coffee before retiring. Eve circulated among the guests. She was speaking to Mr Ford when Sir Rutherford joined them. She thought him good-looking in an austere fashion, his sharp, aquiline features reminding her of a hawk.

'Mrs Wakeman,' he began. His heavy-lidded eyes looked penetratingly at her.'We have spoken little this night. I believe you were the victim of a robbery by these damn bushrangers, on your wedding day, no less. Ah yes, well I can assure you that if any man will stamp them out, he stands before you now.'

'Hardly a victim, Sir Rutherford, they took nothing from me.'

'Surely your husband's loss is yours, madam?'

Eve was saved from replying by Mr Ford's interjection. 'There is too much of it. Far too much of it. The roads used to be safe. But one's not sure any more.'

Sir Rutherford nodded enthusiastically. 'Ah yes, Mr Ford, it is my task to bring our roads back to safety. As I was saying to Mr Wakeman over dinner, this centralising control of the police force in Sydney is a foolish move. It's allowing these wild colonial boys full reign. But then the force has asked for my expertise, and in that they have offset the madness of centralisation. The outlaws are becoming cocky, almost arrogant. Only a month ago, the police magistrate in Wagga Wagga, what a quaint name that is, was held up by a fellow I'm sure was this damnable Dan Morgan. Ah yes, I'm working on a trap for him right now. I have posted two hundred and fifty pounds reward on him. And though Frank Gardiner has disappeared, we've not heard the last of him. Just between us, he's gone north if I've guessed correctly.'

Eve did not like this subject. More and more, bushrangers were the topic of conversation and while she could not explain the reason, it unsettled her.

She had been delighted when John Stuart had seated Sir Rutherford next to him, far away from her, at dinner, for Sir Rutherford's main purpose in life seemed to be to annihilate the bushrangers from the earth. She wanted desperately to escape this conversation and was looking around for the means when her husband joined them and lifted her arm through his, blocking any hope she had of leaving.

The saturnine Sir Rutherford smiled at John Stuart. Even when he smiled, he seemed sombre. 'We are discussing the bushranging vermin again.'

'Having experienced a hold-up, we are all for ridding the country of them, aren't we, dear?' John Stuart looked down at his wife.

Eve attempted a smile in answer.

Mr Ford looked sympathetically at them.

160

Sir Rutherford's keen gaze passed from one to other of his three listeners. 'Do not worry. These characters all make mistakes in the end and I'll be there when they do. As for pardoning the devils like they did with Martin Cash in Hobart town just last June, damn foolish, encourages people to break the law. Break those who break the law, that's my motto. And as for printing letters written by them! I must say the *Lachlan Miner* has much to answer for. To have truck with such as "Darkie" Gardiner, as his mates call him, and to print his boastful reproaches, now that is plainly foolish.' His voice had been filling the room and Daydee, Roy and David Elrington moved closer to listen.

'Ah yes, it is mostly greed that leads them to become outlaws. Yet they all believe they've been forced into it. More often than not they simply have grudges against society which they translate as grievances. This Ben Hall blames the world for his wife's running off with another man, so he becomes a bushranger. And Dan Morgan's another one, a thief who loses a finger in a prison quarry and holds it against the police. Then Frank Gardiner, "prince of Tobymen" as he so pathetically calls himself, has Aboriginal blood he can't forget. Ah yes, "Darkie", not only is he illegitimate, but holds it against his mother for being a half-caste it seems, so he takes it out on decent law-abiding folk.'

'That's terrible,' Eve said.

'What, dear?' asked her husband.

'Frank Gardiner's holding a grudge against his mother because of her Aboriginal blood.'

John Stuart nodded thoughtfully, while the police detective answered. 'You are right, madam. It is terrible. But with a man like him, if it were not that it would be something else. Ah yes, they've all got their excuses.'

Eve listened uneasily. She was thinking how positive Sir Rutherford was of his own judgment. She wished she could be as sure of anything as he seemed of everything. There was little doubt that he was highly intelligent, but as she watched she wondered what the reason for his actions were. What was it that made him believe he was this seer of incontrovertible reasoning?

Daydee stood next to John Stuart, and in an attempt to gain the attention of the expert on the bushrangers she tossed her hair back over her shoulder and lifted her hand daintily towards him. 'So what of the gang who robbed Uncle John Stuart? At dinner you agreed it was Alan Fletcher; tell us more about him.'

'Ah yes, Miss Daydee, now that damn blackguard, he and his men have been on the run for ten years as I mentioned at table. Made his way south from the Moreton Bay area a decade ago, but he is a different case. Though he was a convict, ah yes indeed, a lifer, a killer, he is the educated one, runs his men like a military operation. He will be harder to take than the others but they all make mistakes in the end.'

He turned to Eve, alight with excitement at the information he passed on. 'Do you know, Mrs Wakeman, he was from a vice-regal family? Ah yes, his mother's father was a Braintree, spent years in Lahore as Governor of the Punjab. What a scandal it was, his grandson a murderer. And his father was old Sir Graham Fletcher, a squire in Somerset, knighted for his work with the public hospitals, a philanthropist. Ah yes, Alan Fletcher would have inherited the lands and farms, some of the richest in England. He'd had a ship of his own in the Royal Navy, he was someone in society. What a disgrace it—'

'Excuse me, Sir Rutherford,' Eve broke into his monologue, 'but I . . . have left something in the dining room. Please excuse me.' She turned from the group and walked away.

Her husband's eyes widened in surprise, and the detective policeman watched her for a few seconds, an expression both puzzled and curious on his face, before he turned back to his remaining listeners.

Fifteen minutes later they had all retired to their rooms and the housekeeper Mrs Smith and her staff were tidying up. It was close to half past one in the morning and the night had been a huge success.

John Stuart turned to his wife as he took off his shirt. 'Evelyn?'

'Yes, dear.'

'The way you walked out on Rutherford when he was so engrossed in telling us about that bushranger, Fletcher, well, darling, it was a little rude, don't you think?'

'Oh sweetheart, I am tired of all the talk of bushrangers. The man eats and sleeps them.'

Her husband smiled. 'Well, yes, he does at that. Nevertheless . . .'

She came to him and placed her hands on his naked chest, looking up at him. 'Darling, please let's not talk about this any more.'

'All right, my love, you are right, I suppose. He does go on a bit.' He bent down, and enveloping her in his arms kissed her and immediately forgot about Sir Rutherford.

'Perhaps,' she said as he lifted his mouth from hers, 'I could ask you for one more gift?' Her eyes invited him; her half-open lips allured him; the pressure of her breasts against him tempted him.

'I gave it to you before dinner,' he replied with a smile. Then as his mouth found hers again he murmured, 'But as it's your birthday . . .'

162

Afterwards, John Stuart fell quickly to sleep and by the hour of two, Mayfield House was quiet.

But Eve lay awake as the hours passed. Alan Fletcher . . . Alan Fletcher . . . Why did his eyes rise out of the blackness around her? Son of a knight! Grandson of a Governor! Born to wealth! But a convict, a killer. A killer! No, he could not be! She did not want him to be. She felt cold. She felt hot. She could not get comfortable. What had happened to her that afternoon at the coach door? Or had she imagined it all? The man had only looked at her, for Heaven's sake. She must forget him. This was madness! With a murmur of frustration, she nestled closer to John Stuart and, finally, she fell asleep.

The next morning she went down to breakfast nearly two hours later than usual. She found that Sir Rutherford and his assistant Mr Elrington had left hastily after news had been brought early by messenger. It appeared that Ben Hall's gang had made a daring raid on the town of Orange forty-eight hours before and, the same night, patrons at a ball in Forbes had been bailed up. The Fords acquainted her with the news as she arrived in the hall outside the breakfast room. They had already eaten and were about to return to their rooms to pack and take their leave.

'We think we'd best be on our way, Mrs Wakeman,' said the voluble Mr Ford. 'Make sure everything's all right at home. Don't know where the rabble will strike next!'

'Yes, yes, of course.'

Roy looked appealingly at his father. 'I'd like to say goodbye to Daydee first, Father, before we rush away.'

Mr Ford nodded and Eve looked understandingly at the young man. 'I think Daydee may still be in her bed, Roy, but you go over and see, by all means.'

The young man left with a lively walk.

John Stuart had ridden out to his day's work long before. He was supervising fencing over an hour's ride from Mayfield House in the north-west corner of the property, so Eve found only Mother and Father in the breakfast room. They had obviously eaten at a leisurely pace, waiting for her arrival.

'Have you heard about the hold-ups, dear?' Mother asked as Eve sat down opposite them.

'Yes, the Fords informed me just now.'

Mother sighed. 'Ah me, it seems the whole country is in fear of the outlaws. I wonder where it will end.'

Father was silent and Eve noticed he looked as if he, too, had not slept well. He seemed pensive and quiet. Mother in her passive, calm way also seemed more than usually thoughtful. Surely the news of the bushrangers was not having this effect, there must be something else.

When finally the serving girl and Baines left the room at the same time, Eve asked, 'What is it that makes you both so preoccupied this morning? Are you tired after so amusing a night or is there more to your reflective moods?'

The cleric looked apprehensively at his wife. She nodded in reply to his unspoken question. His pale eyes were lit with concern and he leaned across to where Eve sat, and touched her hand. 'Darling, there is a letter. I have been carrying it since we arrived, but didn't want to give it to you until after your birthday. Let us meet in the garden when you have finished breakfast.'

Eve now looked thoughtful herself. 'Yes, dear, of course. We shall go to the garden bower, by my rooms, no one will be there. Will you come, Mother?'

'No, Eve love, I have promised Thelma to go with her to the mothers' sewing bee this morning and it is better that you and Father have the time alone. I must hurry or I'll be late.' She kissed them and left.

'What is the letter, Father?'

'I do not know, my love. It is from Adelaide. I shall get it and meet you in the garden in five minutes.'

As he descended the few steps from the verandah into the garden and walked towards her, she looked so lovely, he felt a tremor in his chest. He stood perfectly still for a few seconds looking at her. She was sitting on a wooden seat, wearing a warm mustard-coloured gown and matching shawl. The early blooming wattle tree beside her had brought forth the first of its golden buds. The morning sun filtered through the branches onto the soft fairness of her hair. To his eyes, the scene had an unreality about it, as if it were a painting where the artist had completed his picture, then covered his canvas in gold. He sighed as he touched the letter in his pocket and walked towards her.

While Eve waited, she had thought about the letter. It was undoubtedly from Clare. To think how often her sister had been in her thoughts yesterday and Father had been holding a letter all the time! When she had written to her sister the day after she had agreed to John Stuart's proposal, she had told Clare to reply to the parsonage and now, at last, it had arrived. She had posted another letter off to Clare only two weeks ago when she had been in Cowra for the day. She knew she should have told John Stuart about his sister-in-law by now. She felt so guilty, but how was she to explain the free spirit that was Clare? Still, she must soon. It was not fair to him. She would steel herself and do it. He would understand. Perhaps Father and Mother were anxious that the letter would somehow mar her happiness. How very like them to be concerned.

She moved to make room for him to sit and he withdrew the envelope from his pocket, large and official looking. His voice was soft as he handed it to her. 'It came a week ago, Evvy, and as I knew I was coming here, it was timely for me to bring it. It is marked "Adelaide General Hospital and Sanatorium"; I have not opened it.' He handed her the envelope.

'But Father, what can this mean?'

All he did was shake his head.

A look of apprehension came into Eve's face. She turned the letter over in her hands, not wanting to open it. It was very quiet here under the trees and when Father gave a small cough, it sounded loud to his own ears. He patted her arm, saying, 'Perhaps you would rather read it in private, darling.' He began to rise.

Eve stayed him with her hand. 'Please, Father, no. I'd much rather you were here with me.'

It was addressed to Miss Evelyn May Herman. Her hand trembled a little as she opened the envelope. There were two pages and as she read them she made small sounds of disbelief and her eyes blurred with tears. She completed the two pages and turned her distraught face to Father. She tried to speak, but the words caught in her throat.

'My dear, dear Evvy, what is it?'

Silently she handed the papers to him.

The first was on official paper from the Superintendent of the Adelaide Hospital. It was dated 9 September 1863 and it read:

Dear Miss Herman,

It is with great reluctance that I find it my sad duty to inform you of your sister's death.

Sarah Clare Herman passed away in my hospital on this day of Our Lord, September eighth, 1863. The cause of her demise is listed with the Crown Coroner's Office as pulmonary consumption. Miss Herman was admitted to the care of this institution only one week ago. She was beyond medical help and only through the painstaking nursing of my staff did she endure these seven days.

She named you as her only kith and kin and what possessions she brought with her are here for you to claim.

Yours faithfully,
Michael Lusher, Superintendent.

The second page was a short letter from the Reverend Albert Durst of St David's Church of England, River Road, Adelaide. It had been written three days later and it read:

Dear Miss Herman,

Allow me to offer my deepest sympathy to you on the sad passing of your sister.

Your sister Sarah Clare Herman requested, and was given, a church burial according to the last rites of the Church of England. She lies at rest in the East cemetery, Adelaide, C of E section, grave no. 245. God rest her soul.

There were funds enough to cover her burial but very little else I am sorry to inform you.

I knew her not but deemed it my responsibility to inter her as one of the flock after conversing with her in the Adelaide Hospital where she took Communion shortly before she passed away.

Yours sincerely,
Albert Durst, Rector, Saint David's Parish, Adelaide.

When Father had finished reading, he prayed quietly, 'God Almighty, suffer the soul of Clare Herman to reside with you in Paradise this day, in the name of the Father and of the Son and of the Holy Ghost.' Then he turned to face the pallid woman beside him. Her lovely face was streaked with tears and they continued to run in a stream down across her cheeks. Some fell from her chin, staining the mustard gown. She looked pathetic and childlike in her grief. He opened his arms and she flung herself into them, the misery and confusion and pain she felt for Clare all bursting from her now.

He held her safe and patted her hair and whispered words of comfort that parents say to their suffering children, and yet she cried on. She sobbed for all that had been Clare. She sobbed for the wayward little girl, mischievous, fickle, yet captivatingly lovable. She sobbed for the beautiful, wilful young woman, full of spirit and defying social standards. She sobbed for the frivolous grown woman who had used her sexuality as her only resource in a man's world. And then, at last, she sobbed for her sister, the soft, sweet, disillusioned Clare, whom only she, Eve, had ever known, blood and flesh of the same womb, her alter ego, herself.

And so they sat on the bench in the sunlight, Eve suffering, and the man who held her suffering with her. When ultimately her tears ceased, they sat silently together for a long time, drawing a kind of solace from each other.

Finally, Eve spoke. 'Oh, Father, and I still have not told John Stuart about her. How right you were. I should have told him before our marriage. It has lain like a shadow over me, and now . . . now she is gone.'

He looked at her lovingly. 'My child, at last she is at peace. Now there can be no shadow. Why is it that you have never told John Stuart?'

Haltingly, Eve recounted the story of her wedding day and John Stuart's reaction to the poor woman in the street in Blayney. She told him that she realised John Stuart held a very low opinion of most women and she knew he would be outraged to have a sister-in-law like Clare, that he hated his mother for the sort of woman she had been and he would consider Clare the same, perhaps worse. Thus, for the months since her marriage she had kept silent. 'For I have been terribly afraid that he would somehow see it as a reflection upon me; that I would lose his love.'

When she had finished, he put his arm round her shoulders. Occasionally she still shuddered with the aftereffects of the sobbing and he spoke quietly but firmly. 'Eve love, you are no doubt correct about John Stuart's attitude. I am not a graduate of the new psychiatrics but it seems to me his feelings towards his mother may be the key to his position on women. But you are his wife. He married you. Not the poor woman in Blayney or your sad departed sister, but you. John Stuart loves you. Promise me you will now tell him of Clare. She is gone. Not even John Stuart's pride can be injured by the departed.'

Eve's eyes brimmed again with tears. He dabbed them with his already wet handkerchief. 'Cry no more, my love. She is in Paradise. No matter what Clare did here, she will be in the arms of the Lord now.'

Eve then looked pleadingly at this man she loved and admired so much, and asked for reassurance like a child. 'Do you really think so? Will she be with the Lord? Really, Father?'

'Undoubtedly. Don't you remember that Our Lord forgave and loved Mary Magdalene? No, my child, dear Clare will not be judged in Heaven as she was on earth.'

Eve smiled a small quivering smile. 'Oh Father, if only she could have known you, I think her life would have been so very different. All those times you wrote to her and asked her to come and live with us.'

'Yes, Evvy, but her last letter to me showed that she was firm in choosing the road she trod.' He had received a letter from Clare in February in which she had thanked him for his letters over the years.

She pointed out she was not dissatisfied with her lot, and she had a 'new friend' now, whom she could not leave. She thanked him for his charitable attention. She asked him to take care of 'her dearest Evelyn', and to understand that she was able to take care of herself.

Eve nodded. 'Yes, I know, but if only she could have met you and Mother . . .' She broke off and the tears welled again in her eyes.

'Perhaps. Thank you for the faith in us, my Evvy. Now please, no more tears. I want a commitment you will not upset yourself like this again.'

'I don't know if I can commit, but I will try,' she said wiping her eyes. A torturous sigh vibrated through her as she rose from the seat. 'I think I will go for a ride on Moonlight. I feel I want to be out in the bush, by myself. Do you understand?'

Father stood up beside her. 'Yes, Evvy love, I understand. I will walk down to the stable yard and have a chat with Jack Hennessy and then wave you off on your ride.'

She hugged him again. 'I will see you there.'

She left him and walked towards her bedroom, passing close to the beautiful poinciana tree that dominated the garden. It was an umbrella of bright green, dotted with the first of the buds that would become brilliant orange-red flowers within a few weeks. He watched as she stepped onto the verandah, her voice drifting back to him as she called to her maid Stephanie. Then he looked skywards for a long moment into the eternal blue and, folding the two pages he still held in his hand, he put them in his pocket and left the garden.

He had been in Jack Hennessy's office for about ten minutes when Eve joined them. She had changed her mustard gown for a warm jacket and a flared, brown riding skirt. She wore a small dark hat tied beneath her chin with a red ribbon.

'Morning, Mrs Wakeman.'

'Good morning, Mr Hennessy, I'm taking Moonlight out for a ride.'

'Very well, m'lady, and are you accompanying the mistress, Reverend?'

'No, Mrs Wakeman prefers to ride alone today.'

Jack Hennessy would have preferred her to have an escort, but he offered no argument and gave orders for Moonlight to be saddled.

Father helped her to mount. She rode astride as she always had.

'How long do you think you will be, my love?'

'I'm not sure. John Stuart is out with a team fencing near the bluff to the north-west, Daisy Ridge. I may ride over there and join him.

Perhaps even take luncheon with him. Don't wait for me if I'm not back by one o'clock.'

Father was pleased. He hoped she would go to her husband and tell him of Clare. 'Good. Perhaps you will spend the entire day in his company.'

'Oh no, he'll be too busy for that. I will ride back directly after eating. I'll be home by three o'clock.'

She bent down from the saddle and touched him on the shoulder. She smiled bravely at him. 'Thank you, Father dear, thank you for everything. Words cannot express my gratitude.' Then she smiled briefly again and turned the skittish Moonlight out of the stable yard onto the path that led to the road and down to the Lachlan River.

She turned once to wave, a small dark figure on the white stallion.

The road took her over Larmer's Crossing, Moonlight's hooves thudding loudly on the planking. She rode steadily for a long time, stopping now and then to open gates in fences that separated the huge paddocks and fields. When at last she met a gate in a fence that kept cleared land from the bush, again she dismounted to open it. The wind plucked at her skirt and the sun was suddenly covered by cloud. She looked up. Rain threatened. She did not consider returning but led Moonlight through the gate and closed it behind her. She stood deliberating for a few seconds before she nodded to herself in decision. Then, remounting, she turned Moonlight's head in the opposite direction to where her husband would be fencing and rode at a goodly pace south-west towards a large escarpment which was beyond a series of hills some miles away, on the other side of the extensive valley.

She had resolved not to find John Stuart. Today, she preferred to be alone. She needed some time to adapt to her sister's death. She wanted the wind in her face and the clean smell of the bush around her. To remember her sister and their years together. To recall Clare's happy, impetuous ways, her laughter and high spirits, the good and dear things about her. She didn't want people and talk and explanations. And that's what it would be if she joined John Stuart. Tonight, yes; she would explain Clare tonight.

She let Moonlight have his head and her hands went a little slack on the reins as she rode on in the quickening breeze.

It so distressed her that Clare had been dead and buried and she had not known. Tears rose to her eyes, but remembering her promise to Father she tried to hold them back. He and Mother were the only people she had told about her sister. At first she had been apprehensive and simply mentioned that her sister lived in Adelaide, but later when she knew them better and realised the extent of their compassion, she had told them everything. That was when Father had begun to write to Clare.

She tightened her hands on the reins and looked up. Clouds chased the sun across the sky. The day was turning colder. It looked like rain to the north.

Down towards the Boorowa River she went. Near the bank rose several small mounds alive with black ants. She steered Moonlight away from them and entered the water; its course through this part of the valley was more like a creek. Midway he drank, his sleek long neck reaching down to the water. She detached the small water bottle at the side of her saddle and she, too, drank. Both refreshed, she urged him onwards. She rode at a quickening pace over the undulating ground, her red ribbons trailing from under her chin over her shoulders in the wind. The open air and the freedom banished some of her misery. She impelled Moonlight to accelerate, and the nimble-footed horse responded, his hooves pounding through the tall paspalum grass, his white tail flying behind in unison with her red ribbons. On and on she went, her mind freeing itself of the pain and sadness of the morning.

When at last she came to the far side of the valley she checked Moonlight and looked about. She had been riding for over two hours south-west. She knew approximately where she was, for she had been brought this way a few times before; she was under the cliff that ran some miles along the valley and formed a natural portion of the western Mayfield border. The clouds seemed to sit upon the cliff top as she looked up, and suddenly she wanted desperately to be there, above the world, looking down. She remembered that a rough track led up the side somewhere. Eager to find it, she rode south for another half-mile or so, examining the steep rock face.

Then she saw it. It was a sharper ascent than she had remembered. She knew if she continued on for a few miles the ridge yielded and met the valley in a much gentler incline. But today she felt like taking risks; she would go up the face of the escarpment. Moonlight was as sure-footed as any horse ever born. Taking a deep breath, she urged the stallion forward and up onto the uneven ground. For the next fifteen minutes, they picked their way up the trail. Once or twice she faltered where passage was nearly impassable, the drop to her right almost sheer. But fear has no reasonable pattern, and though she feared to speak to John Stuart of Clare, she was intrepid in this physical danger.

Finally, Moonlight brought her to the top and, dismounting, she stood looking down across the valley. She felt elated and satisfied. She could follow the dark line that was the meandering course of the

Boorowa River she had crossed. The wind blew more fiercely up here and the sense of being alone excited her, stimulated her.

She supposed it must be almost luncheon-time. Oh well, her darling husband would not miss her. He had no idea she had considered joining him, and Father and Mother would not concern themselves, for they would think she was with John Stuart. She felt quite pleased knowing that she was at liberty for hours yet. Even so, she must turn back soon to be sure of being home by the hour of three.

A bandicoot scampered round a dead branch to her right hand and disappeared into the scrub. She jumped and then laughed in surprise. Moonlight snorted beside her and lifted his head, sniffing the wind. She hugged his thick neck and remounted, heading through the bush and scrub which ran along the ridge towards the long easy slope to the low ground.

To left and right, the green-grey of the scrub was highlighted with the crimson of the first waratahs and bottlebrushes pushing out of the undergrowth. She could smell the penetrating odour of the lemon-scented eucalyptus on the air. It was fresh and clear. The sun had come out from behind the clouds to offer a mild warmth through the cool wind. She sighed a small sigh and smoothed Moonlight's long white mane. He gave an answering whinny of pleasure.

Abruptly, the picture of the bushranger flashed into her mind. She could envy him in a way; his life in the unrestricted bushlands, his freedom. But of course he lived in constant danger. He was not really free at all. Who was? Weren't there always restrictions and rules and obligations for everyone?

She shivered. She must stop reflecting this way.

She took Moonlight forward. Her pace needed to be a little quicker or it would be late by the time she got home. The horse moved easily into a fast trot.

Her course took her between the towering gums. Birds flew from their hiding places and the smaller bush animals departed at the sound of the advancing hooves. Mostly the ground was even, but here and there it was striated and dead branches and small rocks occasionally blocked clear passage, yet unerringly the stallion avoided these. He moved up into a canter. Eve's ribbons trailed once more in the wind. She rode well and the horse responded. She could feel the surge of strength under the saddle as the animal accelerated.

But even the unfaltering Moonlight could not sense the approach of the big red kangaroo that had been startled by a falling rock down a narrow gorge to their right and now came leaping in fear and panic towards them. On and on came the powerful animal in giant strides towards the woman and the horse. On and on came Eve and

Moonlight, moving at a steady pace, hidden from the kangaroo.

Inescapably, their paths crossed.

Eve became aware of the kangaroo at the last moment, but too late. She tried vainly to pull back on the reins as the enormous animal jumped directly into Moonlight's path, smashing with all its force into the horse's forelegs and breaking them instantly.

There was a terrible sound and Moonlight reared up in shock. His head was thrown back and his mane hit Eve in the face. She lost hold of the reins and was lifted up and out of the saddle. Her right foot caught momentarily in the stirrup and she was dragged forward and upward by the rearing horse. Her hat flew off and landed in the bracken. Her body twisted in mid-air and her head caught the trunk of a silky gum. Then her foot dislodged and she fell heavily to the ground.

As the kangaroo shot past and crashed into the scrub, continuing on its way, Moonlight's shattered limbs collapsed under his body. The last thing Eve remembered before she lost consciousness was the sound of him, so like a human scream, high-pitched and piercing, expressing his pain. The poor animal continued to whinny in shrill suffering and terror while his mistress lay still and silent, the blood oozing from the wound at the back of her head turning the collar of her dark jacket a murky red.

CHAPTER TEN

'Hold me but safe again within the bond
Of one immortal look.'
'Eurydice to Orpheus', Robert Browning, 1812–1889.

It had been an early morning for Alan Fletcher.

He had taken a watch on top of Nelson's Boulder looking down from Treehard Hill as was sometimes his way when he woke before the sun, a habit from his shipboard days.

There was a chill wind blowing up the valley and the day had broken with lemon rays across a cloudy sky. Just after dawn, Daniel, wrapped in a greatcoat, came to call him to his breakfast. They sat together in the tiny kitchen and Alan ate the hot oatmeal Dan had prepared while the others slept. Daniel was always the early riser, mostly up before six o'clock. He was the self-appointed cook and his meals were plain but palatable.

Treehard Hill was 'home'.

It had been Lawless who said, 'Let's call it Treehard, mateys, for it's covered in trees and hard to find.' Years had passed before they had fashioned the sturdy wooden house that nestled now on the flat, tree-covered plateau between the wall of rock and the sheer drop of hundreds of feet to the valley floor. There were four rooms: two bedrooms, a large kitchen, and a fourth room for storage of their clothes, saddles and equipment.

It had been hard but pleasant toil to build a home, a goal for the men to work towards during the long weary weeks between deployment. They had stumbled upon Treehard Hill almost four and a half years before. Alan had been searching for just such a natural stronghold for years. By chance they had made their camp near the thicket of trees that hid the entrance to the narrow tunnel through sandstone boulders. They had been there for over a week before Daniel, wandering deeply in through the trees to find firewood, had discovered the well-hidden entrance.

In those early days after finding Treehard, they had camped out until they had built the first roughly hewn structure.

Even now a shudder ran through Alan whenever he remembered

173

the hundreds of tarantula spiders that had lived between the slabs of bark that were the hut walls. Of all the insects and animal life of the bush, and there were many, sometimes deadly, tarantulas were the ones that he found the most distasteful. They had been their constant ugly companions. Masses of them had nested within inches of their heads as they slept and no matter how hard they fought them, they could not clear the spiders from the bark. But since they had replaced the bark with weatherboard and lined the rooms, the hairy, unsightly creatures rarely troubled them. Of course there were the ever-present hazards of living in the bush, like the death adder snake that had killed Patricia June. It was always possible on a hot night to see a length of scale slither across the doorstep. But the danger of one falling on a sleeper had gone since they had made the dwelling weatherproof. Their latest refinement was to begin to build a proper verandah along the front of the kitchen, and Alan had plans for an additional outhouse where they would bathe, and a real stable for the horses.

He was thorough and imaginative. Other bands of bushrangers simply played cards, gambled and became irritable and bored in their hideouts, but Alan's men were not idle. They had their relaxation but it was in the evening like normal working folk, and they enjoyed it all the more, for it was the natural pattern of life.

How often Alan had heard of other bands disintegrating because of ill temper, drink and women. He could control the first two but could do nothing about the third. Daniel and Sam were not interested in women. Indeed Daniel was happy simply to take care of the cleaning and cooking at Treehard. And Sam? There were times when Alan wondered if females had ever occupied Sam's mind. With Lawless it was different. He had loved Patricia June with the energetic passion of a young man, and when he lost her on Christmas Day 1858, he had mourned her a long time. But recently Alan had noticed he was once again enjoying the company of women. Yet it was only Jordan who made a priority of tarrying in the safe houses, the wayside taverns and inns where the owners were sympathetic to the 'wild colonial boys'. Jordan O'Day, who had come amongst them because of his sister Patricia June, Lawless's wife, mild mannered and sweet through all her adversities.

Alan finished his breakfast, pushed his plate away and stood from the table. He was going hunting for fresh food and Daniel followed him out into the yard as he saddled Freedom, his grey stallion. Daniel handed him the reins of the second animal, Waterloo, Lawless's horse, which he took to carry the game.

'How long will you be, son?'

'It depends on my luck, Danny. We're low on provisions. Perhaps the best part of the day.'

'I'll not be easy until you're home,' his faithful companion commented.

Alan smiled at him with affection. 'Keep the boys working on the verandah, Danny.' Then he waved and rode off round the house, disappearing between the walls of the dwelling and the corrugated iron tank that held their water.

Eight yards from the back of the house rose the first huge limestone boulder. Alan circled it and entered the narrow passage. It was broad enough for a man on horseback to pass and was the only opening that led from their 200-yard-wide ledge to the outside world. At the end of the passageway he rode through the thicket of eucalyptus, white cedar trees, and scrub, looking impenetrable from the outside.

Daniel had followed part of the way down the sandstone passage to the rocky lookout they called Nelson's Boulder where he had free vision across the hillside and watched Alan until he vanished into the silent bushland.

Frost had settled overnight, covering the lower glades in a fine grey carpet, and Alan turned in the saddle to see the double line of prints left by Freedom and Waterloo. He smiled to see them, the only telltale sign that this lonely place had been disturbed. As he rode, with the dexterity of one who has ridden from early childhood, both he and the horses blew little white clouds in the air with every breath. He was dressed in a durable, sheepskin jacket and as he lifted one sunbrowned hand to turn up the collar, it made a dark line across his cheek, setting off his striking profile against the advancing day.

Alan was a lover of the bush, just as once he had been a lover of the sea, and he looked with appreciation at the landscape around him. He and his men were forced to live mostly off the land. They ventured into towns only when grain, ammunition or information was needed. Many of the bushrangers were foolishly imprudent, and in cavalier fashion took little precaution. Some, like Dan Morgan and Johnny Gilbert, carelessly disdainful of the police, allowed too many people to know their whereabouts. Alan thought it could lead to their downfall in the end.

Last year, Frank Gardiner had asked Alan to join in the now notorious Eugowra gold robbery. He had gone to meet Gardiner even though he deprecated taking from other than the Government, the police or, infrequently, the exceptionally rich. He had met Ben Hall, Johnny Gilbert, Alexander Fordyce and Johnny O'Meally. There were four others in it but they were not present. Alan had refused to unite with them to rob the Forbes gold escort containing hundreds of bank notes and gold from the Lachlan diggings. Apart from his overriding reason, he did not like the way it was proceeding. Ben Hall's had been the single voice that agreed with him.

Alan's judgement was proven correct. Most of the gold had now been recovered. Two of the bushrangers in the action were gaoled and one had been hanged. Frank Gardiner had disappeared, and Hall, O'Meally and Gilbert were very wanted men.

The Fletcher band's operations were kept absolutely secret. It was the only way to survive. The single individual Alan trusted apart from his band, was their proven friend 'Bluey' Williams. Bluey's real name was Edmund, but in colonial fashion he was called Bluey, an inexplicable but accepted nickname for red-haired men. Bluey idolised Alan. He was an itinerant odd-job man who plied between Bathurst and Young and called home a wooden hut in the bush. He had the knack of making people laugh, although he was an imaginative and thoughtful man. It was through Bluey that Alan knew police movements and much of the information that had kept himself and his men out of harm's way in the last few years. He was a trusted go-between and it was he who had brought Alan the news that Frank Gardiner wanted to see him about the planned Eugowra robbery in 1862. But even Bluey did not know the location of Treehard, more for his own protection than anything else.

The morning advanced. By ten o'clock he had three rabbits slung across Waterloo's back and by noon he had added a wild boar. They were extremely dangerous animals, and had been known to kill a man, but they were delicious eating; Daniel would be delighted with it.

Alan's face softened in thought. Daniel was sixty-nine now and the hardships of convict life and living out in all weathers had taken its toll on him. There was no doubt his health had suffered. He tired quickly and was sometimes out of breath. Alan smiled as he visualised his dearest friend singing Irish ditties and going about his daily routine at Treehard Hill.

When his thoughts came back to the present, he reined in Freedom and took stock of where he was. He had ridden a little further than usual, in fact some miles further. He was in bushland leading up to the bluff that overlooked one of the valleys of Mayfield. A lone kookaburra on a broken branch to his left laughed. It was a mocking sound and it struck him like a jeer. He turned to look up at the bird before he urged Freedom forward up the slope. He would complete the ascent to the top, then strike west and return in a circle to Treehard. He had painstakingly studied this part of the country and his judgement in direction was unerring. He read the signs of the bush as well as he had once read the wind and the sea.

He cantered uphill and along the ridge. The wind still blew although the sun had come out from behind the clouds where it had hidden most of the morning. He was about to turn and head west when he heard the crashing noise of an animal in the scrub to his right. Reining in the horses he saw a huge red buck kangaroo, its haunches massive, bounding in mighty leaps through the trees. And then through the bush came another sound, faint yet discordant, and not a bush noise.

He nudged Freedom forward into a walk, and Waterloo, whose reins were tied to the back of Freedom's saddle, moved automatically. All the instincts of the hunted man became alert. His right hand dropped the reins and found his rifle. He tensed in the saddle and his mind cast about for the fastest route of escape.

Then he gave his full attention back to the cry, for that was what it was, high-pitched and sharp. It was coming from in front of him, directly north. He realised it was a horse in agony.

Traps for bushrangers were set in the most bizarre fashions.

'Be ready, Freedom, Waterloo,' he said, 'we may have to run for it.' And Freedom, seemingly in reply, stiffened beneath the saddle. Alan turned the horses in a full circle, all the while scanning through the trees. He saw nothing, but the pained call still continued. He sensed there was nothing to fear, so he urged Freedom on towards the sound. It was shrill and urgent, the suffering like a scream. A minute later he saw the stallion. A beautiful, white creature writhing on the ground. And, almost instantaneously, he saw the figure beyond.

He dismounted and led his horse forward. The form on the ground was a woman.

He peered through the trees again in every direction. No one in sight and no noise of riders. What was a woman doing out here alone? Her hat hung crazily in the scrub, its red ribbons blowing in the wind as she lay face down at the base of a gum. There was blood in her fair curls.

Delicately, he turned her over.

John Stuart Wakeman's wife!

He felt the warm breath from her mouth and a sort of relief shot through him; for a moment he had dreaded that she was dead. Her pulse seemed normal although she was unconscious. He took off his jacket and covered her with it.

Then he turned to the unfortunate Moonlight. His dignified head moved up and down in pain and his continuous whinny of fear and agony was loud in the wind. It was obvious that both his front legs were broken.

Alan spoke to the animal; quiet, soft, soothing words, and as he spoke he levelled the rifle at the regal head and shot Moonlight through the brain. The explosion brought a strangled noise from Freedom and a sound of returning consciousness from Eve. He moved back and, kneeling beside her, positioned her so that she lay against him. There was dirt down the side of her cheek and in her hair, but it was the wound that concerned him. He wiped some of the blood away with his handkerchief as she moaned again.

He felt the cold through his cotton shirt, yet the sensation was as if it belonged to someone else, for his whole attention was given to the woman, so amazed was he to find her here like this, alone.

As the blackness receded, Eve felt someone holding her. Her head throbbed and there was pain in her arms and legs.

A voice said, 'Can you hear me? How do you feel?'

The sound cut through her confusion. She opened her eyes and began to focus. It was then she recognised the eyes above her and a shocked sound escaped from her lips. She drew away from him, and yet at the same time she registered the wonderful look of him, the sunbrowned face that she had actually dreamed about seeing.

It was outlandish. How could the bushranger be here? She shuddered as he bent down towards her and replaced the handkerchief against her wound.

There was alarm in her voice. 'You! It is not possible! How can you be here?'

'You have cut your head,' he said quietly, disregarding her question. Then taking her right hand and placing it upon the handkerchief against her head he added, 'Here, hold this. I must bandage it.'

She could feel her heart thumping. She was still aware of pain in her head and soreness in her limbs, but the astounding reality overwhelmed her. She had begun to tremble and was unable to stop.

'You fell from your horse,' he was saying, 'hit your head on this tree, no doubt. You are fortunate. The wound is not deep.'

Then she remembered Moonlight. She looked around but could not see him. Alan had placed himself in the way.

'Moonlight? Where is Moonlight?'

His tone was gentle. 'If it is your horse you speak of, I'm afraid he had smashed both his forelegs. He was suffering badly. I'm sorry, lass, but I had to put him down.'

Oh no! Her princely Moonlight gone! Her eyes filled with tears.

'There, lass,' he said quietly. 'He's better off. He could not be mended.'

He stripped off his shirt and tore it in pieces. She feebly protested when she realised what he was doing, but he wound the shirt bandages round her head until he had covered the handkerchief and checked the bleeding.

The early afternoon sun, gaining some mastery over the day, shone down through the straggling clouds and the wind, bringing a capricious warmth to the two people. Fallen leaves blew by them in the grass and bush birds watched from the scrub.

To Eve it seemed as if he studied her, looking not merely at her but down into the depths of her. Unnerved, she averted her eyes.

'Is the pain bad?' he asked.

'No, not bad. It throbs a little.'

'Sit still.' He rose from her, and she noticed the L-shaped scar exposed on his left forearm. It looked an old wound. It was the only imperfect thing about him, and somehow it heightened the symmetry of the rest of him. She felt light-headed, a sensation unrelated to her injuries, as if she were intoxicated. She stared at him as he walked from her to his horses, her eyes riveted to the rippling, muscular nakedness of his back.

She could not believe this was happening. It should not be happening. It was not feasible that it was he who had found her. How could he be here? She was fascinated by him, and the overriding fear she had experienced earlier was fading. With relief she realised she had ceased to tremble, but her amazement was blocking her ability to think clearly. She was only able to acknowledge the confusion that this man stirred within her. Did he feel any of these emotions? She was flooded with guilt.

He stood with his back to her as he removed a water bottle and a rolled blanket from his saddle.

Could it have been as recently as last night that Sir Rutherford had been discussing him? It seemed so much longer.

He turned to her and she watched him cross the space between them. His arms came down towards her. She was highly aware of his hands pressing through her clothes as they touched and lifted her to where she could lean against a rock.

She drank a little from the water bottle, and with shock she realised that the thought filling her mind was not that the water refreshed her, but that his mouth too had covered the opening of this bottle.

Her heart was still beating rapidly. She observed him silently as he placed the blanket over her and retrieved his jacket. He stood and

179

put it on and she focused on that part of his chest which the jacket did not cover, the brownness of him beneath the hollow of his neck.

When he had buttoned his coat, he bent down, half kneeling, right knee on the ground, resting his left elbow on his left knee and surveying her. 'Is there anywhere else that causes you pain? You will be bruised in many places.'

He was so refined, everything about him extrinsic to the type of man Sir Rutherford described as a bushranger. Son of a knight, from a vice-regal family, naval captain, convict, killer, lifer. It was all fantastic. She replied to his question. 'My ankle hurts too, I think.'

He moved over to her. Gently he took off her riding boot and looked at her leg. It was swollen but it moved back and forth without great pain.

'I would guess there is nothing broken, probably just badly sprained.' Then his face broke into a smile. 'You'll not dance on it for a few days.'

It was the first smile she had seen from him and suddenly her aches and discomfort dissolved in a feeling of well-being, and she smiled involuntarily back at him.

He began to ask a question. 'Were you . . .' And to their surprise, both of them completed the sentence in unison. 'Riding alone?' they said.

'Yes, I was,' she finished.

For some time they were both silent.

'What happened to make you fall?'

'It was a kangaroo, enormous . . . it seemed to come from nowhere. Moonlight reared and I fell.'

'Yes, they can be dangerous, the big ones.' He guessed it was probably the huge buck he had seen in the bush moments before he heard her horse's cry.

She looked down at her hands. 'How is it you are here?'

'I was hunting, as you can see.' He pointed to the bounty on Waterloo's saddle.

Often in the months to come, when her mind drifted from the daily routine of her life, she would sit again on this bush floor, here with him.

Freedom lifted his head from where he was chewing grass some ten yards distant and whinnied. Waterloo answered.

Immediately, Eve thought about Moonlight again and tried to look in his direction. The man opposite shook his head. 'Don't think on it, lass. He is gone. There was nothing else that could be done.'

The tears came again. 'Yes, I know. It's just that he was so . . . beautiful.'

180

Then he said the thing she somehow did not want to hear. 'I must get you home. Won't people be looking for you?'

'What time is it?' she asked.

He lifted his hands to shade his eyes and looked up at the sky. 'Between one and two o'clock, closer to two I think.'

'I must leave soon, but I would rather rest a little longer here.' Then she added, 'If you don't mind.'

'I do not.'

She dropped her eyes lest he should see what she was thinking.

'My head does not hurt as much but I must look a fright,' she said.

'You do,' he replied.

She looked up quickly and there was amusement in his eyes.

'You have the startling appearance of a female pirate after battle; your hair tied in a bandana made from the shirt of a victim no doubt. All you need is the eye patch!'

She laughed then. And he laughed. And above them a kookaburra laughed. This time there was no mockery in the sound.

He seemed to be studying her. 'Why is it that the mistress of Mayfield rides alone and so far?' he asked.

'I sometimes like to ride alone. But I have never been this far before, I . . . wanted expressly to be alone today.' She looked up into his eyes again and now she felt no fear of him at all. How could this man be a killer? It was not possible!

They sat in silence again for a short time.

Then she sighed and said, 'I wished to be by myself today because I had some terrible news. Sad news. My only sister, she is dead.' Tears came again to her eyes and clouded her vision.

He looked compassionately at her. 'We all must die, lass. And I'm sorry you are so sad. But what has occurred can't be changed. Nothing can bring her back. Perhaps it is good you experience the pain of her loss so keenly now and rid yourself of much of the grief.' Briefly a distant look came into his eyes. 'I have known those who lived daily with grief, and that is not living.'

'She was so misunderstood, so very misunderstood.'

He nodded. 'If you say so, no doubt she was.'

Then she felt an urgent need to exonerate Clare. She did not know why, but she wanted to explain to the bushranger. It made no sense; she was aware it was ridiculous. And yet from somewhere within her mind came the bewildering knowledge that this man would understand and that she truly wished him to know the truth.

'Don't upset yourself more. You have a head wound and have jolted yourself badly. You need rest and care.'

'But I honestly feel all right and . . . I would like to tell you about my sister. That is, unless you must leave now?' He regarded her some moments. Was that a hint of a smile?

'No. I do not need to leave.'

So Eve told the story of Clare to Alan, the stranger and yet not the stranger, sitting on the ground in the bush surrounded by the cold of this September day. And he listened, calmly and impartially, with great attention, to what she said.

She related their childhood in Boston and their three years in San Francisco; Clare, erratic and loving, spoiled and sweet, the enigma that had been her sister. She explained how her mother's illness, the coughing and wasting disease, followed by her death, had changed their lives. How her father had made the decision to bring them to New South Wales, only to die on the journey.

When she told him of her arrival with Clare in Sydney, alone in a strange land, he nodded thoughtfully. She spoke of the Maggses and the Ship Inn and the sailors; of Father Billings and the gold watch and the sewing business. And when she came to recount the morning Clare had left she halted a moment and looked up to the sky. The old sadness and the hurt filled her and now she felt the soreness in her limbs and the pain in the back of her head more.

He leaned towards her just a little. 'You have told me enough. There is no need to continue.'

But she wanted to finish. In him, she felt she had found a sympathy that perhaps not even Father could meet. Her voice was tentative. 'I . . . I feel as if I must finish it now.'

'Then you must,' he said in his disarming fashion.

'It was in October eighteen fifty-six. The day she left me, I mean. We lived at the back of our shop, a shed in Hunter Street. I had worked late the night before and Clare had been out with Harry, the man she had been seeing lately. Try as I might I could not like him or his companions. He was a writer. Seemed to work only intermittently and boasted openly of his itinerant life. He was handsome enough. Clare's men were always handsome. I was in bed late that morning. I had not heard her come in the night before. I remember I had a sense of foreboding as I went into her little room. It was empty. All her clothes were gone. Then I found it, the note I mean.'

'And what had she written?'

'That she had gone with Harry to Adelaide. He had acquired some position with a newspaper. He said he'd marry her when they got there, though he never did. Clare's was a malignant star. Men were always promising to marry her. And now she is gone, from consumption they said.' She bent forward and held her head in her hands.

Quietly he moved to help her to her feet. 'Come now, lass. You were the best of sisters, I have no doubt.'

She stood with his help. 'But it was all wrong! The last time I saw my sister she was working in a barroom again, another tavern. Clare, so elegant and graceful; it broke my heart.'

He stood looking down at her. 'Now, lass, it was her life. She made her own choices, whether she found what she searched for or not. But then aren't we all searching for what few of us find? Let her rest in peace now. For my part, I cannot judge her.' He gave a sound like a laugh in his throat but there was no humour on his face. 'It would be presumptuous, indulgent,' he finished.

'Yes, perhaps,' Eve replied in a faint voice. 'But there are those who don't quite understand, and who would judge harshly.'

'I claim no close association with the Bible,' he answered, 'but "Judge not, that ye be not judged". My mother used to say that, a thousand years ago.'

She looked intently at him and wondered about his mother. What would this man's mother be like? Did she know what had become of her son? And what about him? What was the truth? All she knew was what Sir Rutherford had said. What had really happened to bring this cultured, urbane man to bushranging in this wild land?

An impetuous anger rose within her towards Sir Rutherford and all like him. Suddenly she was positive that Alan Fletcher was good and incorruptible and fearless, no matter what they said about him. She knew this with an unquestionable certainty, and it brought her heart to racing again. She was filled with a torrent of confusing sensations as she stood there looking up at him. She would remember the intimacy of this strange afternoon. And she realised with a terrible surge of guilt that she would miss this man for ever after, now that she had experienced this time with him.

He knew he must return her to Mayfield; she belonged to Wakeman. She appeared so distressed, and with her head bandaged and her jacket torn where it had caught in the undergrowth, she looked almost waifish. He found himself wishing that he did not have to take her home. Then he moved abruptly, saying, 'We must leave now.'

She looked over to where the lifeless Moonlight lay.

'I will return and bury him,' he assured her.

Relief flooded her face. 'Will you? Thank you . . . oh thank you. Goodbye, Moonlight. I am so sorry, so very sorry.'

Alan took her arm and steered her towards Waterloo. 'Can you ride alone?'

Now that she was standing, she felt very dizzy and was conscious of the aching in her limbs. 'No, I'm afraid not.'

'Then we shall ride upon Freedom.' He took Waterloo's reins and tied them loosely to a small tree. 'You wait here,' he said to the animal. 'I will come back for you.'

'Does he understand?'

'Better than some humans.'

He helped her up on Freedom and mounted behind her.

'Thank you for listening to me,' she said. 'Somehow I feel a completeness about Clare's life now. I know I must have appeared . . . that is, I hope you didn't think me impertinent.'

Then she thought she sensed him laugh and a flush rose to her throat as he replied in her ear, 'Impertinent? No, I did not think that.'

They moved off through the grey bush at a walking pace and he said, 'Sometimes we need to speak that reality which is our inmost feelings, and perhaps it is easier to tell it to a stranger, as you have done today.'

At these words she felt sorrow catching in her throat. The feeling bordered upon injury. The reason she had told him was she had wanted to tell him. *Him.* Because she knew in her heart he would understand. She knew it was outrageous, but she did not think of him as a stranger. She did not want him to think of himself as a stranger. Yet all she answered was, 'Perhaps.'

Her head hurt badly now and she wondered if she would ever learn the truth about his life. She thought about John Stuart and how she loved him and how hurt and horrified he would be to know what she was thinking. This made her head throb even more.

She considered something as they rode the next few miles. Then decidedly she took a deep breath. 'I know who you are. I know you are Alan Fletcher. And there is a man, a tenacious, brilliantly clever man, Sir Rutherford Blake. He was at Mayfield only last night. He is working with the police and is out to capture you. You and all the others!'

She was mounted in front of him, his body against her back and his arms round her, holding the reins, so she could not see his face. He was silent for some seconds as if deliberating, then he replied, 'Yes, I know of him, he wishes to be the nemesis of the bushrangers.'

She was again alarmed at herself, but could not help saying, 'I am afraid of that.'

'Don't be,' he said.

An hour later they were crossing the valley floor in the biting wind. They had been travelling steadily in a north-easterly direction.

He had been watching the dark and threatening horizon and could see that it was raining some miles in the distance, although for the present there was no sign of it here. He held Freedom still for a moment, his eyes covering the landscape.

Neither had spoken for a long time and recently she had begun to feel alternately giddy and sick. At the beginning of the ride she could not help but be excited by the closeness of him, but after all the emotion her head throbbed badly, while the aching in her arms and legs now extended to her back.

He was troubled. She felt hot in his arms, yet the day was now quite cold. He feared, too, that she could have suffered concussion from the blow on her head.

'How do you feel?' he inquired. 'We are within Mayfield. I see a gate up ahead, although it will be some hours before we get to the homestead.'

A sharp thought hit her through the haze of her distress. 'We?' she began anxiously. And she admitted to herself that she was afraid for him; that he was in danger inside the Mayfield border. Her fear for him brought her to say what she truly felt. 'But you must not come into Mayfield. It is not safe for you!'

'I will take you home.'

She felt too weak to argue but she summoned up her strength. 'What is the time now?'

'Around four o'clock.'

'Then they could be out looking for me. You must leave me if you see riders. Simply set me down and ride away. I will be all right. It is not safe here for you.' She sat up a little to be forceful, but began to sway. She felt him steady her as she continued, 'You will do as I ask, won't you? You have been so . . . kind. I do not want you in danger. Please?'

To calm her he replied, 'Fear not, I will take no risk.'

Her feelings overcame her, she lost her composure and now she was stammering. 'Y . . . you see, th . . . they will t . . . take you prisoner. Th . . . They do not understand. It is too d . . . dangerous.'

They had come to the gate in the fence and he gave a command to Freedom who knelt down slowly.

As her guardian lifted her out of the saddle and placed her delicately on the grass, Eve was becoming incoherent, mumbling something about Father being the only one who might be sympathetic. Alan opened the gate and led Freedom through, returning for her inert body. This time he lay her across the saddle so that she rested in his arms, her head upon his right shoulder.

He feared she was becoming delirious, but all he could do was to continue on towards the Mayfield homestead. There would surely be a search party out for her by now. Alan supposed they would have a black tracker at Mayfield who would inevitably be following Moonlight's path. He looked skywards. Fortunately it appeared the rain was not coming towards them but holding position to the north. He rode with Eve in his arms for another hour while evening fell. He forded the Boorowa River and continued on in the chill bleak twilight. He talked softly to her, trying to keep her awake, asking her questions about Mayfield and about who might be out looking for her, but Eve had slipped into complete unconsciousness half an hour before. He was very concerned. He had seen enough men in his time with head injuries to know this could be very dangerous. The last time she had spoken, she opened her eyes briefly and looked up at the blurred face above her. She had fought to bring him into focus. But the blackness was enveloping her. 'Alan Fletcher . . .' she said as she drifted into nothingness.

The man above her had looked down and for a few moments his face changed. He was not on Freedom's back in this bleak, cold dusk, but elsewhere; elsewhere with this woman in his arms. His exceptional eyes clouded wistfully before he shook his head and a resolute expression crossed his face as he accelerated Freedom forward in the wind.

Suddenly, he peered absorbedly, a frown of concentration on his forehead. He heard sounds, almost inseparable from the bush noises, but not quite. Horses and men! Yes, ahead and to the right, maybe two or three riders.

A living trail of orange lifted itself from the darkness of the scrub and flew skywards. In being disturbed, the parrots had established for him what he had guessed.

They would be Mayfield men. No one else would dare ride this far inside the boundary; the homestead was sited only miles away.

He pulled Freedom's head towards the noise of the newcomers. The wind whipped at him as he rode forward, the knuckles of his right hand turning white, so tightly did he hold the reins. The three men who appeared in the twilight each rode about ten yards apart and scoured the country as they came. The one who saw Alan first carried a telescope in his right hand and the reins in his left. He shouted and spurred his horse forward and the other riders followed. The man was Joe Larmer. Alan halted and Freedom stamped his feet as they waited in the lee of a large boulder while Joe skirted a gully between them. Alan recognised him. This was the man who had ridden shotgun on the Mayfield coach five months before. He must be careful. They did not allow strangers on Mayfield land.

It was not until Joe was past the gully that he saw there was a blanketed figure in the arms of the rider. Alan waited, eyes alert to every move of the men who rode up. Joe came straight to Freedom's side.

'Eve!' he said. 'Thank God! Do you realise who you carry, man? This is Mrs Wakeman.'

Alan did not reply.

'Is she badly hurt? What happened? Where did you find her?'

Avoiding Joe's eyes, Alan answered briefly. 'She fell and hit her head. She is unconscious now. I found her some time ago.' He waved his hand in a vague fashion behind him.

'Where's her horse?' Joe continued.

'Dead. He had two broken limbs. I shot him.'

Later, when Joe was composed, he would analyse this encounter and recall that he had been given very little information. But now he was too filled with relief at finding Eve to notice. He turned to one of his companions. 'Fire the signal, Barnes.'

The man fired two rifles, one after the other into the air. Then, on the count of ten, he fired two more.

Eve did not flinch during the explosions. Joe turned back to the man who held her. There in the wind he caught the man's eyes. He had the uncanny feeling that he was being seen through and that he had experienced this once before, but he had no time to concentrate and the sensation passed. He held out his strong, solid arms for Eve. 'Give her to me.'

As Alan lifted Eve's inanimate body over to Joe, out of her subconscious came one word. It was loud and clear and all the horsemen heard it plainly. 'No!' she said.

Joe was startled into thinking she was regaining consciousness and began to speak to her. 'Eve! Eve! Are you all right?' But then he realised she was insensible. 'Well, I'll be darned!' he exclaimed and shook his head. He looked across at the rider opposite, but his eyes were on Eve.

Then, anxious to be away, Joe said to the stranger, 'I know Mr Wakeman will want to give you a reward for finding Mrs Wakeman. If you call or write any time to Mayfield House, there will be something there for you. Meanwhile, here . . .' And he took from his pocket two gold sovereigns and a guinea. 'It sure isn't much for getting the mistress back, but it's all I have on me.'

For a moment contradictory expressions seemed to vie for supremacy on the stranger's face. Then he spoke quite softly. 'You are right, I'm sure the value of the woman you hold is positively more than three pounds. And a gift of money, in my line of work, is so seldom as to be never, yet I must refuse. Just get her to care as fast as you can.' And he dismissed the offering with a wave of his hand and looked directly at Joe again, just for a heartbeat. Then he dropped his eyes another second to Eve before turning his horse round in a brisk movement to ride away.

Two galahs lifted from the branch of a gum and swooping low flew almost in unison with his retreat across the intervening country, until he was lost in the cold of the murky, swiftly falling night.

On the ride home, as Tommy Barnes led, compass in hand to be sure of their way, Joe thought of the stranger repeatedly. He still felt his presence, and he continued to have the indefinite feeling that the man was someone he knew. He was vexed with himself too. There was so much more he should have asked the man. He didn't even know his name. Then he would remind himself that most importantly they had found Eve and were taking her home to Mayfield. She returned to semi-consciousness a few times on the slow ride home and murmured against Joe's chest. But for the majority of the long ride she lay unmoving in his powerful arms.

CHAPTER ELEVEN

'But the waiting time, my brothers,
Is the hardest time of all.'
'Psalms of Life, The Hardest Time of All',
Sarah Doudney, 1843–1926.

It was well past three o'clock before Father rode down to the Lachlan to look out for his darling returning from her ride. Instead of Eve he met John Stuart and the fencing party coming back from the north-west where they had abandoned their task having been caught in a downpour.

The clergyman told John Stuart of his wife's ride; how she had left that morning a short time after ten o'clock and had not yet come back. 'She said she might take luncheon with you and that is why I did not worry until the time had passed the hour of three.' But he did not reveal what had prompted Eve's departure nor in what state of mind she had been.

'Damn!' replied John Stuart in the manner of the preoccupied businessman. 'Eve should have more sense than to ride a long way alone.' But by the time they had arrived at the stables and found she was still not home, he was concerned for her and convinced that a search should be mounted.

At quarter to five, more than six hours since Eve's departure, the search party rode out. They had to rely on spreading a net of men in the general direction Eve had taken, for the Aborigine, Charlie Lightfoot, Mayfield's best horsebreaker and black tracker, was away in the southern hills with a team, extending one of the connecting roads.

The men rode in groups of three, Father and the Mayfield owner riding together, with Richard Lane from the dairy. John Stuart would have preferred to ride with Joe, but understood that the experienced men needed to be separated. He looked worried, signs of real concern showing as nightfall advanced, and the crease between his eyes became permanent. The wind intensified and the limited warmth of the day evaporated. The horses' tails danced in the cold air as the men drew their coats more firmly about them.

About dusk they heard the gunshots. Faintly audible they came, two shots followed by a ten-second interval, then two more shots.

'Mrs Wakeman must have been found, sir!' said Richard Lane.

'Yes,' John Stuart replied closing his eyes in release from the strain. 'Thank heavens! It's getting so dark I was beginning to despair.'

'Praise be to the Lord!' Father said.

John Stuart coughed, then turning in his saddle shouted, 'Let's go, so we can be there waiting when whoever has found her brings her in.'

As the miles disappeared beneath the bellies of their mounts the wind that had whipped them on their outward journey showed an inspired fury on their way homeward. It was turning into an icy night. At last their horses' hooves rang out on Larmer's Crossing and they sighted the fires near the buildings on the far side of the river, looking like command headquarters of the Duke of Wellington on the battlefield, with people coming and going in the firelight and men sitting and standing around. When they neared, some came forward to meet them, including Thelma and Mother.

Jack Hennessy held John Stuart's horse as he dismounted and Thelma said, 'Thank goodness she's been found. We're prepared for her.'

'I'm sure you are,' John Stuart replied as he dismounted. Then to those men who had returned from the search he called, 'When you have taken some refreshment, retire for the night, men. I thank you all for your help.'

'Thank you, sir!' sounded the general reply.

A few minutes later, Father took his wife's arm and moved her aside. 'The news of Clare upset Eve badly and I fear she has had an accident. I'm sure she would not have delayed her return until nightfall without a mishap.'

She looked gravely at him. 'We'll know soon enough, my dear.' And she stroked his sleeve and said optimistic and comforting things for she knew he blamed himself for letting Eve go out alone.

An hour later, fourteen groups had returned, all without Eve. Some of them had not even heard the signal but, as ordered, had turned round when night fell. When five more groups rode in empty-handed, Father Billings knew unquestionably she was injured. Only with an injured person would the pace of return be so slow. Even John Stuart's inclination to be confident faded with the passing of time. The frown returned to his forehead and he sat in the lively firelight, his back straight, his eyes fixed on a point across the river.

It was Joe Larmer's party that remained missing and Thelma, ever cheerful, gave thanks that it was her Joe who had found the mistress, for as she put it, 'He's a great man in an emergency, has the strength of two!'

A little after nine o'clock Father went and sat by John Stuart in the glow of one of the fires. The master of Mayfield turned to look at him. It was still cold, but blessedly the wind had dropped and the fires could burn unhindered.

'John Stuart, we know the way they will be returning. Why don't you and I remount and ride to the other side of the river? We will see them coming and, besides, it will give us something to do.'

John Stuart examined the man beside him. It was a concentrated look and it lasted many seconds. Perhaps he saw the reverend gentleman clearly for the first time, for when he spoke, it was from the heart. 'I know you love her,' he admitted. 'And so do I, with all my being. I don't know what I'll do if she's badly hurt or . . . She's the purest, most special of her kind. I knew it the moment I saw her in the park in Bathurst. She was ethereal, chaste, not like other women.' He turned his head away and stared into the flames.

'I know, John Stuart, I know,' the older man said placing a hand on his shoulder. 'She is a good woman.' He sighed, and moving slightly closer added, 'Do not think I take a liberty when I say simply love her for herself.'

John Stuart's eyes came back to his companion's. For a moment Father read indignation in them, and then to his surprise they altered almost to entreaty. 'Whatever do you mean? Do you not think I love her? For herself?'

For the first time Father felt sorry for John Stuart. And following the sorrow came affection. For all his wealth and grandeur, master of so much and so many, he was as all men were, in need of confirmation, of support, even of advice.

'Son,' he answered, 'I do not suggest you do not love Eve. I believe you do, and deeply. All I say is love the essence of Eve which I know is remarkably good. Do not weave a dream about her.'

In the flickering firelight, the two sat quite close looking at each other. John Stuart recognised the conviction in the older man's eyes and for some moments he rested his chin on his fist, evaluating what had been said. He came to the conclusion that even the cleric did not really see Eve properly, though he undoubtedly loved her. No, it was only he, John Stuart, who knew her for the unparalleled woman she was. He smiled at Father Billings. 'I do not weave a dream about her,' he answered.

Father sighed and nodded, his face ruddy in the fireglow. He patted John Stuart's shoulder. 'Come then, do as I suggest, let's ride over the river.'

In the darkness they rode over Larmer's Crossing and waited together on the far bank.

At last they heard the unmistakable sound of horses coming from the south-west and they rode towards it. It was indeed Joe's party, and John Stuart hailed him with the words, 'Is she all right, Joe? Do you have her? What happened?'

'I have her. She fell from Moonlight, m'boy. She has a head injury and is unconscious. Methinks I should hold her steady until we get to Mayfield House. Best I carry her the same way I have these past hours until I place her on a bed.'

'Yes, yes, of course,' agreed John Stuart. He was filled with anxiety. He had his darling wife back but she was hurt. He followed Joe up to the house feeling very helpless.

The doctor from Cowra had been sent for when the search parties had gone out, and while they waited for him, John Stuart brought a large gilt-bound medical book from the library. He looked up 'unconsciousness' and 'brain concussion' and informed the women that the wound should be dressed and the fever kept down with cold compresses.

'Shame she went to sleep. Best to be keeping them awake when it's concussion,' Mrs Smith declared to Thelma in the hall later.

Dr Campbell from Cowra corroborated the medical book's advice and prescribed a medicine which he instructed was to be mixed with water and administered once she was conscious. When he examined her, he found her swollen ankle which he ascertained to be unbroken. The head wound itself he deemed not to be deep which was a good sign, although the fever could be dangerous. He assured them that as long as they kept the fever in check and there was no brain damage, she would be as good as new in a week or so.

'But how in hell do we know there is no brain damage?' John Stuart interjected.

'We don't yet, sir,' replied Gordon Campbell, a sensitive, inventive medical man for the times. 'Not until she wakes.'

'We shall get our own doctor,' John Stuart declared to Joe when they knew there was nothing more to be done at present and had moved out of the bedroom. 'In emergencies such as this, we need our own man here.'

'I shall see to it,' the other replied calmly.

'Where did you find her, old man?'

'It was not me who found her, m'boy.'

'What do you mean not you?'

'A stranger found her. We came across him well inside the Mayfield boundary. He was some miles this side of the Boorowa. He rode a fine grey and he carried Eve. Said that Moonlight had thrown her and he'd found her.'

'And what of Moonlight?'

Joe shook his head. 'The fellow said he had to shoot him. Two broken legs.'

'What could possibly have happened?'

Joe shrugged. 'I don't know. I'm disgusted with myself. Didn't even request his name. My main concern was to get Eve home. There was a lot I did not ask and I should have.'

'No.' John Stuart was firm. 'You did correctly. Bringing her here without delay was the critical thing. Thank you.'

Joe was thoughtful. 'You know, I had the oddest feeling about that man. As if I knew him. Eerie really.'

The night passed with Dr Campbell often at the bedside and John Stuart mostly holding Eve's hand and sleeping fitfully in a large armchair near her. Eve rambled softly now and then, but for the most part she seemed to sleep deeply.

Father spent the night in the library, coming intermittently to the bedside and praying for Evelyn. Mother had urged him to go to bed but he would not, so she sat up with him, silently comforting, through the long hours of lamp-light.

Morning broke and the news was better, as it always seems to be in sick rooms when, with the coming of the day, comes optimism. The doctor said the fever had almost passed.

Soon after, Eve fell into a calmer, more rhythmic sleep and the doctor felt she would probably wake soon. But she slept most of the morning away. John Stuart, Thelma, Father and Mother were all in the room when she at last gave signs of returning consciousness.

As she moved slightly beneath the covers and murmured, Dr Campbell spoke. 'If Mrs Wakeman is coherent when she wakes and remembers what happened, then there is no danger of her brain being harmed.'

Half a minute later, she opened her eyes. She saw her loved ones round the bed, concern in all their faces. Then the doctor came into her vision and lifted her wrist to take her pulse. 'Is there any pain, Mrs Wakeman?'

'My head is sore . . . and my leg. My back hurts a little, but I think that is all.'

John Stuart knelt and took her hand, the frown of worry that had been a fixture since last night deepening as he spoke. 'Eve love, what happened?'

She did not answer immediately. Then she remembered. 'I . . . Oh Moonlight. Poor Moonlight. It was awful . . . the huge kangaroo.'

'What kangaroo, dear?' queried Father leaning forward towards her.

John Stuart looked appealingly across to the doctor who nodded reassuringly.

'The kangaroo that jumped in front of us . . . and Moonlight. Oh poor Moonlight! He threw me. He could not help it.' She closed her eyes as tears welled up in them. 'He broke both his forelegs. It was too terrible!'

'So that was it. A kangaroo,' John Stuart sighed. 'My poor darling.' He leaned across to kiss her forehead and she lifted her hand and stroked his hair.

'The patient seems normal enough to me,' said Dr Campbell, 'but I think we should let her rest now, sir, if you don't mind.'

She smiled up at them. 'I feel a little hungry,' she said to the delight of them all.

That night as the grandfather clock in the hall outside her room chimed seven, Eve lay propped up by masses of soft down pillows. Stephanie was administering her medicine and Thelma sat tatting a doily in the lamplight.

Eve was thinking of Clare. Poor Clare. She had promised Father she would tell John Stuart. Oh dear! She did not feel well enough now. It would be best if she waited until she were well. She needed all her strength to make him understand. Yes, she would wait . . . in a week or so.

The door clicked and her husband's frame filled the opening.

Stephanie and Thelma departed, and Eve put out her hand to her husband who took it and sat on the side of the bed. He smiled down at her. 'Darling, there are some questions I would ask you if you are not too indisposed.'

'Yes, dear,' she replied, her eyes stark against the paleness of her face and the pillows.

'Reverend Billings told me you had proposed to ride to me for luncheon yesterday. Why didn't you?'

She looked down. 'No real reason, I thought you would be busy fencing and I might be in the way.'

'I see, and the accident, where did that happen?'

Here she hesitated for just a second or two. 'On one of the ridges across the Boorowa.'

'Which one, sweetheart? There are a number.'

'Oh, John Stuart, I don't know the country like you do.'

'No, that is true,' he agreed. 'Were you inside or outside our boundary?'

'Outside, I think. Why?'

'Oh, Eve!' he reprimanded gently. 'You should never ride outside the borders. As if there is not enough of Mayfield for you to ride upon. There are some tribes still living in this area.'

'Now, John Stuart,' Eve answered, mildly reproving. 'The Aborigines are harmless, you know that.'

'Yes, perhaps.' He took up her hand from where it now lay in her lap and kissed it. 'But there are other dangers. I want your promise that you will never ride alone again.'

'Without Moonlight, I don't think I want to ride ever again.'

'Yes, poor Moonlight. That brings me to the man who had to shoot him. He carried you on his horse until you met Joe?'

'Yes. He was very . . . kind.'

'I am so grateful to him. Were you conscious when he found you? Do you know who he was?'

Eve gently removed her hand from her husband's and drew it across her eyes. This was her husband, the man whose life she shared. She wanted to be honest with him, she was already withholding the fact that she had a sister. 'Yes, John Stuart, I do. He was the man who stopped our coach when we were coming here.'

For a moment John Stuart was so amazed he could not speak. He just sat there looking at her. Then he stood from the bed and the outburst came.

'Well, I'll be damned! The bloody bushranger! I can't believe it! The bushranger!'

Three weeks later on an October day, Eve and John Stuart sat on the verandah looking south enveloped by the warm spring sunshine. They had finished lunch and before returning to work John Stuart was keen to show his wife a plan he had detailed to shift water from the Lachlan to the furthest orchards on the southern side of the river. He spread out the plans on the table in front of them and Eve leaned forward concentratedly.

She wore a sweet tiny posy of flowers attached to the bodice of her dress, which John Stuart had pinned there. Since her fall, no matter how busy he was, he had arrived back at the house between noon and one o'clock and they had taken lunch together. He often brought her a small bouquet or a posy, as he had today, and during the first week of her convalescence he had come to her with his boyish smile sitting charmingly on his face, and in his hands a covered basket tied with a red ribbon. On lifting the cover, Eve had found the most beautiful, tiny white kitten. She had delighted in its big green eyes and fluffy fur and had named him Velvet. The little fellow had become her companion and lived mostly in their rooms and the garden outside them to avoid coming in contact with John Stuart's dogs.

John Stuart was tracing an imaginary channel across the paper with his long, sunbrowned finger. 'I want to move water through here. The pump I am using, a type of hydraulic, ram pump, can move the volume I need without difficulty, but I'm concerned about the length of the channel I'll have to cut to feed the new field.' His eyes lit up when he mentioned the pump, he revelled in things scientific. He moved his finger along the edge of the orchards pointing out where the channel would need to go. 'Unfortunately, it will have to be pretty long, and will be expensive. I wish I didn't have to run it quite so far.'

Eve was watching earnestly. Suddenly she had a thought. 'But darling, does the new field have to go there?' She tapped on the plan where he had pointed.

'Yes, I think so. It's the soil. Joe and Jack say it's the best there is for miles.'

'You haven't planted it yet, have you?'

'No, we haven't, Joe will start next Monday.'

She touched the plan. 'Would the branding yard here, west of the orchards, have the same sort of soil?'

He nodded. 'I expect so.'

'Then I have a thought. I know I'm not as knowledgeable as you and Joe about crops, but it seems to me if you put the new field here,' she pointed to the branding yard beside the existing orchard, 'and not further south where you have planned to put it, the water channel wouldn't need to be half as long.'

John Stuart bent forward thoughtfully, his eyes on the drawing.

Eve moved her finger across in front of him. 'And there is a gradual rise there, so the water would flow down easily across it, wouldn't it?'

Her husband did not reply but continued studying the plan, bending over it studiously. Eve waited. Finally, he looked up and smiled. 'Darling, I think you're right. The orchard could go where you say. It will be even better on a gentle rise. We could take the branding yard down on the other side of the corn storage sheds where it would still be close to the river.' He folded the plan and put it under his arm. 'Eve, you're amazing. You continually surprise me. Wait until I tell the boys who thought of this. Thank you, my clever girl.'

He kissed her lightly on the lips and bounded across the verandah and down the steps to where Diomed waited at the railing.

An hour later, Eve and Thelma were in the park taking their

customary afternoon walk. They had been watching old Bartholomew Frith, one of the ticket-of-leave men who had been assigned to Arthur Wakeman in the twenties, and who had stayed on and made Mayfield his home. Bartholomew was cutting the grass, bent over the scythe, his aged back rounded by long years of this very occupation.

They came to a stone seat under a row of tall beeches that Arthur Wakeman had planted twenty-five years before, and just as they went to sit, a large goanna lizard ran from beneath it. They exclaimed in fright and then laughed as it disappeared under a hedge.

Eve settled onto the seat. 'The creatures of this novel land will always fascinate me.'

'Now that is truly odd,' exclaimed Thelma.

'What is?'

'What you just said. It's exactly what Sir Arthur used to say. I can see him standing in this very garden saying, "The creatures of this novel land will always fascinate me".'

Eve shook her head in surprise. 'Why, that is indeed odd. You know, I do sometimes wonder about him. John Stuart seems to have worshipped him.'

Thelma made a soft affirmative sound in her throat. 'That's true enough, and he's like him in many respects. Arthur Wakeman was not afraid to work side by side with his men, long and hard, to see Mayfield rise, and nor is John Stuart. Neither have ever played the lord of the manor.'

'I like the look of Sir Arthur in the paintings of him in the house, the one in the library particularly. There is something in his eyes. Perhaps it's the skill of the painter, but there is a fanciful expression. He seems to be insinuating not to take things too seriously, as if life amused him.'

The other woman looked thoughtful. 'That painting was the last to be done, not six months before he died. That is the older Arthur Wakeman. He had changed, indeed he had. There was a mildness about him then. Not a weakness, don't misunderstand, but a composure and contentment of a kind. And yes, it's possible life amused him, I'm not sure.' Here Thelma closed her eyes in recollection and a frown lodged in a V at the top of her nose. 'Though life did not amuse him in his youth, of that I'm absolutely certain.'

'How do you mean? Was it because of John Stuart's mother?'

'Yes.'

'Once or twice I have asked John Stuart about her,' Eve said. 'He was very abrupt. Said she had left when he was small, that really you had brought him up and he did not wish to speak of her, for she was nothing to him. He has no respect or affection for her at all as far as I can gather. Any mention of her disturbs him, so I don't speak of her.'

Thelma nodded, sadness and regret settling into her face.

Eve saw the expression. 'Father said John Stuart's mother had left years before he ever met Arthur Wakeman, that there had been a terrible scandal and she had returned to Scotland.'

'Mmm, that's right.'

There was silence for a few seconds. Eve watched Bartholomew move rhythmically away between the flower beds, and the familiar sound of the dogs barking in the distance drifted to her.

Then Thelma began. 'Perhaps I should have told you before, but because of the way John Stuart feels, we avoid the subject. Oh, his mother was a beauty right enough.' Thelma's mouth pursed. 'Caroline Burnett. Arthur brought her out from Scotland. All eyes and hair she was, dark eyes, just like John Stuart's really. She was from the landed gentry, youngest daughter of a laird up Fort William way, near Ben Nevis. The property is still there, I suppose. Arthur married her in the late twenties after he had been granted land here years before. The beginning of Mayfield.' She made the last statement wistfully and Eve realised that Thelma was imbued with the love of this place just as John Stuart was, as all those who lived on Mayfield seemed to be.

Thelma continued, 'John Stuart arrived eleven months after the marriage. We weren't here then, didn't come until late 'thirty when Arthur went into breeding cattle. Gosh, but Joe and I were just young things, you know, lucky to get the job. Well, pretty soon after, you could tell things between him and her weren't working. Why, we weren't here more than six or seven months when she left and went back to Scotland. In those days, there was a convict settlement near where Cowra is now. You wouldn't know that being from America and all. Well, there was an army major in charge. Joe said he was a ladies' man right enough, and he was.'

Thelma paused and considered her next words. 'I suppose, what with him being the only proper company for eighty miles, the major I mean, Arthur Wakeman invited him here to Mayfield quite a lot. Too much, as it turned out. Caroline Wakeman and the major . . . It went on a long time before Arthur realised. I remember she seemed so frustrated with everything, so unhappy. She used to say how she hated this country and the heat and the flies, and perhaps she did, coming from Scotland and all. Yet, I got the definite feeling that she put it on for our benefit when she knew she was to be sent back. It was artificial like. Poor Caroline. I got to know her, though. She loved John Stuart dearly. Still does, I'm certain. What mother wouldn't? Broke her heart to leave him, yet he doesn't know it or want to.

'Well, she went back to Scotland. I'll never forget it. Seems like only yesterday. It was early morning in May, an overcast day, a dreary day you might say. Young John Stuart was just over three years old. Arthur Wakeman stood up there.' Thelma waved her hand in the direction of Mayfield House, then her face crinkled into sadness. 'I watched from the window. It was a smaller house then. He held John Stuart in his arms as she mounted the coach. Yes, we had a coach at Mayfield even then although not as grand as the ones now, and the roads, oh they were terrible! Well, she never once looked back as she entered that coach, her back stiff like a ramrod. I could feel the tension in that woman through the window. Then as the door closed Arthur Wakeman held John Stuart out, extending him towards the coach, close to the window, as if to let his mother see him for the final time. It was harrowingly formal, I can tell you, the child sort of hanging in the air. I wept for all three of them.' She sniffed softly as if she were weeping again for them, there in the sunny afternoon over three decades later.

Thelma took Eve's hands in hers and was quiet for a few moments before she shook her head disconsolately and finished her account. 'So there you are. A proud man was Sir Arthur Wakeman. And that, Eve love, is why John Stuart will not speak of her. Methinks he has not forgiven her for cuckolding his father and for leaving him as a wee thing. He is deeply offended by what she did to his father and on top of that he feels she abandoned him, scorned him. Although I'd say she didn't have any choice about leaving him behind. Fact is, I know she didn't, poor thing.'

Eve nodded. 'Thank you for telling me, Thelma. I understand John Stuart a little more now. It is natural that he feels as he does, yet I'm sure it would be better if he could speak of it and settle it within himself somehow.'

'Yes, dear.' Thelma patted Eve's hand. 'Perhaps you are right. I'm only a bush woman, but it seems to me that somehow he cannot face that which has hurt him all his life. He's held this sort of mental penalty against his mother all these years. I don't suppose he's about to stop now.'

Eve nodded. And because of these feelings he had placed his wife above other women. He glorified her, idolised her. His illusion was of his own making. He deemed her perfect. How she wished he could love her for herself, the way she loved him. For she did love him and never wanted to hurt him or affront him, but she also wanted to be honest with him, and there on the seat beside her friend she determined to steel herself and tell him that very night about Clare.

After dinner, she sat with her husband in the 'blue room', a lovely parlour decorated in varying shades of blue and violet, with an eastern aspect. Eve was waiting her opportunity to speak to her husband. There had been none at dinner for the servants kept coming and going. Now, as Baines served coffee, John Stuart spoke. 'Darling, Joe and Jack were impressed with your idea for the new field. I told them you are getting to be an expert about Mayfield and they agree.'

She smiled, and Baines who was pouring out the tea murmured approvingly.

John Stuart took up a sweetmeat. 'When you said today that the branding yard was on a gentle slope, however did you know? I hardly recalled that myself.'

'Oh, I was there yesterday. Remember, I accompanied Thelma to the picnic for all the wives and the small children not of school age.'

'So you did, I had forgotten.'

'Do you know we have twenty-nine married couples here on Mayfield now?'

John Stuart grinned. 'Yes, I think I was aware of the number.'

'We went up on the hill behind the corn storage sheds where the jacaranda trees are; it's lovely and shady up there. One of the small children wandered off and Thelma and I went down to the branding yard to look for her, and that was when I noticed the ground there is a long incline.'

'I see. Did you find the child all right?'

'Oh yes, she was picking field daisies over near one of the sheds.' John Stuart smiled. 'Good.'

Eve was waiting for Baines to leave. At last the door closed behind him and she swivelled round on the sofa to face John Stuart. 'Darling, I have something I want to tell you.'

At the very same moment that she spoke, John Stuart uttered a thought of his own, so their words were delivered concurrently. 'Who was the child?'

'What was that?' Eve replied, her mind now engrossed in what she was about to tell him.

'Who was the child who wandered away from the picnic yesterday?'

'Oh, Mrs Kinnock's little daughter, Katy.'

John Stuart's face clouded. He rose to his feet muttering a sound of censure, his mouth tightening in disapproval and a frown lodging between his eyes. 'Her? Kinnock's wife? She's trash. Kinnock's leaving at the end of the month, I'm pleased to say. What the devil was she doing at the picnic?'

A spasm of dismay ran through Eve. 'John Stuart, dearest, she is one of the wives of the stockmen. We do not discriminate between them. And in any case, what's wrong with her?'

'Forget it, Eve.' He turned from her and placed his coffee cup on the table. 'It doesn't matter.'

But Eve was sick with apprehension. She had to know. 'John Stuart, please, what is it about Mrs Kinnock that vexes you?'

He moved back and sat down beside her, placing his hands on his knees and sighing. 'Oh Eve, I do what I can to keep Mayfield pleasant for those who live here, as my father did before me. And I try to find the best of men, decent, moral men, with wives the same, to be my workers and my stockmen. I don't like to speak of these things, but sometimes a man brings a woman here who does not fit, who is, like her, a bad type.' He lifted his hands up to hold them over his face momentarily, adding as he did so, 'Like my mother was.' Then he turned his face to her. His eyes were pained and he blinked as if to remove the expression from them. 'Anyway, Kinnock's leaving soon, so let's say no more about it.' He stood. 'Now, why don't we have a gentle walk through the park before bed?'

Eve felt prickling sensations up and down her spine. She had been about to explain Clare, had actually started to speak, and now this had happened. She found herself asking, 'John Stuart, why do you feel this way? Oh darling, why do you cause yourself pain and say Mrs Kinnock is like your mother?'

A rumbling sound of frustration escaped from John Stuart's lips. 'Eve, Eve, these women are all alike; they bring only pain. They're worthless. Kinnock is a fool. When he came here, it was to make a bit of money; he's on his way to Queensland to start afresh. Joe and Jack felt sympathy for him and so I agreed. But the woman was to keep to herself and now I hear she's out at a picnic with you. It's common knowledge amongst the men that the child you went searching for is not Kinnock's; it was born down in Yass, before she married him. I don't know any more than that, nor do I wish to. All I do know is I am angered and affronted that you are forced to keep company with such low-class trash. The sooner she leaves Mayfield the better.' He moved a few steps. 'Now, please, are you coming for a walk or not?'

Eve stood. She felt quite lifeless. Automatically she put her hand on the arm he extended towards her. They went into the front hall and across the verandah in the lamplight. The luxurious scent of the first spring jasmine blossoms floated headily around them. As they passed down the stone steps John Stuart asked, 'Darling, didn't you say you had something to tell me earlier?'

And Eve responded, 'Did I? No, dear, I don't recall anything.'

CHAPTER TWELVE

'If we do meet again, why, we shall smile;
If not, why then this parting was well made.'
Julius Caesar, William Shakespeare, 1564–1616.

It was the twenty-third day of November and Joe and John Stuart were riding in, tired and dust-covered, after a hard day of mustering and counting two of the eastern herds. Their topic of conversation was the menace of the bushrangers, as was so in most of the west these days. The previous Saturday, bushrangers had held up a group of Roman Catholic churchgoers at a fête in Cowra.

John Stuart shook his head. 'It is fortunate Eve is not Catholic, for she might have been there.'

'True, m'boy, at least no one was hurt.'

'This particular raid might deter her from running to Cowra to church services with Thelma every fortnight.'

Joe looked doubtful. 'It might.'

'Eve and I don't exactly agree on religion, but you know that.'

'I do. You have always been the one to be reading about science. Even as a child you seemed to choose your own book-learning. Puts you a little out of step at times with your contemporaries, not to mention your wife. You cannot expect her to understand. Why, I hardly do myself when you talk about all that natural – ' he hesitated – 'natural selection, is it?'

John Stuart's mouth turned up into his half smile. 'Yes, Joe, that's it. Do you ever read any of the literature I give you?'

Joe turned in the saddle towards him. He raised his eyebrows in a look that was slightly offended. 'Of course I read it. But it's hard for a man nigh on sixty-five, as was brought up strictly in the Methodist Episcopal Church, to believe it, even though I admit it makes sense at times.'

John Stuart said no more but leaned across to Joe and patted him affectionately on the shoulder.

When they neared the stables, Jack Hennessy waylaid them with the news that there had been a raid on David Campbell's property, a small sheep station at Goimbla, thirty miles from Forbes, a tiny township to the north-west. 'It was the Hall gang, last Thursday. They've become more game since their raids on Bathurst and Canowindra last month. Set fire to a barn, we're told. Terrorised them, by all accounts, though the homesteaders put up a good fight for one of the Hall gang was shot and killed.'

'Good enough,' remarked Joe. 'Pity more of them weren't shot. The whole countryside seems to be alive with the rabble. Sir Rutherford has his work cut out, that's for certain.'

That night at dinner Eve talked of many things pertinent to Mayfield. She and John Stuart were in evening dress, as was the tradition of the upper classes, and they were seated in the small dining room which was adjacent to the breakfast room. It was not as imposing or as luxurious as the grand one, but it was a striking room nevertheless and Eve preferred it. She had spent the day with the new doctor, Gerald Douglas, whom John Stuart had insisted on getting after her fall. Eve was organising his cottage and surgery and had been working as his helper since he arrived, although he was training Betty Watson who showed a great aptitude for medicine. Her brother Stephen was one of Mayfield's managers. John Stuart had been reluctant to agree to Eve's helping to nurse the sick for it meant tending the children and the general staff, and he argued she was not really back to health herself. He had been adamant at first but Eve had persuaded him; for secretly he was quite proud of the way she cared for Mayfield and those who lived here.

Towards the end of the meal, she leaned towards her husband. 'John Stuart, I have to go into Bathurst to do a little more Christmas shopping – small things for the workers' children and the staff, and I must order some medical supplies for Dr Douglas. While I am in Bathurst I would like to stay a few days with Father and Mother, if you agree.'

John Stuart frowned. 'Certainly not, darling. While I understand your wish to work with Dr Douglas, I still think you've hardly recovered from your fall, and after what's been going on in recent months, I should think you would want to stay off the roads.'

'Oh, John Stuart, you know I am absolutely well again. Young Betty Watson is learning so fast with the doctor that I feel quite happy leaving for a week, and as to the roads, there have only been a few isolated incidents.'

John Stuart shook his head. 'Isolated incidents! Evelyn, we hear of someone being robbed or harassed by bushrangers every other week. And this latest business of attacking a small and ill-protected homestead is awful!'

Eve sighed. 'John Stuart, there must be more to the Campbell raid than we know about. It's probably some kind of feud. In any case, there aren't enough bushrangers to be on every road in the colony. I am not concerned.'

Her husband was unconvinced. 'Your mathematics are at variance with mine, Eve. There is danger in travelling and I don't like it. And you choose to go to Bathurst, when it was Bathurst that was raided only last month. It is not a town to be visiting.'

A determined look came into Eve's eyes. 'On the contrary, John Stuart, it is more than probable that Bathurst is the safest town west of the Blue Mountains for that very reason. Anyway, it is the only town that has decent shops, so please, my love, don't be difficult.'

John Stuart's expression was sceptical. 'And coincidence only that a certain cleric and his wife abide there, no doubt.'

'Yes.'

He did not speak but returned to eating.

She watched him. 'Oh, John Stuart, you exasperate me. After all, I will be in a Mayfield coach, thoroughly well-guarded.' She had almost added 'damn it' but had caught herself in time.

He did not look up. 'You are too much of an emancipated spirit, my darling. That is how you came by that trouble the day after your birthday and were forced to associate with such company.'

The indirect reference to Alan Fletcher brought disquieting memories. John Stuart had never mentioned him since the night on her sickbed. She fell quiet.

After a little time, he broke the silence. 'You see, Eve, I am not pleased that my wife has had two encounters with a wanted man, a notorious outlaw.'

She took a deep breath. She knew he was only concerned for her welfare, but she did not like the tone of reprimand in his voice. 'John Stuart, I am desiring to go to Bathurst to shop, order medical stores and to visit some loved ones, not to have an encounter of any kind with any outlaw.'

'Enough!' He said it so sharply that she started in surprise. 'I will not have you speaking this way, it is too flippant.' His voice was rising. 'You are my wife. It is not fitting that you have been in association with such a man, unconscious for most of it or not.'

Her chin lifted and she returned his gaze. There was a note of defiance in her tone as she reminded him, 'He did me a kindness. Even more, he probably saved my life.' She was thinking how alarmed John Stuart would be if he knew that she had been conscious for hours in his company; that he had held a long conversation with him; that she thought him honourable and moral and kind.

John Stuart's fist came down on the table in exasperation. 'Oh

Eve, you try me! All right. You go on the conditions that Thelma and Daydee accompany you and that you are in Bathurst no longer than a week.'

Eve agreed readily. She did not mind Thelma being with her, in fact she would like it, though the thought of Daydee was not so attractive.

Daydee was enthusiastic to make the journey, for a close friend from her school days now lived in Bathurst. As the vehicle rolled across Mayfield towards the outer world, she leaned in the corner reading *The Moonstone*. She gave her attention to the two women intermittently, passing from petulant to gay, moody to talkative. Eve was well aware that Daydee disliked her. She had made many overtures towards the girl in the previous months, only to be rebuked one way or another. Essentially, this did not concern Eve for Daydee was difficult with many people. She was a spoiled girl with little on her mind except reading and painting and indulging in genteel pastimes. She was like all wealthy graziers' daughters, doing very little once their schooling was over, living in a sort of hiatus between school and marriage. Eve thought it understandable that the girl was infatuated by John Stuart, she had plenty of time to indulge in fancies. Consequently Eve dismissed most of Daydee's attitude towards her as girlish jealousy and optimistically hoped it would pass in time.

They made the journey in easy stages and by nightfall were in the settlement of Blayney where they stayed the night at the Albion Hotel in the main street, in the only street. Mrs Osmond, the proprietor, waited on them herself. It was an honour to have Mrs Wakeman under her roof for a whole night.

During the evening meal, Mrs Osmond knocked and entered, curtsying at the door of the parlour. She carried in the sweet tray and put it down. 'Excuse me, Madam,' she said. 'There be a gentleman stayin' under our roof who says he knows ye. He is desirous of taking tea with ye after the meal if ye would be so generous as to favour him.'

Her pronunciation derived from the Cockney, a distinctive pattern set to become the Australian accent in another generation.

Eve looked inquiringly up at her. 'Really? And who is he?'

'He says to give to ye Sir Rutherford Blake's compliments.'

Sir Rutherford Blake! Oh dear, he would only succeed in making her feel uncomfortable. He spoke of nothing but bushrangers as far as she had experienced. She felt inclined to refuse.

Suddenly Daydee, whose face had lit up at the mention of Sir Rutherford, spoke. 'Oh good, it would be ever so nice to see him

206

again! Maybe he's caught a bushranger!'

Eve motioned to the woman at the door. 'Could you wait outside, Mrs Osmond, we will just be a moment.'

When the door closed, Eve turned to Thelma and Daydee. 'I had thought to retire early as we have the trip on to Bathurst tomorrow. I'm feeling rather weary. What do you think, Thelma dear?'

'Oh no,' interrupted Daydee.

'Quiet, Daydee, please,' her mother remonstrated. 'Eve, I don't really know what to think. What would John Stuart want you to do?'

Daydee interrupted again. 'Uncle John Stuart would expect us to see him, of that I'm sure! Why, Sir Rutherford is a friend of his.'

Thelma looked skywards and shook her head. But Daydee's point had sailed home and ten minutes later the police detective made his entrance. He wore a fashionable dark-blue frock coat, neat checked waistcoat and spotted cravat tied in a bow at his throat. His lean features took on an almost cheerful aspect as he said, 'Ladies, ladies, a pleasure.' He bent over the extended hands.

He soon ascertained they were on their way to Bathurst. He tapped his finger on his saucer. 'Bathurst, ah yes, it's been getting a little attention lately from the lawbreakers. Well, I'm to be giving the township some attention of my own. I will be setting up my head-quarters there in the New Year, ladies, with an assignment of two dozen troopers.'

Daydee's face was full of interest. 'Why have you chosen Bathurst, Sir Rutherford?'

'The telegraph, missy, the telegraph. The line ends there, and it allows me to be in communication with the Inspector General in Sydney on almost a daily basis.' Then he gave one of his mirthless grins. 'I can honestly say I'm not concerned about your entourage, Mrs Wakeman. In the Mayfield coach with the four sturdy guards I saw downstairs in the bar, you'll not be troubled. But if you were travelling alone or even in a mail coach, ah yes, a different matter.'

Daydee's eyes were wide. 'Oh, do tell us, Sir Rutherford, what is the latest adventure you've had? What did you think of the church fête in Cowra being robbed and the Campbell station raid?'

Eve shivered. The conversation would be wholly of bushrangers, just as she had dreaded.

'Ah now, missy.' Sir Rutherford drank from his cup and clinked it down in his saucer. He dabbed his mouth with the napkin and rolled back his eyes. 'The three things you have asked me are all of a one. The latest adventure of mine has been on Campbell station itself. I've been there to scrutinise the scene, you might say. Why, they put up a good fight, you know, the Campbells, shot dead John

207

O'Meally! The Hall gang is disintegrating. Micky Burke's dead, we got him in October, and I have John Vane in custody, surrendered in Bathurst the very day of the Campbell raid. Leaves only Benjamin Hall himself and Flash Johnny Gilbert. Ah yes, now when—'

'Have some more tea, Sir Rutherford,' Eve interrupted.

There was a distant expression in his eyes for a moment, then he grasped what she had said. 'Ah yes, tea. Thank you, Mrs Wakeman, a little more.' He held out his cup and Eve poured.

'Please go on, Sir Rutherford,' Daydee requested avidly.

He knew he had one ardent listener, and that was enough for the police detective. 'My dear Miss Daydee, the facts are such that I'm feeling confident about taking the two surviving rascals. But your other question of the Catholic church fête,' he coughed, 'well, I'm on my way to Cowra now to discuss the matter with the victims. I think it must have been Old Joe Daily or Dan Morgan. I'm sure it wasn't Alan Fletcher for he acts quite differen—'

Eve's cup rattled loudly in her saucer. All heads turned towards her.

'Oh, do excuse me,' she said as she leaned forward and with both hands placed her cup down on the table.

'Of course, madam,' Sir Rutherford answered. He pursed his lips in thought before he went on. 'I've decided it wasn't Fletcher for it was not the sort of job he does. The women were robbed and he doesn't rob women and I've never known him to rob a church or the needy. In fact, it's more the Government he goes after, or sporadically the very wealthy.' He looked directly at Eve. 'As you would be aware. Ah yes, now he is so interesting,' he was warming to his subject, 'operates in various parts of the country, all over, hard to track, has strategy.' He gestured with his elongated, middle finger towards Daydee. 'In my experience, outlaws, pirates, brigands, bushrangers, call them what you like, operate from a central point. Fletcher has acted as far north as Wellington, as far south as Young, as far east as Bathurst and Crookwell and as far west as Forbes. And the centre of those places is—'

'Canowindra!' interjected Daydee.

He turned almost a smile to the girl. 'Ah yes, excellent geography. Months ago I combed the plains around Canowindra for ten, fifteen miles and there is no sign of a hideout there, young lady. No. Alan Fletcher is clever, and what is more his men are devoted to him.'

Daydee was leaning forward, her face attentive, her small mouth an O of excitement. 'And who are his men, Sir Rutherford, do you know?'

'Ah yes, missy, I know. There are five in all. Three escaped with him from Moreton Bay back these ten years. Samuel Cooper, Lawless Drake and Daniel Dwyer, convicts with Alan Fletcher to a man. The fifth member of the band is Jordan O'Day, a horse thief, ah yes, as so many of our wild colonial boys are.'

He had opened his mouth to continue when Daydee spoke again. 'But you don't know, Sir Rutherford! Aunt Eve fell from Moonlight on the day after her birthday, and it was Alan Fletcher who found her in the bush.'

Sir Rutherford's eyes seemed to bulge, so large did they grow. 'What? What is that?' He looked to Eve for verification.

Eve steeled herself. 'I cannot tell you much, Sir Rutherford. Very simply, the man found me after my fall and returned me to a search party led by Mr Larmer. That's all.'

'But my dear lady, there must be more. It is invaluable information to me. Anything about that man is. I am anxious to hear, excited to hear. Please tell me all. What does he look like?'

A prickling sensation ran across her shoulders. She gathered herself and looked in his eyes. 'I'm sorry, Sir Rutherford, but I was injured at the time. I cannot tell you.'

He was looking at her with disbelief 'Cannot? But . . . you were with him. Actually with him! Why—?'

'I repeat, sir, that I was injured. I was unconscious.' Her voice was cordial but uncompromising.

Thelma took Eve's hand and in doing so took her side. 'Yes, Sir Rutherford, Eve was unconscious; she had a head wound. You would do better to talk to my Joe; he saw him too.'

Eve stood. 'I'm sorry, Sir Rutherford, but we are continuing our journey tomorrow and a good night's sleep would be welcome. I don't mean to seem ungracious, but I hope you will excuse us.'

'Mrs Wakeman,' her guest exclaimed rising to his feet, 'I've been unmannerly. I become so zealous given opportunity to learn about these ruffians, I forge ahead. Forgive me, madam. Please.'

Daydee's mouth turned down. 'Oh no, don't stop. I'm enjoying it.'

Thelma broke across her daughter's words angrily. 'Please, Daydee, have some manners.'

Daydee looked peevishly at her parent, but said no more.

Eve extended her hand to her visitor. He bent over it formally. 'Your servant, Mrs Wakeman, and as your husband has been good enough to invite me to Mayfield for the Christmas week, I will be in your delightful company again in a very short time.'

Eve had not known of this, but she covered her surprise with a polite smile.

He took Daydee's hand. 'And we will continue our conversation then, Missy, will we not?'

Daydee smiled agreement up at him. 'Oh yes, most definitely.'

He bowed to Thelma and walked to the door, turning back to say, 'I certainly hope you are entirely recovered from your fall, Mrs Wakeman.'

The door closed and Thelma rounded on her daughter. 'Daydee! You really are the rudest girl. How dare you dispute Aunt Eve. Apologise!'

With half-closed eyes she looked from her mother to Eve. 'I'm sure Aunt Eve would not want me to apologise simply because I was enthusiastic.'

For a few seconds Eve steadily returned the girl's gaze, then patting her on the shoulder replied tolerantly, 'No, Daydee, I would not.'

Outside in the corridor, Sir Rutherford hesitated. It was astounding that the woman had encountered Alan Fletcher. Almost too hard to believe! And her reluctance to speak of it? Fact was, she was not simply reluctant, she had refused. He shook his head in thought and continued on to the barroom.

The next morning, Eve had her two companions up early and on their way out of Blayney at eight o'clock; the Mayfield coach passing like some gilded, shining, precious thing, at which ordinary folk could but stare. Two guards rode in front, one behind, and Leeroy Barton up beside Deke Edwards the driver. As Thelma put it, 'With all this protection, I wouldn't blame the bushrangers if they think we carry diamonds and gold. Merely draws attention, if you ask me.'

The journey over the great expanses was uneventful. At times the lonely coach wound its way through a counterpane of deep-purple flowers. Known by the settlers as 'Patterson's curse', they grew here in prodigal numbers. The travellers arrived in Bathurst at half past eleven that morning.

Mother Billings had been gardening. Her face glowed under her wide-brimmed sun hat as the coach drew up. She took off her gloves and hat and laid them on the grass at her feet, her lovely, placid features breaking into a happy smile. 'My dears, my dears,' she exclaimed as she hurried through the gate, arms open, to greet them.

Inside, they were taken to their rooms. Eve had her old room back, the green room, and Lottie followed by Jennie soon came in, fussing to help her unpack.

'Oh, it's so good to see ye, Miss Eve,' Lottie began, then stopped. 'Oh dear, I'm sorry, I meant to say Mrs Wakeman, but in the excitement and all . . .'

'Don't be silly, dear Lottie,' smiled Eve. 'I'm very happy to be

210

Eve and it's wonderful to see you, too.'

Father returned from his visit to the outlying farms and cottages late in the afternoon. Eve watched for him on the verandah, cooling herself with a Chinese silk fan. As soon as he rounded the corner in his sulky, she saw him and he saw her. The vehicle was well cared for and had been highly polished when he left that morning but now, on his return, it carried the dust of the bush roads all over it.

She ran down the steps and across the lawn to meet him. He jumped down to meet her as briskly as a man thirty years younger and lifted her from the ground like a child into his embrace.

'Only two months since I saw you, my love, and here you are once more! Ah, what good fortune I'm having.' He held her at arm's length to look at her. 'Beautiful,' he whispered. 'The fall from poor Moonlight did not harm you a bit.'

He did not mention Clare until Eve had been with them five days. He finally brought up the subject when they had been into the church to set up the altar for evening prayer. As they came out onto the church porch, he turned to her, his brow wrinkling in the afternoon sun. 'Have you told John Stuart about Clare?'

She looked guiltily at him and shook her head.

'Ah,' was all he replied.

Some seconds passed. Two sparrows flew in and landed on the beams of the porch above their heads. They perched close together, their small grey bodies almost touching as they performed a sort of kissing action with their beaks. Eve looked up and seemed to be watching them as she said, 'I cannot find it in myself to explain to him. He will never be able to accept her as I would need to describe her.'

Father still did not speak.

She drew her eyes down from the birds. 'Whenever I have been going to tell him, there is always something that prevents me. Just a few weeks ago, I had truly decided. At the very moment I was about to speak of Clare, he informed me of his opinion of one of the married women on Mayfield. She had a child out of wedlock and he looks down on her. He said she was a bad type like his mother. Once again, he confirmed how he despises women like that – women like his mother, women like Clare. I am always fearful of how he will react, of how he will be hurt, if I tell him the truth. I love him so.' Her eyes were full of entreaty. 'Would it be better if you told him?'

Father considered what she had asked before he answered. He was deeply concerned for her and understood her fears, but it would be wrong to intercede in this way. 'No, it is for you to tell him, my Evvy. It is your responsibility. And one you must acknowledge. My intervention would not be a kindness to you. He cares deeply for you and I believe he will accept what you say. Delay no longer, and when you have told him, I would like you to let me know.'

Eve managed a smile she did not feel as he looked encouragingly at her. She knew he was perfectly right. He was not letting her down. He never had, never would. She was accountable. She had the strength. It must come from her. She was John Stuart's wife and must live up to that, not have Father interceding. But she knew in her heart what her husband's reaction would be.

She nodded and took his arm, and they walked in silence to tea.

The following morning she went to inspect the twenty small cloth dolls she had ordered from the seamstress on Rocket Street. The day after would see the week in Bathurst gone and they would make the return journey to Mayfield.

Mother and Thelma accompanied her to the shops. Eve was now much less of a spectacle in the settlement. A week had satisfied the inquisitive and dulled her power to draw eyes on every corner. She passed through the streets almost as Eve Herman would have done. Where George and Lambert Streets joined, they separated. They would meet again at Mrs Ayres' Tea Room, a cosy little shop run by a friend of Lottie and Bathurst's premier cook.

Eve proceeded diagonally across the road to enter the park. Her destination was on the far side. Her mind lazily surrendered to the warmth of the day. She remembered that this was where John Stuart said he first saw her. She smiled at that, feeling the heat of the sun on her face and the backs of her hands. Her gait slowed.

The park was empty. Usually there was a mother and child, or a stockman in Bathurst for the day resting under the trees, but as she looked around she saw no one. Then suddenly, over to her left, a man issued through the trees carrying a box of ammunition upon his shoulder, and walked at right angles to her.

Instantly, she halted. There was no mistaking that form, that walk. Alan Fletcher! Here in the middle of Bathurst.

The memory of their afternoon together burst into her mind, his face, his eyes, his body. The warmth of his arms encircling her as she slowly slipped into unconsciousness. She remembered praying that she would see him again. And here he was, like a miracle. Gone was the lassitude of a few moments before. All the sensations of the time she had spent with him rose inside her. And with them rose guilt, terrible guilt. What was it John Stuart had said? 'You see, Eve, I am not pleased that my wife has had two encounters with a wanted man, a notorious outlaw.' And she had replied she was not coming here to have an encounter of any kind with any outlaw.

And now here he was. Right here.

She stood stock-still as the seconds passed and he walked on. She must turn away and leave; he had not seen her yet, she was sure. Let him go. It was best. It was fortunate that he had not seen her.

But was it? There was a panicky feeling in her chest. How badly she wanted to call out to him.

Then as she watched he glanced sideways through the trees. With reckless anticipation she saw him catch sight of her and halt. Then very slowly he rounded to face her.

Daily, Alan had hoped she was unharmed. And now here she was, just yards away, apparently fully recovered and all by herself again. For a moment he thought to tip his hat and continue on to where Lawless waited with the horses. But too often in recent weeks he had recalled John Stuart Wakeman's wife. He had remembered her face as it lay against his chest on that long ride in the wind. On the odd times since, when he had danced with women in the safe houses, he had thought of the feel of her body in his arms. This was his chance to dispel the emotions he was beginning to associate with her.

He began to walk towards her in his easy way.

Eve's heart raced. A small vein in her neck pulsed visibly and she took a deep breath to calm herself. She even looked quickly to right and left as he advanced, but the park was still empty.

He advanced to within a few feet of her. 'I am surprised to see you here,' he said, tipping his hat.

'And I you,' she replied.

She watched him smile faintly at her, an odd smile. There was something in it that made her uneasy and as he smiled, he asked, 'How is it you are here in Bathurst?'

'I am visiting the rectory for a few days, the Reverend and Mrs Billings are like parents to me. But you, why are you here?'

'Supplies of ammunition cannot be bought in the same store too often in my trade, else the shopkeeper might ask too many questions. Hence, we often travel far afield.'

She nodded in understanding. 'But is it not dangerous here?'

'Lass,' he spoke the word from deep within his throat, 'there can be danger in the most innocent of places. It is not something I dwell upon. But danger aside, I am pleased to discover you are well with no apparent ill effects from your fall.'

'Thank you. Yes, I am quite well again.'

As they stood together in the middle of Bathurst town they were unaware that they were being observed. Daydee, on her way to her friend's house, had crossed Lambert Street and entered the park behind Eve, just in time to witness the meeting.

213

She stopped and watched across the bushes. At first there was mere interest in the sight of Eve being spoken to by a strange man. But then her small dark eyes narrowed. In the attitude of the two before her there was a certain quality that heightened her curiosity. She began to advance across the grass towards them.

As she did Eve continued to speak. 'For a few moments I felt that perhaps you did not wish to see me.'

'And perhaps you were right; it may have been better if I had not. But as I have, I am not unhappy about it.'

She smiled at these words, delighted, confused, mystified by her feelings for him. She had forgotten everything in the nearness of him. His proximity brought only wishful thoughts.

He still held the box of ammunition on his shoulder and now he swung it down to hold it under his arm. As he did so, involuntarily she said, 'We have so much ammunition at Mayfield, I wish I could give you some.'

The statement was catalytic. The intimacy that had come to his expression died. He seemed to withdraw himself from her while he still looked straight in her eyes. There was hardness now. He took a step away from her. 'Yes, no doubt you have many things at Mayfield. And Mayfield is where you belong. I must leave you now. It would have been better if this meeting had not taken place. This is all incomprehensible to me and yet you speak and act as if it were commonplace. I am a bushranger, Mrs Wakeman.'

The statement found her quite unprepared. She felt a stab of pain and the smile faded from her mouth. Her hands hung awkwardly in the air. She stared at him in bewilderment.

At that very moment Daydee's voice exploded at her shoulder. 'Hello, Aunt Eve!'

Eve started and turned towards the girl. She said nothing. There was a dazed expression in her eyes and she seemed to stare right through Daydee, unseeing. This only served to make Daydee more suspicious. She turned from Eve to Alan inquiringly.

Then Alan spoke. Now his voice was raw and hard, the tones of a bushman, totally unlike his own. 'Why thank ye again, ma'am. I reckon I'll be able to find my way now.' He tipped his hat and bent forward in a slight bow.

Automatically, Eve turned, white-faced, to watch him walk away.

'Aunt Eve, who on earth was he?' asked Daydee sharply. 'I don't think I've ever seen such a man. His eyes are just . . . wonderful.'

Eve's confusion was obvious. She did not answer but moved off in the opposite direction.

'Aunt Eve,' the girl began again, walking beside Eve, 'I said who was that man?'

This time Eve replied, though she did not look at her. 'I don't know. He just wanted some directions.'

Daydee had missed little. 'Then why is it you were so upset when I came along? To me it looked as if you knew him well, as if he had told you something that distressed you.'

'Daydee, please.' Eve was trying desperately to sound normal. 'I have told you what happened. I do not know him and he did not upset me!'

The girl was watching her as she spoke. Watching the telltale flush on Eve's throat and noting the agitation beneath the imposed calm.

'Where did he want to go then?'

'What?'

'Where did he want to go then? The man. What directions did he want?'

Eve stopped walking. When she answered there was anger in her voice which she tried unsuccessfully to quell. 'Daydee, you really are the most inquisitive pest. I do not have to explain myself to you. Don't you have your friend to meet? I am going.' And with those words, she left the girl standing there.

On the far side of the park Alan mounted Freedom, and with Lawless rode out of Bathurst town.

Three hours later found Eve alone in the back garden of the rectory. She sat on the grass under the jacaranda tree where she had lunched with John Stuart on the day of their first meeting. Her head was bowed and her hand rested on her chin. Among her disordered thoughts ran many of her husband, and between them, intermingled with them, thoughts of Alan Fletcher. As always, the guilt was uppermost. Why was he so significant to her? Why was she so instinctively drawn to him? Why? Why? Why? Her head spun, she felt ill. What was it he had said this morning? 'Mayfield is where you belong. It would have been better if this meeting had never taken place . . . I am a bushranger.'

It had hurt her for they were statements she had not wanted to hear, but of course he was right. This feeling she had for him was wrong, unseemly. It was deceitful. She was being false to John Stuart. John Stuart.

She knew him so much better now. Seven months at Mayfield had given her many insights into her husband. He was a complicated man, wise and often surprisingly kind, and always generous. He seemed to ignore his wealth, but then he owned all things material,

215

so perhaps it was easy to disregard them when they had always been there. He was learned and articulate, especially on things scientific. He worked hard, too hard, twelve or thirteen hours a day were not unusual for him. From the top managers like Jack Hennessy and Stephen Watson down through the ranks to the foremen and ordinary workers, he was held in high esteem. He had won their respect by his ability, his constant performance, deeds and actions. In fact some almost revered him.

His personality was complex. He hated what he considered loose or immoral. He had been irreparably wounded by his mother's conduct, Eve was positive of that. He only mentioned her to decry her, although almost daily there were proud references to his father.

There was no doubt that he placed her, Eve, above all women, for he had decided she was different. John Stuart created that which he wanted. As she thought of it now, it frightened her, for while she felt equal to any challenge that could arise in her role as his wife, she did not really think she could ever live up to his saintly estimation of her. If only she could. It would remove the guilt that rose within her every time she thought of Alan Fletcher.

She closed her eyes. Her head was so hot, she felt feverish. 'Oh God, how to do that, how to stop thinking of Alan Fletcher? Please, please let me think of him no more.' Still with eyes closed, she stretched out her hands in supplication.

At that moment Father stepped from the back porch to the grass and he saw her gesture. Tears rolled down her cheeks as she opened her eyes.

'My love, what is it that troubles you so?'

'Oh, Father dear, you are back so soon, I was not expecting you yet.' She tried her best to smile.

'I can see that, Evvy love. Please answer me. What is it that troubles you this way?' He knelt on the ground in front of her.

Eve was about to reply 'nothing', when the love and understanding in the eyes that looked into hers overwhelmed her and she took his hands saying, 'Father, there is something I must tell you. Something I do not comprehend at all. It is within me and overshadows many of my waking hours . . . My sleeping hours too,' she added softly as an afterthought.

Father eased himself to the ground and sat beside her in the hot, dry, afternoon breeze, and she told him of Alan Fletcher. She spoke of the first time she saw him, her wedding day. Of the inexplicable feelings she had experienced.

At first Father was clearly startled. Although he loved the woman beside him more than himself, he was a Victorian man, and a man of God. He had married Eve in the sight of his God and now she was telling him of a strange and mysterious association with a known and wanted outlaw. He was amazed and frightened for her. He thought she must be hallucinating. But as the story progressed and she told of the day after her birthday and the fall from Moonlight, he knew she meant what she said.

He did not interrupt her with remonstrance or argument. Instead he listened with all the calm and reason of his rare intelligence. Slowly his face changed. He could not acknowledge what she said as real, but he began to see that it was truth for her.

She came at last to the meeting that very morning in the parkland. When she told him of Daydee's intervention, he said nothing but he did not like what he heard. He had summed Daydee up quickly and though he was generous by nature, he could see little in her to inspire confidence.

Eve finished her story with the words, 'You see, no matter what men say, I know Alan Fletcher is not bad. I know he is moral and courageous and good, just as surely as I know that you are. But I am almost deranged, Father. I feel as if there is a battle going on inside me. I am muddled and confused. I don't know why all this is, but it is, and it's not as if I don't love John Stuart. I do.'

And only then did he speak. His fine brow wrinkled and there was concern in every nuance of his voice. 'Eve, I have heard all you have said. And perhaps this Alan Fletcher is as you describe him. Nevertheless, no matter what you feel or have felt in his presence, you are married to John Stuart, inextricably and for ever. You say you love your husband. There is no future in thoughts or dreams or whatever it is you have. You must forget the man! Even if he were not outside the law, any connection would be fantastic. You are Mrs Wakeman. You must realise what that means, Eve. You are no longer the girl I met in Sydney, nor the determined teenager of the sewing business, nor the Bathurst music teacher; you have been elevated. Settle. Be still with your position. There is no more important woman in the colony, not even the Governor's wife.'

Eve was watching him, and she listened carefully. As he finished she said, 'Yes, Father, I know you are right, but there is so much turmoil. I . . . I love John Stuart. It is not that I wish it to be any other way. I do not. I am very happy as his wife. Only it is as if there is an outside force reminding me constantly of Alan Fletcher. I have been in his presence in the most freakish of circumstances, and no matter what, it is beyond me to govern how I feel. Even if I never see him again I think it will always be there.' She looked imploringly at the man beside her. 'Oh, I am so confused,' she finished hopelessly.

'Eve, what the bushranger said to you this day is beyond doubt. Even he sees the ridiculous nature of the most tenuous of associations. Only you can divest yourself of these thoughts. It is up to you, no one else. "Therein the patient must minister to himself." I love you and the notions you mention worry me deeply. It is a path to destruction. I pray you will never see this Alan Fletcher again. Return to Mayfield and your husband. Work at your marriage.'

As he completed his words, she sighed and murmured. 'Thank you,' she said softly, 'thank you for not judging me. I love you so.'

His eyes glistened as he answered her. 'It is not for me to judge anyone, and where you are concerned, my Evvy, I could not judge. But ask God's help. Close your eyes now and we will ask together.'

So there on the lawn, surrounded by the blue fallen blossoms from the jacaranda tree, they closed their eyes and Father's voice softly began,

'In thee O Lord, do I put my trust: let me never be put to confusion.

Deliver me in thy righteousness, and cause me to escape: incline thine ear unto me, and save me.

Be thou my strong habitation, whereunto I may continually resort: thou hast given commandment to save me; for thou *art* my rock and my fortress.

Hear our prayer O Lord, and give Evelyn May the help she needs to dismiss this man from her mind. Return her to Mayfield and happiness.

Hear our prayer O Lord. For thou art our hope O God. We ask this in the name of the Father and the Son and the Holy Ghost. Amen.'

CHAPTER THIRTEEN

'Laugh and be merry together, like brothers akin,
Guesting awhile in the rooms of a beautiful inn,
Glad till the dancing stops, and the lilt of the music ends,
Laugh till the game is played; and you be merry, my friends.'
        'Laugh and Be Merry', John Masefield, 1878–1967.

John Stuart missed Eve while she was away in Bathurst. His days were full and busy from dawn to dusk, but the nights without her were dull and lifeless. He had been conscious of the lack of laughter and the absence of the sound of her voice. He had missed her touch and her sweet company.

Each evening, he and Joe ate together and after dinner they talked business, sitting on the verandah or walking across the park in the warm December nights.

'It seems strange with Eve gone,' John Stuart confided to Joe. 'I really miss her. I hadn't realised that I would, old man, but I do. I keep reaching for her in bed at night, only to remember she's in Bathurst.'

Joe smiled. 'Yes, m'boy, it's the same for me without Thel, even after all these years. Women have a way with them. Sneak into your heart and damn it if you don't miss them when they're gone.'

They both laughed. As always they were content and comfortable with each other, and these days Joe's heart rejoiced in the knowledge that his boy had a good wife and one whom he loved dearly.

It was no accident that they were both working in sight of the road across the property on 9 December, the day their wives were coming home. When the coach came into sight, John Stuart turned from Jack Hennessy and Stephen Watson who stood with him in the foundations of the new silo, and mounting Diomed, shouted to Joe, 'The coach comes, old man! The coach comes!'

By the time Deke Edwards brought his horses to a halt at the front steps of Mayfield House, John Stuart was at the side of the coach.

'My darling,' he said as Eve stepped down into his arms. 'How I've missed you.'

Thelma smiled to see their delight, but Daydee's face was peevish, regarding the reunion with bitter unhappiness. When John Stuart at last turned from hugging his wife to greet her, she forced a pretty smile to her mouth. 'And I have missed you,' she said, looking meaningfully up into his eyes.

'Yes, it's good to have you all back,' he answered, not noticing her earnest expression as he bent to hug her slight frame.

At that moment Joe arrived and soon the Larmers departed to their own home and John Stuart and Eve entered theirs, where Mrs Smith, Mr Baines and Stephanie waited. As soon as the greetings were over, John Stuart turned to Eve and hugged her again in front of them. Eve laughed. 'I see you truly have missed me, my love.'

While Stephanie unpacked for her, Eve and John Stuart walked down into the garden bower off their rooms. The poinciana tree was in full bloom; its glorious blossoms a sunshade of bright crimson above them and the fallen ones a carpet of glowing colour beneath their feet.

'So tell me, darling,' John Stuart said, bending down and breaking off a small cluster of chrysanthemums and handing them to her, 'what did you do in Bathurst?'

Eve took the flowers. 'Thank you, kind sir.' They smiled into each other's eyes and Eve was reminded how very attractive his genial half smile was. 'Oh, we were busy. It was lovely to be with Mother and Father and I helped Mother with the altar flowers as I used to do. And Thelma and Mother and Lottie and I went to the church social evening, and we pottered in the garden and took luncheon under the jacaranda tree. Remember our first meal there together? We did all the things that we did when I lived there.'

His mouth drew down in mock disappointment. 'I see, Mrs Wakeman. You did not miss your husband at all?'

She threw her arms up around his neck. 'No, sorry, Mr Wakeman, I did not miss you at all.' And then she burst into merry laughter and running a few steps from him called, 'Well, perhaps I did just a little.'

He sprang across the space between them and catching her up in his arms pressed kisses upon her eyes, her cheeks, her hair. Then holding her face in his hands, he whispered, 'You tease me, Evelyn May, and it is not fair.' He bent down and kissed her lovingly on the mouth, and at the touch of his lips a little thrill ran through her, for she had missed him too and was glad to be back in his arms.

They spent the remainder of the short afternoon together and later, when they were dressing for dinner, they discussed their plans for Christmas. When John Stuart spoke of the guest list, Eve told him of her meeting with Sir Rutherford in Blayney on her way to Bathurst;

how he had taken tea with them and informed her he was coming to Mayfield for the Christmas week.

John Stuart nodded. 'Yes, darling, I'm sorry I didn't tell you. It slipped my mind, I should have. But I thought he and young Elrington would make a fine addition to our house party.' Then he asked a most innocent question. 'Did you run into anyone else you knew?'

A sharp chill ran across her shoulders and down her spine. Anyone else? Oh, Lord, yes, she had run into someone else. What should she do? Tell him? He would be so upset. She had thought a great deal about Alan Fletcher since her meeting with him in the Bathurst park, but she had come home determined to reject the inexplicable feelings she had for the bushranger. John Stuart was looking at her with his dark, sincere eyes.

'Darling?' He wondered why she had not answered him.

'Yes, I ran into a lot of folk I knew; after all, I lived in Bathurst five years.'

'Of course.' He turned into the dressing room to choose his jacket.

She felt quite sick. How desperately she wanted to be honest with him, about everything, always. She felt guilty. She took a deep breath, her heart was racing and a flush had crept up her neck. 'John Stuart?' Her husband turned and faced her. 'It is almost unbelievable, but I did run into someone else. Accidentally. I saw the bushranger, Alan Fletcher.'

John Stuart's face became blank, totally blank, as if his mind had gone elsewhere.

She held her breath. The seconds passed.

'John Stuart?'

With an obvious deployment of will, he refocused his eyes upon her.

'John Stuart, I know it's a surprise to you. It was to me; and of course I was astounded to see him there . . . just as you are astounded to hear it.'

'Astounded?' The word broke from his mouth with such force she started. 'I am outraged! How can this be? How in the devil's name can my wife go to Bathurst for a week and manage to fall in company with that man again? It is not possible!'

'Darling,' Eve hastened to him, 'it was the most unlikely event. I was in the park and there he appeared in front of me. I was amazed. I think he was too. Our conversation was very brief. In fact, Daydee came up and he lifted his hat and walked on.'

'Bloody hell! You mean you had conversation with him? Have you lost your reason? He is a bushranger. Don't you understand?' He moved away. 'Are you stupid?' A few seconds later he added,

'Daydee? The child didn't realise who it was, did she?'

'No, no. I said he was someone asking directions. It was none of her business.'

'Is that all?'

'Of course it is all! For goodness sake, I left him and heaven knows where he went.'

John Stuart was still in shock. He walked by her through to their bedroom and over to the window where he stood leaning with his hands on the sill. For a full minute he did not speak. When he turned and spoke again his voice was almost normal but a strange expression lingered on his face. 'So, you were alone when you met him?'

'Yes, John Stuart, I was.'

'What did he say to you?'

'I think he said good day . . . and that he was pleased to see that I had recovered from my fall.'

'Bloody impudence. He's got a hide being in Bathurst. Up to no good, that's for certain.'

Even though the news had greatly angered him, Eve was relieved she had told him. She felt better for it. She sighed. 'My dearest, I knew you would not like it.'

For some seconds he stood staring at her, then he moved swiftly and wrapped her in his arms. Her cheek was against him and his voice sounded almost stridently in her ear. 'No, I do not like it. I hate it. It's terrible that you had to face another encounter with such a person, for you are different, my Eve, different. And you are mine. I hate to think of your having met and conversed alone with any man, let alone a blasted outlaw. Why, I am even jealous of Reverend Billings sometimes.'

'Oh, John Stuart,' she retorted, her face pressed against him, 'you are a silly thing.'

'I know,' he answered, 'but it's how I am.'

As he continued to hold her close, she looked up at him. 'Come, darling,' she said. 'Please. Let's forget about it.'

Christmas 1863. Many of the inhabitants of the Australian cities were without work. Conditions in Sydney and Melbourne were poor, both cities still passing through a 'shanty town' stage. Despite the land available, overcrowding was as bad as in Europe. Much of this was due to the rapid increase of population during the gold rush of the previous decade. Land settlement remained difficult, and those who did leave the cities found it as hopeless to find employment in rural areas as in the towns. But there *were* bastions of well-being and prosperity, and perhaps the most flourishing of these was Mayfield.

Christmas Eve was hot and humid. Rain clouds threatened but did not deliver.

Eve had been working with Dr Douglas and Betty Watson the last two days, for three stockmen had been injured curbing a stampede near Daisy Ridge, and two were very ill, needing constant care. One of the dairy maids had come to relieve Eve but still she had not arrived home until after three o'clock in the afternoon to find a concerned John Stuart. 'Darling, you are not minding your guests. You will be late for the children's Christmas tree.'

But she was not; she was ready just in time to join the exhilarated party that made its way along the macadamised road leading from Mayfield proper across the river to the workers' cottages. The Governor, Sir John Young, had taken a week from his worries, and he now laughed with his wife at some private joke as they rode side by side with John Stuart and Eve. Behind them came a chequered group. Sir Rutherford rode with Daydee and the Governor's aide-de-camp. David Elrington separated Mr and Mrs Stanley Ford, while their son Roy rode with Thelma and Joe. The rear saw John Stuart's barrister Robert Robinson-Pike with the district's Member of the Legislative Assembly, Stan Payne, and his wife Barbara.

Strapped to each lady's saddle was an umbrella in case the menace of rain became reality.

It was four o'clock in the afternoon and the Christmas tree ceremony for the workers' children was to begin in half an hour with a concert on the green in the workers' village.

The party from Mayfield House was welcomed with a cheer. Near two hundred were in attendance, for not only were the married workers and their families present, many of the single workers had come to enjoy themselves as well.

They all took their seats and the concert commenced. The last to appear was the eldest child on Mayfield, Jack Hennessy's son, Peter, a fair-haired boy of ten. He recited the first four verses of John Milton's 'On the Morning of Christ's Nativity'. It was a mammoth task and the child did a splendid job.

Sir John Young leaned across to John Stuart. 'You have some promising seedlings here, like this young boy. The future of your fair valleys and hills seems ensured.'

'Yes, I hope so. I pay their parents ample money and look after their needs. My hope is that the children will follow in their fathers' footsteps.'

'A good and sensible desire. If only there were more Mayfields, the current slump would be soon over,' replied the Governor seriously. 'There is much to talk with you about before I leave. The economy is overwhelmingly based on sheep now that the gold is petering out. You alone are creating a beef industry, for which I and Australia thank you. The Premier and I are concerned about all the divergency in land laws and tariffs between the colonies, not to mention the foolishness of the different railway gauges between each colony. I wish there were more stable and successful heads like yours around.'

'Thank you, Sir John.'

At that moment, the children and their teacher presented themselves on the stage. There was a round of applause and the gift giving began. The delight and excitement of the children was infectious. Eve and Thelma were soon surrounded by a sea of Christmas paper and laughing young faces. In the midst of all the happy noise and clamour, Eve lifted her head to look over to her husband. At his side stood Daydee. A crease lodged between Eve's eyes but soon she felt her hand taken by a small one and she turned to the children.

Daydee was on a mission. 'May I sit a minute with you, Uncle John Stuart?'

John Stuart smiled up at the girl. 'Of course, Daydee, sit down.'

'We don't talk like we used to,' she said, her dark eyes trained on him.

John Stuart laughed. 'Well, my Daydee, it's a grown woman you are now. I can hardly swing you on my knee and banter as before.'

Daydee sighed. 'I didn't mean when I was little. I meant . . .'

John Stuart turned in his chair towards her. He brought her chin round to face him and looked into her small, intense face. He would have been horrified if he had known the joy she felt at the touch of his fingers.

'Ah Daydee, don't be like a child. I am happy to talk to you but I am a busy man and now that I am married things have changed.'

'I know.'

'Come on, give me a smile, it is Christmas Eve, you know. What about the famous Daydee Bronwyn Larmer smile?'

And Daydee complied. Her mouth broke out of its stiff line into a radiant smile. She looked so young and virtuous that John Stuart bent forward and kissed her on her forehead. 'Merry Christmas, Daydee,' he said.

'Merry Christmas,' Daydee replied, and under her breath said, 'my love.'

'Now tell me,' continued John Stuart innocently, 'how did you enjoy your recent sojourn in Bathurst?'

A shiver of glee ran through her. John Stuart had asked the one question she had prayed he would. Her mind ran over what she had prepared to say. 'Well it was fun, really,' she began. 'I saw my friend Connie French every day and oh how we laughed about our days at St Catherine's together. We had a grand time.'

Just then, John Stuart's attention was taken by something else and she fell silent until he turned back to her. 'Now, what was that, Daydee?'

Her face brightened as she continued skilfully, 'We all had a lovely time, actually. Aunt Eve is so fond of Reverend Billings, it was quite a delight for her to be back in Bathurst, I'm sure. She no doubt caught up with lots of past acquaintances. Yes,' here she laughed a harmless, merry laugh, 'like that strange man she remained with for so long in the park that day.'

John Stuart frowned. 'In the park? With a man?'

'I don't know who he was. It was surely someone Aunt Eve knew very well, for they were standing ever so close as they talked. Although she swore she didn't know him at all. Funny, for they were so very familiar.'

John Stuart tapped on the side of his chair. Was Daydee speaking about the bushranger? This was not as Eve had told it to him. He was silent for some seconds. Then he asked, 'How is it you know of this, Daydee?'

Daydee, pretending not to notice anything amiss, answered gaily, 'Oh, I chanced upon them. You would say it was amusing really, the way they didn't even know I was there until I came up and spoke. I'd been watching them for ages. They were sort of staring into each other's eyes.' She gave another innocuous laugh. 'I dare say there were other friends Aunt Eve re-acquainted herself with, although that gent did seem extra special and he was so very handsome. I can't understand it really, when she swore she didn't know him.' Intuitively artful, Daydee turned away as she finished her sentence.

John Stuart coughed to cover his emotions. 'Ah, well, that's interesting, Daydee.'

She smiled as she looked away. She let a little time pass, then she turned back to him. 'I do so wish we could see each other like we used to; you never ride with me any more and our rides were such fun.'

'Ah, Daydee, you've turned into such a fine young woman.' His hand went out and patted her hair absently. 'It is not me you should be spending time with, it's the likes of young Roy over there.'

At that same moment Roy looked over and smilingly beckoned Daydee.

'Go on, my dear,' John Stuart touched her shoulder, 'go and join the young man, he dotes on you.'

'Silly old Roy,' came Daydee's scathing judgment, 'he's such a child.'

'Don't be so harsh on him. Off you go and see what he wants.'

'All right then, only because you ask me to.' But she knew it was time to leave.

Robert Robinson-Pike, champagne in hand, joined John Stuart. He chatted with the barrister, outwardly calm, and passed through the happy crowd, his troubled thoughts hidden. Of course Evelyn had told him of the meeting, naturally she would. She was good and chaste and honest, wasn't she? But little, innocent Daydee had seen the encounter as intimate, very intimate. 'I'd been watching them for ages. They were sort of staring into each other's eyes.' The way Eve had told him, it was brief and dispassionate. Surely Eve would not lie to him.

At half past six, the children's refreshments began and the Mayfield party mounted their horses and rode back to the big house. There they were to dine in two hours' time followed by their own gift giving.

The following morning, Christmas Day, the Mayfield chapel that Sir Arthur had built would be opened, and under sufferance John Stuart would attend while the Governor read a short service, for it was unthinkable to have a Christmas in this reign of Victoria without at least one religious gathering.

From his earliest memories, John Stuart had been interested in the earth and the universe, fascinated by science, and natural and physical phenomena. At five years old, his first tutor had encouraged him to collect ants and moths, beetles and butterflies, and together they had studied them for hours. His library was vast and carried much biology, Asa Gray's manuals on botany, scientific works by astronomer Sir John Herschel and such noted dissenters as Charles Lyell and Thomas Henry Huxley, the most recent addition being Huxley's *Evidence as to a Man's Place in Nature* specially ordered from London. John Stuart was in communication with the British Association for the Advancement of Science in England, and it was through this body that he received his publications. On his visits to Sydney he had lectured to the group of colonial amateur scientists who called themselves 'Friends of the Royal Society'. His last paper had been a treatise on Charles Darwin's *On the Origin of Species by Means of Natural Selection, or The Preservation of Favoured Races in the Struggle for Life* which had been published four years before. Most of his peers, hidebound by their beliefs, thought John Stuart highly eccentric. They tolerated his views only because of his great wealth and personal charm.

But for all his logical thought where the origin of species was concerned, he was as a machine when his emotions were involved. When the riding party returned to Mayfield House and retired to rest, bathe, and dress for dinner, John Stuart was silent and preoccupied.

Eve had noticed he seemed a little distant on the ride home and as they entered their suite she turned to kiss his cheek, saying, 'John Stuart, you have been very quiet, is something wrong?'

His heart was racing. Daydee in her innocence had implied that his beautiful, saintly wife had been in the Bathurst park with a man who was more than a friend, and he knew that man was Alan Fletcher. He felt dejected, disappointed, and it showed in his eyes. 'When you told me about meeting the outlaw in Bathurst, you did not tell me you were in his company a long time.'

Eve was taken aback. 'What do you mean? Who has said I was?' Then she realised. 'It's Daydee, isn't it? What has she been saying to you?'

He took her by the shoulders and gazed into her eyes with a weird, concentrated expression. 'She said you were in intimate conversation. That you stood so closely to the man you almost touched him. That she watched you a long time and you were so engrossed with each other that you didn't even know she was at your side until she spoke. Evelyn, tell me she is wrong.'

Eve was disconcerted. Daydee was trying to harm her, that was certain. Her husband looked so hurt, she felt terrible. 'Darling, of course she is wrong. Daydee saw the astonishment I felt at running into the bushranger, and misinterpreted it. I was not going to explain myself to her, it was none of her business. I was not in his company very long. Daydee is greatly overdoing the situation. She tends to do that. Everything is dramatic with that girl. The whole thing was entirely accidental as I told you.' She stood on tiptoe and kissed him. 'John Stuart, don't you know I love you?'

His peculiar expression faded. His hands slid down her back and crushed her to him; he hugged her so tightly he hurt her. 'Oh, darling,' he whispered, 'how could I doubt you for a single moment? What a jealous fool I am.'

Later, when everyone assembled in the drawing room, Mrs Smith glided deferentially into the room, making her way to the master. She was a thin, wiry, severe little woman who had been transported for seven years in 1834. In 1839 she had been sent as an assigned servant to Arthur Wakeman and when she became free, she remained, rising from scullery maid to housekeeper. She was fiercely loyal to the Wakeman name and had transferred her worship of Arthur Wakeman to his son. She appeared now in a grey gown pressed stiffly

227

to perfection, her hands almost the same colour clasped together in front of it. 'Sir,' she said quietly, 'we are ready.'

Arm in arm, John Stuart and Eve left the room. In the front hall were assembled the Mayfield House staff.

As Eve surveyed the scene in front of her, she felt overawed as she had so often since marrying John Stuart. All this he took for granted and it was like some magnificent dream to her. The huge hall was decked with holly and stars and great spangles of gold, the servants all assembled in their best – Stephanie all smiles with the chamber maids, the head cook Mr Free, the apprentices, the parlour maids, Timothy and the valets, the girls from the scullery and laundry, the servers, Mr Baines the butler, and proudly at their head Mary Smith.

They all bowed in unison.

'Ladies and gentlemen all,' John Stuart began amid genteel applause, 'I am once again happy to wish you a merry Christmas. This year, I stand with my wife at my side.' Another short applause. 'Mayfield thrives and you thrive with it, for that which is cared for lovingly returns a bounty to those who care. Mayfield is yours as much as mine, and I am happy and proud for us all. Mrs Smith, Mr Baines, you have brought your staff together in your usual unparalleled fashion. Congratulations. The compliments of the season to you all.'

Louder and more vibrant approval sounded now and Mr Oldfield, John Stuart's secretary, came forward with the first basket of Christmas gifts. As he handed them out, John Stuart spoke to each servant. He knew them all by name and could refer to something specific in each person's life of the last twelve months. There was genuine interest in his face as they answered him, and Eve felt great pride in the way he cared about them and gave them such obvious pleasure. She, too, spoke with each of them and they wished her a happy Christmas, for she was as popular with the house staff as she was with the wives and families.

At the end of the ceremony, there were three cheers for 'the Master and Mistress' and John Stuart and Eve returned to their guests.

Dinner was a splendid six courses. During the meal Eve was aware of Daydee watching her. Daydee was eager to see what effect her words with John Stuart might have made. She smarted at the evident harmony between Eve and her husband and had to admit that apparently she had gained nothing.

Daydee hated Eve. It was a simple, uncomplicated hatred. Eve had taken John Stuart away from her. She was jealous and vicious in her jealousy. All her life she had played make-believe games where

John Stuart was hers. In her mind John Stuart belonged to her. Eve had changed all that.

When Eve smiled at her down the dinner table she could not force herself to respond in kind; instead she turned away and spoke to Roy who sat beside her.

The gift giving afterwards was an odd affair. Eve found it strange to give to, and be given by, people she hardly knew. She watched Sir Rutherford as he came over to her carrying a parcel wrapped in shining silver paper. His footfalls were certain, firm, almost heavy. He was a man in charge of himself. She felt that he was an honourable man, a man with a strong sense of justice and duty, but there was little humour in him. His laughter was never the hearty laughter of a man who knows joy. She wondered why that was as he sat stiffly down beside her, and she answered herself by supposing that his occupation was not one which led men to be cheerful. They exchanged gifts. Politely they thanked each other, and he moved away to speak to Lady Young.

But there was ease between herself and Sir Rutherford compared to the feeling she had as Daydee came over. The girl had thanked John Stuart for her present by hugging him until he had to extricate himself from her arms. Eve looked up at her as she approached. For a second, the eyes in the face above were icy, then as Lady Young turned towards them she said, 'Merry Christmas, Aunt Eve,' and dropping a box in Eve's lap turned sharply away.

When Eve untied the ribbon and opened it, inside lay a book. It was an atlas of New South Wales. A card lying on it said, 'In case you are asked directions in the future. From Daydee.' Eve replaced the lid and put it down with a speculative expression.

Sir Rutherford had missed none of this. His usually reflective look deepened as he turned back to conversing with Lady Young.

Suddenly, a hand rested on Eve's shoulder and she looked up to find her husband standing beside her, his familiar, slanted grin lighting up his face. Her heart quickened, for his smile gave him such a boyishly handsome look.

'Now it is my turn.' He handed her a small package, tied with yellow ribbon. She opened it with a beating heart. Inside was a miniature painting of Mayfield House. It was mounted in a gold and amber frame, and made into a brooch. It was exquisite.

'John Stuart, it's too beautiful.'

'Nothing is too beautiful for you,' he answered serenely. He pinned it to her breast and she felt a swell of love for him.

Later, when sleep had descended on the many rooms of Mayfield House, the hostess lay awake, listening to the fall of rain outside and reflecting on the day's events. When John Stuart had questioned her tonight about the meeting with Alan Fletcher, once more she had felt terribly guilty. She would always be confused about her feelings for the outlaw, even though now she was consciously subduing them. Her husband so adored her, he could not even bear to think of her in company with another man. She recalled the way he had pulled her into his arms and held her as if never to let her go, and the wonderful look of love from him a few hours later with his words, 'Nothing is too beautiful for you.'

He had made love to her tonight aggressively, thrusting hard into her as if somehow to purge them both of the bushranger. She had not minded that, she had found it exciting, erotic, and their orgasms had been simultaneous, long and intense. Their lovemaking was always good. His hand still rested on her bare stomach as she listened now to his soft breathing beside her. She moved and kissed his hair as he murmured in his sleep. She did love him, now and for always, and she must forget Alan Fletcher.

And Daydee despised her. The girl was showing it increasingly. She had grown up in luxury and was spoiled and peevish, but why didn't the girl realise how foolish she was? John Stuart did not take Daydee seriously. He was twice her age and thought of her as not much more than a child. For a minute, Eve thought of her own teen years. The likes of silly little Daydee didn't know they were born. She sighed.

The barbed message with the atlas came to her mind and the way Daydee had sought out John Stuart to tell him of her version of the meeting in Bathurst. As surely as she could, the girl had drawn battle lines. Well, Eve would give her no satisfaction. She would not allow herself to be embroiled in an artificial fight with a spiteful, teenage girl.

Eve underestimated Daydee Bronwyn Larmer. There was nothing artificial in the attitudes of Daydee. To her, Eve constituted a real and ever-present threat. She was not simply a spiteful, teenage girl. She was an insanely jealous, viciously effective, hand-to-hand combatant who would never forgive Eve for capturing John Stuart's affection. She was as unyielding in her hatreds as the Moor, and self-interest was the motivating force behind all she ever did.

Eve assessed Daydee with reason and there was no reason in Daydee.

It rained overnight, and the bright cloudless sky of Christmas morning proclaimed a warm, dry day. The service was at ten o'clock and the entourage walked the three hundred yards to the small chapel in clear sunlight. Sir John Young read the service in a fine, loud voice, and Eve thought of Father in Bathurst doing the same. They sang one hymn only, 'Hark the Herald Angels Sing', to Mrs Myrtle Ford's accompaniment on the harp, and soon after issued back out into the sunshine.

On the walk back to Mayfield House Sir Rutherford left Mr Payne's side and fell in step with John Stuart. Taking his arm in confidential fashion, he asked, 'Have we time to take a ride across the Boorowa and get up into the hills to look where that blasted bushranger found Mrs Wakeman? Ah yes, I'd really like to see that part of the country.'

John Stuart looked at Sir Rutherford. 'I doubt it, those hills are well over two hours' ride. Tomorrow we could, but today I think not.'

His guest nodded. 'Tomorrow is just as good. Better even, for I would like to have your wife accompany us and show me just where it was she was found.'

John Stuart's pulse quickened at this suggestion. He was not happy about taking Eve along. There was a place in his mind where the number of her encounters with Alan Fletcher rankled and festered, and this coloured his response. 'No, Rutherford. I think not. I don't . . . want her in any possible danger.'

'There will be no danger. With a few good men like Jack Hennessy and Mr Larmer carrying the Sharp's carbines I saw Hennessy cleaning yesterday, the danger will be to what or whom we come across, eh?'

'Nevertheless, I do not want Eve to be reminded of it. I prefer she remains at home.'

Rutherford was grave. 'Just as you wish. But perhaps you will allow me to question her. I will cause her no distress.' He turned his head to gaze at the classical profile beside him, his eyes narrowing.

John Stuart acquiesced. 'All right.'

When dinner was over and they had all assembled in the drawing room, Sir Rutherford detached himself from his group and moved in long strides across the room. 'Well, mine host, so we ride out into the hill country tomorrow?'

'Why yes, Rutherford, that is what we agreed.'

Eve sat looking up at the detective policeman.

'And you, dear lady, since your husband prefers you not to ride with us, I would like permission to ask you a few questions.'

John Stuart patted Eve's hand. 'Yes, sweetheart, Sir Rutherford wants to ascertain the area you were in when you fell from Moonlight. He has a few questions for you.'

Eve had opened her mouth to answer when Sir Rutherford went

on, 'It's just that I want to examine that part of the country for myself, scrutinise it. Ah yes, to see if there's anything to see, you might say.' He rocked back on his heels a little, a self-satisfied expression on his face, and gave an imitation of a broad smile.

Looking up at the towering form, Eve answered as dispassionately as she could. 'I don't want to disappoint you, Sir Rutherford, but it would be absolutely useless to question me. I have no idea where I was that day.'

Sir Rutherford's face lost its amusement. 'Not even an idea of which way you went?'

She met his eyes, and for a moment he saw the strength of character there. 'Of course I know which way I took from here. It was south-west across the Boorowa. But I have no sense of direction after that, possibly because of the fall, I don't know. But it is useless to continue this conversation, utterly useless.'

The expert on the bushrangers nodded slowly; Mrs Wakeman was far more interesting than he had thought. 'In that case, dear lady, I shall leave you in peace.'

Eve felt cold even though the breeze through the open door was warm. Her husband patted her hand again, then rose and moved away in conversation with Sir Rutherford and Joe.

Eve watched them. She pitied any outlaw that came within the police detective's grasp. Suddenly she found herself praying silently for the only one she knew. She dropped her eyes and prayed that Alan Fletcher would be spared. That he would never be caught; that no signs of his whereabouts would come to Sir Rutherford's notice; that he would stay free and unharmed.

As she looked up from her lap she noticed that the detective policeman was watching her over her husband's shoulder, looking at her speculatively, studying her with thoughtful eyes. And just beyond Sir Rutherford, Eve saw Daydee. The girl was playing cards with Roy and David Elrington. She held her cards up in front of her, and above them, her dusky little eyes were trained on Eve maliciously.

Eve was absent when the riding party left the next day to search the hills. She was once more with Dr Douglas and his able helper, Betty Watson, in the small surgery building they called the 'hospital', down by the river. As well as the cattlemen, they now had two children to attend to, a brother and sister who had fallen from a tree early that morning and had broken bones.

Eve held the little girl in her arms while the doctor set her leg; she kissed the tiny, tear-stained face, and when she looked up she saw the riders through the window as they turned and passed the orchards before heading south-west away from Mayfield proper. Daydee was one of the riders. Eve shook her head in thought as they disappeared from view.

After the riding party had crossed the Boorowa River they stopped to refresh themselves. The horses drank from the river and the humans drank from leather water bottles. While they were partaking of the hamper of food Jack Hennessy had opened, Daydee approached Sir Rutherford.

He smiled at her. 'And how do you enjoy the ride, Miss Daydee?'

'Splendid, I find the whole notion exciting.' She returned him a wide smile.

He tapped his riding crop on his shiny brown boots as he studied her. 'Ah yes, you are a gallant sort of a girl. Methinks you'd even enjoy a scuffle with some of the wild colonial boys, eh? Unlike other ladies.'

'Unlike Aunt Eve, do you mean?' came Daydee's quick retort.

'Well now, I didn't exactly mean that, Miss Daydee.'

Daydee's smile broke into a little laugh. 'Oh, come now, Sir Rutherford, I understand much more than you think.'

Sir Rutherford was looking quizzically at her. 'Do you now, young lady?'

'It seemed odd to my way of thinking that she could not help you with your questions last night.'

The police detective said nothing.

'Perhaps,' said Daydee lightly, 'she sympathises with them.'

Sir Rutherford's eyebrows rose. 'No. I'd not believe that, missy.'

Then Daydee gave him one of her long, slow looks. Sir Rutherford had never been the recipient of one before and it excited his curiosity.

'She certainly doesn't like to talk about them,' Daydee remarked before she walked away.

He watched her very carefully as she moved through the men to her horse. So, the girl wanted him to believe that Mrs Wakeman commiserated with the bushrangers. He already suspected there was no love in Daydee Larmer's heart for John Stuart's wife, and this seemed to confirm it. Ah yes, an interesting subject was Miss Daydee, and so too was the object of her dislike.

Four hours later, the riders descended from the high country and returned to the banks of the Boorowa. They had enjoyed the ride and had shot some of the game that abounded on the upland, but as for finding any indication of the bushrangers' whereabouts, there had been nothing. Even so, Sir Rutherford was not disappointed. For in finding nothing he had found something, as he pointed out to John Stuart as they had passed along the ridge overlooking the river valley.

'For you see,' he said, 'we know the bushranger Fletcher was here, we assume on this very height, the day he found your wife. Today we have discovered nothing to suggest he dwells in this vicinity or frequents it. Ah yes, so I am led to guessing why he would be here. No coaches run here. No gold passes from the goldfields here. No settlement or town is here. No farms are here. So why was he here? Well, there is one thing that is around . . .'

'Food,' broke in John Stuart. 'There is an abundance of game.'

'Ah yes,' replied Sir Rutherford. 'I see you are abreast of me. Fletcher was most probably hunting and if I am right, it means he does not rest his head a very great distance from this spot, for it is unlikely he would ride more than a few hours to seek food. Also, I believe he is not nomadic any more. It is my view that the notorious Alan Fletcher who has evaded the law these many years dwells within ten or at most fifteen miles from us at this very moment. I am elated, my friend! Excited in the extreme! Ah yes, it is a start, a real beginning, you might say.'

John Stuart turned in his saddle to face Sir Rutherford and the question that came from him gave voice to the doubt in his face. 'That certainly sounds a rational deduction, but is it not an impossibility to find his hideout in the vast sameness of this country?' He waved his hand in a wide curve at the endless gum trees.

There was a hint of smugness in the look Sir Rutherford returned. 'As I have said before, my friend, they all make mistakes in the end. Ah yes, and each piece of knowledge I gather will turn into the completed patchwork quilt at last. Then I shall have them one and all! Ben Hall and Flash Johnny Gilbert are still running free and easy, and some public opinion even supports the beggars. But too many people have dealings with them and in the too many will be one or two for me. One or two who will inform. Ah yes, the same with Morgan, Gardiner, Daily, Dawson, Fletcher and the lot. This first bit of information I have gleaned about the "Governor", as they call Fletcher, excites me. Up to this time, he's been like a phantom. It's a start, ah yes!' Sir Rutherford made a rumbling sound in his throat, and then he laughed, hollow as it sounded, pulling back his lips to show his gums above his front teeth.

'You know,' he added, 'I did not get much help from Mr Larmer when I approached him for a description of Fletcher. Seems he was so happy to find your good wife that day he took little notice. Ah yes, it was your man Barnes who was the most helpful. Good man that, recalled Fletcher as slim and sunbrowned, wearing a sheepskin jacket. Said he was what a person would call handsome. Strong jaw line, light brown hair, penetrating gaze. Astride a grey stallion. Now, it's not as good as having seen him myself, but it is the first description I've ever had of the devil, for, would you believe it, the old convict files could not be found. Typical,' he finished.

John Stuart looked thoughtful. 'I see it is a slow and steady game you play. I doubt that I could be so patient.'

It was later that night before Eve heard about the ride in any detail. She had been eager to know what had happened but did not dare ask John Stuart. After dinner, she managed to catch David Elrington lingering on the terrace when the other men had gone in to play billiards. He was enthusiastic when she asked him if they had learned anything from their ride.

'Yes, a great deal, madam. Although we found nothing tangible, Sir Rutherford has a suspicion that Alan Fletcher's hideout may be in the hills beyond your border somewhere. He calls it a start. You see, other gangs of bushrangers roam the territory and stay in nomadic fashion with those who will have them, which makes them easier to trace, I am happy to say. Whereas this Fletcher keeps himself to himself, and his men the same, so any clue to his hideout is most significant.'

'But how can it be a clue if you found nothing?'

'It is our opinion that he was hunting for food the day he found you. Our leader believes, that is, we believe, the outlaw was probably only a few hours' ride from his hideout when he came across you. Sir Rutherford says it is really thanks to you, madam, we know these things.'

'Oh dear!' Eve said.

The young man looked strangely at her. 'I beg your pardon?'

She coughed. 'I mean oh dear it all seems so dangerous.'

'That's true,' replied David Elrington with an eager expression. 'But that's the exciting part. And thanks to Tommy Barnes, one of your foremen, we have a fairly reasonable description of Fletcher.'

Eve was feeling cold again. 'What? When did Barnes see . . . the bushranger?'

'When they found you in the bush; he was in Mr Larmer's party.'

'I see,' she was trying to sound impartial, 'that is interesting. Would you excuse me? I think I shall get some air.'

'Certainly, Mrs Wakeman. Lovely chatting to you, madam.'

It was a hot, still night and low clouds hung sluggishly in the dark sky, yet Eve clasped her arms round her body and shivered. She was feeling fear again, and her lips were pressed together tightly. Her fingers tapped nervously against her body as she walked. Every sense told her this reaction was irrational. After all, Sir Rutherford only suspected where Alan Fletcher's hideout was. He did not *know* anything. But the description . . . oh dear God, it was all her fault that they had his description.

Then suddenly she stopped walking and the ever-present guilt rose again. Why am I thinking of Alan Fletcher? Why, when I pray so hard to forget him? My husband is a wonderful man, remarkable, respected, rich almost beyond my understanding. We are happy together, we have a wonderful marriage, we exult in each other. He loves me and I love him. I hate this feeling I have for the bushranger.

Her eyes lifted to the pale light of the billiard room and the figures that moved within.

My duty is to the man who has given me more than I ever dreamed of having, both materially and emotionally. I can fight against my thoughts. I have the desire to, and are not desire and will akin? Doesn't the inclination send us half upon our way? Ah God, that it did.

She leaned against a tree and sighed so deeply that a shudder ran through her. Then she gathered her skirts and returned slowly to the verandah.

The following day was cheerful. The men played cricket while the ladies basked in the sun watching. John Stuart was the outstanding bowler, taking five wickets for fifty. Eve felt a happy glow of pride in her husband's prowess and surprise at herself for the satisfaction she felt when Sir Rutherford was clean bowled for only two. She actually had to stop herself from smiling at him as he stamped from the field.

When the house party ended on Monday, 28 December, most of the guests departed before the hour of nine in the morning. Eve was so sorry for Roy as the young man looked wistfully at Daydee, who in haughty fashion gave him a brief goodbye.

Sir Rutherford and his assistant were the last to leave. They were travelling south to join their troopers in a camp on the Sydney road. Eve held John Stuart's hand as Sir Rutherford bent from the neck to say goodbye to her. Perhaps it was imagination that made her feel as if he were inspecting her closely.

'Goodbye, Mrs Wakeman, all the best, madam, for the coming year.'

'Thank you, Sir Rutherford, the compliments of the season to you.'

CHAPTER FOURTEEN

'She's beautiful and therefore to be woo'd,
She is a woman therefore to be won.'
Henry IV, Part I, William Shakespeare, 1564–1616.

Daydee awoke. It had been an exhilarating dream. She had been kissing John Stuart. The kiss lasted a long time and she murmured aloud and moved in her bed. She opened her eyes and sighed.

It was still dark. There was a cool breeze coming through the slightly open window and she pulled the blanket up round her shoulders. If only her dream had been real!

Damn Eve, damn Eve to hell! How she hated her! John Stuart could have been hers; would have been hers. She had come home from school in November of 1862 and he had just begun to notice her as a woman when he left on that cattle drive in March the following year. Then he had come home in April to tell them he was getting married! She had been so shocked. When she heard about it, she had felt so ill she had locked herself in her bedroom and cried and cried.

In the eighteen months since *she* had come here, the woman had ingratiated herself with all the Mayfield people. Her own stupid mother thought *she* was wonderful. Daydee was so sick of hearing 'how good', 'how kind', 'how thoughtful' Mrs Wakeman was. It made her want to vomit.

She looked at the black uprights of the bed posts and smiled wistfully, for there was still the odd time she did have John Stuart to herself, totally to herself. In recent months three or four times she had waylaid him on his way to the summerhouse to read his journals on a Sunday afternoon and he had allowed her to come and sit with him and read her own book. She pretended that they were married and that *she* was not at Mayfield at all, that *she* was not even alive!

The most terrible thing of all was that Father and Mr Ford had been communicating recently. They wanted her to become engaged to Roy. Well, she never would. Never. Hot tears ran down her cheeks. She had turned nineteen a month ago and she wanted excitement. She noticed how some of the hands watched her when

237

she went riding or was down at the stables. There was unveiled admiration in their eyes. Mr Watson's grooms stammered awkwardly whenever she spoke to them. Why couldn't John Stuart see how lovely she was?

Many of the men desired her, she was sure of that. What about that cheeky stockman about John Stuart's age? He had been sent up to the house to call her father out to one of the yards a couple of times. He was only a 'short-timer', as they called men put on to help out at busy times, but he had a way about him. He had looked straight at her with his impudent smile and said, 'You're a good-looking woman, Miss Daydee.' Of course she had given him one of her 'how dare you' looks and walked away. But she could not deny there was something about him; he was truly handsome and he actually reminded her of John Stuart. She had found out his name. Lake he was called, Nathaniel Lake.

She swung her legs down onto the floor and into her slippers, dragging the counterpane from the stool at the foot of the bed. Wrapping it round her shoulders, she made her way to the window. She looked out into a pre-dawn September morning. Her dark hair hung in waves down her back and her small pert face was smooth and fresh. Her lips were a cupid's bow of deep pink and her long eyelashes circled her eyes like a frame. As she rested her hands on the sill and looked out, her firm young body pushed her breasts up enticingly beneath her warm white nightdress. There was no doubt that the grooms would stammer if they saw her now!

From her window she could see the evenly planted windbreak of firs and beeches that lay along the side of the house. Through a gap in the trees to the south-west, her youthful vision made out the lights in the bunkhouses a mile away down the gentle slope. She stood for a time looking towards them.

While she watched, men were tumbling out of their bunks and making their way to the good smelling cookhouses where breakfast was already being laid. Early morning in the hands' quarters was a time of good-natured banter, and now at fifteen minutes past five in the morning, a long-time employee, Jason Fowler, was complaining loudly in one of the wash-houses. He lifted an empty bucket in the air. 'Damned if I can get these short-timers out o' bed. Methinks I'll be goin' and fillin' this bucket and douse me a few o' them.'

'I'm a short-timer, but I'm up, old man,' replied a handsome individual who looked up from a washbasin, his face dripping water.

'Sure ye be, Lake, but ye don't follow any pattern as I can notice. Never see'd a man who could drink as much as ye at night and be gettin' up smooth as silk at cocky's crow, as I note ye've done once more again.'

Lake laughed and returned his face to the water. He was very popular with the other men. He was always ready with a quip or a joke, and never moody. As Fowler said, he drank too much, he knew that, but it did not affect him. A long drink of water and five or so hours' sleep and he was as good as new.

This was the second time he had worked a spell on Mayfield. He had spent three months here in fifty-eight, six years before, on his way north from Adelaide.

He liked his way of life, no ties to anybody, and only working when the money ran out. Another thing, you didn't get caught by one woman this way! Spread yourself around them all, that was what to do. Well, yes, there had been a few 'ladies' he had entangled himself with for a time. And one he had lived with nigh on a year, down in Adelaide. She had been a looker right enough, but he didn't like town-dwelling and had moved on when the time was right.

The problem at Mayfield was the lack of good-looking women. The only available girls were the dairy maids and those up in Mayfield House; all the others in the cottages were married. They didn't like anything going on that was not 'proper' here. Stemmed from the self-righteous Mr John Stuart Wakeman, no doubt. Now everybody said his wife was a beauty. Wonder what a woman would have to be like to catch old Wakeman. She'd have to be pretty good to beat some of his women.

If none of the girls here gave him any loving, well there was always the publican's daughter in Cowra. On his way here, she had been real nice to him, Elizabeth Jenks had. Bit of a slut, and thick ankles, but nice eyes, and he had always been a one for eyes. Yes, he could put up with the ride into Cowra on his day off if none of the Mayfield girls gave him what he wanted.

Nathaniel Lake began this day much the same as all the others, with a bowl of porridge, thick buttered toast and bacon, and a laugh. Then he and fifteen other stockmen were sent over to the yards southeast of the river to begin branding the calves that had already issued from the huge spring calving now taking place. There were hundreds of 'ready' cattle, about to calve. Teams of men had been tending the mothers night and day for the last week. It was tedious work that left the men blood-soiled and tired. Lake was pleased he had the branding, he preferred that.

During the afternoon rest when the billy was boiled and the men took a short respite from their back-breaking work, Lake and two companions wandered down and sat on the river bank. They were joking and Lake slapped his friend Larry Cadee on the shoulder. 'You know, Cadee old son, these Herefords remind me of some women I knew on the goldfields at Sovereign Hill near Ballarat.'

'Why's that, Lakey?'

'Well, they stand five feet high, got thirty-two teeth, they're stupid and take nine months to bear a young 'un.'

This they found very amusing.

'Ye be a wag and no mistake, Lake,' said Tillert, another short-timer.

'And you're a poet and don't know it,' retorted Lake which produced more laughter.

The Lachlan River was not wide at this point and there was a natural ford which joined this side to the home pastures on the other bank. A few minutes passed and then riders appeared in the distance through the trees and made their way to the ford.

'Here comes Mr Wakeman,' said Tillert.

'And Mr Larmer,' spoke up Cadee.

'Yes, and that looks like her, Mrs Wakeman, with them.' Tillert pointed with his mug. 'Fancy gettin' a visit from the mistress. Wanted to see the wee lambs, I'll be bound.'

The men watched the riders come to the ford and begin to cross. In silence, they observed the group ride by. Joe waved a greeting to the three men as he passed.

'Well, what d'ya think o' the mistress, Lake? Mrs Eve Wakeman, that's her. A real beauty, ain't she?' asked Tillert turning towards Lake and striking him playfully on the arm.

Lake did not speak.

'What's up, Lakey boy? Struck dumb by the lady fair, are ya?'

'Hey, Lake, ye be turnin' white as a ghost,' said Cadee.

Lake made a strange strangled sort of sound and then coughed.

'Are ya all right, Lakey?' inquired Tillert. 'Ya do look a bit peculiar an' all.'

Lake took a couple of deep breaths and stood up. Finally, he spoke. 'Yes, I do feel slightly odd. Must have eaten my luncheon too quickly, a bit of indigestion most probably.'

Cadee nodded. 'I bin tellin' ya that ya eat too fast.'

Just then they heard the call to resume work.

'Come on,' Lake said turning from his mates. 'I'm all right. It'll take more than eating quickly to stop old Lakey. Here, let me tell you a joke I heard on the Yuralga goldfields . . .'

Eve was fascinated by the calving. John Stuart had preferred her not to ride down among the cows, so she remained sitting on a tree stump on a knoll some seventy yards away. Even at this distance she could see the pain and the blood of birth, and hear their plaintive bellows in the air. They were two pure-bred herds of beef cattle, the black, compact Aberdeen-Angus and the red and white, low-set Hereford. There had been two other calvings since she had come to Mayfield but this was the first time John Stuart had allowed her to come. Before when she had asked, he had said, 'It's no place for a woman.' Though why it was no place for a woman, when women had been giving birth since the world began, she could not fathom.

Where there were cattle there were flies, and she spent much of the time waving her hand across in front of her face and hitting at them as they came to rest on her. When one bit her on the arm, she struck out at it saying, 'Go to blazes, damn you.' Then she laughed, her brown eyes twinkling with mirth, for she had not said such a thing for years.

Over to the right, away from the calving, she could see the branding taking place. The calves that were healthy and strong were being marked and then returned to their mothers, before being loosed to graze.

When John Stuart returned up the hill in long strides, he was alone.

'Isn't Joe coming?' Eve asked.

'No, he'll remain awhile.'

As they rode away, one man looked up from where he squatted holding a branding iron over the fire. His body was tense with excitement. He had looked up to where Eve waited on the mound a hundred times in the past hour, and now he regarded her departure. 'Well I'll be damned!' he said to himself. 'Imagine my finding "her" again. And she's set herself up as the mistress of Mayfield, nothing less. Calling herself Eve, eh? God, fancy that!' He took his iron from the fire and repeated half-aloud, 'Well, I'll be damned!'

'What was that, Lakey?' asked Larry Cadee who held the calf beside him.

Lake's face twisted into a self-indulgent smile. 'Nothing, mate, nothing at all.'

It was only four days before the cattle drive to Penrith, over one hundred and fifty miles away by road, was to begin.

Eve had risen early to breakfast with John Stuart. She wanted to spend as much time as she could with him until he left on the drive, for he was not coming straight home afterwards. He and Joe were continuing on to Sydney, Melbourne and Adelaide. The barrister Robert Robinson-Pike was accompanying them for he had set up some land deals in the towns of Melbourne and Adelaide.

John Stuart was a man of vision as his father had been, and even though his love was the open land and the unbridled spaces, he knew too that the commercial future lay in the expanding metropolitan areas. He and Joe would journey by sea and on the new railways between some of the towns, taking them away from Mayfield for perhaps six weeks.

Eve came to the breakfast room just as John Stuart folded a newspaper and placed it on the table beside his latest scientific journal. He pointed to the paper as she sat down. 'There has been a great battle in Pennsylvania at a place called Gettysburg. It was a decisive defeat for the south, it seems, and may even be a turning point in the war that divides your country.'

'I must read it. When was the battle?'

'It lasted three days from the first of July. The southerners fought gamely but collapsed. Your northern blood should be pleased at that, my dear.'

'No, John Stuart. I'll be glad when my homeland is no longer at war with itself. There are even families divided, it's awful.'

Her husband's expression was sympathetic.

'Perhaps it will be over soon. Let us hope so. Lincoln appears to know what he's doing and since he issued that Emancipation Proclamation in January, the north seems to fight to free slaves as much as to preserve the union. Still, you read it for yourself, my darling.' And he handed her the paper.

After breakfast she did read the long article and it left her heart heavy for her countrymen. Her thoughts were consistently of the tragic war all morning as she went about her household chores. After lunch, she went down to the hospital. All was quiet there and Betty was sewing cloth arm-slings for broken bones. She did an hour's work on the latest medical inventory before taking her daily walk. Since the incident the year before, when little Laura Dale had almost drowned, John Stuart preferred Eve to have a companion on her walks and Stephanie or Thelma often accompanied her; but the girl did not enjoy the long walks so Eve did not always take her, and today Thelma was in Cowra, so she walked alone.

She took a path that followed the meandering course of the Lachlan and soon she was in a secluded part of the valley where the first blossoms of native heath were in bloom. As she often did, she gathered some of the clusters of the red, bell-like blooms, using the small silver scissors that dangled on a ribbon from her waistband.

As she bent to cut the stems, her mind played the trick that it often did, and flashing to her thoughts came the day she had sat with the bushranger. Somehow she did not feel as uncomfortable with his memory out of doors. She did not have so much of the sickening guilt out here. For a few minutes she stood holding the bunch of heath and remembering. So much had happened to the bushrangers this past year and she read the newspapers avidly for any account of them. She knew all the well-known names: Ben Hall, Johnny Gilbert, Dan Morgan, Old Joe Daily, Lefty Dawson, Jake Crane. Lately, a new one had appeared, a man from Queensland, James Alpin McPherson. There had been some sort of a duel between him and Sir Frederick Pottinger, the police inspector under Sir Rutherford. Eve could not help smiling when she read that. Sir Rutherford would have been livid.

Mayfield had seen two brief visits from the detective policeman in the past six months. He brought the news of the notorious Frank Gardiner's capture at Apis Creek in Queensland. Sir Rutherford had always maintained that Gardiner had fled to Queensland. The bushranger had been jailed for thirty-two years in July. Among the almost weekly tales of the outlaws, she lived in fear of hearing of Alan Fletcher's capture. There had been a bank hold-up in Goulburn in August, which at first had been blamed on Alan Fletcher, but later it was found to be the work of Flash Johnny Gilbert. Gilbert and Johnny O'Meally had been the first men ever to rob a bank in Australia, a year ago in Carcoar.

Then earlier this month had come definite news of the Fletcher band. The Government gold diggings at Theresa Town had been their quarry. The whole town had been held up and Government gold taken, and a Chinese thief set free. It was all the more notable for Sir Rutherford Blake had been there; he was held prisoner along with his troopers. All the gossip said he was made to look a fool. There had been no injury, except to Sir Rutherford's pride, she guessed, and a new reward of a thousand pounds had been posted for Alan Fletcher.

The world was indeed a very mess as Clare had so often said. Her home country was at war with itself, men killing each other, sacking cities and pillaging; and here in her adopted home men used force and disagreed and were given to hatred of their fellow man just the same.

She sighed. Men! No doubt it would be a better world if women ran it! She had proved in her own life that she could be self-reliant and plucky; a lot of women she had known could have been leaders, even Clare if she had been given the chance. But Clare lay in a graveyard Eve had never seen. She, Eve, was the lucky one. She had so much, not least John Stuart, a man so worthy, so upright and moral. She must be more mindful of him, more contrite, stop thinking of other things. How many times a day did she say this? Life was so difficult!

She turned to continue on her way. She had been standing so still in reverie that a platypus had come up behind her out of its burrow in the riverbank to rest in the warm grass. The water on its ebony, mole-like fur glistened in the afternoon sun as his webbed front claws opened and closed. When Eve turned, the movement of her skirts brought him to life and in seconds he was gliding swiftly beneath the water.

She branched off the river path and headed up the wooded hill to a spot where she looked back. She always did this, it was such a pretty view through the trees to the Lachlan.

What she saw pushed all thoughts from her mind.

Not sixty yards away, down through the trees, she saw a man and a woman standing close together, his arms encircling her waist. The woman was Daydee. The man pushed back her dark hair with his hand. He was much taller than the diminutive girl. Eve could not make out his features but she could see he was a stockman and had a shock of dark hair falling to his collar. He was the general size and shape of John Stuart. As she watched, he bent forward and kissed Daydee on the mouth, lifting her from her feet into his embrace. Then he put her down and they walked away, hand in hand.

Eve turned on her heel and hurried along the path.

The two people, oblivious of her presence, strolled along by the river shallows.

'Well, you are the cheeky one,' said Daydee. 'When did I give you permission to do that?'

'Ah, permission now, eh? Is that what I have to ask for?'

He stopped and, turning to her, took her hand and bent over it, saying in mock servility, 'Dear Miss Larmer, would you be so kind as to lend your lips to a passing wayfarer, as he has never seen any as beautiful as yours in his whole life.' Then he looked up at her and winked.

She began to laugh, 'Oh, Nathaniel Lake, you are the joker.'

He stood straight and putting his hand over his heart said, 'Yes, ma'am, I cannot lie, I am. But I'm serious about your lips,' and taking her again by the waist pulled her to him.

After the kiss, she moved away. 'How could you be sure I would meet you here today?'

'I couldn't be,' he answered, leaning back on a rock and looking her up and down, 'but it's a chance I had to take. I'll bet there are a few boys back at the quarters who would give a week's pay to be here in my place.'

Then Daydee turned sharply back towards him, fear in her eyes. 'You won't say anything, will you? You won't tell anyone about this?'

This amused him. 'Will you?' he countered.

'No, of course not.'

'Then neither shall I. Come.' He grasped her hand and gently pulled her over to their tethered horses. From the back of his animal's saddle he took a rolled blanket and, placing it on a grassy spot secluded in the undergrowth, he motioned for her to sit. They spent half an hour on the blanket and when the time came for Daydee to leave, he persuaded her to meet him again the following afternoon.

And so she did. She lied to get away as she had done the previous day. Down to Larmer's Crossing and over the bridge she galloped, past the orchards, round the river paddocks and along the cliff paths that ran high above the river. She rode swiftly, descending to the low path through the scrub and finally emerging at a shallow part of the Lachlan, surrounded by thick bush. Here she forded the river and found him waiting.

He kissed her many times and between the kisses he asked her questions about Mayfield House. She understood his interest, for the cattle and stockmen were never allowed past the great hedge boundary enclosing the big house and the park, unless it was an extraordinary occasion.

The wetness of his tongue thrilled her. He ran it back and forth across her teeth and searched her mouth. The only thing she did not care for was when he asked her to drink some brandy from the flask he carried. It had made her feel peculiar. But when he saw she did not like it, he brought fresh water from the river in his water bag. After she had drunk some of that and eaten an apple, she felt better.

The next day, she arrived before him. She sat on a small rock on the edge of the river waiting. She certainly found this Nathaniel Lake diverting. He was the first man she had ever agreed to meet and it was exciting. At last there was something in her boring life that was exciting.

She liked his talk and the way he made her laugh. Physically, he reminded her of John Stuart; she thought them roughly the same age. They were both big men, but long and slender too and both very handsome with dark eyes and moustaches. She liked the way Nathaniel's moustache felt on her mouth. She pretended he was John Stuart. Suddenly she felt a terrible longing for John Stuart and she clasped herself tightly round the waist as she bent forward on the rock.

Then she heard the sound of an approaching horse on the far side of the shallows. She sat up straight and tossed her hair back over her shoulder. There was no doubt this sort of thing was amusing. She could learn from 'Lakey', as he referred to himself. But she would not go too far. Oh no, she was not silly! She just needed to have some experience. She needed experience for John Stuart.

He placed the blanket down as he had the last two days and they sat on it as usual. He did not have the brandy flask today and his mouth tasted fresh and wonderful. She was lying in his arms and he was playing with the ribbon on her dress when he said, 'I'll not be able to come tomorrow.'

Daydee made a sound of disappointment. 'Is it because of the cattle drive?'

'Yes, it starts the day after tomorrow and some of us will be on duty with the herd all night. The following day, now that'll be different. We've already been told that once the drive begins at seven o'clock, those of us who worked the night shift will have the day off.' He kissed the tip of her nose. 'We can see each other a lot of that day for certain.'

'How do you know you'll be one of the men who has the day off?'

He laughed and kissed her on the earlobe, whispering, 'Lakey will make certain of it, m'dear.'

She put her arms up round his neck and a tiny frown creased her brow, 'Oh, darn it,' she said. 'That will be Monday and I have two hours with Mrs Cadman who comes out from Cowra to give me piano lessons. She stays to lunch, the old crone. It'll be well after two o'clock before I can get away.'

'Never mind, I'll be here,' he replied. 'There's plenty of the day left after the hour of two. Where are you supposed to be now, by the way?'

She smiled at him. 'Why, that is the best thing about having one's own horse. It has to be exercised, you know.'

'Clever girl,' he said, and he kissed her again, their firm bodies pressed together. She let him undo the ribbons on her bodice and camisole to feel her breasts as he had done the previous day, and today she did not stop him when he pushed back the material and covered her nipples with his mouth. His hot wet tongue aroused all sorts of sensual feelings in her.

The final year at school, some of the girls had spoken about love and loving. It was always at night. They would gather on one of the beds and whisper about it. Daydee remembered how one girl's mother had said a man must never be allowed to touch a woman's breast, even with his hand; it was profane. Well, if this was profanity, Daydee liked irreverence. But later, when his hand strayed beneath the skirt of her riding habit, she sat up straight saying, 'No, Nathaniel.'

'Oh, come on, love,' he whispered holding her close, his voice thick with passion. 'Come on.'

'No,' she said again and pulled away from his embrace.

'All right, all right. I understand. But come on, girl, give old Lakey a kiss, if nothing else.' He pulled such a comic face of entreaty that when he came across the rug to her, she kissed him as he asked.

Later, he lay back with his hands behind his head and asked her more about Mayfield House. 'So, it was built by Mr Wakeman's father, was it?'

'Yes, Sir Arthur, he began with one wing, which now contains the kitchens, sculleries and pantries.'

'And that's the side nearest your house, is it?'

'Yes, that's right. But why is Mayfield House so interesting to you?'

His face creased showing the tiny dimple in his left cheek. 'Well, love, to be honest, I was an architectural student before I took to this easy life, and that place is the finest example of design I have ever seen anywhere.' He took a deep breath and rolled on his side to regard her. 'I suppose the master and mistress live above the kitchens, eh?'

'Oh, Nathaniel, are you ever serious?'

'About you, yes.' He leaned towards her. 'So, tell me then, what part of the house is theirs?'

'The wing furthest from our house on the far side. It was added at the time Sir Arthur was dying. I was only little, but I remember it.'

'To me, it's like a U with a tail. The tail is their wing, eh?'

'Yes, that's right, I suppose. There's the walled garden all along to the front of the house. Aunt Eve uses the garden as hers, it's private.'

Lake did not miss the spite in the words 'Aunt Eve'.

'Don't you like her?'

'Who?'

'Come on, Daydee, you cannot fool old Lakey. Your Aunt Eve.'

He saw the anger rise in her eyes and she gave the habitual toss of her head. 'No, I don't like her. It's different since she came.'

'It would be.'

'How do you know?'

'Let's just say I do,' he replied enigmatically. 'Now tell me, they say she's from Bathurst. Is that right?'

Daydee did not want to talk about Eve, her answer was reluctant. 'Mmm . . . she was a music teacher there.'

Lake smiled, remembering how he had only heard her play a few times in public houses. But how she could play! Her fingers had darn well skimmed across the keys. She had made the thing talk.

'And this was only last year, the boys tell me. They say the master met and married her all in about a month.'

Daydee's mouth turned down in distaste. 'Yes, it's true. He met her at Easter time and married her five weeks later. And, if you don't mind, Nathaniel, I did not come here to talk about *her*.'

His arm went out round her and he pulled her to him. 'No, and nor did I.' He kissed her again, long and hard, fondling her breasts with his right hand. His mouth was moving down to her nipples again when she broke from him and stood.

'It's getting late, I must return.'

He drew the back of his hand across his eyes in disappointment before he clasped his knees and sat regarding her as she smoothed her riding habit. While she tied the bow on her bodice, he asked, 'And so, my pretty Daydee, I'll see you here the day after tomorrow at two o'clock, eh?'

'It will probably be later than two o'clock, but I will come.'

'Make a good excuse so that you can stay a few hours.'

'What will I say?' she asked him, sounding suddenly very childlike.

He looked closely at her. So youthful and innocent did she appear standing there in the gentle light of the dying afternoon that he almost told her not to come at all. Instead he heard himself saying, 'Ah, Daydee love, I have no doubt you will think of something.'

She nodded. There was one good thing, her father would be gone on the cattle drive and she would only have her mother to contend with.

When she had ridden away, Lake mounted his horse and crossed the Lachlan deep in thought. He was playing a reckless game, he knew that. If any one in authority here knew he was seeing Daydee Larmer, he would be thrown off the property and in all likelihood never get a job on any station or farm in the colony again. But hadn't he taken risks before?

Tomorrow, the cattle drive would begin. Old Wakeman was leading the drive again as he always did, they said. It was one of the things his men admired about him. God! If it hadn't given him a start when he saw Wakeman's wife ride by last week. She had not noticed him, he was sure of that. She had been looking straight ahead, so high and mighty too. Sitting tall in the saddle with the same straight back he recalled so well. And still as beautiful as she had been – what was it exactly? Five? Six years ago? Eighteen fifty-seven? Yes, that was it, eighteen fifty-seven. It was not so surprising really to see her married to Wakeman. She had multifacets to her character, that one! And wouldn't she be fascinated to know he was here, working on Mayfield? Somehow, he might just have to let her know.

God, weren't women amazing?

He smiled broadly as he rode along the bank of the Lachlan in the dying day.

CHAPTER FIFTEEN

'And lovelier things have mercy shown
To every failing but their own;
And every woe a tear can claim,
Except an erring sister's shame.'
'The Giaour', George Gordon Noel, Lord Byron, 1788–1824.

It was the night before the cattle drive was to take place. Darkness had fallen when John Stuart returned to the house and his evening meal.

Eve had been a little tired the last day or two, sometimes the monthly change in her system affected her that way. So when John Stuart stood from the table to return into the night and make a final check on the herd, he simply said, 'You go to bed, dearest, don't wait for me. I shan't be late.' He smiled at her, adding, 'I must be up before dawn, anyway.'

But Eve surprised him by answering, 'It's a perfect spring night and I feel much better. I would like to come with you.'

Her husband looked thoughtful. 'All right, I'll be there only briefly, for Joe has everything under control, I'm certain. But are you sure you feel able to take the ride? It's over two miles to the herd.'

'Yes, John Stuart, I would love to come.'

He sounded pleased. 'In that case, I'll take the phaeton, the road is good enough over to the holding yards.'

Half an hour later, Eve and John Stuart sat in the light carriage on the drive at the front of Mayfield House. Deke Edwards held the reins in front and Jack Hennessy and Tommy Barnes were mounted on horses beside them. It was a clear sky and two large lanterns attached to either side of the carriage would give plenty of light to see their way. Nevertheless, Jack Hennessy insisted on riding in front. 'I've got good night sight, Mr Wakeman, sir.'

Out of Mayfield Park they went, round by the Larmers' front door and down across the incline of the valley. Eve and John Stuart were silent for the first part of the ride. Her hand lay in his and every now and then he would squeeze it gently. There was one moment when he leaned towards her and whispered, 'I could be away as long as six or seven weeks in all and I shall miss you every day.'

She turned to him and kissed his cheek. She heard him say, 'I love you, Evvy.' He had never called her that before. A tingle of surprise ran through her, for it was Father's pet name for her.

'Yes, John Stuart,' she replied in a voice so quiet he bent his head to hear her, 'I love you, too.'

It was a balmy night, much warmer than the previous September, there was no wind and spring was in the air. The stars shone above and there was a soft stirring in the trees as they passed. There was something perfect about this ride, as if the night were unblemished and their peace with one another unqualified. She felt there was no intolerance or possessiveness in the man beside her now, he was the essential John Stuart, the kind and generous one, the noble one, the one she loved with all her heart. He moved in the seat and turned to her, and as his mouth came down on hers, she kissed him and only him; there was no ghost of Alan Fletcher anywhere in the night around her. It was a long, loving kiss and afterwards she laid her head on his shoulder and was completely content. How she wished he did not have to go away, especially for such a long time. She would miss him awfully.

'Talk to me, John Stuart,' she said quietly. 'Tell me more about your journey, about the land you will buy and the places you will go.'

John Stuart, too, felt the complete union between them and did as he was asked. Eve listened carefully to him, questioned him and attended his replies. There were moments when they laughed softly together, murmured intimate things, and all the journey he had his arms round her and three times more his mouth found hers before they reached the herd.

Over the brow of a hill, they saw the glowing dots that were the fires of the herdsmen. Eve wondered how seven hundred cattle could be so quiet. It was not until they were close that the muffled, plaintive bellows drifted to them.

'Why is it that so many steers make such little noise?' she asked.

'Cattle usually settle down with the sun,' her husband explained, 'and even though they are gathered here in a great number, they will be relatively peaceful until the morning light. Then, my darling, it will be a different matter.'

As they approached, it was hard to make out the individual cattle, but Eve could distinguish the mass of bodies ringed by the fires of the men who watched them. When they left the road and came closer, she could discern the steers were held inside a large fenced area somewhere near one hundred and fifty yards square. Inside were other fences separating them into four groups. Some lay, others stood, and a few milled in circles amid their brethren. There had been grass here during the day when they had been mustered, but by tomorrow morning when they moved out it would have vanished, trampled by the two thousand eight hundred hooves.

They halted about twenty yards from one of the fires near a huge, silky-bark gum and John Stuart alighted. As Deke tethered the phaeton's two horses to a small stringy-bark sapling, John Stuart leaned back into the carriage to Eve. 'You wait here, darling.'

'But I should like to accompany you.' She really wanted to be with him tonight, every minute.

His slanted smile formed on his mouth. 'Evelyn . . .' In the faint light she could see his amusement. 'You "cannot" come down among the stockmen, I really can't agree to that. Edwards will stay with you.'

She watched him stride across to the fire followed by Jack Hennessy and Tommy Barnes. The six or seven stockmen there stood respectfully as he arrived. He spoke briefly to them and then moved on to another fire.

A few minutes passed. Deke Edwards was not a voluble individual and when she asked him the occasional question, he answered monosyllabically. Soon she dropped into silence. She could feel the eyes of the men round the camp fire looking up at her. There was a wealth of difference between a man and a woman in this world, and a chasm between 'Mrs Wakeman' and the stockmen. She climbed down from the carriage.

'Are you all right, Mrs Wakeman, ma'am?' called Deke Edwards promptly.

'Perfectly, thanks, Mr Edwards. I'm just going a few short yards to look at the stars.'

When she was out of the radiance of the carriage lamps, she turned and looked back towards the men and their camp fire. One man stood slowly up. He moved almost languidly, his back towards her. There was something familiar about him. He bent and spoke to his companions before straightening his long body again and detaching himself from the group. He moved outside the rim of light and did not turn round. Perhaps he was one of the stockmen she saw regularly. But somehow she understood it was not that; he was familiar for another reason. Then he was hidden in the darkness beyond the firelight.

There was a breeze drifting gently across the valley past her towards the cattle and she fancied she could smell the sweet scent of the yellow box and the faint, tangy smell of the tee tree. She smiled to herself; she was starting to learn about Mayfield and the bush, and that gratified her.

A few minutes later she heard John Stuart calling goodnight to the men at the fireside. When she joined him and the others at the phaeton, he hugged her. 'See, darling, I wasn't long.'

As he helped her up into the vehicle, she was observed by the ring of stockmen round the flames. The one who stood outside the light of the fire watched her the closest.

'Now, I wonder if you noticed me, tonight, "Mrs Wakeman", my love?' Lake said softly to himself as he lit a cheroot. God she was a goodlooking woman. Wouldn't he love to lie with her again? Wakeman, the lucky bastard . . . if only . . . but there was no chance of that; he'd have to content himself with little Daydee. He sighed and drew deeply on his cheroot.

On Monday, 12 September, the morning of the cattle drive, it was a beautiful sight as the daylight broke over Mayfield. The colours were exceptional. The whole valley was awash with the tints of rose and gold. A single cloud hung in a vermilion streak along the horizon and the trees behind Mayfield House were lit like sharp yellow brushstrokes on the hillside; the house itself, usually a clean white glow, shone golden.

John Stuart and Eve came though the front door just as their horses were being brought to the steps. Before Eve could mount, her husband took her by the hand and walked her south-east across the carriage drive over the wide lawn, still damp with dew, through a thick screen of tall Norfolk pines and native shrubs to the summerhouse nestling by a trellis covered with climbing rose.

The sun was higher now and the yellow glow that had bathed the house and its surroundings had turned to a vivid light.

The summerhouse was John Stuart's favourite spot; he read his scientific journals and the latest copy of the London *Times* here, and it was a natural place to say goodbye to his wife. He turned to her and kissed her, holding her tightly to him. 'I hate to leave you, Eve; the other drives were soon over, this is not the same. I shall be away many weeks. Take care, my love.'

Then he held her from him at arm's length and looked into her eyes. He seemed to have difficulty starting to speak again and when he did, he spoke slowly. 'It is hard for a man to say this, but I loved my father above all things, Evelyn, and when he died, well . . . I know I love Joe, for he has been the constant in my life, but it is not the same as you. Someone to love of my very own, my wife. You are special, you are virtuous. Different from so many others.' The tone of his last sentence grew slightly hard.

His words made her sad, so very sad. A feeling of shame shot

253

through her for the moments when she had not been able to be honest with him. She took a deep breath and answered gently, 'Do not make a saint of me, my dearest, I am but a woman.'

'You are without parallel,' was his reply.

Standing there looking up into his face, a small shiver ran through her. She removed her eyes from his. Then, to her surprise, he took a small velvet box from his coat pocket.

'This is for your birthday. I am sorry I will not be here to spend it with you.'

'Oh, John Stuart, you are always so generous.'

He spoke softly. 'I like to be, my Evvy.'

The box had a small silver catch at the side which she opened. Inside lay a gold chain and pendant. The links of the chain were heart-shaped and the pendant was a large gold heart covered entirely with tiny diamonds and dark red rubies. The rubies spelled out the words: *'EVE, I'LL ALWAYS LOVE YOU'*. She had never seen anything so beautiful. She was speechless. She looked from the sparkling heart to John Stuart's face and down to the heart again. 'Why, I . . . I . . .'

'Don't you like it?'

She found her voice. 'Like it? It is . . . magnificent. I have never seen anything so perfect, darling. Thank you, thank you.'

He turned her and clipped it round her neck. She felt the cool touch of the metal on her skin, then his hands on her shoulders as he brought her back to face him. From inside his coat he took a small hand mirror. She looked at the jewellery lying on her skin, gleaming.

'Why do you always spoil me so?'

'Because, my Evvy, I want to, and you must let me, for you are my pure love and perfect and thus must wear perfect things.' He smiled a quiet smile, a possessive smile.

The sickness of guilt rose in her again. She wanted to cry, 'No! Please don't say these things, you make me feel so guilty. I am culpable of digressions from the truth. I am wicked because of my thoughts of Alan Fletcher. I am not sinless and spotlessly pure like you say. I have hidden my sister's experience from you out of fear. I am just me. God, that you would love me as myself!' But instead, she smiled. It was a sad smile but John Stuart did not see the sadness. He smiled happily back at her and then drew her arm through his and they left the summerhouse.

When they reached the herd, it seemed that all of Mayfield was there.

This was only the third drive Eve had witnessed and each time she marvelled at the pride the people of Mayfield took in such things. All around were men coming together and chatting and passing on, calling out to their mates and gesturing to one another over the incessant noise of the herd. On the fallen needles beneath a clump of tall casuarinas gathered many of the household who had been brought over in a number of drays. Of the thirty stockmen going on the drive, most were already in the saddle but there seemed well over a hundred others to see them off. If there had been acrobats and coloured stalls, Eve would have taken it for a fair.

A little distance beyond the bustle of activity, sitting in a chaise on a rise covered with long grass, was Thelma. She saw Eve riding up the incline towards her and she waved and beckoned her younger friend.

'Good morning, Thelma, there is always something thrilling about it, isn't there?'

Thelma nodded. 'Always, my dear. I have watched them leave from this spot for nigh on thirty years.' She laughed. 'It's above the dust, that is why I chose it.'

'You must have seen the size of the herds grow immensely,' Eve remarked as she dismounted and tied her horse to the back of the chaise.

'Not just the herds, dear. In the early days when I used to have John Stuart here beside me watching Joe and Mr Arthur leave, we were the only ones to wave goodbye.'

Eve laughed. 'What a difference.'

They spoke loudly for the bellowing steers almost deafened them. Eve thought the noise significantly like a protest, as if the cattle knew somehow what their destination represented. They moved and jostled each other and their heads seemed to be in constant collision with the backs and sides of their companions. They were massive animals, all finished steers, solidly fat with brisket full and muscle firm down either sides of their tails.

Eve climbed up beside Thelma just as the gates were pulled back and the cattle issued forth in a rumbling, undulating motion.

John Stuart and Joe galloped over to say their final farewells. There was a slight flush of enjoyment already in her husband's face. It was plain he was stimulated by the scene around him. He bent over from his mount, his mouth twisting into his characteristically slanting smile. He looked wonderfully handsome this morning and her heart-beat accelerated as she looked up at him.

'Goodbye, darling, keep Mayfield beautiful for me.'

'Goodbye, darling,' she answered. 'I will.'

Then he leaned over to her and brushed her mouth with his lips. Then he took her left hand and, turning it over, kissed the palm. As his lips touched her she had the most unnerving sensation. She felt as if she were losing him. Last night had been so wonderful, why did he have to leave now? She wanted to stop him, to beg him not to go. There seemed to be a weight on her shoulders. She felt horribly strange. As he lifted his face from her palm, she raised her right hand to touch his cheek longingly. He smiled his engaging smile once again and then moved his horse round the carriage to Thelma.

She watched him, seeing him distinctly, with a heightened clarity: his perfect features, his dark hair under the hat, his olive skin and his irresistible smile, the sunbrowned part of him where his shirt opened at the neck, the long fingers with the oval fingernails, the gold buckle of his belt peeping from under his leather waistcoat, his polished brown boots. And then for a second he changed. The clarity was gone. He was without definition. She was staring at him . . . and imagining Alan Fletcher. John Stuart's face was Alan's face, his body Alan's body. He sat there on the horse on the other side of the chaise bending towards her friend Thelma.

Eve gave a startled sound, but with the perpetual noise everywhere it went unheard. She closed her eyes and shook her head and refocused, and now it was her husband she saw. The figure was John Stuart. She saw him take Thelma's hand. She heard him say, 'Goodbye, Thelma, take care of my darling Evvy,' and he raised her hand to his lips and kissed it briefly.

The older woman's eyes filled with tears, but none of those near her saw, for her husband and John Stuart had already turned and ridden away, and Eve, in the seat beside her, was consumed by the images of the two men in her mind. Eve did not see John Stuart and Joe stop in front of the groups of Mayfield staff and call goodbye to a resounding cheer that could just be heard over the dissenting bellow of the steers, and she did not see them ride back to the moving herd. She sat staring until Thelma came out of her own reverie and said, 'It's a rare sight to see, isn't it?'

'Yes,' Eve replied coming back to the present, 'that it is.'

It took the cattle a long time to disappear along the valley. So great were their numbers that they spilled over the sides of the narrow road, up the banks and down the gullies, a sea of black, russet and white, surrounded by the mounted cattlemen keeping them in loose formation. Finally, the encompassing din had gone, and all that could be seen was a great cloud of dust in the distance representing the men and animals. The onlookers began to withdraw.

In the distance, Eve saw Daydee riding round the fences. The girl had remained on the far side of the herd all morning for she had no wish to be near her mother or Eve, particularly Eve. When she had said her parting words to her father and John Stuart, they had hugged her and she had clung to them both a long time as she always did. John Stuart had kissed the top of her head, and she had prayed that one day soon he would kiss her mouth.

She did not catch sight of Nathaniel Lake until half the cattle had departed. He was on the inner fence at the third of the yards, opening the gates for his section of steers to leave. He did not make any sign that he had seen her but he had. It had been harder for him to make out 'Mrs Wakeman' but finally he spotted her in the chaise on the far hillside.

As the cattle moved out along the valley, he and his comrades wandered round the outer fence and over to their tethered horses. They came closer to where Thelma's chaise was and now he could clearly see the two women seated in it. He wished she would look his way and see him. But never once did she turn in his direction. As he and his companions mounted their animals and rode away, he saw Daydee ride up to the chaise. Behind him, Eve and Daydee spoke briefly.

Eve began in friendly fashion. 'Did you enjoy the spectacle, Daydee?'

'It was like any other drive departing, no different.'

'Well now,' her mother broke in, 'back home to a cup of tea, Daydee, before Mrs Cadman arrives for your music lesson.'

'Yes, Mother, you needn't remind me. But afterwards I'm going to take my paints and a picnic and I'm going up to Chinaman's Hill to spend the entire afternoon.'

Eve smiled amicably. 'On your own?'

'Yes, on my own. I enjoy my own company.'

Eve nodded. 'But Chinaman's Hill is a long ride, Daydee, especially alone.'

The girl's expression was supercilious. 'You of all people shouldn't worry about that; after all, last year you rode so far that a bushranger had to bring you back.'

'Yes, Daydee, I know, but that was foolish of me and I am very careful now.'

'But you go for long walks on your own,' Daydee argued, 'I know you do.'

'Don't be so rude,' Thelma broke in. 'How dare you speak to Aunt Eve this way! It's dreadful.' She turned to Eve. 'I'm so sorry, dear, forgive her.'

Daydee sat sulkily on her horse, looking away.

'No, Thelma,' answered Eve tolerantly, 'Daydee's perfectly right. I set a bad example by riding out so far alone last year, and as for the walks, Daydee, they don't take me great distances.'

Daydee's reply was a sullen glance. Then she said, 'But Daddy agreed that I may go to Chinaman's Hill to paint. He gave me permission. It has the prettiest colours in the whole valley, and if he said I can, why should you stop me?'

Her mother eyed her sceptically.

'Then you should take one of the housemaids with you,' Eve said slowly.

'None of them can ride,' retorted Daydee quickly, 'and painting is a solitary occupation. I could not bear to have anyone with me. I always paint alone.'

'But you always paint in the park,' her mother countered, 'so the question does not arise.'

'But Father said I could do it. He said yes,' the girl persisted plaintively.

Thelma looked to Eve and sighed. 'Ah, Eve, forget all this. Let's go home and have a cup of tea.'

It was half past two when Daydee rode away alone in the direction of Chinaman's Hill. She had won. She passed at a trot through Mayfield Park and the east gate. Because it was so surprisingly warm this September, she wore only a light riding habit and soft leather boots. When she emerged from the trees at the appointed place, she was delighted to see him standing in the shallows of the Lachlan, his corduroy trousers rolled up to the knee. Of all things, he was fishing! He had a small branch of sapling with a line on the end. He stood there smoking a cheroot and grinning broadly, looking so deliciously odd and agreeable that she laughed and waved as she approached him.

'Well, love,' he called as she dismounted, 'I had to fill in the waiting time somehow. Look at this.' He pointed to a small boulder and there on top of it was a minute fish; the poor little chap was hardly six inches long. 'My reward for an hour of toil!' he laughed.

'Oh, Nathaniel, you are the one, you really are.'

'Come in, get your feet wet, it feels wonderful.'

She laughed again and sitting on the bank drew off her boots and stockings and entered the water. He held out his hand and she took it. The cool water on her feet and legs was delightful and she made small appreciative sounds of pleasure.

When Lake splashed her riding skirt, she took it off and laid it on the bank in the sun. Then she pushed her pantaloons up over her knees and went back into the river. They spent a merry half an hour in the water, fishing and laughing, sitting on rocks and dangling their legs in up to their knees. Finally, Lake said, 'Daydee, love, would you go in totally?'

258

She looked at him questioningly. 'What do you mean, totally?'

'Well, it's quite warm, isn't it? With all your clothes off.'

Her amazement showed in the soundless 'O' her mouth made.

'Will you?' he asked quietly.

'No, Nathaniel, I will not,' she answered, all imperious lady, and with that she left the river shallows and lifting her now dry skirt from the bank, put it on.

'Shit,' he said softly as he followed her.

They ate the picnic that had been prepared for Daydee and fought off the hungry flies. Afterwards, she painted some flowers and trees to take home with her and she did a sketch of him. It was not a bad likeness really. She gave him the picture and he folded it and put it in his saddle bag.

Later, they took a walk along the river bank and Lake carried the blanket. In a shaded glen between some candle-bark trees and mint bushes where the soft scent, similar to the mint herb, pervaded the air, they lay down in the undergrowth and he kissed and fondled her again. He was very aroused this afternoon and he grew angry when she would not let him go further than her breasts. He was getting tired of this 'child's play'. He moved away from her sullenly and sat with his back to her, looking down at the river.

It was her turn to coax. She ran her fingers playfully through the hairs on his arm. She kissed him on the ear and told him to give her some time to think about it.

'How long do you want?' he said moodily.

'I don't know, Nathaniel. It's something I must consider. I . . . I'm a little frightened,' she confessed.

He turned back to her and took her in his arms saying, 'Oh love, it's not easy for me to be with you like this. I want more of you. You are so beautiful, Daydee, and damn it I think I'm . . . in love with you.' He was looking straight into her eyes.

She felt a tingling sensation all over her body. No man had ever said such a thing to her, well, not a real man; silly old Roy had tried to say it at Christmas time but that didn't count. She did not know what to reply. She longed to hear John Stuart say it, but he was far away on the cattle drive and Nathaniel was here in her arms and he was so handsome, so much fun.

Suddenly she realised that it was very dark in the glade. It must be nearing dusk, and a breeze had blown up. Her small face filled with concern. 'Nathaniel,' she said in a worried tone, 'I have to go now. It must be very late.'

'Oh, all right.' His tone was resigned. 'Come on.'

As he bent to pick up the blanket, a thought occurred to him. His eyes half closed in deliberation. 'Love,' he said in a more cheerful way, 'what time are lights out at your establishment?'

'What do you mean, Nathaniel?'

He took her by the arm and headed towards the horses. 'I mean, what time of night does everybody retire at your house?'

'Well, while Daddy's away, I suppose about ten o'clock or half past. Our manservant Leith goes to bed around that time I think. Bess and Rosy the maids and Beth the cook usually go to bed and read. Why?'

He was setting a goodly pace back to the animals now and hurrying her along. 'Saturday night, can you get out of the house and meet me? The nights are so pleasant lately. Not cold at all. I often leave the smoky bunkhouse and go outside about the hour of eleven and it's wonderful.'

Daydee stopped walking and he almost shot past her.

'Hey? What's wrong, love?' he asked, turning quickly back to her.

Her small eyes looked knowingly at him. 'Nathaniel Lake,' she began in a severe tone, 'are you suggesting I meet you in the middle of the night?'

Biting his lip, he returned her gaze, a hopeful expression in his eyes.

She wagged her finger at him. 'Mind you,' her tone was milder now, 'I don't say it's a bad idea; it should certainly be an adventure. I suppose I'd like to, if I can, for it's been very hard to keep coming here in the afternoons on my own. They're all so keen on chaperones all the time. It's a wonder I'm sane.'

He sighed faintly and smiled. 'Ah, but you are, love, and clever too. Now come on, let's work out things as we go.'

They hurried on, and Daydee, excited now, reminded him, 'We shall have to be careful of the night patrol. Mind you, if we meet inside the park, we'll be safe, for they only ride through once about midnight. Yes, that's it. It will be easy for me once I'm out of the house, for we have a private gate from our back garden into the park.'

They reached the tethered horses. He retrieved the paints and pictures from where she had left them to dry and put them in one of her saddle bags. He gave her a significant look. 'I'll meet you inside the park. I will wait near your gate in the hedge. I'll be there by eleven o'clock on Saturday night. Now, don't forget.'

She bent down to him from her horse and he kissed her.

'I'll see you Saturday night, Nathaniel,' she called over her shoulder as she disappeared into the twilight. Her heart beat quickly as she rode back. She had stayed too long. God! What if they had sent Leith to find her? There would be the devil to pay! How she hated not ever being able to do as she liked. How she hated her mother and Eve. They forced her to this subterfuge. It was their fault!

Nathaniel had said he loved her! Did he really? He was so different from the others on Mayfield. He was handsome and well-bred, educated too, not like a common cattle man. Of course he was not as refined and wonderful as John Stuart, but then who was? No, there was no man in the world like John Stuart. That was why she had to know things; these things about loving that Nathaniel was showing her. She felt so thrilled when he kissed and fondled her. Perhaps she should let him go a little further on Saturday.

Daydee saw them as she rode up to the house. They were down near the front hedge waiting for her. She had ridden directly to the house, specifically to let them know she was all right. Did they have to stand there accusingly?

She really did hate them. Her mouth pulled down as she rode up to them, but as she came near and they could see her face, her expression changed completely and she began to smile at Thelma and Eve who waited for her.

'I do hope I didn't worry you, Mother,' she began. 'I was having such a good time, I painted some pictures I'm very pleased with. I didn't realise how late it was. I do feel so sorry for having concerned you, really sorry.'

Thelma shook her head in exasperation and Eve answered, 'At least you're back now and safe.'

'I'll not have you riding out alone again,' her mother added. 'I don't care what your father said. We've been so worried.'

Daydee edged the horse away from them. 'I'd better take Boots down to the stables.'

When Daydee returned over the field from the stables, it was almost dark. She was close to her front hedge when she saw Eve waiting for her. The girl started in surprise.

'Daydee, I want to speak to you.'

'What for?'

'Ah, Daydee,' Eve spoke quietly, 'whoever he is, he's not worth it.'

'What do you mean?' the girl said, throwing her head back and tossing her hair over her shoulder.

'I mean the man you have been meeting. You were not at Chinaman's Hill painting today.'

Daydee's face became defiant. 'So, you've been spying on me, have you? How disgusting!'

261

'No, Daydee, I have not been spying on you. I had no need. I knew you would not be there.'

The girl's eyes were cold, contemptuous, loathing. Suddenly Eve realised the depth of Daydee's hatred; she saw that the girl really detested her. The knowledge was frightening. This was not something she could continue to ignore. She went quite cold, so much did Daydee's expression impart. Never had she suspected the girl's antipathy was so malevolent. For those moments there in the dusk, Daydee Larmer was ugly. The hate inside, manifesting itself upon her face, actually altered her features. Gone was the dainty look with the pert upturned nose; it was pitiless, coarse, vindictive. Eve was alarmed.

'What is it you want with me?' Daydee said belligerently. When Eve remained silent, the girl prompted, 'Well?'

With an effort, Eve managed to speak civilly to the venomous face. 'Daydee, I am not trying to hurt you. I want to stop you from doing something indiscreet. Although the more I look at you, the more I wonder if you're worth it. I am not judging you, just warning you. If anyone finds out you have been secretly meeting this man, it will be the talk of Mayfield and it would not just stay inside our borders. In your position it would be a disgrace. You would hurt your parents dreadfully.'

'Will you inform on me?'

Eve shook her head, 'No, Daydee, I will not inform on you. Unlike you, I do not act maliciously. I'm not interested in telling tales to people. All I ask is that you consider what I have said. Think of the shame you would bring on those . . . who love you.' Daydee's face continued to be so hostile, Eve shook her head in disgust and swiftly walked away.

The girl's voice sounded after her. 'I shall do as I please. Just go away and leave me alone, damn you! Oh, how I wish you had never come to Mayfield. How I wish you would go away for ever.'

Daydee wondered how on earth Eve could have known she was meeting Nathaniel. Eve obviously did not know who he was or she would have said his name. Daydee could only suppose that somehow Eve had guessed what was going on, though she was at a loss to work out how. The only result Eve's warning had was to make her decide to be more cautious. This meeting at night was a far better idea; for a start she did not need to make excuses.

As Friday passed, she became more and more alert. She was positively excited about it. Her walk, normally bouncy, was positively jaunty; and on Saturday, in expectation of the meeting, her disposition became more pleasant by the hour.

That night after dinner, Thelma announced that she was going over to the big house to play cribbage with Eve. It was all Daydee could do not to laugh with delight. She read a little but her mind was not on the story. At twenty to ten she put out her lamp and sat by the window looking down through the trees to where Nathaniel would be. She heard the grandfather clock at the foot of the staircase chime ten times, and about fifteen minutes later her mother's footsteps on the stairs. She heard the rustle of her gown as she passed down the hall, then the sound of her bedroom door opening and closing. Good, she at least was out of the way.

The next half hour was the slowest of Daydee's life. She paced the room in a nervous excitement. She dressed in a sweet concoction of pink and white, with bows and ribbons. She brushed her long black hair and tied a double bow at the back.

Ten minutes before the hour, she took her shawl and opened her bedroom door. The house seemed still. She made her way down the staircase and, turning right, crept towards the kitchen.

Suddenly she stopped, every nerve on edge. There was lamplight in the kitchen. God! Leith must still be up, damn him. Trust him to be here tonight. She could not go out the back door now. What to do? She went out through the long french windows in the dining room and crept along the side of the house and round to the hedge gate. It was a calm night, no wind, just a gentle coolness in the air – exhilarating. A pale wraith, she slipped silently through the shadows.

The lamplight from the kitchen threw a wan beam across the back garden as she stole to the hedge gate. She opened it gently; it squeaked just a little. Through she went. How she hoped Nathaniel had not forgotten.

He had not forgotten. Yet it would have been best if he had, for the one thing Nathaniel Lake could not do was to stay sober until eleven o'clock at night. He was an habitual drinker once the sun went down, and often when he was drifting from place to place he found himself drunk in the afternoon.

He had tried to drink lightly tonight, he had thought he could; but after all, he had finished work at five o'clock in the afternoon and six hours was such a long time to wait! He could walk and talk well enough. Perhaps he slurred a little, but he knew what he was doing. He remembered he had to meet that delicious little Daydee at eleven o'clock in the park. Anyway, a few drinks did a man good, made him feel like a man. Still, he had to be careful; make sure no one knew where he was going. Make sure no one saw him enter the park.

He left to walk to the appointed place at quarter past ten. It was a glorious night. He took a blanket and a bottle of rum to keep him company while he waited for Miss Pretty. She certainly was that, firm, round little breasts pushing their way out from her chest, pushing their way right into Lakey's mouth. How many dear little breasts had pushed their way into Lakey's mouth? Ah, but this one was a virgin, he was absolutely sure of it. Good family, quality, upper circles of the colony, young. Nineteen? Twenty? It was a long time since he'd had a virgin. Had he ever? Buggered if he knew. He felt somewhat heady out here in the air. Never mind. What had they said to him as he left the public room in the recreation house with his rum under his arm? 'Going to bed early with a good friend, Lakey?' Funny, that. If only they knew.

He had come diagonally across the fields and for a few minutes he was confused about direction. Then he oriented himself and took a path north-east towards Mayfield Park. He could walk through the west gate easily enough. There were no guards or anything like that. Everyone trusted each other on this property, thank goodness. Even the night patrol was more to keep a watch on things being peaceful and to check that no fires started, than to police the place. Still, there was a lamp in both of the great pillars at the gate, so it was just possible someone could see a man enter. He would be careful. Careful, Lakey boy, that was him. He giggled.

In the deep shadow of a clump of ash trees not far from the gateway, he stood looking left and right, in front and behind. He could not see the Larmers' house from here, trees obscured it, but it was just over there about a hundred yards away.

His boots made crunching sounds on the gravel but he was soon through the light at the gate and onto the grass again. He still felt a bit giddy from the night air but that was all right, he had felt like this before.

This was the first time he had been inside here. Couldn't see much at night with all the trees and gloom, but he could see well enough to make out that the gardens looked like they belonged to a palace. She had come up in the world, his old love had, to be calling such as this home. But then she always did have a good head on her shoulders, that girl. Now, where was this gate little Daydee had told him about? He followed the hedge and a few moments later came to it. Then he found a bench. How convenient of old Wakeman to put a seat here. He sat down. Come on, Daydee love. Speed it up a bit, old girl.

He waited a few minutes and while he waited he swallowed a sip of the rum. Then a minute later he had another.

The starlight gave a gentle, moody vagueness to the trees and shrubs. He liked it here, but where the devil was Daydee?

He laid the blanket on the ground at his feet. Then he heard the gate open. He stood and turned in the direction of the sound. A pale figure glided through the trees. Good girl.

Daydee called softly, 'Nathaniel, Nathaniel?'

'Over here, love.'

She ran forward to him. He had enveloped her in his arms before she realised the state of him. She pulled back, an expression of distaste on her face. 'You're . . . you're drunk!' she said in a loud whisper.

'No reproof, love,' he countered, pulling her back to him. 'Give me a kiss.' His mouth covered hers. His tongue pushed deep into her, bringing with it the sour taste of stale alcohol, so opposite to the sweet kisses of the afternoons. She was shocked; he was so different. She was repulsed by his coarseness.

She drew her face away from his. 'Don't, don't!' Her voice rose out of a whisper. 'Nathaniel, I don't like it. I don't like you when you're drunk.'

'Well, I like you,' he replied holding her more tightly in his arms.

'Please, Nathaniel, you're hurting me.' She was scared, yet she did not dare to cry out. She was tugging to get out of his arms but it was useless. She was so light and tiny, he easily pulled her down to the ground with him. He had her now. His hand went beneath her gown, his eager fingers pushing up between her legs, his mouth searching for hers.

'God, Nathaniel, someone comes!' she said in a voice of fear.

He stopped and looked around in surprise. 'Where?'

In the moment that he loosed her, she rolled away and gained her feet. She ran swiftly over the grass and the flower beds and through the gate, and was gone before the befuddled man realised it was a trick.

'You bitch, Daydee, you bloody little bitch!' He said it loudly.

Then he gathered his senses and moved quickly over to the bench and picked up the bottle of rum. Mustn't leave that here. Then as fast as he could he went back towards the park gate. He was about to step out onto the gravel when the idea came to him.

Of course!

He smiled widely there in the night. He would go to the one up there in Mayfield House. She would have him. She had always been in love with him. She wouldn't change, not that one. She was just like him, always ready for a good time. They were two of a kind really. He could still hear her saying, 'Nathaniel, you're the one I'll always love truly.' All he had to do was get into that private garden. It led directly to her bedroom. And Wakeman was away.

God, he could feel her heat beneath him already.

Drunk, the little hussy had said he was. Well, he might be a bit. But he knew exactly what he was doing. He knew exactly where to go to get the loving she wouldn't give him. What damn good was a fucking virgin anyway? He laughed softly at that. A fucking virgin, what a contradiction!

He moved through the darkness of the trees at the edge of the carriageway towards the pale radiance of the house in the distance. There were lamps lit on the verandah. It looked positively awesome. And to think she was in there.

The three carriage drives opened up into a large gravelled half-circle surrounded by lawn in front of the house. He kept to the line of trees until he crossed the roads, his boots again crunching loudly in the still air. At last, he stood beneath the stone wall that enclosed the garden. The top was only a couple of inches above his head. A man could almost climb it if he hadn't had a drink. He moved along the wall a little way. Now what had that bloody Daydee said? Yes, that's right. She said there was a wooden gate here somewhere. Where the devil was it?

In front of him loomed a shape. Oh, only a tree. That was better. He could climb it if he had to. He moved on, and yes, the girl had told him correctly, here was the gate. Latched on the inside! Bugger it! Back to the tree.

To his amazement, he climbed it easily. He dropped down on the inside and as he did so he felt the rum bottle fall. His hands groped around in the grass. He found it and, uncorking it, took another swig.

It was bigger than he thought, this garden, and bloody dark, but soon his eyes adjusted and he could make out the shapes around him. There were many small trimmed trees and hedges. He found a path. Quietly, he walked along it. His gait was unsteady, but his direction was unerring, straight towards the verandah.

He halted under the only large tree in the garden. It was an umbrella-like shape, he could tell that. He took another swig of the rum bottle and ever so gently laid it at the foot of the tree. He leaned on the trunk looking over to a wide verandah where a kerosene lamp, on a marble table, threw a benign light across hanging baskets full of flowers and a climbing rose trailing along the railing. Fancy living in a place like this. God! Hadn't she come up in the world?

Then as if the thought of her made her a reality, she issued through the long casement windows onto the verandah in front of him. She looked just as he had seen her so many times: her body covered with a film of nightgown, a light shawl round her shoulders and her burnished curls hanging down her back; his eyes lingered on her bare forearms and the fullness of her breasts.

Ahead of her scampered a white cat.

Eve had said goodnight to Thelma about ten o'clock. They had enjoyed a quiet, pleasant evening playing two-handed cribbage and after a glass of port and some sweetmeats, Thelma had gone home with Leith who had waited for her.

Around eleven o'clock, Eve bade Stephanie goodnight. 'As it's Sunday tomorrow, I shall sleep in a little, Stephanie, so don't wake me early. And you sleep in too,' she added as the girl closed the bedroom door.

She had been reading for some time when Velvet ingratiated himself into the bedroom through the door from the sitting room. 'Oh, Velvet, is that where you've been?' He stretched his long, supple limbs, arching his back, before he made his way to the casement windows and began to scratch on them.

'You are a nuisance, you know,' she said playfully, climbing from the bed to open the casements and let Velvet scamper through.

The night was still. She walked across the verandah to lean against a colonnade. In the soft lamplight, she noticed that on the lawn below, Velvet had hold of something in his front paws and was teasing it.

'Velvet,' she called. 'You naughty boy, what have you there?' She hurried down the stone steps and across to him. In his claws was a small lizard.

'No, no, sweetie,' she said pushing the cat away with one hand and rescuing the tiny reptile with the other. It seemed stunned and Eve could feel its heart beating. Keeping Velvet behind her with one hand, she walked to a garden bed near the poinciana tree and put the creature in among the flowers. 'There you are, little man,' she said softly, 'away you go.'

Then she turned and lifted Velvet in her arms to keep him from following the lizard. It was as she stood up with him that she heard the voice.

'Clare,' it sounded thickly, 'Clare, love, I'm here.'

She was petrified with shock. She stood stock-still, unable to move. Velvet half fell, half jumped from her, dragging her shawl with him, as a hand took her arm and turned her. She looked into a face she

267

did not know. Ice-cold fear shot through her limbs.

The mouth was on hers in an instant. She pulled back in automatic resistance.

'Clare, Clare,' he said again. 'It's me, Nathaniel.'

At last, something like a strangled sound came from her throat. 'No! Please . . .'

He pulled her tightly to him and kissed her again. The taste and smell of liquor was revoltingly overpowering. He was staggering slightly.

'Come on, old girl. What the devil's wrong? Too good for your old lover?'

She managed to lift one hand and push at his face. 'No! No! Don't!' She turned in his arms and tried to escape. Her elbow swung sharply up into his ribs as she thrust herself away.

'Not you, too,' he muttered angrily as she writhed out of his grasp. His hand slid down her arm as she pulled away and, grabbing at the flimsy material of her nightgown, took hold of it. At the same time, he lunged with his other hand, striking her shoulder as she moved away from him, knocking her off balance. As she fell, she felt her nightdress rend, the weight of her body helping the fine material to tear.

She was aware of her nakedness and then the weight of him as he fell on top of her. The fumes of alcohol were overwhelming and he was mumbling, 'Come on, love, come on.' She rolled to the side but he had his arm round her ribs and he pulled her back under him. She pushed at him, digging her fingers into his throat and twisting her body to slither from beneath him.

For a moment, he hesitated, growling in anger, 'What the hell's the matter with you? Clare, have you gone mad?'

Swiftly, she squirmed sideways, kicking and reaching out to free herself but he recovered and dragged her back down, flattening her with his body, his hands on her breasts, his hot, alcoholic breath filling her senses.

She tried to scream but the horror had made her dumb. There was nothing but blind panic in her now and the only sound that issued from her throat was a gurgling sound of terror. His mouth thudded onto hers, the sweat from him mingling with her tears, her thoughts reeling with shock and horror. Everything she did was instinctive. She pushed his head back and hit at his face.

He yelped and rose slightly from her, giving her a chance to push at him and to lift her knee as she tried to turn and snake away from beneath him.

This man was not just angry now, his voice was crazily excited and urgent. 'So, you want to fight? Good, I love to fight,' he cried, smashing a heavy blow across the side of her head and driving it round into the grass. The impact dazed her but she was aware he was trying to pin her arms to her side. She heard him call her Clare over and over again, and through the blur of terror she managed to force her right hand up out of his grasp to claw at his face and draw her nails down across his cheeks. With a growl, his head jerked back. He was in a frenzy, hardly knowing what he did, stimulated by the alcohol and aroused by her resistance, intent on fulfilling the need that had brought him here. He struck out with his fist, punching her in the face and at the same time wrenching his legs up to straddle her body. As he held her pinned under him, she lifted herself in an attempt to drag her body out from his, but he cuffed her across the face again, knocking her backwards.

She was writhing, kicking, swamped by the appalling reality of what was happening. With all her will, she drove the top half of her body upright again, throwing her hands up to take him by the throat and dig her fingers deep into the flesh of his neck.

'You bitch!' he growled, knocking her hands away and grabbing her wrists, pushing her arms down back to her sides.

She was fighting for sheer survival now, blind, fierce survival, her brain screaming for her to fight, scratch, kick. With a mighty effort, she forced one hand from his grasp and thrusting it up to his face found his lips, nose, cheeks. She tried to drag her fingernails across them again, but he tore her hand from his face as his body snapped backwards and momentarily he slid sideways.

'Clare, you fucking bitch!' he shouted as she shoved him from her as hard as she could. He lost his balance and for a moment his bulk was toppling, but his big legs were still encompassing her and his arms were already lashing back to grab her. She began to yank her body from beneath his but he regained his balance, his determined hands reaching out and groping for her naked arms. She felt his long, thick fingers find her shoulders and take hold. He had her now, he was back on top of her, her body pinioned beneath him, his solid weight riveting her to the ground. He jerked her shoulders up towards him and then smashed her head down to the ground, once, twice, pounding her into senselessness. Was he going to kill her? As she thudded backwards she knew she was trying to scream, but had no idea whether any sound came from her mouth or not. There was a part of her violated mind that told her no one would hear her anyway, they were all far away in the other wings of the house.

As she plunged into unconsciousness, she thought she actually managed to say, 'I'm . . . not . . . Clare!' The last thing she felt

269

before her mind went completely dead was the force of him down between her legs and the brutal pain of his entry into her body.

She was insensible to his noises as he moved over her limp nakedness, panting and groaning. At last, he released himself, completing what he had come for. She was unconscious for the minutes he used her.

Awareness began to return just as he gave his final, carnal grunt. She became conscious of the cessation of movement within her and his heavy body rolling away. His breath was coming in short gasps. He made strange sounds as he half rose. She saw his hand come back towards her and she gave a sharp, terrified intake of breath. But his fingers only touched her mouth. It was absurdly like a caress.

'Oh God!' he said. 'Who are you?'

She closed her eyes and her only answer were her tears.

He made a hopeless attempt to cover her with the torn nightdress, then she heard him lurch to his feet.

'Damn you!' he said. 'Why did you let me believe you were Clare? Look what you've made me do!'

She heard him move across the garden mumbling things she could not understand. She heard him unlatch the gate, heard it open and close.

Then nothing, only the pitiful silence of the night.

CHAPTER SIXTEEN

'O call back yesterday, bid time return.'
Richard II, William Shakespeare, 1564–1616.

As she rose and gathered her nightgown and shawl to her, her foot touched something cold. A bottle . . . alcohol. She took it in her shaking fingers and, gaining her feet, stumbled back to the verandah.

The clear sounds of horses' hooves on the gravelled drive drifted to her in the stillness. The night patrol were riding through. Was it only midnight? It seemed so long since she had climbed from bed to let Velvet out.

She locked the casements and mechanically drew the curtain. She wrapped the tatters of her nightgown in an old petticoat. The numbness that was her mind told her tomorrow she must dispose of it somewhere.

She looked in the mirror. Two eyes looked back, glazed eyes. Clare's eyes? The woman in the mirror had blood coming from her nose and the edge of her mouth, and her lip was swelling. There were dark, red patches and scratches on her face and breasts, and marks which would be bruises showed near her eyes. She bent her head. Some of the skin had been rubbed from her thigh, knees and elbows. She could not feel any pain. Her body seemed as paralysed as her brain.

She sat down to gather strength, then with trembling fingers wiped the blood from her nose and mouth with a handkerchief.

Slowly, very slowly, she put on her dressing gown and, taking her pitcher from the washstand, made her way out along the corridor towards the small room where she could tap the water cisterns used for this side of the house. Fortunately, she did not have to go over to the kitchens and scullery. She passed along the corridor like a barefoot automaton, not feeling the rich carpet beneath her feet. She filled the pitcher and returned.

With deliberate movements, she bathed her cuts and bruises and put on a fresh nightgown; then once more she made the walk along the corridor to empty the dirty water. She could have opened her door and poured it in the garden, but the irrational fear that he may

271

still be out there filled her mind. She picked up the bloody handker-chief she had used. She would throw it away with the remains of her nightgown.

Now she began to feel things. Her joints ached and a little muscle in her groin twitched uncontrollably. Her right hip bone and upper leg were tender and her face and neck felt as if they had been twisted in a vice.

Finally, she was between the clean sheets of her bed again and she began to have some coherent thoughts.

How in the Lord's name could this have happened? How could she have escaped this very act by her wits and wiles when not much more than a child at the Ship Inn, a rough sailors' tavern, with no one to protect her, only to be assaulted here among all this splendour with dozens of servants in the same house?

She was sobbing, pitiful sounds of outrage and misery filling her whole being. She was battered and beaten and everything ached, and with the awareness of the physical pain returned the horrible images of him, his noises and his contact. She began to shake uncontrollably and, sinking her face into the softness of the pillow, she drew up her legs and curled into herself, until at last she drifted into blessed sleep.

Poor Velvet took the blame for the swelling on her mouth and the abrasions to her face. She was drawn into intimating he had accidentally tripped her on the verandah steps and she had fallen heavily to the ground.

Stephanie and the household were all compassion and concern. Mrs Smith prepared an old herbal remedy for the relief of swelling and applied it to Eve's mouth, while Mr Free cooked a special beef broth for her.

Eve had lain ever since she woke, thinking of what to do. There were moments when she burst involuntarily into tears, and others when she had an almost ungovernable desire to scream.

It was unthinkable, sexually attacked in her own secluded garden by a man who had mistaken her for her twin sister. Firstly, no one knew she had a sister! If only she had told John Stuart long ago as Father had advised her. Everything now was so horribly complicated.

A woman in her position could not be raped; it would reflect on John Stuart, it would reflect on Mayfield. She had always known that John Stuart would be appalled to learn of Clare. But how could he contend with the knowledge that his wife was the twin of a woman whose lover had found his way to Mayfield and assaulted her? It was a nightmare. How her head ached. What was she to do? Visions of John Stuart and Alan Fletcher rushed simultaneously to her mind.

How she longed to be held, hidden and safe, away from this ghastly reality.

But there would be no holding, no minding, for neither were here . . . and the one, even were he here, would have difficulty understanding; while the other, though he were understanding, could never be here. But perhaps she was wrong. John Stuart would understand; of course he would. When he returned, she would tell him everything. He would be as he was in the phaeton the night before he left. He was so dear, so gentle and so loving. God in heaven, why hadn't she told him about Clare? If only he were here. How desperately she needed him.

Then her confused brain screamed, no, she would never tell. She would remain silent. People looked up to her. She was 'the mistress' and 'the mistress' did not get raped. Society believed only harlots and unfortunate girls in slums and poor houses were raped. There was the most shameful stigma to being sexually attacked. She had no choice; she must uphold all that she and John Stuart stood for, to keep the dignity of her husband and of his position as master of so much and so many. No one must ever know. She began to sob again. Thank heaven Dr Douglas was not on the station to examine her. He had accompanied the cattle drive and would attend an annual assembly of medical men in Sydney.

By midmorning, the news of the accident was all over the household and had stretched to the gardeners and via them to the Larmers' kitchen and Thelma. Thelma wasted no time in coming swiftly to the big house.

'Oh, my dear, my dear, I feel terrible,' Thelma began as she entered the room. 'Why didn't you wake the servants and send for me immediately this dreadful thing happened? When did it happen?'

Smiling wanly, Eve replied, 'Last night after you had gone.' Eve avoided her friend's gaze and lay back, closing her eyes. 'I'll be perfectly well in a day or two. It looks much worse than it is, Thel.'

'It looks terrible,' her friend stated. 'As if you'd been beaten, not fallen.' She came over and sat on the edge of the bed and in doing so touched Eve's side. Eve winced.

'Why, you are hurt in your body, too!' Thelma exclaimed.

'It's nothing, dear. I must have twisted as I fell.'

'Oh Eve,' the older woman's face creased in sympathy, 'I fear you are in more pain than you say.'

'No. No. It's nothing serious.'

Thelma looked sceptically at her. 'I shall send to Cowra for Dr Campbell and we'll find out.'

Alarmed, Eve looked up quickly. 'But it was only a fall.' When she saw the older woman was not convinced, she began to panic. 'Thel, please. If I'm not feeling better in forty-eight hours, then yes, send for him. But you must let me decide what is best. Please.'

'I don't know what John Stuart will say, he only just gone and this happens. I won't blame him if he holds us all responsible.'

Eve gave a trembling sigh. She hated this subterfuge. Looking up at her friend from where she lay, her lovely brown eyes bruised and swollen, she had an overwhelming desire to tell Thelma everything. But no, she suppressed the inclination. How unfair it would be to burden her good friend with such a horrible, shameful secret.

Thelma left to let her sleep, and at five o'clock Mrs Smith arrived.

'Mrs Wakeman,' she began, 'the gels have brought hot water and I have a little remedy to go in the bath. It will help.' She patted her apron pocket.

'Mrs Smith, thank you. Please leave the remedy with Stephanie and explain its use. I shall be only too happy to try it.'

'Very well, m'um, ye know best.'

Eve realised that Stephanie would have to see her body. As her personal maid, the girl saw her in the bath now and then. She and Stephanie spent a great deal of time in each other's company and there was a bond between them. So when the others left, she asked the girl to come to her.

Stephanie stood looking down at her mistress in bed, her big, round face sympathetic and concerned.

'Stephanie, you will need to help me bathe. You will see that I have other marks, bruises on my body. It was a very bad . . . fall. I have not wanted to worry Mrs Larmer or the household, so I ask you not to mention them to anyone. You understand?'

'Yes, ma'am. But Mrs Wakeman, shouldn't you send into Cowra for Dr Campbell?'

'No. Stephanie, I'm going to be all right. I just want you to be prepared for what you will see.'

But for all the warning, when the girl saw her body, she exclaimed, 'Oh no, Mrs Wakeman! Oh Lordy me!'

It was not until twenty-four hours later that Eve learned what her attacker had been doing on Mayfield.

When Thelma came to sit with her the following morning, she chatted away and told her many things to pass the time. 'You know, love, Mrs Hennessy told me a strange thing this very morning. She brought over some pound cake, the dear, she do make that a treat, you know, the best cook on Mayfield, if you ask me. Well, it seems Mr Hennessy had one of his short-timers just up and go the night before last. In the middle of the night too, would you believe it?'

Eve stiffened.

'Well now, it seems this short-timer was a real one for the women. Notorious in the bunkhouses, they say. Name of Lake, Nathaniel, I think she said.'

Thelma could see that Eve was paying attention and so she went on enthusiastically, 'As I say, my dear, in the middle of the night he went and took his horse from the stables. Didn't take his wages, nothing. Mr Hennessy says that in all his years on Mayfield he has never known a short-timer leave without his money. Says he's mystified. But Mrs Hennessy and I say it's obvious. Only one thing makes a man run in the middle of the night.'

Eve could not help herself. 'And what is that?'

'A woman. Sad but true. We have no doubt he's running from a Mayfield girl. Stands to reason. As Mrs Hennessy said herself "There's some poor girl here on Mayfield as is in the family way, mark my words." And you know, Eve, she'll be right. No blighter runs off in the middle of the night like that for nothing. And to be sure, we'll find out who the poor soul in trouble is soon enough.'

Eve's heart was racing, she could feel the thump of it inside her chest.

Her friend continued, 'We've had more than one marriage here on Mayfield as where a bairn has come before its time. Oh yes, we've had a few seven-month babes and one six-month indeed; but that is one thing. When the man lights out and leaves the woman it's another altogether. Remember when poor Sally Collins got herself into trouble?'

Eve shook her head.

'No, love, of course you wouldn't. You weren't here then. It was proper disgraceful. He was a Mayfield man too, no short-timer! And he lit out as soon as he knew about the babe. John Stuart did right, I believe, after all, yet, I was a mind to being a touch more sympathetic to Sally at the time.'

'Why, Thelma, what do you mean?' Eve asked, her voice sounding a little unsteady to her own ears.

'Well, yes, I do believe he did right, after all. The father had gone, as I mentioned, and the girl, Sally, well she hid her problem until she was nigh on six months gone. Heavens knows how, for those girls often sleep two and three to a room in the larger bedrooms, as you know. Now, when John Stuart found out, he was more than a mite outraged. He doesn't hold with immorality, but I don't need to tell you that.

'None of us knows exactly what John Stuart said but she came out of his study crying her heart out. Although he was more than kind really. Many a man in his position would have been heartless and sent her away immediately, no pay, nothing, but John Stuart has principles. Well, she stayed on here until the baby was born, and the child was removed from her at birth. She didn't lay hands on it at all. That's what I felt was a touch hard at the time, but when I look back on it, I'm more of a mind to reckon it was kind, for she had no chance of being attached to it. And so the baby boy, for it was a boy, was taken from her the minute of birth. We kept it over at my house the first three weeks. Dear little angel, it was.'

Thelma closed her eyes in memory. 'Then a minister, a Reverend Theodore, came and took him away. I asked John Stuart where he was going and he said – you know, Eve, I remember his very words: "It's not the poor infant's fault, Thelma," he said. "It's the degenerate pair that begot the child who are to blame. It would have been branded a bastard but I have done the best I can by it." He had found some couple somewhere that couldn't have a child of their own, and that Reverend Theodore, yes, well, he delivered it to them.'

Eve couldn't help asking, 'And what of Sally, the mother?'

'Sent away as soon as she could travel. Oh, John Stuart made sure she was given plenty of money to tide her over until she could place herself somewhere again, but that was it. He was only concerned with the welfare of the child. That's the way John Stuart is, he has no time at all for fallen women.'

'No,' Eve shook her head, 'he hasn't.' A sickening chill rippled through her.

When her friend had gone, she began to tremble. So Lake was his surname? Into her mind came the fearful memory of his voice. 'It's me . . . Nathaniel.' She even remembered which one of Clare's menagerie he had been; the very one Clare had been living with when she went to her in Adelaide in 1857. She had never seen him, but she remembered his name, Nathaniel. Oh God, the irony of it all. Your lover, Clare. And he had run away. Of course he had, he didn't want to get lynched. At least he was gone, never to come back, and she had time to consider how to broach things when John Stuart came home.

Dr Campbell was never called because she said she felt better each day and by Wednesday morning she had convinced Thelma and Mrs Smith that she was well enough to leave her bed. It was uncomfortable to walk but her lip was back to its normal size and even though she had a black eye and abrasions, some of the soreness had left her limbs.

She wanted desperately to be normal and in the morning she insisted on working with Mr Oldfield in John Stuart's study, checking lists and supervising accounts, but by noon she had gone to her bedroom where she washed herself all over. She lay on her bed seeing the horrible, mad images of Nathaniel Lake in her head. Suddenly, an overwhelming anger took hold of her, and she sat up, consumed by indignation and resentment. She moved swiftly to the door and across the verandah and down into her garden bower. 'Damn you!' she called aloud, smashing her fist into the indifferent trunk of the poinciana tree. 'Damn you to hell!' Then as quickly as her rage had risen, it died. She sagged forward, overcome by fear. She needed compassion, understanding and love. But she was quite alone once more in her life.

When she was called to luncheon, she forced herself to eat something so that the household would not be concerned, and the afternoon she spent taking gentle walks and resting on the verandah at the front of the house.

She thought of Father. If only he were here. Perhaps she should go to him, stay with him and Mother while John Stuart was away. Being with them would calm her and she would find the strength to combat this. Yes, in a week or so she should be able to travel. The very memory of the two dear folk in Bathurst brought a small measure of cheer into her misery.

Suddenly, out beyond the Norfolk pines, something pink caught her eye. It was a parasol bobbing up and down and under it the jaunty walk of Daydee passing through the grounds. As she bounced along, the girl looked over towards her.

Realisation hit Eve like lightning.

Lake! Nathaniel Lake! He was the man she had seen kissing Daydee that afternoon by the Lachlan. He was the man who had stood up from the camp fire on the night before the cattle drive and walked into the darkness. Another cold shiver rippled through her. He was the man she had warned Daydee not to see! It was like some fantastic, morbid jest being played upon her. She had to lean on the railing in front of her for support as every nerve end screamed. She felt physically ill.

Daydee, too, had learned that Lake had gone. Not that she cared. She was glad. She hated him for the way he had fooled her. How she had wept last Saturday night when she returned to the safety of her bedroom. She had been awake and worried all night because she realised she had left her shawl in the park. The next morning she had sneaked out just after daybreak and found it, and a blanket. But she had learned something from her experience with Lake, and even though she hated him, in some ways she was grateful to him. How she loved John Stuart, perhaps more than before if it were possible.

And now, as she passed through the park with her book *Agnes Grey* under her arm, she looked sideways and saw Eve on the verandah.

Daydee had a feeling that all was not as it appeared with Eve. She hardly knew what she thought, but it was to do with Eve and the fall and Lake. Lake had disappeared from Mayfield in the middle of Saturday night. Disappeared without a trace, no pay, no goodbyes to anyone. She was positive he had not left because of what he had done with her in the park, unless he was worried that she would inform on him. No, he would have known better. She would have disgraced herself by her own misconduct. It was something else that had made him run. She had this irrational suspicion. She had seen Eve up close, and the woman looked more like someone who had been beaten than someone who had fallen. But even Nathaniel would not have dared; drunk as he was. He was a mere working hand. *She* was Mrs Wakeman. Nothing made sense, yet the suspicion lingered. She must be watchful and possibly she would find something out.

As the days advanced, Eve's bruises faded, her lacerations healed and the soreness all but disappeared, yet she could not heal the wound inside or throw off the feeling of being dirty. She washed herself two and three times a day, feeling the horror and the shame of Lake's assault crushing in on her. She felt weighed down by guilt. If only she had told John Stuart about Clare, perhaps this would not have occurred. Could it be that the attack was some sort of retribution for her falseness?

Sometimes she told herself she was stupid, that she was not the only woman in New South Wales to be attacked, that she had to conquer all these emotions; but no sooner had she thought this, than she would weep uncontrollably again.

She postponed her idea of going to Father and Mother; for as much as she desired to see them, something told her to wait here at Mayfield for John Stuart. How she missed him and how much she needed his warm arms round her and the feeling of security she knew his presence would bring. Finally, after all her soul-searching and reasoning, she decided she must try to accept the degradation of it all and tell John Stuart everything the moment he came home. She felt sure he would understand and help her. It would be a new start, no secrets or doubts between them. All would be right.

Once she had made this decision, she forced herself to begin walking again, good-natured Stephanie trailing her over hill and dale, and with her belief in the future, her spirits lifted a little. She dreamed often about her husband and sometimes about the bushranger. Occasionally she noticed an aching in her teeth and tenderness in her breasts, but she took little notice, thinking it was the aftermath of the trauma.

On her birthday, she had grown strong enough to have a small luncheon celebration with Thelma, Mrs Hennessy and Mrs Watson, and while there were still the moments of ungovernable depression and guilt and misgivings, for a short time her feelings became more stable.

Then five weeks after John Stuart had left, a message came to say he would be delayed until at least mid-November. It seemed the buying of land was going so well he wished to visit other places that interested him.

From the moment the news arrived, Eve felt odd. It had nothing to do with the news itself, it had to do with her. As each day passed, the apprehension ebbed and flowed. She sublimated these feelings until the day came when she could no longer keep the indefinite imaginings away. Though the aching in her teeth had gone, she could not ignore the soreness in her breasts nor the slight dizziness she felt now and then.

It was seven weeks to the day that Nathaniel Lake had bludgeoned into her life, that she was sure she carried his child. Her cycles were always regular. This time she was weeks late and had awoken ill and dry-retched into the marble dish on her washstand.

No, not his child! It was too obscene. She had irrational thoughts. Firstly, she thought to kill herself. Better to be dead than to carry his child! She would cut her wrists and be out of this appalling misery. No – suicide was not the answer. Evelyn May Herman was stronger than that. Then she thought to brazen it out, pretending it was John Stuart's. No, she could not do that either, it would be a cruel, cowardly deception.

She remembered the story Thelma had told her of Sally Collins, and John Stuart's judgment on the woman in the Blayney street on their wedding day. Long ago, John Stuart had decided Eve was virtuous beyond all women. His vision of her was of his own making, and his vision was immaculate. Why had she let him retain this irrational view of her? But could she have stopped him? Whenever she had tried to temper his opinions of her, he had disregarded her words as if they had not been spoken. Yet she had allowed it. It was her fault as much as his. She had been cowardly and dishonest.

She began to spend more and more time alone. She ate solitary meals in the garden. She kept her appointments with Mr Oldfield and continued to do those things which were her duty, but any social engagement she tried to avoid and often told the staff she had headaches, which indeed was mostly the truth.

279

She still took walks, long walks, but now she returned to taking them alone. When Stephanie asked why she did not wish her company, Eve was sharp with the girl for the first time. 'I do not need a servant questioning my actions. Do not dare to interrogate me again.' Stephanie looked as if she would cry as she turned to leave.

Feeling immediate regret, Eve called, 'Wait, Stephanie!'

The girl turned back and Eve spoke wearily. 'I'm sorry, truly sorry, I did not mean to speak so cuttingly. I am unwell lately.'

She grew thinner and the tiny lines near her eyes were more obvious. Her half-crazed thoughts led her to avoid Thelma. She made up excuses for not spending time in her friend's company and when Thelma called by to pick her up to ride in to church, Eve met her on the verandah with the pretext she was tired of the long journey to Cowra. Thelma stood at the bottom of the steps, one foot tapping the sandstone as she looked up at Eve with an expression of concern. 'I see, love, I'm sorry you feel this way.' Eve turned from her and Thelma called, 'Eve?' She looked back. 'Then I shall stay home with you, the good Lord won't miss me.'

But Eve quickly replied, 'No, Thel, I don't want you staying home on account of how I feel. Please, I insist you go.' And she turned swiftly and re-entered the house.

Thelma's frown of concern deepened. She shook her head sorrowfully before she mounted her gig and drove away.

One November morning, Mr Oldfield came to Eve holding in his hand a telegraphed message from the Mayfield man stationed at Bathurst. His bright young face was aglow.

'Mrs Wakeman,' he began as he opened the door, 'I've some grand news at last.'

Eve lifted her drawn face from the papers in front of her and asked with dread, 'And what is that, Mr Oldfield?'

'The master comes home at last. The Mayfield coach is to be at the Penrith railhead by December first. He hopes to join it by the following afternoon and to be home by the fourth. And Mrs Wakeman,' the young man went on zealously, 'as it's the twenty-eighth today, it had better leave straightaway to get there in time.'

'Yes, yes, of course it should.' She tried to smile, to inject some eagerness into her voice. 'You will see to all that, will you?'

'I will indeed, ma'am, with pleasure.'

When he had gone, Eve stood from her chair. So, within a week she would be reunited with her husband. She shivered. Now that his return was imminent, she could not help feeling the cold chill of fear. She had heard there were people who knew how to bring about miscarriages, but who were they and where could she find them?

And even if she knew such a person, could she go through with such an act?

She went to her room and through it out onto the verandah where she stood looking down into the garden and the poinciana tree, a glorious parasol of scarlet shading the manicured lawns and flower beds. She began trembling as the mad, terrifying memories tumbled through her mind. How could something so ugly have happened here in the midst of this serene beauty? She went back inside, stripped off her clothes and washed herself from head to toe.

In the late afternoon she decided to leave the house and go riding in the fresh air in an attempt to clear her troubled head. She rode to the north for twenty minutes or so, on Betsy, a smallish roan mare, steady, reliable, and good-natured. She reined in on a gentle slope, and for a time she wandered aimlessly through the wild field daisies that grew in abundance here. She sat down on the ground and looked at the tiny white flowers, wondering at the miracle of harmony that they were, the perfection of the petals and the rich, plush yellow of the centres. She felt an overwhelming sadness for these beautiful things which would soon be dead, and for some minutes she sat and touched each small flower within her reach with the tip of her finger in some vain, pointless game, as if the ones she touched would not die.

She began to reflect on her life, recalling all the contingencies that had brought her to this day, and how she alone might have changed it. A tear broke over her eyelid and ran down her face. She wiped it away and lay down on her back in the grass, looking up at the infinite sky, and for a time tried to think of nothing.

There was a large, grey cloud above, that seemed to be like a human profile with a handkerchief across the face. Immediately, she thought of the bushranger, recalling again the first moment she had looked into his compelling eyes. Where was he? Did he ever think of her? And then her brain did what it often did and across her thoughts of that man came thoughts of the other, and she imagined John Stuart, her husband, looking down at her with his irresistible smile.

She noticed the sun getting low in the sky and she climbed back on Betsy and returned to Mayfield.

Adrian, the head groomsman, was there to take her horse, and as she brought Betsy to a halt, she saw Thelma at the entrance to the stable yard. She felt a rush of sadness and guilt. It was obvious her friend waited for her.

Thelma had been worrying daily about Eve. She knew there was something very wrong indeed. She had first noticed the change in

Eve a few weeks ago when she had made an excuse not to go to the monthly mothers' meeting, and subsequently, it had become obvious that Eve was avoiding not only Thelma, but others too. Eve usually worked in the hospital every Tuesday and Wednesday, but the last three weeks she had sent messages she could not come. Then two Sundays ago she had made that lame excuse about not liking the long ride to church in Cowra. A few days ago, Thelma had gone to the big house to talk to Eve, and Eve had refused to see her. She was deeply concerned, and today when she had received a written note from Eve giving a 'continuing headache' as the excuse for not being able to adjudicate at Mayfield's annual eisteddfod she had decided enough was enough. On receipt of the note, she had gone over to the big house again, only to find her friend not at home. She had been informed that Eve was out riding, so she had come here to the stables to wait for her.

When Eve dismounted, she looked over to the older woman. Thelma had an expression on her face that said she could not be avoided this time.

'Hello, Thelma.' It was a reserved greeting.

Thelma's face crinkled with an encouraging smile. 'Hello, dear, they told me you were out riding, so methought I'd come and meet you. Walk home together. We've not done that for a week or two, eh?'

'No, Thelma, that's true.'

They joined the path that led up towards their homes, walking in silence for half a minute or so, then Thelma said, 'It's turned nice, hasn't it, after the heat of today?'

Eve knew her friend was concerned about her. She looked into Thelma's kindly eyes. 'Yes, it's pleasant in the breeze. I like this time of the day, the twilight, although it makes me sad, somehow.'

They continued on a little further without speaking until Thelma took Eve's elbow and steering her off on a side path that led to a wooden seat said, 'Come on, love, let's sit here a minute or two and watch the sunset.'

Behind the seat, a small clump of banksia grew and shooting out above them two flame trees. The seat was covered in red fallen flowers and Thelma bent to brush them away before they sat. Eve picked one up and sighed. 'I have just been up on the northern plain a little way. The ground there is covered with wild daisies. Flowers are miracles, aren't they?'

'Yes,' her friend answered, 'wouldn't trust a person that didn't like flowers.'

They sat, and Thelma took Eve's cold hand and held it between her own. 'What is it, love? I've watched from afar for weeks now. Don't keep me at arm's length any more, please tell me what's wrong.'

Eve could see the sympathy and tenderness in the face beside her. She listened as Thelma went on, 'Eve dear, I know there is something terribly wrong. I've tried to let you know I want to help you. Don't continue to push me away, please. Whatever it is, if I can do anything to assist you, I will.'

Eve felt terrible hiding her guilty secrets. 'Oh, Thelma, dear Thelma, I know you will.'

At that moment Daydee appeared through the trees from the direction of the river path that led over to the workers' cottages. She was accompanied by Rosy, the maid; they had been to a painting class in the schoolhouse and were walking home. Rosy carried the paints.

The two women fell silent until they arrived. Thelma smiled, 'Hello, girls, shouldn't you be home? It's getting late.'

Rosy agreed, but Daydee asked, 'Aren't you coming too, Mother?'

'No, Daydee, we've things to talk over. I'll be along in a minute. Off you go.'

The girls went on by and were soon out of sight.

Thelma turned back to Eve. 'Now, dearest Eve, please tell me what troubles you.'

Eve looked silently at her friend. For weeks now she had yearned for love and compassion, needing the tolerance and love of Father; imagining wild and fantastic compassion from the bushranger, hoping that her husband would come home and listen to her explanations with love and understanding. She had told herself over and over that she was strong and self-reliant, but now as she sat looking into the sympathetic hazel eyes of her friend, all she really knew was that she was confused, bewildered and terribly alone.

'Ah, Thel,' her voice was thin and weary. 'I know you are kind and sympathetic, so much so that I wish not to burden you with my worries.'

'You are no burden, no burden at all. Tell me.'

Suddenly, Eve could hold it in no longer. 'You remember when you told me of the man . . . the man, Lake, the short-timer who ran away from here in the middle of the night some two months ago, the night of my fall.'

Thelma nodded, puzzled.

'You recall you said no doubt some poor, unfortunate woman was the cause of his flight?'

Thelma nodded once more.

'I am that woman.'

Thelma's face dropped, her eyes grew large in her sunbrowned face. She stammered. 'But I . . . I . . . Eve, love, I don't understand.'

The leaves behind them rustled in the breeze. In the distance an owl hooted.

Eve shuddered a sigh. 'That man Lake got into my private garden on that night. I did not fall, he assaulted me. He called me . . . by another name. He mistook me for someone else.' She raised her hands palm upwards in a gesture of hopelessness, then they fell heavily back into her lap. Even though she was relinquishing part of the dreadful secret at last, she still held back about Clare. She was convinced that her husband must be the first to learn of her sister's existence.

'Oh, my dear, my poor dear,' Thelma said, taking Eve in her arms and pressing her tightly to her breast.

'But that is not the worst of it,' Eve went on, bringing herself gently from her friend's embrace. She could not stop talking now, did not want to stop talking now. 'You see, Thelma, I don't know what I am to do. What troubles me and makes me almost insane is . . . I am carrying that man's child.'

'Oh dear Lord God in heaven!' Thelma cried. 'You poor, poor girl, are you certain? Certain it's his?'

'I'm certain.' She lifted her eyes to look directly into Thelma's. 'The very time that John Stuart left me makes it impossible for the child to be his. It was during my period, and he will remember. He will know immediately, and he is due back home within the week.'

Thelma did not speak, she simply clasped Eve to her again. After a little while, she spoke gently. 'Oh, darling, no wonder you were so badly hurt. And keeping this to yourself all this time. It's an outrage. He must be caught and punished. Why, oh why, didn't you tell me before?'

Eve drew back to look at her friend. 'I did not want to worry you, to burden you. Oh, Thel, I was so confused. I did not know what to do. I still don't. God, it's just so awful.'

'Eve, love,' Thelma replied patting her hand, 'please do not be discouraged.' Her face broke into a comforting smile. ' "A worry shared is a worry halved." My old mum used to say that and I believe it. I know how you must be feeling, the fear you must be experiencing, thinking about John Stuart and all. But you are his wife, I know he loves you and I'm certain he will know what to do. You poor child, fancy suffering all these weeks on your own. It makes me sick to think how you must have been feeling. Now, love, what say we go home? I made some fresh scones this very afternoon. We shall pick them up and then go directly to the big house for a good natter and a cup of tea. Dinner can wait.'

'Oh, Thelma,' was all Eve could say, but relief trickled through her and there was the flicker of a smile on her lips, for at last she felt a small swell of hope.

As they rose from the seat, Thelma went on brightly, 'Yes, we'll have some time together, get away from Miss Nosy Parker. We have better things to do tonight than be bothered with Daydee.'

Eve managed a smile and the two women moved off arm in arm.

Behind them in the dim light, the leaves of the banksia trees rustled again. The slight figure which had stood silently there and listened for many minutes turned and slipped speedily back the way it had come. It ran to get ahead of the two women. It darted across the path and into the wooded field beyond. It ran again until, flushed and triumphant, it entered the front door of the Larmers' house.

'Is that you back, Miss Daydee?' called Rosy as she came downstairs.

'Yes, Rosy, pour me some tea, will you?'

CHAPTER SEVENTEEN

'There is a method in man's wickedness –
It grows up by degrees.'
'A King and No King', Francis Beaumont, 1584–1616,
and John Fletcher, 1579–1625.

The evening passed as Thelma had promised. The two women enjoyed a few quiet hours and Eve slept peacefully for the first time in weeks. Although with the coming of the day and the imminent return of John Stuart, she did not feel as calm as she had in her friend's company the night before.

The next days passed in the same way. When she was with Thelma she felt more sure that all would be well; when she was alone her security left and her fear fashioned dread.

'Tell him, love, without a moment's delay, as soon as he arrives,' Thelma advised her. 'He is a good man according to many lights. He loves you and is great and powerful and will know how to bring evil to justice.'

Why was it she believed this when Thelma said it, and disbelieved it later?

Just after twelve o'clock on Sunday, 4 December, one of the stockmen reined in his horse outside Jack Hennessy's office shouting to alert the homestead of the approaching coach. It had been seen two miles from the property border and the estimated time of arrival at Mayfield House was half past the hour of one. Adrian was despatched immediately to tell the household.

The feeling of expectancy that had pervaded the big house for the last few days expanded into excitement and the large rooms echoed with the sounds of raised voices.

Thelma was with Eve when Stephanie came running to alert them of the imminent arrival. From the moment Eve had told the older woman of her worry on the seat at sunset, Thelma had been her constant companion. It was a shocking thing that Eve had told her and she prayed consistently that all would be well. Eve had suffered an appalling, brutal attack from that unspeakable man Lake. Thelma felt sure that John Stuart would bring him to justice, thank the Good Lord above.

It was a hot, airless afternoon and Eve changed into a pale rose muslin dress. She wore a crinoline as was the fashion and she had Stephanie pull back her curls and pin them with a pretty olive branch haircomb that John Stuart had given her. When she and Thelma finally sat together on the front verandah with most of the household milling below them on the grass and half a hundred wives and children and cattlemen beyond, she had calmed herself. But the moment the children began to call, 'It comes! It comes!' she stood up, all nerves.

Half a minute later, the coach came into view swinging up the drive. Eve noticed a single, riderless horse tied to the side of the coach. Beside her at the top of the steps, stood Thelma. All around waited the staff, Mrs Smith and Mr Baines in front, then Mr Free, and clustered behind him in general order of importance the others, a black and white bevy.

Before the vehicle came to a halt, a figure leaned out of one of the windows, hand raised in a happy salute. It was Joe, a broad grin on his face. People called and waved in greeting and as the coach halted, he opened the door and jumped to the ground.

Eve waited for John Stuart to follow, but instead the next figure to alight was female. Eve was so surprised that it took a second or two to recognise Daydee as she bounced down into her father's arms. She heard Thelma whisper at her side, 'Daydee! So that's where she's been.'

The girl looked happy, in a cream riding habit and neat, feathered hat. She turned to the carriage. 'Come on, Uncle John Stuart.'

A burnished boot followed, and the master of Mayfield unfolded from the coach. There, a few short yards in front of Eve, stood her husband, and the chill that she had felt so often recently settled down along her spine.

An hour before, when Eve had been dressing, the Mayfield coach was making solid progress along the sealed, north-west road within the property. It moved along in the face of a hot breeze, and Deke Edwards working to keep the horses at a steady eight miles an hour called encouragement to his charges. The only hindrances to the speed of the coach were the stops to open the successive gates dividing some of the huge paddocks. Creaking, the weighty vehicle slowed in front of one of these. It was just after noon and the summer heat rose in a haze from the surrounding hills, when down the nearest slope, Joe saw a horse cantering towards them from the south-east. He turned to John Stuart who gazed out at his beloved Mayfield with a gratified look. 'A rider comes from this side.' Then with realisation of who it was, Joe continued, 'Why, it's Daydee come to meet us.'

It was indeed Daydee and she hailed them with the wave of a hand and a call as she brought Boots to the other side of the gate where she dismounted and stood waiting, determination in her face and a mean, supercilious smile hovering on her mouth. Her eyes were hard and scheming and her small, gloved hand tapped the gatepost restlessly as Leeroy Barton jumped down from where he rode beside Deke and Timothy to open the gate. Then, as her father and John Stuart alighted, an immediate change came across her features and her small mouth broke into its widest, most innocent smile. Her eyes lost their meanness. The haughty air was gone. 'Father dear, I have come to meet you both. I could wait no longer.' She threw herself into her father's arms.

'Yes, it's been a long time, sweetheart, nine or ten weeks to be sure,' her father replied, hugging his daughter.

'More like twelve, Dada, I have counted.' She turned to John Stuart, 'Oh, how simply wonderful it is to see you,' she said embracing him. 'It's so good to have you come, Uncle John Stuart, so good.'

He smiled affectionately as he withdrew from her embrace. 'Thank you for coming to meet us.'

'Is it all right if I ride inside with you?'

'Of course.'

Soon Boots was tied to the carriage and it ambled forward. Inside, Daydee laughed with excitement and chatted, her father and John Stuart listening to the events of Mayfield since their departure.

'And what of the calves? Any losses after we left?' her father asked.

'No, not a one, and you should see them now, great beasts they are growing into.' For a few minutes, she told other snippets of information, then she said, 'We have all been so excited since we knew you were coming. I went out to Nervy's hill right after breakfast with the lookouts; we were positive you would arrive today, and when we sighted you through the telescope, I rode on to meet you.' Here she turned to John Stuart who sat beside her. 'No doubt Aunt Eve would have ridden out to meet you as well . . . except for her condition.'

John Stuart looked alarmed. 'Her condition, Daydee? Whatever do you mean?'

Daydee's face registered surprise at the question, before she answered, 'Well, I mean the baby, of course. You must know, Uncle John Stuart, the baby Aunt Eve's having.' Then she paused, and with a look of concern said, 'You do know about the baby?'

For a few seconds, John Stuart's face was expressionless, he and Eve had not planned to have children yet. What was this about? He was confused, but at the same time he smiled. 'Ah, Daydee, I cannot say that I did, but it's good news all the same.'

'Now, Daydee,' her father said reprovingly, 'you never were one who could stay quiet about things.' Then clasping John Stuart's hands in both his own continued, 'Well, well, congratulations, m'boy. What wonderful news.'

The coach continued its steady pace and so too did the conversation, only now John Stuart only half listened. He was considering what Daydee had told him. Sometime later, he asked, 'Daydee, is Eve ill? She's not abed, is she?'

To which she replied, 'Oh no, she is very well. Most days she goes out walking, or riding alone, goodness knows where, for hours on end.'

A frown creased his brow, and it sat there on and off for the remainder of the journey.

Daydee watched him closely. Outwardly, she continued the picture of harmlessness, nattering away, but inwardly she regarded him with satisfaction. Daydee, the manipulator, was full of glee. She had been determined to tell him ever since she had eavesdropped on her mother and Eve and heard about Lake and the assault. She guessed he should be very upset by the time he reached home.

And all went as she hoped, for by the time the coach reached Mayfield House, John Stuart had clearly remembered the day of his departure; he had remembered the time of the month; and he had realised that it was impossible for his wife to be carrying his child.

When he stepped down from the coach behind Daydee, the people gathered raised a cheer of welcome. He responded with a smile he did not feel. There was no telltale sign of the inner conflict as he mounted the steps and kissed Eve upon the cheek. She smiled at him, her mind so engrossed in her secret that she did not feel the lack of warmth in his touch. And when he turned back to his people and spoke, it was only Daydee who suspected he was troubled, even though his speech was a good deal shorter than it normally would have been.

'Thank you one and all for being here. You have waited for us in the hottest part of the day and given us a Mayfield welcome. I have looked forward to returning home to the very faces gathered here. Mr Larmer and I have travelled a great deal since we last saw you and we have seen much of this fair country, but nowhere has the landscape pleased my eye as much as it does here with you. Again, thank you all.'

Another cheer, and John Stuart turned on his heel and entered his home.

Thelma caught her daughter's arm. 'And now, miss, why did you not tell me you were going to ride on from the lookout to meet your father? I gave you permission to go to the lookout, not to waylay the coach.'

Daydee's eyes narrowed. 'How could I tell you when I didn't know myself. I only decided to meet it when I saw it coming.'

Thelma sighed. What would she do with this girl?

'Mother, please don't be difficult,' her daughter said as she pulled her arm from Thelma's grasp and moved away to her father.

Thelma shook her head unhappily. 'Ah, Joe Larmer,' she said aloud to Daydee's departing back, 'we've truly ruined that girl.'

Once inside the house, John Stuart turned stiffly towards Eve. She moved quickly to him to enter his arms, but to her amazement he stepped away from her. It was now she saw his uneasiness and the tension in him.

'Evelyn, please join me in the library in twenty minutes, will you?' It was a command.

Mrs Smith entered. 'Sir,' she began, 'I have luncheon ordered for you. Will you eat now?'

'No, Mrs Smith, I wish to bathe and change clothes first.'

John Stuart walked away as soon as Mrs Smith had turned from them. Eve was dismayed. What was wrong? She had so much to tell him. So much that needed a sympathetic, loving John Stuart; not this strangely severe man.

As the minutes passed, she began to think that Daydee must be behind whatever troubled him. Daydee had travelled with him in the coach. What had she said to him? What could she say to him that would make him this way? Eve felt cold, she felt hot, she felt sick. Surely, Lake had not told Daydee that he suspected she was Clare, surely she couldn't know anything. But why was John Stuart so cold and distant? It was Daydee, she was sure of it.

Swiftly, she returned to the front of the house and looked through the windows. The coach had gone and the people had dispersed into smaller groups. Joe and Thelma were still there and so was Daydee, talking to Mrs Hennessy. The bright sunlight lit up the girl's features as she threw her head back in laughter.

Disconsolately, Eve toyed with the fringe on the heavy tassel of the sash securing the curtain, her fingers moving back and forth nervously. Then coming to a decision, she hurried through the front

290

door across the verandah and down the steps.

'Daydee,' she said as the girl turned to her with a puzzled look. 'I want to talk to you. Excuse us, Mrs Hennessy.' She took the girl's arm, steering her across to the steps, up onto the verandah and into the house. 'Follow me,' she said, crossing the hall and into the blue drawing room. She closed the door and faced Daydee, 'What have you told my husband?'

Daydee feigned amazement. 'What on earth do you mean?'

'Don't pretend, Daydee. You have told him something. I know you have.'

'I have told him nothing. Why would I?'

Eve's eyes met Daydee's steadily. Once more she read the patent hatred in them. She knew the girl had caused her husband's strange withdrawal, it was obvious. 'Daydee, I don't know why, but your demeanour betrays you.'

The girl's expression was contemptuous.

A frown creased Eve's brow. 'I fear you are much more evil than I could possibly have imagined. I have underestimated your wickedness.'

Daydee's voice sounded smugly in reply. 'Your opinion of my character means nothing to me.' Then her eyes hardened as her violent hatred finally found release in words. 'You make me sick. You don't belong here. You never have. You don't deserve him, he's wonderful and you're nothing. I despise you.'

Eve's heartbeat quickened as she forced herself to step a pace closer to the repellent expression trained upon her. 'Daydee,' she spoke slowly and deliberately, 'you waste your time thinking you can ever take my husband's love away from me. You are a mean, selfish child.' She saw Daydee flinch at the word 'child' and she continued, 'Yes, child is what I said and child is how my husband thinks of you. He will never take you seriously; you are merely a joke.'

Daydee's mouth opened in injury and rage. Tears of resentment sprang to her eyes. 'He does not think of me as a child. I'm a woman,' she spat angrily as Eve turned away and walked to the door. 'Damn you, damn you to hell!' she shouted at Eve's back.

Eve opened the door, and halted. She did not look back. She had seen enough of that face. Her voice came steadily. 'And you, Daydee Larmer, are not worth damning.' Then she closed the door and walked away.

Eve felt the cold chill of increasing fear again and the lost and lonely feeling of the previous weeks rose like a net of despondency to cover her. John Stuart must listen to her, he must, no matter what Daydee had said.

Entering the library, she stood behind one of the gold brocade Louis Seize chairs, clutching the enamelled wood framework. Sunlight came through the windows now in broad beams and she noticed the minute particles of dust dancing in them. For the first time, she observed the complicated bas-relief of small carved angels at the top of the bookshelves and how they were repeated in a pattern round the skirting board. Near the casement windows hung a portrait of John Stuart's father. This was the one she liked, showing a strong though tired face. The expression appealed to her; it was almost amused, a somewhat droll smile played around his mouth as if he saw that things were not as important as poor mortals made them.

Thelma had said he was a different man in his later years. But he had not seen the lighter side of things in his youth, and he had sent his wife away forever, because of her transgressions. For a moment, real sorrow welled inside her for John Stuart, never to have known his own mother. The thought of her husband threw her back to the present. If only she had told him of Clare before this. If only, if only . . .

The great walnut door swung back and John Stuart entered. He wore a suit of dark gaberdine, but he had not changed anything else; he still wore his unhappy expression and moved in a rigid, formal fashion.

Eve moved towards him holding out her hands. 'John Stuart, darling, I—'

He raised his hand to stay her, bewilderment and confusion showing plainly in his face. 'Evelyn, is it true that you are with child?'

Eve started. 'But how can you can possibly know?'

His face paled. 'Then it is true?'

Eve fell silent. Now she too was hopelessly confused. Who had told him? Daydee? Of course it had to be her, but how could she have known?

He waved his arms in a lost, helpless movement and his voice rose a little. 'How can this be? I have been gone for twelve weeks and we both know the time of the month that I left. Eve, how is it possible that you are carrying a child?' John Stuart could not believe this was happening. Since Daydee had told him he had been confused, mystified, uncertain. He had been looking forward to seeing his wife for so long, his beautiful, pure wife, and to be told in the last half-hour before joining her that she carried a child, a child that could not possibly be his – it had eaten into the core of him. His own mother had cheated and made love with others behind his father's back. She had been immoral and despicable.

With terrible fear, Eve saw the shock and horror in his face. Panic rose constrictingly to her throat and fighting desperately to keep her voice calm she said, 'Please, John Stuart, listen. You must listen to me. Let me explain. It is not simple.'

'Simple?' he whispered the word, but it would have been better had he yelled it, so ominous and sinister did he make it sound. 'What has been going on here? What has happened in my absence?'

'Dearest, this is not how I expected it. I don't know what to say. It's Daydee, isn't it? What has she told you?'

He moved forward and pulling her to him held her tightly. 'Eve, please, what has happened? Answer me!' He seemed to be slipping out of control. She knew there was no hope of explanation as she had planned, but she must try, she must.

She lifted her hand and touched him gently on the face. 'There was a man. Nathaniel Lake. He was hired, extra help. You know, a short-timer. He mistook me for someone else . . . One night soon after you had gone, he . . . he was in our garden . . . He attacked me . . . assaulted me. The child . . . I . . .'

John Stuart dropped her arms as if they were molten lead. The look in his eyes terrified her. 'No! It cannot be.' His voice was desolate. 'It is obscene. Tell me it cannot be.' His eyes were begging her to deny it, but all she could do was to look back at him beseechingly. He was silent for many seconds, looking at her in disbelief. She made small imploring sounds which he did not hear and then in misery, he cried, 'The swine! I'll kill the swine! I'll kill him!'

She looked up at him and clutched him. 'Please, darling, listen!'

Bringing himself under control, he removed her hand, not roughly, but deliberately. There was a sick, malevolent look in his eyes. 'Evelyn, where is he now?'

'I . . . I do not know. He is gone from Mayfield.'

He turned and left the room.

There was no sympathy in him as he strode down the corridor. He was past understanding. His mind was a blur with pain and the need for revenge. How dare the man touch her! How dare he even look at her! That he had sexually assaulted her was beyond endurance. He did not hear her cries calling to him as he stamped away. He did not hear her shout that there was more he should know. He heard nothing but the singing in his ears of his own damaged pride.

Eve rushed after him down the long corridor. As she came to the door leading to the hall, she heard a crash and the sound of broken glass.

When she reached the bottom of the wide staircase, he was already striding across the front verandah. Stephanie and one of the chamber-maids stood on the stairs staring, their eyes wide with amazement, but Eve did not even see them. She hesitated. The glass of the locked gun cabinet in the hall was smashed and two Enfield rifles were missing. There was blood on some of the pieces of glass. He must have smashed the glass with his fist. She went out onto the grass at the front of the house. She could see him in the distance striding swiftly away.

She must follow him. Explain everything. He was appalled, yes, and hurt. But what could he do? Lake was gone. He would of course send immediately for the police, probably enlist even Sir Rutherford. They would find Lake and he would go to trial and all the sordid details would come out. Everything. Clare, her liaison with Lake. Could John Stuart bear it? Could she bear it? What should she do? She felt sick, sick to the pit of her stomach. 'Come back, John Stuart, please, please . . .'

At that moment Mrs Smith's high-pitched voice called from the house. 'Mrs Wakeman, Mrs Wakeman, the broken glass . . . can I help you?'

Even turned back and began to speak, but Mrs Smith spiralled into a dark shape, Mayfield House went black and the whole, giddy world spun up at her face. The housekeeper just managed to run forward and catch her before she hit the ground. Her cries soon brought others from the house and Eve was taken immediately to bed.

It was in some ways best that she was oblivious of what was taking place in Jack Hennessy's office.

John Stuart had stopped a rider just outside the park gates and taken his horse. When he reached the offices, Jack Hennessy was not there but Stephen Watson was. (He handled Mayfield's records and correspondence.) There was a grave look in his intelligent eyes and his freckled brow dimpled with concentration as he answered John Stuart's questions, for he could see his master was enraged.

'So you employed this man Lake for six and a half weeks?'

'Yes, sir, he left as I told you, the night of the seventeenth of September, with pay owing to him. It's all here, sir, in the day book.' Stephen Watson tapped the ledger lying on the desk in front of him.

'Do you know where he went?'

'No, sir. But some of the boys might.'

'Get his mates immediately. Send for them and bring them to me at Mr Larmer's home.'

'Yes, Mr Wakeman, sir.' And he ran from his office shouting loudly for Adrian and the grooms in the stable yard.

When John Stuart arrived at the Larmers' front door, he did not wait for Rosy to take him into the parlour, but went straight past the girl down the hall, calling for Joe.

Thelma had been all nerves since Joe and John Stuart had come back. On their way home across Mayfield park after the gathering outside the big house, her husband had taken her arm and said, 'Isn't it grand that our boy is to have an heir? Wonderful news, eh?'

She had stopped walking in astonishment. 'How on earth did you know?'

Joe laughed indulgently. 'Ah, Thelma love, you know our little Daydee, can't keep a secret. Told us in the coach on the way here.'

'Then . . . then John Stuart knew before . . . he got here?'

'Yes, love, I just told you our little chatterbox let the cat out of the bag.'

Thelma had not said any more. She felt ill. How could Daydee have found out? Her daughter was such a troublemaker. She felt a flood of anger towards the girl and guilt and sadness when she thought of Eve. She remained sick with apprehension, and when John Stuart arrived in her dining room looking fit to kill a man, she was not surprised.

Joe stood from the table, his napkin in his hand and a look of consternation on his face. 'Whatever is it, m'boy?'

'I'm glad you've eaten, old man, we've a ride in front of us this day.' The ominous note in his voice was unmistakable and Joe had not missed the violence in his look and the guns in his hands.

It was then Thelma saw the blood on his fingers. 'What have you done? Let me bathe it.'

'It does not bother me, Thelma,' he replied, but she went to get hot water and a bandage just the same.

As soon as she left, John Stuart moved to Joe. 'We ride to kill a man, Joe. It's hard to believe or comprehend, old friend, but my wife was raped while we were away. It is not my child she carries. You and I ride to track down an animal called Nathaniel Lake, the cur responsible.'

Joe's mouth dropped open, but he left immediately to get his gear together.

When Thelma came with water and bandage, John Stuart protested but he allowed her to dress the ugly gash on his hand. As she tended his wound she watched him from beneath her eyelids. She prayed to God that Eve was all right but she said nothing, and he too said nothing. His pulse raced and there was pain in his chest as if a band of iron had been welded round his heart.

Soon, Timothy arrived with the master's riding clothes and he and Joe were waiting ready to leave when Jason Fowler rode up.

'Good day, Fowler,' Joe began as the man raised his hat. 'I want you to tell me of Nathaniel Lake, a short-timer who disappeared a few weeks back. Do you have any idea where he would have gone?'

'Well, sir, I do and I don't.'

John Stuart broke in sharply, 'Then just tell us what you *do* know, man.'

'Yes, sir. Well, 'e might have gone to the goldfields. Always said 'e was goin' there after 'ere. But there be a mate of 'is, Larry Cadee, 'e might know more cert'in like. 'E's tendin' the servicin' of the bulls down in the furthest of the river paddocks, sir.'

'He's been sent for?' asked Joe.

'That 'e has, sir.'

Jack Hennessy had arrived with the saddled horses and the spares before Cadee and a second man came galloping up.

'Afternoon, Mr Wakeman, you wanted to see us?'

Joe answered. 'Yes. Tell me what you can about where Nathaniel Lake would have gone after he left here.'

The two men looked at each other. Then Cadee spoke. 'It's hard to say, sir, but he said oft times he was goin' to the goldfields.' The second man nodded in agreement.

'Did he ever mention which one?'

'Well, not in so many words, Mr Larmer.'

'Is there anyone other than yourselves who would know?'

Both men shook their heads.

'Damn!' John Stuart exclaimed.

Then Cadee spoke up again. 'Well, actually, sir, there is someone as might know, or as might hazard a good guess.'

'Who, man, who?' asked Joe.

'She's the publican's daughter at the Fitzroy Arms in Cowra. See, he always said he was goin' to her for a bit when he left here. Mind you, he might not have as he went in a hurry like. But he was all for stoppin' with her at one time.'

'Her name?'

'Elizabeth Jenks, she's the barmaid there.'

John Stuart was already riding away as Joe turned to Jack Hennessy and said quietly, 'You'll manage things until we return, Jack?'

'That I will, Mr Larmer,' the man answered in the same quiet tone. 'Haven't I been doing that very thing for the past three months already?'

'Aye,' nodded Joe.

As they rode out, Daydee walked in the back gate with Leith. They had been out to the strawberry gardens and they carried two baskets full of the bright red fruit. Thelma stood watching the men leave.

'What's happened?' Daydee asked.

'Nothing that concerns you.'

'Well, where are they going?' Daydee persisted.

'I don't know,' answered Thelma walking by her into the house, 'but come with me. I want to speak with you.'

Daydee followed her mother reluctantly.

Inside, Thelma rounded on her daughter. 'How did you know Eve was with child? Tell me the truth, Daydee. I am very serious.'

Daydee was prepared for this. 'I heard you talking together about it one day. I didn't mean to listen, I just couldn't help it.'

Thelma was exasperated. 'How dare you eavesdrop on other people's conversation and then go and repeat it to your father and Uncle John Stuart. It's terrible.'

'Why is it terrible?'

Thelma looked at her in disbelief. 'My goodness, Daydee Bronwyn Larmer, if you don't know the answer to that, there's no hope for you.' She shook her head. 'I don't think you're my daughter at all,' she said angrily, before she turned and walked away.

In a little over two and a half hours, John Stuart and Joe tied their horses to the hitching rail outside the Fitzroy Arms, one of the two hotels in the tired township of Cowra. The summer heat rose up round the cluster of wooden huts and buildings. Semblances of life were few. A dog lay some ten yards away on what served as a footpath and down the street a little way, dust rose in the air as Father Tooley swept the wooden stairs of the Roman Catholic church.

The Fitzroy Arms was a typical bush hotel, one storey only of roughly hewn timber covered with a cast-iron roof. The wooden planking of the verandah squeaked as if the footfalls of the newcomers were some kind of invasion of the barren silence.

Inside, weary movement passed for activity. Three men played cards at a small table in the corner and a couple of old-timers lolled spiritlessly at the bar. Behind the bar, a jaded-looking person of twenty-nine or thirty, dark hair pulled on top of her head, looked up from washing glasses as the door swung open. She had an ordinary face, her nose was not a pretty shape and her chin receded, but her eyes were large and striking. Her figure was heavy-bosomed and beneath her gown her legs were thick and unshapely, but she was still in the last stages of the appeal that comes with youth, and before it finally passed there would be those who would find time for her. When she registered the presence of the two arrivals, a glimmer of interest showed in her face, for while she had seen him only a few times, she thought she recognised the master of Mayfield.

At the door, John Stuart sniffed the air as if he smelled something offensive then crossing to the girl asked, 'Are you Elizabeth Jenks?' He spoke in the abrupt manner of the person used to having immediate answers.

When she hesitated in replying, Joe said, 'Come on girl, what's your name?'

One of the men at the bar turned towards them and in mocking tones said, 'She don't often get called Elizabeth, it's a bit highfalutin for ya, ain't it, Lizzie?'

'Oh, shuddup, you,' the girl said and, turning her eyes on John Stuart, answered, 'Yes, I am Elizabeth Jenks, and why is it of importance to you?'

Joe answered. 'Can we speak away from here, is there anywhere private?'

She pointed to an opening in the wall beyond the end of the bar. They passed through into a mean sitting room.

As the woman entered, Joe began. 'We believe you know a man called Lake, Nathaniel Lake. We want you to tell us if you know where he is.'

Her demeanour changed slightly. She swung her hips round to them and with arms akimbo looked knowingly from one to the other. 'Why? What's he done?'

John Stuart viewed her with contempt. He had judged her and found her wanting. 'Just tell me where I can find the man. I've little time to waste with you.'

She stared back at them for a second or two, then shifting her glance so she did not meet their eyes replied, 'Tell me why you want him first.'

John Stuart was barely containing his temper, but Joe intervened. 'We are not going to tell you, so it's useless your asking, but here, this may help your memory.' He handed her a gold sovereign.

She turned it over in her hand and a grin passed across her face. 'Do you have more of this, for I deem you want the information very badly?'

John Stuart grunted angrily, but Joe calmly handed her a second gold coin.

She stood there unmoving, looking insolently at Joe, her arm still extended, the two coins lying in her palm.

He dropped another beside them. 'That's all there is,' he said quietly.

She smiled and closed her fist round the coins. Then putting her hand inside the pocket of her dress, clinked the three sovereigns together. She had an exquisite feeling of joy as she felt the metal rub, it was a deal of money. 'Yes, he was here for a few days in September. Worked for you before that, didn't he?' She looked at John Stuart who averted his eyes. 'Promised to marry me, he did.' She gave a small, disdainful laugh. 'Well, he's gone. Wouldn't say where he was going 'cept to say he'd try his hand at mining, so I'd say he's gone to the goldfields.'

'We know all that, damn it,' broke in John Stuart.

'Come on, girl,' went on Joe calmly, 'you've told us nothing we don't already know.'

She considered a second or two, her eyes moving from one to the other. 'Well, you won't know this. He didn't say nothin' about his destination but he left with a fella that I happen to know was going to the goldfields at Tanner's Rock. So, I'd say if you looked there, you just might find him.'

John Stuart turned on his heel and left without further communication. Joe tipped his hat to her and followed. As they departed, the girl was still clinking the coins in her pocket. She stood there saying to herself, 'Yes, he did, said he'd be back and marry me . . .'

Tanner's Rock was a small goldfield seventy-odd miles south-west, and towards this John Stuart rode with one thought dominating his head; to kill Nathaniel Lake. It was not that he did not think of Eve, he did, although he was so blinded by his own need for revenge that he did not begin to comprehend her suffering. He did think that perhaps he should not have left so hastily, that he should have told her not to worry, that everything would be all right. One thing he could not bring himself to consider was the baby. He must deal with this abominable man before he could allow his mind to come to terms with that.

They rode another four hours. The night was one of those Australian summer nights where the heat almost stifles the thought processes. By the time they reached the small outpost of Mogongong, both men and horses were exhausted. They slept on the verandah of the single dwelling, a tiny inn, and the next morning set off into the searing heat once more to ride the forty miles to their destination.

If it were possible, John Stuart's determination had grown with the passing of the night. Yes, he would be the judge and jury and convict and kill this animal. No man in the colony would blame him. He would find Lake, wherever he was, he did not care if he had to ride around Australia. But in fact, he did not have to ride around Australia, Tanner's Rock would be far enough, for that was where Lake was, confident that no one was following him.

He had ridden away from Mayfield a shaken man. Ever since he had seen her ride by at the ford that day, he had been absolutely positive the Wakeman woman was Clare. The likeness was uncanny. He had been totally convinced, until he had her on the ground; then he had realised. He should have stopped then, he had been a bloody fool. Still, what was done was done. But who the devil was she? She was identical to Clare. He remembered Clare had once or twice spoken of a sister. She had come to Adelaide when he was living with Clare, though he had never met her. Could that be it? Were they twins? They had to be. God! You couldn't even believe what you saw these days.

He had ridden straight to Cowra and the Fitzroy Arms, to Lizzie, the old tart. She had taken him in. They had been four really good days with her, at it morning and night, safe in the knowledge that Wakeman was still on the cattle drive. Of course he had moved on smartly before Wakeman returned. He knew that if the woman told what had happened he would be a dead man one way or another. He'd have no hope against Wakeman. He'd be hanged. But his strong belief was that she would remain silent. Lots of women did that, to avoid scandal. And what a scandal this would be! It would stagger the whole colony! Being married to Wakeman she would surely avoid the humiliation and the sneers and gibes if she could. And so he counted on Eve's silence, and perhaps he even could have, if there had been no pregnancy.

Nathaniel Lake was in essence an indolent creature and when he reached the goldfield and found there were women, voluptuous, easy women, he stayed. Even so, he spent an anxious week or two and he had panicked when two policemen rode into the settlement a few days after he arrived. But it turned out they were just looking for a horse thief, thank the Lord. And now? Well it was over two months ago . . . hell, two and a half. Yes, she had stayed her tongue, whoever she was. He had been relaxed for weeks now. His apprehension had disappeared and his self-assurance had returned.

As he made his way along the single, dusty street which was Tanner's Rock, in the gathering dark of this December night, he whistled a bawdy tune and walked with jaunty tread. His mind filled with the pleasures that awaited him later tonight in the tent down the street. There was one there he really liked, Leslie-Jane, more skilled than the others, with big eyes and big tits – his type. He grinned, reliving the moments of the night before with her.

A touch of breeze had sprung up. It gave a bit of release from the oppressive heat. It had been a bastard of a scorcher today out prospecting. Found nothing, too bloody hot; perhaps tomorrow would be cooler. He was heading for the tavern, he could see the lights in the bar ahead. This place was a pile of bark huts and tents that straggled along the only thoroughfare. Miners lived in tents, traders mostly in bark huts. There were as many Chinese here as there had been in the Victorian fields, damn queer lot with their odd habits. They could put you off the goldfields. He had seen one of them combing his hair out this morning, down to his waist it was. Fancy a bloody so-called man with hair to his waist! They were a clean bunch though, he would say that for them, not that you could say much more.

He was within fifty yards of his destination and looking forward to an ale when he heard his name spoken from behind. He stopped whistling and turned. 'Yes?'

The blow in the mouth sent him staggering backwards. In the darkness, he had not even seen the man who hit him. As he recovered his balance, he realised there were two figures in front of him. It was then he discerned the guns. Fear clouded his mind as he tried to make out the faces of the two men. They were not police, he could see that. He held his right hand to his mouth as blood seeped from his lip where his tooth had cut it. 'What the devil . . .?' he began, then froze as he recognised John Stuart Wakeman. After all this time. No, it couldn't be! Why? What had gone wrong? Even in the darkness, he could see John Stuart's eyes were wild.

'You swine,' he heard the master of Mayfield say, 'I'm going to kill you. I am going to execute you.'

Lake's mind went blank. In horror he watched the gun being levelled at him. Then the thoughts came. Oh God, so she had told him after all. After so long. Why? He heard words come rushing from his mouth, extemporaneously, all uttered to delay the firing of the gun. 'Please, you don't know what you're doing! There must be some mistake. Mr Wakeman! Sir! Please, what have I done? Please? Why would you want to k . . . kill me?'

'My wife, you animal! For what you did to my wife.'

Lake's mind raced, looking for something to say that would ensure survival. 'What do you mean, did to your wife? I don't know what you're talking about, sir. Please—'

John Stuart hit him again and this time the blow had such force that he dropped to the ground.

'You know exactly what I'm talking about.' The menace in John Stuart's voice took on a new sound; there was killing in the sound. 'That an animal like you even touched my wife is not to be borne. But that you assaulted her is abominable! And for that, I am going to kill you, now.' John Stuart once more levelled the rifle.

Ice-cold with terror, Lake heard the click of the hammer cocking. Instinctively he began to speak. 'I did nothing to your wife. Nothing

301

she didn't want. She knew me well. She asked for it. I swear before God.'

John Stuart's sharp intake of breath sounded loudly on the night air. In the weak light, his face tightened and the rifle barrel edged up just slightly. 'What do you say? Knew you? Asked for it?'

Lake went straight on. 'Look, I knew her long before she married you. She wanted it. She asked for it. She's that sort of woman, she led me on.'

Joe spoke for the first time. 'I don't believe it. John Stuart, he's lying. She would not do such a thing! She's a good woman.'

Thoughts tumbled over themselves in Lake's racing mind, his head throbbed. Impulsively he rushed on with the lies that preserved him, and they had the ring of truth to them, for he only had to imagine that woman to believe she was truly Clare.

'I'm telling the truth,' he cried. 'As God's my judge, I knew her in Adelaide years ago. She was my *de facto*. When I met her she was with another bloke. Look, she knew lots of shady characters, shacked up with them too, I swear. When she came to live with me she called herself Clare Herman.'

As he said Clare Herman, John Stuart blanched.

There was just enough light for Lake to see the impact of his words on the faces of the two men above him. They were amazed, disconcerted, that was clear. Ah, sweet providence. He must cement their misgiving, quickly.

Slowly he raised himself from the ground and then stood, his arms open from his body, palms out towards John Stuart.

Now that he could think more clearly he spoke with the expertise of the congenital liar.

'Look, sir, I would never have told you all that. Never! But you were going to kill me a few moments ago. It is not a thing that one talks about, sir. I realise how you feel, Mr Wakeman. That is why I left Mayfield, sir. I mean, after all Clare is married to you now, and mistress of so much. I was only confusing her, bringing up her past. I don't know how she told it to you, sir, but there was no assault. I swear it. There was no need for assault, if you know what I mean. I'm not saying Clare . . . ah, excuse me, Mrs Wakeman . . . is a liar. I wouldn't. But I swear on the Bible, she was not opposed to it.'

John Stuart looked towards Joe. He lowered his gun and retreated a step. There was shock in his face and a dazed look in his eyes; they implored Joe to help. He bent forward as if he had received a body blow and he seemed much smaller than his six feet one. His demeanour showed total defeat; all the pride and anger were gone.

Joe hated to see the suffering in him, but all he could do was to ask him, 'Do you know if she was ever in Adelaide, m'boy?'

'No, I . . .' The words were lifeless. 'There's so much I don't know, it seems.' Then his eyes returned to Lake, upright now with some of his former perky air returning. He was dabbing the blood from his mouth with a handkerchief and he watched them closely.

With a visible effort, John Stuart brought his feelings under rein. 'This time you speak of in Adelaide. When was this?'

'Oh, some six or seven years ago.'

'What year? Tell me.'

Lake was quiet for a second or two, then answered. 'I suppose it was fifty-seven. Yes, it would have been fifty-seven.'

'And where had she come from? This Clare you speak of?'

'From Sydney,' Lake replied and then added in a perceptively brilliant afterthought, 'I think she went to live in Bathurst after we separated, taught music. She could play the piano like a dream.'

The feeble light gave enough illumination for him to see John Stuart step back as if he had received another blow. Then he watched as the master of Mayfield turned his head slowly to Joe. 'There is no more to be achieved here.'

Almost in charge of his feelings once more, Lake watched them walk towards their horses. He was free to go now, wherever he wished. A smile of real satisfaction curled his still-bleeding mouth. Now he would make good his escape, get as far away from this bloody place as he could. Perhaps, even get back to Sydney and hop a ship. He had heard there were things to offer a clever man in New Zealand these days.

He watched the two distant silhouettes mount their horses. He had saved himself and brought destruction upon Eve.

CHAPTER EIGHTEEN

'If you have tears prepare to shed them now.'
Julius Caesar, William Shakespeare, 1564–1616.

John Stuart had left Mayfield in a passionate fury; he returned in a passionless self-possession.

In the three days since they had ridden away so hurriedly, Mayfield had been astir with gossip from the scullery to the bedrooms, from the dairy to the orchards, from the cottages and living quarters to the stables and beyond.

Those people in positions of rank like Thelma and the heads of staff would say nothing and have nothing said in their presence, but they were few against the tide of common talk. The speculation was endless. On and on it went. That Lake had stolen something very valuable was the popular belief, and what he had stolen varied, depending on who told the tale.

Mrs Wakeman's swooning in Mrs Smith's arms was something no one was really sure about. Some said Mr Wakeman had blamed her for allowing the theft to occur and she had collapsed in mortification, others said she ran after her husband in such a temper that she fainted, and some even averred she must be with child.

Daydee had soon found out that her father and John Stuart had gone after Nathaniel Lake. She and her mother were the only ones who in fact comprehended the pursuit. They alone knew of Eve's pregnancy. But neither knew the complication of Clare. Had Thelma known, she might have been able to help the situation; had Daydee known, she would have been delighted instead of merely happy.

The girl's thoughts were filled with what must become the staggering scandal of Eve carrying Lake's child. Surely this would ruin the marriage? The marriage could be annulled. She had read somewhere about a marriage that was annulled by the Archbishop of Canterbury. The husband had been at sea for a year and had returned home to find that his wife carried another man's child. Well, this was like that really, just like it. Daydee was so pleased, she went around singing to herself.

When Eve fainted, Dr Douglas, the Mayfield doctor, had been

304

sent for immediately. He had come from the bedside of a sick child over in one of the river cottages, and while she said she felt quite normal, he had insisted on examining her and confirmed what she already knew. She asked him not to say anything to anyone about her condition.

He smiled gently. 'Of course, Mrs Wakeman, as you wish.'

Eve was so ashamed for John Stuart. The knowledge of the child she carried would emasculate him in the eyes of the world and, worse than that, in his own. Again, she thought to commit suicide. Perhaps that would release John Stuart. He had created the myth about her; he alone had made her a Lucretia. Should she kill herself as Lucretia had done?

When she remembered the agony in his face after he had learned of the assault, she cried for him. She thought of Alan Fletcher and his compassion that day they had spent together in the bush. If only John Stuart were more like him, they would survive this. Then she would muster all her strength and tell herself that together they would survive; no matter what, she and her husband could weather all this and face anything. Their love was strong enough to ride out any disparaging slander of the misinformed. Once she had convinced herself, the thought of the child would make her uncertain again.

Thelma continued to comfort her like the good friend she was. She hardly spoke to her daughter, so angry was she about her behaviour, but that did not trouble Daydee.

So the days passed, until John Stuart's return.

When John Stuart and Joe had left Lake standing in the street of Tanner's Rock, they had ridden ten miles back to a rundown tavern in an area known as Billabong Diggings. In this they spent an uncomfortable night, surrounded by human flotsam and jetsam. The next day they rode on and that night they slept again on the verandah of the inn in Mogongong. There was little said between them and when they did speak, it was of business and Mayfield concerns.

From Mogongong to Mayfield, John Stuart seemed to dawdle, halting for rests on the hour and riding slowly. His excuse was the heat, and although it was enervatingly hot, it was no hotter than the previous days. It was as they reined in for one of these pauses, near a single clump of mulga trees that made the only shade on a long, dry flat, that Joe decided to speak his thoughts.

Joe Larmer was a weatherbeaten sixty-seven, his pale eyes made so by the constancy of over forty years in the heartless Australian sun of the bush. He barked commands to the hands on Mayfield as a general would to his troops, but there was an honest, downright respect for him pervading the attitudes of all the men. There was no one more reliable in times of trouble; no one more knowledgeable about the hard country they sought to tame. He could converse in his objective, unassuming fashion with gentry or common man, and neither would take him for a fool. He was a man of his times, steady, moral, loyal to Mayfield, Queen and country.

Yet, inside this modest, discerning man lay an intensity of emotion completely alien to one so stable. Where his daughter and John Stuart were concerned, he was governed by blind love. They could do no wrong, and any who hurt them were his enemies. Consequently, all his feelings told him to hate Eve as an immoral impostor. Yet somehow he hoped there was an explanation, something that would counter Lake's words and show her in a better light. He wished this most of all for John Stuart's sake. John Stuart's pain was Joe's pain; it had always been so.

Ever since they left Lake, he had felt sorry they had not dealt more severely with him. He had disliked the man intensely. He sighed now as he spoke. 'M'boy,' he began, 'I've a feeling you move at a sluggish pace because of what is ahead when we get home.'

John Stuart did not answer but, turning his dark, morose eyes to Joe, slowly nodded.

'I know how shocked to the core you are. We both are. It's a blow few men could take. But there is something I would caution you to do when at last you face your wife.'

'It seems she was never wife to me.'

'Now, m'boy, that's as may be, but what I'm saying is this. That man back there was scum, albeit he spoke like an educated man. And while he condemned Eve, there may be more in the explanation when she tells it.'

John Stuart made a sad, scornful sound. His head ached from the heavy thoughts that sat in gloomy judgment there. 'Joe, I recognise the man was worthless, but there were too many things he said that fitted too precisely for them not to be true. He said he knew her in Adelaide. That she had come from Sydney and that after being his *de facto* wife in eighteen fifty-seven, she went to Bathurst.'

'Aye, lad, I'll admit that sounded bad, but he could have learned she lived in Bathurst from the men on Mayfield.'

'But the date fits, he knew when Eve went to Bathurst that she was a music teacher, and he knew the name Herman. He knew her maiden name, Joe, how do you account for that?'

'Well, now, John Stuart,' Joe was struggling to find a reason, 'it's not impossible that some of the Mayfield hands knew her maiden name.' He frowned in thought. 'Nevertheless, it was strange he called her Clare Herman, why wouldn't he just say Eve?'

John Stuart had dismounted as Joe spoke and now he tied his horse to a low branch and stood with his back to the older man. Without turning he said, 'That is the very thing that helps to damn her.' He stood silently for a time while Joe dismounted. When he turned around his eyes wore the expression of the convinced, and his movements were those of the life-weary.

'There are two things I must tell you. Then you will see what I see, and know what I know.' Briefly, he leaned on Diomed's saddle, as if gathering strength. 'At one stage she must have called herself Clare Herman.'

'Why sonny? How do you know such a thing?'

'Joe, I have never mentioned this, for at the time I thought it unimportant. It was a few weeks after I brought her to Mayfield. I remember she was out somewhere and as I was passing through her sitting room, I dropped a collar stud – you know how darn finicky those things are. At that time, she still had a trunk with music books in it. The lid was up and the stud fell in, down into the sheets of music, and as I moved them some splayed out onto the floor. I saw that one had the name Clare Herman written on it. I looked further and there were others with the same name. The handwriting was hers, I know it was. At the time, I assumed it was the name of a relative. Now I know differently. There was a time when she called herself Clare and I fear that time was when she was in Adelaide.'

'Ah,' said Joe, 'I see.'

'And there is the other thing.'

'What is that, m'boy?'

'I have had much time to remember things on this ride, Joe, and much has fallen into place which I would have preferred did not. You will recall that when Daydee met us in the coach on our way home three days ago . . . was it only three days? She said that Eve had been taking long walks and long rides alone while we were away. Well, I have got to thinking about those lonely walks and rides.'

'What do you mean, m'boy?'

'You remember Lake said she had known a lot of shady characters in her time.'

Joe nodded.

'It was a "shady character" who held up our coach on the day we married and we both recall who it was that brought her back to Mayfield the day after her birthday when she rode beyond the Mayfield borders.'

'Yes, we do, but what has that to do with things?'

'You recall she went to Bathurst a month or so before last Christmas?'

'I do, m'boy, with my Thel and Daydee.'

'She met the same shady character there, a third time, in the Bathurst park.'

The expression of amazement that rose to Joe's face remained as John Stuart continued.

'Oh, she told me about it right enough, I now fear only to put me off the track of what in truth occurred, for our own innocent little Daydee told a vastly different story to Eve's.' John Stuart brought his eyes to Joe's. 'Eve's account of the meeting was brief. She said she ran into the bushranger accidentally. That she was shocked to see him, as he was to see her, that he asked her how she was and that was the end of it. I believed her. Daydee said that Eve and the bushranger were in close and intimate conversation in the Bathurst park. She said she happened upon them and they were so involved with one another that they didn't realise she was beside them until she spoke. She said they talked for a long time.' He sighed, a painful sound. 'I ask you, would straightforward little Daydee lie?'

Joe shook his head. 'She wouldn't. She would have no reason to.'

Darting back to John Stuart's mind were Eve's words: 'I do not go to Bathurst to have any encounter with any outlaw.' It seemed she had been fooling him all along.

Joe's expression was melancholy. He was considering all this. He put his hand on his boy's shoulder. 'The sum total of all this is not good, is it?'

John Stuart's voice was lifeless. 'Joe, the sum total of all this, is bad.'

When they finally rode through the gates of Mayfield Park and up to the house, John Stuart had decided on the course he must take. Before he dismounted, Joe leaned across and took his arm. 'If you need me, I'll be waiting.'

'Thanks, old man.'

He stood on the threshold of his home. He did not enter immediately. He was still thinking. I must not let her charm me. Her immorality is unbelievable. She is corrupt, just as my mother was.

He had dwelt much upon his mother during the long ride home. He did not remember anything of her and he had hated her all his life. No, perhaps that was not so. When he was very small, he remembered crying into his pillow at night and wishing she would come back to him. But he had always known she was bad, even though his father refused to speak of her. He had known it, from the time he was about eight years old when he had heard the ticket-of-leave men discussing her. In those days, in the thirties, there had been convict servants and a lot of ticket-of-leave men on Mayfield, convicts who had been granted a form of freedom to work for themselves or find paid employment. John Stuart had been playing alone in the foundations of Joe and Thelma's new house where the ticket-of-leave men were doing the building. He had overheard them talking and when they mentioned his father's name, he had stood still and listened.

'Yeah, I wuz here when Mr Wakeman sent her away,' one said.

'What wuz she like?'

The man had laughed. 'A beauty right enough, black hair, flashin' eyes, big tits forcin' themselves at yer.'

They had all laughed at that.

'Yer cud see she wuz openin' her legs for that Major Breely right from the start. Don't know how the master didn't cotton on to it for so long. I mean, we all knew she was whorin' with the major, all of us knew that.'

'It's the kid what I'm sorry for,' another voice had said.

'Who? Young John Stuart? Don't be sorry for him. Gawd! He's goin' ta be ya landed gentry even if his mother was a whore.'

John Stuart had no idea what a 'whore' was, but he knew it must be very bad. He had slipped away unseen and cried alone for a long time after that. It was about three years later that he found the painting of her. He had been playing 'dress up', as he used to call it. At the time many old trunks and boxes had been stored at the top of the stairs above the east wing of the house. He had found some more old clothes and had been rummaging through them when he came across a portrait brooch on an old velvet coat. A funny thrill passed through him as he looked at it, a painting of a beautiful lady with black hair to her shoulders.

Something had told him not to take the brooch to his father, so it was Thelma he had approached. He had taken it from his pocket tentatively. She took it and gazed at it, then she hugged him. 'This is your mother, darling. Perhaps you should give it to Daddy.' But he had not, he had hidden it and he used to take it out at night and look at it. He knew she did not love him, just as she did not love his father, and he had begun to really hate her and to wonder if all women were bad like she was.

After his father died, they had held memorial services for him in Sydney. Sir William Denison had recently succeeded to the high office of Governor. He had been a friend of Arthur Wakeman as had many Governors before him, and he treated John Stuart in fatherly fashion. Sir William had given the young man a transcript of what was to be inscribed on a plaque to be laid in St James's Church in honour of his father. John Stuart had taken it to show to Joe and Thelma. When he arrived at their lodgings in a town house in George Street, Thelma was there alone. He sat down with her, and gave her the composition to read:

SIR ARTHUR FRANCIS WAKEMAN

Younger son of Mabel and Douglas Wakeman, born Mayfield, England, May 15th. 1798, deceased Mayfield, New South Wales, Sept. 17th. 1855.

Entering in youth the service of his country he travelled to the colony of New South Wales. His life was one of integrity, useful devotion and toil, wherein he created cultivation and industry out of a wilderness. His ability and public zeal extended to his many acts of charity and benevolence to the poor of this colony. By his generosity he endeared himself to all those who knew him and to a great number where he was not intimately known. His many gifts for the promotion of education and science will long be remembered by those fortunate to be in beneficiary. He lived his life as do those dedicated few, the good and kindly. He won the praise of those whose praise was honour. His memory is of a man of God who in Christ helped others.

Thelma sighed. 'Those are fitting words, a fine description of his life.'

John Stuart nodded. 'I hope I shall be as fine and capable a man as he was.'

'No reason in the world why you shouldn't.'

And then he had asked her something he had wanted to since the morning they found his father dead. 'Thelma, on the night of his death, why do you think he wore the wedding bracelet my mother had given him?' He said it awkwardly, playing with the cushion at his right hand.

She shook her head before replying and plucked at her skirt, avoiding his eyes, but she gave him an honest, straight answer, as she always did. 'I think he knew he was dying and at the last he somehow wanted to have Caroline, your mother, with him like. And you see the bracelet was all he had.'

Inscribed on the inside of the band were the words: *'To my dearest Arthur from your own wife Caroline.'*

John Stuart was confused. 'But I never knew he had such a thing. I thought he had disposed of everything that had been associated with her.'

'Yes, that's what we all thought but now we know otherwise, don't we? He had always kept that, her wedding gift to him.'

'I don't understand it. She left us. She was . . . bad. He hated her. Why would he want to wear her bracelet at the last?'

And Thelma in candid fashion replied, 'Perhaps he didn't hate her after all.'

'But he did,' countered John Stuart. 'He would never speak of her, never. In all my life we have never communicated with her nor she with us.'

Thelma had smiled a sad smile and leaned forward towards him. 'John Stuart, what lies in the heart is sometimes different from what a body shows to the world. And she did communicate with you, although you never saw the letters.'

'What do you mean?'

'I would never have told you while your father lived, but now perhaps you should know. Each year for your birthday a letter came from her, until you were about fifteen.'

John Stuart was amazed. 'How do you know?'

'You may remember that before your father employed a private secretary it was I as did such things for him. When I fell with Daydee, Mr Arthur said it was too much for me. I'd had four stillbirths before her. We are lucky to have her . . . I suppose. Anyway, until those letters stopped coming from Scotland, I handed them to Mr Arthur myself.'

John Stuart stood up defiantly. 'I'm glad he did not give them to me.' His tone was angry, adamant. 'Her behaviour was appalling, it disgusts me. I wish no communication with her and I'm sorry she was my mother. I'm ashamed she was my mother.'

And now, pausing on the verandah of his home, all this returned to his mind, and he saw his mother and Eve as one. He stood there, his eyes cold and glassy, his mouth a grim line of anguish and bitterness.

When he entered the hall at last, Mrs Smith stood patiently waiting.

'Good afternoon, sir. Welcome home. Is there anything I can get you?'

'No, thank you. Where is . . . Mrs Wakeman?'

'In your private garden sir. I have sent a gel to tell her of your arrival.'

As John Stuart strode away from the housekeeper, he noticed the smashed doors of the rifle cabinet had been removed and unconsciously he rubbed the cut on his hand. He passed swiftly through the house now, the lethargy gone, and when he stepped on to the verandah, Eve walked towards him across the grass. She had been down on her knees planting some seedlings.

She had been thinking about him. In fact he was all she had thought about. Her love for him was strong, surely his was the same for her. Couldn't they fight this together? She had been planning to start afresh, tell him of Clare, everything, and he had rushed away from her in pain and anger to find Lake. She had analysed his reaction over and over and she sympathised with him; she knew he had been stunned to his very core. He could not help his Wakeman pride and she truly understood the reasons that had taken him in blind fury from her. And now, here he was back again, and whatever had occurred, she would right things. She smiled compassionately as she came forward to him.

He watched her as she came out of the shadow of the poinciana tree. She was wearing a white dress and a rose-coloured apron. Her sleeves were rolled back to the elbow exposing her forearms and in her hand she still held the small trowel she had been using. Her hair was tied back in a ribbon, but some stray curls had fallen forward. She was smiling.

He halted. His heart was beating rapidly. Why, oh why, did she look so simple, so pretty and so good? For a second he wavered. How could one who looked this way be bad? But then had not his mother been lovely too? Perhaps evil women were all beautiful.

They faced each other across the host of blooms that filled the garden.

She spoke first. 'John Stuart, I'm glad you are home again.'

As he came closer, she saw the remoteness in his face. But his distant expression hid the mad pounding in his head. '*She was my de facto . . . she knew lots of shady characters, shacked up with them too, I swear . . . called herself Clare Herman . . . shady characters . . . fifty-seven, yes, it would have been fifty-seven . . .*'

He did not answer her greeting, he simply asked, 'Eve, when were you in Adelaide?'

'Why do you ask?' she replied, puzzled. He was so different from the last time she had seen him. The pain and anger had been replaced by a dead coldness.

'Answer me!' was all he said.

'Please, darling, tell me why you want to know.'

'Eve!' His voice rose. 'If you do not answer me, I shall simply turn and leave, and will have no further conversation with you now or at any other time in your life.'

There was no doubt he meant what he said. It was terrible. She did not know what to do. She had been awaiting his return with some trepidation, but she had brought herself to feel confident that things would be all right; she was not ready for this. For a second she faltered, before she said, 'I was in Adelaide briefly some years ago. I know this has something to do with that man Lake. What is wrong? Did you find him?'

He seemed without emotion, like an automaton. 'It is important that you answer me truthfully. What year were you there?'

She looked blankly back at him.

'What year?' he asked again, more loudly, yet his eyes seemed to look through her, to be trained on the garden wall.

'I . . . I . . . Why does it matter? I simply went to visit—'

'Tell me the year!'

'This is silly,' she remarked.

'By your evasion, I will take what I have been told to be true.'

This frightened her. 'John Stuart, this makes no sense but it was late eighteen fifty-seven.'

'Oh God!' he said.

She had never heard him say 'God' in all the time she had known him. It was so alien to his whole persona, that she froze with fear. She did not understand what was happening but she was aware there was no time left. She must act quickly, say the things that needed to be said immediately, without hesitation.

She dropped the trowel and stepped closer to him. As she did so he backed away.

'John Stuart, John Stuart,' she began, 'please, all this is a dreadful mistake. There is much I have to tell you. Much you don't know. I should have told you long ago and I am truly sorry that I did not. But it is not too late. I am heartbroken that you have been hurt so, but I have been hurt too, badly, and I want to tell you now. Please hear me. You see, when I was born I was one—'

He was not listening and he cut her off with the words, 'Yes, there is much I don't know! I have given you everything. Elevated you from nothing to mistress of Mayfield. Thought of you as purity itself and all the time you were just like my . . . my filthy whore of a mother! Your own words condemn you. There is so much I know now, things have all fallen into place, things that I would have preferred to die before I knew. You lived with Lake. You are mean and depraved, just as my mother was!'

Eve was shaking her head as she heard his words and she came towards him with her hands outstretched to touch him. There was a pitiful entreaty in her voice. 'But that is not true, please believe me. It was not me who lived with him.' She could see he found her repulsive. As she touched him, he pushed her away and she stumbled sideways into an ivy-covered seat and only gained her balance because of it. Her face was white with despair and the look of shock and fear that passed across it was to live in his mind.

'Please, please listen, I beg you,' she beseeched.

'Do not speak!' he commanded, the conviction of her immorality making him feel ill. His hand rose again as if to strike her. Then he checked his voice and kept it awesomely steady. 'Listen carefully, woman, for I will never again repeat what I say this day.' His words numbed her mind and chilled her to the bone, as if she stood in an arctic wind instead of the heat of this draining summer day. 'I know you carry the child of your old lover. You lied when you passed off your association with him as assault. One of many lies I fear you've told me. Lies about your meetings, your associations, your liaisons. You must live with that, but I shall not. The vileness is yours, the dishonour will be mine. Until your child is born you can remain here. I will move into other rooms today.'

He fell silent for a second or two although his eyes still were locked with hers. The sick pain of what he now believed made him almost unsteady on his feet.

'I shall expect you to leave here as soon as you are able, after the birth. In the months ahead, I ask you to have the decency to avoid me.' He took a deep, shuddering breath. 'There will be no need for us to speak to each other again. Should there be reason to communicate it will be through Mrs Smith. I do not wish to see you. Do you understand?'

Understand? She understood nothing. It was like some monstrous nightmare. She stood paralysed, looking blankly at him.

'Do you understand?' he asked again and when she did not reply, he waited no longer. 'I assume you do,' he said as he turned from her and walked away.

She was petrified. She could not think. Her eyes were the only parts of her that moved as they followed his departure. The seconds passed. Then suddenly she began to tremble uncontrollably. How desperately she had needed his love, his sympathy, his care, his understanding, and instead she had received this.

He never turned back so he did not see the helpless shaking nor hear her stammering like a child to explain herself to the empty garden. He did not see the hopeless gestures her hands made or the tears that broke from her eyes to run down her face.

And there were things she did not see. She did not see the despairing misery that replaced the severity in his face as he strode away from her. She did not hear his pitiful whisper, 'Oh God, how I loved you,' and she did not see his tears, the first tears that had

314

fallen from John Stuart's eyes since his father had died nine years before.

Three hours later, John Stuart dictated messages to each of the people he had invited to Mayfield for the Christmas week. He was cancelling the invitations.

Mr Oldfield sealed the letters and departed from the library without any show of emotion. His place was taken by Mrs Smith who entered as he left.

'Sit down, Mrs Smith. You have been here at Mayfield how long?'

'I came in thirty-nine, sir. Twenty-five years, twenty-six next March.'

'Yes, you are an important part of Mayfield.'

To this she gave a rare smile.

'You have been in the position of housekeeper all my adult life.'

'Since forty-eight, Mr Wakeman.'

John Stuart nodded. 'It is a position of great trust and because of that I have something to tell you. Something which causes me undeniable pain.'

Mary Smith edged forward slightly in the chair.

'It is impossible for me to relate this in the particular, Mrs Smith, but I must tell you that while I was away Mrs Wakeman's conduct was such that dishonoured me and her position as mistress of Mayfield. From this day forth, we will live separately. She will stay in the master suite. I will live here in the south wing.'

The first glimmers of emotion stirred in Mrs Smith's sedate features.

John Stuart was attempting to sound in control, but every now and then his voice trembled. 'Mrs Wakeman should still be attended by the girl Stephanie, and yourself. I do not wish her to have general access to the rest of the staff. She is not to ride or to walk beyond the gates of the park. She is not a prisoner, you understand, and is quite free to move within the limits I have mentioned, but it would be best if she were not seen by the majority of Mayfield's employees, for there will be . . . a child born, and after that she will leave here.'

The severity of Mrs Smith's expression softened in sympathy as she listened. She was hurt and mortified for her master. How could such a thing have happened to this wonderful man? A child born and not his obviously! It was too dreadful. She had loved Arthur Wakeman with a passion. He had taken a poor convict girl and had given her dignity, self-respect and position. She had worshipped him with an undying loyalty and his son had been the natural heir of her affections. She was honoured by his trust and she would not let him down. 'And what of Mrs Larmer, sir? They have been very friendly up to now.'

'I would not restrict Mrs Larmer's movements under any circumstances. She may come and go as she pleases.' He motioned that the interview was over.

Mrs Smith stood. 'I understand perfectly, sir.'

After she had gone, John Stuart sat with his head in his hands for a long time. The tears dripped through his fingers to make strange shapes as they soaked into the blotting paper on his desk. When he stood, twilight had fallen.

He ate a solitary meal he did not want, and later he walked alone in the park. He slept little that night and when he found himself awake at sunrise, he rose and was down in one of the river paddocks breaking horses when Joe arrived there at seven o'clock.

As the hours passed, they worked side by side. And at midmorning when the men stopped for their tea break, John Stuart and Joe moved apart from the others. They walked out of hearing range of the men to a rocky outcrop along the side of the paddock. As they gained the first of the boulders, Joe touched John Stuart affectionately on the shoulder. The younger man tried to smile but his expression remained grim. There was a forced animation in him this morning.

'How are you, m'boy? I've been very worried.'

'I'm all right now, Joe.' He made an unhappy sound. 'It was just as we thought, old man,' he said in a small voice for such a big man, 'she had been in Adelaide with Lake.'

'I'm sorry, lad.'

John Stuart put his mug of tea on top of a large weather-worn stone and looking back towards the men who rested from their work, he recounted what had passed between himself and his wife.

When he finished, Joe said with resignation, 'I truly would not have thought it of her, but we shall get by, m'boy. We always have.'

'It's so hard to believe this is happening to me. You know, I actually looked forward to an heir of my own some day, but I thought it best to have a few years alone with her first, just the two of us, before we shared ourselves with a family. Can you believe that? How stupid I was.' He laughed, a wretched sound. 'And now,' his eyes closed, 'all there will ever be is the poor bastard issue from her.'

Joe nodded, leaning forward to hold John Stuart's shoulder. He spoke quietly. 'You could get a divorce.'

John Stuart did not answer for a few moments, it was obvious he had not thought of this. When he replied it was slow and considered. 'I think not, Joe. While I know there are men that have done it, divorce is long and difficult and there will be enough malicious gossip attached to the Wakeman name. No, I must stay as I am, for now anyway. It is best.'

'But there may be another woman somewhere, one who would make you happy.'

He gave a melancholy smile as he answered. 'No, Joe, old man, I would never trust another, not in this world.'

As they spoke, Thelma had just come down the steps of Mayfield House to join Eve in the walled garden. It was a hot, cloudless morning and the sun's rays lit Eve's hair to a golden sheen in contrast to the white, desolate face she lifted to her friend. She had spent a night in the depths of misery. After John Stuart had left her in the garden, she had stumbled to the steps and across the verandah to her bedroom. She could not believe what had occurred. Over and over again she pictured his face, the look of cold, remote despair in his eyes and the loathing on his face. She sobbed for a long time alone in her room. Her life was shattered, nothing mattered any more.

It was almost dark when she heard a gentle tap on the door. She dragged herself to her feet to find Stephanie standing in the doorway, a look of concern on her face. She sent the girl away saying that she needed nothing and preferred to be alone for a time.

Why hadn't her husband given her a chance to explain? Why was he so ready to believe Lake? Did he really think that all women were deceivers? Yes, he probably did, that's why Lake could convince him. John Stuart could not help himself. She was shocked to her soul that he could believe something so vile of her. She was not like poor Clare. But then she had only herself to blame for not telling him ages ago of her sister's existence. For that she was entirely culpable, but she was not responsible for the ease with which John Stuart fell a ready victim to Lake's lies. Did their love mean so little to him?

Then she thought of the bushranger and suddenly she saw that John Stuart might have misinterpreted her meetings with him and believed they were not accidental. With John Stuart's willingness to see women as being like his mother, he probably had added it all together to form some kind of misguided proof, and in doing so condemned her. He had not allowed her to speak, had rejected her before she could defend herself. How could he have such little trust in her? How angry she was at his lack of trust. How hurt and dejected she was by his repudiation. How badly he had treated her when she needed him most.

Thelma came across the lawn to her and hugged her. 'Oh love,' the good woman began, 'whatever has happened?'

Eve sighed, a broken sound. 'He believes I was Lake's woman and that I consented to lie with him.'

Thelma looked baffled. 'But that's impossible, you didn't know the man. How could John Stuart think such a thing?'

Eve slowly shook her head. 'Seems he found Lake . . . somewhere. Lake said he lived with me. Swore that I was his woman, in Adelaide, years ago. Eighteen fifty-seven. And it's true, I was there to visit that year, Thel, I . . . John Stuart would not listen to me. He seems to think I have had meetings, liaisons. Whatever Lake said, he convinced John Stuart absolutely.'

'Oh dear, this is terrible. I must go to him, tell him he's wrong.'

Eve waved her hand tiredly. 'No, Thelma, love, you must not. He will not want to hear what you have to say. He does not want an explanation. He hates me as he hates his mother.'

'But I know you are innocent,' Thelma insisted. 'I must help you. This is too outlandish. How is it possible the man is so blind?'

Eve stood up from the seat and moved across the grass. There she remained motionless, looking up into the stark brightness of the day. Should she tell Thelma the whole truth? For a few seconds she was truly tempted for she was so very badly in need of help. The sunlight hurt her eyes and she squinted as she stood there thinking. No, it would not be fair to her good, true friend, not fair at all. It would place Thelma in a terrible position. She turned back to her friend and now her inner strength shone in her eyes and her chin tilted determinedly.

'I should honestly prefer you did not, my dear Thelma. He now believes that I am as bad as he once thought me good. John Stuart Wakeman's accusations and self-appointed judgments are not all his fault. I see many things I did not see before and somehow, now, I think possibly it is better that he believes what he does. He is a good man according to his own lights, it is simply that perhaps they are not mine.'

Nevertheless, for all Eve's resistance, Thelma could not let such a dreadful injustice occur. She had to defend her. Thelma was not a particularly articulate woman where her deepmost feelings were concerned. She was like the majority of the bushwomen, wonderful, hardy souls that they were. She could chatter all day with her own kind where she felt in harmony, but she found it almost impossible to express her sentiments clearly if she felt uncomfortable or out of her depth. So it took her twenty-four hours to find the courage to approach John Stuart.

Her step faltered as she was given entry to him, for it was a long time since she had been alone with John Stuart. She had fondled him, nursed him, fed him, mothered him until he was five years old. Then a series of nannies and tutors had taken him from her, although her influence had still remained during his childhood. But as the years had passed and adolescence had changed to manhood, he had slipped from her and passed from the candour of youth into the self-possession of the adult aristocrat.

He looked over as she hesitated at the door of the blue room. It was a hot, still night and he sat in gloomy silence with his dogs. 'Yes, Thelma, what is it?'

'I have come to speak to you on an urgent matter, John Stuart.'

'Come in, sit down.'

She did so.

'Well, what is it?'

She took a deep breath. 'I believe you have come to a terribly wrong conclusion about the delicate matter which concerns you and Eve.'

'And why is that?'

'I was here. You were not. I saw her the day after the attack by that . . . man. She was in a dreadful state, bruises and goodness knows what. Eve is a good girl, she is innocent. Please forget all this and go to her and—'

'Thelma!' he cut in, his tone icy. 'You speak from your feelings, you do not know the facts. You are being duped. I do know about the bruises she suffered from her fall. Mrs Smith told me everything.'

'But that is not so, it's Mrs Smith don't know the truth,' Thelma argued.

'No, Thelma, you don't know the truth. I know so very much more than you.' He rose to his feet and his voice became louder as he continued. 'This is all distasteful, my tolerance is breaking down. I tell you she has fed me a series of lies, lies you know nothing about and in your good-natured fashion you have allowed her to fool you. I have let you speak because of who you are and your long association with me, which gives you certain privileges, but I will not tolerate discussion of this again, not from you, not from anyone. I forgive you only because you are not in full possession of the facts.' He turned away from her, signalling for her to leave.

She stood. The insides of her hands were damp from the tension; he was intimidating her just as she had known he would. She was aware that she could not be successful. That all she was doing was aggravating him. There was little arbitration with John Stuart once his stand had been determined. She knew he wanted to hear no more, but she was a strong bushwoman for all that, and so with beating heart she made one last attempt. She spoke to his unyielding back.

'John Stuart, you have made it clear that I have dared to speak when I should have held my tongue, but as that is so, I shall brave a little more. This is a terrible mistake. I do not share your view of Eve, no matter what evidence you believe you have. I will respect your wishes and never mention it again, but one day you will see for yourself her innocence and the error you make, although I fear there will be much heartache 'tween now and then, for there's none so blind as he who will not see. Ah, John Stuart, my heart is heavy for you both.'

He did not speak. He did not turn round.

She sighed and left him standing there.

There was a sick feeling in his stomach and his chest felt tight. He walked out through the open doors onto the whitewashed terrace. The strong scent of jasmine hung in the warm air about him. How he wished his life were different. How he wished he had never seen her that night in the Bathurst park. Oh, how good and pure she had looked in the twilight. But she was iniquitous. To think he had cared for her, touched her, kissed her, loved her. His mother and his wife, blasted whores! His bitterness rose to his tongue like bile.

He looked about him into the darkness, and out of the night echoed the mocking refrain of Lake's words: *'When I met her she was with another bloke. She knew lots of shady characters, shacked up with them too, I swear . . . was my de facto . . . knew lots of shady characters . . .'*

Poor innocent little Daydee meeting those two in Bathurst park so unsuspectingly. Briefly he felt a flashing tenderness towards the girl. At that very moment he turned and walked over the doorstep into the sitting room to see the door to the hall open and a maid announce Daydee and Joe.

'Uncle John Stuart,' Daydee began, 'I have wanted to show you my paintings for ever so long, and at last Father has finally succumbed, so here we are tonight to entertain you.'

Although he would have preferred to be alone with his melancholy thoughts, his recent reflections had left him feeling fondly towards the girl. He manufactured a smile. 'Good, Daydee. I would be happy to see them.'

She had a certain talent, and her watercolours of parts of Mayfield were quite well done. When John Stuart remarked favourably upon them she preened. Later, while the two men talked of Mayfield matters, Daydee became engrossed in a pile of journals and newspapers.

After a time, Joe asked in a low voice, 'Was that Thelma of mine here this night?'

'She was, she came to tell me that she did not share our view of

320

my . . . of Eve, but she shall speak of it no more.'

'That's the trouble with women these days,' Joe commented, 'they've got minds of their own. I'm sorry, m'boy.'

John Stuart shook his head. 'It matters not, Joe. She has been deceived a little longer than we have, that is all. She knows not to mention it again.'

A whistle from Daydee broke into their conversation.

'Now that's a very unladylike thing to do,' her father remonstrated.

'Listen to this.' She lifted the *Sydney Morning Herald* in the air. 'It's about Sir Rutherford and the bushrangers.' In an excited voice she read, 'In a recent interview, Sir Rutherford Blake, the New South Wales police adviser on the apprehension of bushrangers in the colony, made it known that an outlawry act would be passed in the New Year, a Felons' Apprehension Act, which would give police the power to shoot known bushrangers on sight.

'Sir Rutherford made it clear that there would be long jail terms for anyone known to have assisted or harboured an outlaw. He also said he had issued orders via Sir Frederick Pottinger, police inspector of the Southern and Western Districts, for police to carry firearms even when off duty.' Daydee lifted her finger in the air. 'People say Sir Rutherford has little time for Pottinger.'

'Yes,' her father agreed. 'It'll be Sir Rutherford that will do all the catching, if you ask me. He is the bloodhound. I'd hate for him to be tracking me.'

Putting the paper aside, Daydee stood and came forward to John Stuart's side. 'Will he be coming again for Christmas, Uncle John Stuart? I do like him. He's so diverting.'

Her father looked up hastily; he had told Daydee not to mention anything sensitive.

But John Stuart did not look alarmed, he merely stretched his hand out to her and she came quickly into the arc of his arm.

'No, Daydee, there will be no visitors I'm afraid, only us.'

'Oh, that's perfectly all right,' the girl said. 'In fact I would really prefer it like that.'

CHAPTER NINETEEN

'If we could read the secret history of our enemies, we should find in each man's life sorrow and suffering enough to disarm all hostility.'

'Driftwood', Henry Wadsworth Longfellow, 1807–1882.

Sir Rutherford Blake twisted in his chair.

'How extraordinary! How damned extraordinary!' he exclaimed aloud as he folded the letter that had caused the outburst and turned to look thoughtfully out on the unseasonably moody, wet, December day.

The letter had been lying on his desk in wait for over two weeks while he had been reconnoitring out west in the hill country where it was said Johnny Gilbert had been sighted. He had found no trace of Gilbert but he had caught a horse thief and made friends of many of the country folk thereabouts, and that was tantamount to making enemies for the bushrangers. He regarded it as time well spent.

The letter was from John Stuart Wakeman and the contents were shocking to say the least. John Stuart was not to hold his customary house party for the selected few this year. It would appear that there was some scandal involving Mrs Wakeman. The innuendo was that John Stuart had been cuckolded! It seemed hard to believe, for while the woman had a comely body and fine features, he would not have thought her flighty or immoral. She seemed to have an eternal disinclination to talk to him but he did not think she lacked inner strength. Sir Rutherford rubbed his thin top lip in thought. Today was four days before Christmas. He had been planning to leave for Mayfield early tomorrow morning. Well, now he would ride south to the town of Young before Christmas instead of waiting until afterwards as he had originally proposed.

There were times when he wished his headquarters were in the south somewhere and not in Bathurst; but the telegraph only came as far as here and he needed to keep in touch with Sydney and the Inspector General of Police. He had little respect for Frederick Pottinger. Bushrangers had slipped through their fingers more than once because of his incompetence. It was only because he, Sir

Rutherford, had ridden long and hard covering the territory making friends like the parish priest Father McCarthy in the township of Carcoar that they had ever caught the likes of John Vane of the Hall gang. The parish priest had talked Vane into surrendering, and when Sir Rutherford had said if Vane talked, he would not swing, he had kept his word, and things like that impressed the bush folk, priests or not.

There had always been bushrangers. Right from when the colony began. They had been in the main escaped convict scum, bolters. It was not until recently the class known as 'the wild colonial boys' had developed, free malingerers with a grievance against the public. Well, he would break them all in the end, bolters or not.

He had studied each of them in intimate detail, in an attempt to find some sort of pattern in their movements. And the amazing thing was, he thought he had found something. That was why he wanted to be well south of here and established with a goodly force of police troopers in the heart of bushranger territory by the coming January. In all his research he had noticed that each and every gang had made a major hold-up shortly after Christmas, usually early in January. Certainly they robbed in other months, any month. But the one month they all had in common was January. Perhaps it was something to do with the excesses of Christmas. Even as far back as the 1820s a robbery had taken place in January. In recent years, the very same had occurred, all south and west of Bathurst. This year, there had been three significant January robberies: Johnny Gilbert and a man called Collins at Goulburn coaching office, Dan Morgan at two home-steads ouside Lambing Flat, now renamed Young after the Governor; and Alan Fletcher and his gang at the magistrate's ball in Wagga Wagga. Ah yes, Alan Fletcher, the one who had been evading the law the longest, the one Sir Rutherford wanted the most.

He tapped his fingers rhythmically on the windowsill at his right hand.

How many long nights he had sat by the light of the kerosene lamp here in his office contemplating Fletcher. The man always took from the Government, the sole one who operated this way. It was as if it were some sort of revenge. Next month he would have evaded capture for twelve years. Amazing! He was unique. Since his escape in fifty-three, he had held up Government officials, police and magis-trates all the way from the Darling Downs in Queensland south in a rough spiral to the township of Orange. The last of these linked crimes appeared to have been in January 1859. That was why he believed Fletcher had found a permanent hideout. He was no longer on the move. Since fifty-nine, robberies accredited to him were all over the place, no pattern emerging.

He looked over to the map of New South Wales that dominated his wall. Ah yes, he had a feeling about Fletcher's hideout. Ever since Mrs Wakeman had been found by Fletcher in the bush that day, he felt sure it was somewhere south of Cowra outside Mayfield's western border. He had been given a passing fair description of Fletcher from Tommy Barnes, but not good enough to recognise the fellow in the street, and that had held true until two months ago when he had the disagreeable but invaluable experience of meeting Alan Fletcher. Now, he knew what most of the bushranger's victims noticed; it would be a man of little observation who could look into those singular eyes and not recognise them a second time. Ah yes. But now he knew the man's habitual movements, his height, the way he held himself, the rhythm of his walk – all priceless. He would most definitely recognise him if he saw him again.

Sir Rutherford could barely wait for the New Year and the Apprehension Act. The Chief Secretary himself had promised it would be tabled and passed by parliament early in the coming year. Sir Rutherford was using his influence to get a twenty-year jail sentence included in the Act for anyone found aiding the bushrangers. That would check scum like Morgan from strutting into inns and ordering drinks all round, and it would put a stop to the 'safe houses'. Ah yes, they all used 'safe houses', even one as skilful at avoiding the law as Fletcher.

He lifted a paper from his desk and read the description upon it. 'Fletcher, Alan: About five feet eleven, medium–muscular build, slim, light brown hair and brows, skin browned from the sun, well-spoken, long fingers, blue-grey eyes.' Beneath this in pencil he had scribbled, *'haughty, aristocratic, impudent, also unusual eyes'*.

The memory of the October day when he and Mr Elrington and six police troopers had been at the Theresa Town gold diggings brought a flush to his face.

He had taken his men there on a lead to the whereabouts of Ben Hall. It was known that Gilbert and Hall had parted company for a time but were back together again and doing holdups with the help of three others, one an eighteen-year-old delinquent called John Dunn, nicknamed 'the jockey'. There had been two robberies in six days just south of Theresa Town, both by them.

Theresa Town had a Government mine in operation as well as being open to public diggings and soon after his arrival Sir Rutherford was informed that there was a Chinese miner turned petty bushranger, who was robbing travellers on the road to the south.

'They say he lives in a cave and that Ben Hall himself has been seen with him.'

Now the expert on the outlaws knew that this could be just 'bush gossip' but nevertheless he took Mr Elrington and his six police south from the diggings disguised as miners. They separated and walked in groups. The plan worked. Sure enough the Chinese robber, Foo Yong, held up the third group and after a fierce struggle the police detective took his prisoner.

Sir Rutherford quickly realised that Foo Yong knew nothing of Ben Hall; nevertheless, he was one more law breaker in custody.

That night was the monthly miners' dance and Sir Rutherford was guest of honour out of gratitude for the capture of Foo Yong.

Applause broke out as Sir Rutherford entered the room. He bowed from the shoulders in reply to the acclamation and stalked through the guests to his seat beneath a picture of Queen Victoria peering gravely down upon the raucous laughter and noise of her colonial subjects.

The entire European population of Theresa Town, all two hundred and fifteen of them were here, spilling out of the bar over the verandahs into the heat of the October night.

The merrymaking was in full flight when Sir Rutherford's sharp senses registered something odd. There was something wrong outside. He stood from his chair and began to move to the nearest window. He had taken no more than two steps when the swing-arm doors of the bar slammed back loudly against the wall.

The music stopped. Everyone turned in amazement to look as two men, with faces covered and rifles levelled, thrust themselves to each side of the door and trained their weapons on the gathering. 'Hold still you lot!' Then a third masked man in dark clothing and carrying a gun entered to stand midway between the other two. 'We're sorry to interrupt, ladies and gentlemen, but it is necessary from our point of view. We will not keep you long.' The voice had total authority and the nuances of sound were of a class not usually heard in the outback.

He lifted his hand to keep the crowd quiet and then called over his shoulder, 'Inside here, everyone, I'm sorry you will have to be overcrowded for a few minutes, but please be patient.'

The men who had been out on the verandahs and in the street, under the encouragement of the rifles, filed in through the door. As they came in, the two who had stood to either side of the door moved through the crowd to the back of the room. One, whom Sir Rutherford carefully noted had the semblance of a limp, mounted the bar. The other, a very big man, pushed two chairs together and climbed upon them. From their strategic locations they menaced the gathering with their rifles.

The leader called to one of Sir Rutherford's party who was moving away as the men from outside swelled the numbers inside. 'Constable, you there! Forward here beside me, please.' He pointed with his rifle through the swelling crowd to the other police near the bar. 'And you others, over here as well.'

'Move as ye're told!' shouted the man on the bar brandishing his rifle.

In a few minutes the room was overfilled with the two hundred and fifteen souls of Theresa Town and the visiting troopers.

Then the leader turned his head and called out through the open door, 'Send in the other members of Her Majesty's Police Force.' And he moved aside, as two constables, one who had been guarding Foo Yong, and one who had been guarding the shed of Government gold, entered. Behind came two more armed men looking dangerous.

'Over with the others now like good policemen,' the leader said to the troopers as a titter ran through the crowd.

It was then Sir Rutherford could be quiet no longer. 'Blast you!' he shouted pushing men aside as he advanced to within a few yards of the intruder. 'This is an outrage! What the hell is going on?'

'Stand fast you!' the stranger answered taking a step forwards and halting Sir Rutherford with a threatening movement of his rifle, 'I shall do the questioning here, not you whoever you are.'

Sir Rutherford fell momentarily silent as he registered the warning in the eyes he beheld, but as the man turned from him to look over to his companions, he could not contain himself, 'I demand to know what is happening here, this is a gross violation of the law!'

In contrast to Sir Rutherford's shout the man's reply was quiet, icy quiet. He spoke with his back to the police detective. 'I can only assume you are Rutherford Blake.' Then slowly he rounded to face him. 'The trooper guarding the prisoner said you were here. You act like one whose supreme arrogance could at times outweigh his rare cunning. You should control that part of your nature, it is not conducive to clear thinking.'

Sir Rutherford wanted to strike the man. No one had ever dared to say such as this to him. With a tremendous effort of will he calmed himself and his answer brought murmurings from the fascinated crowd. 'I will remember what you say . . . Alan Fletcher!'

For a second an expression of mild surprise appeared in the eyes of the stranger. The look was so fleeting that all except Sir

Rutherford, who was close to him, missed it. Then ignoring the conclusion to his identity, he continued speaking to the police detective, 'I must ask you to join your men, here beside me.' He motioned with his gun.

Sir Rutherford did not move.

It was then the small wiry man next to the leader, who had mustered those from outside, spoke up. 'Move, man, as the guv'nor says . . . now! Or I'll not be accountable for what me rifle does.' He stepped forward agilely and cocked the trigger on his gun. Sir Rutherford noted he was probably Cooper.

Shocked sounds escaped from the inhabitants of Theresa Town and Sir Rutherford, mindful of his safety, did as he was told.

'Now,' continued the leader, 'there will be one more here I had better be aware of; which one of you is Elrington, the companion of Rutherford Blake? His secretary assistant, I fancy you are called.'

All eyes turned automatically to look at David Elrington, who stood in the midst of the gathering towards the front of the room. He had been among the people from outside.

'So you are the apprenticed "police detective". Over here, young fellow, I would like all the vigilant law enforcers together.'

'Yes, over here with yor mateys,' said the small man gesturing towards Sir Rutherford's group, 'and now we'll be havin' that pistol I be noticin' in yer belt, son.'

David Elrington gingerly took the gun from his waist and handed it to the speaker who added it to the arsenal in his own belt. 'Nice of ye other gents to come unarmed,' he said as he looked back to the leader and winked.

The leader now moved back into the doorway. 'Understand this. We are not here to harm any of you. Most of you are honest men hoping to find your fortune. It is with the Government of this fair colony that today we are at variance.'

Sir Rutherford's eyes greedily followed the man's every movement. He would remember everything about Fletcher.

'There is a little matter of the shipment of Government gold that is being held in the shed down the street. We come to alleviate you all of the worry of holding it here. Once it is gone you will be able to sleep soundly, knowing no bushrangers will be coming to invade this little scenic spot, to take it away.'

Some of the ordinary diggers laughed. They found it amusing that the Government gold might be stolen. It gave them no pleasure to see the Government working the mines they thought should be freehold.

'So,' he went on, 'I will have the key please, which my police guard informant tells me Constable Boehm is holding. Forward please, Constable!'

Just then there was a clicking sound from the man at the door; everyone looked in his direction as the leader asked over his shoulder, 'What is it?'

'Looks like some Chink chappies peeking over the hilltop.'

'The Chinese are an intelligent and sensible race,' answered the leader. 'They will look, but they shan't interfere. Worry not.' Then he turned his attention to Sir Rutherford. 'Which constrains me to tell you of your prisoner. The poor chap was under some impression that you were going to hang him.'

'He is a prisoner of Her Majesty, a criminal and a thief. Justice will be done!' Sir Rutherford broke in angrily.

'But not as soon as you would wish. You see I have given him a horse and told him to put as many miles as possible between here and where he hopes to set up trade again.'

Now, the police detective shouted. 'Damn you! I'll see you hang as high as any of them in time, ah yes, I will!'

Just for an instant, Sir Rutherford fancied he saw the leader stiffen with distaste before he replied, 'My boys and I will continue to defer your pleasure as long as possible.'

The big man on the chair called angrily, 'Shut Blake's filthy mouth now, boss, with a bullet!'

'Constable Boehm,' regressed the leader, 'the key of the shed please or I shall have to let the more aggressive of my crew have their way.'

The constable handed him a large lock key from inside his jacket.

'Thank you, so much better than chopping down the door.' He strode out followed by the man Sir Rutherford had guessed to be Dan Dwyer.

Sir Rutherford began speaking as soon as they had gone, 'Listen, you men,' he said, lifting his hands in appeal to the remaining three bushrangers, 'don't you realise the risk you run? If you will only listen to me I will . . .'

He got no further for the man on the chair swung his rifle in the air and discharged it into the ceiling. The crowd in shock fell away as bits of wood dropped down upon them.

'Now, shutup, shutup I say!' he growled as he took a pistol from his belt and brandished it at Sir Rutherford. 'I will not shoot the bloody ceilin' next time, I'll shoot you, Blake, with the mouth as large as a hog's.'

'Steady, friend, steady!' counselled the man on the bar.

'Just disciplinin' Blake, guv'nor!' shouted the little man at the door out into the inky street.

Sir Rutherford, realising he was getting nowhere, decided that discretion was indeed the better part of valour and fell into a bitter silence. Some six or seven minutes elapsed while the captives murmured and sweated in the closeness and heat, and then they heard the leader's voice. 'All right lads, we have accomplished what we came for.'

The bushranger on the bar waved his rifle in an arc over his head. 'Right then, back up ye lot, nice and tight I say!' Then he jumped down while the people made passage for him and the big man who passed back to back along the opening to join the little man at the door. There they were met by the leader from outside. Sir Rutherford thought he could perceive a smile beneath his mask.

When his men were all outside he did a startling thing.

He was holding a ten-pound bag of gold in his hands and had untied the string. He bent and poured a line of nuggets across the doorway, saying, 'I would like to share some of the Government's gold with you, my friends . . . for your patience and good humour.'

With that, the bushrangers left as a man and were on their horses and riding away within ten seconds, while behind them the pandemonium that Alan had counted on broke out as men scrambled for the gold falling over each other and shouting in their haste.

Sir Rutherford grimaced as he remembered all this.

He had pushed the reward on Fletcher up to £1000 after Theresa Town. How badly he wanted him. Damn the man.

A knock sounded on the door. It brought his head up in sharp awareness.

David Elrington entered carrying a paper in his hand. 'Sir, I have just now received this telegraph message. It is from Sir Frederick. He cannot meet you here today as planned. He will join you in Young after Christmas.'

The expert on the bushrangers made a contemptuous sound. 'Then we shall miss him for we ride to Young tomorrow.'

'But, sir, we do not go to Young until after our Christmas at Mayfield.'

Sir Rutherford shook his head. 'Mr Wakeman is having troubles of his own. Our Christmas there has been cancelled. Instead, we will ride south tomorrow. So go ahead, Mr Elrington, leave me, you've much to prepare.'

'Sir, it is raining pretty heavily for a long ride.'

'What's a drop of rain, man? You won't melt!'

329

As the door closed behind his assistant, he turned to the window, a preoccupied expression on his face, and his gaze on the falling rain.

CHAPTER TWENTY

'A still small voice spake unto me,
"Thou art so full of misery,
Were it not better not to be?" '
'The Two Voices,' Alfred, Lord Tennyson, 1809–1892.

Eve stirred. The patter of rain sounded in her ears and for a moment dream and reality blurred, then thunder rolled in the distance and the verandah door rattled in the wind and she was awake.

She shivered. She was cold even though it was stuffy in the closed room. Ever since the assault, she had been afraid to open the windows at night.

What a strange dream, Alan Fletcher and John Stuart together, in the San Francisco of her girlhood.

The thunder rolled again. What a night to be out. She supposed some poor souls would be. Where would Alan Fletcher be on a night like this? She wondered where he lay his head and if he were dry and comfortable. Could he hear the same thunder she heard? Sir Rutherford seemed to think he dwelt not far from here. Ah, but that was a year ago.

She rolled over and lay on her side. She would have liked to lie on her stomach, but that was no longer comfortable. The life that grew within her was almost fourteen weeks old now. There were only four days to Christmas. What a sorry Christmas it would be at Mayfield this year. The master and the mistress estranged. The whole property talking about it. What would John Stuart do? She knew he had cancelled his invitations for the Christmas week. Dear Thelma had told her that. And the children's tree? Would he go to that, putting on a brave face? Even though life hardly seemed worth living, there was yet a corner of her heart that was sorry for John Stuart. His dream had been shattered. How could their love and their lives have come to this?

She had passed two wretched weeks since her husband had returned, waiting to see if he would come to her. But the days had gone by without his face and the nights had stretched into long, lonely hours. Each morning, she had awoken with the hope that today he would come and make amends. Yesterday she had even waited on the verandah knowing the time of his return to the house. She thought that if he saw her, he would soften and come to her, that perhaps she could speak to him. Surely his love for her would overcome the horrible belief he had? When he had appeared on the carriageway astride Diomed, she had come down the steps towards him, lifting her arm in gentle greeting, but when he saw her, he had stopped momentarily, then turned the horse and ridden away. She had lost all hope when she saw that. There was little doubt he found the sight of her unbearable.

How very alone she was. Her eyes filled with tears. All the frustration and anger and pain and suffering raged through her again. For some moments she was back in the garden, on the ground being battered by Lake. The nightmare was still there, living in her head. She sobbed, consumed by an awful, empty ache. How could John Stuart have believed that vile man? How could he have treated her this way? Finally, she pulled herself up on the pillows and wiping her eyes with a handkerchief said aloud, 'Come on, Eve, what are you going to do?'

Her future appeared as interminable months of day-to-day confinement. Oh, she would have Thelma, that brave lady had not let her down, and she had the company of sweet Stephanie. But that would all end when the baby was born. John Stuart intended to send her away.

'No!' she spoke aloud in the darkness again. She would not allow that. How dare he! She would leave of her own volition, in her own time, and soon, when he would not suspect it.

Go to Father. Yes, that was it! Of course! Father and Mother would stand by her. She could deal with any scorn if she were by Father's side. She would be strong in the face of all the indignity of what was to come. John Stuart did not want to know the truth. He probably never would be able to contend with the truth. Let him continue in his misbelief.

She had been sick again these last few days, had not been able to keep food down, but perhaps she would be well enough to travel soon. Yes, she must be. She would tell no one. She would leave at night and go to Bathurst. But she must wait until after Christmas Day. Christmas Day was one of the two busiest days of the year for Father. She would leave in the early hours on Boxing Day when the house was asleep. She would ride to Cowra and be there to catch the mail coach at nine o'clock in the morning. It ran to Blayney every day of the year except Good Friday and Christmas Day; and from Blayney, she could catch another to Bathurst.

332

That was what she would do. She would stay here no longer.
It was her decision, no one else's, and it was made.

Christmas Eve was a quiet affair.

There was an unseasonal chill in the air and because of the rain they had been experiencing on and off for days, the children's Christmas tree was held in the schoolhouse and was a much smaller affair than usual. John Stuart made only a token visit for the concert and departed before the gift giving.

When he left the hall in company with Joe, Daydee followed him out onto the verandah, disappointment on her face. 'Uncle John Stuart . . .'

Her father answered. 'What is it, love? We're in a hurry.'

'Oh, Uncle John Stuart, I . . . I just wanted to say, I think it's just wonderful that . . . that you came here this evening and, merry Christmas.'

John Stuart smiled gently as he came the two paces back to her. He took her tiny shoulders in his hands and bent and kissed her forehead. 'Merry Christmas, dear,' he replied.

Her small eyes followed him longingly into the covered landau. Then as Deke Edwards, wrapped in leather cape and hat against the rain, urged his horses forward into the damp twilight, she blew a kiss after him.

'It looks like we might have some flooding on our hands if this rain keeps up, m'boy,' Joe remarked as the landau moved off, 'although I would say we're only experiencing the edge of it. It's worse to the north and west. Bathurst is getting it bad, they say. Did I tell you we had a message from Cowra yesterday? It was the second day the northern mail coach hadn't gone through. Had to turn back before it reached Blayney, seems the Belubula River broke its banks and the low lands are flooded on and off for miles.'

'In that case, Joe, we'd better watch our Lachlan. It doesn't seem to be rising as yet, but it can happen quickly and if it does, the river paddocks, the dairy and the closest cottages would be in trouble.'

'Right. In fact I might take a ride out in the morning, just check upriver a few miles, see what she's doing.'

'I'll come with you,' replied John Stuart.

When Christmas Day morning broke, it was raining only lightly. There had been a deluge during the night for many hours, and just after dawn John Stuart and Joe rode up the Lachlan to where it joined the Boorowa.

The river was running at speed, not surprisingly, for it had taken a lot of water from the hills in the past days, and had swelled in some places enough to be in danger of breaking. If the rain stopped in the next twelve to twenty-four hours, probably all would be well, but if it did not . . .

It was close to noon when the two riders, in wide-brimmed hats and long leather capes, returned over Larmer's Crossing. As they neared the stables, Joe broke the silence. 'So, we will see you tonight, m'boy?'

'Yes indeed, we shall have a great dinner, I'm assured.'

'You know, m'boy, it is not necessary.'

'I want to have it, old man. I want the backbone of Mayfield at my table this night.'

Joe smiled. 'Very well.'

After coming home from the children's Christmas tree the previous evening John Stuart had made a late decision to have a Christmas dinner at Mayfield House even under the present circumstances. First thing this morning, he had despatched messengers to some of his trusted staff. His guest list was going to be unusual, but certainly one his father would have approved. This year there would be no governors or colonial secretaries, no knights or members of parliament or lawyers or officials. This year his table would be graced by Mr and Mrs Jack Hennessey, Mr and Mrs Stephen Watson, the three Larmers, Mr Oldfield, and himself.

John Stuart stayed the entire afternoon down in the stables grooming his horses. It gave him satisfaction to be close to the animals, brushing them and examining them. He even cleaned out the stalls, working so hard that while the temperature had dropped greatly, he still stripped to his waist. The physical work eased him and as it was Christmas Day no one was there; he was alone, exactly as he wished. The married men were with their families and the unmarried were having their own banquet in the recreation hall. That was something he was very proud of: Mayfield had the best housing and facilities for working men in the entire country. Yes, Mayfield was unique and those lucky enough to live and work upon it realised it.

Why hadn't the woman he had elevated to mistress of it been worthy?

A sharp picture of her face as he had seen it that terrible day in the garden came to his mind. It made him feel uneasy. Unhappy and uneasy. He dropped the hoof pick he had been using. Diomed and his stable mate whinnied as he moved out into the rain.

She had waited for him a few nights ago, he had seen her coming down the steps of the house towards him as he rode up in the dusk. She had waved and he had steeled himself to turn and ride away. She was corrupt, he knew she was, yet he could not control that part of his mind which continued to see her face and hear the sound of her voice. For some time he stood in the cobbled yard wondering what she might be doing.

At the same time, alone in her room, Eve was standing in silent consideration. She was thinking of him and what his reaction would be when tomorrow he heard she was gone. Would he be sorry? No, probably not. Perhaps he would not care at all.

Stephanie had told her he looked gloomy and sad. Strange, but to hear that had brought her no joy.

What a fool he was! And what a fool she was! Why hadn't she told him long ago about Clare? How many times had she been over this in her mind? It would not have mattered anyway. It all would have ended in this fashion. She would have been assaulted by Lake. She would be carrying his child and John Stuart still would not be able to contend with that. He would need to be a different man altogether. Perhaps like . . . Alan Fletcher. Momentarily, she imagined the two men standing on the bush road, side by side, as they had done on her wedding day, John Stuart and Alan. She made a small sad sound, clasping herself round the waist, holding herself tightly.

Velvet brushed her skirt as she stood unmoving. She bent and lifted him to her arms. 'I will miss you darling boy, but Thelma and Stephanie will take care of you. You like Thelma.'

There had been no service in the chapel this year although it had been open for anyone to use. For the first year ever, none of the Mayfield folk had gone to church or Mass in Cowra, the weather was too terrible.

Thelma had spent the morning here with her. Eve had been glad of her kindly companionship for she had given Stephanie the day off to attend the festive staff events.

It was now close to four in the afternoon. What an awful Christmas Day. It was all unbearable, unbearable to her and unbearable to him. Well, she would be away from all of it tomorrow. Home with Father soon. The first smile for weeks hovered on her mouth.

Outside, the wind blew rain across the verandah. The smile left her face as she noticed it. She returned Velvet to the floor. What if it were raining when she left in the morning? Oh, please God let the rain stop! At a sensible pace it could take almost four hours to ride into Cowra. The mail left at nine o'clock. She had better allow herself six hours, for some of the ride would be in the dark of night. She would leave her bedroom before three o'clock in the morning. If it continued to rain, there was nowhere to shelter on the roadside. She would just have to pray that it did not.

If only she could feel better. Her head was often dizzy and she felt

335

sick on and off all day. At least she had not vomited for a few days now.

'Ah, poor thing within me,' she said aloud, holding her stomach. 'I am truly sorry.'

Then, rousing herself, she crossed to her dressing table. Out of one of the drawers she took a large jewel box. She opened the lid. She did not touch the important gems that John Stuart had given her. Instead, she lifted out a few simple pieces Mother and Father had given her over the years, and put them in a gilt trinket box that had been a gift from Billy Tompkins. She sighed. Poor Billy.

Then she put the trinket box in the soft carpet travelling bag she would take with her. Her eyes returned to the diamonds, rubies, sapphires, emeralds and gold, all fighting for supremacy. She lifted out the diamond heart with the ruby message *EVE, I'LL ALWAYS LOVE YOU* upon it. It was so exquisite, she sighed with that certain touch of pain that can come when beholding something perfect; and then, with an acute thought of the imperfection of the love of the giver, returned it to its place.

Suddenly, she had a short sharp pain. She felt faint and a little squeamish. She crossed to the bed and lay down. She must have fallen asleep for she awakened to a light tapping on her door. Thinking it must be Stephanie with her evening meal, she called, 'Come in!'

The door fell ajar and John Stuart's frame filled the doorway.

She sat up in surprise. She had expected to leave tomorrow without seeing him. Fear shot through her. What if he knew of her plan?

When he spoke she realised he knew nothing of her scheme.

'It is Christmas Day,' he began, his voice low and controlled. 'I believe you asked to be allowed to go to the chapel.'

It was true, she had asked Mrs Smith this morning but had been told that John Stuart was not at home, and since then she had heard no more. She lifted herself from the bed.

He noticed how thin she looked and a small tremor of sorrow rippled through him. He had overheard Thelma saying she ate very little. He attempted a smile, his look was almost gentle. 'I am sorry to have disturbed you.'

'You do not disturb me. Yes, I did ask this morning if I could use the chapel, but I was given to understand you were from home.' She sounded polite, distant, but her pulse raced. How she prayed he had come to put things right.

He advanced a few steps into her room. He made an awkward gesture with his hand, explaining, 'I rode along the river to note if it had risen anywhere. All the rain, you know I must keep watch.'

She nodded. 'Of course.'

'This afternoon I worked down at the stables. I was unaware of your request until my return here this evening.'

'It doesn't matter.'

'Yes, it does, and of course you may use it. Eve, I told you, you are not a prisoner here. The chapel has been unlocked all day for those of the staff who wished to go in. You did not need to request formally. You simply could have gone there. It is inside the park, you needed no one's permission.'

'But I did not wish to embarrass you by visiting at a time when there might be others there.'

'Really?' he replied, and for a second, his expression softened. At the change, a ray of hope shot through her. Then other thoughts rushed to his mind and, unable to help himself, he made a sneering sound. 'I would have thought that embarrassing me was a knack of yours.'

Her chest constricted. 'Oh, John Stuart,' she answered dejectedly and closed her eyes.

There was silence between them.

He took another step into the room, and before he could check himself said, 'Do you go to pray for the forgiveness of your sins?'

She walked away from him round the bed to the far side of the room where she stood silently looking out into the gloomy light. It appeared to have stopped raining.

Now, he felt sorry he had spoken so hastily, and as she turned from him he actually lifted his hand towards her. There was a sickening torment inside him; he wanted to take her in his arms, to hold her, to kiss her, even to forgive her, but his arm dropped without touching her and she was unaware of his intention.

When she turned back to him she looked drawn and ill. What was the point in prolonging this? John Stuart hated her. It was obvious.

'I am tired, John Stuart, tired, do you understand? You seem to have come here simply to mock me. Well, this is your house and as that is so, this is your room, and you can be here if you wish, but as for me, I was happy with the understanding that we would lay eyes upon each other no more.'

'Yes, I can see that.' Now his voice was bitter.

'And as it seems you are not ready to leave this room, I shall go to the chapel and you may stand here as long as you like.'

She came forward and picked up her pelisse that lay on the end of the bed. As she did so he said, 'Why? Why have you done all this?'

She stood at the end of the bed facing him. Her eyes dominated her face.

The air was heavy with tension.

'I have done nothing to be ashamed of,' came her deliberate reply.

'Nothing to be ashamed of?' he echoed her. 'Nothing . . .' He shook his head. 'Oh, Eve.'

She brushed past him into the corridor beyond.

He moved to the door intending to call, 'Eve, come back!' But he only got as far as 'Eve' and then in frustration he shouted, 'Damn you!' smashing his hand upon the open door.

And, 'Damn *you*!' came her answer flying back to him from down the corridor.

He stood in the doorway watching her disappear. He was in torment. He smashed his fist into the door again and into his head came Thelma's words. 'Eve is a good girl, *she is innocent*. I saw her the day after the attack by that . . . that man. I was here. You were not . . . I was here. You were not . . . Eve is a good girl.'

With a tortured sound he strode away.

As Eve made her way to the chapel, her heart ached. A fine rain was falling and when she arrived, all was quiet and empty. While she was there, no one else came in. Alone, she offered up her prayers and alone her tears fell.

An hour later, when she returned across the lawn towards the western entrance of the house, the rain was still falling and so too was the night. Only a few hours more and she would be gone, and what happened here on Mayfield would not concern her. She felt a powerful pang of tenderness.

Mayfield!

Her eyes filled once more, but this time with sentimental tears for this beautiful retreat that had been her home. In the twenty months of her marriage, Mayfield had insinuated itself into her heart. Never had she loved anywhere like this. She walked back across the verandah and resting her hands on the rail looked through the rain over the lawns and neat garden beds that lay in geometric patterns in front of her, their magnificent summer blooms cheerfully tingeing the failing light with colour. She looked to the left where the rows of stately pines grew along the carriageway, and to the right where above the park and over the cool, green beeches along the perimeter, she could see the black ranges in the distance. With the rain and the clouds, the whole scene, darkening swiftly as she stood there, had an energy of its own. The very atmosphere of Mayfield would move any heart. She did love this place! It was no use to pretend she wouldn't miss it, she would, always.

When she returned to her rooms, the lamps had been lit.

It was Mrs Smith who brought her dinner. Eve was disappointed. She had hoped to see Stephanie a final time.

'Now, Mrs Wakeman, ye yerself knew she was to have the day off.'

Eve sighed. 'Please, Mrs Smith, I would like to see her. I have a gift.'

Mrs Smith yielded. 'Oh, then I shall send her to ye directly.'

Eight minutes later Stephanie's gentle rap sounded on the door. 'You wished to see me, Mrs Wakeman?'

Eve rose and came towards her. 'Merry Christmas, Stephanie,' and she handed the girl a small package.

'Oh, ma'am,' she began as she opened it, 'you shouldn't have.'

Inside lay a velvet pouch and inside the pouch a delicate bracelet of jet and pearls inlaid with gold. The girl had never thought to own anything so lovely and tears welled in her eyes. 'Oh! I . . . it's so beautiful and . . . genteel!'

In a spontaneous movement, she hugged her mistress, and Eve, glad of the opportunity to hold her, hugged her too. Then, abashed, the girl drew out of the embrace, saying, 'Oh, pardon me, Mrs Wakeman, I . . . ought not to have done that.'

'Fiddlesticks, Stephanie dear, I wanted to hug you just as much as you did me.'

'Really?' the innocent girl asked.

'Really,' said Eve. To prove it, she hugged her again.

'Would you like me to stay with you, ma'am? I'd be as pleased to be here with you.'

'No, that won't be necessary. I would like to think you were enjoying yourself. What are the staff doing? You usually have a treasure hunt in the park on Christmas night, don't you?'

The girl's eyes lit up. 'Yes we do and we were going to as well, except it's been cancelled as it's raining again. Mrs Smith got special permission from the master to use the ballroom and we're going to have a dance and a party. It's about to start.'

Eve actually smiled. 'And there you were, my dear, about to give all that up to stay with me. I wouldn't hear of it. Off you go and have a lovely time and wear your new bracelet.'

All smiles, Stephanie left. She would miss Stephanie, the girl had been a dear companion.

Later, Eve sat and wrote a parting letter to Thelma. She had desperately wanted to tell her friend she was leaving but had decided against it. It was not a long letter.

Christmas Day, 1864.

My dearest friend Thelma,

I cannot stay here. Estranged from John Stuart, the sadness of each day is such that I think I will die if I do. Instead I go to those others who love me.

Thank you for the help and care you have shown me. And thank you for your continuing belief in me. Seldom have I met a heart so true as yours.

Perhaps one day we will meet again, I do truly hope so, with all my heart.

Do not worry about me. I feel quite sure of what I do. I will always remember you with love.

Your friend,
Eve

She would place it on her pillow when she left.

She must wake before three o'clock. Please Lord, don't let it be raining; please let it stop and don't let it rain on the journey.

Her heart beat quickly. She looked across to the large ormolu clock on the table by the bed. It was after eight o'clock. Six hours to go.

She slept fitfully, constantly waking to check the time, and on each occasion she listened for the rain and gratefully sank back on her pillow when she heard none. She felt she was not strong enough to ride in the rain. But she must get away, she must.

At twenty past two she rose, and walking to the doors looked out into the night. She could actually see the moon, watery looking and filtered through restless clouds though it was, and it gave her heart.

She dressed and soon she sat for the last time at her polished rosewood dressing table and brushed her hair in the lamplight. She studied her reflection a moment. She looked older. Her face was much thinner and the lines near her mouth a little deeper. Then suddenly thinking of what might be the reaction to her empty bedroom in the morning, she smiled. She looked better when she smiled, so she smiled again, determinedly. A moment later she rose and took up her pelisse and carpet bag.

She felt mildly unwell but not as bad as she had so many times in the past weeks. Taking a deep breath she went towards the door.

As she opened it a whim took her and she turned back. Crossing to the dressing table she took up a delicate gold and jade ornamental haircomb that lay there. It was the olive branch pin John Stuart had given her in the first days of their marriage. She often wore it in her hair when she twisted her curls up on top of her head.

Swiftly she went to her davenport and taking paper, pen and ink wrote, 'John Stuart, I'm sorry,' and placing it on her pillow alongside the note for Thelma, put the olive branch on top of it. As her fingers left the hairpin, the hurt and sadness at John Stuart's rejection rose like something solid to her throat. She gasped and coughed.

When she was calmer, a tear welled over her lid as she spoke aloud to the room. 'While I am leaving you, John Stuart, I am sorry for all that has happened and I do wish you peace.'

In eerie fashion her words seemed to hang in the air after she had said them. The great long drapes over the windows, the massive bed, the tall pieces of furniture, the shadows between all seemed to echo her words like living things. 'Peace' they seemed to whisper, 'peace'.

Prophetic word. John Stuart was to enjoy little enough of it as time passed.

She took a last look at the room where her husband had loved her so many times, before she closed the door behind her and moved silently down the passage. There was no sign of Velvet anywhere; being nocturnal he was probably out in the park.

It was a simple matter to leave the sleeping house.

Although it had not rained for a few hours, the ground was damp and muddy in places. She followed the carriageway and then the road that led down to the stables. She was in the stable yard by quarter past three. Feeling tired from the walk, she sat a few minutes on the wooden seat under the sheltered entrance to the yard. It was black inside the stables, but she knew where the lanterns were and soon had one lit. The hardest thing to do was to saddle the horse. She was weaker than she had thought and lifting the saddle fatigued her. She struggled to secure the girth under sweet-natured Betsy, and the animal stood quietly for her.

Then leaning against the wall, she took a few seconds to catch her breath before she put out the lantern, mounted Betsy, and set her bag of belongings in front of her. The animal's hooves clanged loudly on the cobbled yard, but no one heard except her stable mates.

A fresh wind had sprung up in the damp air, the night was not hot as December nights were, so much rain had brought the temperatures freakishly down and she was glad of her warm pelisse. Betsy sniffed the air and Eve shivered as she looked skywards. Drifting clouds at times hid the moon, but there was enough light to see, and while the sky looked mean and threatening, no rain was falling.

She was soon on the north road leading across the property. It was an easy ride to the Mayfield boundary for the road was mostly macadamised. When the sealed road ran out, it would be muddy and difficult in places. Fortunately, much of the continuing roadway was high ground. She could feel her heart beating and she felt bitter and sad, but there was also a feeling of exhilaration in her now that she had broken away. She had made herself an outcast by her actions, she knew that. But hadn't she been through hard times before? She was strong. She still believed in herself, just as she always had.

Her mouth tightened with resolution. Firmly, she brought Betsy to a trot and rode on.

She who had always held respectability so precious, now seemed destined to live without it. In the end, it appeared the Herman twins would be regarded as identical in everything.

CHAPTER TWENTY-ONE

'Nothing that is can pause or stay;
The moon will wax, the moon will wane,
The mist and cloud will turn to rain,
The rain to mist and cloud again,
Tomorrow be today.'

'The Potter's Song', from *Keramos*,
Henry Wadsworth Longfellow, 1807–1882.

Alan Fletcher was awake. At the door of the solid wooden hut he stood cross-legged leaning against the frame. His arms were folded and he surveyed the night. Above the tree tops, he watched a moody sky of rain-laden clouds pushed by a fast wind. It was cool tonight, cooler than it had been since the winter, from the week of constantly recurrent rain.

It was the small hours of Boxing Day and he had found it hard to sleep. He was not an insomniac. Normally he slept very well, but the last few nights he had been restless and troubled. Lawless had gone yesterday to visit Patricia June's grave, alone; Alan had always accompanied him before. It was a regular habit at Christmas ever since the girl had died exactly six years ago. No doubt subconsciously he was worrying about Lawless, yet too, there had been discomfiting thoughts of her, the woman who was married to the richest, most influential man in the land.

He thought of her often and he had lain awake thinking of her tonight, until impatiently, he had risen and, not wanting to wake Daniel who shared his small room, had donned a jacket and gone to meditate by the kitchen door. He stood now wondering about her. Why did he wonder about her? He had no answer to that.

He could hear Sam and Jordan both snoring in their bunks and he moved across the verandah. His fingers clutched the rail as he breathed in the damp air.

Tomorrow, he and Jordan would ride down to Lyon's Tavern on the road south of Cowra and there they would wait for Lawless to join them. Lyon's Tavern was one of the safe houses. It stood alone slightly off the main road in the area known as Wattamondara. Henry

343

Lyon was an ex-convict, a big, good-looking, congenial man who, like many of his ilk, disliked the 'traps', as the police were commonly called in the bush. He was a man of his word and when he knew Alan was coming, which was not often, Alan did not frequent the same places regularly, he would close his doors to other travellers. Alan had agreed to meet Lawless there for Jordan's sake. He was the youngest of them and looked forward to his visits to the taverns and particularly Lyon's, for he was sweet on Bridget, one of Henry's three handsome daughters.

It was a rarity for an argument to occur at Treehard and when one did, it was usually because Jordan wanted to go and meet a woman more often than the others thought was wise. At these times, Samuel was the one to console Jordan. He would talk him round and then remind him he was an outlaw with a price on his head and that his only true friends were here with him. When Jordan calmed, he would look over to Alan with his big eyes so reminiscent of Patricia June's, as if desperately seeking the leader's exoneration and Alan would invariably nod and smile and things would quieten. After all, Jordan was young, it was understandable.

When they did visit a safe house, it was one of a very few that Alan knew had a reliable owner, one like Henry Lyon. Sometimes they would stay the night, Jordan with a girl of his choosing; and while Alan was meticulously careful that they never mentioned their trade, the publicans possibly guessed. There were always girls ready to be charitable to good-looking bushmen and if they too presumed the profession of those they entertained, they had, up until now, kept silent. At Lyon's Tavern it was different, for Henry and his family did know their identity, although they had no idea where Treehard lay.

In early 1859 when Alan's band were making their way south, he and Lawless, alone out hunting, had come upon two men screaming fit to bring the gum trees down around their heads. It had been near a tributary of the Lachlan in a part of the low country at the bottom of the Sugarloaf Mountains. When they investigated, they found a man deep in quicksand and a second, in trying to help the first, in trouble himself. They had rescued both men and in the years since, Henry Lyon and Edmund 'Bluey' Williams had become their friends.

Alan had arranged to visit Lyon's Tavern tomorrow and to drink of the spirit of Christmas with the few trusted folk who would be there. Nevertheless, these days there were more troopers abroad and it was a concern to him that he had to frequent safe houses at all.

Daniel and Samuel never accompanied them on these visits, both preferring to stay in the seclusion of Treehard. Daniel, at seventy, was as sprightly as ever and his mind as keen as when they had met, but he caught chills easily and had a chronic cough.

Alan folded his arms and moved slightly against the railing, continuing his thoughtful study in the damp air. Straight ahead of him were the stable and outhouse they were presently erecting and behind them towered the tall iron-bark gums, their thin trunks scattered like pale wisps in the vague night light. They stood dotted across the top of Treehard Hill to the edge of the escarpment where the land dropped dramatically away to the valley floor. For perhaps another fifteen minutes he watched before rain began to fall, and giving a final glance to the gloomy scene he returned to bed. Sleep came quickly now, and it was to the sound of Daniel's voice that he awoke.

'Come on, sonny,' he heard the affectionate, familiar tones, 'breakfast is on the hob and tea's made to your liking. It's nearly the hour of six and you are to meet our Lawless by half past nine of the clock.' It was a ride that could take close to three hours.

'I'm coming, Danny, I'll be but a minute.'

Half an hour later, Alan and Jordan, wearing leather capes and wide-brimmed hats, mounted their horses that Samuel held steady in the lightly falling rain.

Daniel sat watching on the verandah. He was feigning offence at not going with them and called merrily, 'So it's an old man I am now, eh? Leave me home with me keeper and all, is it?' He pointed to Samuel.

Samuel laughed, 'No, old man, it's not that, it's ye be too unfit to go out in the rain.'

Daniel stood in mock insult, arms akimbo. 'What's that? Unfit to go out in the rain, is it? I'm telling you, Sam, my man, I'm from Ireland. I was weaned on rain.'

'All right, Dan,' his small friend called stepping away from the two riders, 'and we'll have more fun here at Treehard with our bottle of rum than they will have with the like o' foolish women botherin' them down at the tavern.'

'That's true enough,' agreed Daniel, 'and you two, if you're coming home tonight be back by nightfall, otherwise we will understand that Bridget has enticed Jordan, in which case we shall see you definitely by nightfall tomorrow.'

Alan waved as he pushed Freedom forward. 'Yes, that's the plan.'

'Don't expect us tonight, mateys!' shouted Jordan as he entered the passage.

Samuel laughed.

345

'I'll not breathe easily until they're back,' said Daniel to himself as he turned and entered the kitchen.

The riders wended their way through the trees, undergrowth and scrub outside the secret passage and soon were riding down the long slope to the Cowra road. The track was slippery and muddy in parts but it was mostly a moderate incline, so water did not lie on their path.

As they gained the road, Lawless was on it too, but he was some sixteen miles to their north on the near side of the township of Cowra heading towards Lyon's Tavern at Wattamondara. He had skirted Cowra even though it was early morning on the Boxing Day holiday; it was second nature to him to take no risks. He too wore a flowing leather cape as protection from the rain and wind. Waterloo, his horse, was making slow progress up a long muddy incline where rainwater lay in the undulations every few yards along the unsealed road. He was looking forward to reaching Lyon's. The guv'nor would be there and they would enjoy the indulgence of a shot of whisky in their stomachs and their feet resting in a warm dry room.

He hated to leave Alan, even for a day. Alan was the voice of sanity in his life. He was like his mother, father, and own best friend. And to think the guv'nor was gentry and he, a child of the London slums, could count such as him his lifelong friend! He often thought there should be a better word than 'friend', for it just denoted a sort of middlin' standard that one could reach with many people, whereas Alan was so very much more.

Always before, the guv'nor had accompanied him to visit Patricia June's grave. That was the guv'nor all over! But somehow, this year, Lawless wanted to go on his own and he had decided this would be the last time he made his Christmas pilgrimage. For yesterday, as he stood in the lonely valley named Coral Way where she lay, he had experienced an odd sensation. He felt he heard her saying, 'Lawless, love, ye do not need to stand over a pile of dust and pretend it is me. I am livin' in yer heart, love, that's where I am. Remember me, but let me go, don't mourn.' And he had nodded and replied aloud, 'All right, Patricia Junie, I understand.'

Yet he was pleased to think she had a proper resting place and he smiled sadly as he thought of the inscription carved on the tablet of stone.

> Patricia June Drake,
> Sweet Wife of Arnold,
> Sister of Jordan,

'O for the touch of a vanish'd hand
And the sound of a voice that is still.'

Alan had given him the lines of poetry, they had been written by someone he had actually met at home in England. Lawless had carved the inscription lovingly, for it said what he felt so exactly.

And to think they had gone and found Treehard only a few months after her death! How she would have loved Treehard. Just as Swiftie would have. He missed Swiftie too and yet it was twelve years in February since he had gone.

Lawless tilted his wide-brimmed, cabbage-tree hat forward against the windblown rain. He had met no other traveller on the road since he had left Mike Dunphy's safe house at dawn, and so it was with surprise that he lifted his eyes to the brow of the hill to see a single rider coming down the gradient towards him. Always cautious, he reined in his horse and looked right and left and then behind the way he had come.

No one in sight. He moved Waterloo forward at a walk.

The lone rider was perhaps a hundred yards away. It looked as if the person leaned forward in the saddle. Then he realised with surprise that it was a woman. As she came closer, he could see she did indeed bend forward. She wore a rain-sodden cape and the hood had blown back to reveal her wet face.

They drew abreast and he hailed her. 'Good morrow to ye, mistress. Where are ye headed on such a terrible day as this? It be no weather for ridin' out, I'm sure.'

The woman focused weary eyes upon him, a glazed expression in them. Her sodden hair fell limply to her shoulders, her whole demeanour one of fatigue. She replied in a voice that held a soft accent. For a moment, he thought she was Irish. He wondered about her. He fancied he had seen her before.

She tried to sit up straight as she replied, 'Good morrow to you, sir. Can you tell me how far I've yet to ride to reach the village of Cowra?' She sagged slightly forward again as she finished speaking.

'Ah, ye be almost there, m'lady. It's less than a mile straight ahead.'

'Thank you, I must get there soon. My journey has taken me longer than I thought. I must . . . catch the nine o'clock mail coach north.'

'I'm sorry, but ye won't be catchin' the mail coach north, mistress.'

'Why . . . yes . . . I must.'

'But it has not run for days, ma'am. The road is greatly flooded

347

just south o' Blayney. I know this for I've been north of Cowra myself, since yesternoon. The mail has not been goin' through these three or four days since, and they don't know when it will be runnin' next again, for there's heavy rain continuin' to the north and general floodin' many places.'

The woman slumped further forward in her saddle and then she rallied, slowly forcing herself upright.

It was then Lawless recognised her. Mrs Wakeman!

He had seen her only the once in his life when they had held up the private Wakeman carriage by mistake, but he was sure. What in heaven's name was she doing here alone and bedraggled like this?

'Oh no!' she whispered.

Lawless was out of his depth. He did not know what to do. He did not know what to say. She looked so ill. Involuntarily, he put his hand out to her and almost touched her before he withdrew it, saying, 'Mistress, you seem unwell. You need help. Go on and find the doctor. There's one in Cowra.'

She was frightened now and sick. But she must rally, must go on. She had to find strength. She looked at the traveller, he seemed kind. It was good just to be with someone after the hours of lonely riding in the night and the wind and rain. She forced herself to think clearly. 'Can . . . you tell me then . . .' she began falteringly, 'if the afternoon coach runs? The one that goes south to the township of Young? Does the flooding affect that one too?'

Lawless did not know for certain. 'It might be runnin', mistress, for there's no floodin' there as I know of. Yet ye'll recall that the southern coach only travels but three times in one week. I fear ye shall not be findin' it runnin' today.'

Then the alarm in her was obvious. 'Oh dear,' she began, and he noted her bring herself together with an effort of will. 'I must get away. Perhaps there will be someone I could pay to take me where I need to go.'

In this, Lawless knew he could help her. 'If it's private transport ye be wantin', mistress, why old Ronald Richards will carry ye in his dray, I'm sure; for a shillin' he'll take ye to the moon, they say. But he'll be unable to take ye north, there's no hope o' that.'

'Oh, thank you, and where will I find him?'

'All in Cowra knows him, he lives in an old place hard by the food and grain store.'

She lifted her eyes to meet his. 'You are very kind. Do I know you?'

'No, m'lady, but I know who ye be. And it's strange an' all for the mistress of Mayfield to be abroad in such a sorry state.'

'Yes . . . I suppose it is. Thank you. The man's name was . . . Mr Richards?'

'Yes,' Lawless called after her as she edged her horse forward, 'Ronald Richards, but do see the doctor first, Mrs Wakeman.'

He watched her for a minute or so wondering if he should accompany her. If he did, he would be late for the guv'nor and that would mean he would worry. His loyalty was to Alan not to some rich woman in trouble.

He urged Waterloo forward and continued on.

Christmas night had passed slowly for the master of Mayfield. He had eaten his dinner, conversed with his guests, smiled goodnight to them on the verandah and seen them to their vehicles in the wet air; all this with his mind elsewhere. When his guests had driven away, he remained on the verandah, standing unmoving in the darkness.

Since seeing Eve that afternoon, he had experienced conflicting emotions. The fact was, he had been feeling conflicting emotions since the ghastly day in the garden bower and this afternoon had only increased his torment. He had been startled this afternoon to see how sick and pale Eve looked. He had not expected that. It worried him.

And he had recalled many things. Today, when he had said to her, 'Why have you done all this?' she had replied, 'I have done nothing to be ashamed of,' in the firm, deliberate fashion of the guiltless. He had not meant to say the things to her in the way they had come out of his mouth. He kept seeing her drawn face, and he kept feeling . . . sorry for her. But there were other things that disturbed him greatly, and lately, he had spent many long, unhappy hours looking out on the December night skies and remembering.

When he had been convinced by Lake, he had come home a changed man and confronted her in the garden, condemning her. The sick import of what Lake had told him and his recollections on the homeward ride had festered inside his head until he was consumed by the belief in her guilt. Enough time had passed now for him to analyse Lake's words. To analyse Lake.

When he tried to remember what Eve had said in her defence, he realised he had allowed her to say little, and what he did remember, concerned him more and more. And while that terrible day his conviction had rung in his ears disallowing him to really hear, he thought he recalled some things like: '*John Stuart, all this is a dreadful mistake*' . . . '*It was not me who lived with him*' . . . '*There is much I have to tell you. I should have told you long ago.*' It all danced crazily around now in his mind, and there was something else that he could not recall at all, it floated at the edge of his awareness, but he had not listened. That was the part which troubled him most.

So he stood alone near the verandah railing deep in thought, hardly feeling the dampness or the chill surrounding him. At last he sighed unhappily and turned with leaden footsteps to enter his home.

He was sitting in the long drawing room staring at a painting of his father when the watch rode through in the rain at midnight. He could hear the music drifting from the ballroom. He smiled wanly. The Mayfield celebrations were still going.

A minute or so later he heard sounds on the front verandah. He stood and walked to the hallway door. The ornate, white cedar front door opened and there stood Joe in wet leather cape and hat. He removed them before he crossed the threshold.

'Joe, what brings you back?'

'You, m'boy.'

John Stuart looked questioningly.

'I am troubled. What is going on in that head of yours?'

'Ah Joe, how well you read me.' He turned and the older man followed him back into the drawing room where they sat facing each other. It was a full minute before John Stuart spoke and Joe sat watching him, arms folded on his chest.

'I have been thinking, old man, constantly thinking if the truth be told. I am confused . . . and unhappy.'

'I know.'

'I remember your words when Lake convicted Eve. You said, "He's lying. She would not do such a thing. She is a good woman." '

The older man nodded.

'I have deliberated over and over on it, old man. I am . . . that is . . . I find I really want to believe that I have made some sort of . . . mistake.'

Joe unfolded his arms and leaned forward. 'But what of *the proof*, m'boy, the things that persuaded you at the time? What of Eve's meetings with the bushranger?'

Once again, John Stuart fell silent for a long time. They could hear the wind on the verandah outside, and the sound of the last waltz at the Christmas party floated from the ballroom through the corridors, to them.

'I saw her this afternoon, Joe, and while I don't understand any of it, I do know how . . . I feel about her. I want things to be all right again. I want to believe the meetings with the bushranger were accidental.'

'And what of Adelaide in eighteen fifty-seven? The year she said she was there?'

'She said she went there to visit only.'

'And Lake's words that she encouraged him to make love to her?'

'I don't want . . . to believe them.'

'And the name, Clare Herman?'

'That I do not understand, but now I realise I want to hear what Eve has to say about it.'

Joe was silent for a time. 'And what of the baby? What of that?'

John Stuart did not reply immediately. He sat looking at his hands, deliberating. When he brought his eyes up to Joe's, he answered, 'I don't know, Joe, I'm so confused.'

The older man bent forward to pat John Stuart's arm, a frown of concentration lodged between his eyes. 'Look, m'boy, you need answers, and the only person who can supply them is your wife. We should sit here no longer. It is clear how you feel. Go to her now, this minute.'

'No, old man. When I saw her this afternoon, I was shocked. She was . . . so pale and sickly. It is far better she sleeps the night through.'

'Then go to her first thing tomorrow, and I shall bide impatiently to hear what happens.'

An hour later, John Stuart was still awake, peering through his window at the restless clouds tossing past the milky moon. He drifted briefly into sleep and was awake again to hear his bedside clock strike half past two. Some time later, as he was drifting once more into a heavy sleep, he imagined he heard a door open and close somewhere in the house . . .

He awoke to a gentle tapping on his door and a bleak Boxing Day morning of winds, chill and rain; he sat up in bed.

Timothy entered. 'It is a quarter to eight o'clock, sir. Are you all right?'

'Eight o'clock!' He jumped out of bed. 'Great heavens, Timothy, I have never slept so late in my entire life.'

Five minutes later, he strode down the corridor to the bedroom he had shared with Eve. There he hesitated. Momentarily, all the considerations rushed through his mind again . . . all Lake's arguments. But the overriding feeling now, was his love for her. He loved Eve Herman Wakeman. Loved her with a deep, abiding passion. He wanted to hear what she had to say, wanted to believe in her.

He knocked gently and opened the door.

'Eve? Eve.'

The big draped bed was empty.

Swiftly, he went through the dressing room to the large sitting room beyond. 'Eve?'

Would she be outside? Surely not, it was raining heavily. Nevertheless, he went out onto the verandah and down into the walled garden. Where could she be? A feeling of apprehension rippled through him.

He returned to her bedroom. It was then he saw the things upon the lace pillow. His face went white.

He picked up the olive branch hairpin he had given her and read the words on the paper underneath: 'John Stuart, I'm sorry.' Next to it was an envelope addressed to Thelma.

He stood there re-reading the words. *'John Stuart, I'm sorry' 'John Stuart, I'm sorry'.*

He ran down the corridor and through the massive hall out onto the verandah in some vain hope that perhaps he would see her in the park. But all was quiet except for the constant pattering of the rain. Down the steps and across the park he ran, leaping small flower beds and avoiding bushes. He threw open the Larmers' back gate and bounded up the steps and into the kitchen calling, 'Joe! Where are you?'

Leith looked up in amazement from where he knelt on the hearth lighting the fire.

'Mr Wakeman?'

'Quickly, Leith, where is Mr Larmer?'

The man sprang to his feet and was soon calling, 'Mr Larmer, come quickly, sir, the master is here.'

Joe had been up since five o'clock when it had begun to rain heavily again. Shortly before seven he had ridden down to the Lachlan. He had come home and changed and was about to go up to the big house to tell John Stuart that the river was rising around the crossing. He had just put his foot on the top step to come downstairs when Leith shouted to him. He came swiftly down and was met by John Stuart at the foot of the stairs.

'M'boy? What the devil is it?'

Leith diplomatically withdrew.

'Joe, Eve is gone!'

He listened calmly as John Stuart explained.

'Ah, m'boy, this is serious.'

'She left this for Thelma.' He withdrew the envelope from inside his wet corduroy jacket. 'Where is she?'

'She is just now dressing, what with it being a holiday morning. I shall get her.'

As Thelma came down the stairs she saw John Stuart. 'Oh my Lord, you're soaked. Change your clothes. I shall get Leith to—'

'No, Thelma, that can wait. Read this, please, if you will.'

She opened the envelope and read the letter. With a deep sigh she handed it to John Stuart. 'You read it for yourself.'

He did so. He lifted his eyes to Joe's and shook his head as he handed it to the older man.

'So, there we have it. She goes to "those others who love her". The Reverend Billings?'

'Yes, m'boy, I would guess so.'

Thelma said nothing. She could see that John Stuart was distraught. It was patently obvious that he had changed his mind about Eve and she thanked God for that.

'Eve could not get far in this dreadful weather,' Joe went on. 'What do you wish to do?'

'Ride after her, of course. I must bring her back.' His bewildered eyes found Thelma's as Joe's arm went round his shoulders.

'All right, son, we shall find her.'

When Lawless rode into the back yard at Lyon's Tavern, he smiled. Freedom and Jordan's horse were tethered there. He dismounted, and before he gained the threshold of the door Alan was there to meet him on the small verandah. Their hands met and held.

'Journey go well?'

'Aye, guv'nor. The ride up was wet on and off but the ride back has been wet all the way.'

'Come on then, lad, inside and warm yourself. Mrs Lyon has provided us with dry shirts and an excellent toddy that no doubt shall interest you.'

Lawless extricated himself from his watersoaked cape and hung it on the pegs alongside the others, then he took off his boots and followed Alan.

Inside, a ring of happy faces looked up and smiled their greetings.

'Good on yer, Lawless!'

'Happy Christmas!'

'G'day, Lawless. Sit 'ere. We've kept the seat dry specially for ye.'

Soon, Lawless in dry shirt and stockinged feet, sat down next to Alan. Opposite sat Henry Lyon, side by side with his wife Edna, a pretty-faced, corpulent, middle-aged woman with grey hair, and beside her, their old ostler handyman, Felix. Behind them, near the bar, stood Jordan with his arm round Bridget Lyon, a small girl with a voluptuous body and wide mouth. They were in conversation with her two sisters, Christina, tall and captivating with smooth olive skin and long hair, and Marilyn, slender with dark, sensuous eyes and a matching smile.

'So, this is the company, then?' asked Lawless.

Henry shook his head. 'Not quite, we're expecting Bluey.'

'Good,' answered Jordan, as he squeezed Bridget. 'It's a while since we've seen old Bluey Williams, isn't it, boss?'

Alan nodded, and Christina said laughing, 'Me too.' She was Bluey's girl.

Henry Lyon patted his wife on her massive arm. 'How about some music, mum, my sweet? Get the party started.'

She nodded and soon the first chords of 'Paddy Finley' rang out on the piano. Jordan and the girls joined her at the piano and began to sing.

Lawless drank a mouthful of his toddy and settled back in his chair. 'It was a long ride I made.' He turned his eyes to his glass and took another mouthful.

'Indeed,' agreed Alan, 'and it's good to see you here. I don't like your making any long journey alone.'

'Aye, I know that, guv.' Then a thoughtful look passed over Lawless's face as he took another drink. 'I had a strange meetin' on my way here.'

'And what was that?'

'Oh, no trouble or nothin'. It was real odd though. I was comin' up the long slow rise that leads to Fagin's Pass just south of Cowra, ye know the place, when I see a woman alone on horseback, ridin' towards me from the other way. She was all wet and she looked mighty tired and sick. She stopped by me and spoke with an accent I've scarce been hearin' before. Now, she wants to get to Cowra and the northern mail coach. I told her it wasn't runnin' because of the floods and she carries on all upset like. Then I realised who it was, guv'nor. I mean I was truly amazed and all, for it was Mrs Wakeman, Mr John Stuart Wakeman's wife. Well, I can tell—'

'What?' broke in Alan. 'She was alone, you say? And ill?'

'Aye, that she was. Talked like she had to get away from somethin'. Quite queer an' all, really.'

Edna Lyon was playing another boisterous tune on the old upright piano. Jordan, Bridget, Christina and Marilyn were rocking in time to the music and Felix was beating his hand on the bar. Henry Lyon, whisky in hand, had turned towards the merrymaking.

Lawless looked up in surprise as Alan took hold of his arm. 'Lawless, lad, you say she was going to Cowra? Are you sure? Are you certain she was alone?'

'Why yes, guv. I told her to be seein' old Ronald Richards, said he might drive her where she wanted to be goin'. But what does it mean to ye?'

Alan dropped his friend's arm. 'Fagin's Pass and in to Cowra. Yes, all right. It's raining, the roads are slow. If I leave now, possibly I'll be there in an hour and three-quarters, two hours.'

Alan stood and so did Lawless, in bewilderment.

'What is it, guv'nor? What's wrong?'

For reply, Alan took his friend's arm again and led him out onto the back verandah. The others were all enjoying themselves singing and laughing. Marilyn's deep hazel eyes were the only ones to notice them leave.

Outside, the rain was still falling and the air was still chill.

'Lawless,' Alan looked him in the eye, 'listen carefully to me. This is of major importance. I have no time to explain to you now, but I will, lad, I will. That woman is . . . it's hard to tell it simply. Suffice for me to say that she means something to me. I have seen her more than just the one time we held up the coach. I did not tell any of you for I believed it could have no meaning in our lives. But now . . . Tell me again. You're sure she was alone and sick and she seemed to want to catch the coach north?'

'Aye, that is so. I saw no one at all but herself, all the way here.'

Alan bent down and began to draw on his boots.

'In that case, I be comin' with ye.'

'No, Lawless, it's a celebration in there. Jordan has been looking forward to it for weeks, as no doubt the others have. You must stay here and wait for me.'

Rarely had Lawless ever questioned a decision of Alan's, but he did so now. 'Guv, this lot here are goin' to have a fine time whether I be stayin' or no. But where ye be goin' is dangerous territory. Now, I don't understand all this ye be sayin' about the woman but that's as may be. What I do understand is she belongs to Mayfield and she'll be drawin' attention like Ben Hall would at Government House. There may well be all sorts out lookin' for her now for all we know, maybe even police. Ye'll be needin' a second string to yer bow goin' chargin' off like this. And me, I'm that second string.'

Alan smiled. 'You're right, of course, Lawless, and I thank you.'

Marilyn's soft voice sounded from the doorway, 'Oh no, Alan! You are not leavin'? You just got here.'

'Sorry, lass,' Alan replied. 'But there's something we must do, and immediately.'

'What?' She looked up at him with ill-concealed affection, her hand on his arm.

Alan touched her gently on the chin. 'Now, Marilyn Lyon, you know better than to ask such a thing.' And with that, he moved inside.

Edna stopped playing as Alan approached the piano. Jordan looked down at Alan's boots. 'Going somewhere, boss?'

'Yes, Jordan, though it doesn't concern you, lad. You stay here and enjoy yourself.' He looked round their faces. 'Lawless passed a traveller on the road who is an old friend of mine and might need help. We're going to ride out now and assess the situation. We'll be back.'

For a moment, Jordan looked quizzically, for he didn't know of any 'old friend' the boss had, but he was too taken up with Bridget to consider it for long. He squeezed her to him and kissed her cheek. 'No need to hurry, boss.'

'Don't listen to him, Alan,' said Marilyn looking provocatively up at him. 'I'd like you to hurry.'

Alan smiled at the girl and touched her hand in farewell. 'You wait here, Jordan. We will return for you, understand?'

'Absolutely.'

'And bring Bluey back if you see him,' instructed Christina.

Henry Lyon came close to Alan. 'Sorry ye be leavin', mates. Is there danger in this?'

Alan shrugged. 'It is best you know nothing, Henry.'

'Aye,' agreed the publican, 'now that's true . . . but be careful.'

They made good time to Cowra considering the doggedly falling rain and muddy, sodden roads; when they entered the wide, deserted street of the township, it was fourteen minutes before twelve noon.

On the way north, Alan spoke little. He had thought to explain himself to Lawless and then changed his mind. Time enough to do that if they found her and it became necessary. When Lawless had ventured a question, asking, 'Why is it we are ridin' out to find the woman, guv'nor?' Alan simply replied, 'Trust me, lad, I'll explain in time.'

Lawless looked over to him through the rain, replying in his uncomplicated fashion, 'I do, guv, always have, always will. But I'm thinkin' it's a powerful magnet and all she has, to be drawin' us towards her on a day such as this.'

And Alan turned his head and smiled at his guileless, yet discerning friend.

They crossed the decrepit wooden bridge that lay over the Lachlan and soon were riding up the gentle slope of the main street of Cowra. There was little to see. After all, it was the Boxing Day holiday and it was raining. They soon found Ronald Richards' small dwelling, but no one answered their knock.

Alan looked at Lawless, a frown between his eyes. 'She would have reached here hours ago, but let us go to the coaching office anyway.'

'Aye,' agreed Lawless, 'but in a township this small there's nary a person who won't know she's been here. If we have no satisfaction at the coachin' office, we've but to walk the settlement and ask.'

'And that's exactly what we will do, lad, and keep a ready eye on the street, we don't want to be surprised by men we have no wish to meet.'

As they mounted the steps to the coaching office, they saw figures moving inside. Umbrellas were open and dripping near the doorstep and three small children played noisily at flicking water on each other. Two men and two women stood with their backs to the door, while a fifth was kneeling down in front of a woman lying prone along the wooden seat.

As they entered the small dank room they heard some of the conversation.

'Oh dear, she's out to it. What will we do now?'

'We shall just have to carry her to my place, in this rain and all.'

The people turned to look at the newcomers and Alan saw immediately that it was Eve who lay upon the bench. He felt his pulse quicken as he estimated the situation swiftly and spoke immediately. 'Ah, there is Mrs Wakeman. We have come for her. Ridden on ahead. The carriage comes behind.'

His educated voice made the men and women look at him with respect. One of the men stepped forward and Alan noticed the reversed white collar of a priest. The brother's face broke into a smile. 'Oh good,' he said, 'we are pleased to see you. So, er, you are Mayfield men?'

Alan did not reply but came forward to the group. Eve was unconscious. He moved through them and, lifting her in his arms, turned to leave.

The priest looked alarmed. 'Now, now! Surely, er, Mrs Wakeman should wait for the carriage. She has fainted. It amazes me how, er, she got here in the first place!'

But Alan was already moving to the door.

'Hey, wait!' shouted one of the men. 'Where is Mr Wakeman?'

'He follows in the carriage,' Alan called over his shoulder, not stopping but continuing out of the building and down the steps.

The group inside followed. It was still raining and it kept the women and children back, although the priest and the two men came out. 'Earlier we sent to Mayfield for Mr Wakeman,' the priest called. 'Andy Leeman rode out. Did you come across him on your way?'

Alan passed Eve to Lawless and mounted Freedom. Then Lawless lifted Eve up into his arms and he enclosed her inside his cape, protecting her.

'Hey, did you see Andy Leeman?'

357

Looking down, Alan replied, 'No, he must have gone by the north fork.'

'Gawd, guv'nor,' said Lawless quietly, 'what the devil does that mean?'

At that moment one of the women called from the door, 'Mrs Wakeman's purse bag!' Lawless ran back for it.

'Hey, er, steady on,' called the priest coming across the footpath. 'I really don't think this is proper. Mrs Wakeman should wait for the carriage. She is obviously quite ill.' Now his voice was stern. 'What sort of instructions did, er, Mr Wakeman give to you?'

By this time, Lawless had moved round to Waterloo and Alan answered, 'Don't worry, sir. You can be sure we shall take care of her.'

Lawless had now mounted.

The priest opened his mouth to speak again but without waiting for further consultation, Alan spurred forward.

Brother Michael turned to his companions. 'Now, er, what on earth do you make of that at all?'

One of the men answered. 'Well, I be gatherin' they be from Mayfield sure enough, Brother Michael, else why would they have come here for her at all? Rivetin' sort o' eyes on the fellow that did the speakin', eh?'

'Yes, er, I suppose so,' replied Brother Michael. 'But I feel there is something queer about it, I do. What in our good Lord's name did he, er, mean by missing Andy on the north fork? There are no forks in the road to Mayfield! I do, er, wish Mr Wakeman were here.'

But they were not to see Mr Wakeman until well after one o'clock in the afternoon, in company with Andy Leeman whom he had indeed met on the way into Cowra.

Some few hundred yards south of the rustic Cowra bridge over the Lachlan, the road turned left and ran through a dense growth of white cedar trees, their ancient limbs almost touching across the road. They provided partial shelter and Alan brought Freedom to a halt beneath them while Lawless reined in beside him.

Eve's face had been exposed to the falling rain and it had served to revive her. She moved slightly in his arms and opened her eyes. In her weakened state she could not believe that it was Alan who held her, she thought she must be dreaming. Tears broke over her lids and ran down her face to mingle there with the dampness from the rain. 'It cannot be,' she whispered.

'Ah, lass, don't weep, please,' he said gently. 'Listen to me. Listen carefully. We found you in Cowra, and now we have a long ride ahead of us no matter which point we travel towards, but there are some questions I must have answered.'

'I don't understand . . . I've been . . . all alone. How can it be you?'

'We found you in the coaching office. You had fainted. I don't understand how you come to be alone and ill in Cowra. Should you not be at home? Am I now to return you to Mayfield once more?'

'No! Oh no!' she answered, gathering her strength. 'I've been riding away from Mayfield all through the night. I was on my way to . . . to Father in Bathurst. I must get to Father.'

He was in a dilemma. Nothing was clear.

'Do you mean the minister?'

'Yes . . . Father. Reverend Billings. I must go there. I must.'

He could not take her to Bathurst, the roads were flooded. Besides, even if they could, by a miracle, get round the inundated land, she was ill, and Bathurst was over a seventy-mile ride. If he could get her to Treehard, then, when the flooding subsided, he could take her where she wished to go.

But for this moment, he savoured the miracle that had occurred. She was here. But she was exhausted and unnerved. They must be careful with her.

'All right, lass. You can tell me all about it later. But I must repeat, should I not return you to your husband and your home?'

She moved in his arms and turned her face to his, 'No,' she said again. 'You are . . . my friend. Do not do that. I will not go. Oh please, I will not.'

'But I cannot take you to Bathurst, lass. The roads are covered with flood water and there seems to be no abating in the weather. We may not be able to make that journey for weeks.'

Her voice became a little stronger, more resolute. 'Then . . . then can I stay. . . . with you, until I can get through the floods?'

Alan did not answer straight away, he was deciding his next move.

Lawless looked across to him and there was doubt in his eyes. 'Are ye thinkin' to take the mistress home to Treehard, guv'nor?'

'I don't see we have an alternative, Lawless. We cannot leave her here. Would be best if we could find a doctor.'

She straightened a little in Alan's arms, saying, 'I do not want a doctor and I can make the ride. I can make the ride.' Then she looked over at Lawless and seemed to see him for the first time. 'Why, it's the traveller I met on the road.'

'Aye,' answered Lawless, 'it's me. I'm Lawless, yet my real name be Arnold, and when I told the guv'nor here we had met, we were promptly on the road again to find ye.'

Vague comprehension dawned and she managed to smile at him saying, 'Bless you, thank you.'

Alan put out his hand. 'Give me your blanket, lad. We had best move on, but first we must protect her face from the rain.'

'Where are we heading, guv?'

'For Bluey's. It's a long ride for her, but it's the nearest, safest place.'

As they rode on, she settled in his arms. She did not feel really ill any more. She felt a euphoric sort of peace. Some prodigious marvel had brought her to him and that was all that mattered. He would take her to Father, she knew he would. The well-being transferred itself from her psyche to her physical self and with an effort she remained conscious throughout the ride.

John Stuart had mobilised swiftly and ridden in haste from Mayfield with Joe and Jack Hennessy by half past eight in the morning. Joe was worried about the Lachlan rising, and about getting back to Mayfield through the low lands around Cowra, but he knew that right now Eve was the most important thing on John Stuart's mind.

The ride into Cowra was slow and difficult, much harder even than when Eve rode through a few hours before, for the constant rain now brought mud slides in places. John Stuart pushed them hard, and even harder after they met Andy Leeman, but it still took them five hours to make the ride. As the sodden group made their way through the mud to the coaching office, John Stuart's heart was beating swiftly. She was here. Thank heavens for that. Now he could talk to her, let her know how he felt, take her home.

They dismounted and leaped up the steps into the waiting room.
Empty.

Andy Leeman pointed down the street. 'They probably took m'lady to the doctor's home, sir. They was discussin' doin' that when I left here.'

They made their way along to Dr Campbell's home. The street was deserted, for the rain was coming down in sheets. Outside the wooden cottage covered in climbing vine with a small sign over the door announcing 'Gordon Campbell M.D.', they reined in. Mrs Campbell was in the parlour and through her front windowpane saw the arrivals. She hurried to the door.

'Oh my Lord! Mr Wakeman, sir, what brings you here?'

'Isn't my wife here?'

The woman looked mystified. 'Oh Lordy. I . . . but isn't she with you by now?'

Joe took off his rain-soaked hat and stepped closer. 'Mrs Campbell, we understood from Mr Leeman here that you were taking care of Mrs Wakeman.'

'Well, we were, sir, down in the coaching office, until your riders came in and took her away.'

Joe and John Stuart looked at each other. Joe responded. 'Riders? What riders?'

'You mean you didn't send them?'

'What the devil—'

Joe lifted his hand to John Stuart's shoulder; it was a calming gesture. 'Mrs Campbell,' he said, 'could we come in? Then perhaps you can tell us exactly what has happened. Is there anyone else who knows anything?'

'Why yes, Brother Michael was at the coach waiting room too and Dick Barovill and . . .'

Joe turned to Jack Hennessy. 'Get the priest and bring him here, Jack.'

Ten minutes later, they had heard the entire tale from Brother Michael.

John Stuart sat in silence, his brow furrowed, his right hand up to his chin. He had asked no questions during the interview and had left it entirely to Joe. To Mrs Campbell and the priest he appeared quite calm, but the truth was that his heart thumped crazily against his chest and his mind was in sick turmoil.

Joe reiterated, 'And so they rode out to the south, you say?'

Brother Michael nodded. 'Yes.'

'And the man that did the talking was educated?'

'He was. Spoke like nobility, you might say, not fancy or priggish, mind, but upper class, no doubt. That was really why we let them take Mrs Wakeman.' He looked to John Stuart. 'Er, we could not stop him really, he, er, just whisked her away.'

John Stuart's expression did not change, except for the subtle hardening of his mouth.

Joe went on, 'What did the man look like?'

Brother Michael peered seriously at them from behind his spectacles. He was the lonely representative of his church in Cowra, an outlying district of the parish and very small. He was in awe of these two eminent men, he could not help it. He did not know what to make of Mr Wakeman; he was a heretic, if one believed what one heard. He sat now in gloomy silence opposite, an imposing man. It somehow surprised the priest that Mr Larmer was speaking for him.

Brother Michael was a kind, principled young man, and while he accepted this was none of his affair, it all confounded him. He answered Joe's question, seeing again in his mind's eye the man who had taken Mrs Wakeman away. 'Well, he was taller than me, perhaps five feet ten or eleven, clean-shaven, firm jaw line, sunbrowned, and, er, Dick Barovill, who was with me, pointed out he had singular eyes.'

John Stuart stared straight ahead, expressionless.

Joe nodded thoughtfully. 'And the man with him limped, you said?'

'Yes, he did, I noticed that, didn't you, Mrs Campbell?'

'Yes, I did.'

'And Mrs Wakeman was unconscious the entire time?'

'She, er, certainly was; had fainted just before they came in the door.'

Abruptly John Stuart rose from the sofa and extended his hand to Brother Michael. His pulse was still racing and his mind was leaping from conclusion to conclusion. 'Thank you,' he said and turned to the door.

On the small verandah with the rain pattering loudly on the corrugated iron roof, they joined Jack Hennessey who pointed to the horse tethered to the railing. 'We found Betsy, sir.'

Joe nodded and faced round to John Stuart. 'What do you make of all that, m'boy?'

There was real pain in John Stuart's face and he seemed to consider his words. 'Joe, these men, who were they? Why would they ride in and take an unconscious woman?'

Their eyes met meaningfully. Both men were thinking of the description, thinking of the only man they knew who fitted it. Neither of them spoke their thoughts aloud, but both knew what was going on in the other's mind.

'What do you want to do, son?'

'I must follow, Joe. They've got my wife!'

'But, m'boy, that was two hours ago and with the heavy rain we have little hope of—'

'Joe, I must.'

Joe said no more. They jumped down the steps and rode into the rain.

It was over two long hours later on the road south of Cowra, in the mud and slush, that Joe put up his hand and halted. He turned to John Stuart, rain dripping off the brim of his hat. 'I'm now very concerned for those at home, m'boy. This rain is constant. The bridge at Cowra was close to overflowing when we rode over it hours ago. Now, we don't need to cross it again to get home, but it was a sign of how quickly the Lachlan is probably rising on Mayfield.'

'What are you saying, Joe?'

'M'boy, we have seen nothing to indicate that Eve is even on this road. Just because she was taken from Cowra on it this morning doesn't mean she's still on it. She could be anywhere.' He leaned over and took hold of John Stuart's arm. 'I do not want to be the one to say we are riding in a futile search, but . . .'

John Stuart looked at Joe, his determined face set against the weather. He turned in his saddle to Jack Hennessy who sat with water running in rivulets down his cape into the mud below his drenched horse's body. The horses were obviously tired, and while they had been fed and watered in Cowra, it had been a long difficult ride. These two men would continue on with him, he knew that, but it was unfair, unfair to them, and unfair to those who depended on him at Mayfield. Joe was right, of course, the Lachlan would be rising there now. But, by all that was sacred, his wife had been abducted!

'Perhaps I should go on and you should turn back.'

'I will not allow you to go on alone, m'boy.'

He was torn. He knew he had a pressing duty to those at home. He looked up to the leaden sky. Yes, this downpour would continue.

He sat in indecision.

Joe was right, Eve could be anywhere. Anywhere. And he knew exactly where those others were for whom he was also responsible.

He felt a nauseating lurch in his stomach. When he spoke, his voice quavered slightly. 'We return to Mayfield,' he said, pulling Diomed's head round.

CHAPTER TWENTY-TWO

'When the traps give chase (may the devil take his power!)
He can ride ten miles in a quarter of an hour.'
'A Bushranger', Kenneth Slessor, 1901–1971.

Edmund 'Bluey' Williams' eccentric little two-roomed shack could
be missed easily by the unknowledgeable. It stood a mile or so north
of Lyon's Tavern, well back from the road through a thicket of small
trees, its rickety verandah nestling against a clump of shrubbery,
beyond which an outhouse for the horse and dray leaned at an angle
against a picket fence covered in vine.

For the first few miles of their ride from Cowra, the heavens had
shed only light rain, but now as they arrived it was falling heavily
once more.

Lawless climbed down first, calling as he did so, 'Bluey! Bluey!'
There was no reply and he came round Freedom to help Eve down.

Alan dismounted. His arms were stiff from holding her and he
rubbed them as Lawless helped her onto the verandah.

Eve leaned heavily on Lawless as he called again, 'Bluey? Bluey?'

Alan walked ahead and pushed on the front door. It swung open
although there was obviously no one home.

'No doubt he's at Lyon's,' Lawless decided.

'Probably,' agreed Alan. 'Let's get the lass onto a cot.'

They divested themselves of their capes and boots and helped Eve
inside, where in a number of places Bluey had placed large buckets
to catch the water from the leaking roof.

Alan nodded to Lawless. Lawless nodded in reply and returned
outside to house the horses. As he exited, Alan gently steered Eve
to a chair. 'You must take off your damp clothes and lie down while
we are here.'

'I . . . but . . .'

'Come on, lass, your shoes and stockings are sodden, and the rest
of your clothes are damp, it's no time for modesty.' He knelt at her
feet as he spoke and relieved her of her shoes. Then he began to
unbutton her jacket. She rallied and pushing his hands away said,
'I'll do it.'

As she undressed, he turned away and found an ancient kettle and some firewood. He busied himself getting a fire burning in the grate and the kettle on to boil. When he turned round she was lying under the blanket on Bluey's iron cot with her eyes closed. 'Good girl,' he said lifting her clothes and taking them close to the fire to dry.

There was a gentle knock at the door and Lawless entered. He crossed to the fire with their waterlogged boots and stood them near the grate.

'A cuppa, guv'nor,' he said, 'that's what we all be needin', a sweet, strong cup of tea.'

He managed to find some salt beef and damper that had been put safely away from the ants and when the tea was made they ate some of it. Eve ate sparingly and lay back down, falling quickly into a deep slumber. Both men, too, were fatigued. They had ridden hard and long in cold, wet weather and soon they also fell asleep.

Bluey's hut became silent, the only sound, other than the rain on the iron roof, the steady breathing of the three fugitives.

Alan woke first. He looked swiftly around to see if she were here and not a figment of a dream, and yes, there she lay, fast asleep, not five feet away. He guessed he had slept perhaps an hour. He walked out onto the leaking verandah and avoiding the worst of the drips went to the rail and looked at the sky. Reading the time in an overcast sky was hard, but he discerned it was somewhere between three and four o'clock. He was correct. It was in fact some fifteen minutes to four and on the Sydney road leading back to Cowra, three riders turned round and headed back to Mayfield.

It would be inky black tonight and very difficult to travel beyond nightfall. They must leave for Treehard soon. For a moment, he visualised the two men waiting there and he smiled gently.

But could the woman inside make the ride?

From what Lawless had told him, the heart of the deluge was to the north; yet this local rain was wearisomely constant. His years of familiarity with bush weather told him there was no chance of its stopping. Abate it might for a short time, but there was a lot more rain to come, he was certain.

He returned inside. Noiselessly, he crossed to where Lawless lay on a blanket by the primitive hearth. He knelt down and touched him softly. Lawless's eyes opened instantly, full of alarm; the alarm of the hunted man woken. But it disappeared as he focused on Alan's composed expression. 'Nothing to worry about, matey,' Alan spoke quietly. 'All's well, but one of us will have to ride to Lyon's to tell Jordan and inform Bluey we're here.'

'I'll go,' said Lawless rising. 'I'm ready.'

'I would not have you go, lad, except that it's probably better I stay here with her. If she wakens, it may be best it's me who's with her.'

'I reckon, guv,' Lawless smiled.

Alan continued in an undertone, 'There's no need to bring Jordan back here. I've decided to bide here the night and he'll be happy to stay where he is until tomorrow.'

'Aye, he would be counting on that, I'd say.'

'And you stay there too, don't bother to come back in this weather. Just make sure you're both here by eight or nine o'clock on the morrow.'

'I'm not concerned about that, I'll take the news to Jordan and Bluey and I'll return to ye here, guv.'

Alan smiled. 'All right, lad.'

Once more Lawless attired himself in his long leather cloak and wide-brimmed hat and pulled on his still damp boots.

Alan walked with him onto the verandah. It was time to be honest with his faithful companion.

'Lawless,' he said taking his arm, 'I should explain to you about her.'

'It isn't necessary, guv'nor. I be seein' for meself ye be attached to her.'

'Yes, Lawless, that is true, but you have a right to know more now that it seems we will be in company with her for a time.'

He took a deep breath and began to speak of the complexities he did not understand himself. 'I am at a loss for the right phrases, my friend, but somehow she has become important to me.' And he recounted the happenings of the day he had found her injured in the bush and Lawless replied, 'Well now, so that was what happened! Never could account for why ye were away so long, us worried and all, thinkin' the traps had ye, and at last ye come home in the black of night, thoughtful as an Oxford dean.'

'After that day, naturally, I thought never to see her again, but I did. It was in Bathurst before Christmas last, when you and I bought ammunition and supplies. We met briefly. She seemed so pleased to see me and I realised that I, too, was pleased to see her. Yet it seemed absurd . . . I spoke unkindly to her. Any association at all seemed ludicrous. I was angered by the way I had begun to feel. A sort of amorphous feeling that I could not control. But now here she is with me again, this time brought to me through you, my friend. She's called Eve and when I think of her, it's not as the mistress of Mayfield, simply as Eve.'

'A nice name that, Eve,' Lawless remarked.

Alan fell silent and Lawless's face grew grave. 'Well, guv'nor,' he began, 'the way she be comin' into yer ken, it's like somethin' out of one of those plays or poems ye read. And it's all of a surprise to me and no mistake. But that's as may be, and for whatever reason the Almighty has, she's here and that's the way of it.'

Alan pulled affectionately on the brim of Lawless's hat and smiled. He watched Lawless mount up and leave, a strong, capable bushman. As Alan lifted his hand in a wave, he remembered the bone-thin young man with pallid complexion who had been sentenced a convict for pilfering a meagre living in the London slums. The horseman who now disappeared through the trees held no resemblance to that street youth of long ago.

Alan sighed. Life was not just; he knew that. Life was mysterious, and rarely just. If there were equity, the mild, steadfast man who had just ridden away would have been born of happy parents in a prosperous English town, made a career for himself and had sturdy sons, never knowing the shock of prison or what it was to run a hunted man.

And the others?

Diminutive Sam would have lived an even, settled life, a farmer on the Surrey downs. Swiftie would not have died a convict, shot in the back at twenty years of age, but would have turned his wit and sensitivity to some lucrative trade. And Daniel, dear Daniel, would never have been pushed to the brink in times of poverty. His sweet Audrey would have lived, and they would have grown old together in tranquillity.

Jordan? Fate had dealt harshly with him, too. If he had not lost the farm his parents had worked all their lives, he never would have held the grudge that led him to horse-stealing and thus placed him outside the law.

And himself? Alan Fletcher? If life were fair, where would he be? He would be at Long Moss House among his tenant farmers, embroiled in the pleasant destiny of English country life. And in his peaceful moments, he would be writing of the sea and reading his books.

And if such had been? He could not answer for his men. But for himself, he would rather be here. Here, living this strangest of all existences, with the knowledge that trust and faith flourished in the hearts of the men who were his comrades. Here, with her asleep inside. The only thing he would change would be the death of Swiftie. And yes, too, the death of Patricia June.

He turned and went back inside.

She still slept. Her face was drawn and tired, there were shadows under her eyes and her pale, full mouth looked almost too large in her thin face. He wondered what had happened to make her look this way. The blanket had slipped down from her shoulders exposing her hand which lay across her breast. He lifted the blanket back and as he did so noticed there was a cut on her forefinger.

Contradictory emotions circulated inside him as he stood looking down at her, but the one sensation he recognised as pervading his being when he was with her was tenderness. He found it hard to believe she was here, real and breathing, beside him.

He smiled down at her sleeping form and moved away.

The fire had gone out. The hut was chill again. He stacked more wood in the fireplace and relit it. Then he sat at Bluey's table considering the next moves and the next days. The sound of the rain on the iron roof was soothing, mesmerising. All was peaceful, when into his thoughts came noises, distant noises heralding the arrival of riders.

He looked sharply up and across to Eve. She still slept.

His hand went automatically to his rifle as he rose and moved swiftly to the door and onto the verandah. Through the wet trees he could discern the shadows of the coming figures. They were riding very fast, almost too fast, in the thick scrub. There appeared to be only two; it was Lawless and Jordan. What was Jordan doing here?

Out of the trees into the clearing they came, Jordan's horse sliding a little in his rider's haste to bring him to the hut.

'Trouble, guv'nor!' shouted Lawless as they reined in.

'We'd best get out of here and fast, boss!' added Jordan.

'What is it?'

'Bloody countryside is crawlin' with traps,' answered Jordan, dismounting and landing on the verandah in one leap.

Lawless followed. 'There have been two robberies, guv, one in Warraderry yesterday at Christmas noon, a man was wounded; the other at the Redley station, near Landsdowne, this morning. They be blamin' Dan Morgan for the one in Warraderry.'

'And the bastards are blamin' us for the other,' broke in Jordan. 'Seems they wore masks. They've mobilised every bloody mounted trap for forty miles, in this rain and all, and Bluey's mate, Tinker, says a policeman was shot dead at Redley's and the troopers are headed this way. Bluey thinks they might come here.'

'All right, lads, now calmly,' answered Alan. 'How did you hear of all this?'

'From Tinker, guv'nor, Bluey's mate. He came precise at the time I arrived at Lyon's. Isn't that right, Jordan?'

'Yes, he'd been in the tavern north o' Greenthorpe this afternoon when five troopers rode in and surrounded the bloody place. Seems the traps had word that we were there celebratin'. They questioned everybody and then Tinker left, ridin' the eight miles cross country on the bush track by Gorman's farm to Lyon's, bringin' the news to everyone as he passed.'

Lawless nodded. 'It were only chance he came to Lyon's, thinkin' to find Bluey and ask him if he knew of it. Gawd, guv, lucky we were there and all, for Bluey says they'll be sure to come here to his hut, havin' a fair idea he's more than friendly with such as us.'

'Right then,' said Alan calmly. 'So they're laying the blame on us for shooting a man?'

Lawless grimaced. 'Aye, and we've never done no such thing, it's disgustin'! What'll we do, guv'nor?'

Alan's mind was racing. He was thinking of her, inside. Where could he leave her, so she would be safe? She had fallen into his life again, was now his responsibility.

Damn the rain, and yet the rain could be their friend. Troopers might ride abroad to catch a bushranger in the dusk of a warm, starry night but he did not know of a trooper in New South Wales who would be willing to try to chase one on into the inky blackness of a cold, wet night.

But night was still a couple of hours away. They had best move out. It was not right to commandeer Bluey's home any longer.

'We'll leave from here as soon as we can,' Alan said.

Lawless looked to Alan. 'I haven't told old Jordan about . . . the mistress, guv. There were no time, ye see, he bein' ready to hightail it over here as soon as Tinker dropped his news.'

Jordan looked to Alan. 'What's that?'

Alan unconsciously stepped back to bar the door. 'A friend, a lady you met once before, is in the hut, Jordan. Mrs Wakeman.'

Disbelief spread across Jordan's face. 'What?'

'It's a tale I'm not going to relate to you now, lad,' Alan went straight on. 'It's enough to say she's here with us. She's exhausted and sick and I find myself accountable for her. I will explain it all to you when we arrive at Treehard.'

Jordan was confounded. His mouth actually dropped open. The boss had gone completely bloody mad! He looked to Lawless to have this absurdity contradicted but all Lawless did was nod his head. 'Aye, she's in there and all, Jordan, old son.'

Jordan's arm went out to move Alan aside to see for himself but Alan stayed his hand with his own. 'You'll have to take my word for it, lad. She's asleep. I'm going now to wake her. Then we'll wait out here while she dresses. After that, we make the ride to Treehard. Is this all clear to you, Jordan?'

'No, it isn't, boss, not bloody clear at all, yet I hear the words you say.'

'Then that will have to be sufficient for the time being.'

'Come on, then, Jordan, matey,' said Lawless, putting his arm round the big man's shoulders and dragging him back a step. 'We'll wait here and give the horses a drink, eh?'

'Bloody strange!' commented Jordan as Alan went inside. He moved out of Lawless's armhold. 'So it's true then? The flamin' mistress of flamin' Mayfield is in there?'

'Aye, that she is, Jordan, old son, just as we told ye.'

'I thought you two rode out to help a friend of his. Someone he heard was in trouble.'

'Aye, Jordan, that's true.'

'Her?'

'Aye, her.'

'Bloody defies imagination,' stated Jordan shaking his head.

'Aye, that it does, and no mistake,' agreed his companion, taking up his cape again and throwing it round his shoulders. 'Come on, let's water the horses. It's them as have to carry us on the road again.'

As they moved down the steps, Alan was shaking Eve gently. 'Lass, wake up now, I'm sorry but we must depart this place.'

Coming out of her slumber, Eve felt weary and her bones ached but seeing his face above hers brought a smile to her mouth. 'Why, it's you,' she said trying to remember how it was they were together.

'We may need to ride on soon,' he said quietly. 'Are you well enough?'

She nodded.

'Are you sure, lass? It's raining outside and I cannot promise you a comfortable ride.'

'I'm sure,' she said with more determination in her voice than she felt in her heart.

There was silence for a few seconds, then she sat up. 'After our last meeting, I had feared we were no longer . . . friends.'

He looked searchingly at her for a moment and shook his head. 'Ah, lass. I remember. But that had naught to do with whether we be friends or not. Do you understand?'

'I . . . I think so.'

He smiled at her reply. 'I shall stoke up the fire and leave you to don your clothing.'

'Where are we going?'

He had already moved to the hearth and responded with his back to her. 'To my home, the place we call Treehard, in the hills some hours' ride from here.'

She was holding the blanket up to her breast. 'I fear it is not proper,' she said softly.

He heard, and after a heartbeat turned round.

'You are right, lass.' There was the tiniest hint of disappointment in his voice. 'It is quite improper and I am more the fool for ever suggesting it. Forgive me.'

'What do you mean?'

'There is a tavern but a mile or so down the highway where there are rooms for travellers. I will take you there and you can wait for the flooding on the roads to subside, afterwards continuing your journey to Bathurst.'

Fright rose in her. He was going to abandon her! 'Am I too much trouble?'

'Ah, lass, you confuse me. No, I am not thinking anything such. I want you to keep your reputation. This way, I believe you can. It's more seemly.'

She gave a small laugh, thin and tired though it was. 'I assure you I have no reputation to keep.' Sadness crept into her voice. 'But if you think it best, then of course I shall go to this tavern. I would not have you in peril for me.'

Alan came back the few short feet between them and there was a note of severity in his tone. 'I would not deposit you at any tavern and leave you to yourself to ease complication in my life. I am ready to do whatever it is you want, but you must not be tempted to trifle with me.'

'Forgive me,' she said, 'I do not trifle with you. There is much that I must explain. You see, I cannot go back to Mayfield. My marriage is over. Dreadful things have happened. When I said it was not proper, it was merely an automatic observation. I was thinking of what the people I know consider to be right and wrong. It has naught to do with my real wishes. Please take me to your Treehard, do not leave me alone in some tavern. When the floods go down I can make the journey to Bathurst; you need but get me to a mail coach. I know you live a life full of danger and I would not add to your worries for any length of time.'

She had said what she truly meant and he knew it. He nodded. 'Very well. Then I should tell you it becomes imperative to ride on soon. There are police troopers in the district.'

'Oh no!' she said, 'then we must make haste.'

'I will leave you now and when you have dressed, we will journey on.'

She still felt weak and very lightheaded, but better than she had when they arrived here. Her clothes were dry and she was just pulling on her bodice when a sharp stabbing pain seized her. It took her breath away. She bent forward grasping herself and made a small moaning sound. This was no good, they were in a hurry. She must not have pain now! There were police in the district. Oh dear. She must hurry . . . but the pain. She eased herself onto the bed. Oh dear! Oh dear! Come on, Eve. Half a minute lapsed and the pain passed. She righted herself and pulled on her dress. To think he had been going to take her to the inn had she wanted to go and there were police in the area . . . the risk to him, the terrible risk!

She was buttoning the dress across her breast when a knock came on the door followed by his voice above the constant sound of the rain. 'Are you ready in there, now?'

'Yes, please enter.'

He came in followed by Lawless and a very big man who looked at her intently, disbelief in his eyes.

Alan waved his arm in the direction of the fire and said, 'Jordan, Lawless, a minute by the flames to warm yourselves, then we shall douse it and be on our way.'

As the two men moved the short distance to the hearth, he spoke again, 'Mrs . . .' There was just the slightest hesitation after this word, '. . . Wakeman. You already know Lawless, this is Jordan O'Day.'

'How d'you do,' Jordan said.

'Pleased to meet you,' Eve replied.

Alan lifted her small bag of possessions. 'We must ride in tandem again, and although it will be cold and wet for the next few hours, I can promise you a warm, dry reception at Treehard.' He smiled at her and once more she experienced the inexplicable happiness that came over her in his presence.

On Bluey's worn and pitted table, Alan left two gold sovereigns.

As they moved to the door, the wind gusted with such force that the tin roof rattled and water came though the leaks in streams.

Outside, Jordan hesitated. 'The night's goin' to worsen, boss. Do you think the stinkin' traps will continue searchin' in this weather?'

'It depends on who leads them. Most wouldn't. But a man such as Rutherford Blake would continue his ride if he thought to capture us. Until nightfall, there is some risk.'

'Aye,' spoke up Lawless, 'Batty Blake would ride on. He's got a score to settle with us and the way I be thinkin', Jordan, we better be gettin' on the roads and makin' good time homewards.'

'You're right, Lawless,' agreed Alan. 'Unfortunately there will be mud slides on the trails we would normally use, so we must ride by the road a little way. You, Jordan, lad, ride ahead until we reach the main track and keep a lookout. If you see movement in the distance, return to us immediately. You, Lawless, keep a constant watch behind us, for I cannot turn in the saddle as you can.'

The rain was steady, enduring and perpetual. The temperatures were the lowest for a summer day ever in the colony of New South Wales. The sodden band rode on. They covered the mile to the turn-off near Lyon's Tavern without catching sight of any other travellers. As they passed the corner that led down to the inn, Jordan looked warily in that direction but all was deserted.

'I bet they're having fun down there,' he grumbled to himself, 'and here I am out in bloody weather as is not fit for a dog!' He had been lying with Bridget in the little room behind the bar when Lawless and Tinker had arrived and he was not one who enjoyed interruptions to his lovemaking. He got to do it precious little as it was. Blast the traps! They were being blamed for a raid they didn't even make! The bloody injustice of it all. And now hours of this riding in the cold and wet. Christ, what a man had to put up with! It was all right for the boss and Lawless, they didn't seem to mind goin' ages without females. Yet what the devil was going on with the boss and this Wakeman woman? Now, that was something unbelievable. Takin' her to Treehard, no less! Oh well, no doubt the boss knew what he was doin'. Anyway, he hoped so.

He rode on, his thoughts tumbling over each other. No doubt that was why he did not see the troopers until they came out of the dip in the ground not a hundred yards in front of him; five police on horseback pushing their mounts at a goodly pace over the mud and pebbles of the road, in the moody evening.

He froze, pulling back hard on the reins of his horse.

Alan and Lawless were behind him round the bend and could see nothing yet. Too late to ride back and warn them.

This was the first time in his life outside the law, that he had ever been taken unawares. Alan had always delivered him from such as this. There had been only three occasions when he had been faced with police and each time they had been at the disadvantage, being the victims caught in one of the band's movements.

His mind went blank. He could not think. And so he panicked. And with panic came frantic, startled movement. He pulled his horse's head sharply round and plunged into the bush. The animal jumped forward and almost lost its footing as it staggered on water-logged brushwood. But it righted itself and with Jordan holding on for his life and spurring him, the horse continued to crash through the undergrowth to the trees beyond.

The troopers had not expected to see anyone on the road this late in the day. After all, it was Boxing Day and raining. They were tired and had been riding for many hours in fruitless search for the Fletcher gang, first in the bush around Landsdowne and then in a raid, without result, on the inn north of Greenthorpe. Sergeant Samuel had pushed them on through the tiny community of Koorawatha, promising that they would lie up for the night at Kiddley's place, one of the only two inns between here and Cowra on the Sydney road. At last, the inn was not far ahead, they could already taste the rum heating their throats and they smiled at the thought, swallowing it in their imagination and bringing a little solace to the chill damp eating through them.

The man on horseback on the road in front of them came as a surprise, and they gaped as he brought his horse to a violent stop at the sight of them and then pulled the animal round and lunged into the bush. Sergeant Samuel was the first to gather his wits. 'After him, boys!' he shouted at the top of his voice. 'Forward!'

Their horses rallied to the touch of their spurs and the troopers shot forward at as fast a pace as the water-drenched road allowed.

'Halt!' shouted one of them to the swiftly disappearing Jordan, and the sergeant lifted his rifle from beneath his leather cape and fired into the air.

The discharge sounded exactly as Alan and Lawless came round the bend to see troopers charging towards them.

'Oh Gawd!' exclaimed Lawless. 'Oh Gawd, guv'nor!'

Eve sat bolt upright at the noise of the gunshot and she felt Alan's body tense.

The five troopers saw the newcomers and three of them halted while the others continued off the road into the scrub after Jordan.

Alan took it all in immediately. He looked at Lawless. 'Ride forward at the same speed,' he said. 'We are farmers, I will do the talking. We have been to my parents for Christmas Day. Lawless, you are Anthony Miller, my farm hand, and I'm James Trent.' His arm tightened around Eve.

'Hold there!' cried one of the police. 'Who are you and where are you going?'

In the voice Eve had heard him use in the Bathurst park when Daydee had surprised them, Alan answered, 'Afternoon, sirs. We be travellin' south to our farm. Bin to me mother's for the festivities, yet we are thinkin' we ought to have bided home, the weather bein' so blasted sorry.'

Sergeant Samuel rode up as he finished speaking. 'Who do we have here, Crystal?'

'They say they be farmers, Sergeant.'

'Farmers, eh? Well, what the devil are they doin' ridin' out on a day such as this?' He looked hard from Lawless to Alan. 'Explain yerselves!' Then he noticed Eve. 'Ah, good afternoon, madam.

Dreadful weather to be ridin' out in, I'm sure.'

'That it is,' she replied softly, her pulse quickening.

'We bin to my mother's,' Alan explained again. 'This be my wife and my farm hand Anthony.' He nodded towards Lawless.

'G'day,' said Lawless.

'And who are you?' asked Sergeant Samuel.

'James Trent at your service, sir,' answered Alan.

'Did you see a rider ahead o' you at all? A man just dashed off into the bush at sight of us.'

'Well, I saw your troopers just this minute goin' into the bush. Chasin' a man, eh? Now I thought at one stage I be seein' a rider and then ye understand at another stage, I wasn't certain. Did ye see a rider, Anthony?'

Lawless sat staring ahead.

'Anthony!' Alan repeated, turning in the saddle and raising his voice. 'Did ye see a rider ahead of us?'

'Oh!' answered Lawless with a start, remembering his name. 'Er, well, in this rain, ye cannot be sure of such a thing, it's hard to tell and that's definite.'

'Ride on carefully, then,' said the sergeant, 'for I've reason to believe he was a bushranger. I hope my men catch him. It's gettin' so it's not safe on the roads.'

'Aye,' said Alan, 'terrible an' all, I know. We often say how terrible it be.'

'We've been chasin' our tails all day,' went on the good-natured sergeant. 'The Fletcher gang robbed Redley station early this mornin' and we've been on wild goose chases all day since. Mind you, this here fellow takin' off into the bush like that gives me heart. Maybe we're closer to them than we know.'

'Maybe,' said Alan nodding his head sympathetically.

'Y'know, madam,' the sergeant looked to Eve, 'seein' a lady such as yourself out on the roads ridin' so close behind what could have been a robber, now, it's a worry it is.'

Eve smiled bravely.

'For weeks we been settin' up for Sir Rutherford Blake to arrive and then low and behold the rain. He's stuck in Blayney until the floods subside and we down here with all the worries. Ah well,' he sighed.

Alan dearly would have liked to know more of Rutherford Blake's impending arrival but he was concerned that at any moment the two troopers might return with Jordan in their charge. He could not take the risk of being here with Eve if that happened, and if Jordan were actually taken, he would work out some plan to help him afterwards.

'We'll be gettin' on then, Sergeant,' he said. 'The wife's a little poorly and this blasted weather be no help in the matter.'

'Oh, I'm sorry,' answered the sergeant moving his horse to let them by. 'Where did you say it is? Your farm?'

'Down well past Bendick Murrell,' replied Alan.

'Oh,' spoke up the trooper called Crystal, 'near Fetteringham's hut then.'

'Further south.'

'Aye,' nodded Lawless.

Before another word was spoken, a gunshot sounded through the trees.

'Hope that was one o' our boys gettin' the lout,' said Crystal looking towards the noise.

Alan edged his horse by them. 'Well, goodbye, Sergeant.'

'Yes, best you get on home,' said the kindly policeman, 'out of this flamin' soul-destroyin' weather. Never known so much rain.' Then he looked to Eve and half saluted. 'Good evenin' to you then, Mrs Trent.'

'Goodbye, Sergeant. Nice to meet you.'

They rode past at an even pace, leaving the three policemen in the middle of the road, and Eve marvelled at how calm Alan and Lawless had remained during the questioning. They were soon out of earshot and yet no one spoke. It was not until they were some two hundred yards away from the troopers that Lawless said, 'That blasted Jordan, why the devil didn't he see them comin'?'

'Yes, I wonder,' answered Alan.

'And actin' up like that and rushin' off into the bush. He might have been shot! We might have been shot.'

'No doubt he panicked, but let's hope he wasn't hit. That would be bad.'

'Aye, it would.'

'But don't judge him yet, Lawless, we all make bad decisions sometime. Let us hope he's home and safe when we get back.'

'Yes, so I can punch him in the mouth,' said Lawless angrily.

'No, lad, I shall do the disciplining. Now, let's hurry on to the track. The sooner we are off this highway the better.'

It was over three hours later when they found out about Jordan.

They avoided mud slides and continued in the merciless downpour, the damp chill biting through their capes. They rode the last mile uphill towards the entrance to Treehard in almost total darkness.

Alan was very concerned about the woman in his arms. Her breathing was laboured and she was making soft moaning sounds against his chest.

About a hundred and fifty yards before they arrived at the trees and rock face that hid their home, they reined in. Lawless tilted back his head and gave a high, piercing call indistinguishable from the screech of the parrot. In the distance, two calls came back in answer, to which he replied.

'All's well, guv'nor, that was Sam's answer and no mistake.'

'Aye, and it makes me think Jordan is already there, for it seems like Sam was waiting for us.'

'Yes,' said Lawless, urging Waterloo forward.

Sure enough, Samuel was waiting inside at the end of the rock passage as they came through in single file. He was covered from head to toe in a durable leather cloak similar to those that Alan and Lawless wore. He stood holding a large umbrella in one hand and a hurricane lantern beneath it in the other. With his sharp features, lit in the glow of the lantern, he looked like some mischievous goblin.

'Thank heavens ye be here safe,' he shouted above the wind and rain. 'Jordan arrived as bedraggled as could be. He's had the devil of a fright and was not able to tell us what had become of ye. Says we been blamed for a hold-up. Daniel and I been worried sick. It's more than a body can take, ye've no idea, and what's all this about a woman?' he scolded.

'Now, now, Sam, hold the scathin' tongue, a lot has happened,' Lawless said as they dismounted in front of the cabin.

Alan handed the semi-conscious Eve down to Lawless and he carried her up the steps to Daniel waiting on the verandah.

'Thank the good Lord Jesus, I see you both safe and sound,' Daniel said, holding out his arms to help Lawless with Eve.

Sam held the reins of the two horses while the leader dismounted. 'My, my, so I see it's true what Jordan said.'

'Look after the horses, Sam,' Alan replied. 'I'll explain it all later. First we must take care of the woman, she's ill.'

Sam shook his head as he led the horses away, clicking his tongue and mumbling to himself. 'That's all we need, I'm sure, a sick woman. Oh, and not just any woman! We but must be pickin' on the most notable.'

Eve was too weary to help herself. She was aware that she was stripped and put to bed. Her whole body was fatigued and there was a dull ache in her pelvis, but when the blankets covered her the warmth of the bed made her rally a little and she opened her eyes. A sort of strange peacefulness rippled through her, for there was the bushranger looking down at her. It all seemed quite fantastic, like a dream.

'Will you be able to take a little hot broth, lass?' he asked quietly.

'I will.'

She watched him leave the small room in the light of the lamp beside her bed and it was not long before he brought her the soup in a cup. She raised herself enough to drink it.

He waited silently. When she finished, he asked, 'How do you feel?'

'Worn out.'

'Then sleep, there will be time for talking later.' He smiled at her and the sensation of well-being ran through her again.

'Goodnight,' she said as he closed the door. As she drifted into sleep, she could hear voices in the next room.

When Jordan had arrived at Treehard to find Alan and Lawless still not back, he had avoided explaining to Daniel and Sam what had happened. All he would tell them was that there had been a robbery for which they had been blamed; that they had run into troopers on the road and he had become separated from the others. To their consternation, he added that Mrs Wakeman of Mayfield had been travelling with them. He said he knew nothing about it and for them to 'ask the boss'.

Since arriving at Treehard, Alan had not spoken to him and he had kept to the room he shared with Sam and Lawless. When Alan was sure that Eve seemed quiet for the night, he requested Jordan to come from his room and gathered his men round the kitchen table in the light of the fire and the oil lamp.

'But you be needing something warm to eat, Alan,' Daniel protested. 'Jordan and Lawless have partaken but you haven't.'

Alan shook his head. 'No, Daniel, food can wait. There are things for me to explain to you and I will do so. But firstly there is something else which concerns us all.'

Jordan sat surveying his leader, the thick forefinger of his right hand tapping on the scrubbed wooden surface of the table.

The rain drummed loudly on the roof as Alan spoke. 'We shall keep our voices low because of the woman. I would prefer to have this talk elsewhere, but there is nowhere else to go. We were on the main road south of Cowra this afternoon when a sergeant and four troopers appeared. You were riding vanguard, Jordan. Why is it you did not warn us?'

Daniel and Sam reacted with surprise.

Jordan's eyes narrowed as he looked down at his hand. He had been waiting for this. It really wasn't fair. When he had left the road in panic, some of the troopers had followed. He couldn't tell how many, but his horse, thank God, was a beauty. She had ignored the bracken and the branches that caught at them, threatening to bring them down, and charged onwards. Luckily there was open country of sedimentary rock after about a hundred yards and he had made good speed across it. In a sense he knew where he was, whereas the troopers did not. One had discharged his rifle at him. It had near blown his flamin' ear off! He knew he had lost them when half a mile or so later he no longer heard their shouts. But he had been mighty scared and had continued overland not daring to return to the road. He was pretty sure of his course but it had been sheer luck that he had missed any swampy ground and come at last to the valley that led to Treehard Hill.

And now the boss was angry. Well, he was sorry he had panicked and doubtless it had put the boss in an awkward position, but Alan had got through just as Jordan had suspected he would. So what was all the fuss about? No harm had been done.

He raised his big soulful eyes. There was silence in the room.

Lawless looked accusingly at him.

Sam looked unhappily at him.

Daniel was not looking at him. His eyes were directed to Alan.

And Alan waited. 'Jordan?'

'Well, it's easy for you to be blamin' me for what happened, and I'm sorry. But none of you nearly had your bloody head blown off like I did!'

'Serve ye right, indeed,' Lawless spoke up, leaning across the table in anger. 'Ye damn near had us taken, ye bugger.'

'Not so loud, lads, keep it down.' Alan's tone was even. 'But Lawless is right, Jordan. The only thing that saved us from a hopeless situation was our companion.' He gestured towards the room in which Eve lay. 'We said we were farmers and if we had not been with a woman whom I misrepresented as being one of us, I doubt we would have passed by the sergeant so easily.'

'But you did,' Jordan defended himself. 'You're here and unharmed and I've said I'm sorry.' His voice had risen.

Lawless brought his fist down on the table. 'How can ye disregard what ye did like this? Of course ye should be sorry, ye were supposed to warn us, damn ye!'

'I couldn't help it! You would have done the same!' Jordan cried, standing from the table.

'I would not!' countered Lawless, jumping to his feet.

'Silence!' Alan's voice was hard. Silence fell. 'Now, sit down.' Alan's voice was even again. 'And for the last time, keep your voices down.' He looked from Lawless to Jordan. 'This is an issue which you, Jordan, seem to be taking too lightly. It is very serious and affects each of us. If we cannot rely on one another to do as we plan, our whole future is placed in even more jeopardy.'

Jordan spoke sulkily. 'Damn it, boss, I panicked, can't you understand?'

'Yes,' Alan replied. 'I can. We all make mistakes. You have no monopoly on that. It is not about the panicking that I'm speaking. That's quite natural. What I am talking about is reliability. Your job was to watch the road ahead, to miss nothing, and you managed to miss five mounted police until they were nearly on top of you.'

Jordan opened his mouth to speak but Alan went on. 'You are one of a group and we must all be able to rely on each other. Yet, enough has been said about this, for as you earlier observed we are all here and safe. No one was harmed, so this can be the end of the matter;. but it *must* not happen again. Understand?'

Jordan nodded.

'Ye be too easy on him,' Lawless mumbled.

'Now then,' Sam spoke up leaning forward and patting Jordan's forearm, 'come on, me old sod, let's have a tot o' rum.'

'A minute, Sam,' Alan restrained him. 'There is just one more thing I want to say, but before I do . . .'

He stood from the table and went to the door of the room where Eve lay. He opened it gently and looked in. He could see her face in the lamplight. Although her breathing was still laboured, she was deeply asleep.

He came back to his men and stood at the end of the table holding the back of the chair in front of him, considering them for some seconds before he began speaking.

'In accordance with my promise, I will tell you about Mrs Wakeman.'

The eight eyes were trained on him.

'She will stay until the floods on the northern roads subside. Then I shall put her on a mail coach to Bathurst where she has dear friends. As you have seen, she is sick. I do not wish to speak at length about my association with her, but you all should know that I met her twice after we had stopped the Wakeman coach. Once in the bush some months later when I was hunting. I spent some hours with her and came to know her. I think of her as . . . a friend, and as you must all be aware, she regards me in that fashion also.'

'But how is it that she comes to be with ye at all?' Sam asked.

'For some reason she has left her home . . . and her husband. I know nothing of that, except that it is patently obvious she has no intention of returning. Lawless came upon her on the road on his way to Lyon's. It was sheer chance. We rode back to Cowra and found her.'

Lawless nodded. 'Aye, she was ever so pleased to see the guv'nor. She wanted to come to Treehard, there's no mistake about that.'

'So there you have it,' said Alan. 'I hope it will not inconvenience any of you.'

'Won't inconvenience me,' Lawless replied quickly.

'Me neither,' said Daniel. 'Nice to have a lady about for a bit.'

'Hope we can trust her,' murmured Sam.

Jordan did not speak.

Alan sat down. 'Now, my good companions, where is the food you spoke of, Danny? And that tot of rum of yours, Sam? Let us have them.' Then he smiled at Jordan. 'Come and sit by me, Jordan,' he said.

CHAPTER TWENTY-THREE

We cannot tell the precise moment when friendship is
formed. As in filling a vessel drop by drop, there is at last
a drop that makes it run over; so in a series of kindnesses
there is at last one which makes the heart run over.

Life of Johnson, James Boswell, 1740–1795.

The skies were dark when the bedraggled troop of John Stuart, Joe
and Jack Hennessy wended their way into Mayfield Park, fighting
the rain, only their total familiarity with the property bringing them
the last few miles in the ebony night.

They were met at the front door of the big house by Thelma who
had kept watch in the west drawing room, where on a clear night
the long windows allowed view out to the carriageway. In the wind,
rain, and inky blackness, she had seen nothing until the men had
indeed ridden by the window where she sat surrounded by lamps.

'Thank God, you are home. Where is Eve?'

'Not now, love,' her husband replied. 'We could not find her.
Let's leave it at that for the present.'

Mrs Smith and a number of the staff materialised to remove their
soaking capes and hats and to see to the horses, and the weary riders
crossed the threshold into the hall to find Stephen Watson and two
of the foremen waiting.

'Sirs,' Stephen began, looking round their faces, 'we fear the Lachlan is rising on both sides of Larmer's Crossing.'

As the Cowra road led directly west off the property and Larmer's
Crossing was to the south, they had not come home near the river.

Joe answered. 'Is there any likelihood of it breaking tonight?'

Stephen shook his head. 'No, but more'n likely by tomorrow noon,
she'll go.'

John Stuart looked to Jack Hennessy. 'The river cottages?'

'Aye, we'd best evacuate at first light. I'll be getting home there
now, Mr Wakeman.'

'Right,' said John Stuart. 'It's first morning light we evacuate.
Goodnight.'

★　★　★

When Alan sensed there was something amiss, it was the small hours of the morning.

They had all retired early after the anxieties of the day.

Eve was in Daniel's bed, so the older man had set up bedding for himself and Alan in the small fourth room of the cabin, the utility room where they kept the guns, saddles and equipment. Alan had fallen almost immediately to sleep, but woke with a start. He lay listening to the rain falling loudly on the roof. What had woken him? He slid down from the makeshift bed on one of the wide shelves that housed the saddles. Daniel slept soundly nearby.

Swiftly, he pulled on his trousers in the darkness and, feeling for the lamp on the floor, took it up and went through to the kitchen. In the glow from the dying embers, he lit the lamp. As he did so, he saw the blanket-draped figure in the doorway. She leaned against the frame gasping and doubled up in pain.

'Oh, lass,' he said, coming swiftly to her, 'what is it?'

'I . . . I . . .'

He caught her as she began to crumple to the floor and lifted her in his arms. As he did so, he felt the dampness of her. She was covered in blood!

'Eve!' he exclaimed, using her name for the first time in his shock. 'What is wrong?' He carried her back to bed.

She began to tremble. Her words came convulsively. 'Baby . . . baby . . . I fear it's . . . miscarriage.'

'Oh lass,' he whispered, as he laid her down. 'Oh lass. Is the pain bad?'

She was breathing in gasps and her words came between the gulps for air. 'Yes . . . bad . . . now.' Beads of sweat covered her forehead.

'Stay still, don't move.'

He passed quickly into the room where Daniel lay. Shaking the older man from his sleep, he said, 'Danny, the lass is with child and I fear she is miscarrying. Help me. I need hot water and cloths.'

Daniel was awake instantly. By the dim beam of the lamp in the kitchen Alan saw his eyes grow wide in amazement, but he was up and pulling on his trousers in seconds. 'Should I be wakin' the boys?'

'No,' Alan replied as he turned away.

In his life, Alan Fletcher had faced many fears. Faced them, and in the main conquered them. His was a natural instinct to accept the untoward, but this plight of Eve's compounded his deeply complex emotions. Recently when he had thought of her he had longed for her physically and he had deliberately put from his consciousness her intimacy with John Stuart Wakeman. But now as he tended her, cleaned the blood away, heard her moaning barely able to suppress the cries that rose inside her, he was forced into catharsis, confronting all that he had suppressed.

And in doing so, saw that it had no significance. It was his hand she held; his eyes she looked up into; his strength she drew on.

And finally, his name she cried as if symbolically with the coming of the shapeless foetus.

Her single cry woke Sam, though not Lawless and Jordan. He rose and found Daniel in the kitchen heating water.

'Did I hear that woman call Alan's name?' he asked, his eyes bleary with sleep.

'Aye, Samuel, and I'm to be taking this here water in now.'

'Oh?'

'It seems the mistress was with child.'

The frown line between Sam's eyes deepened.

'And but a few minutes ago she lost it. Now, excuse me, matey,' he said, moving by his friend towards the door, 'for I'm helping Alan.'

'Can . . . I be doin' aught?' Sam asked, the words catching in his throat.

Daniel stopped and turned back to him. He shook his head. 'No, you had best be returning to your bed.'

Sam retreated, relieved.

At last, Eve slept.

Daniel brewed tea and, as the leader issued from the bedroom, he handed him a mug. 'You look tired, laddie.'

There was strain on Alan's face and tension tightening the corners of his mouth. 'I'm concerned for her, Daniel. She's as weak as a kitten and has little stamina left to fight.'

'Aye, lad, she's been through a great deal and 'twould seem obvious that there was worry and stress in whatever it was that took her away from husband and home.' He sipped his tea, then pursed his lips in thought before he asked, 'Son, this woman may bring trouble upon us. Is she worth it?'

Alan looked hard at his old friend before he answered slowly, 'She's worth it to me, Danny.'

'Then . . . she's worth it to me,' the older man answered.

They were silent for a time, until Dan spoke again. 'Alan, my son, what we have been through, eh? There we were, you, me, Samuel, Lawless and Swiftie, living in the cramped nightmare of the *Mount Stewart Elphinstone*. And you, the most honourable and courageous . . . in the box, ah, how wrong.'

He put out his hand and covered Alan's with it. 'And all of us in the chain gang, beaten and chastised, then to be escaping only to have young Swiftie shot. I do remember the look on his sweet, young face, lying in your arms. Remember how we rode across six hundred miles of country, no place as was permanent for six years, until Treehard. There's many a time I've been scared.' He patted Alan's hand beneath his. It was still dark and the continuous hammering of the rain sounded all around them. He withdrew his hand and Alan smiled at him, a close intimate smile.

'All this has passed through my head as I've tended the mistress with you, this night.' He sighed. 'I know she has a singular interest for you, my son, and that is why I pray the Lord has the notion to save her for you.' He closed his eyes momentarily. 'We've lived the dangerous life of the ostracised and kept from being taken thanks only to your wits and skill, right down to this here night; this dark, freakish cold, wet December night, bringing with it what it has.'

He took a deep breath and stretched out once more to cover Alan's free hand with his own. 'Take no notice o' me, son. It's but the ravings of the Irish.'

Alan put down the mug he held with his other hand and placed it over Daniel's. And finally Daniel added his free hand on top.

There they sat, hands on hands and no more words were necessary.

For the remaining few hours of the night, Alan slept fitfully in a chair by Eve's bedside.

Dawn entered the cracked window-pane as a melancholy light showing Eve's drawn, grey face.

He moved to her and felt her pulse. It was feeble and her hands were clammy. He felt her forehead. That too was moist and sticky. As he knelt there, she opened her eyes. They were bloodshot and glazed.

He remained on his knees, motionless, as she lifted her hand and touched his face. It was a touch of love, unconstrained, and he felt it. There was a tremor in his chest as he saw the tears run from her eyes.

She saw him through a haze.

'Alan Fletcher,' she said, and his name was a caress.

'Fight, lass. Fight,' he whispered to her. 'I want you to.'

He was not sure but he thought she said, 'No . . .' as she closed her eyes. And now, fear rose in him.

He could hear Daniel moving once more in the kitchen. He was always the first to rise, no matter how little sleep he had. Alan guessed it was about six o'clock.

He came to a decision. There was nothing else he could do for her. It was evident, she had been so physically spent before he had found her that now she had no endurance left. She appeared to be drifting into death. There was only one man he knew who may be able to help.

Daniel looked round from the hearth as he came into the kitchen. 'How is she?'

'Worse, Dan. I think there is little hope unless I can persuade Womballa to see her.'

Daniel closed one eye in thought. 'But aren't they on the move? Last time I saw any of them was months ago.'

'When they're around here they invariably camp over on the high plateau. I'm going to ride over to see.'

Daniel shook his head. 'I doubt he will come here even though he thinks the world of you. It'll be the devil's own job persuading him.'

'Perhaps, Danny, perhaps not.'

Ten minutes later, Alan brought Freedom out of the rock passage through the trees beyond and turned south. There was a bleak light and the rain continued. He rode as swiftly as conditions allowed and an hour later rose onto the southern plateau.

The man he sought was an Aboriginal elder of the small Welba Welba tribe. Alan had stumbled upon the camp four years before while out surveying the territory around Treehard. The Aborigines had seen Europeans, but had studiously avoided contact with them. They greeted Alan's arrival with shock and fear. He remembered how Womballa had stood in front of Freedom shaking his spear in defiance and shouting. When he had not thrown the spear, Alan had sensed his curiosity and for a long time had not dismounted. Long enough for them all to realise he was alone and for some to come from behind the trees where they had run in fright.

Alan had seen Aborigines in the settlements. Poor desperate creatures, neither Europeanised nor in their natural state. A few others worked on homesteads as stockmen and they were often used by the police to track runaway convicts and the like, for they were magnificent bushmen and could follow signs that white men could not even see.

Womballa's tribe still existed in the same condition as their ancestors had for perhaps five hundred generations. They had come to terms with their environment as no European could ever hope to do. Alan saw them as the great Captain James Cook had seen them almost one hundred years before, '. . . . living in a tranquillity which is not disturbed by inequality of condition . . . coveting not magnificent houses but sleeping as soundly in a small hovel as the king in his palace . . .'

That first day he had been with them, Alan gave them some honey

386

he had collected from a yellow box tree. It turned out to be a most acceptable gift, for it was a favourite delicacy of the Aborigine. He remembered how Womballa had marvelled at the jar that held the honey, and was as happy to have the container as to have the honey itself.

In the years since, Alan visited the tribe whenever they were here and he continued to bring them gifts. They went away for they were semi-nomadic, but being territorial, the Welba Welba returned to the same plateau two or three times a year. Womballa always remembered him and so did the others. He had learned much about this ancient race and their complex social and religious disciplines. In hot weather, both sexes went naked, but in the cool winters, they wore cloaks of kangaroo or opossum skin.

Womballa had learned a smattering of English words and could make himself understood, albeit haltingly: one of the children, a boy called Odoono, picked up phrases quickly and could chatter away in English quite well.

Womballa's face broke into a grin showing broken and blackened teeth whenever he saw Freedom approaching. He and Alan had formed an attachment for each other although his culture was Stone Age and he had no way of understanding Alan's world. He was an artistic, peaceable, old man in touch with the harsh land and the elements in which he survived, and the reason Alan rode to him now was because of the old man's skill with tribal medicine.

As Alan brought Freedom through the trees towards the place where the camp should be, he felt his heart quicken with hope. A minute later he saw through the drizzling rain the *gunyahs*, the bark dwellings of Womballa and his people.

Coming to a halt on the edge of the encampment, he heard the familiar tones of Odoono calling, 'Fletcher he come! Good you see, Fletcher!'

A few faces peered at him from beneath the scant protection of the *gunyahs*.

Odoono and another boy of nine or ten braved the rain to run excitedly towards him. 'Oh, Fletcher,' gabbled Odoono, 'good plenty you come, hey?'

Alan dismounted and took the children by the hand.

'Where Womballa, hey?' he asked.

'You come, you come,' the boy called excitedly. Then he shouted in his own tongue as he led Alan towards one of the *gunyahs*. All were on rocky ground slightly higher than the floor of the plateau, so the water would drain away.

Alan bent and entered beneath the sheets of thick bark and

branches. In the centre of the shelter, Womballa sat by a small fire smoking a wooden pipe made from a hollowed-out branch and wearing a hat Alan had given him. His black eyes under thick dark brows welcomed his friend. He blew smoke out of his wide nostrils and nodded, smiling. '*Orana*, Clever Fletcher.'

Beside him sat his wife Datta, who, as was the custom of the Welba Welba, had come from another tribe. In tribal terms she and Womballa were old, although Alan suspected that they were both only about his age, and possibly even younger, the harsh rigours of their existence dictating their life span.

Womballa's children and grandchildren clustered around him. One of his daughters, a girl of about fifteen, sat clutching a newborn in her arms. She was particularly lovely. Her jet black hair hung in tousled curls across her forehead, her long black lashes sweeping her cheeks as she blinked. Her nose was broad but was in complete symmetry with her high cheek bones. Her teeth gleamed white against the deep purple of her ample lips. Whenever Alan saw her, Gray's lines ran through his mind: 'Full many a flower is born to blush unseen,/And waste its sweetness on the desert air.' She smiled at him now in welcome, as they all did.

Alan knew some of their language. His vocabulary was passable, although he had difficulty with the syntax. The structure was often by the suffixing of markers onto the first word of the sentence, or onto special particles to indicate the subject and object of the verb. He began now in a mixture of their language and his own to explain that he came for help.

Interest flickered in Womballa's eyes. Perhaps he found it intriguing that Clever Fletcher, as he had designated Alan, was in need of help. Alan said how Womballa made 'good medicine' and Womballa nodded his craggy head in agreement. Alan explained that in *yargunyah* he had a very sick woman, perhaps near to dying, and that Womballa's medicine was the only way to save her.

Womballa puffed silently on his pipe, then to Alan's surprise came the question, 'This woman, your woman?'

'Does it make a difference?'

Womballa studied Alan impassively. Then he handed his pipe to Datta and folding his arms said, '*Paluna*.' Yes.

'Then she is my woman,' he replied.

The old man nodded. 'Womballa bring medicine Clever Fletcher woman.'

The other elders of the tribe were called and soon Womballa's body was being ritually painted, as were the stones on the floor of his *gunyah*.

Alan wished they could leave and be on their way but he knew the significance of these rites so he sat waiting in the dwelling of Gumulu, one of the other tribal elders, while the chanting drifted over to him through the sound of the rain. Womballa's medicine had already begun for the ritual painting and chanting were part of it.

An hour later they left. Womballa would not ride. He walked and ran beside Freedom in company with one of his sons, Mulgatta, who came to 'guard' the elder.

As they neared Treehard, Alan explained that he must give a bird call to his friends to let them know who came. He made the parrot sound and the replies came, telling him all was well and to advance. Womballa and his son burst out laughing at the sound of the cries, for to their subtle hearing, the noise was nothing like a true parrot call.

The rain had almost ceased on the journey to Treehard but now as they passed through the hidden passage it began in force again. Sam met them in his customary outfit of long cape and umbrella. Alan had explained to Womballa that there would be other white men he had never seen before, as well as Daniel whom he knew.

Womballa pulled on his beard and hung back as Alan dismounted and Sam took Freedom.

Daniel waited on the verandah and signalled welcome to Womballa and his son. The two stood together in their kangaroo-skin capes, their long, thin legs painted with white ochre, their faces painted blue and white, water dripping from them and merging the colours. Men out of a timeless place, coming fearfully into modern culture, to help a friend.

'Come please, Womballa, come please, Mulgatta,' said Alan mounting the steps.

But only Womballa came. Mulgatta had come as far as he intended. He had accompanied his father to 'Fletcher *gunyah*' as he had been told to do, but nothing would induce him to enter the place.

'The boy cannot be standing in the rain,' said Daniel. 'It's not proper. He's come so far.'

Alan shook his head. 'I'm afraid he won't come in, Danny.'

Daniel looked grave. 'Well, I'm not having him getting wetter than he already is, he looks waterlogged, now, he does.' And with that, Daniel strode down the steps and went to Sam who was tending Freedom in the stable lean-to. He took Sam's big umbrella, opened it and advanced towards Mulgatta saying, 'I know you don't understand me, laddie, but I want you to hold this.' He placed the handle in Mulgatta's right hand, and the boy, quick to comprehend the protection, stood there under it. While his father followed Alan into the house, the spectacle that was 'Mulgatta with umbrella', stood outside waiting in the falling rain.

Inside, Lawless and Jordan had gone to their room, reasoning that Womballa would not want to be surrounded by so many white men. Certainly Womballa entered the building with trepidation. He even trembled a little to be inside such a construction. In awe, he looked upon the furnishings, but when Alan spoke and thanked him for his friendship and his courage, the old man managed an unsteady smile.

'This way, my *waminda*,' Alan said.

Eve lay as she had when he left her, the dark circles under her eyes even more pronounced, the bones in her shoulder exposed above the blanket.

Alan gestured to her. 'There was a child come. The child was dead.'

'The magic strong,' Womballa stated, looking round the small room.

'Can you help?' Alan asked.

Womballa did not reply. Instead, he sat on the floor and unwrapped a piece of folded leather he had carried from his camp. Inside were five or six different substances. Alan recognised a small amount of manna, the sugary matter from insects that collected on the leaves of the candlebark tree. There were three large waratah leaves and what looked like two blackbean pods and two dead flowers which resembled blooms from the hakea shrub, plus a few more items Alan did not recognise.

The craggy old face looked up at him from the floor. '*Nabilla* . . . water, need water.'

Alan went to the kitchen where the worried faces of Daniel and Sam greeted him.

'Womballa wants some water.'

'Hot or cold?' asked Daniel.

'Cold, I imagine.'

When Alan returned with it, Womballa was bending over Eve. 'Bad *ungawilla*,' he stated.

Alan knew the term meant black magic. He watched in silence as the Aborigine felt the veins in her neck, then put his hand under the blanket and felt her stomach.

He took the dish of water that Alan held out to him and returned to his position on the floor. On each of the waratah leaves, he mixed a number of the substances together with drops of water that he made by putting his hand in the bowl and letting the water drip from the ends of his fingers.

Alan moved to the bedside and he lifted Eve's inert arm with the intention of taking her pulse. Womballa reacted. *'Tauo!* No! Fletcher no touch. Clever Fletcher heart close with woman heart. *Awulla adina.* Womballa takes badness.' Alan moved away from the bed. 'If badness go,' he added simply.

Womballa rose and lifted back the blanket placing one of the waratah leaves on Eve's navel, the mixture against her skin. He had broken open the two seeds that looked like blackbean pods and he put one in each of her armpits. Then he lifted her head up just enough to feed her from the other leaf.

She moaned but did not open her eyes.

With a gnarled finger Womballa pushed the mixture into her mouth but in her semi-conscious state she did not swallow. Alan noticed that he put pressure on a spot in her neck and, automatically, she swallowed. He did this until she had taken all the mixture, then he returned to his position on the floor and began to chant.

Alan stood watching. His mind turned to all the formidable events that had occurred in his life. He was sure that the outcome of this one was more important than any of the others. He did so want this woman to live. He knew now, that whatever happened, this was his greatest wish. Last night he had finally admitted to himself that he loved her as she so obviously did him. He acknowledged it had begun for him the day he had found her in the bush, inexplicable though it was. He had thought to live out his life without the admission ever passing between them, but the touch of her hand on his face during the night had been her confession and the saying of his name her embrace.

Eve had believed she was dying. She could feel the coma of death begin to wash over her and had brought herself to show her love. Alan did not know what to make of it or to do about it; all he knew was that he wanted Womballa to make her well.

After a long time, the Aboriginal elder stopped chanting and rose and went to the bed.

Eve was perspiring profusely and the blanket was wet.

He removed the two pods from beneath her arms and replaced the waratah leaf on her stomach with the one he had not yet used. He glanced sideways at Alan. 'Leaf stay on woman one dark sky.' Then turning to face his friend, he said, 'Womballa go now. Medicine *nguldin*. Clever Fletcher woman hot like fire. Good. Some badness go.'

Alan smiled anxiously. 'Will she live?'

Womballa did not respond immediately. He seemed to think about the question. Then he said with finality, 'Spirit leave . . . going skyworld. It come back, she live. It no come back, she die.'

'How will I know, my friend?'

Womballa concentrated, again finding the English words. 'Woman live two dark sky, she come back . . . speak with Clever Fletcher.'

'Thank you, my *waminda*.'

They returned to the kitchen.

Womballa was the most intrepid of his tribe and perhaps the most intrepid of all his race. In the kitchen he looked at Daniel and Sam with interest, his coal-black eyes intense. He had done all he could to help the woman, she would either live or die depending on how strong the magic was. His son waited for him outside, but he was here, in this wonderful dwelling, where Clever Fletcher and his father, for that is how he thought of Daniel, lived. He wished to look at the possessions of the white man, for he would never again be able to. If he had known the word, he would have regarded it as an 'opportunity'.

Absorbed, he walked slowly round the small room. He touched the table and to the amazement of Alan and the others sat down on the edge of one of the chairs and placed his hands flat on the table. He sat this way for perhaps half a minute looking around, and when he rose he went to the old wooden dresser in the corner. He lifted the cups and plates and turned them over in his hands. He clinked two of them together smiling at the noise. The pots and pans, he touched and rubbed and he stood in front of the hearth looking at the fire and the iron cooking plate on which the billy was now heating. He took up the poker and felt the weight of it.

There were wooden shelves down beside the door to the outside and on these were all manner of things: towels, books, newspapers, containers, scissors, even a small pendulum clock that had belonged to Patricia June. He looked at these for a long time, touching each in turn and mumbling softly to himself. Finally, he turned to the wall of the room where Lawless and Jordan were concealed. On this wall hung a decorated shield he had given to Alan. It obviously delighted him to see it displayed. His face broke into a wide smile. He slapped his thigh with pleasure and said, '*Numurkah*,' meaning 'war shield'. Then abruptly, as if he had decided he had seen enough, he walked out onto the verandah.

Alan followed him.

They stood facing each other silently, the ochre-painted, time-worn, Aboriginal tribesman and the sea captain aristocrat, the bush-ranger, Alan Fletcher.

Beyond them, in the constantly falling drizzle, Mulgatta sat on the tree stump they used for chopping wood, still holding Sam's umbrella.

Alan took off the leather coat he wore and handed it to Womballa. 'For Womballa, my *waminda*.' As he helped him to put it on, Womballa's face lit up with pleasure. Sam and Daniel watched enthralled through the unshuttered kitchen window. Then Alan took off his belt which had attached his hunting knife in a sheath. He had given the tribe knives before and it was something he knew they used and highly valued. He fastened the belt round Womballa's waist.

'Thank you,' said Alan.

The Aborigine scrutinised him, his head on one side. Then with the guileless logic of the innocent, he said, 'Woman die, gifts come back, Clever Fletcher.'

'Womballa,' Alan answered, 'I give in friendship, I do not want them back.'

'*Tauo!* Woman die, I bring. Woman live, I keep,' came the conclusive reply. It was not to be argued with and Alan nodded.

As Womballa went down the steps to his son, Samuel called through the window, 'Tell the boy to keep the umbrella. I'll get another somewhere,' and he nudged Daniel beside him, 'from someone.'

Alan went to the end of the passage with his friends and there took his leave of them.

While Jordan and Lawless had been alone in their room little had been said for a long time.

Then, after about an hour, Jordan asked, 'How much longer is this farce goin' to be?'

'Now, what is the meanin' of that?'

'I can't understand the boss bringin' a flamin' black here to try and cure her. She will either live or die without him and all his mumbo jumbo. And what bloody well happens, if she does die? Mrs Bloody high and mighty Wakeman dead in a bushranger's hideout. Strewth, one more thing they will hold against us.'

'Jordan,' replied Lawless looking up at him from where he sat on the floor cleaning his saddle and boots on newspapers. 'Ye be a . . . what is it? A "pessimist" that's it! Truly, that's what ye be. Now, first and foremost, if the guv'nor thinks that Womballa can save the mistress, then ye know what, Jordan? That's bein' my opinion too. And as for what happens if she dies, no doubt we shall face that if it comes upon us.'

'And him,' said Jordan pointing out to Mulgatta who had taken up his vigil on the tree stump. 'Too flamin' stupid to come in out of the rain.'

This time, Lawless did not look up. 'Ye be a hard man, Jordan O'Day. That bloke out there might be stupid as ye be referrin' to him, or he may not be. All I know is what the guv'nor says. They be a gentle folk, not given to human sacrifice and never killin' for the sake of killin'. Nor be they in the habit of rapin' their women, nor of torturin' their prisoners, nor of murderin' their enemies' children. Now, they may not live in houses nor have the wherewithal to be buildin' bridges and steam engines and be a sailin' in ships, but so what, Jordan? So what?'

'Ah, there's no point in discussin' it. Your mind's clouded with the opinions of the boss. You've no mind of your own,' Jordan answered.

Lawless shook his head. 'That is not true, but were it so, it would not be the worst thing to happen to a body.'

His companion groaned.

When at last, they had seen the Aborigines depart, they went from their room to the kitchen.

Soon, Alan returned inside. 'Womballa has done all he can. I shall go in and watch her. He says if she holds through tonight and tomorrow night, she will live.'

The relentless rain continued. The weather was dank and cold, yet Eve perspired so much, that in those first twenty-four hours, she soaked three blankets. Over and over, Alan wiped her brow and her cheeks and her neck. Her features etched themselves on his memory for all time as he sat and watched her; the shape of her mouth and the gentle curve under her lower lip, the tiny creases at the corners of her eyes, the long lashes like her mother's, the fine line of her eyebrows and the shape of her nose and chin. Sitting helplessly, his feelings continued in turbulent disorder. There was an unreality in the little room, like some weird play where he acted the lead and said his lines but did not know the ending. Sometimes she would murmur and his heartbeat accelerated hopefully, then a violent tremor would run through her and his hope would sink.

His thoughts were complicated. There was some bizarre force at work in his life. This woman was John Stuart Wakeman's wife. She said she was estranged from her husband. What was that all about? It was best he did not think about that. The reality that she was here was enough for him.

Time passed, and Danny drifted in and out, a comforting, helpful aide. Finally, a wan, misty light filtered through the rain outside the window and it was morning. Alan removed the waratah leaf and the mixture from Eve's navel and noticed that it had changed colour. When Womballa had placed it there, it was a pale, murky yellow, now it was a deep orange-brown.

The next twenty-four hours were slow to pass, but Eve murmured quite often and began to move. Now, Alan's confidence rose. Shortly after dawn broke on the second morning following the two 'dark skies', she opened her eyes and spoke.

It had been exactly as Womballa had predicted and Alan praised the old man in silent thanks.

By eight o'clock the rain had stopped. It was the twenty-ninth of December and there were windows of blue sky in the clouds where the sun broke through. It had been the greatest deluge in New South Wales since the colony had been founded in 1788. All the rivers for nearly one hundred miles had broken their banks: the Macquarie, the Belubula, the Lachlan, the Boorowa, the Campbell and the Fish; and what had been water holes had become great lakes. All over the countryside, there was devastation. In the low-lying areas, homes had been flooded and water lay across the roads. Telegraph poles and wires were down, so that communication was lost. In some towns rescuers rowed in boats through the thoroughfares that had become canals to save stranded householders. Trees were uprooted and live-stock went swirling by in raging currents. Bridges gave way and men and women had been drowned.

But at Treehard, there was no destruction. Hundreds of feet high clinging to the top of the escarpment, it had been remote from the ravages of the floods. The only thing to overflow had been the water tank and the nearest they had come to water damage was from the leaks that had appeared in the roof.

And now Eve was awake.

She was weak and infirm and would need many weeks of convalescence but she was alive! She was remembering many things. Things which a week ago would have embarrassed and abashed her. She was sipping broth, lying back on a pile of pillows in the man's undershirt she had found herself wearing when she woke.

He had saved her. Somehow she had not died and she had been so sure she would.

Suddenly, she remembered the child and knew it was gone. She put down the broth as she was overwhelmed by the loss, even though she admitted she had not wanted it. She whispered, 'I'm sorry.' It had been forced on her in a most savage assault, but it had been part of her and now it was gone. There were so many anomalies in her emotions. Tears welled over her lids and she wept for it.

Some time later she became conscious of what was around her and she began to notice things. The sun streamed through a broken and cracked window to her left. She was in a proper bed, a wrought-iron one with all manner of design in the bedstead at her feet. There was another in the room but it was just a wooden stand with a mattress and blankets, without framework. It was a neat room painted white with pale blue around the window frame. Clothes hung from a wooden clothes-horse in a corner and there were shelves along one wall with many books and papers upon them. Beside both beds were small tree stumps polished and smoothed to pass as tables, and beside the bed in which she lay was a chair with a yellow pillow on the seat. She knew this must be Alan's room and he obviously shared it with someone.

The door opened and she looked round.

He entered, closed the door behind him, and stood looking at her.

She had difficulty finding her voice after her days of silence. 'Thank you for making me well,' she managed to say.

He shook his head. 'It was not my doing but the skill of a great friend of mine. His name is Womballa and he is a native of this land.'

Eve marvelled at such a thing.

'I fear it will be many weeks before you are truly over your ordeal and able to travel.'

The circumstances of her presence here rushed to her mind. 'Oh yes, I see . . .'

A grave expression settled on his face as he moved to sit in the chair beside her. 'I do not wish to tire you, but there are things I must understand.'

'Of course.'

'You see, lass—'

'Perhaps now,' she interrupted, then hesitated. 'Perhaps you could call me Eve, for I know I have called you Alan.'

'Perhaps,' he answered quietly, before he stood and moved to the window where he turned back to face her. 'As I was saying,' he resumed, 'to the world it will seem as if you disappeared. You were in Cowra and two men came and whisked you away. There could be a search mounted. Your . . . husband, with all his resources, will be a hard man to avoid if he decides to find you.'

'He will not,' she replied simply.

'How can you be so certain of this?'

Then she explained to him: beginning with her failure to tell John Stuart about her twin sister and afterwards of her fear to do so when she realised his attitudes; the mistake Lake made in her identity and the rape, and John Stuart's reaction, followed by his pursuit of the man; of Lake's lie that she was Clare and John Stuart's belief in the lie, his censure and his ultimatum to her.

She was wondering what he was thinking as he leaned on the

window-sill gazing at her. After a few seconds' silence, she said, 'At least I will bring no more shame upon him or Father and Mother. Now the world can only say I left my husband. There will be no poor, innocent infant to suffer, and to cause others to do the same.'

'Yes, that is true.' It hurt and angered him to know how she had been used and how she had suffered. He thought her gentle and beautiful and resourceful and resolute. Her husband appeared proud to the point of insensitivity, yet he would not be judgemental about John Stuart Wakeman; he was obviously a complicated, complex individual. The one thing Alan Fletcher was grateful for, was the miracle of her presence.

He listened as she finished in a weary voice. 'So you see, I left but half a year before I was to be turned out. Our marriage is finished. John Stuart will not give chase. I *know* he will not.'

He came back towards her and sat down on the chair beside the bed. 'And what of Reverend Billings and his wife? You were going to them. Will they not worry when they hear of your disappearance?'

Eve thought of the two dear people and her face became troubled. 'Oh yes, they will be distraught and it will be so long before I can . . . travel to them and tell them what has happened. If they hear before I can tell them, it really will be too dreadful.'

He tapped his lip in thought. 'You must rest now and not concern yourself, for I know a way to apprise them of your whereabouts. Tomorrow, when you are not so tired, I will discuss it with you.'

She closed her eyes and smiled. She felt so warm and secure here. 'You seem to be able to do anything,' she murmured. She heard the door close gently behind him and soon she drifted into a comfortable sleep.

While she slept, outside the bright new day was glaringly light after the many days of sombre skies. With the coming of the sun, the temperature rose again and by midday it had climbed to within ten degrees of what was normal for the summer.

Alan worked side by side with Lawless sawing wood and hammering nails for the new stable, while Samuel tended his waterlogged vegetable gardens helped by Daniel; and Jordan, up on the roof, checked for the places where the water had leaked through. Thus, life at Treehard went on, although all were conscious of the woman who had come amongst them.

In the evening after their meal of damper, vegetable soup and eggs, Alan gathered them together out on the verandah in the pleasant night air. Lawless sat on the stone steps looking at the sky. Daniel was moving gently to and fro in the rocking chair that Lawless had made for him a Christmas ago. Samuel stood leaning on the rail smoking an old wooden pipe and beside him Jordan lay full length on a bench, feet up on the rail smoking a cigar. They all turned heads to look at their leader who stood in the doorway, lamplight behind him.

'You all know I go to the height near Camara's Creek for the arranged meeting with Ben Hall a fortnight this day, Thursday the twelfth of January to be exact.'

'Lor', I'd forgotten,' admitted Lawless.

'I remembered,' said Jordan between puffs of smoke. Jordan never forgot a chance to visit a safe house and they would be stopping at one or two on the long ride to the appointed place.

'I shall keep the appointment. After which, I will continue on to Bathurst to let the Reverend Billings, who has been father to the lass inside, know that she is all right.'

'Gawd, boss, how do you know you can trust him?' asked Jordan.

'The little I know of him is enough to know that I can.'

Sam clicked his tongue. 'Don't like that at all, guv'nor.'

Lawless shook his head. 'Nor I.'

'And this meetin', is it not with blasted Morgan and some of the others?' Sam continued. 'The ones with a price on their heads?'

Daniel spoke up. 'Yes, that's what Bluey said when he gave us the message. It's to be a meeting of all the leading 'rangers.'

'But we've never been 'afore,' argued Sam. 'Ye've always refused to meet them when they've asked 'afore, guv'nor.'

'I know, Samuel and I would not go this time but that Hall has arranged it, and in him I see some qualities lacking in the others. Besides which, lads, it's the right time for a meeting of this kind. The newspapers are full of this coming outlawry act, the Felons' Apprehension Act they seem to be calling it. I have no doubt parliament will pass it and perhaps an overall strategy agreed to by the bands is what is called for now.'

Jordan swung his legs down off the railing and sat up. 'Do you think they'll make it law to shoot us on sight, boss? Like the papers say?'

'Probably, Jordan, and then at last you'll understand why I have maintained our disguises all these years. Why I do not even like such as Henry Lyon and his family knowing what you all look like.'

'Aye,' agreed Lawless, 'it'll be hard to shoot a man on sight, Jordan, if the troopers don't know what he looks like.'

'What else do you think will be in the Act, Alan?' asked Daniel.

'I only know what I've read, Danny, but the mood of the people has changed little in the last six months. There was still sympathy abroad when they brought the heavy sentence down on Frank Gardiner last July. But since, what with Gilbert's shooting of Sergeant

Parry and the mad way Dan Morgan's behaved killing two police in the last six months, not to mention those he has wounded, opinion is changing.'

Samuel clicked his tongue again. 'And now we know there was another shot on Boxing Day, that we've been blamed for!'

Alan stepped down onto the verandah and walked to the railing to stand beside Sam. 'Yes, Sam, so the Apprehension Act will make it mighty hard on those folk associating with bushrangers. I think they will get gaol sentences, and heavy ones.'

Lawless looked up quickly. 'Then why is it exactly that ye've agreed to go and meet with the others, guv?'

'Because I have an idea that could lead to our survival for many years yet. I will put it to them at the meeting.'

'And then, ye'll go on to Bathurst?' asked Sam looking sideways at him and puffing on his pipe. 'As I say, that I do *not* like.'

Lawless nodded vigorously. 'Yes, Bathurst's a hot-bed of troopers now that blasted Blake has his headquarters there, guv.'

Alan nodded. 'I have decided it is my responsibility to inform the clergyman. And as Camara's Creek is within twenty miles of him, I have made the decision to combine the two.'

'Decided then, is it?' remonstrated Sam. 'Decided indeed? I see, and what if somethin' happens to ye, Alan Fletcher? Eh? What about that?'

Alan laughed. The sound rang on the night air. 'Ah, Samuel Cooper, your sharp tongue hides exemplary sentiments which I do not pass over lightly.' He put his arm round the little man's shoulders. 'I promise, I shall take whatever care is necessary not to leave any of you orphans.'

At that, they all laughed. All except Sam who puffed furiously on his pipe mumbling about 'people not listenin' and takin' foolish risks'.

The following day, Eve sat propped up on pillows, her eyes closed, when the door opened and Alan came in. She opened her eyes and smiled as he came forward and sat once again on the chair before her bed.

'I must go close to Bathurst thirteen days from now.'

She looked concerned. 'But I fear I shan't be well enough by then. It is a long journey, a week or so more—'

'No, you misunderstand me. It will be three or four weeks before you should consider travelling. I go because there is to be a meeting between Ben Hall and myself.'

Now she looked surprised. 'But he has killed people,' she whispered.

Alan shook his head, 'No, he has killed no one. It is those he has kept company with who have done the killing.'

She was lying back on the pillows watching him. The reality of what he had to do, the people he knew, how he survived, struck her. She was looking at a fugitive, a man who met and spoke with criminals, who took things at the point of a gun. And yet, she knew as incontrovertible what seemed a perverse truth, that he was just and honourable, and that there were few men who had ever lived who were as good. A lump of sadness settled in her throat; she swallowed and quickly looked away, holding back tears.

He continued speaking. 'The meeting is to take place on Thursday the twelfth of January some twenty miles from Bathurst and your Reverend Billings. I will deliver a message from you to him. It is unlikely that word about you will have reached him by then, as the flood waters alone will take a week to subside.'

She looked back at him. 'But won't it be dangerous? Why must you meet this Ben Hall?'

'Because I said I would. He has desired to meet me many times and always I have refused.'

'Then why did you agree this time?'

'Because the request to meet is earnest as well as timely.' His mouth twisted in a grim smile. 'Thus, I will see Hall at the appointed time and place and after that I will let the minister in Bathurst know that you are safe.' He stood to leave. 'I go now to my friend Womballa to tell him of your recovery.'

'I should like to thank him for myself.'

'Yes, and sometime you will.' He turned to leave.

'Before you go,' she said, holding up her hands to his back, 'there is something I must ask.'

He turned around. 'Yes.'

She had been wondering about this for twenty-four hours. 'You do not think the less of me, do you? For what I related to you yesterday?'

Then he smiled broadly. 'Hardly, lass.' And he bent and touched her hand before he left the room.

On the way to the Aboriginal camp-site, he found himself thinking back through his life. It was a long time since he had done this. He was not a dweller on the past, although he recognised that there were moments from it that he cherished, like his childhood at Long Moss House. He recalled his father striding through the farms arm in arm with his mother, while he and Sophie, hand in hand, trailed happily behind.

And his youth in the Royal Navy; the weeks at sea and the tales the old salts told. The transition from naive midshipman to captain of the HMS *Coral Regis*. The respite in the ports, the almond-eyed Arab girl in Aden, and the women of his adulthood, the blue-eyed daughters of naval captains, the chocolate-eyed ones of the Indies and the strong, supple women of the bush here in New South Wales.

Then, he thought of Eve and how she had come into his life. She was the one he had never thought to find, the one he could love as he had loved no other. Intuitively, he knew that she understood him without knowing any detail of his life. There was an Italian word he remembered learning which he thought exemplified their feelings for each other so perfectly: they were 'simpatico'. She had always appeared to trust him, right from when he found her in the bush. That the feeling had become love was clear, she had shown him that when she believed she was dying. It had been like a completion between them, coming before they had ever spoken of their feelings.

But he wanted to be careful with her, mind her, help her to get really well, for while he recognised the strength of her, that inner quality of spirited self-reliance that had enabled her to find her way to Cowra, she had suffered and been through physical terror, shock and pain.

He was not a fatalist, although with his past it would not have been surprising had he been. He believed more in individual responsibility and in self-determination of the course of one's life. Yet he accepted that external influences sometimes left a man little choice. He saw the arrival of Eve in his life like this. For even though he had been willing to acknowledge that she was John Stuart Wakeman's wife, forever beyond his reach, it seemed that fortune had decided differently. When, by all that was logical, their first meeting should have been their last, it had not been. After the hold-up, she had been kept visible to him – the fall in the bush, the meeting in the Bathurst park . . . to Lawless's encounter with her on Boxing Day, and her arrival in his life.

But he did not think it could last. The fact remained, she was married to John Stuart Wakeman.

He considered the master of Mayfield and remembered the indignation in his eyes. Alan did not think him vainglorious but it had been obvious that John Stuart Wakeman was perhaps too proud. It now appeared he was uncompromising when he had made a value judgement. But Alan thought he had recognised principle and a strength of character in the man that day during the hold-up. He shook his head; it was not comfortable for Alan to think of John Stuart, just as it was not comfortable for John Stuart to think of Alan.

He brought Freedom to a halt. He could taste the dampness in the air not yet dissipated by the morning sun. He looked at the rain-soaked bush, the small pools of water on the ground around him, the leaves on the trees bright green and fresh with recent moisture. The world sparkled with a lustrous light and smelled sweet to his nostrils. And she was alive, the woman he loved was in his room at Treehard. For how long mattered little. It was this way, now.

He smiled and the world around him smiled back as he took Freedom forward towards Womballa.

CHAPTER TWENTY-FOUR

'It's all in the day's work.'
Anonymous, current since the 1700s.

Eve sat on the seat in Nelson's Boulder watching the riders disappear. She strained her eyes to catch the last glimpse of the grey figure that was Alan, as the bush enveloped him. He and Lawless and Jordan were going to meet Ben Hall.

She was feeling much better and each day in Alan's company had been like a revelation. There was a concord and tranquillity here at Treehard unlike anything she had experienced before, and it stemmed from Alan Fletcher. Security and calm emanated from his very presence and all those who lived here felt it. The only times she had felt this sort of peace before were now and then when walking across the great open spaces of Mayfield.

She sat staring at the patch of grey-green bush that had enveloped Alan, feeling an emptiness now that he had gone. Ever since she had awoken in Daniel's bed after her miscarriage, he had been there. Each day had brought his face and his smile and the look of care in his unforgettable eyes. When Alan's gaze lingered on hers and when he touched her in the course of their daily lives, she knew a joy that was beyond anything she had ever experienced.

She thought of John Stuart, and all that had occurred, for even after everything she could not erase the feelings she had for him; but they were different and there was deep pain attached to them. She had given vows before God to love and cherish him. Her heart raced when she thought of that, for there was so much about him that was worth loving and cherishing, but he had rejected her and scorned her. She felt guilty and yet, at the same time, set free.

She recognised that while she had loved John Stuart, she was 'in love' with Alan Fletcher, had been ever since their eyes had met at the carriage door on her wedding day. She was sorry that John Stuart had spurned her, that he hated her, but his actions had created the circumstances that had delivered her to Alan Fletcher. There was great confusion in her heart about John Stuart, perhaps there always would be, but there was no confusion about her feelings for Alan, none at all.

While no mention had been made of their love since she had thought she was dying, she knew he loved her; it was apparent in all he did. In the two weeks since he had brought her here, he had tenderly nursed her back to health. She thought she would be well enough to travel in another week or two, and then she would go to Bathurst to Father and Mother. She knew that she dearly wanted to stay with Alan Fletcher, and it was agony to think of leaving him, yet it was not fair to him and those with him to remain here. They were wanted men, no matter how harmless they appeared to her, and her presence was one more problem in their lives, a continual pressure for them which she alone had the ability to remove. For the sake of Alan and his men, she must leave and go to Bathurst. But, until she did, she intended to be helpful, to assist the men who lived here. They were strangely diverse characters, but each one, in his own way, appealed to her.

Daniel was a caring man, generous and attentive to her. He was the father figure. She liked the way he hummed Irish ballads as he went about his work. Samuel had a veneer of severity. He could be daunting at first meeting for he chastised everyone, even Alan in a fashion, but beneath the arrant chiding Eve had soon realised he was the softest, most good-hearted of men. Lawless was as agreeable a man as she had ever met, sunny-natured and cheerful, and in the evenings he often sat on the verandah step and played to them on his old mouth organ. Jordan was the youngest, and in that role was boisterous at times, introspective at others. He was closest to Samuel, but Eve had noticed how Jordan behaved with Alan, and she suspected he badly desired Alan's approval.

It was odd to be living with five men in a small, wooden house hidden on a ledge above the world; strange but marvellous. Here, she could be Eve Herman again, really justifying her existence and showing her gratitude for the sanctuary these men had given her. The last few days, she had felt well enough to help Daniel in the kitchen and while Sam had objected to any assistance in the garden, she was determined as time went by to be of service to him.

She took her eyes from the sea of bush and looked down at the rock surface where her hand rested. Tiny black ants were running backwards and forwards, round in circles, meeting one another, stopping and going again. There seemed to be no pattern in their movements but they looked mighty busy. She smiled; that's what she should be, busy, then perhaps she would not miss Alan so much. Besides, she would feel better working, it would take her mind off all the disturbing memories living in her head.

She stood up, and with a last, longing look down across the hill where Alan had disappeared, she left Nelson's Boulder and climbed down the stone steps that led to the passage back into Treehard.

John Stuart wiped his brow with his handkerchief, then flicked it at the flies that buzzed incessantly around him. The heat of the sun was intense. He lifted his arm to rest it on Diomed's saddle. Suddenly, he flinched and withdrew his hand as it came in contact with the metal studs, burning hot from hours of exposure to the sun.

He was waiting for Jack Hennessy and Stephen Watson who advanced towards him up the mud-dried slope from the pile of bricks and wood that had been the dairy. The smell was vile down here where the water had lain and everything that had been mud-covered delivered up the stench.

It was a fortnight since the rain had stopped. How different this scorching hot day was from the cold and rain of such a short time ago.

When the Lachlan had begun to rise after their return home on the night of 26 December, they monitored it closely. It had broken its banks and continued rising for another seventy-two hours, even after the rain had stopped, so much water had come down from the upper reaches. Where the Boorowa and the Lachlan joined, a lake almost half a mile wide had formed. Fortunately that was many miles from Mayfield proper, although they had taken their share of destruction. The Lachlan broke its banks in the Mayfield community just after mid-day on the twenty-seventh as Stephen Watson and his foremen had predicted, but never had they been ready for the ruin the raging waters had brought.

As the water rose swiftly to inches beneath the bridge of Larmer's Crossing, all the families in the river cottages had been evacuated and housed in the recreation hall. Early that same morning they had begun moving the livestock to high ground, but even so there were cattle drowned and now, as John Stuart looked about him, his nostrils quivered as he recalled the days when he had worked side by side with his stockmen in the cloying mud to bury the remains of carcasses.

Over to his right across the now normal Lachlan, men were working on the river cottages that had been under water, rebuilding them and cleaning away the debris deposited by the flood. The rushing water had wreaked havoc on the cottages and the dairy, and had annihilated much of the orchards. Most of Eve's fence along the Lachlan had been swept away and trees had been torn up along the banks and been brought down to lodge against the bridge of trunks that was Larmer's Crossing. Finally, the bridge could hold no longer and it had been washed entirely away. The tree trunks had been thrown around like straws in the swirling current that took them downstream.

There had been only two human casualties, and for that John Stuart was grateful, although it saddened him to think of them. One was a married worker called Shaw who had become separated from his group while leading a team of steers to high ground. He had disappeared and they still had not found his body. The other was young Peter Hennessy. John Stuart had blanched when he received the news. Unbeknown to his parents, the child had gone back to their cottage after the family had been evacuated, perhaps to get a precious possession. He had been cut off by the rising water. When the flood finally receded they had found his little body lodged in the hallway of their half-demolished house. His mother had fainted when they told her.

They buried little Peter beside the Mayfield chapel.

John Stuart sighed as he watched the child's father walking up the hill towards him now. He was remembering Peter's recitation just two Christmas Eves ago and how Sir John Young had called him a 'clever seedling'.

The two men he watched stopped momentarily to discuss something, and Stephen Watson lifted his hand in a wide arc expressing some point of view. It was Stephen Watson that John Stuart had sent to Bathurst after the flood.

Immediately the flood waters had gone down and a man could ride through to Bathurst, John Stuart had sent for Joe, and the older man had influenced him not to leave his property and his people, at this time. So Stephen Watson was sent and had returned with disquieting news.

John Stuart had known in his heart it was a *wild goose chase* as they said of an improbable quest here in the west, but he had sent Stephen in the forlorn hope that somehow Eve had gone north to Bathurst and that he would indeed find her with Reverend and Mrs Billings.

In fact, Stephen had not even needed to go into the little township to see if Eve were with the minister, for he had met Dr Marcus Walker at a cross-way six miles out of Bathurst. He knew the medical man for he had grown up in Bathurst.

'Dr Walker, goodday to you, sir.'

'Helloa there, Stephen, what brings you so far from Mayfield?'

Now Stephen was a loyal Mayfield man and he was loath to discuss his reason, a delicate one in his opinion, and one he had been told to be discreet about so he merely answered, 'I am come from Mr Wakeman to see how Bathurst fared during this great flood we have experienced.'

'Oh, yes, dreadful, wasn't it? I've had many sick from the effects of it. And some have died. Why, two of Bathurst's best were taken. Mrs Jackson the alderman's wife went on Christmas night, died in childbirth stranded in their homestead, and Mrs Billings was drowned on Boxing Day in Clearfield Creek which rose without warning.'

'What? Mrs Billings of All Saints' Church?'

'Yes, Stephen. She and the Reverend were out helping the farmers when they got caught. She drowned, and I'm sorely afraid he did himself such harm in bringing her to the bank that he will soon follow.'

'Oh, my Lord, how terrible.' Stephen paused. 'So the Reverend is very ill, you say. Is anyone with him?'

'Yes, good Mistress Thatcher is taking care of him. I was only just attending him before I rode out here this very morning.'

'Then he has not had a visit from anyone?'

'Actually, he has had many visitors, all the town is worried about him.'

'But there is no one staying with him? Other than Mistress Thatcher, I mean.'

Dr Walker looked quizzically. 'What do you mean, staying with him? There's nobody in that rectory other than himself and Mistress Thatcher. Oh, and young Jennie, who is soon to leave, I believe.' Now the doctor looked stern. 'What on earth are you talking about, Stephen?'

Stephen realised he did not need to go into Bathurst town now. He doffed his hat to the doctor and thoroughly astonished him by saying, 'Well, sir, it is grand to see you again but I must be moving.' And he turned his horse's head and trotted back the way he had come.

'Now what the devil was all that about?' Marcus Walker asked himself as he watched Stephen along the road.

John Stuart was saddened by the news of Mrs Billings' death and concerned about the clergyman. He truly hoped the man would live.

Eve. There was a nagging ache through him whenever he thought of her, which was almost all the time. Why had things gone so fatefully, dreadfully wrong?

He moved away from Diomed to greet his men. 'Hello, boys.' He looked to Jack Hennessy. 'How is Mrs Hennessy?'

The furrows in the man's brow deepened as he positioned his feet and folded his arms. 'Well, sir, she's taken it hard. I find her crying when she thinks none see. Yet, we have the other two and they are a solace to her. She's a real Mayfield woman and strong. She will rally.' Then he took a deep breath and added, 'Now me? Work is my cure.'

John Stuart's eyes met his. He gave the suggestion of a nod. 'Work is my cure too,' he said very slowly.

The two men looked sharply at him.

It was the first time John Stuart had ever referred to his own situation in front of anyone other than Joe. This was John Stuart's deliberate offering to his faithful employee. The statement proposed kinship and Jack Hennessy recognised his master's gift. The man did not speak, instead he smiled in empathy, and in appreciation he tipped the wide-brimmed hat he wore.

John Stuart nodded gently and the moment passed.

They began to talk of other matters.

'So, how extensive are the losses?' John Stuart asked.

Jack answered. 'It will be itemised for you at the meeting you have called of the section heads this afternoon. This morning Mr Oldfield gave me the latest estimation on cost of the damage. It comes to ten thousand five hundred and sixteen pounds and that is without the expense of replacing Larmer's Crossing.'

John Stuart whistled.

Jack Hennessy sighed. 'Aye, it's a fortune, sir, that it is.'

'Aye,' agreed Stephen Watson.

'All right, I shall see you both at three o'clock,' replied the master as he mounted and rode away.

When he arrived back at Mayfield House, he left Diomed hitched to the verandah railing and strode up the stairs into the house. As he did so he met Daydee exiting the blue drawing room. He was unaware that she had been waiting there watching for his arrival. Baines had informed her he was coming home for lunch today and she was determined to have conversation with him.

'Uncle John Stuart, what a nice surprise. How are you?'

'Passably well, Daydee, considering everything. And yourself?'

'Oh, I'm happy enough, thank you, although everyone's been so busy since the flood, there's so much to do.'

'Work never hurt anyone, Daydee.'

Daydee did not agree but smiled at him anyway.

He patted her on the shoulder and moved down the corridor.

The encounter had been far too brief for Daydee. She was thoughtful for a moment then decided to find her mother. She wandered down the tall corridors looking in the open doors of the rooms, but nowhere did she see Thelma. She was about to turn and go back to the kitchens to watch the cooks preparing the day's food when she stopped. She stood in indecision then, smiling to herself, hurried down a side hallway and turned into the corridor that led to Eve's rooms. Outside the door of the bedroom she hesitated. Then ever so gently she turned the knob. It was not locked and opened to her touch.

The sun's rays came through the heavily draped windows, lighting up the interior. It was a beautiful room and Daydee sat on the white lace bedspread and looked around. Oh to be John Stuart's wife and to sleep here with him. Sighing, she reached forward to caress the pillow with her small hand.

Then she swung down from the bed and passed into the dressing room where two massive walnut wardrobes stood in state. Gingerly she opened one of the mirrored doors. Inside were all the beautiful gowns that Eve had worn. Standing on tiptoes she reached up and lifted out a black silk gown with embroidered sleeves. She held it in front of herself, smiling all the while.

Then her features tightened in hatred. She knew that John Stuart had ridden out to find Eve on Boxing Day. Even now her father said he wanted her back. How could he? She threw the dress from herself to the floor in fury. 'God, how I hate you! You are so ugly!' she said aloud. With aversion lingering on her face, she went through to the sitting room where Eve's books and music and other personal possessions lay as she had left them.

To her right was a wicker table on which dozens of sheets of music lay. Daydee riffled through a few of them and found 'The Meadow Green' which she had ordered from Sydney months before. The music shop had written to say they were out of it and would have to order from London. Her expression changed to delight. She picked it up and turned to leave with it in her hand. Then the smile on her mouth died as she drew in her breath in shock. 'You . . . you . . . startled me!'

'And what is that ye be holding there?' asked the sombre figure of Mrs Smith who stood eyeing her from the doorway.

'Oh . . . it's music . . . "The Meadow Green". I have been wanting it for ever so long. I shall take it.'

Mrs Smith's face hardened with disapproval. 'And what is the meaning of that?' She made a severe gesture to the black silk gown lying crumpled on the floor behind her.

Daydee stood her ground. 'I don't know.'

Mrs Smith did not approve of Daydee, always dressed in silks and lace and acting as if she owned the place. She was a spoilt brat, to the housekeeper's way of thinking. 'I was in here earlier and there were no dress lying in a heap on the floor and no wardrobe door open.'

'Well, I know nothing about it.'

Mrs Smith's expression called Daydee a liar, but she said no more. Instead she pointed to the sheet of music in the girl's hand. 'Who has given ye permission to take that?'

'No one, exactly,' said Daydee, 'but I know Uncle John Stuart would let me have it if I asked him.'

Mrs Smith flicked her hand at the girl. 'No one, exactly, eh? So, "Miss" Daydee ye had best be receiving permission to have it very quickly indeed. For I'm under instructions from the master himself to lock these rooms, and that means what's in them stays here. Put it back.'

Daydee's face was full of fury, but she dared not take it. After all, Mrs Smith was the housekeeper and the old witch was a favourite of John Stuart. Her chin shot forward aggressively but she put the sheet down slowly on top of the pile.

'I shall get permission,' she said with deliberation, 'and I would not lock up with too much haste if I were you.' Then she turned on her heel and left the room. 'The witch! The old witch!' she kept saying to herself all the way down the corridor. She headed towards the kitchens. Baines was coming along carrying a silver tray with a single covered platter upon it.

'Is that for the master, dear Mr Baines?' she asked.

Baines looked down his long nose to the girl barring his way. He liked Miss Daydee: she was such a pretty girl and had a charming turn of phrase.

'It is, Miss Daydee, he eats alone in the morning room, just a salad plate is all it is. I do wish he would eat more.'

'When you go in, would you please ask him if I could but have a brief word with him. Please.'

'All right, Miss Daydee.'

He was not long. He smiled. 'The master says go in.'

'And what is so urgent, Daydee, that it has occurred since I saw you in the hall?'

'Dear Uncle John Stuart,' she began, 'it's but a mere pesky happening and I would not have troubled you but it is urgent you see.'

He smiled tolerantly at her.

'There's a piece of music, "The Meadow Green", I've been waiting on it for simply ages to come from Payne's music store in Sydney.'

'Mmm.'

'Well, just now I saw a copy of it. Mrs Smith is in the east wing, and . . . I . . . popped in there. It is on a table among a lot of music.

I know Mrs Smith is right to refuse to give it to me, but it seems a shame to let it lie there when I would get so much pleasure from learning to play it.' She looked down at her hands. 'Especially as Aunt Eve is no longer here to play it.'

John Stuart closed his eyes for a brief moment. 'Mrs Smith is only doing her duty as she sees fit.'

Daydee's face dropped.

'But at the same time,' he smiled, 'she is often strict.'

'So I may have it?'

He nodded. 'I'm sure Eve would like to know her music was being played. So, yes, you may and if there are one or two others you especially like, I think she'd want you to take those, too.'

She had won as she had believed she would. She broke into her loveliest smile.

'Now, you go and get your music, and I'll explain to Mrs Smith.'

Ten minutes later, Daydee was sitting on the floor in Eve's sitting room sorting through the music when Mrs Smith returned from the master. The girl lifted her head and, tossing back her hair over her shoulder, smiled with open satisfaction. Mrs Smith did not look at her, but as she swept by said, 'Be swift with yeer choices, "Miss" Daydee. I want no delay. This room is to be cleaned and locked before the afternoon is out.'

When Daydee had sifted through the stack of music on the wicker table she noticed more on a shelf below. She continued on through these. Some had no name written on them, others had 'Eve' or 'Eve Herman' or 'Eve Wakeman' in neat writing. Then her eyes widened in surprise as she came to one sheet that had 'Clare Herman' written on it in the same hand. So, Eve's other name! Or at least the one she had used when she was with Nathaniel Lake in Adelaide.

Daydee knew all the story of Eve calling herself Clare and living with Lake in Adelaide. Her father had told her and her mother about it when he and John Stuart came back after finding Lake. Her mother had not believed it and maintained that Eve was good and respectable; but then her silly mother's opinion did not matter.

It seems Lake had convinced her father and John Stuart of his intimacy with Eve, and that the baby was a result of their love-making. That was why Daydee could not understand the reason John Stuart ran after Eve on Boxing Day. Why had he changed his mind? It made no sense. No wonder Nathaniel had always been so interested in her! All those questions he had asked. All the time he had known her!

Daydee was now definitely sure that Lake had gone from her to the big house the night he was drunk in the park. She was also sure that he had assaulted Eve, although she was telling no one about that. In the state he had been in, he was capable of assaulting anyone, past lover or not. It had almost been her in Eve's place! How Daydee hated both Eve and Lake. She had always suspected there was something to know about Eve. Yet she had never for a moment considered that Eve was playing false to John Stuart. It just went to show how devious people could be. Especially *her*.

She was so happy that Eve had gone. But her father told her John Stuart was going to continue to search for her. How she prayed he would not find her. Then as time passed he would forget her. Yes, please Lord, let him forget her! How badly she wanted him for herself.

She took the piece of music that had the name Clare upon it and added it to those she had chosen. She picked them up in her arms and passed again through the empty dressing room. The black silk gown still lay where she had thrown it. Huh! she was not going to pick it up. Let the damned servants do it.

She caught her reflection in the mirrored door and stopped to look at herself. She bent down and put a pile of music on the floor, straightening up to swirl round and admire herself. She made a few haughty faces and imagined herself as the mistress.

It was as she bent again to retrieve the music that her eye caught something lying just beneath the wardrobe. It had obviously fallen there unnoticed. She reached under and lifted it out; it was a grey cover with silver embossing. She had only ever seen a few of them; they contained photographic likenesses. Her mother and father had obtained one of themselves in Sydney a few years before and they had taken it out of the cover and placed it in a frame on the mantelshelf over the fireplace in the drawing room.

She opened it.

Her mouth dropped open in shock. For some seconds, she did not grasp what she saw. She knelt on the floor holding it in front of her. Then understanding came and her heart raced as her mind leapt from conclusion to conclusion.

What she held was a picture of two girls, two identical girls. Twins, of about fourteen or fifteen, and underneath was written, 'Evelyn and Clare, San Francisco, 1852.'

Oh Lord! Eve had a twin sister. This was Clare!

Suddenly, she understood so much more.

Nathaniel had mistaken Eve for her twin sister. It was Clare he must have lived with in Adelaide. He had gone to Eve that night thinking she was Clare. Eve was the innocent victim after all! And where was this Clare? It was obvious John Stuart knew nothing about her.

For some reason, Eve must never have mentioned her twin. How strange. Or perhaps not so strange. For it was scandalous, living in a *de facto* relationship. It was something only harlots did. Daydee was enthralled. Her eyes darted this way and that.

'What are ye doing there on the floor, Miss Daydee?' The clipped tones of Mrs Smith sounded behind her.

Startled, Daydee grabbed her music to hold it against her body and to hide the photograph.

'Nothing, nothing,' she said as she stood.

Mrs Smith looked suspiciously at her as she backed out of the room, saying, 'I'm going now, I've much to do this afternoon.'

Ten minutes later, Daydee sat in her room with her door locked. She had taken a metal dish from the scullery as she came upstairs. She placed the photographic likeness in the dish and took out of her pocket one of the long matchsticks and a piece of stone that Leith used to light his pipe. The matchstick ignited as she rubbed it on the stone.

She was so intent that her hand shook ever so slightly as she touched the flame to the sepia photograph.

Then her black little eyes gleamed and her face filled with satisfaction as she sat and watched it burn until it was a small pile of ashes in the bottom of the dish.

Twenty minutes before three o'clock, John Stuart sat behind a large mahogany desk in the west drawing room. Fifteen drawing room chairs of Regency type had been placed in three rows in front of it and in front of them an armchair for Joe. John Stuart awaited the leading men of Mayfield to discuss the aftermath of the flood and the details of rebuilding and repair. His right hand toyed with an inkwell decorated in coloured flowers and gilt.

He was thinking of his wife. The words she had written to him and left on her pillow and the gold and jade olive branch hairpin were both in his jacket pocket. Ever since he had found them, he had carried them there.

What the devil was going on? He must find her. It was driving him to distraction. How dare the bushranger ride into Cowra and . . . remove her, just like that. Rutherford was not the only one who wanted Alan Fletcher now. John Stuart Wakeman wanted him too. He knew it was the bushranger who had abducted her, had been absolutely convinced since he had spoken again with the priest who had come to Mayfield to hold a service for little Peter Hennessy. Mrs Hennessy was Catholic, and young Peter had been christened in her religion.

He shivered and stood from the desk.

It had been only two days ago, a stiflingly hot afternoon, and after the service, Joe had brought the priest up to Mayfield House.

John Stuart had gone ahead and waited for them. He had decided to take tea out on the verandah where the confining heat of the day was not as bad as inside the stuffy, airless house.

They sat facing each other on white painted chairs with lattice backs.

Brother Michael still did not know what to make of Mr Wakeman. No doubt, he held unorthodox beliefs. Perhaps that was why the man had not invited him inside to tea but instead had served him here on the verandah. Well, that didn't matter. He could turn the other cheek, just as the good Lord had done.

Joe broke the silence. 'When we spoke to you in Cowra, you said Mrs Wakeman had arrived wet, tired and ill.'

'Yes.'

Joe nodded. 'And you tried to persuade her to stay and see the doctor?'

'Yes, indeed. She, er, had some idea she was waiting for Ronald Richards to appear and to, er, take her somewhere in his dray.'

'And then you said that Mrs Wakeman fainted and the two men turned up and carried her away, pretending to be Mayfield men.'

'You are right. They were so forceful. That is, the one who carried her off.'

John Stuart's expression did not change but Joe sensed him stiffen on the chair beside him.

'The one that carried her off was well-educated you said. Would you repeat his description for us?'

'Well, he was taller than me, perhaps five feet ten or eleven. I recall he was clean-shaven, a firm jaw line, sunbrowned, and I think he had light brown hair. There was a real authority about him.' Here he looked to John Stuart. 'As I think I told you at the time, that is why I believed he was, er, one of your men.'

'And his eyes?' Joe prompted.

'Er, yes, his eyes. Dick Barovill thought they were unusual. Penetrating, I think he said, er, bluish sort of colour, from memory.'

There was silence for a few seconds during which time Brother Michael built up courage to ask a question of his own. 'Do you know who they were?'

John Stuart spoke at last. He uncrossed his legs and stood up. 'We have our suspicions,' he said. 'I am grateful for your help.'

The priest smiled. 'I, er, it must be a terrible worry. Yes, sir, I can quite understand how you must be feeling.'

John Stuart stood holding the back of the chair he had just vacated. He looked down into the cleric's eyes as he said quite deliberately, 'On the contrary, Brother Michael, I do not think you have the remotest comprehension of how I feel. Yet, you are correct in your assumption that it is a terrible worry.'

Then he bent forward and offered his hand to the startled young man, who took it in an automatic reaction, as John Stuart finished, 'I am indebted to you. Goodbye.'

John Stuart sighed now as he moved to the wide window of the drawing room. It definitely appeared the bushranger had carried his wife off somewhere. Where, oh, where? The torment he went through when he thought of that! How in the devil's name had Alan Fletcher been in Cowra on Boxing Day?

Eve, where are you? Damn it! Damn and blast it! Where in hell are you? I must find this bloody bushranger, and bring you home.

Through the trees he watched Joe, papers clutched beneath his arm, stride across the lawn towards the house, and forty or fifty yards down the carriageway a dozen or so of his men came riding up to Mayfield House together. Soon the meeting would begin and he would be given details of the flood damage and the cost of repairs. Then tomorrow he would lead out the search party to find his wife.

He returned to his desk and moving the armchair for Joe around nearer his own, thrust the concerns of Mayfield uppermost in his mind.

At the same moment that John Stuart prepared to meet his staff, one of the subjects of his recent thoughts sat on a boulder on the flat top of a sandstone hill near Camara's Creek, three miles from the Bathurst road. He waited to meet Ben Hall and the others.

The arrangement, made through Bluey before Christmas, was to meet at this spot, at four o'clock in the afternoon on Thursday, 12 January, 1865.

Alan, Lawless and Jordan had spent the previous night under Bluey's roof in his little hut and risen before dawn to make the ride here. Bluey's robust voice had followed them through the bush as they rode away, 'And let me know the outcome, Governor, my ally,' he had shouted. 'Oh! And don't turn your back on Mad Dan!'

They had arrived at the meeting place over an hour early. The hill was the same one where Alan had met some of the bushrangers in sixty-two when Frank Gardiner was plotting the Forbes gold escort robbery.

Ben Hall had been lucky that time. Although he had been taken by the police in an initial rounding up after the robbery at Eugowra, they had been unable to prove his involvement and he had been freed.

Jordan looked over to Alan. 'Boss, there's somethin' I still don't quite understand.'

'What's that, lad?'

'You've always maintained that we didn't need to mix with the others. That the likes of Dan Morgan and Johnny Gilbert and Lefty Dawson are to be avoided. That their killin' need never have happened and you found them offensive.'

'Yes,' answered Alan.

'Then what are we doin' here?'

'Firstly, Jordan, we have been asked here by Ben Hall, whom I classify slightly differently, although he sleeps in tainted company. Secondly, even though Morgan, Gilbert and Dawson, to describe them kindly, be impetuous fools, we need their agreement to what I've decided to propose today.'

'And what's that?'

'When Ben Hall sent the message, he asked me to come here if I had any ideas to foil Rutherford Blake. He specifically expressed that he did not, and he was in fear of what the coming Apprehension Act would bring. We are here because I do have an overall plan, which you will hear when they all arrive.'

'What time is it?' asked Lawless who stood above them atop some rocks that gave him a vantage point to watch the plain below.

Jordan took out the gold fob watch and chain he had taken from John Stuart almost two years before. 'It's coming up to twenty-five minutes after the hour of three. There's more than half an hour to the appointed time.'

Lawless nodded. 'Oh, well, if I be rememberin' correctly, it was Benjamin Hall as was early when we met here before. It was dead Henry Manns and live Johnny Gilbert as were the tardies.'

'Yes, Gilbert was very late,' laughed Jordan. 'Maybe that's why he never robs coaches these days. You have to keep to a schedule to do that, don't you, boss?'

Alan nodded, smiling.

Lawless grinned. 'Aye.' He took a small telescope from his belt and scanned the countryside. A minute or so later, he said, 'Well, Jordan, Gilbert be earlier than his schedule today, for I reckon it be he and Hall comin' through the trees down there now and, if so, it'll be but five minutes before they're here.'

Alan and Jordan stood up.

'Is it only two, Lawless?'

'No, guv, I'm wrong, another comes behind. It be three. Yes, Hall all right, and Gilbert. The third I've never seen before.'

Alan looked thoughtful. 'Probably the eighteen-year-old they've been riding with just of late.'

Lawless continued to watch through the telescope. 'Aye, he looks pretty young from what I can see of him.'

'Johnny Dunn, isn't it?' said Jordan climbing up beside Lawless to look.

Lawless handed him the telescope. 'I think that's his name. Joined Ben after he lost Dunleavy and Mount last October. Ben's partial to partners called John, it seems.'

'Yeah, this'll be the fifth or sixth, won't it boss?' Jordan said looking through the eyeglass. Then finding the riders, he announced, 'Yeah, that's them. Dunn looks nothin' more than a slip of a kid.'

As Lawless had predicted, five minutes later, the newcomers stood facing Alan and his men.

Ben Hall was one month off twenty-eight. He was of medium height and walked with a limp from a broken leg he had suffered years before. Johnny Gilbert stood beside him, slight, thin and good with a gun; one might say 'too good'. The third man was indeed the new recruit, Johnny Dunn.

'It's been a few years since we met,' Alan said, offering his hand to Ben Hall.

He enthusiastically took Alan's hand in both of his. 'Yes, it is.'

'Too right,' spoke up Gilbert. 'Eugowra, wasn't it, guv'nor? You were sensible to stay outa that one.'

'Yes, Johnny, and that be the reason we did stay out,' Lawless informed him from his position some six feet above.

Gilbert looked up with a grin. 'Hello, Drake. You, is it?'

'Aye,' answered Lawless, 'it be me, Gilbert.'

'Good to see you all,' said Jordan.

'This is "the Jockey" Johnny Dunn,' introduced Hall.

'How do you do,' Alan said.

Johnny Dunn's eyes were wide open, and that was something of a feat, for he had tiny eyes which in their natural state were half closed. He was actually facin' the famous Alan Fletcher! The guv'nor. Strewth! The man was a flamin' legend. There were so many stories about him among the bushrangers – Why, they said that he was of flamin' noble birth, a cousin of the Queen yet, and had been an admiral in the Navy; that he could disappear into the bush like a bandicoot. And the old-timers said there was a certain look from his eyes that could affect a man's bloody breathin'. Johnny Dunn, finding his voice, replied, 'All right, thanks.'

Ben Hall too was looking hard at Alan. In truth, he was almost as much in awe of Alan Fletcher as was young Johnny Dunn, but not for the same reasons. Hall was a thoughtful man who was lost in admiration for one who had kept himself and his men free from capture twelve years, when most who took to the road were imprisoned or dead within a quarter of the time.

He was appraising Alan now. Fletcher did not appear as old as they said he was. Hardly looked much older than himself, really. But then, all the Fletcher band were getting on, even Jordan O'Day must be near thirty. Rumour had it there was a seventy-year-old with them, one of the men who had been a convict with the Governor. The oldest Hall had ever known were James Mount and Dan Morgan. James Mount, a partner of his briefly, had been over forty and Dan Morgan, they said, was thirty-five. But the great majority of bushrangers were in their twenties, and a lot of them taking to the road lately were like the Jockey, bits of boys in their teens.

Everything about Alan Fletcher fascinated him. No one knew where his hideout was, for a start. It was suspected to be south of Cowra. The story was that Jordan O'Day had said so when in his cups one night at a safe house. It was rumoured that the Governor only used safe houses to appease O'Day's need for women. And his men were never seen unless he decided they would be. It was told that he had been an intimate of the Prince of Wales, was of gentle birth, had been very rich, and had been a Captain in the Royal Navy, and all manner of other things.

Hall had despatched the message to Fletcher through Bluey Williams, a good bloke and trustworthy. He had sent communications before but always Fletcher had rejected his proposals. So, when Bluey had returned this time with an affirmative answer, he was very pleased and surprised.

How like Fletcher to be here and waiting! Ben had been sure he would be first by coming some thirty minutes before the appointed time. But no, the Governor had beaten him. He was deeply impressed by the man opposite and he stood looking at Alan now, as if by scrutiny he might learn how to be like him.

'So we await the others?' Alan said.

Ben nodded.

'Who else will be here?'

Gilbert replied. 'Dan Morgan said he'd be 'ere and we got an answer that James McPherson would too. Do ya know 'im?'

'We do not.'

''E's all right,' Gilbert said.

Alan smiled.

Hall was still looking at Alan. 'Old Joe Daily will be here, and Lefty Dawson said he'd come.'

'What about Crane?' Alan asked.

''Aven't ya heard?' broke in Gilbert. ''E's bin shot. Bloody Rutherford the rat took 'im near Flat's Creek a week ago.'

'Shit!' said Jordan.

Alan looked to Ben Hall. 'Where is that, Flat's Creek?'

'Just south of Orange.'

''E was caught there in camp with his girlfriend, a darkie, just after midnight,' Gilbert explained. 'Seems they surrounded 'im and shot 'im dead, and no sign of his partner, Billy Dunken.'

Ben Hall nodded. 'There was some talk that Blake tried to ride south before Christmas with a pack of traps but was held back by the flood. Apparently as soon as the flood subsided, they went west instead and caught Jake Crane.'

'We reckon Billy musta informed,' stated Gilbert.

'It sounds likely,' agreed Jordan.

No one spoke for a few seconds, then Lawless's voice announced from above them, 'Here comes dangerous Dan with two young fellows in tow, and if I'm not mistaken there be horses ridin' in from the west as well.'

Alan climbed up beside him. 'How far ahead is Morgan?'

'He be comin' directly from the north, a few hundred yards nearer than the others.' Lawless handed him the telescope.

'Good,' uttered Alan putting the instrument to his eye, 'we don't want Dan making a mistake and shooting any of those who are coming here.'

'Too right,' agreed Hall.

Alan found the riders in the telescope. 'I believe it's Daily and two riders coming in from the west.'

By ten past four o'clock, all the bushrangers had arrived. James McPherson was the only one who came alone. All the others had one or two companions each.

The meeting place had been chosen because of its uninterrupted view on all sides to the plain below.

Lawless was asked to stay in his position as lookout with clear vision to the north, east and west, and one of Joe Daily's men took up a station where he could see any movement to the south. Both were well within hearing of the conversation which took place in the inadequate shade of a few straggling gums.

They sat forming a rough circle, sharing two fallen tree trunks and various small rocks and boulders.

A chequered group they were. Directly below where Lawless kept lookout, sat Dan Morgan with two teenage boys as cohorts. He eyed the group morosely from where he hid behind his long black beard. Next to him was Ben Hall quietly dressed like a farmer, sharing a tree trunk with the Jockey and Johnny Gilbert who had dressed for the occasion and wore a flamboyant red shirt and knee-high boots. Over from them squatted James McPherson who called himself 'the wild Scotsman', his lean face pensive, hands clasped round his knees. Beside the Scotsman settled on the other trunk was Old Joe Daily, pipe in his mouth, nicknamed 'old' because his hair was pure white although his age was only twenty-nine; and, beside him, one of his partners. Next to them were Alan and Jordan. Jordan's blue shirt was unbuttoned to show a yellow kerchief tied round his thick brown neck. Making up the circle were Lefty Dawson, a big, lumbering man in a cabbage-tree hat, and his brother Kenny smoking a cheroot.

It was to be the last and the largest gathering of bushrangers ever on the Australian continent.

Exactly one month later, James McPherson would be captured, only to escape and be recaptured a year later and sentenced to fifty years' imprisonment. He, in fact, would serve only eight.

Within three months, Dan Morgan would be shot dead.

Within four months, Ben Hall would be shot dead.

In just over four months, Johnny Gilbert would be shot dead.

Within nine months, Lefty Dawson would be caught and within twelve months hanged, and his brother would be gaoled for fifteen years.

Before the year was out, the Jockey would be caught and within eighteen months hanged.

One year later, Old Joe Daily would be captured and subsequently sentenced to thirty years' imprisonment. He would serve sixteen.

But on this hot, humid, January day, they were all very much alive and they sat weighing each other up as the minutes passed.

'Tell us why we be here, Ben?' Old Joe broke the silence. 'It was from ye that I received the message.'

'As we all did,' spoke up James McPherson.

'I know I asked you all to come,' Hall began in his quiet voice, 'and I'm not sure why 'cept I thought perhaps we might be able to help each other, as it seems the traps close in upon us under this mongrel Blake.' He stopped speaking and looked to Alan. 'Is there not usually a chairman or something when there's a meeting?'

'Aye, guv'nor,' called down Lawless from above, 'we need a chairman.'

'Yes, perhaps it is necessary to have someone to conduct things,' agreed Alan.

'Then it had best be you,' suggested Hall deferentially.

'Yes, boss,' agreed Jordan.

'That's right,' Daily nodded, pointing with his pipe. 'Ye do it, guv'nor, "old boy". It's ye as are the one who has had the experience with genteel matters like chairmen and all.'

Everyone laughed except Dan Morgan who moved uncomfortably and repositioned himself on the rock.

Alan smiled. 'Your hair was brown the last time I chaired a meeting, Daily, but I'll indulge you.'

There was more laughter and even Dan Morgan grimaced this time.

'Thus we will all offer any opinions we have, shall we?' Alan said looking around the group, 'and I'll begin by thanking Ben Hall for bringing us together. It was a difficult event to arrange.'

'True,' murmured Old Joe.

'You say you thought we might be able to help each other, Ben,' Alan continued.

'Mmm, that's right, Governor,' replied Ben Hall. 'It was simply a feeling I had that if we all sat around and talked, someone might have an idea.'

'Does anybody?' Alan asked.

No one spoke.

'Well then, is there anything that anyone would like to discuss?'

'Yeah,' said Gilbert, 'I'd like to discuss how to shoot bloody Blake, that'd get rid of our biggest problem straight off.'

There was general amusement at this recommendation and a few lewd suggestions about which part of his anatomy the bullets should remove.

'Come on, fellas,' called Ben Hall over the noise, his expression solemn, 'we're not here to talk about Blake's balls. Let's talk serious.'

Kenny Dawson dug his brother in the ribs and Lefty Dawson responded by saying, 'In any event, what about this here Act that's becomin' common talk? That sounds bloody serious to me.'

'Yeah, what about that?' asked Gilbert. 'Ominous, I'd call it.'

Alan bent forward, elbows on knees. 'Yes, I believe much will change when parliament passes it. What Lefty refers to, is the "Felons' Apprehension Act". No doubt you have read about it.'

'I can't read,' spoke up the Jockey.

'Shaddup,' replied Gilbert.

Alan continued. 'It is an extreme measure they take against us. It is an "Outlawry Act" dating back many centuries and I assure you if they bring it into force it is because they see the state of things as an emergency. The Government cannot allow us to continue as we are.'

'Yeah, the bastards are afraid of us,' spoke up McPherson.

Alan nodded. 'Yes, I think you are right, but men in fear do not behave moderately.' He looked around the ring of faces. 'One of our problems will be that "safe houses" will no longer be safe, and men we have all trusted will no longer be able to be trusted.'

'Why do ye say that, Guv?' queried Daily.

'Everything I've read points to heavy gaol sentences for helping outlaws and worse for harbouring. Fear alone will close their doors to you.'

'But some say such an Act is a long way off,' declared McPherson.

'Na,' retorted Gilbert, shaking his head, 'they'll pass it soon, the bastards.'

'It won't make no difference ta my mates,' said Lefty Dawson. 'They'll stand by me.'

'Mine neither,' spoke up the Jockey, 'they'll be true blue.'

McPherson agreed. 'Yes, I can count on the blokes that have helped me in the past.'

'Gentlemen!' said Alan.

They fell silent.

'You don't seem to understand. There may be as heavy a sentence as fifteen or twenty years for these "mates" of yours if they so much as point you in the direction of water, and the most extreme measure of any Outlawry Act is to make it legal to shoot outlaws . . . us, on sight. If that becomes law, it will be a different world.'

'Strewth! Is that goin' in this bloody Act?' asked the Jockey turning to Gilbert.

''Fraid so, Jockey, old son.'

'Holy bloody hell,' opined the boy.

Alan looked grave. 'Thus, Ben Hall was right to call us here to see if there might be any way to prolong survival.'

'Do you think there is?' asked Hall looking hopefully at Alan.

'Yes, do ye believe there is?' repeated Daily in the same way.

'Possibly,' answered Alan.

Quiet descended.

A slight breeze had sprung up taking some of the steaminess out of the hot, summer air. It blew in tranquil change across the company on the hill. The horses snorted and moved their hooves as if in enjoyment of the difference.

Gilbert removed his hat and his long wavy hair lifted gently back over his shoulders.

Alan looked round the strange group. 'I think there is perhaps a way we might avoid Rutherford Blake's net, if we all agree on it. We know that the police force is centrally controlled in Sydney.'

'Do we?' asked the Jockey.

'Shaddup,' ordered Gilbert.

'The police districts are often too large for the numbers of police to enforce the law properly, and even Rutherford Blake is not autonomous, he has to get his plans agreed to by the Inspector General in Sydney. Now all that is time consuming, and while he has the telegraph system, Blake is hidebound much of the time in Bathurst, for it ends there. Hence, his forays out into the country are only when he seeks to get one of us, and that is usually after a major raid.'

'What the devil's the point ye make?' thudded the heavy voice of Dan Morgan who had held silence until now.

'The point is this,' Alan continued, looking now directly at Morgan, 'if we used an agreed stratagem—'

'What the hell is that?' broke in Morgan again.

'A plan, a scheme for obtaining an advantage,' explained Alan, 'where we divide the colony up into districts in a similar way to the way the police have done, and each keep to within our allotted areas.'

Ben Hall was listening closely, his pleasant face earnest with concentration. 'Go on,' he prompted.

'Then don't you see we would keep the police divided. Blake simply would not be able to mount the large search parties he has in the past, for we all would be operating at extreme distances. Let me give you an example. Although we all have acquaintances who pass on news to us, our own bush telegraph if you like, it's not always as swift or as reliable as we need. So, if I had known that you,' Alan motioned to Ben Hall, 'had done two robberies near Theresa Town last October, I would not have ridden quite so casually into the gold-field to remove the Government gold. It was a little disquieting to find eight troopers in residence instead of two, as well as Rutherford Blake himself. Now, I'm not saying our raid was not successful, it was, but perhaps a raid elsewhere would have been safer for my men.'

Hall was absorbed in Alan's words. 'I see what you mean.'

'And so too if you, Dan Morgan, had not done the Cootamundry race track robbery four days before you, Old Joe, held up the Cootamundry mail, or vice versa, then you would have four men in your band today instead of three, Joe.'

'True,' nodded Old Joe, 'I'da never done the bloody coach if I'da known there was traps around lookin' for ye, Morgan.'

'Yes,' agreed Ben Hall. 'I *do* see what you mean.' He turned to Lefty Dawson. 'That goes for us as well, we wouldn't have done Dry Flat if I'd known you'd been there a couple of days before. Traps almost took us there.'

'Yeah, bloody bullet actually grazed me,' said Gilbert holding up his hand to show the mark.

'So . . . if we each took a division of land, and the areas are quite huge enough for all of us, and kept our own efforts within them, the large raids would be so separated that such as what we have just discussed, could never happen,' argued Alan, 'and Blake's force would be so divided, he would have real difficulty maintaining any sort of pressure upon us.'

'But, boss,' spoke up Jordan, 'there are always the petty thieves and they will still be robbin' all over.'

'They do not mount police search parties for them, lad. We are the ones they want. There is not a man here who doesn't have a price on his head and Rutherford Blake wants us all. This is the one way I believe we can make it hard for him.'

Every eye watched Alan. He turned his smooth, sun-browned face away from the assembly to look up at Lawless. He was a prepossessing figure meticulously dressed in dark grey with boots brought to a lustrous shine. He had spoken well and articulately, exactly as Ben Hall had hoped he would. It was a good plan and workable.

There were mutterings of agreement.

'Yes, I like it,' said Ben Hall, 'and so what sort of areas do you think we should—'

He got no further, for suddenly Dan Morgan jumped to his feet in a blind fury and pulling a revolver from his belt fired it indiscriminately in the air. The explosion reverberated through the bush stillness.

Lawless who stood above him yelled in fright as the bullet shot straight past his face.

Alan started as the others jumped to their feet in amazement.

'What the fuck. . . .'

'Shit!'

'Christ, man, are ye mad?'

'Bloody 'ell!'

Dan Morgan stood violently shaking his revolver in the air.

Alan recovered quickly; there was resignation in his voice. 'Have you something to say, Morgan?'

'Too bloody right!' Morgan screamed. 'I'll not sit 'ere and be told by a bloody upper-class dandy where and when I may go abroad.

I've been doin' all right the way I am. Ye'll not point at a map and tell me where to live. Ye're a bastard!' he yelled waving his revolver at Alan. 'And no doubt in this carvin' up ye've saved the best for yeself!'

'Drop the revolver, Morgan, or I'll be puttin' a bullet through yer mad dog's brain this second!' shouted Lawless who had regained his senses and now trained his rifle on Morgan's head.

'He means what he says, Morgan!' Alan's voice was icy now. 'We don't hold with killing but we shall exempt you from that policy.'

Morgan was panting with fury. Saliva ran from the corner of his mouth to lodge in his thick black beard. He looked resentfully round their faces. 'Bastards!' he exclaimed, dropping the revolver to the ground.

'I gather you don't agree with our proposal,' Alan said quietly.

Ben Hall shook his head. 'You're a fool, Morgan, a bloody, stupid fool!'

'I'll not be told what to do!' Morgan answered, shaking his now empty hand in the air. 'Not by ye or any fuckin' man. Arrogant arseholes! Now, I be ridin' out o' here and me boys with me.'

'Then walk steady, fellas,' called Lawless loudly, 'and mount real, real slow. I can make a proper mess of each one of ye at this range.'

Morgan and his two associates moved to their horses. Alan picked up the revolver and emptied it of its bullets.

'I'll die game, I bloody will!' Morgan stated as Alan handed him up his empty gun.

'No doubt,' answered Alan.

A few seconds later, Morgan spurred away down the hill to meet his fate.

Old Joe Daily watched his retreating figure. 'No wonder they call him mad dog.'

Ben Hall spoke almost to himself. 'He's a mindless fool and we will all pay for his stupidity.'

'For a minute, I thought we was goners,' philosophised the Jockey.

'Yeah, he's bloody mad enough for anythin'!' commented Lefty Dawson.

McPherson came back a few paces from where he had watched Morgan ride away. He hesitated before he spoke. 'Look, you blokes, it's not that I'm in agreement with Morgan, for he's an odd bugger, no doubt about it, but I'm a bit of a free spirit meself. I work alone or I pick up an assistant jest for one job, you see. It's the Scot in me.' He smiled. 'Like to keep the rewards for meself. I prefer to cover great distances and if the truth be said, although the idea is sound that you put forward, Fletcher, I'm not denyin' that, actually . . . I'd rather not be a part of it.'

Kenny Dawson looked speculatively at his brother. 'Yeah, he could be right, Lefty, might still be better to work the way we have, I reckon.'

Ben Hall sighed loudly, a very dejected sound.

Fifteen minutes later the hill was quiet. The bushrangers had all departed.

When Alan said goodbye to Ben Hall they were both on their horses ready to ride away. They looked at each other in silence a few seconds.

'It was a brave idea you had, Ben Hall,' Alan said.

'Yes,' he answered, 'and it was a good and feasible plan you had.'

'Be careful,' Alan said leaning forward and offering his hand.

Ben Hall took it in both of his as he had done earlier, but this time held onto it for a long time.

When at last he let go, he said, 'Thank you.'

CHAPTER TWENTY-FIVE

> 'I pray thee then,
> Write me as one that loves his fellow-men.'
> 'Abou Ben Adhem and the Angel',
> James Henry Leigh Hunt, 1784–1859.

That night, after the meeting of bushrangers, Alan, Lawless and Jordan made camp in a long shallow valley beside a creek running high with water.

As the night closed in and Lawless lit the camp fire, Jordan said, 'I reckon you might have saved the boss's life today, Lawless, old son.'

Lawless looked over to where Alan stooped to fill a water bottle from the creek. 'I doubt that even Mad Dan would have pulled the trigger on the guv'nor.'

'I dunno about that,' Jordan argued. 'He ain't called Mad Dan for nothin'.'

'Yes, Lawless,' answered Alan coming back to the fire, 'with Dan Morgan, anything is possible, and I thank you for being so alert.'

'Well, he damn near shot me for a start. I wouldn't fancy to be ridin' with him. Didn't he kill his first partner, "German Bill", in sixty-three?'

Jordan nodded. 'So they say. Anyway, he ruined your plan, boss, for I reckon McPherson and the Dawsons might have gone along with you if Morgan hadn't caused the ruckus.'

'I think Ben Hall was the most disappointed; he really hoped that something might have been worked out.' He lifted a branch and put it on the fire. 'But there will be other plans for us which will have no need for consent from men like Morgan.'

Lawless looked up quickly. 'What do ye mean, guv?'

Alan looked across to the two men with him, the dancing firelight reflecting in his eyes, and briefly both Jordan and Lawless thought they saw his gaze soften as he regarded them.

'I mean, Lawless, that I have an obligation to you, to you all, and I have other ideas in my mind. They are but visions yet and I will explain them when they are more substantial.'

427

'Gawd!' said Lawless.

'Always thinkin', the boss,' murmured Jordan in awe.

Alan smiled. 'But now I have a duty to the woman who recuperates at Treehard and so tomorrow night I will fulfil that trust.'

'And we'll wait for you at the North Star Inn as we agreed,' said Jordan, images of the buxom women there filling his mind.

The following evening, close to the hour of six, Alan was riding across country towards Bathurst. In his breast pocket was a letter from Eve to Father.

It had been another hot day with sun searing down from a cloudless sky, the opposite of a few weeks before. All around him on the plain grew the purple Patterson's Curse, so named by the pioneers. It had burst into bloom after the flood, and Freedom thudded now through a sea of deep-violet flowers.

When he gained the road, it was dark, stars dotted the still cloudless sky and the moon had not yet risen.

He came to Reverend Billings at night for he was very aware that as Bathurst was the headquarters of Sir Rutherford Blake, there could be as many as twenty-five troopers billeted in the town at any one time. On entering the township, he avoided the police paddock at the end of Russell Street where the troopers kept and trained their horses and made his way to George Street. Opposite the park, where he had met Eve and where John Stuart had first seen her, he dismounted and hitched Freedom among the twenty or thirty horses collected at the side of Buckle's Ale House, a popular place which stayed open until late.

'Wait here, my beauty,' he said softly and the animal gave the gentlest of whinnies.

Bathurst was a straggling settlement. Like any country town of the time, there were no lamps in the wide, unpaved streets; illumination came only from the moon and the indirect light of the buildings. The streets were all but deserted, yet the ever pervasive smell of dust and horses hung in the night air.

All Saints' Church and parsonage were in the next block to the gaol, but rather than walk by it and the policeman at its entrance, he took a circuitous route and came back towards his destination from the opposite direction. He was some hundred yards from his objective when a door not far ahead opened in a stone wall and two men came out and turned to walk towards him.

Alan instantly saw the police uniform one wore, but continued on at the same pace. As he passed them, the man nearest him who wore mufti greeted him.

'Good evening.'

'Evenin',' Alan replied, recognising Sir Rutherford Blake.

To gain the parsonage, Alan had to cross the road and turn the corner, but he dared not go towards it. Instead he continued straight ahead.

Meanwhile, Rutherford Blake had stopped dead and turned to watch Alan's receding figure.

'What's wrong, sir?' asked Constable Crystal, his thick eyebrows raising.

'Now who is that man? He's not a local. Where have I seen him before?'

'Dunno, sir.'

Alan did not accelerate although every nerve in his body strained to do so. He concentrated on reaching the corner and turning it.

Sir Rutherford's mind was calculating his dark form and the way he moved.

By now Alan had almost gained the corner.

Suddenly, Sir Rutherford remembered. 'Halt!' he called loudly. 'You there! I wish to speak with you!'

As he shouted, Alan reached the corner and, turning it, ran as fast as he could down Russell Street away from the town.

Sir Rutherford was now certain of his identity. 'Damn it, Crystal! That man is Alan Fletcher! Quickly, this way!'

They raced to the corner in time to see Alan leap a fence and run across an open paddock towards the back of the houses in the next street.

'Stop! Stop!' Sir Rutherford and the constable shouted in unison as they ran after him and jumped the fence in pursuit.

Alan's figure could be seen reaching the side of one of the houses some fifty yards away.

'Give me your revolver, man!' shouted Sir Rutherford who was one of the best small-arms' marksmen in the colony.

Constable Crystal handed the revolver he carried in a pouch at his waist to his superior, who took aim in the poor light, steadying his right wrist with his left hand. The gun exploded as Alan disappeared down the side of the house and was lost in the trees.

'Did ye hit him, sir?'

'I'm not sure. Come on.'

The noise of the discharge brought people out of their homes and as Sir Rutherford and the constable raced down the side of the house where Alan had gone, people appeared at the front.

'There he goes,' called the constable pointing as Alan crossed the street and leaped a fence.

'Stop, thief!' shouted one of the men who had come out into the street in time to see Sir Rutherford charging after Alan.

Others appeared across the street to see what all the noise was about. One of them carried a lantern and as Sir Rutherford and the trooper ran up to them, in the light of the lantern, they saw blood on the white-washed fence where Alan had leaped over.

'Ah yes,' Sir Rutherford cried. 'See that? I've winged him.'

Alan could hear the hue and cry after him. The bullet had ripped through his jacket and shirt, opening the flesh at the top of his arm and continuing on to lodge in a tree trunk. He ran, all his senses intensified, vaulting fences and careering down streets and lanes.

Sir Rutherford was loudly deputising as many of the townsfolk as he could to search for the bushranger. The shouting and yelling seemed to come from all directions.

It was almost impossible to keep track of where he was. On he ran trying to attend the buildings he passed and always moving away from the noise of pursuit. Finally, when he could no longer hear the voices, he took stock of where he was. With relief he realised he was in the lane behind the hay and corn market which was only a block and a half from All Saints'. Luck had brought him round in a circle. He ventured to the lane's end. Down the street some few hundred yards to the right he could see figures carrying lanterns but they were moving in the opposite direction.

Stealthily, he crossed the uneven road and walked on. He turned into the small street that ran in front of the church and the parsonage.

All was silent here.

He was breathing heavily and he moved inside the church grounds and came to rest in the church porch. He stood a minute to regain his breath.

From the distance, shouting drifted to him.

He put his hand inside his coat and felt the letter he carried. Then he took a handkerchief from his pocket and wrapped it as best he could round the wound, knotting it with the use of his teeth and his right hand.

He crossed the church yard. His boots crunched on the gravel between the gravestones. He looked to right and left. No one in sight.

He jumped the small stone wall that divided the church yard from the rectory.

As he did so, Martin Carlyle, the church warden, closed the side door of All Saints'. He had been in to return the altar silver which his wife polished at home once a week. The warden saw the dark shape bound across the stone wall and watched it move noiselessly into the shadow of the trees at the side of the parsonage. Curiosity led Martin to hurry to the street in time to see Mistress Thatcher speak to the figure and stand aside to let it through the front door.

She had come to the door when Alan knocked. 'Who is there?'

Alan replied, 'I come on urgent business to see the parson.'

She opened the door and saw the stranger. Her face grew stern. 'What business can ye possibly have with the Reverend?'

'I must see him, lass.'

Lottie looked at him keenly. 'Where are ye from? Ye're not from hereabouts.'

'No, I come from far afield to carry a message to Reverend Billings. It is imperative that I speak with him now.'

A rueful expression came to her face. 'Then, ye don't know?'

'Know what?'

'The Reverend Billings is very ill, it's not but ten minutes since the doctor's been. So I cannot allow ye in and that's all there is to it.' She went to close the door but Alan held it open.

Lottie could look formidable when she chose and she chose to now.

Alan looked into her eyes. 'Please, lass, I entreat you to stand aside for it's imperative I see the clergyman, ill or not.'

There was something about the man that made Lottie waver. 'Why?'

'I bring a message from Mrs Wakeman.'

Lottie's mouth opened in surprise. 'Oh! In that case come in.'

In the light from the hall lamp, she saw the bloody handkerchief wrapped round his left arm. With a sharp intake of breath she said, 'Oh, ye're hurt!'

Alan shook his head. 'It is but a graze. Unimportant. It's seeing the cleric that's important. Is he able to speak?'

Alan saw now that her eyes were puffy from crying.

Lottie nodded and tears rose to her eyes. 'Though Dr Walker says it's but a day or two he has left. He is . . . dying.' Then she regained a little of her severity. 'Ye haven't come to atrouble him, have ye?'

'No.' His voice was sympathetic. 'Can you tell me what happened?'

'Oh, it were all too dreadful. In the flood Mrs Billings and the Reverend were out atrying to help folk as was homeless . . .'

The tears now brimmed over her lids and Alan said gently, 'There, lass, I'm sorry to distress you.'

She sighed deeply. 'They got . . . caught in a flooded arm of the Macquarie. Mrs Billings drowned, ye see. Oh, it's terrible, and the good Reverend in atrying to save her . . . which he did though she be dead when he got her to the bank . . . harmed himself so greatly that he took mortally ill. Oh, it's too terrible.'

431

Alan patted her on the shoulder. 'Take me to him, lass.'

'Ye won't disturb him too much?' she asked as they halted outside his door.

Alan shook his head. 'I hope not, and I will be as brief as my message allows.'

'I will tell him ye be here. What's your name, sir?'

'Just tell him I come from Mrs Wakeman.'

Lottie looked intently at him again.

'Please, lass.'

She sighed with resignation and went in; shortly to reappear. 'I will await ye in the hall. Go in.'

Alan entered and closed the door behind him. The room was lit by two lamps, one on a table by the bed, the other on a mantelshelf on the far side of the room.

In a four-poster bed lay Father. He was propped up on pillows and his face was gaunt. Beads of perspiration covered his high forehead. His look was troubled as he brought his eyes up to regard the visitor.

Alan came close beside the bed. 'Reverend Billings?'

'Yes.'

'I bring a letter from the one who regards you as her father. Are you able to read it, sir?'

'Eve . . .' He said her name like a prayer. He spoke with great difficulty and his breath was laboured. 'Yes, I can read if it is from my darling. But I do not understand who you are and why you come to me.'

'She is no longer at Mayfield, sir. Please read the letter, it will explain.'

Father pointed to the spectacles that lay on the table in the lamplight. Alan picked them up and as he leaned to place them on the sick man, Father lifted his hand and took hold of Alan's arm. 'And who are you?'

'I am Alan Fletcher, sir.'

'I thought as much, and I see someone has been shooting at you.'

'Rutherford Blake. But it is merely a flesh wound, though it bleeds freely.' Then he opened the letter and held it for Father to read.

> Written at a place of safety,
> 11th January, 1865.

My Dearest Father and Mother,

　　You may or may not know that I no longer live at Mayfield. If you have heard of this then I am truly sorry to have worried you. If not, herewith is the truth.

I left Mayfield of my own free will. I am sadly alienated from John Stuart.

I am with a friend who is the bearer of this letter. He is an honourable man who as luck would have it found me alone and ill, in Cowra, on Boxing Day.

You will know him, Father, for he is the man we spoke about as we sat beneath the jacaranda tree in your back garden when I visited you in November 1863. Understand that he is my dear friend and comes to deliver this letter at great personal danger to himself.

I do not come as I am not yet fit to travel. Although I will come to you some weeks hence and then I will explain everything, my dear ones.

For the meantime, remember that I am well and safe. I trust my life with the man who brings this despatch.

I miss you both and love you very dearly,

Evvy

Father closed his eyes. 'Ah, that it has come to this.' He spoke barely above a whisper but Alan could hear his words. He opened his eyes and tried to raise himself and contemplate the man who stood at his bedside. He did so for a second or two and then sank heavily back upon the pillows.

He reminded Alan of an old lion he had seen on the veldt inland from Natal Bay in the Cape Colony. The lion was alone and dying and as he and his companions approached, it raised itself up on its front paws and shook its craggy head defiantly.

He could see that the clergyman was close to death and he sensed the fine spirit that would depart with the body.

'My darling says . . . she will come to me a few weeks hence. I fear she will come to a graveside. Can you . . . possibly understand what that means to me, Alan Fletcher?'

'I am not sure, sir.'

'Then I must make you sure. My Evvy writes of you . . . as moral and good. Is that how you would describe yourself?'

Alan said nothing for a few seconds and then he leaned down towards the clergyman. 'That is how she sees me and for her sake I would be that.'

Father regarded Alan steadily. He felt his very life ebbing away and he was so conscious of his responsibility to his darling Eve. This was the bushranger, the outlaw, the felon he had heard about, read about, and yet this was the same man his Evvy said she was akin to, the man she 'knew' was fine and good. What had she said? 'You see,

433

no matter what men say, I know Alan Fletcher is not bad. I know he is moral and courageous and good just as surely as I know that you are.'

It was a dilemma for a dying man.

Something terrible had occurred at Mayfield. Something that had driven her from her home and husband. Yet, did the letter not say she was 'well and safe', and if that were so, it was due to this Alan Fletcher who stood beside him. He needed to rally, to find the strength to converse. It was necessary for his Evelyn's benefit and so his God gave him the capacity.

'I had two loves, Alan Fletcher,' he said at last. 'Lillian Gedge whom I made my wife, and . . . Evelyn May Herman who was my long lost daughter.'

Alan stood silently listening.

'The one who was my companion is gone. The other writes to me to tell me things . . . that perhaps I would rather not read.'

'I understand that, sir.'

'Yes, I believe you do.' Father stopped speaking and his laboured breathing lasted for a long time. Then once again he raised himself a little with an obvious effort of will. 'You see, I am but a man. A broken, tired old man. The Lord has seen fit to take my Lily, and thus I too must go, for what am I without her? For Evvy, I wish I could stay, but that is not . . . to be.'

'I am sorry, sir.'

Father nodded.

'I want you to know, sir,' Alan began and stopped short, for the sound of raised voices in the hall outside carried to them.

It was the voice of Sir Rutherford Blake arguing with Lottie! 'I must see the man who is with the parson!' came his shout.

'The parson is very ill,' answered Lottie's voice, raised in irritation. 'Ye must not go in.'

'Let me by!' sounded Sir Rutherford's voice again.

'No!' came Lottie's high-pitched answer followed by a scuffling sound.

Apprehension fleetingly crossed Alan's face. He looked quickly round the room.

Then Father spoke. 'Move, get behind me . . . behind the drapes at the back of my bed.'

There were long, heavy, brocade curtains hanging from a canopy at the back of the bedstead. Swiftly Alan moved behind them just as the door opened and Sir Rutherford Blake burst into the room. He was followed closely by Lottie expostulating on how she had tried to stop him. Out in the hall stood Constable Crystal and another trooper.

'Where is he?' Sir Rutherford demanded as he entered.

Father raised his hand. 'What do you mean . . . by this intrusion?'

'Oh, excuse me, Reverend,' Sir Rutherford apologised. 'I am sorry for the use of force, ah yes, but I am told you had a visitor whom I believe is a wanted man.'

Father's ailing eyes could still flash and so they did now. 'Sir Rutherford, this . . . is unforgiveable!'

The detective policeman was slightly taken aback and for a second or two said nothing. When he again spoke it was in a quieter, more even tone. 'Reverend Billings, I should never have been so brash as to intrude in this manner upon one so ill had I not been told by your own church warden that he saw a man enter the parsonage who fitted the description of the man I chase. You see, sir, at this very minute, my men are searching the town for the bushranger Alan Fletcher.'

Father closed his eyes. 'I see.'

'Ah yes, I hope you do, sir. For it is very important that I apprehend him. I am led to believe there has been a man who fits his description in here, that is, in the parsonage. I must ask you if he has been in this room with you?'

'There was a man here but he has gone.'

'I hate to bring any unnecessary stress upon you, Reverend, but I must ask who he was.'

'A friend, who brought me a letter . . . a very important personal letter.'

'You are a man of God, sir, do I have your word the man was not Alan Fletcher?'

Father opened his eyes. He looked directly into his inquisitor's face. 'You do,' he said.

Sir Rutherford almost groaned in disappointment. 'Then I believe you. The warden must have been mistaken. Accept my apologies for disturbing you.'

Lottie had stood silently in the background, tense with horror. She had been watching a blood-stain on the brocade drape at the back of the bed. Watching it widen!

Sir Rutherford moved back from the bed and as his eyes lifted in the direction of the blood, Lottie's voice sounded unnaturally loudly in his ears. 'This way, Sir Rutherford! Come along, I will see ye out.' With a theatrical wave of her hand she ushered him to the door.

Some twenty or so seconds elapsed before Father said, 'It is safe. You can come out.'

The brocade moved and Alan came to the bedside. 'Thank you, sir. I don't know how to express my gratitude for what you did just now.'

Father looked up into Alan's face and met his eyes. 'I did it for Eve.'

Alan nodded.

'Tell her . . . there is a small estate . . . it is now hers. To see Mr Lees, the solicitor here. There is a matter of some three hundred and fifty pounds, mostly dear Lily's from her parents before her.'

'I will, sir.'

'And give her this.' Father pointed to the leather-bound Bible lying on his bed.

There was a gentle knock on the door. Startled, Alan turned towards it.

'Worry not,' said Father. 'It is but Lottie.'

His body tense, his hand on the revolver in his belt, Alan watched the door open and the woman enter.

Father lifted his hand in a weak gesture. 'Lottie . . . you have perhaps guessed who our . . . visitor is.'

'I have,' she answered, 'and the sooner he be aleaving the better.'

Father beckoned her closer. The exertion had taken its toll and he spoke now barely above a whisper. 'Dear Lottie, this man is our friend . . . he is a good man. He brings news of Miss Evvy. She is in . . . his care.'

Lottie looked up at Alan and considered him. She was a bushwoman, and she took this news in her stride. 'I see.'

'You must . . . bathe his wound . . . help him to leave Bathurst . . . make sure he gets away safely, dear Lottie . . . I beg you.' His voice faded.

'You be tired, sir,' the good woman said, 'leave it all to me. Get some sleep now, dear Reverend Billings.' She tucked the sheet in at the side of the bed.

'Alan Fletcher . . .'

Alan moved closer. 'Yes, sir.'

Father took his hand. 'I don't know how it is so, but I know you have all the . . . qualities that my Evvy says, and I believe . . . you will look after her.'

'I will keep your trust,' Alan answered.

The dying man closed his eyes as Alan followed Lottie from the room.

'Ye be lucky there's only me here,' she scolded as they went down the corridor. 'There used to be two of us maids, but Jennie, the other, has gone just yesterday, to look after the new parson.' She pursed her lips before she added, 'I doubt ye could have trusted her.'

'Then I'm fortunate indeed that it is you who are here,' Alan replied as they entered the kitchen.

As she heated some water to bathe his injury, Alan noticed all the blinds were drawn.

'Take the shirt off, please, Mr Fletcher.'

'You have a great affection for the Reverend,' Alan said as she bathed his wound.

'He is the best man God ever saw fit to place upon the earth, as was the mistress the best woman. And why the heavenly Father has taken her and is ataking him is beyond a mere body like mesel'.'

Tears welled in her eyes again and Alan comforted her, saying, 'Don't be too sad, Mistress Lottie. He will be remembered with love and affection and that alone is the most remarkable of achievements.'

She bound his wound.

He stood from the table. 'You are a kind soul, Mistress Lottie, and I thank you, but I must leave now. I would not have you or the parson at any more risk for me.'

She looked alarmed. 'But that is not what I've been told,' she declared. 'The Reverend was particular that I must help ye and aputting ye out of doors to be surrounded by the troopers is not helping ye, I'm sure.'

'I don't want you in any more peril, I can make my own way now.'

Lottie pulled herself up to her full height and put her hands on her hips, and, in what reminded Alan of Samuel, she pressed home her point. 'Now, Mr Fletcher, I do not know aught of ye but what I've read. And the *Bathurst Times* says as ye are a fearsome robber who terrorises his victims, while such as the *Katoomba Advertiser* writes that ye have never robbed any but the Government and the exceeding rich, which I approve of. *The Plainsman* paints ye as the most romantic and courageous of all the wild colonial boys, while if ye be areading any o' the Sydney newspapers, ye be written as a blackguard and a devil.' She sighed. 'So, who do I believe? The Reverend Billings, that's who! And he says you are good and our friend, and that I must be ahelping ye out o' Bathurst. So ye must wait here until those that do the searching are sure they can find naught. Where's the animal ye came to Bathurst upon?' she finished disconcertingly.

Alan smiled. 'In George Street near Buckle's Ale House.'

'Very good, for that lot in there will be adrinking for hours yet. Now, if ye be our friend, it means that Sir Rutherford is not. Thus, it's the two of us, Mr Fletcher, who will be walking the streets o' Bathurst arm in arm in a few hours' time, for the troopers will be looking for a man alone, not one with a female on his arm.'

437

'You are a forceful woman, Mistress Lottie,' Alan smiled again.

And for the first time in weeks, Lottie smiled back. 'It's thanks to the Lord I be just that.'

Three hours later as midnight fast approached, Lottie and Alan left the sleeping Reverend Billings and made their way through the church yard to the street on the far side of All Saints'.

Alan had gone into Father's room before he left and stood a few moments in silence looking down at the sleeping man, now withered by his mortal illness. Alan knew he would never see him again. What pain this death would bring to Eve. He was sorry he had to bring more grief to her, for she had suffered enough already.

When they left the house, Lottie was dressed in her darkest gown and Alan wore fresh clothes that were the least like those of a cleric she could find. On his nose he wore a pair of Father's eyeglasses. They made their way arm in arm down William Street into Lambert and finally into George. A large dog came out and barked as they passed the Empire Hotel and Lottie's hand tightened on Alan's good arm as she said, 'Oh Lord, I do hate big dogs!'

There was lamplight in the windows of the alehouse, and the noise was almost as loud as it had been four hours earlier. In the hitching yard they found Freedom and on him they returned to the church yard. This time they passed two police on foot carrying a lantern. The men looked up at them, but registering the skirts of a woman they simply said, 'Goodnight.'

Down the side of All Saints' they rode and round the back of the church. After they had hitched Freedom to Father's sulky, Lottie returned inside. When she came out she carried Father's Bible and a small portmanteau of silver.

'Mistress Lottie, you are as brave as any man I know. I thank you for your spirit and your courage. You have done what many would not have done.'

'As it happened, Mr Fletcher, there was no danger at all.'

'That there could have been, was where the courage lay.' He took her hand. 'I fear the good Reverend will not last many days, but be not too sad. He wouldn't want you to mourn, I am sure of that. Where will you go, Mistress Lottie, when that comes?'

'As in all they did there was care and attention. The master has some money to leave, though little else, but he has taken care o' me. I am to engage in the cleaning of the church for a small annuity, and I'm to work two days a week for Mrs Ayres in her tea shop, which the Reverend has arranged. Mrs Ayres is a sweet and generous soul, and will look after me. Truth is, I'm the lucky one, for there be six tiny cottages belonging to the church down by the river and the

438

Reverend has seen to it that one is my home whilst I live. Noble is what he's been, Mr Fletcher.'

'I understand that, Mistress Lottie, and I know of the money you speak, it is a legacy of three hundred and fifty pounds and it has been left to Eve.'

She nodded. 'Yes, that's as what the Reverend told me.'

'Can I ask you to do one more thing?'

She smiled at him again, and now there was approval in her expression. 'You can.'

'It will be a long time before Eve is able to travel here and claim her bequest. If, soon, a letter were to come to you, would you take it privately to the solicitor Mr Lees?'

'Of course I will, certainly.'

'Thank you, Mistress Lottie.' He pulled himself up onto the vehicle with his good arm.

She smiled up at him. 'Please be apassing my love to Miss Eve.'

He looked down at her and in the dim light their eyes met meaningfully in silent good-bye. Then he took the sulky forward into the night.

She watched him leave and could not help herself saying aloud, 'Oh please, do be ever so careful, Mr Fletcher,' before she turned away and hurried inside.

Bathurst was still only a settlement of around three thousand and in a short time Alan came to the edge of town. Ahead of him he could see a lantern standing on a post of a barbed wire fence. In the timid light it threw, two troopers spoke to two riders on horseback, while a third lounged near by. They waved the horsemen on and all turned at the sound of Freedom's approach.

'Halt!'

Alan came up to them and stopped the vehicle.

One trooper blocked his way and the other two came forward. 'Who are ye and why are ye abroad at such an hour?'

'I am Thomas Drew, salesman of fine silver.' He looked down through the spectacles in haughty fashion. 'I am upon the road at this unfortunate hour for I needs must be in Lucknow before breakfast, my friends. There, to make the finest sale of silver this side of the Blue Mountains. Ah ha, I hope so, chaps. By the way, do you want to buy some of the world's best silver, lads?' And Alan leaned down waving one of Father's goblets in front of their noses.

Now, the three constables were looking for a bushranger, on a single horse at best. A man they knew had been hit by a bullet and might be badly wounded. They were not looking for an uninjured, smartly dressed, silver salesman in a gig.

'No, no,' replied the trooper with the rifle. 'Methinks ye fellows would sell to yer own mothers. Write that down, Simmons,' he said over his shoulder to the policeman with the book. 'Thomas Drew, silver salesman.' Then he looked up to Alan. 'Lucknow, ye say? That's to be yer destination?'

'That's right.'

'Write that down too, Simmons.' Then he waved Alan by. 'On yer way.'

Three hours later, Alan arrived at the North Star Inn. Sitting on the front verandah he found Lawless wide awake. The rest of the house had long gone to bed.

'I been worried sick, guv'nor, I have,' Lawless admitted looking in amazement at Father's sulky.

'I knew you would be, lad, but there was little I could do about it.' He put his good right arm round Lawless's shoulder. 'I shall tell you all about it in the morning. Let's get a few hours' sleep and be on our way home.'

At the same time that Alan and Lawless entered the North Star, a wide-awake Sir Rutherford roamed his office in the lamplight. David Elrington sat watching, a frown of preoccupation between his eyes.

The police detective shook his head. 'We've definitely lost him, too many hours have gone by, Mr Elrington.'

'Yes, sir, I'm afraid so.'

'Mr Elrington, how long is it since I sent to England for the transcripts of his trial?'

'Let me think, sir. I suppose it must be four or five months.'

'Is that all? Then it's unlikely they'll arrive here before another four or five. Damn!'

'Let's hope we've caught him before then.'

'Ah yes, Mr Elrington, I like your optimism, but the man has avoided the arm of the law for twelve years, thus it seems feasible to me that even with such measures as the coming Apprehension Act, it is possible he may continue to do so.'

'Yes, he's a jolly sight more clever than the average bushranger.'

There was an expression of bemused admiration on the detective policeman's face as he replied. 'Mr Elrington, Alan Fletcher is a jolly sight more clever than the average "anything".'

Some hours after the evening meal on the following night, in the typical, enervating, still, Australian summer heat, Eve sat on the Treehard verandah with Daniel and Samuel in the pale moonlight.

It was twenty days since she had arrived at Treehard. She felt almost properly well again and was mentally preparing herself to leave this place. Somewhat wistfully she looked at the two men. Daniel sat with his feet up on the wooden bench looking like a weather-beaten, kindly farmer, and Samuel in sleeveless undershirt, smoked his pipe peacefully a yard or so away.

She remembered Alan's words of some days earlier. 'We do not complain,' he had said. 'Society must have rules for the good of the majority, and although there are miscarriages of justice and harsh sentencing, which we at Treehard have all experienced, the British system is still perhaps the fairest in the world. It is some of the men who work within it that I would change.'

It seemed absurd that these two inoffensive men sitting with her under the stars had a bounty on their heads. She looked from one to the other and broke the silence. 'Do you two usually go with Alan when he goes to . . .' She stopped short not knowing what word to use.

'When he goes to do a job?' Sam stated.

'Yes, when he goes to do a job.'

Daniel smiled. 'We do if he needs us. Yet, it's his preference to leave me here at Treehard. And mostly our Sam is my companion. He would rather preserve the elderly, eh, Sam?'

The little man laughed. 'The truth of it, Mistress Eve, is that Daniel here is seventy turned and I be in my fifty-fourth year, and the guv'nor has some silly idea that we be better off at home than on the road if there be the likelihood of danger.'

Dan nodded. 'Wants to keep us out of harm's way and away from the likes of Rutherford Blake.'

Sam took his pipe from his mouth and wagged it in emphasis. 'He'd like to see us all swingin' at the end of a rope, would Blake.'

'Now quiet, Samuel. There's no need for that sort of talk.'

'The mistress is here among us. There's no point pretendin' otherwise than the truth.'

Eve spoke up. 'No, Sam is right, Daniel. Besides which, I have had the dubious benefit of being in Sir Rutherford's company on various occasions and I am not naive. I know that what Samuel says is true.'

'Thank you,' stated Sam, looking reprovingly at Daniel while turning out his pipe and tapping it on the railing. 'He's lookin' to be famous by riddin' New South Wales of the bushrangers. I reckon that bloke's a mile ahead of any other trap I ever heard of; he's sharp and clever, which makes a dangerous law-man. Still,' here he smiled smugly, 'on an even scale our guv'nor would outwit him every time.'

'On an even scale, Samuel,' answered Daniel, 'our governor would outwit anyone.'

'Yes,' agreed Eve softly, 'he would.' A gentle thrill ran through her as she pictured him looking at her with his concentrated gaze. How she hoped he was all right, that he had met with Ben Hall and seen Father and that all had gone well. She lifted her eyes up to the stars and heard the rustling bush sounds and the noise of the hot breeze in the trees. Suddenly, she had the feeling that he was quite close and to her surprise, within seconds out of the night came a parrot call.

Sam jumped to his feet and ran down the steps and round the side of the dwelling to the tunnel mouth where he cupped his hands to his lips and replied twice. Back came a call in answer.

'Thank the Lord God above in his Heaven,' cried Daniel, 'our boys are back.'

A couple of minutes later, Alan and Freedom issued out of the mouth of the passage followed by Lawless and Jordan.

'At last,' said Samuel, 'and not a minute too soon. Good grief, what's this?' He pointed to Alan's bandaged arm.

'A flesh wound only, Sam, I'll relate all about it, shortly.'

Daniel looked concerned. 'Well, come in and tell us, I'll put the kettle on.'

'Whisky for me,' said Jordan, dismounting. 'It's been a hard ride and a hell of a stinkin' hot night. Hasn't it, boss?' he turned to Alan.

'It has, Jordan.'

Sam led away the fatigued horses and the travellers turned towards the steps of their home.

Eve was standing holding the rail as Lawless and Jordan greeted her. She welcomed them. 'It's good to see you back.'

She moved to Alan as he came after them. Her face glowed with the pleasure of seeing him, but she was alarmed to see he was wounded. 'I'm so glad you have returned safely. But I fear you have been in danger.'

'Yes, a little, yet we are through it and here, and that is all that matters. I have news for you, and it is not good, I'm sorry.' He stood beside her now and there was sympathy in his eyes.

A chill ran through her. A look of apprehension replaced the glow which had lit up her features upon seeing him.

'Come inside, lass.' He pointed through the door. 'It's best I tell you in private.'

Her eyes begged for reassurance and he steeled himself. How to tell her? He took hold of her arm and guided her across the verandah.

When they came to her room, he spoke immediately. 'Lass, there is no way to tell you gently. Mrs Billings was drowned in the flood, and the Reverend in trying to save her did himself great injury. When I saw him he had but a little time left.'

She felt an icy coldness run through her. 'Oh, no! It can't be true.'

'I am only sorry that it is.'

'But they . . . they cannot both be . . .' She turned away in shock, trembling, hugging herself. In a dazed voice, she said, 'I must go to him.'

'It would be too late, lass. I fear even now he is gone.'

She brought her ashen face back to him. Father gone! Mother gone! The security of life with them gone! Alan's face was blurred through her tears. Blindly, she put her hands out towards him, reaching, searching and then she stepped forward into his arms.

She clung to him as if he too might leave her. She was the lonely, unhappy, teenage girl again. She sobbed against his chest and he held her close.

'Now, now,' he said tenderly. 'It will be all right.' He swallowed hard as her curls brushed his lips. Every fibre of him yearned to turn her face upwards and to kiss her mouth, to kiss away the tears, to alleviate her pain. He cradled her close and stroked her hair and when she looked up to him with her puffy red eyes and tear-stained face, he thought it was the most perfectly beautiful sight he had ever seen.

'There, lass, weep no more. They were the best of humanity and you were blessed to be one of those they loved. Think of their benevolence, and the way they enriched the lives they touched. That is a thought to bring joy, not sadness. And I don't want you to worry. I will take care of you.'

She smiled sadly. And the veriest sound of resolve came to her voice. 'But I do not want to be a burden . . . not to you, or the others.'

'You could never be that.'

His words had the effect of composing her. She believed him as a child believes and as a woman believes the man she loves. She wiped her face determinedly. Her eyes shone in the candle light and she sighed.

'Don't worry about anything,' he added softly. 'Everything will be all right.'

Some five miles to the south-west, in a wide, sweeping valley beside a swiftly running creek, two men sat in the tent they shared.

They had eaten their evening meal round the camp fire with their twenty-four companions and afterwards some of the men had told tall tales and sung bush songs that echoed along the creek bed in the immense stillness of the endless trees. Around ten o'clock they had drifted off in twos and threes to bed down in their own communal tents.

Now, in the vague illumination of the hurricane lamp that sat on a collapsible table between their two stretchers, the two men talked.

'Well, m'boy, how far have we come from Young in five days?'

John Stuart lifted his eyes from the map he studied and drew his hand across them in a weary movement. 'We've kept up an average of about three miles an hour and the men stretch across about three-quarters of a mile, so with time out for luncheon and turns and things, we've covered six miles wide by fifteen long.'

'Good. So how long will it take us to investigate the area left between here and Cowra? There are a lot more heavily wooded and scrubby patches to the north, you know.'

'I do, old man. And if we keep the same pace, it will be around another eight days or so.'

'Mmm. This searching the bush is all very well and none of the boys mind spending each day doing it, and I am happy to, don't misunderstand. But what if we get to Cowra and we've found nothing?'

John Stuart sighed. 'Then I must search further in from the road. Rutherford is positive the Fletcher hideout is this side of the Sydney road between Cowra and Young.'

Joe nodded. 'M'boy, that will see us well into the month of February. Remember, there is all the rebuilding to complete at home, and the lambing in March and the April drive to organise.'

'Yes, I know. And I realise my responsibilities. I will not avoid them but I must find her.' He lifted his right hand to his forehead as if it were in pain. 'I am shocked at what occurred in Cowra. I am angry, I am affronted, and damn it . . . I *miss* her so very badly.'

There was something very tender in the older man's expression as he reached across to touch John Stuart's knee. 'I know you do, m'boy, I know you do.'

CHAPTER TWENTY-SIX

'Speak to me as to thy thinkings,
As thou dost ruminate, and give thy worst of thoughts
The worst of words.'

Othello, William Shakespeare, 1564–1616.

Sir Rutherford Blake stood from the small table where he had taken a cool drink and doffing his hat to Mrs Ayres behind her cake counter, neat and appealing even in the solid heat, strode to the shop door.

The sun beat down from a cloudless sky with unforgiving intensity, one of those oppressive Australian days where the heat lies like an eternal woollen blanket over the country, with no escape for those beneath. In the thick, still air, the merest physical work brought rivulets of perspiration, and Sir Rutherford ached for the moderate summer days of the northern hemisphere. Nevertheless, his swift stride did not slow and in another minute he was across the wide dirt street and opening the door to his office. Simultaneously, his inner door opened and David Elrington entered.

'Letter just arrived for you, sir. It has the Wakeman seal on it.'

His assistant left him as he took it and picked up his long ivory and gold letter opener.

His face tightened in concentration as he read.

> In camp by the Lachlan River,
> Just south of Cowra,
> 24th January, 1865.

Dear Rutherford,

I write this in my tent just after dawn.

I am halfway through a search of the countryside the like of which, to my knowledge, has never been undertaken before. I, Joe Larmer, and twenty-four Mayfield men began in Young on January eighth and investigated the entire country in a six-mile-wide strip running along the Sydney road north as far as Cowra. I am about to turn round and do the same on the inner stretch, making the width from the Sydney road twelve miles, and touching the Mayfield border in some places.

I know you adamantly believe the bushranger, Alan Fletcher, has his hideout in this strip of country, and I believe you will be surprised when I say that I search for it. But I think you will be even more surprised when I say I do this to find my wife. Yes, Rutherford, I have reason to believe the outlaw has my wife at his hideout!

Eve left Mayfield on Boxing Day and went to Cowra. She was ill and became unconscious. I learned that somehow the bushranger found her there around eleven o'clock in the morning and that he kidnapped her. There was a second man with him who walked with a limp.

I am assuming that the deputisation of myself and Joe Larmer, made when we rode into the hills beyond Mayfield to search for signs of the outlaw, are sufficient to cover us now.

My wife's leaving home is something I deeply regret, and I will explain the many contingencies which bring me to this oddest of quests when I next see you.

I live in the hope that my search will have ended soon and that I have the person dearest to my heart with me again. And, too, that I can deliver up to you at least information about the bushranger.

Forgive the ambiguity of this missive. I repeat, I shall explain the details of this most mixed affair when next we meet.

Your friend,
John Stuart

The expert on the bushrangers did not move when he came to John Stuart's signature. He was thunderstruck. In fact, he reread the letter to be sure he had understood. It was astounding! Mrs Wakeman *kidnapped* by Alan Fletcher in Cowra on Boxing Day? What the hell was this all about? Suddenly, he dropped the letter and brought his hand down hard on the desk. 'Of course!' he said aloud. 'I see it now!'

Rapidly, he passed out into the small corridor and over into the records room. Soon, he was perusing the report lodged by Sergeant Rodney Samuel on the events which took place north of Bendick Murrell on the Sydney road on Boxing Day. Samuel was a good policeman and thorough, and the report was well detailed: '. . . two of my constables gave chase into the bush after the suspect while I and the other two rode forward to meet an oncoming trio. There were two men and a woman, by name Mr and Mrs James Trent, farmers, and their farm hand Anthony. James Trent said his farm is south of Bendick Murrell.'

Sir Rutherford read on eagerly. '. . . continued to rain during

446

interview. Mr Trent said he had been to Christmas with his mother. His wife was poorly. I let them pass . . .'

Sir Rutherford found the descriptions of the people:

Anthony (no last name given): farm hand.
Age: mid to late thirties.
Wore cabbage-tree hat and leather rain cape over clothes. Sun-browned, clean-shaven, long side-whiskers, pale eyes. Neither a large nor a small man, but muscular.
Mrs Trent: farmer's wife.
Age: late twenties.
Spoke little. Looked tired, even ill. Thin face, fair curls, pretty.
James Trent: farmer.
Age: probably older than farm hand Anthony, but uncertain.
Wore bush hat and leather riding cape covering clothing. Sun-browned, clean-shaven. Light to brown hair, what could be seen beneath his hat. Probably well above medium height. Spoke like a bushman yet troop remarked he had a quality of authority. An imposing man. From memory his eyes were not dark. I think light blue or grey.

Sir Rutherford's lips stretched back across his face in a distorted smile. Ah yes, Fletcher and the Wakeman woman! Though Sergeant Samuel could not be blamed for not knowing so. Riding south. And their companion? From the description it was most likely Drake.

The point was, John Stuart and Joe had mentioned only two men. Perhaps the third that ran at the sight of the police was not with the trio at all. Even so, he was sure of the two with the woman. Of course he would ascertain whether there was a James Trent farming south of Bendick Murrell, but he already knew what the findings would be. He would get Sergeant Samuel in first thing tomorrow and go over the meeting with him.

So, Fletcher had been heading south of Cowra on the main road. Yes, John Stuart searched in the right place. He was certain of that.

He returned to his office and moved across to the map on the wall. He ran his finger in habitual movement down from Cowra past the western borders of Mayfield and this time stopped on the hamlet of Bendick Murrell.

He had planned to go south to Wagga Wagga the day after tomorrow anyway, after Mad Dan Morgan. That meant he had to ride through Cowra and Young. With a bit of luck, he might run into John Stuart. He really should talk to him. Perhaps he should get going tomorrow.

He turned from the map with a sigh and sat down at the desk

staring in deep concentration. To anyone looking through his office window he looked as if he sat mesmerised, but the opposite was the case. His astute mind was searching into the night of 13 January when he had chased Fletcher through Bathurst town.

Suddenly, he sat bolt upright.

'Ah yes!' he said aloud to the silent room. 'At last, I see much more.' He brought his fist down so heavily on the desk that the lamp to his left hand wobbled.

Ah yes, it *had* been Fletcher whom the church warden had seen here. Martin Carlyle, nosy parker that he was, was reliable. Alan Fletcher had been here to see Reverend Billings and it was something to do with the woman. She was as a daughter to the clergyman. Alan Fletcher had been in her company since Boxing Day! Had he brought a message to the parson from her? Fletcher had been there with the dying man. And on his deathbed, Reverend Billings had lied to save the bushranger. A spasm of shivering ran through him as he remembered how the minister looked him directly in the eye and said it was not Alan Fletcher who had been there. It was hard to believe that the priest had lied. Why? For the woman's sake? Ah yes, most certainly.

Sir Rutherford shook his head.

And she had been in it too, Mistress Lottie Thatcher, up to her eyeballs in it. It was incredible!

It was all clear at last. When his men had blockaded Bathurst that night they had given him the list of the thirty-nine people they had stopped leaving the town and there had only been one man they had been unable to trace, a silver salesman on his way to Lucknow, one Thomas Drew by name. Thomas Drew? Silver salesman? Sir Rutherford himself had visited each and every homestead and farm in and around Lucknow and no one had been expecting a silver salesman. Yet, his constables had said the man had been dressed in a suit, carried fine silver, wore spectacles and gave no sign of being wounded. And even more convincing, Thomas Drew had driven a sulky. The good parson had died the following morning so there had been no more conversation with him, but when the new Reverend Cornish had moved into the parsonage, the sulky belonging to All Saints' had been missing.

No doubt Mistress Thatcher had helped him escape. She would have bound his wound and given him the clothes and the silver too.

Thus his nimble mind went hard at work. He recalled Mrs Wakeman's attitude whenever bushrangers had come into the conversation. In retrospect, it was an aversion to discussing them. Through his head ran the Larmer girl's words, 'Perhaps she sympathises with them.'

And yet John Stuart said his wife had been kidnapped by the outlaw. And he was scouring the bush to get her back. Really? It all seemed mighty odd to him. She was most interesting that one. He had to know more about all this. Ah yes, he would leave tomorrow and get into the south-west.

When Sir Rutherford called for his assistant and gave the news, the young man was totally bewildered. 'I cannot for the life of me come to believe it, sir. Mrs Wakeman is at Alan Fletcher's hideout? It is bizarre, sir.'

His superior nodded sagely. 'Yes, it is, but so much is clear now that was murky before, eh? It's a pity the Felons' Apprehension Act is not yet passed, else we could put the clever Mistress Thatcher behind bars.'

The young man sucked in his cheeks in habitual movement as he thought. 'Perhaps, sir, we could go to her, question her about it. She might admit to something. She lives down in one of the church cottages by the river now.'

'And warn her that we know something? Mr Elrington, that idea is not worthy of your distinguished intelligence.'

His assistant looked abashed.

'There may come the day when Mistress Thatcher helps us unwittingly, providing she does not know we suspect her. And things may change now that the bushranger has the Wakeman woman with him. Ah yes, Mistress Thatcher was an intimate of hers for years at the parsonage. One never knows.'

'I see exactly what you mean, sir.'

'So what do we do, Mr Elrington?'

'And so, sir,' the young man replied immediately, 'we will keep a vigilant eye on Mistress Thatcher.'

'Exactly,' said Sir Rutherford, smiling almost fondly at him.

Three months later Sir Rutherford sat in his office and patted the *Sydney Morning Herald* of Tuesday, 18 April, with an air of satisfaction. It had taken two days to come from Sydney and it was worth waiting for. He was smiling. It was a smile of real mirth, happiness, even elation. For the newspaper beneath his hand carried the banner, 'WILL BUSHRANGERS SURRENDER?' And underneath: 'All bushrangers are ordered to surrender to the gaoler at Goulburn Gaol by April 29th or be aware that they will be declared "outlawed". Hence, from May 8th 1865, it will be legal to shoot known bushrangers on sight.'

In March, the long-awaited Felons' Apprehension Act had been passed and while he had argued long and well for a twenty-year sentence for any who aided the outlaws, the members of the

Government had seen fit to make it fifteen. Well, he was not unhappy about that. Fifteen was more than enough to scare off the sympathisers. In the main, it had already stopped the free houses from functioning. The scum had nowhere to hang their hats in safety now.

He turned back to look with gratification at the map of the colony of New South Wales that hung on his wall. There were a number of small black and red crosses dotted upon it. The black crosses represented a dead bushranger and the place he had died. The red ones were for captured bushrangers, and the places they had been caught. Sixteen crosses were placed upon the map in 1864, most of them red, for unimportant names, but there were a couple of black ones for Johnny O'Meally and James Jones.

This year was proving to be gratifying. Early in January he had added a black cross for Jake Crane. Billy Dunken, his ex-partner, had informed on him and he had been taken in his camp south of Orange. Unfortunately, Crane had been shot dead. Sir Rutherford felt a touch sorry when his troopers shot and killed. It wasn't the way he liked to do things. It was untidy. He preferred to take them alive and let them face justice.

Then in February he had added a red cross for James McPherson, the wild Scotsman. Thirty miles from Forbes they had surrounded him in his lonely camp and taken him without a fight. A good old black tracker had led him to that one.

The most recent cross he had added was not two weeks since. He had drawn it in with mixed feelings – a black cross and an arrow pointing down from the New South Wales border towards Wangaratta in Victoria. It represented Dan Morgan. Sir Rutherford was greatly comforted to have Morgan on the map, but he felt cheated all the same. Once again, it had been his own ingenuity that had caught the bushranger, for he had maintained his vigilant search parties in the south where he knew him to be. It was in desperation that the criminal had crossed the border into Victoria, where a crack shot called Wendlan had apparently shot him through the throat. Thus, the Victorian police claimed Dan Morgan's head when Sir Rutherford knew it morally belonged to him and his men.

There was an irony in claiming Morgan's head. It had, in fact, been severed from the bushranger's body shortly after death and placed on his chest for the local folk to file past and view. Sir Rutherford's mouth drew down in distaste as he thought of it. And they were already making up songs about it. He had heard Constable Ward singing a gory verse the other day:

There was a rush for trophies soon as the man was dead;

450

They cut off his beard, his ears, and finally his head,
In truth it was a hideous sight as he struggled on the ground;
They tore the clothes from off his back to expose the fatal
wound.

In the same week that Morgan had been shot the news had broken
of the death of Sir Frederick Pottinger. In March he had finally been
dismissed as Police Inspector of the Western District. He had been
travelling to Sydney to appeal against the sacking when at a coaching
stop in the Blue Mountains his revolver went off, shooting him in
the chest. He had died a month later. When Sir Rutherford heard,
he could not help but wonder if Pottinger had committed suicide.
Whatever the truth, the man was gone, and Sir Rutherford was not
hypocrite enough to pretend he had not wanted him out of the way.
Still, he had not wished the man dead, not at all. It was most
untoward.

There was still much to be done, and a law enabling his men to
shoot at bushrangers on sight gave him the advantage he needed.
Most of them, foolishly believing such would never happen, in cavalier fashion had let their faces become well known. Only the Fletcher
gang had not made that mistake. Yet good fortune had given him
the close look at them that night in Theresa Town.

Ah yes, of them all, Fletcher was the one he wanted most. An
aristocrat who had allowed himself to become a cohort of convicts and
outlaws. It was an outrage! Sir Rutherford took it almost personally.

He left his desk and walked to the window where he stood staring
out into the street. Across his sight walked a lively figure. His mouth
set rigidly as he watched the slim back of Lottie enter Mrs Ayres'
Tea-Room. He sighed. Ah yes, Mistress Thatcher, I know you helped
Alan Fletcher escape on January the thirteenth. Just try to help him
again and I shall see you in gaol for fifteen years!

Behind him the door opened and David Elrington came in. His
bright young face wore a troubled look.

'I have the report you requested on the movements of the Hall
gang and the Fletcher gang, sir; those between January first and
April twenty-second.'

'And?'

'There were six Hall gang robberies, sir. On January nineteenth
and twenty-sixth, February sixth and seventeenth, March sixteenth
and April tenth. Deaths were two: January twenty-sixth, Constable
Nelson shot dead; March sixteenth, Constable Kelly mortally
wounded, died three days later. Wounded were two: February seventeenth, Constable Wiles; and March sixteenth, Mr Donald Blatchford

451

JP. Gun shots were fired in each deployment, sir.'

'And the Fletchers?'

'No activity recorded in January or February. Robberies on March twentieth and April eleventh. Each done by three masked men, thus the assumption was the Fletcher gang. Both robberies successful, and no gun shots fired.'

'And what were they?'

'The Government Claims Office at Bushman's was robbed of bank notes and cash and troopers escorting supplies to Goulburn gaol were held up. Six rifles, Terry carbines, were taken.' The young man handed the papers he held to his superior. 'There is much more detail on all the raids here, sir.'

'Thank you, Mr Elrington.'

David Elrington brought his heels together in a sort of salute. 'Once again, the Fletcher deployments were a great distance apart, sir, one hundred and forty-one miles as the crow flies, to be exact.'

His superior nodded sagely. 'Ah yes, I see.' Then he pointed to the chair on the other side of his desk. 'Sit down, Mr Elrington.' Sir Rutherford sat opposite him.

'I have been studying the cases of the two robberies on Christmas Day last and have now closed the case on the Warraderry picnic hold-up. We know conclusively it was Dan Morgan. But the other . . .'

'The Redley station raid?'

'The Redley station raid. Ah yes, then let us see how my instruction has served you. At first it was laid at the door of the Fletcher gang. And what is it that we have noticed time and time again about the Fletcher hold-ups?'

David Elrington frowned and sucked in his smooth cheeks in meditation. He was in fact a voracious learner and listened avidly to his superior. He was intelligent and articulate and all lawbreakers affronted his fastidious sense of fair play. He loved his work and often as they pored over eye-witness accounts of hold-ups and encounters with bushrangers, Sir Rutherford would pat him on the back and quote, 'No profit grows where is no pleasure ta'en; In brief, sir, study what you most affect.' And the young man would smile and nod, for that was exactly what he was doing, and the years ahead were to prove him one of the most famous and, let it be said, fair-minded, judges of the Supreme Court. But for now, he was learning his trade and he took a deep breath and replied, 'Well, sir, the thing that has stood out, with the exception of Redley station, was that the Fletcher gang had never killed anyone; in fact, rarely had they ever fired on anyone.'

'Correct, correct. And yet on Christmas Day we note that a trooper

452

was shot and killed in a most perfunctory manner. Ah yes, and that the reason the eye-witness thought it was Fletcher was that the raiders wore masks.'

'True,' agreed his protégé.

'We know there were four men in the gang that day, and that is odd for Fletcher, is it not?'

'It is, sir, for they work in three or five, mostly three. Since being joined by O'Day, we do not think they have ever worked with four.'

'Ah yes, good, Mr Elrington, and is there anything else that makes us doubt that it was Fletcher?'

David Elrington was silent for a few moments. 'Yes, sir. They have never robbed anyone other than the Government, or very occasionally the vastly rich.'

'Excellent, Mr Elrington.' Sir Rutherford beamed at his protégé. 'Ah yes, and more often than not it is the Government, eh?'

'It is,' reiterated the young man, 'and Mr Redley is neither the Government nor is he in any way rich, sir.'

'I am proud of you, Mr Elrington,' Sir Rutherford said standing and moving to the window where he stood, hands clasped behind his back, looking out onto the street. 'And finally there is a last reason that makes the Redley station raid the work of another gang, and I will not blame you if you cannot tell me what it is.'

David Elrington looked puzzled. Once more he sucked in his cheeks. He thought very hard. He looked at the palms of his hands and then turned them over to study the backs of them, but the answer was not written there. 'I'm afraid I cannot tell you, sir,' he answered, a trifle deflated.

Sir Rutherford turned to face him. 'Never mind that you cannot tell me, but listen well, and remember.'

The young man leaned forward in concentration.

'Because,' informed Sir Rutherford, 'it was ill-planned. Ah yes, Mr Elrington, they never do anything that is ill-planned, which is why their hold-ups are always successful. The Redley station raid was aborted. The outlaws were not successful. This on top of all the other leads us to what conclusion?'

'That it was not the Fletcher gang.'

Sir Rutherford nodded. 'So you see, Mr Elrington, much as I would like to believe that Alan Fletcher is beginning to make mistakes and that he did make the unsuccessful raid on Redley, I know it is not so.'

'Yes, sir, that is evident now, and I shall go immediately to the file and change the record.' As David Elrington stood, he looked at his notepad. 'Oh, by the way, sir,' he added, 'just before I came in

453

I received a message from the Royal Hotel. Mr Wakeman and Mr Larmer will be expecting you for dinner in their rooms tonight at eight o'clock.'

'Ah yes,' replied Sir Rutherford, 'of course, looking forward to seeing them, indeed.' He had not seen his friends since he had met them in Young in February after John Stuart and his pack of Mayfield men had rigorously examined four hundred and eighty square miles of countryside looking for the Fletcher hideout. At least that is what the people of Mayfield and the west had been led to believe, that they were deputised to help Sir Rutherford. Only Sir Rutherford, Joe Larmer and a handful of trusted Mayfield men knew that he searched for his wife whom Fletcher had abducted. And if any others suspected the truth, then it had been whispered and had not reached the ears of the master of Mayfield and his intimates.

When they had been in Young together, Joe had been the one to explain to Sir Rutherford the story of Nathaniel Lake and the consequences. It had obviously been a strain for John Stuart even to listen to, and Sir Rutherford had felt acute sympathy for his friend. He remembered when Joe had finished the account, how John Stuart had turned to him, a terrible sadness in his eyes, and added, 'So, Rutherford, unlike my futile search, there may come a time when you *do* find the bushranger, and if Eve is with him, she will be with child.'

Ah yes, John Stuart had been disappointed in his search for his wife. He was a man full of confusion and unhappiness.

In all their long ride, they had found nothing. Joe had related their fruitless search to the police detective. 'Between Young and Cowra, there is virtually no habitation, no farms or stations, only the police camp at Bendick Murrell, a few inns, and perhaps two or three huts of odd recluses. Other than that, we saw two aboriginal camp sites which were deserted and that's all; yet you have always been adamant that the Fletcher hideout is in that territory.'

'Yes,' Sir Rutherford replied. 'And while you have found nothing, my friend, I still believe it.'

John Stuart had shaken his head, desperation sounding in his voice. 'Hell, Rutherford! We have just spent weeks in minute examination of the very area of which you speak, and it has been futile.'

For reply, the expert on the bushrangers had simply sighed.

Afterwards, he had spent hours discussing their epic ride, marking things on his map and jotting down facts about the few inhabited places and folk they had actually seen. And he told them of the night he had chased the bushranger in Bathurst. He would have spared John Stuart if he could, but felt in all truth that he should know.

Joe had remained calm, 'So when we were three days into the search down here, the outlaw was in Bathurst.'

'Yes, Joe,' Sir Rutherford nodded, 'but he was alone, I'm sure of that. Mrs Wakeman was not with him. From what we know, I'd say she was kept at his hideout as you believe.' He looked to John Stuart. 'May I say how very sorry I am, my friend, ah yes, that this should have been in the stars for you.'

At the time, John Stuart had said nothing; he had simply covered his face with his hands.

And tonight Sir Rutherford would be reunited with his two friends once more. Ah yes, it could be valuable to see John Stuart again.

John Stuart and Joe had arrived in Bathurst in the mid-afternoon and were staying overnight at the Royal Hotel. They were returning to Mayfield after the first of their twice yearly cattle drives. Neither of them had been in Bathurst since Eve had disappeared four months earlier.

The purpose of the overnight stay was to see Sir Rutherford. But there was another consideration that John Stuart did not quite admit until he insisted on their taking a turn round the town in the late afternoon.

He did not care for Bathurst these days. He found it like its counterparts, an ugly, dusty, country settlement of sprawling dirt streets and straggling houses, many of them not more than wooden cottages. He would be glad to be on his way tomorrow.

He directed their footsteps to the graveyard of All Saints' Church, as Joe had suspected he would. It was easy to find the burial place they sought, for the parishioners had erected a substantial marble tablet above the resting place of Father and Mother. It had come all the way from Sydney and been positioned only the week before. The words were painted in gold.

Here lies
The Reverend Leslie Billings, late Rector of this parish,
October ninth, 1794 – January fourteenth, 1865.
His devotion an inspiration,
His very passing caused by his dedication to the people of this
district.
Always remembered.
The Lord is my light and my salvation.

And his good and faithful wife Lillian,
June twenty-sixth, 1800 – December twenty-sixth, 1864.

Lost doing God's work for the members of this parish,
A heart true in all she did,
Thy will be done O Lord.

John Stuart removed his hat and stood silently. He had confused feelings.

He looked past the mint bush at the side of the grave, over the fence to the back garden of the parsonage. There was clear vision across the gravestones to the jacaranda tree where he had lunched with the clergyman and his wife and Eve. The event seemed so long ago and yet it was only just over two years. How briefly she had been with him. He wondered where she was as he did every day of his life. Was she safe? Did she ever think about him? He glanced sideways to Joe who was looking straight ahead.

John Stuart truly did feel sadness at the death of Reverend Billings. He had liked the parson, and his wife. He thought of the night they had waited together in the firelight for the return of Eve after her fall from Moonlight. The man had truly loved Eve. What was it the cleric had said to him, that night? Something like, 'I believe you do love Eve deeply. But love the essence of Eve which I know is strong and good. Do not weave a dream about her.' What good advice that had been. At the time he had not recognised it as such, but he did now. Where are you, Evvy? Where are you?

As he and Joe turned to walk away, he said, 'Would you see this new Reverend Cornish in the morning, old man? We will pay for a plaque to be attached to the walls inside All Saints' in honour of Reverend Billings. Let it speak of him as the good and responsible man he was. Deflect them from making it too religious.'

Joe nodded.

On their return walk to the hotel, they did not speak. They were comfortable together in silence.

Later, they met in the parlour for a drink before the arrival of Sir Rutherford. John Stuart had bathed and changed into a brown velvet jacket and trousers. He wore a soft silk shirt and a dark bow tied at his throat. If it were possible, he looked even more handsome these days for there was a distant look in his dark eyes concealing his melancholy, and somehow heightening his attractiveness. When the barmaid brought their sherries, she stared with unabashed admiration at John Stuart who gave her a brief half smile. It did Joe's heart good to see it, momentary though it was, for it had not sat often upon his boy's mouth in recent months.

John Stuart looked over his wine glass and asked, 'Are you and Thelma still keen for Daydee to marry Roy Ford?'

Joe shook his head. 'Ah, m'boy, it's not pressing or compelling that she marry at all. It is just that the Fords and Thelma and I have always had a sort of understanding that we would like our two children to join together. Roy dotes on Daydee, as you know. The dissenting voice is Daydee's.'

'Yes, I understand that,' answered John Stuart, remembering back to the day only a week or so before the cattle drive when he had met Daydee in the front hall at Mayfield House.

It had been Sunday afternoon and he carried his scientific journals under his arm. He had thrown himself into his work after he had been unable to find any sign of his wife in all his long searches and expenditure of time and money. He had always been innovative, trying labour-saving devices and time-saving theories on Mayfield, and in one of the scientific journals he was carrying was an article about the French chemist, Louis Pasteur, his work on the mysteries of germs and the rejection of spontaneous generation. It was Pasteur's marvellous process of heating to kill germs that John Stuart was eager to apply on Mayfield. He was heading in the direction of the summerhouse to read it all, when Daydee appeared from the corridor leading to the kitchens.

'Good afternoon, Daydee,' he greeted her.

'Good afternoon, Uncle John Stuart.' Her face was unhappy.

'You do not seem happy, Daydee.'

'I'm not.'

He hesitated and asked, 'Why?'

She did not meet his glance but instead dropped her eyes to her hands which she held clasped tightly in front of her. 'Well, it's a mite personal, but I am being pushed in a certain direction and I've no one to talk to, for it's Mother and Father who do the pushing.'

John Stuart succumbed. 'Come and sit with me and tell me about it.'

Happy now, she followed him through the hall and out into the day.

What she had told John Stuart was in fact rather exaggerated, for Thelma and Joe did not 'push' Daydee to do anything, Joe by reason that he would not, Thelma because she could not. But they did from time to time mention young Roy Ford as an acceptable suitor and this, to Daydee, was 'pushing'.

When they reached the summerhouse, they sat opposite one another.

'Now, what is this terrible thing your parents are doing?' he asked.

She moved on the seat and crossed her legs, bouncing her tiny foot up and down and watching it as she replied, 'It's that Roy Ford.

457

They suggest that I should become engaged to him. Oh, but he is such a dreary, I hate him.'

'I think that particular emotion a little strong, Daydee. He seems a nice young man to me.'

She scowled, 'Ah, there it is. Nice, nice, that's what Mother says about him. Oh, Uncle John Stuart, "nice" tires me.'

'Yes, Daydee, I think it does.'

'I will never like him,' she said definitely. 'He is not the type of man I like.' He looked at her with interest and she felt her pulse quicken.

'And so, Miss Daydee, what sort of man is it that you do like?'

She lifted her eyes to meet his. 'One like you.'

He said nothing for a second or two, then he shook his head. 'You flatter me, Daydee; but look not to a man such as me, for I made the worst mistake a man can make.' As he made mention of his personal situation, he found himself wondering why.

'But it was not your fault,' the girl insisted.

He did not want to continue with this. 'I point it out to you only to make you aware of the foolishness of setting another up as the model for what you believe to be perfect.'

Daydee dared to persist, for this subject, of all things, was dearest to her heart. She spoke softly. 'But, now Aunt Eve has gone, cannot we all live as we did before she came?'

He looked at her. To him she appeared unworldly, innocent and virtuous, her youth expressing itself in her simple statement.

'Daydee,' he said, 'as time passes you will learn that it is difficult to ignore strong emotions. Eve . . . is gone, yes. Indisputably so. In fact, she seems to have run away . . . from . . . me. No, I will never be as I was before she came here. It is impossible.'

And then, even though she feared to ask the question, she did so, there in the summerhouse with the sun shining on her jet-black hair. 'Do you think she will ever come back?' She sat looking at him, an elfin-like creature with an intense look on her face. The child growing into a woman that he had known since birth.

The only person who knew how he really felt was Joe. No one else would be audacious enough to ask him about Eve. No one but this fairy opposite him. He would have repulsed everybody else, put them swiftly in their place, but to Daydee he answered, 'She has been gone over three months, and I have not been able to find a single trace of her. No, Daydee, I do not think she will.'

He did not explain any of the intricacies in the torrent of feelings that he had for his wife. He did not say he was still confused by Lake's story and the incidents that had led to his mistrusting her.

He did not say that he wanted, more than anything in the world, to see her and hear her explanations. He did not say that he was hurt and angry with her and himself. He did not say that he had finally admitted to loving her whether she was good or bad. He said none of this for he assumed he spoke to an inexperienced, naive, young woman, and consequently, the plain answer sufficed for the proper one.

But Daydee had heard what she wanted to hear. Eve would not be back. She had dared to ask and he had given the reply she longed to hear. Daydee smiled at him, a heavenly smile.

John Stuart changed the subject. 'Now, this business with Roy,' he said seriously, 'why don't you give the young man a chance? It would please your parents, and you may in time find you do not hate him after all.'

'I don't think I will, you see,' she explained. 'There is nothing about him that appeals to me.'

'Daydee, your parents only want what they believe is good for you. They are the best parents in the world. They would not harm you.'

Daydee did not quite see it the same way, but she did not disagree with him. Pushing her hair back over her shoulder and smiling at him once more, she asked, 'Please, may I stay and read the journals with you?'

'Yes, if you're quiet.'

John Stuart's mind returned to the present and Joe's grave face opposite him. 'Mmm,' he said, 'perhaps you should give Daydee more time. The Fords are not pressing you, are they?'

'Not in any real sense, but Roy is twenty-seven. I had a letter from Stan before we came on the drive. Roy is in love with Daydee at present, but he sees her only four or five times a year. He's earnest and hard-working and a good character; besides, he shall inherit a tidy sum eventually. He is the type of man I want for my Daydee.'

'Yes, but it is better not to mention it to her for a little while.'

'She is always reading those novels, too much fantasy. Doesn't see life as it is,' her father observed as Sir Rutherford entered the room, ebullient in his greeting.

'My good friends, it is grand to see you both. Ah yes, I foresee a pleasant night.'

John Stuart and Joe rose to shake his hand.

As the three friends sat, the police detective could not help observing how well John Stuart looked tonight, ah yes, well, but not happy. His was a sort of smouldering, brooding look, that while it had always been there, now was somehow more so. Sir Rutherford had been quick to notice the looks the serving girls were giving the master of

Mayfield. No doubt, he was most attractive to women.

These days, it was generally known throughout the colony that Mrs Wakeman had departed from Mayfield; it was the scandal célèbre and John Stuart's was the name on everyone's tongue.

The detective policeman sat back in his chair. 'One week from Saturday I must be at Goulburn Gaol to see if any of our wild colonial rabble do, in fact, surrender. Ah yes, I am pleased with the way eighteen sixty-five is proceeding, you know. Two of the worst of the bushrangers out of the way and I feel we get closer to Hall and his desperadoes, every day.'

Joe asked, 'Do you think any will surrender?'

Sir Rutherford actually grinned. 'No, I don't. That mob don't go in for surrender. Now, had it been amnesty, a different matter. It was merely a step in the legal process and had to be announced.'

The meal progressed and they spoke of other things and then of the cattle drive.

'Did all go well in the capital?' Sir Rutherford asked.

Joe smiled. 'Always does. Though this time, we saw to something in particular.' He put his hand in his inside pocket and withdrew an official envelope as John Stuart spoke.

'Rutherford, it seems that my wife has disappeared off the face of the earth.'

'Yes, it does. Mind you, while I do not like to say so, if she is in Alan Fletcher's hideout that is understandable.'

'Because I am so sure she is, and the Felons' Apprehension Act is about to become a reality, I had to do something to protect her. For, even though in the first place she was abducted, she has not reappeared.' He pointed to the envelope Joe held. 'In this is a declaration signed by the Governor, the Premier, and the Inspector General of Police. It states that if you or any of your men do apprehend Fletcher, or any of his men, and she, Eve, is in company with them, she is a Crown exception to the Felons' Apprehension Act. She is not to be arrested.'

'I see.' Sir Rutherford put out his hand for the envelope. 'She is a very lucky woman.'

'Yes, and a pity she didn't know that,' Joe replied, before he had time to think.

John Stuart half suppressed a sigh and shook his head at the older man. Joe was so loyal, but it was not Eve's fault. The whole mess was so complicated.

Sir Rutherford took the envelope, his aquiline features shining in the lamp glow. 'If I find her, what do I do with her?'

John Stuart looked to Joe and took strength from the compassion there. 'She should be taken to a place of safety. A place where there is a magistrate would be best. The magistrate should take care of her until we can come for her. We should be alerted the moment you know, or have any suspicion of where she is.'

Sir Rutherford prided himself on his ability to judge the calibre of his fellow creatures. He had never estimated Mrs Wakeman as a woman of loose morality, no, not at all. Even so, while she had been 'kidnapped' in the first instance, it appeared she had remained with Alan Fletcher for months now. What could one possibly think? He watched his friend opposite him with his despondent, dark eyes. Ah yes, people were very strange indeed, and fascinating. He smiled. 'Of course.'

CHAPTER TWENTY-SEVEN

'See the mountains kiss high heaven
And the waves clasp one another;
No sister-flower would be forgiven
If it disdained its brother;
And the sunlight clasps the earth
And the moonbeams kiss the sea;
What are all these kissings worth
If thou kiss not me?'
'Love's Philosophy', Percy Bysshe Shelley, 1792–1822.

As the three friends sat in the Royal Hotel in Bathurst, the moon filtered a pallid light through the tall gums at Treehard Hill down upon the two figures who walked back along the neat path from the escarpment edge towards the little, wooden house.

'Will you be gone the entire day, tomorrow?' Eve asked looking up to Alan.

'Yes, it's over a thirty-mile ride to the store near McGorman's mine where we shall get the provisions this time.'

It was now fall, as Eve termed it, and the nights were cool and soothing. Even the days were almost pleasant at last. It had been the hottest summer in living memory after the flood and the unseasonal chill of Christmas time.

She had remained at Treehard, there had been nowhere else to go. Besides, she had wanted desperately to remain, and the wonderful thing was, that Alan had wanted her to as well.

She stopped walking and turned to face him. 'Alan,' she spoke softly, 'will you ever leave Treehard Hill?'

'Leave? Perhaps. The climate in New South Wales is changing towards bushrangers, lass, and a time may come when we have no alternative but to leave.' He was looking down at her, his eyes reflecting the moonlight.

She nodded to him in the darkness. He was so discerning and courageous. Being with him was a continuing enrichment in her life. 'The future is always uncertain, isn't it?' she said.

'Yes, uncertain for all of us, any of us. The future is something I must think about, though I try not to dwell on it, for survival is all the future ever can be in a bushranger's life.'

'Are you ever,' she hesitated, 'afraid?'

She thought a brief smile flashed across his mouth. 'Afraid of what, Eve? Of being caught?'

'Yes . . . no. Of the possibility of leaving here, of the future that you mention. I know you will probably think me foolish, but these last months, being here with you and the others. I am perfectly peaceful and happy. Life here is so easy, and yet I feel my hold on . . . this happiness is tenuous, frail.' As she finished, she looked away.

He made a tender sound in his throat and he took her shoulders to turn her back to face him. His touch ran a shiver of pleasure through her. He did not touch her often, although his eyes met hers a thousand times each day. He was caring and warm towards her, but he held himself back, she knew he did, and she knew a great part of it was out of consideration to her, for what she had been through.

'Each human being's hold on happiness is tenuous, lass, that's a condition of being human.' His hand came up to her chin and he held her face, looking down into her eyes. 'Eve.' He elongated the 'e' and the sound was wonderful to her ears. 'If I am afraid of anything in this life, it is that these days with you may end.' All his love and empathy for her filled his words and somehow, magically, they echoed ever so slightly in the night air. Her heartbeat quickened. His head came down towards her. Momentarily, the moonlight disappeared, the world was black and exciting and tremors of delirious expectation ran down her limbs. Then his eyes left hers, his hand dropped from her chin and, taking her arm, he moved her forward along the path.

She had been so sure he was about to kiss her and she had wanted him to with all her being. She knew herself now, knew her strengths and resources, and her vulnerabilities, all the things she should have done and had not. She had made mistakes, but now she saw them clearly and hoped she had learned by them. The months here at Treehard had given her time to examine her life, her losses and her griefs; Lake and the pain she had suffered because of him, the rape and aftermath of the miscarriage. Recently she had realised with a sense of strength that now she could accept what had occurred as part of the fabric of her life. It was seven months since Lake had attacked her and the fearful shadow in her mind had dissipated. And it was all because of the man here beside her, his compassion and understanding and gentility and love. All her experiences had

463

prepared her for this. She knew she was ready now, ready to be loved by Alan Fletcher whom she loved, had loved, always. From all the lives of human time, from the beginning, Eve Herman had loved Alan Fletcher.

Her disappointment seemed to be manifested in the very air, for a breeze came suddenly up over the cliff face blowing her dress sideways to hover around his knees, as if linking them. She knew her hand was vibrating on his arm.

Alan's voice sounded a little unsteady when he spoke. 'Danny will be waiting to brew us tea before retiring, it's time we went inside.'

'All right,' she answered softly.

The next day, around six, as the new dawn's sun hurled forth the brilliance of a flawless morning, Eve stood on the Treehard verandah with Danny and watched Alan, Lawless and Sam ride into the tunnel on their way for supplies. Jordan was still asleep; he was remaining at home with Eve and Daniel.

'We shall see ye, tonight,' Lawless's voice drifted back through the rock opening and she turned to Dan as he said, 'Best way to get through the day is to keep busy. It'll take our minds off worrying about our boys.'

'Yes, Danny, it will be a tedious day, I'm afraid.'

The hours of the morning dragged. She groomed the two remaining horses, a job she had begun since her convalescence, and one she enjoyed. Then she trimmed the vine that grew up the front of the little house and wound along the railing of the verandah. The small, white blooms had died weeks ago and now it looked straggly and leafless. She knew Sam had been meaning to trim it but he had so much else to tend with his gardens and paths and lawns. She remembered how she had seen Thelma do this very job on her own porch at Mayfield where a wisteria wound up to the roof. She often thought of Thelma, her dear, good friend.

Jordan came by as she was working and he stood watching her a minute or so before he said, 'Why don't you let me do that?'

'Thank you, but I'm quite capable, Jordan,' she answered, balancing on the stool and turning towards him, one hand holding the verandah railing. Her hair was tied up in a wide, pink band and some stray curls peeped out from beneath. While she was still thin from the ordeal she had suffered, she looked girlish and pretty, tiny pearls of perspiration on her flesh in the V neck of her gown.

He moved a step closer and gazed appreciatively at her a few seconds before he walked away with the words, 'Just as you like. I shall be over near the cliff face severin' branches from a number of trees we are to fell tomorrow.'

464

Dan had just come out on the verandah in time to hear Jordan's last words. He moved forward to the steps. 'But didn't Alan say to finish digging the ditch for Sam's water pipe today?'

Jordan halted, chewing at the inside of his lip before he answered. 'Danny, my man, I hate diggin' ditches.'

Daniel pursed his lips and with a shake of his head to Eve returned to his kitchen.

At noon, all three ate the vegetable stew that Danny had made and by half past the hour they had returned to their various chores.

Early during the afternoon, Eve went gathering native flowers. It was hard to find blooms for the summer flowers had mostly gone. By the time she had a reasonable bunch, she found herself at the very edge of the north corner of Treehard. She remembered how she used to do this same thing at Mayfield, and unconsciously she looked out over the escarpment across to the north-east where the property lay. She imagined John Stuart riding towards her upon Diomed. He was a handsome, imposing man, brilliant but deluded. She wondered how he was; the months away from him had soothed her anger and despair with him. And yes, she had loved him and in many ways been proud of him. Not the same love or pride that she felt for Alan Fletcher, nothing could be the same as that, but it would have been enough to last her lifetime if his distrust and rejection of her had not driven her away. She was sure John Stuart would be all right. He had Mayfield, and he loved the property with all his soul. There was a sadness deep down inside her when she thought of him, a sorrow spot living there in her soul, perhaps there always would be; but her life with him was over and she was here.

Yet life was constant change, and who knew what tomorrow would bring?

She smiled sadly and turned away. Through the trees to the south she could see Jordan close to the cliff face. He looked over and noticed her, lifting his bushman's hat high in the air in greeting. She waved. Soon, she was back along the path near Sam's tool shed. A large bottlebrush grew here which Sam carefully tended and it had some late blooms on it. It was so top-heavy that it drooped and Sam had attached it with thick twine to the roof of the shed to hold it up. She cut one of the last few red bottlebrushes to add to her bouquet.

When she came back to the house, Daniel was chopping chips of wood for the fire. His features broke into his customary, broad smile.

After she had fed the chickens and swept the small front verandah and drawn water from the tank for their use that night, she made tea and took a mug out to Daniel who now was in the stables.

'I shall take a mugful over to Jordan as well.'

She found Jordan on top of a wooden ladder sawing through a branch, his tall frame bent forward. He wore nothing on his upper body and his brown, muscular chest and arms shone in the streaming evening light.

'I've brought you a drink.'

He completed cutting the branch and it fell to the ground.

He appreciated the tea, warm and sweet, and gulped it down, his big, expressive eyes watching her over the rim of the tin mug. He still could not get over the reality of her being with them at Treehard. The mistress of flamin' Mayfield bringin' flamin' Jordan O'Day a drink! That was the boss for you, though. God, if he wasn't something! It had been plain from the start that this woman loved the boss, and the months had shown how the boss loved her, right enough. Never thought a man would live to see the woman the boss loved, but here she was, right here, bringin' Jordan O'Day his tea. Whole thing was bloody amazin'. She was mighty pretty really, great mouth, and even though she was a bit skinny, a bonzer figure, yeah, real bonzer. He smiled. 'Nice breeze now, coolin' the evenin' down.'

She pointed to the stack of branches. 'Jordan, have you removed all these already?'

He nodded. 'Once I get started, I work fast.'

'You do.'

He grinned proudly. 'Yeah and I'd best get back to it. It'll soon be dark.' He turned from her and strode over to the tree he had been working on. It was ready to bring down; he had cut off all the large branches on the cliff side of it so it would fall the right way. He looked back to see if she were watching as he lifted the saw. She was still there.

He smiled to himself, put down the saw and picked up the large axe they used for cutting down the trees. To Eve's surprise, he swung it back in a wide arc and began to chop into the trunk about two feet from the base. A man alone could cut off branches, but felling a large tree single-handed was reckless.

'Stand back!' he called to her. 'I'm bringing this one down.'

'Jordan, don't! It's dangerous alone! You should wait for Lawless.'

Either he didn't hear or he preferred not to answer, for he continued hefting the blade high in the air and driving it with all his might into the tree. Minutes went by and then with a tearing, cracking sound, the trunk began to break in her direction.

Jordan jumped back, throwing down the axe, beads of perspiration on his temples and a triumphant expression on his face. But the expression died as his eyes widened in fear, for the tree did not continue to fall straight; it slewed sideways and even as Eve shouted a warning, one of the remaining limbs clipped him hard on the shoulder, knocking him backwards. He lost his balance and staggered a few steps. His left boot caught between two stones and to Eve's horror he catapulted backwards across the few feet to the cliff top. His big hands grabbed at the air as he screamed and disappeared over the edge.

For a second, she could not move. Then she ran to the cliff edge, white-faced with dread, and looked over.

To her amazement, he was dangling ten feet below, clutching a dead tree stump which jutted out from the escarpment face, his legs hanging in nothingness like a frantic marionette. There was blood on his arms and forehead where they had hit the rocks.

He was terrified.

She was terrified. There was nothing but hundreds of feet of emptiness below him.

'For Christ's sake, get Daniel!' His voice was desperate.

But even as she went to move, she saw the tree stump begin to tear away.

'Oh Jesus!' he screamed. It was an appalling sound.

She looked wildly around. There was no time . . . no time. It was all heightened in her head, the dreadful sounds of terror from over the cliff, the ladder on its side, the fallen tree. No rope . . . nothing.

Sam's shed!

She ran the forty yards without knowing she had.

String? Useless. Where's the thicker cord? The one he uses for holding up the bottlebrush? Where? Ah, thank heaven, here it is. Will it be strong enough? No time. It must be.

Back to the cliff top.

The stump was cracking now.

Stay calm. Double the twine, tie it round a tree, knot it. Back to the edge. Ignore the cracking sound of the tree stump, throw the cord down to Jordan. Yes, yes, Jordan had it.

She watched in hideous fascination, the muscles of his arms expanding like sails in a wind, as slowly he climbed towards her, his veins appearing like laces of purple string across his deep brown skin.

He groaned in terror as his foot touched the tree stump he had been clinging to and it broke noisily, ripping away entirely and smashing down the sheer drop to the ground below. His eyes were on hers, pleading, begging to be saved as he inched his way to where she could take hold of him and help him up over the edge of the cliff.

'Oh God!' he kept saying. 'Oh God!'

They were both trembling as he lay panting beside her. When at last he staggered to his feet with shaking legs, he mumbled, 'Thanks, I was a gonner without you.'

They made their way back to the house and Jordan went to his room. He remained there, door closed, until the sun went down.

The three of them ate the evening meal together and afterwards Jordan smoked his cheroots and whittled silently on the form at the small verandah's end.

Eve and Daniel cleared away the dishes and washed them. As Dan put the last plate away, he turned to Eve, resting his worn, brown hands on the back of the nearest chair. 'Our Jordan owes you his life.'

'Danny, I was so lucky the twine held.'

Dan nodded before he passed through the door to sit a little way from Jordan in the rocking chair Lawless had fashioned for him last Christmas.

They waited on the Treehard verandah in the comfortable night, all with thoughts of their own, until close to ten o'clock when they heard the bird call.

Jordan jumped to life as Dan too left his chair, shouting, 'They come, they come.'

Within minutes, Eve was enjoying the happy laughter and excited voices of welcome return. They all helped to bed down the horses and carry in the sacks of grain and supplies and soon the kitchen table was covered with provisions for weeks to come.

Eve moved to the leader's side. 'Any trouble, Alan?'

'No, lass, nothing untoward. But I have something of interest to us all.' He took a newspaper from out of his saddlebag and, making room at one end of the table, spread it out. It was the *Sydney Morning Herald* of Tuesday, 18 April, and the banner it carried said, '**WILL BUSHRANGERS SURRENDER?**'

He pointed to the words underneath. 'You will see here that we are ordered to surrender to the gaoler at Goulburn by April twenty-ninth or be declared outlawed.'

Lawless gave a short laugh. 'Funny that, and here I was thinkin' we were outlaws already.'

'Let's see,' said Jordan breaking his long silence and looking round Alan's shoulder. 'Oh, bloody hell,' he continued as he read. 'So it's come at last.'

Then Sam spoke up, for he and Lawless had already read the newspaper. ''Fraid so, Jordan, matey. Yep, the rotten Act's goin' into force. It'll be legal to shoot us on sight from May the eighth.'

All of a sudden, the little kitchen fell silent; the apprehension was like a living thing; the six figures rigid in the candlelight, the only noise the crackle of the fire in the hearth.

Eve became aware that Alan made the first move; he stepped very close to her as his dispassionate voice filled the space with reason. 'That part does not matter to us. The tiny few who know our faces will not shoot us.'

The fatal twenty-ninth of April had come and gone. Eight days had passed since all bushrangers had been called upon to surrender to the gaoler at Goulburn or face the consequences of the Felons' Apprehension Act.

Alan and Sam had ridden off before dawn to cover as much territory as possible to find out how people were feeling towards the Act which would be law tomorrow.

Through the tall Treehard gums, Eve's figure moved gathering firewood not far from that part of the cliff face where she had saved Jordan's life. She was about to bend down to add to her bundle when she heard her name called.

It was Lawless striding through the trees towards her. He had been digging a new garden bed for Sam. She thought him quite charming. She enjoyed his quiet company and it was from him she had learned, at least in part, the stories of their lives, including an account of Alan's arrest and sentencing. He had looked at her and said, 'Fancy bein' duped into believin' the guv'nor could kill in cold blood! Can you imagine it, Mistress Eve?' And she had returned his look and answered, 'No, Lawless, I cannot. Some people will believe anything.'

He was kind and sensitive, never a man of moods, and had become her friend.

'Hello, Mistress Eve.' He gave an amused chuckle and leaned on the shovel he had been carrying. 'This weather is so balmy and nice after the heat of the summer. Do you know there was a time in my life when I had never felt hot . . . no, not at all. The closest I came was bein' warm occasionally. It was a hard life in the Rookery when I was a boy, hard and cold.' He shook his head. 'Though I'm not complainin' now. One of the first things the guv'nor taught us, was . . . The way things are is the way things are. If ye be in a situation ye surely cannot change, then that's the way of it. Ye must accept it, and I be happy enough with the way of things.'

'I know you are, Lawless, and it's something I admire in you, admire in you all. The way you have made a life for yourselves through all the adversity. The way you have kept truth in your lives, truth and dignity.'

'Why, Mistress Eve,' he answered, looking searchingly at her, 'now that's a real nice thing to say.'

She smiled at him and he returned the expression. She was totally comfortable with Lawless, always had been. Lawless and Danny had welcomed her from the start, and since the dreadful experience when she had saved Jordan's life, his view of her had changed, and by that his attitude; so too had little Sam's. Not that they treated her like a man, she wouldn't have wished them to anyway. It was simply a less complex situation, as if she were an equal who belonged at Treehard.

She turned from him and bent to pick up her firewood.

Suddenly, without warning, she was hurtling sideways, knocked off her feet by Lawless's body crashing into hers. She screamed as she fell. Then she saw his arms come down across her, wielding the shovel which he smashed into the brown snake, poised, head up, mouth open, fangs exposed to bite.

'Oh, my Lord!' she cried as he measured out a second blow, severing the head of the stunned creature. Perspiration stood out on his forehead and his face had changed colour. He took the two pieces of the reptile on his shovel and, walking the fifty or so yards through the trees to the edge of the escarpment, threw them over the side. When he returned to her, he was shaking his head. 'Ye cannot be too careful,' he said quietly. 'Although they are worse in the summer, the creatures can be around any time of year.'

'Oh, I know, Lawless, and usually I have my wits about me. I'm so sorry.'

'The brown snake is deadly . . . deadly.' He repeated the word, emphasising it with an embittered sound.

'Thank you for . . . saving me.' She was still shaken.

He sighed deeply, a sigh that came from the depths of him. 'Ah, mistress, I'm but pleased I was here to do so.' Then he looked away as he added, 'Once before I was not in time.'

'I don't understand, Lawless.'

Then, looking carefully about him to make sure they would not be surprised by another of the venomous snakes, he took her arm and sat her down on a log. He placed the shovel at his right hand as he knelt down beside her. 'Ye have heard me speak of my Patricia June.'

'Your wife who died? Yes, I have.'

'Brown snake bite,' he said softly, looking straight ahead.

'Oh no! I'm so sorry.'

He concentrated steadily on the silky-bark gum in front of him. 'She was my sweet angel, saw nothin' but good in me.' He gave a sad smile. 'Why, she even found my limp charmin', she did.'

He was silent a few seconds. 'We met her and Jordan, as ye be aware he was her brother, though they be different as chalk and cheese, north o' Millthorpe in fifty-seven, accidental like. They had just lost their parents' farm, taken from them by the law, debts they couldn't pay. Jordan's never got over it, but Patricia June didn't hold no grudge, weren't in her to be that way.

'I'd say we fell in love right then and there, beside that billabong. The guv'nor is a wise man and clever. He was quick to ken I couldn't go on without her. Well, he kept us in that district nigh on eight weeks and I'd be sayin' it was to see if our feelin's died. I suppose he hoped they would, but no, there it was, me meetin' her every day. Well, what with Patricia Junie knowin' about my way of life, Jordan cottoned on. He was all for joinin' with us straight away. No doubt the guv did a lot of thinkin' and finally he sent for Jordan and interviewed him like.'

'And he let Jordan join you?'

'Truth to tell, I do believe it were because of me and Patricia. He knew I wanted to marry her, and the only way to keep us all tightknit was to agree to let Jordan join with us.'

'I see.'

'She would never have left him behind. Fact is, she doted on her brother.' He shifted slightly to face her. 'The very words the guv'nor spoke to me about my Patricia June were high compliment and I'll never forget them. He said, "Lawless, it's no life for a woman, bein' on the run, and I've always said I wouldn't allow it, but I note that your Patricia is different. She is strong and gallant and has that superior quality of dependability found in so few. If we can find a priest or a clergyman who will marry ye, then I believe it should be done and we should move on from here." ' Lawless lifted his eyes to look straight at Eve. 'The guv'nor were right about her, just as he always is where character be concerned.'

'Yes, Lawless, I'm sure that's so.'

Lawless dropped his eyes and there was the edge of anger in his voice. 'Well, we never did find a priest or a clergyman to marry us. No, none o' them ever would. My Patricia were distraught. How they stood in judgement on her and brought tears to her eyes.'

'Oh dear, I'm sorry,' said Eve gently.

'No, don't be,' his voice lightened, 'for we were married, all real and proper like, in the sight of God by one o' the best representatives the good Lord has ever had on this poor earth.'

'Who?'

'The guv'nor of course!' he answered proudly. 'He was the captain of a ship in Her Majesty's Navy. He had the authority, ye see, the authority, and Patricia June was so merry when I told her he would do it. As for me, what's any old man o' the cloth to me? But the guv'nor marryin' us, now that had meanin', that did. For even though he told me he had lost his rank, and that the marriage would not be recognised by society, it mattered nary a bit. Givin' Patricia June a weddin' was what mattered, and we were married in my eyes and the eyes of Heaven.' He smiled in remembrance.

Eve thought how wonderful it was that this unaffected, ingenuous man beside her was revealing all this. Watching his tender smile, just for a second she was reminded of her own marriage in All Saints' Church. A sad, mixed feeling brought a sigh to her lips.

He too sighed as he had done often during his tale and took up his story once more. 'Well, we had been husband and wife for close on one year when the darlin' told me I were to be a father. Happy day. That were when Alan said we had to find a proper hideout, a real home. But she was never to see it. She had been carryin' our child for just four months when the brown snake bit her. It were Christmas Day and all, eighteen fifty-eight. Don't seem right, does it, that an angel would be taken at Christmas? But she was. We were camped in a dry creek bed not two miles from the Warraderry Inn. Dan and I'd been gatherin' wood for the fire, while the guv'nor, Sam and Jordan were out gettin' us a square meal. I can see her now, staggerin' towards us cryin', "Oh God, Arnold, it were a brown snake . . ." and holdin' up her darlin' wrist for me to see the puncture marks.'

He did not speak for a few moments, then he wiped his hands across his eyes as he finished, 'She was dead in my arms within five minutes more. Both of them . . . dead.'

Eve said nothing. She just sat looking at his profile. His teeth were clenched together and his eyes were wet. She could feel his suffering; she knew what it was to lose those you love, and she wished she could say something to alleviate it. She put her hand on his forearm and held it there.

'Lawless, the love you shared was beautiful, and in that the two of you were blessed beyond most others. I don't think Patricia June would want you to be sad.'

He turned to face her. 'Now, Mistress Eve, ye be speakin' the truth there and no mistake, and that's why I try to keep a cheerful heart . . . for the memory of my angel, and for Alan too, in a way. It's only in the speakin' of it all that I've become melancholy, and I thank ye for the sentiment ye have shown me.'

'You're a fine, good man, Lawless, and I am honoured that you saw fit to tell me.'

472

He was moved by her words and for a short time they sat without speaking, the unmistakable feeling of a bond between them.

He broke the silence. 'I'd been visitin' her grave when I met ye on the road.'

'I see,' she replied softly.

He stood up. 'Well, mistress, we'd best be gettin' in . . . luncheon time.'

They bent in unison and picked up her firewood. As they stood, he cleared his throat and spoke again. 'And you're a fine, good woman. Never truly thought there'd ever be a woman good enough for my guv'nor . . . but ye are.'

'Oh, Lawless, thank you. It warms my heart to hear that.'

Five minutes later, they were on the verandah with Daniel and Jordan.

'Mistress Eve, thank the Good Lord for a lucky escape and all,' responded Daniel when they were told of the snake.

Jordan bent forward, head in his hands. 'Yeah, the bloody things are killers. Did for my sister.'

They were all silent until Eve spoke lightly. 'Well, it's warm enough in the sun, but the wind has a bite in it already. After such a hot summer we could be in for a very cold winter.'

'In more ways than one,' Daniel remarked. 'This blasted Act that comes in force tomorrow will make things awkward to say the least.'

'Oh, I don't know,' replied Jordan, 'I think the tavern at Watta-mondara will stay much the same. I'm thinkin' my Bridget won't let me down.'

Daniel made a disgusted sound. 'Malarkey! Even such mates as Henry Lyon will have to think twice about associating with us now.'

'It's not malarkey, damn it!' argued Jordan. 'All I've been hearin' is Felons' Apprehension Act, I'm sick of it.'

Lawless clinked his spoon on the side of his tin mug. 'Let's be waitin' until tonight and see what the guv and Sam have to say. Stuck in here at Treehard, it's hard for a body to know what the general feelin' of the public be.'

The afternoon dragged and so did the night. It was close to eleven o'clock and Daniel had been pacing the Treehard verandah for hours when Eve heard the awaited bird calls.

Daniel stood near the entrance, relief in his face and in the very attitude of his stance. He called happily, 'It's grand to see you, that it is!' as Alan and Sam issued from the passageway. 'What with the day passing like a slug over silt, it's been a wearing time, I assure you.'

'Now, now,' reproved Samuel, leaning down and cuffing Daniel affectionately on the shoulder, 'don't tell me it's ye as have been a worryin', Dan, now that's not like ye.'

The leader's gaze lifted to the verandah where Eve stood on the top step in the reflected light from the kitchen. She had combed her hair down and it lay in masses of soft curls over her shoulders. She was wearing her 'good' dress, the one she kept as special. Her face radiated happiness and there was a vigour in her that made her skin glow and gave her smile of welcome an effervescence.

She thought it a miracle that it was he who dismounted below and smiled up at her. He thought it a miracle that she stood on his doorstep smiling down at him.

Alan's feet had hardly touched the ground when Daniel was asking, 'Well? What did you determine? How is the lie of the land? What are people saying?'

'Steady, Danny, my friend,' Alan replied. 'It's a grim tale, but the short answer is that Ben Hall has been shot dead and the general feeling predicts little good for us.'

'Oh no!' groaned Lawless.

Daniel sighed. 'Ah me. Ben gone, eh? God rest his soul.'

Lawless and Jordan asked simultaneously, 'When? Where?'

'Now, ye two, leave the guv'nor be,' chided Sam. 'We've been on the road since dawn and ridden nigh on eighty-five miles today. We be tired, the horses be exhausted. First, we should put the animals to bed and then we'll tell ye all there is to tell.'

They had led two spare mounts to give their own horses respite from carrying them all day. When the horses had been fed and watered they all assembled in the kitchen.

Complicated emotions passed across Alan's face as he related the day's events. 'We took the northern trail from Treehard and when we gained the road, we swung north-west, by-passing Cowra, and made for the Canowindra district. There are more inns in that part of the country that we have not frequented, and I thought to get the opinions of the farmers and itinerants as well. We rode on the bush track to the tavern south of the gold mine near Idolwood Creek. That's one place we've not ventured near in all our years at Treehard.'

'I know the place, boss,' said Jordan. 'More like a big, one-roomed shack than an inn.'

'That's true,' confirmed Alan, 'as so many are.'

Sam nodded. 'Filled with lots o' miners, it were.'

'Yes, there were about fifteen or twenty men there. Sam brought up the question of the Act after we'd been there ten minutes or so, and the mood of those men was that it was about time something was done about the safety of the bush roads. As we moved on to the other taverns, their opinion was corroborated. The feeling was for the Act and against the bushrangers.'

'Why,' spoke up Sam, 'one young blood said he couldn't wait for the morrow when it became legal to shoot us on sight. I felt like hittin' the sod in the mouth, but restrained m'self. All I said was, "Would ye be knowin' a bushranger if ye looked one in the eye?" And he reckoned he would, makin' him a liar as well as bloodthirsty.'

'Gawd!' said Lawless. 'Ye've had a day of it all right. What about Ben Hall, guv?'

'Was he the only one killed?' interjected Eve.

'Yes, lass, he was alone, it seems. When Sam and I at last rode into Canowindra it was after one o'clock in the afternoon. The whole town was afire with the news of his death. He was shot yesterday morn at daybreak. Seems he was staying in a hut of a friend called Mick Connolly.'

'I know him, boss,' Jordan broke in, 'he's a half-caste, mother was an Abo; used to live in a shanty near Billabong creek, north-west o' Forbes.'

'Yes,' said Alan, 'that is the place Ben was caught.'

Jordan's eyes narrowed in contemplation as Sam's fist came down on the table in front of him. 'Sounds suspiciously like Connolly ratted on him to me.'

'Aye, me too,' agreed Lawless.

Alan shook his head. 'Whatever the truth, and we've heard a number of versions today, Ben Hall is dead. Gilbert and Dunn were not with him. Apparently he was alone in the hut when a black tracker called Billy Dargin led the troopers in. He died in a hail of bullets.'

'Yes,' Samuel added. 'Some of the blokes were sayin' there were more than thirty bullets counted in him.'

Lawless shook his head. 'Gawd!'

They all looked at each other in silence for a few seconds. Eve shivered. Thirty bullets in him. Her eyes were alight with the fear she felt when she looked over to Alan. He was gazing steadily at her, an expression of encouragement on his mouth.

Daniel spoke first. 'No doubt, we'll be learning soon enough if this Connolly did inform. If he did, he'll not need to be living in a shanty by a creek, the reward money will see to that.'

The others murmured in agreement.

'Ben was not a bad bloke really,' stated Lawless in his straight-forward fashion.

'Yes,' said Alan thoughtfully, 'he was a cut above the rest.'

Eve shivered again. Rutherford Blake was having his day.

Later, when Treehard was quiet, Alan lay thinking, as he often did. His great responsibility was to keep the five people under his roof, safe. He did not feel fear for himself, fear had never been Alan's companion; but he felt something related to it for them. Things were changing in New South Wales. Perhaps if they were careful, as they had always been, the Act would have no effect upon them. No one knew the whereabouts of Treehard Hill and very few law-abiding citizens knew their faces; less than ten in the whole colony. That was except for Jordan; some knew him for he had grown up in the bush, farmed in the bush, and Jordan unfortunately would still want to go abroad. The lad needed the outlet of female company. Alan understood that, but he would have to make sure that Jordan did not see the same girl too often from now on. It would be best if he could talk the boy into lessening his visits to Bridget at Wattamondara.

He continued contemplating for a long time, his hands behind his head, listening to the breathing of Daniel beside him. For a long time now he had been thinking of one day making a run for it to Western Australia. There was pastoral land opening up north of Perth, and no one was looking for them there, over two thousand miles away. They would all like the farming life, especially Danny. But now that he had Eve to take care of, he was not so sure. Another thought was taking shape in his head, for today he had seen something that had stimulated a fresh idea. By the time he drifted into slumber, the idea had formulated into a new plan, one of vision . . . one that would give them a life of real freedom, far from New South Wales.

The next morning Eve came to Alan as he was shoeing Freedom. He looked up at her and smiled. 'You want me, lass?'

She had a quivering feeling around her heart as she smiled in reply. 'I do. Will your friend Womballa be back on the plateau yet?'

'He left shortly after he made you well. Yes, I think by now they will all have returned.'

'Then at last I can thank him for saving my life.'

And so they went riding in the tranquil, autumn afternoon, leaving Samuel and Lawless in the vegetable garden, Daniel pondering over the evening meal, and Jordan whittling in the shade of the gums.

Alan rode Waterloo, for Freedom had carried him much of the immense distance of yesterday. Eve rode Milford, Daniel's mare, a compliant, amenable horse. They travelled south through the bush for perhaps twenty minutes and then began slowly rising towards the plateau. They went at an easy pace and reined in to rest briefly when they gained the roof of the tableland.

She sat gazing at him.

'Why do you look at me like that?'

'What are you going to do?' she asked.

'Going to do?'

'Yes, now that Rutherford Blake is gaining the upper hand. He seems to be closing in on the bushrangers. Ben Hall is dead.'

'Ah, lass, it's not for you to concern yourself.'

'Alan. I know you are concerned and so . . .'

'Yes?'

'So . . . I am too,' she finished.

He smiled. 'Are you telling me you feel what I feel?'

She did not answer immediately. When she did, it was very softly. 'Sometimes, you know I do.'

He made no reply and after a few seconds she said, 'Perhaps we should try to leave the country.'

His eyes lifted quickly to hers. He was contemplating her in the way that made her feel he could see inside her. She felt wonderfully uncomfortable. 'You are very astute,' he answered, and he leaned towards her and took up her hand. 'Perhaps we should. I am thinking that way and there are things I want to talk over with you soon.' He lifted her hand and brushed it with his lips.

'All right.'

He let go her hand and pointed through the sparse gum trees to the left, urging Freedom onwards.

Eve had never seen an Aboriginal camp, so it was with interest and a little trepidation that fifteen minutes later she saw through the trees ahead six or seven dark brown bodies appear as if out of nowhere. They had recognised Alan and so made themselves visible to him. He lifted his hand and two or three signalled back. Then leaping and shouting came a child of ten or eleven.

Alan laughed. 'It's Odoono,' he explained to Eve. 'He's my little friend and companion on my visits here. He's a quick-witted lad and speaks some English.'

'Fletcher! You come! Good! It are good. We no see long time.' The child came running to the side of Waterloo in fearless fashion. He looked with interest at Eve and pointed at her as Alan leaned down and took the willing boy up into his arms and placed him on the saddle.

Through the trees, silently to right and left, Eve saw people all naked, making pace with the horses as they rode by. Some had never seen a white woman up close, and there were disconcerted looks and much mumbling.

When Alan dismounted and lifted the voluble Odoono to the ground, the tribesfolk crept forward from behind the trees and the closest *gunyahs* to look. Their dark eyes were round in wonder, and only after Alan had called to many of them by name did they come within a few yards of the curiosity that was the European woman.

Then there was a hail of welcome. The closest bodies fell back and separated, and Eve looked into the face of the man who had saved her life. He gestured welcome, his thick lips parted in pleasure, his white beard resting on his chest. A wonderfully eccentric figure wearing the hat Alan had given him and the hunting knife strapped round his waist above his long thin legs. There were three or four of his family clustered behind him. He moved forward, hand outstretched. 'Ah, Clever Fletcher, again you come, *waminda*.'

Alan took his hand and shook it in the English manner. 'Womballa, my *waminda*, I come to bring you the woman you make well with good medicine.' He turned to the other Aborigines and praised Womballa, saying that the tribal elder's good medicine had saved Eve.

The old man smiled broadly showing his line of broken teeth. The members of his tribe might be timid in the presence of this woman but not he; had he not been with her spirit in the Dreaming? There was a gleam in his black eyes and mirth in his face as he said, '*Merinda*, Clever Fletcher, *merinda*.'

Alan smiled and answered, 'Yes.' For Womballa had called Eve pretty.

Then the old man beckoned Alan and Eve to follow him.

The whole tribe, having been given the example, came along in unison. They were more vociferous now, for the white woman evidently was not to be feared.

Outside Womballa's *gunyah*, Alan and Eve sat on the ground beside the old man and the other tribal elders, while Datta and Mulgatta and Womballa's other sons and daughters, their husbands and wives made a rough circle round them. The rest of the tribe looked on, Odoono standing proudly behind Alan.

There was movement behind them and something that looked like a long, thin hollowed-out tree branch was handed through the throng and given Womballa. It was covered in all manner of design and he raised it to his mouth. Eve looked questioningly at Alan and he whispered, 'It's a didgeridoo, a musical instrument.'

Womballa filled up his cheeks with air, until they were like two round balls, and began to blow into it as the most amazing stream of rising and falling sound began, and the whole tribe started a soft chant that ebbed and flowed with the sound from the didgeridoo. After a minute or two, the dark, naked bodies began to sway. The swaying lasted perhaps five or six minutes and came abruptly to an end.

Eve automatically began to applaud. Then she stopped for there was total silence. They were all staring at her, their wide faces filled with interest.

Never had they seen anyone clap hands in these circumstances before and they were all curious. A few pointed and gestured.

Alan explained as best he could that what Eve had done was a display of appreciation and gratitude, and Womballa nodded in understanding.

Later, when Alan took six pots of honey from his saddlebags and gave them to Womballa, the old man took them and handed them to Datta and Mulgatta before he turned back to Alan and clapped his hands.

Alan smiled with pleasure.

Then the whole tribe began to clap and in thanks he dipped his head to them.

To say farewell, Womballa donned the leather coat Alan had given him. Side by side they walked to the edge of the encampment, while all around milled the tribe. Enthralled, Eve watched the two friends say goodbye. There they stood on the rocky ground of the plateau, the most incongruous of friends, and yet the most compatible. Alan took Womballa's hand in the European manner, saying, 'Goodbye, my dear *waminda*.'

Womballa shook Alan's hand as he had learned to do and said, 'Clever Fletcher, *yanniwan*. You watch day and night. Stay safe.' And then he lifted his dark, calloused hand and gently touched Alan's face. The movement was tender, even loving, and Eve fancied that the tribal elder's inscrutable eyes clouded over for a moment or two.

Alan drew his eyes away from Womballa's and shook hands with the other tribal elders. Then he took Datta's hand. The old woman giggled with amusement.

Odoono, leading Waterloo by the bridle, had kept up his volatile chatter all the while and he tugged Alan's coat saying, 'You come back soon, Fletcher. You come back soon, bring honey! Yes.'

Eve stood awkwardly, uncertain what to say.

'Say *apo*, lass, it means goodbye,' Alan prompted her. 'That's all that is necessary.'

But she wanted to say more. She looked into Womballa's eyes, making a conscious effort to remember them. It was a significant moment for her. She put out her hand and he shook it as he had done with Alan. She did not let go, but grasped it in both of hers, and he, quick to new ways, grasped with both of his. Later, when she thought on it she was honoured to have touched him. She said, 'Thank you, thank you, Womballa. I will remember you always, all my life. *Apo*, thank you.'

Womballa unhesitatingly answered, '*Apo*, Clever Fletcher woman.'

Alan ruffled Odoono's hair affectionately before they mounted their horses and rode away, waving to the cries of farewell that sounded after them.

As they crossed the densely wooded plateau and began the gradual descent to the valley, Eve was thinking. A short time ago she had rescued Jordan from falling to his death, and only yesterday Lawless had delivered her from the brown snake, and now, twenty-four hours later, she had met the man who a few months ago had saved her from dying. Life could be extinguished in a moment. She looked over to Alan. How she loved him! How long did they have? These wonderful days they were spending together, how long did they have?

They had not gone far when Alan turned Waterloo onto a natural track that led through the thick bush to the east.

'Where do we go?' called Eve.

'Follow, it is worth seeing.'

Five minutes later, the track ended against what looked like dense scrub. He dismounted and she followed. He tied the horses loosely to an enormous banksia.

He led the way on foot over the rough ground. They had to scramble across a few small boulders, through undergrowth and trees. Then as they rounded some rocks, quite suddenly the bush opened up. She stood still in delight. Like some conjurer's instant illusion, a beautiful grassy glade lay before them.

The plateau towered above to her right, a vast rocky image. Down its face a small waterfall trickled into a creek a few yards from where she stood. The water was so clear, so transparent, she could see vividly the diverse browns and yellows of the smooth stones at the bottom. The last of the summer wild flowers grew here, determined, tiny blue blossoms dotting the scrub all around, and the scent of mint bushes was strong in the air. There was an atmosphere of harmony, the serene quality of being untouched. It made her feel released from care and she laughed with pure pleasure. She turned round in a circle looking all about. 'What a truly beautiful place it is. I don't think I've seen anything quite like it before.'

'Yes,' he agreed. 'There is almost a sense of Nirvana if one remains long enough.' Then he smiled in remembrance and added, 'Although here is more rugged, it reminds me of a part of my father's land by Long Moss House. There was a green, mossy hill that towered just as the tableland does above us now, and a stream that ran down the hillside into a clear, rocky pool where I used to play.'

She was watching his face. 'England must be beautiful,' she remarked softly.

'It is.' Then he turned away and looked down the creek. 'But England is my past, this land is my present.'

'And the future?' she questioned his back.

'Who can answer that?'

She ached to hold him then, to move to him and to hold him. She wanted to say positive things about the future, their future; that now she did not care about convention or what was deemed proper; that she wanted to be with him always, whatever the future held. It was exquisite agony this being alone with him, this wanting desperately to hold him and love him. She moved closer and spoke softly. 'Perhaps the future will be kind to us. The fates have seen fit to throw us together. Who would have believed, a year ago, that I would be with you now?'

He turned back to her and there was a coldness in him now. A tingle of fear passed through her. She was reminded of the day in the Bathurst park when he had rejected her.

'Alan,' she said quietly, 'what is it? What's wrong?'

'We should not be alone together.' There was an edge to his voice. 'It was wrong of me to bring you here.'

'But why? It is so beautiful and I want to be alone with you.'

'That is the very reason, don't you see?'

'Then I don't understand.'

His tone was distant. 'You are another man's wife, Eve Wakeman, and you always will be.'

They were standing no more than two feet apart, their eyes locked. The seconds passed in silence.

Then she lifted her hand to his face, and when he did not draw away she said, 'I cannot help what has happened in the past. While I am responsible for many mistakes, and I acknowledge them, all I know is that I love you now, have loved you since the moment I first saw you.'

The late afternoon sun was filtering through the trees. As the sun descended, the light in the glade seemed to intensify momentarily, and for a few seconds the two figures were caught in relief against the shimmering verticals of the sunbeams through the trees behind them. There was something unreal about the moment. Dream-like. Eve felt as if the bush around them disappeared. She was aware only of Alan and the radiating light around them. In his eyes she saw the longing, open, obvious. She lifted her other hand to his face and drew down his head. 'You hold back for many reasons and I know them all . . . and I love you,' she said, covering his mouth with her own.

For a second or two, it was her kiss only; he still withheld.

Then the response to her travelled through his veins like a stream of lava. Gone was his restraint of all the months. As their lips joined, the impact assaulted all her senses. The innocent glade learned the urgency of desire as Alan locked her in his arms, pressing her to him.

At last, at last. She felt his hands moving down across her body, demanding, greedy, wanting her. He was holding her so tightly, she could feel the rippling tension of desire in him as if he were merging with her, body into body. A rush of powerful elation churned through her. She was never more aware, more alive than now. This was what she had dreamed of, waited for, longed for. The feel of him down the length of her, his arms, his body enveloping her.

The wonderful smell of him filled her senses, Alan, the clean, bold smell of the bush, of courage and sunshine, the essence of him. Her skin touched his, her hands were in his hair, on his neck. Her lips opened to the pressure of his, opened gladly, hungrily. His tongue tasted the inside of her mouth, searching, meeting. Know me, Alan, know me, love me.

She made a joyous sound in her throat, the earthy, voluptuous sound of desire, of urgency and victory, and he echoed it from deep within his soul. Sweet sensations exploded in her breasts and her nipples rose inside her dress in wanton expectation.

The shock hit her abruptly when he broke from her. His eyes were clouded with yearning and his voice was thick with the need of her, but he resisted. 'No. We must leave this place.' Suddenly, he grabbed her hand and, turning from her, pulled her after him back towards the horses.

She was oblivious of the rocky ground, the scrub, the birds calling in the trees, nothing but Alan filled her consciousness. She was disappointed, hurt, thwarted, so much did she want him.

At the horses, he paused. She could see the battle going on inside him; his pupils dilated, his mouth set. Then with hands that actually trembled a little, he took hold of her and helped her up into the saddle.

They rode home in silence, and when he lifted her down to the ground from Milford, he still did not speak.

'Well, good morning, my son,' Daniel greeted Alan with a wide smile as he entered the kitchen a little before half past six o'clock the following day.

'Good morning, Danny. Is anyone else awake?'

'No, they all be abed still, but I will wake them soon.'

'Before you do, I want you to hear something. Come outside, will you?'

Daniel followed out onto the small verandah where the autumn morning sun was steeping Treehard Hill in a flood of yellow. The trunks of the great eucalypts reflected a lemon light all around, and rays of sunshine made golden stripes between the trees.

'Ah me,' exclaimed Daniel, 'that does my old heart good to look upon.'

Alan patted him gently on the back. 'Danny, when Sam and I were in Canowindra the day before yesterday, we were there only half an hour, but in that time we learned something of great use. We had just made our exit from the Cat and Fiddle Hotel, and immediately next door is the mail coach depot. The coach was about to depart. We walked over and stood with a few others watching them making ready. The driver was about to mount up when he turned to the guard and said, "My God, what with the news of Ben Hall's death, I clean forgot to get the pay slip."

' "What pay slip?" asked the guard, for apparently he was new to the route. And the driver answered with pride in his voice that it was for the Bathurst bank where he was authorised to pick up the pay for the fifty police, forty troopers and all the magistrates, prison and Government officials and employees stationed in the Central, Western and North-western Districts.

'The guard, obviously impressed, asked, "How often do we do this?"

'The driver continued in boastful fashion that they did it six times a year: January, March, May, July, September and November. He said the money is held in Bathurst over the first weekend in those months, and then distributed. He continued something like, "Our run is Bathurst Orange. We picks up all the money and two more guards in Bathurst on the Monday morn, and delivers it to Orange for noon time." Evidently in Orange the pay gets divided and goes to all the other settlements to the north and west.'

Alan's eyes met Daniel's in the sun of the autumn morning and he smiled at his friend.

For a few moments there was total silence and then Daniel asked, 'All that Government pay, two months of pay for how many?'

'Perhaps two hundred.'

Dan calculated for a minute. 'It could be sixteen hundred pounds. A lot of bank notes, Alan, son.'

'Yes, and added to the gold left from Theresa Town it will be a surfeit for six passages to America and freedom. For that's the destination I'm contemplating. Have been for a long time now. From what I read in the *Lachlan Miner* in Canowindra, the confederate armies have all but lost the war. It shall soon be over. It means a new start for that great country and we can all have new starts along with it.'

Daniel sucked in his breath in surprise. 'Oh, Alan, son,' he whispered. Then he repeated, 'Oh, Alan, son.'

Alan leaned forward. 'That's my plan, Danny. To take the coach in July when it makes its next run.'

'Aye, lad, it sounds a good and workable idea. To take only from the Government, once more, as is your way, but it'll be dangerous in the execution as they all are.' He looked down at the backs of his hands.

'Daniel, my old partner?' Alan said softly and Dan raised his eyes. He could not disguise his apprehension although he truly tried. Alan was looking deep into the pale eyes in front of him. 'I ask you this without the others present, for the journey will be the hardest on you. You *will* make the journey with me, won't you?'

The older man found it hard to answer. He swallowed. 'It will break my heart to leave Treehard.'

'I will not go without you.'

Daniel sighed. 'Ah, then I must come with you, my son, and that's the way of it.'

CHAPTER TWENTY-EIGHT

'All great changes are irksome to the human mind, especially those which are attended with great dangers and uncertain effects.'

'Letter to James Warren', John Adams, 1735–1826.

Alan looked up from the map he studied on the kitchen table. It was a detailed drawing of a section of the road between Bathurst and Orange. His finger rested on the spot where a wooden bridge, only the width of a carriage, had been built across a stream known as Kettle's Creek. At the same time, beside him, Samuel's head lifted from poring over the map.

The strains of singing coming from across the yard drifted in to them:

> To Jack Robertson we say,
> You've been leading us astray,
> And we'll never go afarming any more,
> For it's easier duffing cattle
> On a little piece of land
> Far away from the Numerella shore.

Alan smiled. 'Sixteen years since we were brought to this land and now our lad from the Rookery sings political songs in the Australian bush.'

'True, guv'nor,' Samuel agreed. 'Lawless knows more of this land than the one that bred him.'

'And when our plan comes to fruition, there shall be Eve's homeland for him to come to know.'

A stern expression asserted itself on Sam's face and he rapped with his fist on the table. 'Aye, guv'nor, what ye say is all very well, but it's this job ye must be doin' successfully first, and I don't like ye doin' it with just three. I should be along.'

'Sam, don't grumble. It's very important to me that you remain here. You see, my dear friend, if anything does go amiss then I know I can rely on you to mobilise Daniel and Eve. To take the gold and get them on board a ship to America. I cannot stress this too strongly. Don't you see that, my friend?'

Sam's chin wrinkled and his mouth grew tight. 'All right,' he admitted at last. 'I do. But if anything goes wrong with ye and the lads, do you really think I'd have the heart to go on?'

'Ah, Samuel, but I would be relying on you.'

'Life would have little meanin' without ye in it, but I would do what ye wanted to the best of my ability, as ye know full well I would.' Then the little man stood from the table. 'And if ye don't mind, Alan Fletcher, I'd rather not be thinkin' along those lines in any case, for it's six passages as we will be buyin' on that long voyage to America.'

'That's the spirit, lad, and all the more reason I'll need you here at Treehard to have the bags packed ready to leave when we return.'

Sam managed to grin. 'And as far as my mobilisin' Mistress Eve, why, as she'd be goin' along with ye to rob this darn coach herself if she had half a chance, I fail to see where you get the idea she needs takin' care of.'

Eve had entered the door as Sam finished speaking and she stood smiling behind him. 'You are absolutely right, Sam, I'm not a child.'

Amusement rippled across Alan's mouth as he looked from one to the other. 'You two make a formidable pair.'

Behind Eve came Jordan and Daniel. Eve and Jordan both carried .31 inch calibre Colt pocket pistols and put them on the what-not beside the door as they entered. Daniel had been watching them shoot targets down at the southern end of Treehard where Alan had taught Eve to fire a rifle when she had insisted she wanted to be able to help with the collection of food. She had become a quite reasonable shot and the most recent time Lawless, Jordan and Alan had gone out hunting, she had accompanied them.

Lawless was the last to enter, he had taken a quick look down over the hill from Nelson's Boulder and now he joined them at the kitchen table. Alan explained the method of operation he, Lawless and Jordan would use one month hence, the first weekend in July. After much deliberation, he had decided to take the Government payroll coach that he and Sam had learned about in Canowindra. As always he was explicit. The plan was methodical and precise. The coach was due to leave Bathurst at eight o'clock on Monday morning, 3 July, and should reach Kettle's Creek some time after nine o'clock; on a Monday morning, it would probably be the only vehicle.

Alan had chosen Kettle's Creek for a series of reasons. There was a backwoods track not far from the creek running south three miles through the bush allowing a fast getaway from the area. And while

486

it was within ten miles of Bathurst, and Alan did not like to be so near to the headquarters of Rutherford Blake, the bridge was unquestionably the ideal place to bail up the vehicle. The coach would slow down almost to a crawling pace to cross the narrow bridge and, immediately beyond, the land rose in a long hill allowing no acceleration. This would allow Alan and the others to circumnavigate a huge rock formation twenty-five yards from the crossing, and come up directly behind the coach, easily surprising the guard on horseback and, providing the others were not heroes, it would be relatively simple to take them all.

Sitting near the hearth listening to Alan, Eve found herself considering her life and how it had brought her to this room. She reflected on how lucky she was, how lucky they all were, to have Alan in their lives.

'And as always,' he was saying, 'our argument is with the authorities, not the individuals. We shoot at no man except in self-defence, and even then we fire to wound only. We carry arms to cause submission, not to use. We have never yet resorted to violence. This time must be no exception. Do we all understand?'

There were affirmative sounds round the table.

For the next weeks, Alan went over the plan daily with Lawless and Jordan until each man could recite his part with total comprehension.

At last, the Thursday evening before their Friday departure arrived.

Daniel had prepared a special dinner of pigeon pie and dumplings, and to follow he had made a bread pudding with fresh milk, a real treat at Treehard. Jordan had brought the milk home two days before, after he had been down to Wattamondara with the intention of spending the night with Bridget.

The visit had caused some dissension in the Treehard household, for Alan had not wanted Jordan to go. He had finally allowed it after Samuel had taken up Jordan's cause.

'The boy is twenty-nine, guv,' Sam had said, seeking Alan out in the confines of the stable where he was polishing his saddle. 'He has not been with a woman since you came back from Goulburn in April, and he has not been with Bridget since March. It's near to four months.'

Alan continued working. 'Samuel. Four months? We have known men of his age who went without a woman for four years, even fourteen, so what argument is four months?'

But after Sam promised to deliver Jordan to the tavern himself and straight back the following day, Alan relented.

'Thanks, guv, the lad will be right happy, he will.'

But Jordan had returned unhappy.

In fact he had come home abashed, solemn and hurt. Things were no longer the same at Wattamondara.

'The only good thing to come out of this here visit is the fresh milk they got, and that's a fact,' Daniel said later.

Lawless's opinion was a little stronger. 'He shouldn't have been goin' down there and we all know it. He be a selfish perisher at times, and Sam be wrong in takin' his part.'

Eve said nothing, for, while she agreed with Lawless that Jordan seemed to do as he pleased at times, she could understand how he wanted to see the girl he cared for.

Jordan could not reconcile what had occurred. He communicated very little. It was Sam who told the story.

When they had arrived at Wattamondara it had been a cold grey day and was settling into a sterile dusk. Sam remained on horseback at the side of the inn, while Jordan went around the back. During his wait for the all clear, Sam's eye was taken by a number of posters nailed to a new billboard under the awning.

He felt a tremor in his chest as he read, **'Wanted Dead or Alive!'** The reward for Alan's capture had gone to two thousand pounds! Each of the rest of them were one thousand, and so was 'the Jockey', young Johnny Dunn. A man Sam had never heard of, called Frederick Ward, alias 'Captain Thunderbolt', was five hundred pounds. Old Joe Daily and Kenny Dawson were there at twelve hundred, and a couple of others for smaller sums. But the principal surprise was that such a notice board would be attached to the wall of Henry Lyon's Wattamondara Tavern.

Suddenly he heard yelling and shouting from inside the inn. He jumped down from Milford and came rapidly through the back door to see Jordan holding a chair up above his head, another lay broken against the wall where he had thrown it.

There was only one drinker in the barroom, and he was watching the display apprehensively.

Bridget was standing with her father behind the bar. Henry Lyon was speaking. 'Blast it, Jordan, things are different now, can't you see Bridget doesn't want you here.'

Jordan brought the chair heavily down in frustration. It clattered loudly and lay on its side. 'You tell me!' he shouted, pointing at the girl, 'you tell me yourself, Bridget!'

Sam's head did not come as high as Jordan's shoulder but he moved speedily and took his sleeve. 'That's it, Jordan, laddie. Settle. Ye've naught to gain with force.'

'Stay out of it, Sam!' He shook Sam off like a nuisance fly and strode to the bar.

'Speak to me, damn it, Bridgy! Please. Too bloody good for me now, are you?'

'Jordan, I'm sorry.' Bridget burst into tears.

The young man leaped around the bar and Henry Lyon barred the way between the bushranger and his daughter.

'Don't, Jordan, cut it out, she's confused,' the publican pleaded as the big man thrust him backwards. 'Don't you see what you're doin' by just bein' here? If the bloody traps learn of this . . . fifteen years gaol! You're a menace. Go away and leave us alone for Christ's sake!'

'Jesus!' cried Jordan in desperation.

For a few moments, there was silence, broken only by Bridget's sobs coming from behind her father, then Jordan lost control and smashed his fist into the publican's face. The man dropped to the floor and Bridget screamed.

Jordan made a loud, frustrated sound, and the drinker who had stayed at the bar until now hurried out.

Simultaneously, Henry's wife came running in from the next room followed by Christina and Marilyn, both wide-eyed and frightened. Edna Lyon shrieked when she saw her husband on the floor.

Sam knew it was time to take charge. He lifted his rifle up over the bar and pushed Jordan back away from Henry with the side of the barrel. 'That's it, Jordan. Move out, laddie. We've done enough damage, here.'

And Jordan, tired at last of the scene, moved as he was directed.

'I'm real sorry, Henry . . . Edna,' Sam said.

'Just go, Sam, and leave us alone!' Edna Lyon pleaded.

The last thing Sam heard Henry call after them was, 'Tell Alan, we're sorry too, but it's different now, everything's different!'

When they had mounted their horses Jordan looked over and noticed the milk urn on the verandah steps. He immediately dismounted.

'What the devil are ye doin' now?' Sam asked in agitation.

Jordan did not answer. He took his water bottle from his saddle bag and dipped it into the urn and filled it with milk. Then, wrapping it in his large handkerchief, remounted and rode off.

They arrived back at Treehard in the dark of the cold winter's night.

When Sam had explained everything, Alan took Jordan aside. 'Jordan lad,' he counselled, 'don't brood over what has happened.

Henry and his daughter are not to blame. Circumstances are now beyond their control. They act out of fear.'

Jordan's mouth turned down. 'Yeah and you knew it. How is it that you always know things?'

Alan took Jordan by both shoulders. 'Laddie, I don't. But as I have had a longer time to observe human behaviour, perhaps my predictions come closer to reality.'

'It's not fair, boss. It's just not bloody fair.'

'Life isn't, lad, so let us leave it there. We have much to accomplish in the days ahead.' He smiled encouragingly. 'Just think, if all goes well there is a time coming when you will be free of the scourge of being a bushranger, and will be able to make what friends you like.'

Jordan nodded thoughtfully and attempted a smile.

Since then, there had been a flurry of preparation for the departure to Kettle's Creek, and Thursday had been spent in making sure everything was ready.

The day had been cold, the evening was colder, the southern winter having begun; there was a bitter wind whipping up the valley pushing wispy streaks of cloud across a waxing moon in the deep rose sky.

Alan's preparations were finished, and now he was in a clear patch of grass between the trees, doing his calisthenic exercises. It was a practice he had developed in his naval days when the confines of a ship had checked his riding and walking.

Eve was standing on the verandah. She could not see Alan but she knew exactly where he was. Behind her in the kitchen, Danny lifted his pigeon pie from the hob, the aroma floating appetisingly in the air around her. The others she could see through the stable door, moving in the lantern light.

She tapped her fingernails on the railing. She was here, and he was here, and tomorrow, he would be gone, into terrible danger.

She hurried down the steps and across the yard.

Out of the corner of his eye, Daniel watched her go, a tiny, knowing expression appearing at the edges of his mouth.

Alan in his cotton shirtsleeves, warm after the exertion, saw her coming towards him through the trees in the dying day. She was wrapped against the wind. If only he had known, his reaction was similar to the one John Stuart had experienced when he first saw her in the Bathurst park.

She walked swiftly through the gums. She was thinking about the afternoon in the bush glade, and she knew the titanic struggle that had gone on inside him that day. During their walks since in the soft Treehard twilight, he had never referred to it and she knew why.

490

Oh Alan, what does it matter? I love you. I'm sure you love me. This whole human life is so uncertain, so precarious. I only need you. I am ready, there is no need to hold back in consideration of me, I don't need that. If I have beaten the ghosts of Lake and the miscarriage, and the frustrations of a ruined marriage, why can't you? Why cannot you just love me?

She came up to within three feet of him, her ardent, brown eyes regarding him decidedly.

'Alan . . . I . . . there is something I want to say. You go tomorrow. It will be terribly dangerous.' She dropped her gaze to her hands. She twisted her fingers and rubbed her nails. Then she lifted her eyes back to his and as her words came slowly, deliberately, he recognised again with a ripple of love, the indomitable strength living in her soul. 'Father once said to me that there was a time for truth, and that the recognition of it brings freedom tantamount to flying with the angels. He said other things that I try to live by, but the truth, I think, I have often evaded.'

She took a step closer to him. He did not move away but his look asked her not to come nearer.

'Why are you saying this?' he said.

'Surely, you know.'

'Eve.' His voice was cheerless and he elongated the 'e' sound as he sometimes did. 'What is this truth you talk of?'

'The truth that is "us",' she answered.

'I do not intentionally misunderstand, but what do you mean?'

She took a deliberate step closer and took hold of his arms. He did not move. 'Tomorrow, you go to take a payroll coach. I wait here powerlessly, I know you will have it no other way . . .'

'You are right, I will not.'

'So, I am forced to bide here, until you come back . . . or do not come back.'

'I always come back.'

'Yes, yes, that has been so and I hope with all my heart that it is true this time, that you come back and we all get away to America and freedom. But if you do not, in case you do not . . . I must tell you.'

'What?' The light in his eyes somehow intensified, reflecting the last rays of the departing day, and the wind, which until now had not found the little clearing, whistled in the trees.

Eve shivered and suddenly her eyes welled with tears.

His voice was tender now. 'What must you tell me, my Eve? That you want me to hold you? Kiss your mouth? That you want me to love you physically as I do mentally? Because if I do not do these things and I do not come back to Treehard, our love will not be complete?' He looked at her . . . into her, and she could contain the tears no longer.

'Yes,' she said as they broke over her lids. 'I want all those things, for you are the truth in my life, and the truth is love.' She continued to hold his arms as if never to let him go.

He lifted his hands and now he too held her arms. 'Eve,' he answered and once more he lengthened the 'e', a throaty sound. 'Don't you realise how much I want these things you want? But not now. Not yet. Not here. I *will* come back. I will take you away from Treehard, and when we have left these shores, I will love you as I have craved to love you, from the day I found you in the bush.'

'Then kiss me . . . as you kissed me in the glade.'

'No . . . not as I kissed you in the glade.'

His hands slid beneath her jacket, around her waist to nestle in the small of her back. Her world filled with his eyes, his thick sun-lightened hair, his brown skin, and the feel of him as he leaned down to meet her. Slowly, like the dew settles on the petals of a flower at sunrise, he touched her mouth with his, covering her lips with his own. Seconds passed in vague glory as the all-encompassing pledge of love flowed from him. It was for her and only her, this tenderness, this benevolence, this pure love. Never had she received anything like this, never had she known there was anything to receive like this. A sensation of perfect peace spread through her entire being. It was the most loving contact she could ever recall experiencing in her life.

When he lifted his mouth from hers, he said, 'Now, dry your eyes, my darling.'

She smiled gently, coming back from the blissful infinity. 'I have heard what I wanted to hear, and felt what I had no idea I could feel.'

As night descended, he drew her arm through his and they walked in silence back through the trees.

The following morning, Alan, Lawless and Jordan left Treehard.

It was an optimistic farewell, all talking of the future and their lives in America.

Dan hugged Alan close, his time-worn arms wrapped tightly round him for a long time, so long that Alan could actually feel the beat of the older man's heart. Dan's expression was of deep and lasting love, admiration and trust and when he stepped back to look at Alan, his eyes were wet but his words were confident. 'We will be expecting you back, sonny, sometime during the night on Monday. I'll have the fire going and a billy on the boil.' He mustered a smile.

An uncomfortable shudder ran through Alan as he answered, 'Yes, Danny, my dearest, old partner, I'm sure you will.'

When he turned to Eve, she said, 'I will miss you every moment.'

'And I you,' he replied. Then, for the first time ever, he touched her intentionally in front of the others. He stepped forward and held her a few seconds in his arms as his lips brushed her fair curls.

Samuel slapped them all on the back and was giving stern instructions even as they rode away. 'Now, mateys, remember on Monday, I shall be sitting up in Nelson's Boulder from twilight onwards. Call loudly, Lawless, and for heaven's sake make good time home, as I dinna want to be in that cold hole all night!'

Soon, they had all entered the tunnel, and Sam turned away.

'Aren't you going to the lookout to watch them down the hill, Sam?' Eve asked.

'No, I'm goin' to the garden for a while. I'll go to the lookout later.'

'Well, I'm for watching them now,' Daniel said turning to Eve.

'Yes, Daniel, I'm for watching them now, too.'

Dan took Eve's arm and together they walked into the tunnel to Nelson's Boulder.

CHAPTER TWENTY-NINE

'While that for which all virtue now is sold,
And almost every vice – almighty gold.'
'Epistle to Elizabeth, Countess of Rutland', Ben Jonson,
1572–1637.

Jordan rode behind Alan and Lawless in silence as they made the long descent down the hill to the valley. His mind was in turmoil.

He was still hurt over the events of Tuesday night. He had been so looking forward to that soft bed in the back room where he had lain many times with Bridget, the smooth touch of her skin and her dark, full nipples pressed against him. He could almost taste the wetness of her mouth now. He sighed noisily. The bitch, turning sour on him just because the bloody traps had her and her family scared. It wasn't fair! A man's whole life was changed. God! They could shoot now, anybody could shoot a bushranger on sight! It was awful. If only he weren't an outlaw!

His eyes rested on Alan's back. The boss. So flamin' forgivin' all the time. If only he had never met him. Then, he would still be a man with no price on his head. The others were all convicts, for God's sake! It was natural for them to be outside the law, whereas he had never been in gaol. It wasn't right that he could be shot on sight. It wasn't right his women were turnin' against him.

Sam had said that there were two thousand pounds on the boss's head now. Imagine that, a bloody fortune! On Monday next, the whole payroll wasn't goin' to be that much. Two hundred men's wages for two whole months, and it wasn't as much as what the boss was worth on his flamin' own. And the rest of them, Lawless, Sam, Daniel and himself, worth a thousand pounds each! God! The lot of them were worth six thousand pounds!

Jordan rode on, feeling dizzy just contemplating the amount.

That night they made camp on a small tributary of the Belubula River some twelve miles south of the pretty township of Carcoar, where, in November 1863, Johnny Vane of the Hall gang had talked to Father McCarthy and been induced to accompany the priest and give himself up in Bathurst.

They slept well, for the wind dropped with the coming of the night, and the temperature climbed marginally. They were in the middle of nowhere, as Lawless put it, so there was little need for a watch. Nevertheless, Alan mounted one to keep the fire burning and an eye out for anything untoward. Snakes were unlikely on a winter's night, but there was still the slight chance of a bush animal blundering into the camp. He took first duty from ten o'clock to one o'clock; Jordan the second from one to four, and Lawless, the deepest sleeper, took four o'clock to sunrise, around the hour of seven.

Alan woke a little after three o'clock feeling cold. The fire had gone out and Jordan, who was on watch, was deeply asleep. Alan woke him and stoked up the fire.

'I couldn't help it, boss, really,' the young man argued. 'And in any case we're in the middle of bloody nowhere.'

'Jordan, listen to me. I know we're far from any settlement and there is no chance of discovery here, but that is not the issue. We keep watches for other reasons and you know them well. Now, turn in and I shall stay until it's time for Lawless to take over.'

Saturday morning was cold, and a fine film of frost covered the grass in the low-lying areas when they stoked up the fire to boil the billy for breakfast.

'Where will we camp tonight, guv?' Lawless asked sipping his tea.

Jordan raised his head from his plate of damper and grinned. He had regained his humour and forgotten the incident in the night. 'I reckon we could camp right at the spot, boss, there'll be no one around on a Sunday.'

Alan smiled. 'Yes, lad, we probably could. But we shall take the precaution of removing ourselves a mile or so.'

Lawless laughed. 'Aye, that would be a jest indeed, Jordan, old chap. Us campin' by the boulders at Kettle's Creek and the only person out for a Sunday afternoon ride happens along . . . a flamin' trap.' Lawless stood up and, taking a mock serious pose, pointed solemnly at his companions. 'And who be ye gentlemen and why are ye campin' here?' Hands on hips, he continued. 'Ah, sergeant, we be the Fletcher band and we are waitin' to pay our respects to the payroll coach comin' by in the mornin', so here, sit ye down and we'll tell ye all about it. By the way, how does dear Sir Rutherford these days?'

Alan and Jordan were laughing as he resumed his seat and took up his tea again.

They made gradual progress that morning, keeping to the hills bypassing Carcoar and Blayney, and in the increasing chill of the cold afternoon they continued through the deserted miles of tall, yellow grass, spotted here and there by the muted tints of the eucalyptus trees. By four o'clock, Alan had chosen his camp-site for the next two nights, on the Bathurst side of Kettle's Creek, approximately a mile south of the bridge. The creek was very shallow at this point and the bank lifted in a moderate slope to a level area where a clump of young red cedar trees with their greyish-brown, scaly bark grew in a loose half-circle, and to one side a mound or rocks reached some twelve feet in the air. Between the two afforded a sheltered space. A gully ran at an acute angle from the creek and cut through behind the rocks, an ideal place to tether the horses.

In the hour before dusk, they raised the tent and built the fire. The wind dropped a little with the coming of the night but it was hard work to keep the fire going.

After their meal, wrapped in their greatcoats, they sat in the tent and Lawless played his mouth organ. The melody of 'Bold Jack Donahoo' carried on the wind.

In Dublin town I was brought up, in that city of great fame –
My decent friends and parents, they will tell you all the same,
It was for the sake of five hundred pounds I was sent across
    the main
For seven long years in New South Wales to wear a convict's
    chain,

Then come, my hearties, we'll roam the mountain high,
Together we will plunder, together we will die!
We'll wander over mountains and we'll gallop over plains –
For we scorn to live in slavery, bound down by iron chains.

I'd scarce been there twelve months or more upon the
    Australian shore,
When I took to the highway, as I'd oft-times done before,
There was me and Jacky Underwood, and Warder and Webster
    too,
These were the true associates of bold Jack Donahoo,

Then come, my hearties, we'll roam the mountain high,
Together we will plunder, together we will die!
We'll wander over mountains and we'll gallop over plains –
For we scorn to live in slavery, bound down by iron chains.

Jordan's voice lifted in song as Lawless played the chorus.
Once again, Alan took the first watch, Jordan the second and

Lawless the third. They slept fitfully for it was a very cold night and although the tent was in a protected place, the wind was strong, and the fire, struggling to survive, kept going out. They were glad when the sun came up at last bringing a semblance of warmth to the day.

'The only bloody good thing about this frost and cold is the fact it kills the flamin' flies,' Jordan remarked as he rolled up his bedding.

'Aye, too right, old son,' agreed Lawless.

After breakfast, they rode to the bridge at Kettle's Creek where they rehearsed the operation. Only once did they have to retire to hide in the bush. Lawless came riding back from his lookout to warn that some men on horseback approached from the Blayney side of the hill.

They rode into the scrub and waited. Some six minutes later, they watched from their vantage point with a mixture of amusement, excitement, and some alarm as David Elrington rode by with four troopers.

'Isn't that the silly bugger who was with Blake in Theresa Town?' Jordan whispered as the hooves thudded across the bridge.

'Aye, I reckon so,' answered Lawless. 'What be his name again?'

'David Elrington,' answered Alan.

'That was it. Wonder where they've been, boss?'

Alan looked speculatively after the disappearing figures. 'I imagine Rutherford Blake runs his office and his men with precision. That they go out on some sort of field trip on a Sunday doesn't surprise me.'

Jordan was concerned. 'You don't think we've aught to worry about, do you, boss? You don't think them bein' on the road had anythin' to do with us?'

Alan shook his head. 'No, lad, I'm sure it is merely coincidence. Though it does show us that the environs of Bathurst are more dangerous than most.'

Lawless's observation was a mutual thought. 'Boy, I'll be glad when this job is over and we be back at Treehard, mateys.'

When they returned along the creek to the camp, they bathed in it while the sun was still out and at dusk they lit a fire. After a dinner of rabbit stew, they sat round the blazing fire while Lawless entertained them on his mouth organ once more. Jordan rolled a cigar and lay smoking it, leaning contentedly back against one of the rocks.

Alan regarded the two men with him in the flickering firelight. Lawless was now as fine a man as any who made the laws of the land. He was proud of Lawless, the lad was an example of the enduring good in the human spirit. He was reliable in every context of the word.

Jordan was still young and impetuous, nevertheless he had stood his ground as well as any hardened old salt in the Royal Navy on more than one occasion, and doubtless would again.

Alan closed his eyes and imagined Eve at Treehard in her cotton dress with her hair tumbling in curls over her shoulders. He heard her saying, 'You are the truth in my life and the truth is love.' For a few seconds, Lawless's music was shut out as he pictured her.

And then he thought of diminutive Samuel, a lion-heart, faithful and humble.

And Daniel? At seventy the kindest, truest friend a man could have, and a father to him for sixteen years. For just a moment as he pictured Daniel his pulse quickened ever so slightly. He opened his eyes and moved uncomfortably. Opposite him Lawless still played, and Jordan was stretched out smoking peacefully. Alan stood and moved out of the circle of firelight. He walked down a few steps towards the creek and looked up at the night.

It was moonlight but there were stray ribbons of cloud moving across the sky. He knew the constellations of both the northern and southern skies from his naval days. As he stood now, he easily picked out 'crux', the southern cross, and 'musca', the fly, nearby; then he saw a meteor, or a falling star as it was commonly known. It flashed brightly as it entered the earth's atmosphere, and a long, bright streak resulted.

He felt odd. He was not concerned about tomorrow morning, for while any job could be dangerous, he knew he had planned things as well as possible. It was something else, something intangible.

'Guv'nor!' Lawless called from the fireside.

'Yes, Lawless, what is it?'

'Do we keep the same watches? It fast approaches ten o'clock.'

He returned towards his men as he answered, 'Yes, lad, I'll look out until one o'clock. You, Jordan, take three hours after that and wake Lawless to watch until sun-up. I want to be in position by just after eight o'clock.' He put more wood on the fire and Lawless and Jordan unrolled their sleeping blankets.

It was about fifteen minutes before midnight when Jordan sat up and came out of the tent to find Alan putting another log on the fire.

'What is it, Jordan, lad?'

'I don't know, boss, can't sleep tonight, though Lawless is out to it for certain.'

'Would you like a cup of tea?'

'Yeah, that's an idea,' the young man said putting on his greatcoat.

After Alan had boiled the billy, Jordan made the tea. They sat and drank in the stillness of the vast black silence.

'You may as well turn in now, boss,' Jordan said putting down his mug. 'I'm wide awake, and will stay so until it's time to rouse Lawless.'

Alan looked across at him. He seemed to weigh Jordan's offer. 'All right, lad, I will. Goodnight.' As he moved towards the tent, he stopped and turned back. 'Jordan,' he said softly.

Jordan looked up from the fire.

'There is a flat rock just up there,' he motioned to it. 'A vantage point that gives you a clear view of the tent and the fire, allowing you to see through the cedars up the line of the creek.'

'Sounds good.'

'And if you feel at any time you are dropping off to sleep, wake me, Jordan, for I want a look-out all night tonight, you understand?'

'Yeah, yeah, boss, all right.'

Jordan stayed seated. Trust the boss to bring up the other night! Well, he wasn't goin' to fall asleep tonight, no siree. The trouble with the boss was, he was so bloody perfect; never made a mistake and had to remind others when they did. And he was always bloody right, the boss; look at the way he had known how Bridget and her father would react.

He poured himself another mug of tea. That bloody Bridget. Too good for him now. He wondered how she would have responded if the boss had been there? He always had the feelin' she was sweet on the boss. He knew for certain her sister Marilyn was. Why was it the boss had that way with people? Why was he so bloody irresistible?

His face grew hard in the firelight. He stood up and put some more small branches on the fire. He could hear the regular breathing of the two men in the tent. He lifted his rifle, a breech-loading Enfield he had taken from one of the police at Theresa Town, and moved in the direction of the rock that Alan had pointed out. Suddenly he stopped. Why should he do what the boss ordered? Automatically go and flamin' sit on the flamin' rock because the boss said he should? If he was so damn clever, how come he had two thousand pounds on his head? God! What a man wouldn't give for two thousand pounds! It would set a bloke up for life, that sort of money would. It was a fortune!

An idea flashed to his mind.

He looked back involuntarily to the tent. No, no, forget it.

His eyes moved rapidly back and forth. Why should he forget it? He never should have been a bushranger. It wasn't his fault. He wasn't one of them. Not really. Never had been. And bloody Lawless had never liked him, right from the start. Well, there was a way out; the way to a free life and stacks of money as well. If only he had money! Bridget would be all over him then. All the women would be! Yes, don't be afraid . . . do it. The talk was that Mick Connelly was goin' to get part of the reward money out on Ben Hall and Johnny Gilbert. And when Bart Smithers informed on Ruggy Dick, he got half the reward, they reckon. All that money. And Billy Dunken, now he had turned . . . what was it? Queen's evidence? Against Jake Crane. Yeah, Queen's evidence, that was it. Heck, Bart Smithers and Billy Dunken had both been pardoned and got reward money too!

He looked back again to the tent. All silent.

No, he wasn't really one of them, never had been, not really. A pardon, yes, that's what he could get.

Buck up, Jordan. It was now or never!

He was less than ten miles outside Bathurst. Less than ten miles from Rutherford Blake. This was the best chance he would ever have. The *only* chance he would ever have. Now was the time! He would show the boss who was the cleverest after all. Yes, he would do it.

Stealthily, he crept back and put a solid log and some branches on the fire. He waited a short time to see they took light, his heart pounding and perspiration dampening his shirt even in the wind. Then he picked up his saddle and moved away round the rocks into the gully where he untethered his horse. He even untied the two pack horses and Freedom and Waterloo in the vain hope that they might wander away. Freedom stamped his hooves and gave a gentle whinny.

'Quiet, Freedom boy, quiet.'

He led his horse until he was well away from camp before he mounted and followed the creek until he could see the bridge and the line of the road.

Soon, he was spurring his horse and riding as fast as he dared in the moonlight towards Bathurst township.

Sir Rutherford shifted in his chair.

He pulled the lamp a little closer as he pored over the map on the desk in front of him. He ran his index finger back and forth over a spot on the paper and then leaned back. It was the same area that he always studied. Where the hell was the Fletcher hideout? John Stuart and a troop of Mayfield men had minutely investigated the whole countryside, and he had taken his own men there more than once, but they had found nothing. Why, last month, the master of Mayfield had gone far to the south and even searched in the furthest reaches of the Boorowa River, to no avail. Could the hideout be inside the Mayfield border? No, that was impossible. John Stuart seemed to know every nook and cranny of his property, enormous though it was.

Poor John Stuart, the disorder, let alone the dishonour, that had been brought into his life by the Herman woman. He should never have taken her for his wife. That's what happened when one married out of one's class. It was always a mistake.

Flashing to Sir Rutherford's mind came the unhappy image of a girl in black dress and white apron. She was laughing, her merry, hazel eyes regarding him. She tilted her elfin face and her auburn hair fell to the side. She was lifting her dainty hand up to him. It touched his face. Ah yes, Coralea, you were truly beautiful, and how you loved me! So clearly did he see her among all the other indistinct memories from his past. He shifted awkwardly in his chair and for a brief time his severe features yielded to an uncharacteristically wistful, sentimental expression. Why was she still living in his head, able to haunt him?

'No!' he said aloud as he ran his hands across his eyes. Hadn't he done what was right and proper? She was a servant in his father's house. He could not have married her. He was the heir to a marquisate. She was beneath him. No one should step down out of his class.

He stood from the chair and walked to the window. Ah yes, that was why he hated Alan Fletcher. The man had disgraced his birth. Sunk to murder and the dissolute life of a bushranger. The others were born scum, but Fletcher had made the conscious choice.

He put his hand in his fob pocket and drew out his watch. It was after half past the hour of one in the morning. He should retire. There was no more he could achieve tonight.

He was about to turn away from the window when a figure crossed his vision and to his astonishment a loud hammering began on the door. A voice called, 'Sir Rutherford Blake, is that you? I must see you!'

He opened the door and a large man loomed in front of him.

'Yes, I am Rutherford Blake. Who the devil are you and what do you want?'

Twenty-five minutes later, Sir Rutherford's office was crowded with troopers, mostly half asleep and groaning. While his men had been sent for, Sir Rutherford had questioned Jordan O'Day. He now knew where Alan and Lawless lay sleeping.

'How can you guarantee they will still be asleep, O'Day? The earliest we can make their camp will be after three o'clock in the morning.'

'I cannot, of course, sir. But Lawless sleeps real deep, would never wake on his own. And it's much warmer tonight, so I'm sure the boss won't stir, he was pretty tired.'

Sir Rutherford looked sceptical. 'I pray that your opinion is correct.'

When Jordan had drawn the position of Treehard Hill on the map, Sir Rutherford brought his fist down excitedly on the table. 'I knew it! I knew it! All my instincts told me it was somewhere there. Once more I am proven right!'

'You'd have no hope of findin' it, even knowin' where it is,' Jordan replied. 'The entrance to the tunnel is hidden. You would ride straight by. It's a sort of natural fortress.'

'But we *will* find it, won't we, O'Day? For you will show it to us.'

'Not without your guarantee that I'll be pardoned, I won't, and I want half the reward money like Bart Smithers got for Ruggy Dick Middleton.'

'Listen, you scum!' Sir Rutherford rounded on his prisoner. 'You will do exactly as I say. You will show us where Fletcher is. You will show us where this . . . this . . . Treehard Hill is, and then, ah yes, and only then will we talk pardons and reward money.'

Jordan, undaunted by the barrage, lifted his head and looked defiantly at the detective policeman. 'But am I Queen's evidence? I'll do nothin' if I'm not Queen's evidence. I'm not afraid of you.'

Sir Rutherford sighed. 'You aren't such a thing at present, you cannot be, it's a legal term; but yes, Jordan O'Day, I'll see to it that your information will be.'

The briefing of his troopers had been short and explicit. 'We will ride to Kettle's Creek. There, I and ten of you will surround Fletcher and Drake. Meanwhile, O'Day shall take the rest of you, led by Mr Elrington and Sergeant Samuel, on to the hideout at Treehard Hill. O'Day will show you the secret entry and you will capture Dwyer and Cooper.' He waved his hand towards the door. 'Now mount up and be ready to ride.'

As they went from the room, Sir Rutherford took David Elrington aside. 'We are relying on O'Day's word. There's nothing else we can do. He says that Mrs Wakeman is at their hideout.'

His assistant's eyebrow's rose.

'I must impress upon you the delicacy of this part of the operation. As you know she is a Crown exception to the Felons' Apprehension Act. She must be taken expeditiously to the nearest magistrate's house.'

'That would be Mr Finimore's in Young, sir. Though it's near to a twenty-mile ride.'

'Yes, it is, but that is where she must go.' He handed the young man an envelope. 'And send this with her, it explains to the magistrate that he is to take good care of her until her husband arrives for her.'

'Is it true what is being said, sir?'

Sir Rutherford looked questioningly at the young man. 'What is being said?'

'That Mr Wakeman wants her back at any price.'

The expert on the bushrangers inhaled deeply. 'While it is none of your concern, Mr Elrington, yes, it would appear so. Thus, as you pass the Mayfield turn-off, have Trooper Boehm withdraw and report to Mr Wakeman. He has asked specifically to be alerted of such an event without delay. Boehm is a good man; I shall tell him what to say.' Then he added silently to himself, 'John Stuart's search must have taken him very close to Fletcher's hideout.'

'And you, sir? After you have taken Fletcher and Drake, what then?'

Sir Rutherford actually smiled. 'I will send them under heavy escort to Bathurst gaol and I will ride swiftly on to join you at the hideout. I want to see this place for myself. I've thought of it night and day. Make sure you leave a man on the road to show me where to turn up the valley. And wait at the hideout with your prisoners until I arrive.'

'Yes, sir. And, sir, if they put up a fight?'

'Just make sure you don't kill the woman. It would be more than Mr Wakeman, or the Government, could abide.'

In the cold, dark street among the hubbub of the troopers and a few gathered townsfolk, the leader mounted his horse. Then raising his hand up in the style of the military, and signalling them forward, he shouted, 'It might be two o'clock in the morning of a winter's night, but it's to be a day of glorious victory for us, so onward we ride!'

Two miles outside the settlement, they came to the Orange turn-off.

'Now, O'Day,' Sir Rutherford said, 'when we come to Kettle's Creek, Fletcher is a mile along from the bridge to the south, you say? On this side?'

'That's right.'

'And we can reach the place by following the course of the creek?'

'Yes. They're on a rise near a clump of red cedar and a pile of rocks. You'll see the tent and the glow of the fire.'

Then Sir Rutherford addressed David Elrington and the sergeant. 'Keep up the pace even though you have round a ninety-mile ride ahead of you. Commandeer fresh horses in any place you can. You have a full moon during the dark hours which is a real blessing, ah yes. God speed!'

The noise of those departing soon was lost and Sir Rutherford led his body of men along the road towards the creek. At the bridge, they turned off the road and followed the watercourse. When they had gone half a mile, he halted them.

'We cannot risk their hearing us. Dismount and tether your horses; we go on foot from here. No speaking until after we have them. And remember, if you must shoot at Fletcher, shoot low, to wound only. Understand? I want him alive. Drake doesn't matter.'

On along the bank they crept in the chill of the night air. The scrub caught at their clothes and one or two stumbled but they moved silently enough. After a few minutes, an owl hooted loudly above them and some of the men gasped, startled. Sir Rutherford, enraged, whispered, 'Silence, you fools.'

After five minutes more they could see the glow from the embers of the fire up ahead. When they were some forty-odd yards away, Constable Ward and three others moved out at Sir Rutherford's signal and rounded the hill. The rest spread out to each side of Sir Rutherford who started up the incline from the creek, heading towards the tent.

All was motionless. He could see the tent flap open and he thought he made out two forms sleeping within.

Ahead of him and beyond the camp he watched the dark figures of his four troopers coming through the cedars. When they were ten yards from the tent, he lifted his arms in the moonlight and the two men with him dropped to the ground. He too went to his knees as his voice broke the silence, sounding harshly in the still morning. 'Alan Fletcher! Give yourself up! You are surrounded! Do not try to escape or you will be shot!' There was a tingling sensation throughout his whole body and his hands holding the rifle in front of him shook slightly. 'Come out with your hands in the air!'

Nothing moved.

The tent flap still hung open and all was silent.

Sir Rutherford stood and advanced, his troopers at his side. He was wary, ready for a trap, and his eyes darted this way and that. Still nothing moved.

'Come out, Fletcher! Or we shoot!'

Silence.

He dropped his left hand from his rifle and the men with him fired into the top of the tent. The rifle blasts reverberated loudly in the night. He moved swiftly forward and pushed his rifle in through the canvas opening. But even as he did so, he knew he had been thwarted.

He knew there was nothing here but a pile of blankets. In frustration, he smashed his fist into his rifle butt.

'Damn!' he exclaimed. 'Damn and blast the bastard!'

Alan had fallen quickly to sleep when Jordan took over his watch and for a time he had slept deeply.

Perhaps it was the indefinable feeling of apprehension he had been carrying; perhaps it was that he felt the chill as the fire died, or perhaps it was the loud hoot of the owl in the night; whatever the cause, he woke suddenly with a feeling of alarm. Lawless was fast asleep at his side. He sat up and, taking his greatcoat, moved out of the tent to find Jordan.

Jordan was not by the fire. It had gone out and was now bright cinders. Surely the lad had not fallen asleep again.

He moved swiftly to the flat rock he had mentioned, but he could see no sign of the young man. He looked down through the trees.

'Jordan!' he called softly. 'Jordan, where are you?'

It was then he turned to face the gully, and in the light from the moon saw only four horses. Jordan's had gone!

His mind raced. He looked up at the night sky. It must be close to three o'clock. Where had the boy gone? And how long had he been gone? He attempted to think of good reasons that could have taken Jordan away, but he soon realised the futility of that. A bush-ranger did not take his horse and disappear into the night away from his mates unless he had one thing on his mind. To inform.

Why, Jordan? Why?

Alan leapt down from the rock and was shaking Lawless in seconds. Lawless woke instantaneously. His eyes widened with shock as Alan said, 'Jordan's gone, lad. Don't know how long. Quickly, we must leave now. We must get back to Treehard and warn them.'

'Gawd, guv'nor, the bloody little rat!'

Alan was already lifting his saddle as Lawless came out of the tent, putting on his overcoat. 'Bring your saddle, lad. Simply take your guns and ammunition and anything of value. There is no time to waste.'

'Will we take the pack horses, guv?'

'Yes.'

Rapidly they saddled the horses.

'Ready?' Alan asked quietly.

'Ready,' answered Lawless.

'Wait here.' Alan turned and ran across the gully and up between the rocks. He climbed agilely to the flat rock and looked down through the cedars. There, coming along in the moonlight, less than a hundred yards away, were dark figures carrying guns!

Hastily, soundlessly, he retreated.

Lawless was up on Waterloo.

'They come,' he whispered. 'We will cross the creek here at the bottom of the gully and get away into the bush on the far side. Courage, lad.'

The horses moved down the ravine as if they knew to be quiet. They crossed the stream and were in the bush on the far side while Sir Rutherford and his men were still thirty yards from the camp.

Exasperated, Sir Rutherford kicked at the coals of the fire with the toe of his boot.

'What now, sir?' asked Trooper Ward.

'Well, we don't know how long they've been gone. It could be ten minutes or it could be an hour. By the time we get back to our horses and make the road, there is little doubt we will be the last in the race.'

'What shall we do with their effects, sir?'

'You, Himsworth and Fox stay behind and confiscate them. I'll examine them on my return to Bathurst.'

Trooper Ward's face dropped. He had hoped to continue on to the hideout.

'You three return to town. We need some sort of representation there now as things have turned out. The rest of us will go on and take a look at this blasted Treehard Hill.'

'Yes, sir.'

'Ah yes, and one more thing,' added Sir Rutherford as an afterthought, 'remember to keep an eye on Mistress Thatcher.'

Ward saluted.

'Shouldn't we look about the near countryside first, sir?' spoke up Constable Fox. 'Fletcher and Drake might be hidin' around 'ere somewhere.'

Sir Rutherford looked disdain at the man. 'Good Lord, do you know so little of those you chase, Fox? He is loyal to his men you fool . . . loyal! That means he will ride post-haste to warn those he has left behind of the danger. All we can pray is that Mr Elrington is well and truly ahead of him.' Then the expert on the bushrangers coughed. It was cold out here near this blasted creek. Bloody cold! He pulled his greatcoat more tightly round him and heading back down the hill, shouted, 'We shall breakfast first in Carcoar, then ride as swiftly as we can to Fletcher's hideout.'

CHAPTER THIRTY

'. . . we have found release there,
Where there's no ill, no grief, but sleep has mending,
Naught broken save this body, lost but breath;
Nothing to shake the laughing heart's long peace there
But only agony, and that has ending;
And the worst friend and enemy is but death.'

'Peace', Rupert Brooke, 1887–1915.

Thelma looked up to see the burnished leather boots in her vision. Her eyes lifted. 'John Stuart!' she said in surprise, standing from where she knelt nursing Velvet. Eve's cat spent more time with her these days than in the big house. 'What brings you over here?'

'To speak with you. Do you have time?'

She was mystified. John Stuart never spoke to her alone; Joe was always present. 'Of course. I was about to take lunch. Shall we go indoors?'

'No, let's sit over here.' He motioned to a wooden seat in her back garden, out of the wind between the garden wall and a hedge. When they were seated, Velvet came and rubbed up against his boot. Unconsciously, he stroked the cat's tail. 'Thelly,' he said, and a short, sharp thrill rippled through her, for it was the name he used to call her as a child. She had not heard him say it for over twenty years. 'I want to talk to you about Eve. I know you have always maintained that she was good and not in any way involved with that Lake person.'

'I have.'

His brow puckered. 'I knew he was bad. I knew it at the time. But I just kept seeing her as the mirror image of . . . my mother. It obscured my thinking, all I saw was the one in the other.'

Thelma clasped his arm in compassion. 'Oh, John Stuart, I know that and I am so sorry.'

He turned his head to look at her, to stare at her. 'Thelly, did she ever love me?'

Thelma's eyes filled with tears. 'Oh, my dear, dear boy, yes, she did love you. She just could not stay here when she thought all love

507

had been removed from her; when she saw condemnation all around her. She needed your love.'

He sat up, uttering a bitterly sad sound. 'Yes, but perhaps she needs it no longer.'

'John Stuart, what makes you say that?'

He turned to face her. His dark eyes, a misery, his striking features, clouded with regret. 'There is something you don't know. That only I and Joe, and a few others know . . . when Eve was in Cowra on Boxing Day, she was carried off by two men.'

'Yes, John Stuart, we all know that, she was abducted. That's why you've been so worried and all. It's more than a body can stand all these months.'

John Stuart attempted a smile but it failed to mount his mouth. 'Thelma, I *know* who those men were.'

The good woman looked amazed. 'You do?'

'It was Alan Fletcher, the bushranger, and one of his men.'

Thelma's face dropped in disbelief.

'We are certain. So, you see, I have lived these past months in utter torment.' He bent forward, elbows on his knees, head in his hands.

Thelma shook her head as she placed her hand gently on his back. 'John Stuart, are you sure?'

He continued to hold his head in his hands as he answered. 'Yes, we are positive. So positive in fact, that I have prevailed on the Governor and the Premier to make her a Crown exception to this Outlaws' Apprehension Act.'

'Oh, my Lord above!'

At that moment Rosy's voice called, 'Mrs Larmer, where are you? Mrs Larmer!'

John Stuart sat up.

Thelma met his eyes. 'I shall send her away.' She stood up. 'Rosy, not now! I'm with the master.'

The sound of Rosy's shoes clattered along the path. 'There you are, ma'm. Why, it's the master and all they are looking for!'

John Stuart sighed. 'They can't leave me alone even for a few minutes, it seems. I'm coming, Rosy.'

'Very good, sir,' the girl said, turning back to the house.

They stood looking at each other. Thelma felt closer to him than she had in two decades. 'Thank you for coming here . . . for telling me. Do not give up hope my . . . dearest boy.'

He took up her hand and brought it to his lips; then he left her standing there. She watched him walk away, subconsciously lifting the hand he had kissed to hold it to her heart. Confusions of thoughts

508

ran through her mind. Eve, the bushranger, what did it all mean? How she hoped dear Eve was safe, and how she hoped by some miracle she would return to John Stuart. It pained Thelma to see him so disillusioned.

Inside the Larmer household, Timothy waited for John Stuart. 'Ah sir, there is a trooper over in the big house. He has a message for you from Sir Rutherford Blake.'

When John Stuart came to Constable Boehm, he stood immediately from where he had sat awkwardly on the edge of one of the Louis Seize chairs in the morning room, his honest, open face, serious. 'Mr Wakeman, sir. A message, sir.'

'Yes, trooper, what is it?'

'Sir Rutherford's compliments. He says to tell you, sir, that we know the whereabouts of Alan Fletcher's hideout. And . . . that the object dear to you will be in Young by tomorrow morning, waiting for you at the magistrate's house.'

Eve looked round at the sound of Daniel's voice. He was with Sam moving through the trees near the stables. 'Mistress Eve, come and look. If this doesn't beat all!'

She pulled her coat more closely round her before proceeding down the steps of the verandah towards them.

It was afternoon; the sky was a clear blue, and while it was a cold day, there was warmth in the sunshine.

Sam put his finger to his mouth to indicate silence. She followed them through the trees a little way, and there, in a nest beside a fallen log, was a baby spiny anteater, and a foot or so away, its mother, a roly-poly body of bristling spines clutching a branch in its four claw-tipped paws and licking it clean of termites. Eve looked at the baby with delight. She was enthralled by the strange little creature, similar to a tiny elephant with its long nose and round fat paws for legs. The quills of its coat were just beginning to sprout and it was struggling to leave the nest and mount a small tree limb nearby.

'Oh, the darling,' she whispered.

The two men with her smiled. 'Thought ye'd like this,' Sam said quietly.

The baby's long, probing tongue kept popping in and out. They watched as the mother moved back to her infant and deftly pushed him down from where he doggedly tried to climb up the branch. They remained a few minutes longer, then quietly moved away.

'I've never seen a baby one before,' Eve said. 'Aren't they the dearest, quaintest things.'

'True, mistress, and ye be lucky to see a grown one as they burrow in the earth and hide as a rule,' Sam informed her. 'It's a real surprise to see a babe in winter like this. But they'll be here until the little one's prickles grow long enough, so we could look again tomorrow, eh?'

Eve smiled. 'We certainly will.'

'Well now, I think I'll be goin' to the lookout and have a peek down the hill,' Samuel said as they walked by the stables.

Daniel shook his head. 'But Alan and the lads cannot possibly be back before late tonight, Sam, no matter what.'

'True, I know,' the little man answered. 'But I just fancy a look down the hill, Daniel, my man.' And with that he mounted the verandah and picked up his tranter revolver which lay on the old walnut whatnot. He loaded it and stuck it in his belt as Eve and Daniel noticing, looked at each other.

'Why do you take your tranter, Sam?'

'I just fancy I want to, Mistress Eve. I just fancy I want to.'

As Sam's figure disappeared into the entrance of the tunnel, Daniel shook his head. 'It's a real change for him to be as nervous as me.'

Eve said nothing, she felt the same way.

About half an hour later Sam's head appeared around the verandah rail and, looking in to the kitchen, he hailed them.

Eve came to the door. 'Anything to see, Sam?'

'No, nothin', but I'll pop back up to Nelson's now and then. Just feel I want to keep an eye on the outside world today.' He turned away, and she watched his small figure cross over to the stable.

Daniel's wide mouth contracted as he pursed his lips in thought. 'I wonder if old Aggie or Red have given us the treat of an egg today?' Aggie and Red were hens that Bridget had given Jordan as chicks. They roosted in a wooden coop away in the trees on the kitchen side of the house.

Eve nodded. 'I shall go and see for you, Danny.'

Before she went to collect the eggs she looked for Sam in the stable; he was sweeping out the stalls. The broom was as tall as he was.

'Sam, after I've gathered the eggs for Dan, I shall accompany you to the lookout and sit awhile before I groom Milford.'

He smiled at her. 'Why, goodo, Mistress Eve.' She turned to leave and as she did so, he asked, 'Is America like this country at all?'

She came back towards him a few steps. The little man's expression was earnest.

'Well, they speak English, which is a great similarity for a start.'

'But what about them red Indian folk? I heard a few strange tales about them,' he said, putting aside his broom.

'There are none in the cities, Samuel. And yes, they can be savage, but they are no more so than most men. I fear they are like any people who react in panic, when a more advanced civilisation descends upon their lands.'

He scratched the side of his nose. 'True, I suppose. I reckon the guv'nor could make friends with 'em, but. Look at the way he's a crony with Womballa's crew over there on the upland. There's somethin' mighty uncommon about our guv'nor, there is.'

'Yes, Samuel, there is.'

He was looking at her with one of his faintly stern expressions. He hesitated, then took a deep breath and said, 'Ye are not the only one what loves him, ye know.'

Eve put her hand on his arm and smiled gently. 'Oh, Sam, I know that.'

He sighed and dropped his eyes, his lean face wrinkling with emotion. Then he coughed. 'For sure, I won't mind goin' to America. Though no doubt there'll be drawbacks, for nothin' worth havin' in this life comes easy. It'll be goin' home for ye, won't it?'

'Yes, it will, Samuel. Yet, I have found happiness in this country.'

'What? With the guv'nor?'

'Yes, and with others.'

He turned his eyes up into hers. He spoke very quietly. 'Would us lot be in them others?'

She smiled at him. 'In truth, Sam, you lot would be.'

He gave a strange, comic grin and looked away, then picked up the broom and began to sweep again. The scar on the back of his left hand shone as he gripped the handle. It was where the bullet had gone through his palm so long ago, during the mutiny. Eve noticed it and wondered about it. But she did not mention it, she simply said, 'I'll see you soon then, Samuel.'

She moved away and before she got to the door he called, 'Mistress Eve . . .'

She turned back, 'Yes, Sam?'

He swallowed and took a step towards her. 'I don't mind tellin' ye it's real nice havin' a . . . lady such as yeself here, and I'm lookin' forward to America, I am.'

'Samuel, how lovely of you to say such a thing. Thank you. And I am looking forward to America too . . . with all of you.'

A happy expression broke across his face and he went back to his work as she walked away. He liked Mistress Eve, she was a right, good sort o' gal, really. A feeling quite mellow overcame him and he began to hum an old song he had learned as a boy on the Surrey Downs. It had not been in his mind for years. His grandmother had taught it to him. His voice actually lifted into song as he came to the last two lines:

> 'And a hey and a ho my darlin' love did sing,
> And a hey, and a ho, dorry oh.'

He stopped singing and put down his broom, a frown lodging between his eyes. There were unaccustomed sounds of movement in the yard. 'What's that?' he said coming quickly out through the stable door. His mouth dropped open. A mass of troopers, rifles at the ready, were coming straight towards him.

For a second he was frozen then, coming to life, screamed, 'Traps, Daniel! Traps!' as he pulled his revolver from his belt.

The volley of shots that met his shout actually lifted him in the air before he could pull the trigger. He was dead before he hit the ground, blood spurting from the eight gaping holes in him.

Daniel, in the kitchen, heard Sam's scream and the thunder of the gun blasts.

'What is it, Sam?' he cried in shock rushing out to his friend. His eyes grew wide in horror as he registered Sam's bloody corpse, grotesquely twisted on the ground.

'Oh, Lord God!' he cried.

Three troopers reacted to his appearance. They had seen something in his hand and mistaken it for a gun. As the bullets hit him, he groaned, 'No . . .' before he toppled forward down the steps.

Too late, David Elrington shouted, 'Don't shoot, he's unarmed!'

As Daniel fell, the wooden spoon he held, which he had been using to stir the stew, was thrust down. It stuck in the ground and stood upright like some absurd, erroneous marker beside him, as he shuddered in death.

At the first volley of shots, Eve, who had been sauntering back through the trees with three eggs in her apron, stopped in fright, the eggs dropping to the ground. At the sound of the second discharges, she ran forward in terror. Her heart was beating wildly as she called, 'Sam, what is it? Danny, what's wrong?'

In terrible fear, she headed towards the sounds, and when she broke through the trees into the clearing between the house and the stables, David Elrington screamed, 'Don't shoot! It's Mrs Wakeman!'

'Mrs Trent!' exclaimed Sergeant Samuel.

For a few seconds, she was hopelessly bewildered. She could not understand the scene in front of her. She looked wildly round the faces of the men with guns. Then she saw the two bodies on the ground and the appalling reality of what had taken place hit her.

'Oh, dear sweet Jesus!' she cried.

There were men bending down to the shattered frame that had been Sam, and others moving over to Daniel on the ground near the steps.

She screamed, 'No, don't touch them! No!' She ran to Daniel and, dropping to her knees, took him in her arms and cradled his head to her breast, sobbing, 'Daniel, Daniel, no . . . no.' She rocked him back and forth, clutched to her heart, his blood soaking into her apron and her dress.

It was not true. They could not be dead. They had been so alive. Oh, God, why? They were going to America. All of them together.

She looked up at the killers and to her astonishment she saw a face she recognised and then another. Her mind was so blank with horror that for a few seconds she could not place them. Then she realised one was David Elrington, Sir Rutherford's assistant. And the other? Jordan O'Day, white-faced, his eyes wide with dismay. What was Jordan doing here? He was with Alan!

Suddenly, it registered. Thudding into her brain.

'What have you done?' Her voice was so soft it was almost a whisper but every man heard her. 'What have you done? These men were your brothers, your family. They trusted you.' Her eyes grew large in her distraught face as she remembered the day on the cliff top. 'Oh, God in heaven! I saved you, saved your life for this! For this!'

He could not look into her eyes and turned away.

Then cold terror took hold of her and her voice rose as she clutched Daniel's body more tightly in her arms. 'Alan, Lawless, oh no!'

David Elrington's clipped tones sounded impersonally in her ears. 'Mrs Wakeman, we hope Sir Rutherford Blake has the criminals you mention in captivity. In the meanwhile, please take hold of yourself, madam! This is not at all seemly.'

After that she heard nothing. Her mind was a blur of misery. The world was mad. Danny dead. Sam dead. And Jordan O'Day was alive! She just knelt there sobbing, in a blind sea of tears, clutching Daniel. They had to drag her away from his body in the end.

CHAPTER THIRTY-ONE

'All I can give you I give.'
'The Oblation', Algernon Charles Swinburne, 1837–1909.

Some twenty minutes later, Eve had changed her blood-stained clothing and was trying to force herself out of the stupor that had taken
her mind since the shootings when there was a rapping on the door.
She stood up from the bed as David Elrington entered.

His austere tones rang in the small room. 'Mrs Wakeman, I have
come to ask you to please collect your belongings. You are to be
escorted away.'

'Whatever do you mean?'

'What I say, madam. It is not . . . proper that you stay here. I
have orders to transfer you to the magistrate's house in Young.'

Eve looked confused. 'But that is a twenty-mile ride from here.
Why?'

David Elrington sucked in his cheeks as he appraised the woman
in front of him. He was perplexed by her. He certainly did not
approve of her. His superior had mentioned long ago that if they
found her, she would be with child or have delivered one. Well, there
was no baby around here. Anyway, that was none of his concern. She
had been the mistress of the fabulous Mayfield, and yet, here she
was in this place, the consort of bushrangers. The way she had
behaved, screaming and sobbing, one would have thought the dead
men meant a great deal to her. Mind you, she looked enough in
control now. All of it was truly beyond his understanding.

'Mrs Wakeman, I have my orders and I must ask you to prepare
yourself to leave here immediately. You will be in good hands, I
assure you. You don't need to worry. You shall spend the night in
the police camp at Bendick Murrell and be taken on to Young in the
morning.'

She stood up and faced away from him. So they were sending her
to a magistrate. She asked without looking round, 'Am I then to be
charged with a crime?'

He sighed. He found it very difficult conversing with her. He had
no orders to tell her anything. All he had been told to do was to

make sure she was not killed, and that she was transferred without any delay to Mr Finimore's in Young. 'Madam,' his voice was strained, 'I must ask you to please organise yourself to leave here.'

She was feeling very unsure as she turned to face him. 'Why am I being taken by escort to a magistrate? Why do I not remain here?'

'Mrs Wakeman, it is not befitting that you remain here. Can't you see that? The magistrate's house has been chosen for your welfare. Now, if you would be so kind, prepare yourself. I want you to leave within fifteen minutes, please.'

She looked searchingly at him. She was alone again, dear Danny and tiny Sam were dead, she had no idea where Alan and Lawless were, and she was here in the midst of hostile men. Drawing on all her resources, she met his eyes. 'You are certainly a good apprentice of Rutherford Blake, but let me tell you something. Things are not always what they seem. The two men your troopers killed this day were harmless men forced into a pattern of life simply for survival. You have stood in judgement upon them, without the least under-standing of them.'

He was a little taken aback by this spirited defence of the dead outlaws. 'I have done what I was ordered to do.'

'I suppose you think that exonerates you.'

He turned to leave and she stopped him with the words, 'Do you know where Alan Fletcher is?'

He faced slowly back to her. She really was shameless. Here she was, brazenly asking him about the bushranger, and by all accounts Mr Wakeman wanted her back! He could not fathom any of it. 'Mrs Wakeman, I do not know, and if I did, I could not tell you.' He saluted and left the room.

When, ten minutes later, she came out of her room, the house was full of troopers marking things and noting them down, collating and counting. They had all been astounded by Treehard Hill. They had never seen anything like it. As one trooper remarked, 'It's better'n many a squatter's homestead, let alone a bloody bushranger's hideout.'

'Wish Fletcher could have done up my place,' laughed another.

On her way through the kitchen, she came upon Sergeant Rodney Samuel, the man who had stopped them on the highway on Boxing Day. He was stacking Daniel's crockery in a box. He lifted his eyes to hers as she passed. Of course the good man had recognised her and put the pieces together almost as well as Sir Rutherford. The sergeant had dealt with a lot of outlaws, spent twenty-five years in the company of lawbreakers, and there had been something innately different about that man on Boxing Day, the man he reckoned now was Alan Fletcher. And this woman was obviously a lady. It all served to baffle him. He stood up as she came by him and doffed his cap, saying, 'They are ready for you outside, ma'am.' His brown earth-coloured eyes were full of compassion.

His was the first sympathetic expression she had seen. She acknowledged it gratefully. 'Yes, Sergeant, thank you.'

He stepped aside for her to pass by.

She found David Elrington waiting for her on the verandah. He followed as she went down the steps to halt where Daniel and Sam had lain. Their bodies had been removed, though the ground where Sam had fallen was stained with blood.

The wind whipped across the yard now. The sun was behind the clouds and the afternoon was gloomy and cold, like the desolation in her mind. She knew the eyes of the few troopers in the yard followed her, and she heard their mumbling and their soft, crude laughter.

She turned back to David Elrington before she mounted Milford. 'What will you do with them? Where will they be buried?'

He looked so confident, so convinced of his position as a bringer of justice. His face was smooth and the freckles on his nose made him look even younger than his twenty-four years. He was the picture of arrogant, youthful inexperience. She felt ancient by comparison. He smiled. She found it bizarre that he could smile.

'That will be up to Sir Rutherford to decide. We are expecting him here sometime tonight.'

Then she had to say more; she had to say more in defence of the dead men. It was necessary, whether this self-assured person cared or not. She stood tall and straight now for the memory of Danny and Sam. Her expression was not haughty; it was simply candid and unequivocal. 'Mr Elrington, perhaps most bushrangers need to be brought to justice, but you, your superior, and the government of this colony have all made the mistake of judging the few by the many. Four of the five who lived here were better than those who judge.'

Her listener dropped his eyes and spoke as if he had not heard her. 'Mrs Wakeman, these are Constables Dorando and Peters, they will see you safely to Young.' He handed Peters the envelope. 'Give this to the magistrate. And treat Mrs Wakeman well. Goodbye, madam.'

She turned to mount Milford and as she did so saw Jordan watching her from inside the stable door. He was shaking his head and his big shoulders drooped despairingly. She felt sick at the sight of him and deliberately averted her face. When she was astride her horse,

Sergeant Samuel came to her side. She looked down into his kindly eyes.

'Mrs Wakeman.' He patted the back of her hand holding the reins. 'My compliments. Good luck, ma'am.'

David Elrington looked sharply at him, but he made no comment. Instead, he stepped up close to Milford and looking up at Eve's profile said, 'A question, madam, before you leave. How many years have you known Alan Fletcher?'

She did not know whether to answer or not. Her head ached. She felt very lonely. She was still in shock, sick at heart and troubled. She continued looking straight ahead. 'Mr Elrington, not as many as I would have wanted.'

David Elrington watched her ride away. Sir Rutherford said she had been kidnapped, but after the events of today he did not believe it.

While Eve was riding southwest, down through the trees to the road, from a different angle heading uphill towards Treehard in a southeasterly direction, Alan and Lawless continued uncompromisingly to push Freedom and Waterloo.

No more magnificent horses than Freedom and Waterloo existed in the whole colony. Their effort to keep an even pace all the long, wearying journey was heroic. The two pack animals had tired when less than halfway and Alan had left them within sight of a small sheep station. But now, as they covered the final miles, Freedom and Waterloo were all but spent. Their breathing was laboured and they sweated profusely in the chill air, lifting their hooves listlessly.

All Alan hoped to do was to get to Treehard and remove his loved ones. He did not know that David Elrington was in front of him. Nor that he had the advantages of keeping always to the road, and frequently acquiring fresh steeds, enabling him to arrive over an hour ahead of Alan.

Alan and Lawless had left the highway shortly after Koorawatha and taken a short cut, thus had not seen the trooper stationed on the roadway at the bottom of the valley in readiness to alert Sir Rutherford where to go. They had watered the animals at a small stream and were pushing on over the undulating hills up the gradual rise of the valley, when suddenly in front of them, through the trees, they saw Womballa standing with Mulgatta and two other tribesmen, Gannawarra and Goodool.

'They are a long way from their usual habitat,' Alan said in surprise. 'I've rarely seen them north of the plateau.'

Womballa was signalling with his spear for Alan to stop.

'Womballa, my *waminda*, *booralla* to see you,' Alan said. 'I am sorry I cannot stop to talk.' Quickly he explained that they must hurry to Treehard for there were bad men following. '*Murrunmil yanniwan* Treehard *langunyah, thulga jerribong warreyin.*'

'No!' shouted Womballa with such force that Alan, bewildered, asked, 'What is it, Womballa? What is wrong?'

The old tribesman shook his spear in the direction of Treehard. '*Thulga jerribong* no *warreyin. Thulga jerribong noondha* Fletcher *gunyah.*'

Alan blanched.

Lawless reacted to the look on Alan's face. 'Oh Gawd, guv'nor! What is it? What did he say?'

'He said the bad men do not follow us, lad, they are already at Treehard Hill.'

Panic ran through Lawless, filled his whole body until the tips of his fingers prickled. 'Oh no, guv'nor. How can it be? How can they be here before us?'

'I do not believe they could be, Lawless. It is impossible . . . unless there was a separate party of troopers, other than the men who tried to take us.'

'Oh, no!' replied Lawless in despair. 'Oh, no. What will we do, guv?'

'I'm not sure, laddie, but whatever it is, it must be swift.'

He looked again to Womballa asking in a mixture of English and tribal language how many men were at Treehard, when did they come and what had happened. 'How many *thulga jerribong noondha, langunyah? Ungunuk* did *thulga jerribong* come? *Minna* has happened?'

'Bad magic, *ungawilla*,' Womballa replied, and the others with him murmured and shuffled their feet and waved their hands in spirals. Then the tribal elder gave the sign for rifle shots and, telling Alan and Lawless not to continue on, but to leave this place now, said, 'Clever Fletcher must . . . *yanawa, narranda.*' Then he held up his fingers to show the sign for more than ten men. 'Bad medicine *noondha*, Fletcher *gunyah*. You no go Fletcher *gunyah*!'

Alan shook his head. 'But I cannot leave here, Womballa. I must help my *igeelu*.'

Then Womballa hesitated. His eyes blinked, and looking down he gave the tribal sign for sorrow, before answering entirely in English, 'Father no more. Clever Fletcher father dead, little man dead, Clever Fletcher woman live.'

'Oh Gawd, oh no!' cried Lawless.

Alan closed his eyes. His heart was beating wildly in his chest. For the first time in many years the situation was beyond him. He

518

did not know what to do. Danny, Danny. Sam. He wanted to rush carelessly on, no matter what. To be there with Daniel and Sam, to hold Eve in his arms.

Then Womballa's strong voice broke through his thoughts. 'Womballa and people see. *Thulga*. You no help dead men. In *yamminga* now. Too late.'

Alan opened his eyes. There was sympathy in the old, black eyes looking up at him, and once more Womballa made the sign for sorrow, and so too did Mulgatta and the others.

Alan dismounted, moving spiritlessly, consumed by shock. 'Thank you, my *wamindas*.'

Lawless followed the action of his leader and they both stood facing Womballa and his men. The tribal elder gestured with his spear to the south-west. 'Clever Fletcher woman and *thulga jerribong darwong*.'

Alan looked intently at his friend. 'What is that you say, Womballa?'

'Clever Fletcher woman go *yarraman, yanni thulga jerribong*.'

Lawless's anxious face turned to Alan. 'What is it, guv'nor? What does he say about Mistress Eve?'

'He says she is being taken away on horseback by troopers.'

Lawless sighed. It was a broken-hearted sigh and he leaned on Waterloo hopelessly. 'Jordan!' he exclaimed. 'Blast ye for the evil devil ye be!'

Alan put his arm round him. 'Lawless, lad, perhaps there is a chance to rescue Eve and still carry out part of our plan. We must try, for the sake of our Daniel and Sam.'

Lawless nodded feebly. He was eaten up with pain and anguish for Dan and Sam, and hatred for Jordan, but he would do whatever the guv'nor wanted.

Alan faced back to Womballa and asked how far away Eve was and how many men were escorting her. The Aborigine turned his spear on end which was the sign for not far in a straight line, and said, '*Pulwarra thulga jerribong. Cooranga yangennanock ngauwun.*'

Alan again put his arm round Lawless and there was a faint hope in his expression as he translated. 'There are two men escorting her, and Womballa says it is not far. He can take us through the bush so that we can get in front of them, lad. What do you think of that?'

Lawless had to force himself to be alert. 'Oh Gawd, guv! At least we might be able to save the mistress.' Then he faltered. 'But we can't. Waterloo and Freedom are spent. They couldn't do it.'

Alan knew Lawless was right. With a gesture of defeat, he pointed to the sweating, panting animals.

An inscrutable expression passed across Womballa's face and he turned to Goodool and said something. Goodool nodded and removed his headband, a knotted strip of kangaroo skin. At the back was a folded piece of hide. He untied it and handed it to Womballa. The tribal elder emptied the contents into Alan's palm, signalling that he should give it to the horses. There were eight long seeds lying in his hand. He gave four to Freedom and four to Waterloo. The horses seemed to like the taste, for they swallowed them easily.

Womballa shook his spear. 'Good, good.'

And so it proved to be, for while the animals continued to sweat, their breathing soon eased and it was not long before they were standing quietly.

Mulgatta nudged his father and the old man came tentatively forward to observe the eyes of the horses. He looked at Alan. '*Tee-murra* like *mooltunya, murumba.*'

'The eye must be clear, like a rainpool,' Alan interpreted for Lawless.

And Womballa nodded with satisfaction as he looked into the horses' eyes. '*Marook*. Good,' he said, and Mulgatta and the others muttered approvingly.

The party set off across the valley at right angles, Womballa, Mulgatta, Gannawarra and Goodool running in front of the riders.

They crossed the valley almost due south and then turned south-west. They had covered close to four miles when Womballa held up his hand and halted them. He spoke to Mulgatta and Goodool so quietly that Alan caught only a few words. Mulgatta nodded. Then Womballa turned to look at Alan and there was a weary look on his face. 'Womballa no run more,' he said. 'Good medicine no help old man.' He waved his hand towards a rocky hill in the distance. 'Clever Fletcher woman and *thulga jerribong, yalanga*. Mulgatta, Goodool, take Clever Fletcher.' Then an unmistakable expression of sadness covered his face. He lifted his long, thin arm, the veins raised in intersecting pattern across it, and took hold of Alan's right hand in his. 'Womballa and Clever Fletcher, *yannawah. Womballa yallambee* Clever Fletcher *yanna*. Dreaming come, see Clever Fletcher.' He was saying a last goodbye to Alan.

Alan recognised the look of final parting in his friend's eyes. He knew he would never see this wonderful old face again with the coal-black eyes and the white beard, and the deep, intersecting life-grooves time-aged in his bronze skin. All his sorrow rose as a constricting pain in his throat. He let go the Aborigine's hand and dismounted. For a second or two they stared at each other, then Alan took hold of Womballa's shoulders and gripped them. 'Good-bye, my dear, true *waminda. Yannawah* and thank you . . . for everything.' He dropped his hands and gave the tribal sign for many thanks.

Womballa made a sad, broken sound and touched Alan's face as he had done the day Eve was with them, only this time he touched the corners of each of Alan's eyes as well. It was a moment of unadulterated love. Then he stepped back and said decidedly, 'Good-bye, Clever Fletcher. We meet in Dreaming.'

After a second or two, Alan drew his eyes from his friend's to Gannawarra, who was remaining with Womballa, and took his hand in farewell.

They left the Aborigines standing beneath the tall gums, two gaunt, dark, still figures. Lawless turned in his saddle and waved good-bye to them, but Alan did not look back.

Close to three miles later, Mulgatta called a halt, arm raised as his father had done. They were in sparse bushland on the crest of a long hill. A rocky shelf, some eight feet high, rose at their left side.

The young man indicated for Alan and Lawless to follow. He and his companion quickly scaled the rough rock surface and disappeared. Alan and Lawless followed. Some ten or twelve yards across the striated rock floor, there was a clear view back up the valley to the north and the east. There was nothing to see but gum trees and scrub.

Alan turned to Mulgatta. '*Windarra* Fletcher woman, Mulgatta?'

The young man held up his hand once more, his wide, flat face calm.

'I think he be tellin' us to have patience, guv'nor.'

'No doubt you are right, lad, although my patience has all but deserted me.'

They stood and waited perhaps five minutes before Mulgatta pointed eagerly through the trees, stamping his feet as he did so. Alan and Lawless strained to find what the young man saw, but they could see nothing.

'I see nothing,' Alan shook his head. '*Awulla narcoonah.*'

Mulgatta continued to point, saying, '*Billandry, billandry.*'

Half a minute passed and then sure enough, *far away*, as Mulgatta had been saying, Alan thought he perceived something moving. 'Up there, Lawless. Follow Mulgatta's finger, I think I see something.'

Lawless concentrated. 'Why yes, guv, black dots moving.'

'Aye, three.'

Mulgatta nodded. 'Fletcher voomaan.'

Alan patted the Aborigine's shoulder. 'Yes, Mulgatta, you are right.' Then he looked at Lawless, 'It's likely they will come within yards of this ledge.'

When Alan shook hands with Mulgatta and Goodool, he thanked

them and told them they were strong and brave, that he would always remember them and Womballa, and all the people of the Welba Welba.

Both young men grinned. 'Apo, Clever Fletcher.'

Lawless, too, said good-bye, solemnly repeating, 'Apo, Mulgatta. Apo, Goodool.'

The two young men departed, passing swiftly down the grade on their long, thin legs.

In the minutes left to them, Alan and Lawless worked at speed, tethering the two horses well away in the trees and covering their faces with the dark cloths they always carried. It was perhaps more important than ever that their faces not be seen.

The trees leading up the hill on the side the troopers approached gave ample room for passage. They were tall red gums, ancient trees with great trunks one and two yards thick. Alan stationed himself behind one of these at an angle of seven o'clock from the riders; while some fifty yards away, at an angle of four o'clock, Lawless hid. The oncomers did not divert from their line. One policeman rode in front, and Eve and the other came side by side.

Eve battled defeat. At times during the ride, she had cried softly, the tears running silently down her face as she averted it far from the trooper beside her. She kept seeing Danny and little Sam, twisted like corruptions of themselves in pools of blood. Then she rallied and tried to believe that all was not lost, that their deaths would not be for nothing. For, she knew in her heart Alan was alive, her very soul told her that. She must live in that thought.

Why were they taking her to the magistrate? What did they intend to do with her? Those she loved were dead, or in custody, or goodness knew where. Strangely, she kept visualising Alan and John Stuart side by side, as she often did, but they were both lost to her. She lifted her eyes as they came through giant red gums. Where are you, Alan? What have they done with you?

Suddenly a figure in grey leaped out in front of them and fired his revolver in the air. The troopers' horses both reared wildly but placid Milford did not rise on her hind feet; she merely whinnied and shook her head, then, recognising Alan, doggedly trotted forward to deliver Eve to him. By the time the troopers had taken control of their animals, Eve was at Alan's side.

'Alan! Oh Alan! Thank God!'

Trooper Dorando turned his horse to gallop back the way he had come, but there stood Lawless, his Terry carbine trained on the man's heart.

'Hold still, fella, unless ye be sick o' the planet!'

'Dismount, constables. Now!' Alan shouted, holding Milford's bridle for Eve to do the same.

Eve clung to Alan. He was here by her side. It was a miracle! She felt his hands gently push her to position himself between her and the troopers.

'You cannot do this. Mrs Wakeman is our responsibility,' observed Trooper Peters, a conscientious law enforcer.

Alan ignored the statement. 'I must ask you to remove your boots, and be swift.'

With the incentive of Lawless's rifle thrust in their faces, they did so.

'You'll not get away with this, I know you must be Alan Fletcher,' said Dorando boldly.

'Shut up!' shouted Lawless brandishing his rifle. There was a look of hatred in his amiable eyes, making him more fierce than he had ever been in his life. 'All I be wantin' is an excuse to fill ye with lead after what ye devils have done this day.'

There was animosity too in Alan, and the chilling tone in his voice was more threatening even than Lawless's anger. 'My partner also speaks for me, therefore I should stay quiet if I were you. The lives you and your mates have taken make us feel the need for revenge. So be very thankful it is not you we vent our feelings upon. I shall keep your compass and your horses.'

'But we need our boots,' spoke up Peters. 'We must make poor progress without them.'

'I am counting on that,' replied Alan.

'But we'll freeze,' Dorando insisted, though more tentatively than before. 'It's only an hour to dusk. The night . . . we'll be lost.'

'Who flamin' cares?' retorted Lawless, picking up their boots.

Eve remounted and sat watching as Alan said to Lawless, 'Throw them your horse blanket, lad. It will be of some use to them tonight against the wind.'

Lawless's expression disagreed with his leader's generosity but he untied the blanket roll from the back of his saddle and threw it reluctantly to the troopers.

Half a minute later, Alan led them northwards across the valley. When they were a few hundred yards distant and hidden from the police, he halted. Removing his mask, he turned to look at Eve. 'We know what happened at Treehard. Womballa waylaid us down in the valley.'

She closed her eyes. 'Thank God he did. For there was naught for you to do there except be executed like Daniel and Sam.' Her eyes filled with tears. 'It was horrible.'

Alan nodded. 'Jordan deserted us in the middle of the night. I assume he went to Rutherford Blake. We only just evaded a unit of troopers heading to our camp. I did not know . . . did not realise there was another party ahead of us.'

'Yes, David Elrington led them. Jordan was with them, I saw him. Danny and Sam never had a chance . . . Oh dear Lord!' Eve finished, dropping her head in her hands.

'There, lass,' Alan consoled her, though he felt weighed down by his losses. 'We will not talk of it now, though I must ask you to relate it all soon.' He looked at Lawless. 'We will return on the path we were taking to Treehard. That way we can water the horses in the same stream we stopped at earlier, and leave the troopers' horses there.'

'Where are we heading, guv?'

'I do not wish to place any man in jeopardy, but I must, and as I am positive the one man we can still trust is Bluey, we shall take the chance of heading to his hut.'

'Good idea. Bluey would not see us in need.' Lawless turned in his saddle and looked across to face in the direction of Treehard. He used Alan's name. Eve had never heard him use it before, and it surprised her. 'So, Alan, we will never see Treehard Hill again?'

Alan did not speak, he simply shook his head.

'Good-bye, mateys,' Lawless said softly. 'The world won't be the same without ye.' And he tipped his hat in silent salute.

CHAPTER THIRTY-TWO

'A friend may well be reckoned the masterpiece of nature.'
'Friendship', Ralph Waldo Emerson, 1803–1882.

It was well after dark when Sir Rutherford finally arrived at Treehard Hill.

By the time he had reached the point on the highway where he was to turn east, there were four troopers waiting for him. Sergeant Samuel and two others had come down from Treehard and joined the one left there earlier in the day.

All the long journey from Kettle's Creek, Sir Rutherford had seethed with anger. He had spoken sharply to the troopers with him and had grumbled over minor matters. Frustration and short temper had been his companions all the tedious day. Innumerable times he had gone over the events of the morning. If only he had caught Fletcher, what a coup it would have been. But he had not. Once more he had been so close and once more the infernal outlaw had evaded him.

Then at last, a short time after sunset, he had smiled.

As he approached the camp-fire of the men waiting for him on the highway, they hailed him with the words, 'We got 'em, Sir Rutherford. Daniel Dwyer and Samuel Cooper. We got 'em.' And at this news Sir Rutherford smiled; even though subsequently he had been disappointed to hear they were both dead.

'And what of Fletcher?' he inquired eagerly.

'No, sir,' answered Sergeant Samuel, 'there has been no sign of him or Drake, although we've had men at vantage points up to three miles and more from the hideout since we arrived.'

When he questioned the sergeant he learned that Mrs Wakeman had been there too, and that she had been transferred by police escort to the magistrate at Young as he had commanded. 'Good work!' He beamed in the firelight.

While Sir Rutherford's humour had improved, he was baffled. Where the devil was Fletcher?

The wind accompanied them all the way up the valley to the hideout, and it was with amazement that he rode through the concealed tunnel onto the cliff top beyond. O'Day had been absolutely right, there was no possibility of finding this place unless one knew it was here. He had always known Fletcher was different from other bushrangers, but what he saw at Treehard Hill profoundly impressed him. It was far beyond anything he had imagined.

His troopers had lit fires all round Treehard. He stood in wonder looking at the shapes surrounding him. There was a solid, well-constructed house with a verandah, and there were gardens, landscaping even, and a stable and sheds and a water tank. He, like his troopers before him, could not believe he was in a bushranger's hideout. He recognised admiration in his feelings, and was for a time disconcerted.

He viewed the bodies of the dead men, standing over them some minutes, although there was not much of Cooper to see. The body had disintegrated when they had tried to move it and they had needed to use shovels to lift it. His own motto ran through his head: 'Break those who break the law!' It certainly applied to Samuel Cooper. Standing there studying them, he found himself wondering about Dwyer. He looked the age they said, about seventy. The vague half-truths he had heard in the wayside inns came to his mind. How they said, years before, during a hold-up, Alan Fletcher had taken his whip to a man who had insulted Dwyer; that he had loved this Irishman like a father, and how Dwyer was said to call him 'son'. Ah yes, these men had meant a lot to Fletcher, he was sure of that. Fletcher should turn up any minute.

He wanted more detail about their deaths and asked David Elrington to give him an account of the shooting.

'Ah yes, I see, so it was a wooden spoon Dwyer was holding, not a revolver, Mr Elrington. I fancy some of our men had nervous trigger fingers?'

'I'm afraid so, Sir Rutherford, but of course it is law to shoot on sight now, sir.'

He looked closely at the face of his young assistant. 'Ah yes . . . it is,' he replied almost to himself as he turned away. Afterwards, he gave orders for the bodies to be interred on the clifftop the following morning.

When David Elrington told him about Mrs Wakeman, he was most interested to hear there had been no sign of a child as they had been told; and he listened with serious expression to how she had been devastated by the deaths of her two companions. Ah yes, she certainly seemed to be one of them. John Stuart Wakeman's wife and Alan Fletcher's consort! How very demeaning for the great

Wakeman name. He hoped his friend would not be disappointed when he met her in Young.

He did not speak with the informer, although he was told the man wished to see him. He would interview him tomorrow. He was sorry he had to interview the scum at all. Nevertheless, O'Day might shed some light on Fletcher and thus could be helpful.

He left grumbling lookouts at various posts outside the entrance to the tunnel and wandered all over Treehard Hill in the cold night air with David Elrington carrying a hurricane lamp. He examined everything, even down to the hen house.

He smiled again as Sergeant Samuel showed him the bags of gold from Theresa Town found in a box in one of the rooms. There were perhaps two thirds of what had been stolen. Somehow it made up for the indignity he had suffered that awful night last October.

When at last he was satisfied with his inspection, he ate at Daniel's kitchen table and slept in Alan's bed. He did not sleep well. His rest was troubled by bad dreams and he felt uneasy when he awoke early in the morning. He breakfasted off the Treehard crockery and drank from Lawless's mug.

There had been no sight of Fletcher in the night, which very much surprised him, for he thought he knew Fletcher well enough to be certain he would come back. Unless somehow he had found out what had taken place, and how could that possibly be?

He determined to complete things here this morning and begin the long ride back to Bathurst early in the afternoon. At half past eight he witnessed the burial of the bushrangers near the cliff edge. There was no clergyman, of course, so he said what little of the burial ceremony he could remember. As his men heaped the last sods of earth on the graves, he mused on the eccentricities of life; that he, of all men, should say prayers over the bodies of Dwyer and Cooper. He caught himself wondering about them again.

He turned and walked to the edge of the escarpment and looked east into the morning sun. He should have felt satisfied with the way things were progressing. He was inside the Fletcher hideout where he had dreamed of being; he had two more bushrangers' crosses to go on his map. The Wakeman woman was on her way to Young. It was all very promising, and yet he felt discontented.

There was a film of frost on the grass at his feet and the chill air bit through his velvet jacket. Looking down from where he stood, the view was vast; the morning lay upon the earth like a gauze of lemon over the patchwork patterns of the valley below. What a remarkable place this Treehard Hill was. He turned back to the two mounds behind him; the graves of Dwyer and Cooper, and for the space of a few seconds, he felt glad that they had such a resting place. Then he coughed, almost embarrassed at the thought, and rubbing his hands together strode back through the trees.

He spent a long time studying everything once more in daylight and wrote up his reports at Daniel's kitchen table. Now he must interview O'Day.

He had just called Constable Crystal to him with the intention of sending for the man, when he heard the sound of Sergeant Samuel's voice calling from the yard, 'Sir Rutherford, the troopers Dorando and Peters have just returned. They have been lost all night. They were the men with Mrs Wakeman. Alan Fletcher ambushed them and took her away!'

He actually leaped from the table, knocking over his chair, hot anger rippling through him. He bounded out the door, across the verandah and down the steps. 'Bring the blasted informer to me now!' he shouted. 'And make ready for half the troop to ride.'

Alan, Eve and Lawless had arrived at Bluey's not long after Sir Rutherford joined Sergeant Samuel and the three troopers waiting for him on the highway. They had kept mostly to bush tracks and only ventured onto the highway when there was no alternative. The last few miles they had moved at a plodding pace, for Waterloo had become lame and badly needed new shoes.

Eve looked up at the sky. The moon was now covered with cloud and there were a few spots of rain falling as they came through the dense bush that led to Bluey's hut. The wind blew violently and the horses strained. It was with immense relief that she saw the black shape of the dwelling appear ahead, lamplight flickering invitingly through the broken windowpane.

Alan said, 'Hold here, both of you, I'll go ahead to see if Bluey's alone.'

The fatigue showed in Lawless's face as he reined in Waterloo. 'Gawd, I hope he is, guv, for I cannot go much further this night. We've taken no food since yesterday.'

As Alan rode through the broken fence to Bluey's tumbledown verandah, the front door opened and a rifle poked through. 'Who is it there?' called Bluey's voice. 'Who is travelling on such a night?'

Alan's voice sounded in reply. 'It is I, Bluey, who have need of your hospitality again.'

Bluey's answer drew a sigh of relief from Lawless. 'Oh, it's you, Governor, is it?' He lowered his rifle as he came through the door.

'Come on in, Alan. I'm all alone here. Who is it you bring, my dear ally?'

Eve and Lawless rode forward and as they dismounted, Alan explained, 'I don't want to take advantage of your generosity or place you in any danger, Bluey, my friend, but we're on the run. The troopers are at Treehard. Jordan informed on us.'

Bluey shook his craggy head. 'Oh hell, the bastard! What has happened?'

Lawless answered, all the pain and fury of the day sounding in his voice. 'They killed Daniel and Sam, the mistress here witnessed it. All I be wantin' is my hands round Jordan's throat.' He turned away, making a frustrated sound of fury.

Bluey looked to Alan, shock making his face sombre beneath his beard. 'Oh no, what an awful thing. Quick, my allies, come in out of the rain and tell me.'

Lawless faced back to the horses. 'I must be bein' a blacksmith first, Bluey. I'm hopin' ye have shoes enough for Waterloo. One has come almost entirely loose.' He patted Waterloo's mane. 'They've carried us further than ye'd believe possible from three o'clock this morn.'

'Certainly, certainly,' replied Bluey. 'I've enough shoes in the lean-to to reshoe all the nags 'tween here and Bathurst. You'll find a hurricane lamp at the entrance to work by, and feed in the box.'

'I'll join you, lad,' Alan said to Lawless as he moved Eve forward towards the door. 'Bluey, this is Mistress Eve, please take her inside while we attend to the animals.'

Eve remembered Bluey's home well. She took off her cape and hung it over a chair near the fireplace; then stood warming herself and looking along the titles of his books that lay in disarray on a shelf above. There were a few Dickens titles and volumes of poems by Gray, Tennyson and Arnold. She was surprised to see books she had only ever seen before in the Mayfield library: works of Aristotle and Socrates, and more recent thinkers, Thomas Carlyle, David Hume and John Locke. The latter two of whom she had never heard until she met John Stuart. She turned her eyes from the Scottish philosopher's autobiography to look at the bushman behind her with new interest.

Bluey, who did not see her quizzical gaze upon him, asked without looking up, 'And where do you hail from – Mistress Eve, is it? I think the Governor said.'

'Yes, it is. I am . . . an old friend of his.'

He took a sidelong glance at her. 'Are you now? Didn't know that he had any old female allies.'

Eve came to a decision. She took a deep breath. 'I am Eve Wakeman, Bluey, from Mayfield.'

He placed a leg of beef on the table and stood looking at her. 'So? It's you, is it?'

'Yes, it's me.'

'Well now,' he said thoughtfully, as he started cutting the meat into slices, 'from the majestic mighty Mayfield, eh?'

Eve nodded.

They were both quiet for a time while he continued to prepare the meal, then he put down the knife, looked up, and said decisively, 'It's my opinion that you made the right choice.'

'I beg your pardon?'

'The right choice – between the one you were married with and the Governor. In my opinion, Alan Fletcher wins hands down.'

'It wasn't quite that simple, Bluey.'

'I dare say it wasn't. But then life is not, is it?'

'I see by the books you read that you maintain that point of view.'

He smiled at her. 'Ah, you recognise my soul companions. You know the Descartes axiom? "I think therefore I am." Well, perhaps a solitary man thinks too much, but meditations are my comforts on a cold winter's night such as this.'

Eve liked this strange, isolated person. 'Have you ever been married, Bluey?'

'No, never. Got a girl though, good girl, Christina Lyon of Wattamondara. One of three sisters, but to my mind Chrissy's the pick!'

When at last Alan and Lawless came in, Eve moved to his side as Alan spoke to their host. 'I do not wish to place you in any danger, Bluey, so if you would rather we moved on before first light we will, and if you think it better not to know of this day's events, then we'll hold silent upon them.'

Bluey shook his head vehemently. 'Alan Fletcher, you stay here until you're ready to leave. It's my life I owe you. From the day you dragged me out of the quicksand, you have been my ally. So too were Daniel and Sam and I'm wanting to know about them, so you speak freely in front of me. I don't give a bugger if the police question me, I won't rat on you like Jordan did.'

Alan smiled. 'Yes, Bluey, I know you mean what you say and I thank you for it.' Then he put his hand out to Eve and took her by the arm. 'I have not introduced this lady to you . . .'

'I know who she is, Governor,' Bluey interrupted. 'And as she's with you, there's naught more to say than she's very welcome here.'

Eve smiled. 'Thank you, Bluey.'

Fifteen minutes later, they were all seated around Bluey's small table and Alan had given their host a description of the events that brought them to him.

Eve knew she must tell them what had occurred at Treehard. She took a deep breath to calm herself and began.

She told them how Sam had taken his revolver and worn it in his belt. 'It was so odd, his doing that, both Dan and I thought so.' She related the sighting of the spiny anteater and her conversation with Samuel in the stables. 'We were having such a lovely afternoon . . . and we talked of America. I had only been gone from him for a few minutes when I heard a loud volley of rifle shots, followed a few seconds later by another. I ran back through the trees to find them both lying dead on the ground. Sam was just a . . . a bloody heap and Daniel had fallen to the bottom of the steps. I screamed I think, and ran to Dan and took him in my arms.'

She could go no further for a few moments and Alan took her hands in his. 'There, lass, there.'

Lawless's eyes were wet and Bluey pulled at his beard, his expression grim.

'After I had been taken into the house, David Elrington came in. He told me I was to be escorted to the magistrate in Young. He acted as if I were a sort of embarrassment to them at Treehard. He was very anxious to get me to the magistrate. After having lived with you all for over six months, no doubt I would be charged under the new Act.'

Alan nodded thoughtfully.

'There was a single trooper who had compassion for me. He was the sergeant we met on the road on Boxing Day, remember him? He was sympathetic, kind, wished me good luck. I believe Rutherford Blake was to arrive at Treehard tonight.'

Alan nodded. 'Yes, that makes sense, doubtless he led the party which intended to capture us, Lawless, and after failing, he would have ridden on to Treehard. He's the sort of man who would want to see our home for himself.'

'Aye, guv'nor, he wouldn't be leavin' anythin' to chance.'

Eve turned to Alan. 'There was one thing Sam said to me. How very strange he would say it to me, today.'

Alan was looking questioningly at her.

'He said that I was not the only one who . . . loved you.'

Alan leaned forward and put his head in his hands. He sat that way as the seconds turned into an entire minute and no one spoke. The wind was whipping round the little shack and something was rattling on the roof. Then he ran his hands across his eyes and sat upright. 'And tell me of Jordan, did you see him?'

531

'Yes, he was there with the troopers. He seemed shocked. He was ashen and his face was . . . full of fear.'

'Oh, how I would fill him with fear if I could!' Lawless lashed out, smashing his fist down on the table.

'Calm, lad,' advised Alan. 'Though I feel the same way, there's little we can do to Jordan at this distance.' He shook his head. 'Perhaps Jordan believed Danny and Sam would be taken prisoner, not shot down in front of him. In which case he would not have witnessed what happened afterwards, and he would have been able to rationalise it all.'

Bluey grunted angrily. 'The bloody, stinking rat.'

'Aye,' muttered Lawless.

'I misjudged the calibre of the man, that is certain,' Alan said softly.

Bluey shook his head sadly and then, pointing to his bed against the wall, said, 'I'll be offering you my cot, Mistress Eve. It's a night's sleep in peace you all need.'

'Yes,' agreed Alan, 'we will be on our way early in the morning.'

The rain continued falling on the tin roof and for a time Eve lay listening to it, a sound conducive to sleeping, but no sleep came. She could see the shapes of the three men lying on the floor under their blankets, Alan closest to her. There was a painful, empty place in her chest when she thought of Danny and Sam and hot tears were running from her eyes. Slowly, quietly, she raised herself up and moved the few feet to Alan. She knelt down and he turned towards her. She could not really see in the darkness, but she sensed that he lifted his arms and opened them. With a long sigh, she bent forward and lay down inside them, head resting on his chest. He covered her with the blanket, and she felt him kiss the top of her head. She heard his whisper, 'Eve, my love.' Soon, she drifted into sleep, curled securely against him, while Alan lay staring into the blackness, his eyes fixed, listening to the night rain.

Eight hours later, they sat at breakfast. It was a moodily overcast, cold day, but at least the rain had stopped. They wrapped themselves well against the wind and shortly after seven o'clock said their farewells.

Lawless wound his arms round the bearded man's shoulders. 'There be no one truer than you on the whole western plains. Thanks for everythin', matey.'

'Look after yourself, Lawless.'

Eve put out her hand to Bluey and he took it and bent over it. 'Goodbye, m'lady.'

'Goodbye, Bluey, and thank you for your kindness.'

Alan too put his arms round Bluey's shoulders. 'Thank you, my true friend, for harbouring us again. Stay safe in the future.'

'Yes,' Bluey sighed softly, 'you too, old ally, for I doubt I'll be seeing the fine sight that is your face again.'

Before he mounted Freedom, Alan turned back and put a gold sovereign in Bluey's hand. Bluey looked down at it, then handed it back. 'It's hard for me to say no to a sovereign, but I reckon you'll be needin' it more than me, Alan.'

'Bluey, I want you to have it. It is but small payment for what you've done.'

'Don't want it,' the bushman answered sternly. 'Just don't get caught, that will be ample payment for me, Governor.'

As they rode away, Eve hoped Bluey would marry his Chrissy and be happy, and she turned at the same moment as Alan to wave a last goodbye to him standing there in the thick undergrowth near his fallen fence.

Before they reached the highway, Alan halted them. 'The whole force of police in the west will be after us soon. I still propose to get us away to America, but now we have no money, it leaves us little choice. We need to do another job, Lawless, quickly, and one that will pay us well.'

'What do you call pay well, Alan?' Eve interjected. 'The coach with the wages was to pay a lot of money. But,' her voice dropped, 'now there are only three of us, surely we don't need as much.'

He fell silent for a few moments. 'What you say is true, we could get by with less, probably much less.'

'Well, I know somewhere that we can get three hundred and fifty pounds and there's no risk involved.'

Lawless's face brightened. 'That'll do. But where, Mistress Eve?'

'In Bathurst.'

'Bathurst?'

'Yes, it's my money.You know about it, Alan, the money Father left to me. I wrote the letter to Mr Lees, the solicitor, in February and we sent it to Lottie to deliver. The legacy should be there waiting for me.'

Lawless spoke eagerly. 'Gawd, that's wonderful, mistress. Isn't it grand, guv?'

Alan was less enthusiastic. 'Eve, that is your money, yours alone. By all means get it, but it's not for us to buy passage with it.'

Eve looked severely at him. 'Oh Alan, I will not listen to you. It's my money, yes, to do with as I will. It is wrong of you to once more place yourself in jeopardy to get funds when I have enough for us all. How can you scorn using my money when you were proposing that I use yours? Lawless,' she faced round to him, 'you know I'm right.'

'I think the mistress has a favourable argument, guv,' sounded Lawless meekly.

Alan did not speak immediately. When he did, it was as he urged Freedom forward. 'Perhaps we should head to Bathurst where you can get your money, lass, after which we will discuss this again.'

Eve made a small groaning sound, and shaking her head at Lawless moved Milford after him.

Alan thought it very probable that Sir Rutherford Blake was at Treehard, and once the two troopers who had been escorting Eve found their way back to him, he would start immediately for Bathurst. They did not have much time. Once more in their lives they were truly on the run. Now too, the woman he loved was in danger. She was wanted in custody. Escaping to America was paramount. He wished there was another way where he did not need to use Eve's money. Unfortunately, there was only one place that would afford him the amount of cash he needed immediately – a bank, and he had never robbed a bank and taken from ordinary citizens in all his years as a bushranger. He was not going to do so now.

Nearing Cowra, they avoided the old rustic bridge and forded the river at a shallow spot to the east, skirting the township.

Between two o'clock and three o'clock, they ate a meal near a tiny creek half a mile off the road and not far from Carcoar. When Lawless was dousing the fire, Eve was washing the billy and the mugs in the creek; she lifted her eyes to see Alan regarding her. He looked concerned, and when she came back to the horses he moved to her. 'Eve, I don't want you to sleep out tonight. I have some gold soverigns and one of those will be more than enough to get you a good meal and a bed in an hotel. We will ride into Carcoar and put you on the afternoon mail coach to Bathurst. It gets into that settlement around eight o'clock tonight. Then at least you can sleep comfortably, and we can meet you on the morrow.'

'Alan, I am not made of glass.'

'What is that?'

'I am not made of glass. I shall sleep where you sleep. I do not want to be separated from either of you. I refuse to be put on the mail coach.'

Lawless continued quietly to break camp as she continued. 'And in any event, I have an idea of my own. One which will have us all under a good roof and will cost us none of the sovereigns in your pocket.'

'Oh, and what is that, lass?'

'Lottie. Lottie Thatcher. You said she told you she would be living in one of the church's river cottages. I know she will help us. I could get my money, and then we could go on to Sydney.'

Alan weighed her argument before he replied. 'Yes I agree Mistress Lottie would be willing to help. But you forget there must still be some troopers in Bathurst, and we place all these good folk in dire peril when they assist us.'

'But Lottie would not see it that way. She would want to help. That is the sort of woman she is.'

Lawless, who had listened earnestly to the conversation, broke in, 'This Mistress Lottie, she was the instrument of your escape from Bathurst last January, guv'nor. She has always sounded like a plucky one to me, and reliable. It'll be a roof over our heads for a start.'

Alan looked thoughtful. 'I appear outnumbered. But it's still a thirty-mile ride, and I fear you overtax yourself, lass.'

She shook her head vigorously. 'I can make the ride.'

It was some hours after dark when the three travellers rode down the deserted, windswept streets of Bathurst. They rounded the boarded-up hay and corn market into Durham Street and passing along to Rankin Street turned right. There, on the other side of the open fields, lay the row of river cottages.

They reined in near a clump of young casuarinas that made a tolerable wind break and looked at each other in the pale light of the bleak, winter moon. Eve thought all the emotional strain and physical exertion of the last forty-eight hours echoed in Lawless's voice as he spoke. 'Guv'nor, how in heaven's name are we to know which place is Mistress Lottie's? There look to be a number of cottages over there trailin' along the river. We cannot go knockin' upon doors.'

Alan replied as he dismounted. 'You're right, lad. But there are other ways perhaps of divining Mistress Lottie's home. Wait here.'

Eve and Lawless climbed down as his dark shape disappeared across the field and melded with the night. All was still except for the wind around them. They looked at each other as they heard dogs barking. A few more minutes passed and Eve spoke anxiously. 'He seems to be taking a long time, Lawless.'

'Don't worry, Mistress Eve. Of all the men in the world, he knows what he's doing.'

Alan had passed up and down by the small houses. There were six and he examined everything he could see meticulously, including the gardens, the sheds and the paths leading to the doors. A large dog had barked at the fifth cottage and its cry was taken up by another at the sixth but no one came out to observe the disturbance, and before long they fell into silence.

Alan came back to the very first cottage and walking quietly to the door tapped on it. All was still and he knocked again, a little louder this time. His heart quickened slightly as he heard someone stir inside and a few moments later draw back the latch. It clicked and the door moved ajar some inches. 'Who comes aknocking on a poor woman's door this dark cold night?' asked Lottie, peering out into the blackness.

A mild sound, much like a sigh, issued from Alan's mouth as he answered softly, 'Mistress Lottie, it's Alan Fletcher. I have need of your help.'

The opening of the door widened and he fancied Lottie's eyes widened with it. 'Well I never,' she said. 'Come on in, don't be astanding in the cold.'

'I have Eve with me and Lawless, the last of my band. I shall go and get them.'

'Oh do . . . do,' the good woman replied.

'We're on horseback. Where shall I put the animals so they won't be seen?'

She nodded thoughtfully. 'Now, wait a bit, I'll just pop and get my shawl.' With that she turned back into the house and a few seconds later emerged covered in a long woollen wrap.

They crossed the field together.

'Do ye know,' she said as they walked, 'there was a lot of talk here yesterday morn. Sir Rutherford and all his troopers rode out in the middle of the night, Sunday, and only three returned. The gossip all over was that they were after ye and that Sir Rutherford had gone to a place called Tree Yard.' Her voice dropped as she added, 'Well, I'm going to tell ye, I was aworried about ye, I was. It's a true relief to see ye here beside me.'

'Thank you, Mistress Lottie. Do you know whether any more troopers have come back since?'

'Not as I know of, and I reckon I would be aknowing, for news travels fast in this place.'

'That's a good sign for us.'

'And to think two minutes ago I was areading by the fire,' she continued, half running at his side, 'and now here I am with ye again, Mr Fletcher. What a wonder is this life.'

Eve and Lawless saw the two figures approaching. Eve recognised Lottie and ran forward to meet her. 'Lottie, oh Lottie, how wonderful to see you.'

'Eve . . . Miss Eve,' Lottie whispered excitedly as she took Eve in her arms, 'and how grand it is to be aseeing ye.'

As they joined Lawless, Alan's arm went round his shoulder. 'This is my partner, Lawless Drake, Mistress Lottie Thatcher.'

Lottie beamed at the dark shape that was Lawless and taking him by the hand he extended said, 'A pleasure to meet ye, sir.'

They followed Lottie back across the field to her cottage.

When the animals had been put in Lottie's shed and watered, fed and covered with blankets, the humans collected round her warm fire where Alan gave her a brief description of the important events of the last two days. She bustled about as she listened, getting food and drink for them.

Alan finished his account with the words, 'So we're here for Eve to collect her legacy and then we make haste for Sydney town. We don't want to endanger you or be here when Rutherford Blake and his troopers return.'

Lottie shook her head sadly. 'My, that Jordan O'Day deserves to swing, but of course he shan't now that he's in cahoots with Rutherford Blake.' Then she wagged the knife she was using to cut meat. 'And never ye mind about putting me in danger, I'm an old hand at it. Haven't we been through this once before, Mr Fletcher?'

'Yes,' Alan answered quietly, 'that we have, Mistress Lottie, but now there is even more jeopardy for a friend such as you.'

For reply, she simply smiled at him. Then she asked, 'How on earth did ye know this was my cottage?'

'Yes, guv, how did ye pick it?'

'In the end it was a guess. But I knew Mistress Lottie did not like large dogs, so that helped to discount two places. And this was the neatest cottage of all, the garden beds being tidy and the fence whitewashed. It had the stamp of Mistress Lottie upon it.'

'Why, thank ye, Mr Fletcher.'

Eve moved to stand by Lottie. 'Did you receive the letter I wrote to Mr Lees?'

'I did indeed. Came here to me on February sixth and I opened it and took out the sealed missive inside. Delivered it bright and early to him the following morning. Demanded a private interview and got one,' she finished proudly.

Alan turned to Eve. 'You instructed the solicitor to hold the funds in readiness?'

'Yes. I said I would come at a future time to collect the legacy. That I was not sure when it would be, but for him to do what was legally necessary and hold the money until I came for it. How did he react when you gave him the letter, Lottie?'

'Well now, he read it through in front o' me, looking very formal, and then he says, "Miss Thatcher, do you know the whereabouts of Mrs Wakeman?" And I answered I did not. Then he shook his head and looked a mite absorbed and said, "Do ye know what this letter is about?" I replied once more in the negative and then he bade me good morning and in half a minute more I be back in the street.'

Eve patted Lottie's shoulder. 'Thank you, dear. It's six months since Father's death. There has been ample time for probate to have been granted as it was Mr Lees himself who was to be executor.'

While they sat round Lottie's small table and took the refreshment she had prepared, Eve was thinking she must stay until she had received her money. She wondered what Alan would do. As she looked up to meet his eyes, he spoke as if reading her thoughts. 'Lawless and I shall ride out before dawn, our presence endangers Mistress Lottie too much. As for you, Eve, you will be an object of much discussion in Bathurst once folk are aware of you.' He smiled briefly. 'Now, as you are not on the wanted list, they won't arrest you, and I would be certain the troopers here don't know of the plan to deliver you to the magistrate's hands; that would be something private between Rutherford Blake and his deputy. There's no reason for those here to connect you with us. Nevertheless, we wish to expedite matters, and caution should be exercised.'

'Aye, that be true enough,' agreed Lawless, 'and witless as some of the traps be, they can create lots of trouble.'

Eve's face clouded; she disliked the thought of any separation from them. 'So, you leave first. Where shall I meet up with you? What if Rutherford Blake comes back in the morning?'

'Lass,' answered Alan. 'I do not see how he can possibly be back before tomorrow afternoon if he went on to Treehard but to be sure, I shall take up a position where I am hidden from the highway but where I can observe all who ride into Bathurst from the west. If perchance I see him, I'll be back here to remove you from Bathurst immediately.'

Eve brightened considerably.

'So, while I do expect tomorrow morning to pass quietly, I want you to catch the noontime Cobb and Co. coach that goes to Meadow Flat, Lithgow, Bell and Mount Victoria.' He leaned towards her. 'Leave the vehicle at Lithgow. It halts at the Gibraltar Hotel. I don't believe we can expect to be further ahead of Rutherford Blake than twenty-four hours, perhaps not even that long. If he knows of your escape from the troopers, Eve, you are in danger of being taken. You must avoid being here when he returns. I have little doubt Jordan has told him of our plan to get away to America. Blake will most certainly follow us.'

'But we must be well ahead of him, guv, for we were at Bluey's last night whereas you thought he would be at Treehard Hill.'

Alan considered the point. 'Yes, that may be so, lad, but when the troopers who were conveying Eve to Young appear or are found again, I think he'll ride rapidly in this direction, for he will quickly realise we have had the advantage on him.'

'We should have bound the troopers, guv, we really should have,' said Lawless grimly.

Alan peered into the flames of the fire as he answered. 'No, laddie, that would have been wrong. Roped up there in that isolated valley, they might never have been found. It would have amounted to murder, and we do not deal in killing.'

'Aye, I know in my heart ye be right, but the traps deal in it, they murdered Sam and Danny.'

'They don't see it as murder, lad.'

'I know guv'nor, but it was, it damn well was.'

Alan stood and moved to the fireplace. He lifted the poker and stoked the fire before he turned back to them. Eve felt his sadness. He looked at her. 'Eve, do you know where Mr Lees the solicitor lives?'

'If it's where he used to live, it's no more than a quarter of a mile from here, in Rankin Street.'

'Yes,' said Lottie, 'that's right.'

'I think you should be there before he goes to his office in the morning.'

Eve nodded. 'Yes, I understand. To make certain that everything can be arranged before I catch the noon coach.'

'Right. And if it cannot be, then you must catch the coach anyway. We will decide what to do later.'

Alan regarded Lottie contemplatively for some moments. She returned his gaze with a smile. He seemed to come to a decision and he asked, 'Mistress Lottie, can you ride?'

Lottie looked surprised. 'I can. Used to ride a great deal. Why?'

He motioned for Eve and Lottie to rise. 'Would you both be kind enough to stand up side by side?'

Their interest aroused, the two women did so.

Alan looked to Lawless, 'Am I right to suggest they are the same height, size and coloring?'

'I believe ye are, guv.'

'Then I shall answer your question, Mistress Lottie, although I will understand if you do not agree to my suggestion. I ask if you ride, because if you were to accompany Lawless tomorrow morning and acquire a room at the Gibraltar Hotel in Lithgow, when Eve arrived there, you could be of great help.'

Lottie smiled. 'I'll do anything I can, ye should know that full well.'

539

'Hear me first, Mistress Lottie,' Alan continued as the two women sat down, 'then we shall see if you agree. Tomorrow, Eve wears a hat and heavy veil when she catches the coach, and when she disembarks at Lithgow, she too secures a room at the Gibraltar Hotel. Now, Lawless and you, Mistress Lottie, are already there, having left here at dawn on Waterloo and Milford. You two women then change clothes and hats. Mistress Lottie becomes Eve and decides to quit her room and take the night coach south to Oberon, while the couple that came in on horseback, after a few hours' rest, continue on their way, which is east to Bell and up the Blue Mountains.'

Lawless slapped his hand on his thigh. 'I see it, guv'nor, I see it. And aye, it could be done, for none o' them folk in Lithgow knows as what Mrs Wakeman looks like anyway. Thus, if Blake follows, he chases the woman who's gone to Oberon, that bein' Mistress Lottie.'

Eve's face lit up. 'Oh Alan, it's a good plan.'

'And if I wear a bonnet that covers much of my face when Mr Drake and I arrive to take rooms at the Gibraltar, then they won't see me properly either,' added Lottie excitedly. 'We simply change places. Of course I agree.'

Alan smiled gently. 'Thank you, there is but one thing, Mistress Lottie. You said "rooms". I hope you understand that it will be better if there is but one room, if you and Lawless appear to be husband and wife.'

Lottie blushed. 'Oh, I . . . I see. Why I . . . I've no objection if Mr . . . Drake has none.'

'I have none,' grinned Lawless.

Suddenly, Eve felt apprehensive. 'But Alan, from Bathurst to Sydney there is a telegraph line. Is there a telegraph office at Lithgow? If Rutherford Blake gets back here while I'm travelling in the coach, I could find a trooper waiting when I step down at Lithgow.'

Alan nodded. 'There are telegraph offices at Meadow Flat and Lithgow on the plains, Bell, Weatherboard and Blaxland in the Blue Mountains, and then Penrith, Parramatta and Sydney. All those places have police constables except for Meadow Flat. So you are correct, the Lithgow police can receive a telegraphed message from Bathurst.'

Eve stood up from where she had been sitting and faced the fire. 'Then it means another day of fear, doesn't it? And there have been so many days of fear.' She turned back to look at Alan.

Lottie murmured, 'Oh dear, if Miss Eve were taken by Sir Rutherford, it would be just too terrible.'

Alan moved to Eve's side. 'Yes, it would, and that is a consequence

I must make sure cannot result.' His proximity had the effect of calming her. He inclined his head to Lawless. 'Do you remember the time Old Joe Daily set fire to the telegraph office at Bell so they couldn't send a message that he had robbed the mail coach?'

Lawless's mouth drew down at the edges in thought. 'Aye, I do. It was in sixty-one when the telegraph line only went to Lithgow. We used to say, "Don't do a job behind the line", for fear of the telegraphed messages.'

'Yes, that's right. My idea is similar, though I do not approve of that sort of destruction, and it is something I'm not proud to perform, but I am forced to do everything I can to protect Eve from being seized by Rutherford Blake.'

Lawless was bending forward now, elbows on his knees, a knowing expression on his face.

Alan continued, 'The telegraph poles are nine inches in diameter at the base. A sharp axe and a strong arm will bring one down in five minutes.'

'I'm right with ye, guv'nor.'

'I know you are, lad. You will ride out and choose a point where the telegraph line between Bathurst and Lithgow will come down. Repairs will take a long time, possibly days, for they must locate it and mend it. Meanwhile, the noon coach from Bathurst will have arrived and departed Lithgow, with no chance of the police there being alerted that Eve is wanted by Rutherford Blake. There is no police representation at Mount Victoria, and that is where we three will meet again tomorrow night, to continue our journey to Sydney.'

There was an atmosphere of confidence beginning in the little cottage as Alan went on, 'Meanwhile, Mistress Lottie will sleep the night in Oberon at Stopford's Inn and come home to Bathurst on Thursday. Isn't there a mail that runs through Rockley and Blayney in a circle service to Bathurst, Lawless?'

And Lawless, who knew every coach run in the colony, answered, 'Aye, guv'nor, correct. It runs every Monday and Thursday.'

Lottie's home had but three rooms, a sitting room, a bedroom and a kitchen with a small annexe at the side of the back door where she cleaned dishes, and clothes, and herself. With four people in it, her tiny house seemed very full.

Alan and Lawless washed out the clothes they had worn since Sunday night and dried them by Lottie's fire. Lottie brought out two clean shirts she had been keeping in memory of Reverend Billings and they accepted them gratefully. 'It seems fitting that ye should be agetting them, Mr Fletcher,' she said as she handed them over, 'as ye have worn the dear gentleman's clothes before.'

The two women slept together and the two men bedded down on the sitting room floor.

When Lottie had blown out the candle and they lay side by side in the darkness, snug under the blankets, Eve said quietly, 'Lottie dear, I want to tell you how it is that I come to be in Alan Fletcher's company.'

Lottie's voice came soft in answer. 'You do not need to tell me. He is the best of men. I know that now, and whatever has happened to link ye with him is none of my business. Besides, I do not blame ye for being so in love with the man.'

'Is it that obvious?'

'Yes, Miss Eve, it is.'

'But I want to tell you about it, Lottie, I want to.' And in a voice almost a whisper, she began with the incidents on her wedding day and why she had never told John Stuart about Clare. She explained her mixed emotions and her subsequent meetings with Alan; then the calamity of Lake's arrival at Mayfield. Her discovery that she carried his child, and how John Stuart reacted. How she had been forced to fly from Mayfield only to have the miracle occur when Lawless recognised her on the highway, and Alan came for her. 'My life was saved by an Aboriginal elder from the Welba Welba tribe who is like a brother to Alan, and you see, Lottie, I have been with them all at Treehard Hill ever since.' It was a long story, and Alan and Lawless in the next room were fast asleep by the time she ended.

Lottie lay still. The seconds passed, and loud was the sound of the wind whipping around the small building.

Eve nudged her, 'Lottie, aren't you going to say something?'

At last Lottie spoke. 'What is there to say? It tells like one o' those novels that everyone is areading these days. I've never heard such a tale and it coming from ye, well, it fair stumps me, it does. Mind ye, I was aware ye knew Mr Fletcher from the night he arrived to see our dear departed Reverend, so that part of the tale does not surprise me.'

'Somehow I am bound to him, always have been.'

'Yes, I'd say ye were. Wouldn't have mattered how ye pulled against it. A body's only got to look at ye standing side by side to know that.'

'Really?'

'Yes, Miss Eve, really.'

Then Lottie fell silent again and she moved awkwardly in the bed. A gentle flush that Eve could not see began in her cheeks as she whispered, 'I know I've only been in Mr Drake's company a few hours but I'll always remember him. There's something about him, something special. I'm a little timid about tomorrow.'

'Oh, Lottie,' whispered Eve taking one of the kind woman's hands under the covers. 'I've never known you to be like this.'

'I've never been like this,' murmured Lottie.

Eve shook her head in the blackness. 'What a bother this life is. He is going so far away.'

'To the ends of the earth from here, but that's the way of it,' answered the sensible Lottie. 'As long as he gets away safe with ye to America, as long as ye all get safe away, I'll be happy.'

Dawn broke around seven o'clock, and an hour before first light, Lottie made a hearty breakfast. The bacon and eggs standing on the hob spread an enticing aroma through the cottage and Alan and Lawless ate all that Lottie had prepared, as well as half a loaf of her freshly baked bread.

They saddled Freedom and Waterloo, and Milford for Lottie. Then Alan left Lawless with the animals and returned inside. Lottie and Eve stood side by side in the little kitchen.

Alan gazed from one to the other. 'Eve, when you arrive at the Gibraltar Hotel in Lithgow, Lottie will already be there, and after you have changed places, you and Lawless ride on to Newton's Inn at Mount Victoria. It's a reasonably kept establishment and was run by an ex-convict called Hutchins years ago, though I suspect not now. I will arrive late tonight as I will not depart Bathurst until dark, when your coach will have gained Lithgow.'

She looked concerned. 'Why?'

'We deal with a man who has a mania about bushrangers. He's not as the amenable Frederick Pottinger was. You are the link to us, and if he has a chance of catching you, he won't give up the chase. The ride from Treehard to here is a hundred miles and I don't believe he can be here until sometime this afternoon at earliest. But when he returns and learns your movements, I want to know if he continues the chase.'

Eve was listening carefully. 'And if he does continue the chase? What then?'

'Then I must follow him to Lithgow to see if he learns of "Mrs Wakeman's" continuing journey south to Oberon. To know for certain whether he goes after Mistress Lottie in your guise.'

'But it places you in terrible danger.' She lifted her hand to touch his arm. 'What if he sees you? And during the afternoon you can't lounge in the Bathurst streets. He recognised you here once before.'

He took her hand and squeezed it gently. 'Don't worry, Lottie has told me of a vantage point up in the public reserve land where I can watch Rutherford Blake's office without being seen.'

'Oh, and another thing,' Lottie said, 'ye can see the Sydney road to the east from parts of that reserve as well.'

'We had best be goin', guv,' Lawless's voice sounded from the door, 'it'll be light soon.' He came forward to the two women and put out his hand. 'I'll be seein' ye at the Gibraltar Hotel then, Mistress Eve.'

She let go Alan's hand and took his. 'Yes, dear Lawless, good luck, and be very careful.'

'Do ye have a bag, Mistress Lottie?'

Lottie handed him her small travelling case and he went outside to strap it on Milford.

Eve hugged Lottie goodbye. 'I will bring the latch key and give it to you this afternoon.'

'No, dear,' answered Lottie, 'leave it under the mat.' She turned to Alan. 'Well, Mr Fletcher,' she said trying to smile, 'this, I'm athinking is truly goodbye.'

He took her hand in his and looked down into her brave, grey eyes. 'You realise there is a strong possibility that Rutherford Blake will catch up to you before you return to Bathurst.'

'I realise.'

'Fortunately, he can do nothing to you. He will not be able to prove anything, even if he suspects the truth; but you will make an enemy of him.'

'I'm not worried about such as he.'

'I said once before you were a remarkable woman, Mistress Lottie Thatcher, and I repeat the sentiment. I wish you peace and happiness in the years ahead.'

'That is what I dearly wish for ye in return. Good luck and God bless ye.' She smiled into his eyes before moving to the door and out to Lawless.

Then Eve moved close to Alan. 'Be careful. You will be alone and in danger today.'

He gazed down at her and acknowledged the love in her eyes, then he wrapped his arms round her and held her to his heart. She felt him kiss her forehead, his face pressed in her curls. He turned swiftly on his heel and passed out into the chill morning air.

CHAPTER THIRTY-THREE

'Boot, saddle, to horse, and away!'
'Boot and Saddle', refrain, Robert Browning, 1812–1889.

John Stuart and Joe had ridden south on the bleak wet western plains and arrived cold and miserable at Kiddley's Inn some hours after dark on Monday night.

Joe looked tired, the lines in his face showing clearly and John Stuart felt guilty at having brought him on another long ride in such inclement weather. At breakfast on Tuesday morning, he even suggested that Joe bide at Kiddley's until his return. 'For I can ride on to Young and bring Eve back. I shall be all right on my own.'

Joe shook his head. 'No, m'boy, you do not ride alone, not as long as I can sit a horse. I'm coming with you, and besides, it's not raining this morning.'

When they dismounted outside Mr Finimore's wooden house with wide verandah and whitewashed fence, it was close to noon.

Joe rapped on the front door with his solid fist and a woman opened it.

'Mrs Finimore?'

'Yes.'

Joe gestured to John Stuart. 'This is Mr Wakeman.'

The good woman looked amazed. 'Mr Wakeman? Gracious, sir, what brings you here?'

Joe looked surprised. 'There's no one here, waiting for Mr Wakeman?'

'Good heavens, no, sir. Should there be?'

John Stuart gave a loud, disappointed sigh, grasping the verandah rail in frustration.

Joe spoke again. 'Is your husband in?'

'Yes, sir, he has just come home for luncheon. He is out the back seeing to the cleaning of the dray. Do please come into the parlour, I shall get him for you.'

Mr Finimore was as astonished as his wife. 'No, sirs. I have seen no police or Mrs Wakeman, and I have had no message from Sir Rutherford Blake about anything.'

Joe nodded. 'We shall wait.'

And they did . . . all day, and into the early twilight of the winter evening, until a horse and rider in police uniform came up the dirt road at a goodly pace.

John Stuart and Joe met Sergeant Rodney Samuel at the Finimores' gate. He tipped his cap, his good-natured face serious. 'Mr Wakeman, Mr Larmer, I come with a message from Sir Rutherford.'

'Yes?'

'He says to tell you he is very sorry. He did exactly as you asked. Mrs Wakeman was on her way here when it appears she was stopped by two masked men and carried off again. He believes it was Alan Fletcher.'

John Stuart said nothing. He could not even bring himself to thank the trooper. He turned away and smashed his fist into the palm of his hand.

Joe looked up at the sergeant astride his horse and, lifting his hand, held the man's dusty boot in friendly fashion. 'We are very grateful. Thank you, sergeant, for bringing us the news. Where is Sir Rutherford now?'

'He has ridden on to Bathurst. He has information that Fletcher is on his way to Sydney, sir.'

'Thank you.'

'And, sir?'

Joe, who was in the act of turning away to John Stuart, looked back. 'Yes?'

Sergeant Samuel cleared his throat. 'Sir Rutherford asked me give you this.' He handed Joe a folded piece of paper. Then he saluted and pulling his horse's head round rode back the way he had come.

The crumpled paper Joe held had 'John Stuart Wakeman' written on it. Inside, in the police detective's sprawling hand, was the concise, but adequate sentence, '*There is no child.*'

They stayed that night with the Finimores, though the master of Mayfield was poor company. He stared sombrely ahead of him and replied monosyllabically to his hosts' questions. In the end, they talked to Joe.

As they rode away just after dawn the next morning, Joe looked to his companion's rigid profile. 'What are you thinking, m'boy?'

John Stuart's unhappy eyes came round to Joe's. 'What the hell can I think, old man? She's been six months in his company, and now, he "abducts" her again . . . really? Is that what I am to believe, Joe?' He looked straight ahead. 'Tell me what I should think.'

'Where are we going, son?'

'Home.'

'All right, son, we go home.'

'To get a Mayfield coach and to follow Rutherford. I have to find out once and for all what the bloody hell is going on in my life.'

'Yes, Mrs Wakeman, I think I can have a letter of authorisation written for you this morning,' Mr Lees said, his small eyes growing even smaller with scrutiny behind his tiny spectacles. 'But you realise that because of the nature of the money, being a legacy I mean, you will have to collect it at the principal Office of Bequests at the Bank of New South Wales in Sydney.'

'But why was the money not kept here in Bathurst?'

'My dear Mrs Wakeman,' he answered, removing his spectacles and looking severely at her, 'this was a most extraordinary case. You were the beneficiary, the only beneficiary, of Reverend Billings' will. You were not visible. All I had in my possession was a letter. There was no return address. You were not to be found, and there was only a vague suggestion that you would come "sometime" for your money. I did not know whether the claim would be made this year, next year or the one after. You understand?'

'I think I do.'

'The certificate of verification was delivered, and probate granted, but you were not in evidence to appropriate the monies. Thus it was transferred to the Office of Bequests in Sydney.'

'So all I need to do is take your letter there and they will give it to me?'

'I should imagine so.'

'Then you shall be good enough to write it for me this morning?' Eve finished hopefully.

Mr Lees scratched the top of his hairless head and his eyes found the stuffed and mounted lyrebird reposing beyond Eve near his study window. 'Mrs Wakeman, where have you been?'

'I beg your pardon?'

'Where have you been?' he repeated, still concentrating on the lyrebird. Then his eyes came back to her face. 'These last six months? Is it true what I have read in the newspapers?'

Eve looked steadily back at him. He was a portly little man of around sixty. His florid face was stern as he sat surveying her.

'Mr Lees, I don't know what you have read.'

'Oh, come now, Mrs Wakeman, today is the fifth of July, you have been missing since Christmas. When the wife of the richest, most prestigious man in New South Wales disappears, there is naturally much speculation.' He clicked his tongue in remonstrance. 'Only two weeks ago there was an article in the *Sydney Morning Herald* which

547

insinuated that your husband should make a statement to the people in regard to your whereabouts.'

Oh dear, poor John Stuart. How awful for him. Her eyes met Mr Lees'. 'I did not know. The suggestion seems very insensitive.'

Eve could see that Mr Lees was judging her, as everybody would. How could they be expected to know the intricacies that had brought her to this day. She sighed. 'Mr Lees, I am asking you to do me the great favour of writing my letter of authority this morning, and I will be indebted to you for doing so. Because of that, I will answer you. I have been away with . . . my family.'

His eyebrows lifted in surprise as he sat appraising her. 'Your family? I thought you were from America and had no family here.'

Eve stood up as he said this and, as a gentleman, he was forced to stand also.

'I have always had family here, Mr Lees, even though I did not spend time with them until this year.' She held out her hand to him. 'I am truly very grateful to you and I shall call at your offices for my letter at eleven o'clock this morning.'

'Very well, Mrs Wakeman. When do you believe you will be in Sydney, for I shall send a telegraph message to alert them of your coming. It will serve also to identify you.'

Dismay quivered through Eve. She thought of Lawless on his way to bring down the wire. 'What do you mean, identify me? Will not the letter be sufficient?'

He clicked his tongue. 'I was merely meaning to help you. To give the manager an idea of when you would be arriving, so that he is expecting you, and does not think you happened upon the letter you carry by accident, in the street.'

With difficulty, she replied evenly, 'I shall be travelling there directly, perhaps Friday.'

He smiled perfunctorily, 'Well then, I shall organise to send a telegraph message either today or tomorrow.'

Eve's thoughts raced. 'Thank you, Mr Lees. Would you? That is . . . could you send it first thing this morning? Yes, for in fact I am hoping to catch an express mail coach from Lithgow. It is a recent, a very recent, innovation, continues overnight. I actually hope to be there perhaps as early as sometime tomorrow. Would you be so very kind as to send the telegraph message as soon as you get to your office this morning?'

Mr Lees' gaze had entirely forgone the stuffed lyrebird and was directed keenly at her. What a strange woman she was. He had never heard of this 'overnight' coach from Lithgow to Sydney. Of course he was not up to date on the schedule of the mails, but why hadn't she said so at first? He coughed. 'Are you sure of catching this express mail coach?'

Eve felt so uncomfortably hot she wanted air, and it was a very cold day. 'I . . . no, the express mail does not run every day. I will not know until I arrive at Lithgow, you see, whether I can board it or not.' She coughed. 'I would hate to arrive in Sydney to find they did not have the message, when you were so kind and so efficient to send it. Best to have everything in order, don't you think? You could send it this morning couldn't you, sir? Early this morning?'

The legal gentleman put his spectacles back on, replying slowly. 'Probably I can arrange what you suggest, Mrs Wakeman, even though it is all very hasty and I needs must journey on business to Orange this afternoon. Nevertheless, I suppose it can be done.'

Eve gave him a wide smile of genuine gratitude, 'Oh, thank you, Mr Lees. Until eleven o'clock this morning then? Good-bye.'

He sat down shaking his head. He had heard a rumour that her husband had searched hundreds of miles of bush looking for her. Some people had even said she'd been murdered . . . and here she pops up in his home and says she has been with her family. What a peculiar thing!

Back in the cottage, Eve made a pot of tea. Sitting alone, many things ran through her mind. The deaths of Daniel and Sam. She cried for them again. How her life seemed to be filled with losing those she cared for. Her own mother and father, Billy, Clare, Mother and Father Billings, and now Daniel and Sam . . . and even John Stuart too, in a way. Oh, please Lord, keep Alan safe. She saw him in her mind's eye looking at her . . . into her.

It was an interminable morning but at last fifteen minutes to eleven o'clock arrived and she was ready to go to the solicitor's office. She took Lottie's trap again with Daisy, her horse. This time some people were on the streets and soon she was the cynosure for a number of them.

When she was ushered in to Mr Lees, he was still looking at her disapprovingly, but he had kept his word, and he handed over the envelope to her at six minutes after the appointed hour.

'Thank you so very much, Mr Lees.' And at the risk of sounding unreasonably repetitious, she asked, 'Was all in order with the sending of the telegraph message?'

Mr Lees frowned. 'Actually, I'm not sure. I know young Turner, the office boy, was sent to have it transmitted. I assume it went.'

Eve sighed. 'I see, thank you very much, Mr Lees, and goodbye.' She walked quickly through his rooms to the street. There was nothing she could do. The telegraph message had gone, or had not gone, and she must continue in the hopes that it had.

She drove to Cobb and Co., the coaching company round the corner, to purchase a ticket for Lithgow. Mrs Janklor, the town gossip who sold the tickets, was known as the 'sights and sounds of Bathurst'. Eve took a deep breath as she entered the wooden shop front for she knew the woman would put her through an inquisition. With relief, she saw the face behind the counter was one she did not know. The lack of knowing was mutual, for the woman sold her the ticket without a hint of recognition.

There were forty-five minutes before the coach departed. Back she drove swiftly to Lottie's and unharnessed Daisy. She locked the door and put the key under the mat. Clutching her bag of possessions, she passed out through the gate. She carried her small bag and Lottie's hat and veil beneath her cloak. The hat she would put on before she caught the coach.

A voice called to her but she ignored it.

The streets were blessedly quiet. She covered the six hundred yards to All Saints' Church in just under six minutes. It was twenty-nine minutes past eleven when she passed through the stone fence into the empty churchyard. Fortunately, the fruit and vegetable market opposite the church was closed on Wednesday mornings and so there were no inquisitive eyes to follow her. Her own eyes roved across the graves.

There it was! Over near the parsonage fence beside a native cherry tree, the marble tablet with the cross and the angel carved into the pale stone.

She moved through the row of headstones, her eyes brimming with tears. 'My dearest ones,' she whispered as she read the inscriptions. How truly she had loved them. For a moment she pictured her real mother and father, and then the clergyman and his wife. She saw them all together as one. She closed her eyes and began a prayer.

'Well, glory be!' a strident voice sounded behind her.

She turned in fright to see Martin Carlyle and his wife standing there surveying her with amazement. The church warden made a rumbling sound in his throat. 'Goodness gracious! Where have ye sprung from? Whole colony's lookin' out for a sign of ye!'

'I'm only visiting here briefly. I wished to see the last resting place of Father and Mother.'

Mrs Carlyle's meagre lips pursed. 'My, how thin ye be. Have ye really left yer husband as everyone's been sayin'?' she barked.

'Please excuse me, but I'd like to go into the church now.' Eve moved to the church porch.

'Will ye be here in Bathurst long?' called Martin Carlyle.

Eve turned her head to reply as she continued inside. 'I'm catching the noonday coach.'

'My, going on the noon coach, is it?' the woman looked to her husband. 'And what do you make of that, Mr Carlyle?'

'Well I never,' answered her husband.

'Always was uppity, a real miss,' decreed his wife.

All Saints' was blessedly empty. She passed between the pews breathing in the memories of her happy years with Father and Mother. She stood in front of the altar and fleetingly her wedding day pushed itself into her thoughts. She remembered standing by John Stuart, and the air of excitement all around. She knelt down at the altar rail for a few minutes then rose, and putting out her hand in reverence touched the altar cloth.

As she passed through the porch, she remembered standing with Father on her last visit and how he had asked her to tell John Stuart about Clare. His words came gently to her mind on the winter wind. 'It is for you to tell him, my darling. It is your responsibility . . .'

She sighed and spoke aloud. 'I never could tell him, Father. Forgive me.'

She took Lottie's hat out from under her cloak and put it on securing it with a hatpin, then tied the edges of the long black veil firmly under her chin, covering her face. She looked up to see an elderly lady leave a group of children standing on the far side of the street and come towards her. It was Mrs Wiggers, her old head-mistress, out with some of the girls from All Saints' School.

'Eve dear, is it you under that veil?'

'Why yes, I . . . have been saying good-bye to Father and Mother.'

'We have all been so worried about you; are you staying here long?'

'No, I'm catching the noonday coach. I'm sorry, but I cannot stay and talk, Mrs Wiggers. I would have come to see you had I time to do so.'

The woman nodded. 'I know you would have. Is there aught I can do to help you, dear?'

Eve sighed. 'No, thank you, but it is good to see you all the same.'

Mrs Wiggers stretched out her gloved hand and took one of Eve's in hers. 'Then let me wish you luck, Eve, my dear. It does me good just to see you.'

'Thank you.' Eve's voice caught in her throat. 'Thank you so much, and good-bye.'

She left the charitable lady and hurried into the main thoroughfare. Seeing Mrs Wiggers had lifted her spirits. Yes, there were some good, kind people in the world. But her equanimity was short-lived for standing by the open carriage door, waiting to look at tickets, was the formidable Mrs Janklor. Eve handed her the small blue card and the big woman took it. 'To Lithgow,' she said, but did not hand the ticket back. She attempted to peer through the veil in brash fashion. 'Do I know you? For the life of me, can't see through that thing!' The woman's head came closer.

In a swift motion, Eve plucked the ticket from Mrs Janklor's fingers and quickly entered the coach. Her heart was racing, but she told herself to settle and be still.

Didn't she have the letter from Mr Lees in her bag and wasn't she on her way to meet Lawless and Lottie? And what of Alan? It would be many hours before she knew if he was safe. She leaned back in the corner of the coach and closed her eyes behind her veil. She said a prayer.

There was a sudden lurch and the coach moved forward, rumbling down William Street and out onto the Sydney road, while three quarters of a mile away, a dark figure on a grey stallion cantered from the western road up and over a long slope to the public reserve.

Alan had spent the morning a mile west of Bathurst in a dense clump of white cedar trees, watching the open road. He had seen only eight vehicles and riders in the five hours since dawn, none of them troopers or Sir Rutherford.

Now, just after noon, he found himself a position as Lottie had instructed, giving him clear view across the dirt track the locals called Lort Street to the beginning of the settlement and Rutherford Blake's office. From here was free vision of the Sydney road to the east. In fact, he could just now see the noonday coach disappearing in the distance. It was right on time and Eve would be in it.

He did not fasten Freedom to a tree, there was no need, the animal would not stray. He took out his water bottle and poured some water into the crown of his hat and held it for the stallion to drink. Freedom drank gratefully. Then he put the hat in the sun to dry and unwrapped the food Eve and Lottie had prepared for him before dawn that morning. With his eyes on the settlement, he ate, sharing it with Freedom.

Eve would be safely with Lawless and Lottie in Lithgow by five o'clock. In Lawless he had confidence. By now, he felt sure that the last remaining member of his band would have completed his task and be on his way to the Gibraltar Hotel.

He sat in thought, his eyes on the quiet township, as the cold afternoon passed. His mind returned to Danny and Sam just as it had during the morning. Again, he reflected on the events that had brought their deaths. He tormented himself with the thought that he should have foreseen Jordan's move. Why hadn't he recognised that

Jordan had always been the weak link, always been the risk, right from first meeting the boy? How easily it was in hindsight. He should never have let him join them. But then there had been Patricia June. She had wanted her brother along, and the boy had been so desperate to be one of them. But there was no one else to blame except himself. And in the end it had killed Sam and Danny.

His mouth drew down with emotion and he put his head in his hands. He remembered the apprehension, the shudder he had experienced when saying goodbye to Daniel last Friday, and again the odd feeling on Sunday night, only hours before Jordan bolted. He should have known something was wrong. Why didn't he read the signs? Jordan must have shown some indication of what he was thinking.

There was a constricting feeling in his chest as he thought of Daniel shot dead by the troopers. Ah, Danny, dear Danny. It was the one death he had hoped to spare him. Why hadn't he sent Jordan away years ago?

For the first time in many years, Alan Fletcher's eyes brimmed over with tears while Daniel's voice sounded in his mind: 'We'll be expecting you back sometime during the night on Monday. I'll have the fire going and a billy on the boil . . .' And he heard again truculent, faithful Samuel instructing them in forthright tones, 'For heaven's sake make good time home as I dinna want to be in that cold hole all night!' It was then that Alan spoke aloud. He did not know to whom he spoke, for he was not a believer in a merciful God. How could he be? Yet he addressed his words to his maker. 'Whatever happens, let the last of my men get away. Don't kill Lawless! Let the lad and my darling Eve get away to America. Please . . . God.'

He had taken his eyes from the settlement as he spoke and now he looked back. He sat up taut and alert. Men on horses!

Wide, dusty William Street, vacant a minute or so before had activity in it. He could make out the bright sign on Mrs Ayres' tea shop and opposite it Rutherford Blake's office. Into that building disappeared the five or six riders, men in dark clothing, most certainly troopers.

He looked at the sky and guessed it was now fast approaching four o'clock. In just over another hour night would fall. He sat prepared and watchful. If only he had his telescope! But that had been in the pile of equipment they had been forced to leave behind in the flight from Kettle's Creek. He would have to rely on his eyesight.

Five minutes later he distinguished a single figure come out of the office and run up the street out of sight. What was going on? It pointed to one thing. Rutherford Blake must be back. He could not hope to catch Eve. At this very moment the Cobb and Co. coach would be within an hour of Lithgow, thirty-four miles away. Yet the man was fanatical, and a fanatical man would follow his quarry when others would not.

Another five minutes passed, and more men issued from the building and went in the same direction as the previous man.

He thought perhaps fifteen minutes went by and the door opened again, discharging two more forms along the same course as those who had gone before. He fancied he recognised Rutherford Blake as one of them.

What was happening?

The horses they had ridden into town were all still tethered to the rail outside.

Now, it must be about half past the hour of four. His eyes swung back and forth from the dirt highway on his left to the building in William Street. Daylight would soon begin to fade.

William Street was deserted and there were no riders on the Sydney road.

The minutes passed. Suddenly he stood up in surprise. A Cobb and Co. coach rumbled into his line of vision on the Sydney highway. But there was no coach out of Bathurst at this hour!

Straining to see, he moved through the trees. Two figures sat atop in the driver's seat and behind rode two more in dark clothing.

Troopers? Of course!

Rutherford Blake had commandeered a coach and was continuing the chase.

Alan mounted Freedom. Down across the slope he rode to join the Sydney highway behind the vehicle.

Alan had concluded correctly. Inside the rumbling vehicle, sat Sir Rutherford, beside him was David Elrington, and opposite, Constable Ward. Up in front were a driver and Trooper Himsworth, and behind rode two more mounted police.

Sir Rutherford's severe features were not unhappy this afternoon. Even though he had camped out last night, ridden almost sixty miles since breakfast, and had taken only a hot bath and a change of clothes before continuing, he was not displeased. He closed his eyes in contemplation. What an exciting week this had been. Since Jordan O'Day had come to his office in the early hours of Monday morning he had experienced a gamut of emotions: excitement, anger, disappointment, satisfaction, exasperation, melancholy, confusion, and now again the acute exhilaration and stimulation of the chase. And now that he knew from O'Day that Fletcher's ultimate plan was to leave the country, he realised he had no time to waste. Ah yes, he must get him this time.

He had been devastated to learn on his arrival at his offices that the telegraph line was broken between Bathurst and Meadow Flat. He had been hoping to alert the various police stations over the Blue Mountains of Fletcher's probable movements. It was infuriating! These damn telegraph lines were so unreliable, such a flimsy little wire stretched across such immense areas. Ah yes, the tyranny of distance! It was his greatest enemy. Only his tenacious and uncompromising will kept him going.

When he had heard the news that Mrs Wakeman had been in Bathurst and had bought a ticket for Lithgow on the noon Cobb and Co. coach, his spirits had risen again. She was only hours ahead of him when he had believed her perhaps a day in advance. He discovered she had been seen leaving Lottie Thatcher's cottage this morning. He had called on Mistress Thatcher himself to investigate, only to find the woman not at home. His mouth tightened. That Thatcher woman irritated him.

When he was told Eve Wakeman had visited Mr Lees the solicitor, it had intrigued him immensely. He had sent Constable Ward there to investigate, only to find Mr Lees had gone this very afternoon to Orange.

And where was Fletcher? He had a comforting thought. Ah yes, perhaps Fletcher was beginning to make mistakes at last. He had let the Wakeman woman stay in Bathurst and catch the coach alone. To do such a thing the man must have believed he was a few days ahead of the chase. Briefly, he felt sorry for John Stuart. Eve Wakeman was obviously in cahoots with Fletcher, no matter what her poor, deceived husband thought. He leaned back on the corner cushion and his face composed itself. Ah yes, he would sleep for a few hours. He felt confident again. There was one thing he was absolutely certain of, when he caught up to Mrs Wakeman he would catch Alan Fletcher. They were a pair, he was positive of that now. Ah yes, Alan Fletcher was not far away.

If Sir Rutherford had put his head out the coach window instead of on the corner cushion, he may have detected in the distant dusk a figure on horseback behind the coach.

He was right in one thing. Alan Fletcher was not far away.

Eve stepped down out of the coach. How she hoped that Lottie and Lawless were here.

She followed the four men, her fellow passengers, across the poorly tended lawn to the steps of the Gibraltar Hotel. A man with a leather apron across his sturdy frame met them on the verandah. 'Welcome, welcome. Moody's the name and the Gibraltar Hotel has the fame.' He smiled. 'The taproom is open, right this way.' He pointed along to the left. 'Anyone need a room?'

His smile widened as Eve replied, 'Yes, please.' Today was proving successful; he had five rooms to rent and now three would be occupied, unusual for a week day. A couple who had ridden in on horseback were in number three; wished to have a room for perhaps only four or five hours to have a sleep before continuing their journey. And number one was given over to a leather salesman.

Eve signed the register as 'Mrs Jones', and Mr Moody, jovial and well-mannered, insisted on carrying her small cloth bag down the hall to number six.

When he left her and went back to the desk, he assumed she must be in mourning, what with the heavy veil and the subdued attitude. As the cordial publican sat entering his guests' names in his day book, he would have been astounded if he could have seen the activity taking place in number six.

Eve had been so delighted to see Lottie and Lawless that she had hugged them both a long time, and now she and Lottie were exchanging clothes. Eve put on Lottie's skirt and blouse in exchange for her dress. The velvet coat and scarf to complete her transformation lay on the bed.

'Now, what time does the night coach for Oberon leave?' Lottie said to Lawless's back as he stood at the window looking through the small opening in the faded blue curtains.

'In half an hour, at six o'clock. It's some thirty miles, I suppose. I remember it as bein' a windin' road, though I've been upon it but once. There'll be one stop for change of horses, and all bein' well ye should alight there before midnight.'

'You can turn round now, Lawless,' said Eve. 'We're dressed.'

He came back from the window. 'Ye both fit into each other's clothes mighty well.'

Eve smoothed her skirt. 'Thank you. We've changed over the contents of our bags. I think that's everything.'

'Yes,' agreed Lottie. 'Ye two had best be returning to number three.'

Eve came to her and took hold of her hands. 'Now you know what to do, Lottie dear. Wear the cape and carry the dark hat and veil, and go out to the desk in fifteen minutes.'

Lottie nodded. 'I will and I shall say I've decided to catch the night coach to Oberon. *I shall try to talk as much like ye-oo as I can, Miss Eve.*'

Eve smiled. 'You don't need to be too concerned, Lottie. I said very little when I came in.'

Lawless looked to Eve. 'We should ride out as soon as we know Mistress Lottie is safe on the way to Oberon, for we've eighteen mile of windin' road, much of it uphill, in wind and icy chill, to cover tonight, Mistress Eve.'

'Yes, Lawless, I realise.' Then taking Lottie in her arms she said, 'I am loath to say goodbye, but we must. Dearest Lottie, you have been wonderful. I will write as . . . as soon as we are somewhere safe. You will write back, won't you?'

Lottie sniffed and nodded. 'Bless ye, I will. I truly will, yet my writing isn't up to much. Ye shall have to decipher it, I'm afraid.'

They clung to each other a few moments more, then with tears in her eyes Eve took up the bag she was now to carry and the bonnet to wear, and went hurriedly to the door. She opened it a fraction and peeped out.

Lawless watched her, a frown on his brow; she was leaving far too quickly, he had things to say to Mistress Lottie. He was about to speak when Eve looked back at him. 'Don't hurry, Lawless, I'll be waiting. Come when you're ready.' And she was gone.

Lottie and Lawless stood facing each other.

Since before dawn that morning they had been in each other's company, and yet how speedily the day had gone.

When they had left Bathurst town they made good time on the Sydney road. Lawless had chosen a spot to bring the telegraph down some seventeen miles from Bathurst. It was where the wire ran twenty yards in from the road and was strung across a deep gully.

He had stood still and looked at Lottie rather speculatively as if appraising her. Wondering at his expression, she demanded, 'Now, why are ye aweighing me like that, Mr Drake?'

'Er, well, it's somethin' I don't like to ask a lady like yeself but . . .'

'But what? Go on, say it.'

'All right. If ye were to be climbin' up on top there,' he pointed to a line of rocks running back from the ravine to higher ground, 'ye would be able to have good clear vision both ways on the highway and could tell me if I could use my axe . . . er, excuse me, your axe. But ye don't have to,' he added hastily.

'I'm not made o' glass, ye know, Mr Drake.'

Lawless began to chuckle. 'If that don't beat all.'

Lottie fixed him with a stare. 'Whatever do ye mean?'

'Well, it seems that whenever a man says somethin' that a woman is resentin' she says she's not made of glass. It were the very same thing Mistress Eve was sayin' to the guv'nor on the ride to Bathurst.'

Lottie showed the glimmer of a smile. 'Now, where is it ye want me to climb?'

She was soon perched on the rocks and Lawless lifted the axe. In the five minutes Alan had predicted, the twenty-three-feet-high pole was down. Lawless jumped away and ran as it fell, pulling yards of wire free of the next pole beyond the gully.

Lottie waved her arms. 'There's a vehicle in the distance now acoming from the Bathurst side.'

'Well then, swiftly down, please, and we'll be on our way.'

They lunched together in the shade of some grey gums on the banks of the Cox River three miles from Lithgow.

When they arrived at the Gibraltar Hotel, Lottie waited with the horses while Lawless signed the register as 'Mr and Mrs A. Green'. There was no one in the front entrance hall when Lawless escorted her to their room, and Mr Moody only glanced up briefly from his papers at his desk as they passed.

Lottie lay on the bed and actually fell asleep for a time. Lawless sat looking through the finger-marked window pane, over the strip of grass and weed-filled garden bed, to the roadway beyond. It was too ingrained in him to be alert and watchful; he could not rest. When she awoke, he went out to the bar and bought her a lemonade. They remained in the room for over three hours until Eve arrived on the Cobb and Co. coach. They peeked through the door and saw her enter number six. And when all was quiet, they hurried across the corridor and into her room.

And now they stood face to face to say goodbye.

'I . . . er . . . well, Mistress Lottie. I've had a grand day with ye. And thanks for climbin' up on them rocks for me. It were a real help and no mistake.'

''Twere nothing, Mr Drake.' The hint of a flush began to rise to her neck.

'I heard Mistress Eve mention she would write to ye. Would it be too bold if I wrote too? The guv'nor taught me how, ye know, many a year ago, and I can read as well.'

'Why I would be more than pleased to hear from ye, truly I would.'

'Then I will write, Mistress Lottie, and no mistake.'

She put out her hand. He took it and shook it quite ferociously.

He turned from her and took the five or six steps to the door, then he halted. His shoulders lifted.

She heard him take a deep breath and the words he said rushed from him so quickly, she was not sure of their import for a second or two.

'If, and I'm not meanin' to insult a lady such as yeself, please understand, but if a man were to be sendin' money, proper and respectable like from another country, would ye ever consider doin' him the surpassin' honour of takin' a ship to join with him?' He had not turned round, his face was to the door.

She watched his square shoulders.

She said, 'Mr Drake?'

Slowly he turned back to her.

Their eyes met. They stood looking at each other.

Lottie's expression was singularly grave. 'I am all alone in this world.' She could feel her heart thumping in her chest. 'Yes, I would be considering it.'

A smile broke across his face and seemed to ripple down to extend through his whole body. When he spoke, his voice was lighter, more buoyant.

'Good luck, Mistress Lottie.'

'Good luck, Mr Drake.'

CHAPTER THIRTY-FOUR

'My own beloved, who has lifted me
From this drear flat of earth where I was thrown,
And, in betwixt the languid ringlets, blown
A life-breath, till the forehead hopefully
Shines out again, as all the angels see,
Before thy saving kiss! My own, my own,
Who camest to me when the world was gone,
And I who looked for only God, found thee!
I find thee; I am safe, and strong, and glad,
As one who stands in dewless asphodel,
Looks backwards on the tedious time he had
In the upper life, – so I, with bosom-swell,
Make witness here between the good and bad,
That love, as strong as death, retrieves as well.'

'Sonnets from the Portuguese' XXVII,
Elizabeth Barrett Browning, 1806–1861.

When Sir Rutherford reached Lithgow, the temperature had fallen to near freezing on an icy, moonlit night.

He bade the driver draw up at the Gibraltar, for that was the watering place for the coaches and he hoped to find news of the Wakeman woman. He extricated himself from the confines of the vehicle onto his aching, stiff legs. He was exhausted, but the thought of finding her here in the township put a bounce back in his step.

As there was no coach scheduled at this time, no one was there to receive them. A dim light was thrown in the entrance hall by a wall lantern and the voice of David Elrington vibrated down the passage. 'Innkeeper, where are you? Is anyone in attendance here?'

'Go through to the taproom,' Sir Rutherford instructed.

A minute later, Mr and Mrs Moody came speedily with expectant steps up the passage. The possibility of seven overnight lodgers was a pleasing prospect, and that one of them was Sir Rutherford Blake was a bonus in itself, for his name was as well known this side of the Blue Mountains as the Governor's.

Mrs Moody smiled. Her beautiful, nut-brown, almond-shaped eyes widened in greeting, as did her generous mouth. 'Sir Rutherford, a pleasure, and how is it that we can help you?'

Her winsome charm was lost on him; he had only one thing in his mind. 'Firstly, madam, you can tell me of a woman we believe dismounted the noon coach from Bathurst. I am led to believe she was the only woman in a party of men, although the complement may have changed as the vehicle stopped at Meadow Flat on its way here.'

Mrs Moody looked to her husband. 'You took care of them, didn't you, love?'

Her husband nodded.

'Well?' she prompted.

'There was a woman, all right, dearest. Mrs Jones. Took a room for the night.'

'Ah yes, that sounds right, she would give such a name,' Sir Rutherford decided in an excited voice. 'Which room is she in?'

'Well, she ain't in a room, you realise,' Mr Moody replied.

Sir Rutherford looked irritated. This was all he needed, a publican playing games. 'Explain yourself.'

'She's gone.'

'Gone where, love?' Mrs Moody asked for Sir Rutherford, whose mouth was open ready to do so.

Mr Moody smiled benignly at his wife before he turned his face to the impatient police detective. 'Just after six o'clock she comes out here and says she won't be staying after all. Says she wants to catch the night mail to Oberon. Now, as I have a night's rent out of her and she's a grown-up adult, free to make her own decisions, you realise, I told her where to purchase the ticket and off she goes.'

Sir Rutherford's face grew grim. 'What the devil is going on? Describe the woman, if you please.'

Mr Moody's eyes closed in thought. 'Well, when she arrived she was wrapped up against the cold, you realise, wearin' a cape, dark blue, real expensive-looking though a touch worn, and travelling hat and veil, but I could see she were thin. Average height, I think. Oh, when she were leaving she carried the hat and veil; her hair was fair and curly.' Here he looked down at his wife, and said to her, and not to Sir Rutherford, 'And comely. I suppose a man would have to say she was comely.'

'Really now?' his wife answered, her well-defined eyebrows arching.

'That description fits her, sir,' David Elrington said.

Sir Rutherford had turned away and walked to the door where he

561

stood, arms folded, looking out into the night.

'Will you be stayin', then?' Mrs Moody eagerly questioned David Elrington.

His eyes followed his superior's back. 'I'm not sure, madam.'

'It is a thirty-mile ride to Oberon, is it not?' Sir Rutherford threw the words over his shoulder.

'Aye sir, it is,' answered Trooper Ward.

'What time does the mail coach leave Oberon in the morning?'

'Well, as tomorrow's Thursday there are two,' replied Mrs Moody, 'one at eleven o'clock; it goes to Rockley, Blayney and Bathurst.'

'And the other?' urged David Elrington.

'Noon time, and it goes south to Black Springs, doesn't it, love?' she turned to touch her husband's sleeve.

'Indeed, my love.'

David Elrington moved to his leader's side in the wan light. His face was drained from fatigue. 'We are spent, sir, should we not bide here? We will have plenty of time to reach Oberon before either of the coaches depart from there in the morning.'

'My dear Mr Elrington, have I not taught you better than this? You are tired, I know, and hence I forgive the lapse, but who is to say the woman is catching an onward coach? She may be meeting someone in Oberon and going elsewhere.'

The younger man looked abashed. 'Yes, of course, sir, I'm sorry. But even if that is so, she must sleep somewhere in Oberon this night. She has been travelling since noon, and the coach will not arrive in that settlement until late tonight.'

'Probably midnight, you realise,' interjected Mr Moody.

'Probably midnight,' repeated David Elrington. 'So surely, if we depart here early in the morning—'

'All right, young man, all right. Ah yes, it is true we are drained, consumed by a long day of overtaxing events. We will bide here the night.'

David Elrington sighed with relief and turned back to the Moodys who also sighed with relief. They had thought for a ghastly few minutes that they were to lose their lodgers.

Sir Rutherford stood silhouetted, looking out into the night. If only he had known that the man he reflected upon was a mere fourteen feet away, in the deep shadows of the verandah.

Alan had stood and listened to the conversation, relief too covering his face when he heard they would rest here the night and follow Lottie's false trail in the morning. He, also, was weary, but there was no halting yet for him. He must continue on, up the Blue Mountains, and make Newton's Inn this night.

Sir Rutherford's face was a mixture of emotions as he eyed the black shadows of the night. He stepped aside as the driver moved by him to tend the coach and horses, then he sighed and turned back into the dimly lit hall of the Gibraltar Hotel. At the same time, Alan left the shadows and rapidly covered the distance to where Freedom waited.

It was midnight and sleet was falling when Alan and Freedom finally arrived at Newton's Inn. A figure rose from the old leather couch against the wall and came quickly across the covered verandah as Alan reined in.

'Guv'nor,' came the soft tones of Lawless. 'Thank the Lord ye be here.'

'Hallo there, lad, good to see you.'

'The inn is asleep, all but the mistress who waits within. She would not go to bed.'

Alan was now under the protection of the verandah and he shook the rain and sleet from his coat.

'So all went well then? According to our plan?'

'Aye, it did.'

Alan took hold of Lawless's shoulders. 'Good. I knew you'd do it. Now, lad, where to bed down Freedom?'

'I'll take him round to the stables, guv. It's ye should get inside. The mistress is in number ten, straight up the stairs.'

Thursday morning was bitterly cold all over the west country. Deke Edwards shivered as he brought the Mayfield coach round to the front door of the big house, and beside him, Leeroy Barton, wrapped in a blanket with just his nose showing, complained about, 'Being awake at this God-forsaken hour.'

It was half past three in the morning as John Stuart and Joe crossed the verandah to climb into the coach followed by a half-awake Timothy. Thelma and Mrs Smith stood watching, hurricane lanterns in hand.

'Travel safely,' Thelma called to her husband's wave of good-bye, and the vehicle creaked forward to gain speed down the carriageway. As it swung through the pillars of the park in the weak radiance of the morning stars, over a hundred road miles away, Sir Rutherford, mindful of his problems, was shaking David Elrington awake.

Even though every limb had ached from fatigue and the police detective had fallen asleep quickly, he had woken after a few hours and could not go back to sleep.

'B . . . But Sir, I thought you said we should awaken at five o'clock!' the young man complained.

'I have changed my mind. Up, Mr Elrington, and get Ward and the others on their feet. I want to be breakfasted and away in half an hour.'

Sir Rutherford's orders were carried out and it was just after four o'clock that Mr and Mrs Moody, puffy-eyed, candles in hand, wearing dressing gowns over their night attire, saw off a tired and surly crew.

They made slow progress during the three hours of darkness, for it had rained heavily around midnight and the road was muddy and soft. Twice the wheels caught fast in the mud and they needed to haul the vehicle out. They were not halfway when the sun came up. Nevertheless, the dauntless leader pushed onwards, and as ten o'clock passed, the coach rumbled up the single street of Oberon.

Sir Rutherford was displeased and his men were sullen.

'But if she is catching either mail,' David Elrington ventured optimistically, 'then we shall have her, sir.'

His leader nodded. 'Ah yes, that's true, but there is something odd in it all. That Eve Wakeman caught a coach to Lithgow had sense to it. Lithgow is on the way to Sydney. But that she detoured south to Oberon is odd. Why? That is what I ask. Why is she travelling south?'

'I wish I knew, sir.'

'I attempted to get here earlier in case she was meeting someone and has gone off on horseback, but as misfortune has prevailed, all we can hope is that wherever she spent the night, her landlord was inquisitive. Ah yes, I shall be mighty surprised if she is still here.'

She was not still there, but he was mighty surprised all the same. For on alighting at Stopford's Inn, he was informed that the lady of his description had caught the half past nine o'clock mail directly westward to Rockley.

'Half past nine o'clock?' Sir Rutherford exploded. 'But the blasted thing doesn't go until the hour of eleven!'

'No, that be the summer schedule, sir,' answered the informant. 'We been on winter schedule over a month now.'

'Get us all a hot drink!' Sir Rutherford hurled at Constable Ward. 'These damnable icy days and this damnable chase are beginning to tell on me.'

'They be bloody-well tellin' on us all,' mumbled Ward to himself, after he turned away to do his leader's bidding.

Oberon was a minute settlement, but Rockley was what was called in the west a 'one-horse town'; and the road that joined the two places was narrow and potholed, not much more than a track. In bad weather the coach didn't run at all. But it had left this morning, and Sir Rutherford stood drinking his hot coffee and pondering on the enigma that was Eve Wakeman's movements.

'It doesn't make sense,' he said over and over to himself. 'That the woman catches a coach heading *back* towards the part of the country she has just escaped from. Further south on to Black Waters I might have accepted; but returning west to Rockley? No sense in it. But I must follow her, for she is my link with Fletcher.'

And follow they did, along the twenty-mile track that led to Rockley.

Some of the anger and frustration of the last forty-eight hours disappeared when finally they saw the Cobb and Company coach standing by the verandah of the Rockley Hotel. Sir Rutherford jumped down into the wind, calling over his shoulder, 'You men get yourselves some refreshment. Come on, Mr Elrington, Ward!'

Across the uneven dirt street Sir Rutherford bounded in great strides, to the man watering the horses at the side of the plain wooden establishment.

'Are you the Cobb and Company coachman?'

'No, sir, I ain't. He be in the barroom justifyin' a few pints of ale.'

The expert on the bushrangers mounted the battered steps and proceeded on under the precariously hanging wooden sign that read 'The Rockley Hotel' into the public barroom. David Elrington and Trooper Ward brought up the rear. Sir Rutherford's eyes ran over the few drinkers. 'Who is the driver of the coach outside?'

'I be the man,' answered a bearded individual moving out from the bar.

'I believe a woman who sojourned overnight at Stopford's Inn in Oberon, one Mrs Jones, caught your coach this morning.'

'Aye, a lady boarded there for certain, though, fact is, I picked up two ladies, not just one, sir, and I be picking up another here, for she has need to be in Blayney this day. So, as of when the coach departs, ye can say I have three ladies in my care.'

Sir Rutherford hardly contained his impatience. 'For heaven's sake, man, I am only interested in the one from Oberon. Where is she?'

'Yonder in the parlour, sir. I believe she be partakin' tea.'

Sir Rutherford rushed out of the bar and across the hall to the parlour. The door was weak on its hinges and he thrust it open with such force that one of the joints came entirely away from the wall.

The two women who were taking tea looked up from their cups in alarm.

'Good God!' Sir Rutherford exclaimed as he stopped stock-still, and David Elrington, coming at speed behind him, cannoned into his back, thrusting him forward a pace. 'What the devil is going on?'

The younger man looked over his leader's shoulder and a hissing sound of disbelief issued from his lips as he too recognised Lottie, sitting, teacup in hand.

The other lady, who was a governess on her way to new employment, spoke up. 'Who are you? What is the meaning of this blasphemous intrusion?'

'Ah yes . . . forgive me, ma'am. I am Sir Rutherford Blake and this is my assistant, Mr Elrington. It is not with you that I have dispute.' He trained his gaze on Lottie. 'But with you, Mistress Thatcher, I do. Be good enough to follow me please, I have questions for you.'

To the infuriation of Sir Rutherford and the extreme interest of the governess, Lottie refused. 'Well, that's as may be,' she answered putting down her teacup, 'but I have naught to speak with ye about, and as I am a passenger on the mail which is due to depart any minute, I must ask ye to leave me alone.'

'Damn you, woman!' His voice rose sharply, and the governess glared at him. 'I don't know how you achieved it, but I see the pretty trick you have played me.'

Lottie did not move. Her knees were shaking but that was not in evidence. She replied in a voice sounding much more sure than she was. 'I shan't. There is no law says I have to speak with ye if I wish not to.'

Sir Rutherford's mouth drew tight and his face was beginning to flush with anger. His voice grew threateningly quiet. 'Mistress Thatcher, I do not have a subpoena in my pocket to make you do as I ask, but believe me I shall. Ah yes, your little artifice has managed to deceive me and has waylaid me from my purpose for a time. But I will be back for you when I have caught the Wakeman woman and Fletcher, and then you shall pay. Ah yes, pay with a long gaol sentence when I prove your guilt and the part you have played this day.'

'I don't know what ye refer to at all,' replied Lottie bravely. 'It's a fine thing when a body cannot take a coach trip into her own country without the likes of ye turning up to be a harassment.'

Back out into the street Sir Rutherford strode, rage making his voice high and rasping. 'Get the men from their drinks, Mr Elrington. We turn back immediately. It's Sydney they were making for all the time, and we the bloody fools to be duped!'

It was two o'clock on Friday afternoon when Alan, Eve and Lawless stepped off the train at Sydney's city station in the inner suburb of Redfern.

They had ridden in the biting winter winds and drifting sleet east over the Blue Mountains and down to the Penrith railhead. There they had joined the train and with Freedom, Waterloo and Milford in the horse van had travelled the thirty-five miles into Sydney town.

Eve smiled to see how Lawless was enthralled with the train. He had never travelled on one. Having begun his days in St Giles, that part of London so called, north of the Strand, he had seen them, and had often pilfered from gentlemen leaving Charing Cross station, but he had never been aboard one. He leaned out the window as a child would do, bright with excitement. Only once did his face cloud over sorrowfully. He turned from the delights of the passing countryside to Alan. 'Gawd, guv'nor, wouldn't Sam and Daniel have thought this a treat? How I wish they could have been here. Gee, I miss them.'

'Yes, Lawless, I too.'

Eve turned away and looked out the window, her eyes filling with tears.

At Redfern station they fought their way through the mêlée of travellers, station officials and peddlers and found the animal van. The horses whinnied in a mixture of recognition and joy at release as they were led down the ramp from the carriage and across the platform. Once out of the station, they mounted and set off towards the harbour.

The first requirement was for Eve to find out about her legacy. After inquiring, they were told that the main office of the Bank of New South Wales which held the Principal Office of Bequests was Pitt Street, number one hundred and seventy.

Bright yellow horse-drawn tram-cars, about twice the length of an omnibus, ran along Pitt Street, and they followed one that led them to the brown stone building carrying the right number.

Eve went in alone.

The letter was taken from her and five minutes later a clerk escorted her from the front desk to a large office at the back.

'Would you be so kind as to wait here, Mrs Wakeman? Mr Bull, our bank manager, will see you shortly.'

When Mr Bull entered, letter in hand, his eyes ran over her from head to toe. He was extremely interested in his caller. She was a celebrated 'missing person' and here she was sitting in his office. 'So, you are Mrs Wakeman.'

'Yes,' Eve replied, 'I am she.'

He stood still a few moments looking at her, then gestured her to a chair. 'We received a telegraph message from your solicitor in Bathurst, one Mr Lees. We were expecting you yesterday.'

Eve sighed with relief as she sat. She thought he seemed to be considering her. He pointed to the letter lying on the desk in front of him. 'By this I see you wish to remove all your money. Now, madam, I must ask you to reflect. Are you sure? Is it not judicious to leave some with us?'

Eve smiled. 'Mr Bull, I do not need to reflect. I want to remove all my money, now, this afternoon.'

'Very well, madam, you know best. But it is a great deal of money for one woman to be carrying.'

Half an hour later, after signing numerous forms and being observed and watched by the bank's staff, 'the curiosity, Mrs Wakeman', was outside again.

'I have it,' she said, patting her handbag and smiling jubilantly. 'Three hundred and twenty-eight pounds, twenty-two being the cost of the probate, documentation and fees.'

On horseback once more, they crossed through to George Street. Eve was back in Sydney after eight years. How well she remembered the buildings and laneways, the shops and streets. On the left as they rode along was a store with a sign that read, 'SULLY TOMPKINS' HABERDASHERY'. She felt peculiar reading that.

Down George Street they continued to the General Post Office, now a brick building with keystoned arches, portico and pillars. As they passed it, Eve drew back on Milford's reins. 'Oh Alan, look.'

There, free standing on the footpath set in mortar was the large wooden planked board covered with 'wanted' posters, just as she remembered it. And right in the middle, easily readable from the roadway, was one which announced:

WANTED
DEAD OR ALIVE

ALAN FLETCHER

2000 POUNDS!

FOR BUSHRANGING ACTS

SUNBROWNED COMPLEXION
LIGHT BROWN HAIR
THOUGHT TO BE CLEAN-SHAVEN
AND
FIVE FEET ELEVEN INCHES TALL
GREY-BLUE EYES
KNOWN TO WEAR DARK
OR GREY CLOTHING

Underneath was another poster describing all the members of the band, including Jordan O'Day.

'Makes me sick to be seein' his name with ours,' Lawless said as they rode on by.

'I would not like to be Jordan,' Eve answered. 'Night and day, for ever, he will not be able to escape the memory of what he did.'

Lawless turned in the saddle towards her. 'Do ye really believe he will suffer, Mistress Eve?'

'Yes, I do.'

He shook his head. 'How I do hope ye be right, but I lived nigh on eight years with the rat, and I doubt it.'

An hour later Alan had found them two inns, one a quiet establishment called the Prince of Wales in Grosvenor Street, which was not far from Circular Quay and the central dockyards, and the other, a small but lively place, named Paget's Hotel in the Rocks. They did not go as far as Dawes Point Battery, so Eve did not see whether the Ship Inn was still there.

Lawless lodged at the hotel in the Rocks, and Alan and Eve, registered as brother and sister, at the other. Alan hoped that by separating and staying at two inns they would be more difficult to trace.

All their energies now were concentrated on finding a ship to take them immediately from Sydney.

Most of the shipping agents were located in and around Circular Quay and when the shops and work places closed their doors at six o'clock they had been in them all. They looked at each other with disappointment for there was no ship available to them. There were plenty going to America, and with berths available, but the sailing dates were a week or ten days in advance and they could not wait that long. One of the agents had said, 'You'll not get any ships remaining on our books which are sailing in the next seventy-two hours. They are removed, you see. We need time to get the money in and do the paperwork, and in any case we have more work than we can handle. No, you shan't get a passage now under a week's notice.'

They stood together in the cold night air outside the last agent's door.

Eve looked discouraged. 'What shall we do now, Alan?'

'Don't be despondent, lass. There is perhaps one chance.'

'Aye?' said Lawless. 'And what would that be?'

'Let's walk by the ships themselves. We might find one going where we wish to go, and perhaps the master will take us. Three late fares could be desirable. We must try.'

As they walked along the many wharfs of Sydney town, Eve's mind was filled with her yesterdays. At times she would look sidelong at Alan and wonder what he was thinking.

It was with a confusion of sentiments that Alan strode at her side. All the memories of his past life at sea claimed his thoughts as he passed the vessels tied to the quays. He saw a picture of the *Coral Regis* setting sail and drifting down Southampton Waters towards the Solent . . . He had been a bushranger so long, had lived in the wide empty spaces for so long. He had not been prepared for the gamut of feelings that ships and docks and lapping water brought.

Lawless walked beside them experiencing the same delight that he had felt when travelling on the train, for the ships were wonderful; but he was quiet now, aware that this was a serious quest and their lives rested upon it. But when they passed a single iron steam ship with sharply angled bow and brightly striped funnel with lanterns lighting it from stem to stern, he could not help but remark in admiration, 'Hey, guv, if that don't beat all.'

'Yes, lad.' Alan eyed it appreciatively. 'The steamboat is a wonderful vessel.'

For two hours they walked the docks from Circular Quay west towards Darling harbour. Each and every ship they investigated. Many they had not needed to board for the destination was England, and others were cargo ships, bound only for China and the East. It was after eight o'clock at night when they came to the tall-masted American clipper *Port Dennison*, a ship of the Golden Eagle Line, the American partner to the British Black Ball Line. Long and sleek, measuring over two hundred and fifty feet, it was the last vessel on the Pyrmont Wharf in Darling Harbour.

Alan looked from Eve to Lawless. 'Wait here,' he said.

The glow of its lanterns threw pale light amidships as they watched him up the gangplank. It was very cold now, but there were a few sailors smoking beneath two lifeboats secured beside the mainmast. Alan approached them. 'Excuse me, mateys, but where is this vessel bound for, and when does she leave?'

They answered in unison, 'America.' Then one man removed the pipe from his mouth and added, 'We leave tomorrow on the evening tide.'

'I see you carry a cargo of wool.' Alan motioned to the bales piled aft.

'Aye, wool and the odd passenger,' replied the same man.

Alan's voice lifted slightly. 'Where can I find the master? Or the officer in charge?'

'Why? Comin' with us?' asked another of the sailors smoking a cheroot.

'Perhaps.'

'It's Mr Holmes you need,' spoke up the first man again, tapping his pipe on the hatch beside him. 'He's first mate and he's forward on the upper deck.' He pointed with his pipe towards the raised section of the deck.

'Thank you. What is your destination port?'

'New York, though we sail Auckland, Easter Island, round the Horn to Montevideo, Rio de Janeiro, Trinidad and Baltimore first.'

'And what about Charleston, eh?' spoke up the third man.

'Oh yes, that's right,' replied the pipe-smoker. 'We were just informed this morning. We call in at Charleston, too.'

Alan looked puzzled. 'How is it a northern ship calls in at Charleston, South Carolina?'

The three men laughed.

The one who had remained silent spoke. 'Where have you been hidin'? Don't you read the newspapers? The war's over, friend.'

'I see,' Alan replied. 'I assume the Northern Union won.'

'You assume correctly,' answered the man with the cheroot. 'We did. Fact is, we didn't know it ourselves until we reached here. Seems Lee surrendered to Grant on April ninth, and Johnson to Sherman on the twenty-sixth.'

The pipe smoker laughed. 'We have one of the owners on board, you see. He had a tidy little business in Charleston before the war. Seems he wants to investigate matters on his way home.'

'I see, thank you again,' answered Alan turning away to find the first mate. He found Grantley Holmes, a big man with a moustache and long sideburns, beside the wheel. When Alan explained that they needed three berths to America, the first mate shook his head. 'Our shipping agents are the Bright Brothers, you should book passage through them.'

'We've been to them,' Alan told him, 'but they close off the books and take no more fares seventy-two hours before sailing.'

'Do they now?' said Mr Holmes as if it were the first he had heard of such a thing. 'How do you know?'

'I called on them this afternoon. They say there is more work than they can handle, and it gives them time to get the money and do the paperwork.'

'Is that correct?' remarked Mr Holmes thoughtfully.

Alan smiled at him. 'We would like to come with you to New York. We can be ready tomorrow and we have money to pay. Is there anything you can do?'

Grantley Holmes looked keenly at Alan. 'What is your name, sir?'

Alan looked steadily back. 'Trent, James Trent.'

'How do you do.' Mr Holmes shook his hand.

The first mate had partaken of a pleasant evening meal and four rums and was in good spirits. He was an honest, sensible man and fair-minded. He felt slight resistance to the statement that the agents closed their books three days in advance of a sailing date, for sometimes ships left with only half as many passengers as they could take. Obviously the agents were making plenty of money. Once more he looked closely at Mr Trent. The man was quality, you could see that. He came to a decision.

'Mr Trent, it is irregular and we do not have many berths for passengers, but I will talk to the purser, and try to arrange something. Can you come back in the morning, say eight bells, and ask for me?'

'I can and I thank you.'

Eve saw the look on his face as he came down the *Port Dennison*'s gangplank in the lantern light. So did Lawless, and he whistled with delight.

They had a meal in the small dining room at the Prince of Wales and at half past ten, Lawless was ready to return the short distance to his lodgings.

Alan took Eve's hand. 'I shall accompany Lawless. I won't be long.'

'But I would like to come with you, we could accompany Lawless together.'

Lawless looked towards the window. 'It be pretty chilly out there.'

That did not daunt Eve, and so all three set off together again. The footpaths and roadways were quiet until they reached the noisy taverns and inns of the Rocks. A few drunken sailors passed them, and it was here the drifters of Sydney still slept on benches and down alleyways as they always had.

At the entrance to a narrow lane not far from the cutting known as the Argyle Cut, Lawless stopped. 'I shall say goodnight, here. Paget's is only a few paces along. I shall be at yer hotel in time to go with ye in the mornin', guv.'

Alan shook his head. 'No, lad, I think it is best if I go back to the *Port Dennison* and pay the fares alone, but come to the Prince of Wales, for I would like you and Eve to be together while I'm gone.'

Eve smiled at Lawless. 'We will go out and buy some clothes and items for the voyage.'

'Aye. Then I shall be with ye at half past seven of the clock, Mistress Eve.'

Alan looked from one to the other and added, 'Yes, but we must be careful.'

They waved Lawless up the steps of the passage and Alan drew

Eve's arm through his as they walked away from the hustle and noise of the Rocks.

Suddenly, Alan stopped.

Eve looked up at him and saw an enigmatic expression on his face. She sensed something different in him. Her heartbeat quickened. How she truly loved him . . . for always. She did not care what people thought of her, or said of her. It magnified her soul simply being with him.

He took her arm and walked her across the street to where a dozen clippers lay berthed round Circular Quay. They were a striking picture, their tall black masts reaching skywards in the weak, night lights. Two large fig trees grew close to the dockside and he stopped in the jet black darkness of their shadows. All the ships were quiet. Most of the lanterns above decks had been put out and only the ones below threw dim radiance through the portholes. The hum of the noise from the Rocks in the distance was almost indistinguishable and only the water lapping against the hulls and the side of the quay was plain.

For a time she thought he seemed entranced by the ships; he was staring straight ahead at them. After perhaps a minute, he made a sound, a painful sound, and turned towards her. He lifted his hand and stroked her cheek.

It was the intangible difference she had felt in him across the street. What was going on inside Alan Fletcher? She moved round his body to face him. 'My darling,' she said. 'What is it? I'm so happy to be here with you. Tomorrow, our new life will begin. We'll be together always.'

He made no reply. He was looking strangely at her.

She put her arms up to him, just as she had that day in the beautiful glade. He did not turn away, but brought his head slowly down, his mouth slowly down, to hers.

She was vividly aware of him, his hands in her hair, on her shoulders, moving over her spine. When he lifted his mouth from hers, there were a few seconds when she was unaware of what was happening. The world was a dark, glorious blur for her here under the trees. Then she felt him moving down her body, sinking slowly to his knees, his arms encircling and holding her.

She felt as if her skeleton was expanding inside her frame. His face pressed through her clothes . . . his hands pressed through her clothes . . . he murmured softly against her body. Time slowed.

She became aware that he was standing again and she heard her name, 'Eve . . .' He spoke it in that way he had of elongating the 'e' and the sound was sensual now, 'Let's go back.' He moved swiftly along the macadamised dockside with her hand held tightly in his own.

Her face glowed. Her eyes shone. She knew at last he wanted her, now, this minute, as she wanted him.

When they passed through the door of the Prince of Wales, and by the hotel register where they were entered as sister and brother, and on up the cedar staircase, she was conscious only of him. Ripples of sensation trembled through her stomach up into her chest, and round her throat.

Inside their room, Alan turned from her and closed the door.

In the clear patch of light stretching across the room from the brilliant moon, Eve watched his hand on the knob, his long, brown fingers leaving the brass and cutting in an arc across the space between them to take her shawl and drop it aside. He moved to the fireplace and stoked the dying embers; the firelight and the moonbeam blended and strangely intensified to where Eve saw it as the white light of Alan Fletcher's love as the material world seemed to drift away and vanish.

She became aware he had returned to her. His hands undid her coat.

She did not question why Alan had changed his mind. She did not know what he had seen there at the quayside; all she knew was her own expectation.

She lifted her eyes at the same moment she lifted her hands to the button at the top of his jacket. As she unfastened his coat, he smiled at her, his eyes glinting in the dancing light. In the infinite depths of his eyes, she read all that she had longed for, passion, desire, excitement, need . . . love.

They stepped over the two garments and he drew her closer, his hands gripping her slim arms as his voice sounded huskily in the stillness of the night, 'Eve, I want you always to be happy, remember that.'

In the faint light, his face grew serious; the expression tugged at her heart. He was looking into her again, seeing the soul of her, and she felt herself open to him as if layer by layer. She heard him say the things she had longed to hear, love things, wonderful things, reverent, adoring. She shivered as she brought her hand to his face, the rounded tips of her fingers sliding between his lips and feeling the moisture of his mouth. The wetness on her fingers was arousing, erotic. She touched his strong white teeth. 'Yes,' she whispered, 'yes.'

His arms slid round her body, feeling through her clothes the slender planes and gentle undulations of her, his Eve. To her, this action was the promise of encompassing her forever in his life, and in a promise of her own, she enfolded him in her arms. Alan's eyes closed with yearning and he murmured softly as she whispered another 'Yes', unfinished before his mouth came down on hers to close the word inside his lips.

Desire, undisguised now, rushed up through his body. All the restraint of the past months, Alan threw aside.

The taste of him and the feel of his body moulding itself to hers spread a burning heat through her as if it seeped through her skin into her blood and very bones. Alan's mouth moved down across her neck to rest momentarily at the hollow of her throat, his lips relishing the throbbing within her as they drifted on down the opening in her bodice to rest against the tops of her breasts. She arched backwards as his hands pressed up the sides of her ribs to cup her breasts. She felt the heat of his mouth in nerve-tingling sensation through her clothes, closing over her nipples as they hardened in tense expectation.

She had dreamed about this so many times, the wonder of him and the wonder of his love.

She was aware he had moved away a step and was looking at her, openly, greedily, and she held out her arms, tempting him back to where she might possess him. He laughed, a soft, caressing sound, and knelt in front of the fire, drawing off his gleaming, black boots and then beckoning her with open arms. She glided across the space between them to join him in the warmth of the crackling, licentious firelight. Tenderly, adoringly, he ran his hands up her arms and unfastened her bodice and chemise. Her garments fell away to expose her round, firm breasts and she murmured gently as his head came forward, hiding nothing now, mouth open, eyes wanting, to find her waiting nipples. His iron-hard, brown arms easily raised her, placing her astride him as he rolled back on the rug to tease and suckle her breasts above.

She groaned, a deep sound of pleasure, and lifting herself up from the waist so his mouth left her breasts, she sat upon him while her nimble fingers swiftly removed his shirt and undervest. The blood coursed furiously through Alan's veins as he lay looking up at her naked breasts glowing invitingly in the firelight above him. In urgent movement, he tugged at her skirt and petticoat and in turn she undid the silver buckle on his black leather belt. She murmured and rolled over to lie beside him and her hands eased his grey trousers down over his lean hips to show all of his beautiful body.

Now, he rose above her, like Adonis returned to life. She watched

575

him bending forward, removing her pantalets; she lifted her hips smoothly up for him to slide the garment down. He groaned, a sound of wonderful indulgence as his tongue touched her belly and found the indentation there. Everything about him was heightened in her head, as if she must remember each small detail of him, forever: his sun-lightened hair falling softly forward across his brow, the perfection of his eyes and face, his flawless chin line and neck, the wide, earth-coloured smoothness of his shoulders and chest, his sleek, sinewy stomach, his muscle-hard legs, his slender, brown fingers, the fair hairs glinting on his forearms and the L-shaped scar on his left arm.

He was removing her gartered stockings, and as the clinging material was pulled over her ankles, he kissed the inside of her calf and looked back down at her, his eyes shining with boundless love, with need and longing. She lay like a tantalisingly beautiful, nymph-like creature, her voluptuous lips apart, an expression in her eyes that radiated undisguised love, simultaneously earthy and tenderly sweet. She lifted her arms and his eyes fed greedily on her full breasts, erect, demanding, and below the flat, soft belly. His gaze came down across her abdomen and he lifted her right foot to kiss the inside of her ankle, and to watch the tangle of curls nestling between her legs. There was a crescendo of desire building within him now. This was his Eve, naked, available, explicitly wanting him. Finally, after the long months of starving for her, battling his yearning for her, he was allowing himself to exult in her, to be consumed by the touch and feel of her, his one true love.

Eve gave a small, erotic murmur as their mouths met again, and in the depth and intensity of her arousal, she slid her palms down the back of his neck, savouring the smooth, resilient texture of his skin, delighting in the rigid muscles of his back. He was perfect, he was beautiful, inside and out, and he was hers. How could life have given anyone more? She felt released, free, as if she were floating in the smell and feel of him. Her senses were filled with Alan. She spoke, although she hardly knew she had, 'I am part of you, I am a part of you, my darling, my own.'

And as his hands drifted down her silken skin, adoring her breasts, kneading her stomach, he answered thickly, 'You will always be a part of me.'

Giddy demanding spirals were bursting through his limbs as his fingers stroked across her belly to enter between her legs and explore at last the aroused, wet folds of her flesh. The velvet-soft heat, the wetness invited his fingers to probe carefully wider and deeper. He

576

smiled as he heard her acute gasp of pleasure, a wonderful, wanton sound.

Now Eve's hands found the stiffened length of him, inflexible and hot. Thrill upon thrill rose and descended to knot in her womb and spread down through her as she moved his fluid skin back and forth. Through the paroxysms of pleasure she felt his lips move from her mouth, down across her neck, over her tingling breasts and stomach to lodge in the swell of hair between her legs. His fingers came out of her to part her wetness for his tongue to search and knead. She gasped again; never had she felt like this. She was floating, falling into bursts of light and fire, feeling as if her whole body expanded and contracted in explosions of delight, and all the while her fingers twined the thick, waving hair at the back of his head.

The fire crackled, a prodigal, abandoned, beautiful noise as he lifted his tongue from her opening to find her mouth again. Rippling with ecstasy, she clasped him at the small of his back while she tasted again the wonder of his mouth. She wanted to give, as he had given, please as he had pleased. She drew her lips from his and descended across his firm body to his waist and down to the male hardness of him. She ran her tongue round the tip and he moaned, his breath catching in his throat. She squeezed and stroked him, continuing to tease him with her tongue, until she opened her lips to receive him, the wondrous strength of him, to move restlessly in the burning willingness of her mouth. As he moved, his continuous rumbled moan intensified all the rapturous sensations tumbling in confusion through her limbs.

She felt his hands on the sides of her head lifting her mouth from him. He moved her, laying her shimmering nakedness across the rug, her fair curls near the sensual firelight, and now his breath came in rasping sounds as he reared over her slender, inviting body.

Pushing between her legs at last, he thrust himself inside her, expanding her and filling her. She came up to him, to meet and join, twining her legs round him, every sensation acute, the moist channel of herself throbbing with the ecstasy of at last receiving him, taking him down into the extent of her. She rode with him, exulting in the slow, sliding, delicious pressure of him inside her, while their bodies moulded as one in the glorious, decadent firelight. For some moments, Alan stopped to hold himself still within her, his head bowed into the curve of her shoulder, his lips caressing the side of her throat as his voice came thickly, unsteadily, 'I love you, always.' She heard his words and all the emptiness, all the losses, all the pain and hurt that had been travelling with her, hidden in her heart, burst like a volcano inside her, then dissipated and disappeared. She was no longer alone; it was an exquisite, vivid moment of magnification. She was possessing him and was possessed by him; her answer came with a rush of glorious tenderness. 'And I love you, my Alan, my own.'

All thought and will faded as he began to move again, strong and endlessly enduring. Time lost its meaning. The blood surged through their veins as their breathing shuddered and caught.

There was an awareness of his iron-hard body abrading her breasts and belly and thighs, the pulsating urgency of his plunging into her and drawing back. She tasted the salt dampness of his bronze shoulder against her open mouth. Her fingers skimmed down the sweat on his back, lightly scoring the resilient skin, while the rhythm of his thrusts entered a new and intense harmony. He was merging with her, sweeping her into a blinding light of space and colour, immortal.

There were no thoughts now, their world was only continually connected spasms of thrilling, turbulent energy, and the final explosion consumed them, impelling them into total physical and mental bliss, sensation after sensation, magical, shattering and recreating, violently, beautifully, powerfully.

Time passed.

Eve became aware that he was pressing kisses on her forehead. Her lips were resting upon that part of him, at the base of his throat, which she had first noticed that day in the bush when she had fallen from Moonlight. It had thrilled her then, just looking at it, and from that day she had longed to touch and caress it.

She kissed it now.

CHAPTER THIRTY-FIVE

'He goes seeking liberty which is so dear, as he knows it, who for it, renounces life.'
The Divine Comedy, 'Purgatorio', Dante, 1265–1321.

Saturday, 8 July was a windy, cold winter's day, and the sun shone only intermittently on the straggling collection of buildings and byways that were Sydney town. And while the environs of the Prince of Wales Hotel were the rubbish-strewn streets, Eve's eyes saw none of it, for she had been loved by Alan Fletcher and that had coloured her perception of things.

It was the first morning she had not woken with an ache in her chest for Daniel and Sam, and now as the day advanced, she felt guilty at her happiness. Yet she could not suppress the overwhelming love that lifted from her being and composed her. The night before had brought her all she had wanted and dreamed about from the first day she had looked into his eyes at the coach door.

Alan had gone to the ship as arranged at eight o'clock, and half an hour before, Lawless had joined her.

When the shops opened, the two left the hotel to buy the necessary items for the voyage. As they passed through the front door, a small frown lodged between Lawless's eyes. 'Ye know, Mistress Eve, this mornin' there be somethin' impressin' me concernin' ye.'

Eve, who was holding his arm, turned to look in his face. 'Why, Lawless, what do you mean?'

'It's not as I can say exactly. It be hard for me as don't have the guv'nor's gift with words, like you are calm or . . . or I don't know, there be a grace about ye this mornin'. Now, not as ye are not graceful all the time,' he added, nodding to himself, 'but ye are more so today.'

She was silent for a few moments, then she said, 'Dear Lawless, yes, perhaps you are right. You are such a candid and sensitive man.'

He smiled as if her words were enough explanation, and she squeezed his arm as they continued down to the shops.

By the time the clock on the General Post Office struck eleven times, the two shoppers were returning up the hill of Grosvenor

Street, laden with parcels. They had ordered two travelling trunks to be delivered to the Prince of Wales by noon, and into these they would pack their purchases and belongings.

Alan was waiting for them with good news of their embarkation. 'It is all arranged. We can board the *Port Dennison* this afternoon. She sails with the evening tide, which is precisely at nightfall. The animals are last to be taken aboard, after cargo supplies and passengers. So one of us shall have to return here for the horses later.'

'Aye, guv, I'll do that. Wonder what Waterloo will think of shipboard life.'

Eve turned from her purchases. 'How long will the voyage take, Alan? When will we be in New York?'

He smiled gently at her, lifting his hand to touch her cheek. 'The clipper is a very fast ship, lass. They tell me it will be less than one hundred days.'

Lawless whistled, then he looked thoughtful. 'Come to think of it, the old *Mount Stewart Elphinstone* wasn't too bad then, if these here clippers are supposed to be the swiftest things afloat. She did the journey from the Old Dart in a hundred and fifty days sixteen years ago, and we were blown off course as well.'

'You're right, laddie, she was a good ship.'

A few minutes before noon, the two wooden trunks were delivered and while Eve packed them, Alan and Lawless went to hire a dray to convey them to the ship.

As they returned up the hill towards York Street, Lawless asked, 'Guv'nor, when ye bought passage, what relationship did ye say as the mistress holds to us?'

'I said she was my wife, Lawless.'

Lawless made a sound of approval. 'Good, guv'nor, and that's what she wishes to be and all.'

Nothing else was said for a time, then Lawless spoke again. 'Do you think as a man would be disloyal to the dead woman he loved dearly if he began to like another . . . a mighty lot?'

'You cannot live with the dead, lad. It is fine and proper to remember them with all the love you bore them, and perhaps the places they had are never quite filled again, but life continues.'

Lawless nodded. 'I think Patricia Junie would see it that way.'

Alan smiled. 'Yes, she would, I have no doubt of it. She was of the best there is, lad, and she would approve of Mistress Lottie for you. Patricia June would like Lottie.'

'Gawd, guv'nor!' declared Lawless turning in the seat to face him. 'How did you know?'

Alan smiled again and patted him on the back. 'Lawless, lad, it wasn't hard to guess.'

The younger man grinned self-consciously. Then he shook his finger in the air. 'And here I am goin' to this America and as far away from Mistress Lottie as a man can get.'

'Yes, but at the moment you have no alternative. Perhaps she will join you.'

'Aye, guv, that is bein' my very plan. In fact I shall be writin' a letter to her and post it before we sail.'

'That's the spirit.'

They drew up outside the Prince of Wales and climbed down.

Alan took the younger man's arm. 'Lawless, lad, from now on we must be cautious. It's just possible that if Rutherford Blake followed us, he could be in Sydney this afternoon, though I don't deem it likely. Still, we must remain discreet and wary.'

'Aye, guv, that's as I shall be.' Lawless turned away to fasten the horse's reins to the hitching rail.

'And, lad . . .'

'Yes, guv?' He turned back.

Alan stood regarding him, a tender look in his eyes. A number of intense expressions ran in quick succession across his face before he answered, 'Nothing, lad, it's just that you are the best companion a man could ever have dreamed of having. The best, and the most courageous.'

They were standing looking at each other amid the noise and clamour. People and vehicles were all around and a street vendor shouted nearby, but the two companions were alone, holding each other's gaze, while the wind blew cold down York Street.

The seconds passed.

Lawless swallowed hard. 'If I am that, Alan, my guv'nor, then it's as ye have made me.'

Alan continued staring at his friend, a long look that said so very many things. Then he shook his head. 'Ah, Lawless,' he answered, looking quickly away, 'you pay me too high a compliment.'

By two o'clock they were safely aboard the *Port Dennison*.

This first day, men and women were allowed to roam between decks at will, but once at sea the women would sleep on a different deck to the men. There was to be communal living during the day on the main deck, a major difference from ships that carried passengers exclusively, where they often separated the sexes, keeping the females aft, and only allowing the men and women together on a Sunday.

As Lawless commented to Eve, 'It's good we be on a cargo ship, for I reckon the guv'nor would have been right upset if he could not have seen you but once a week.'

She smiled in answer.

There was a bitter wind blowing steadily from the west and Mr Holmes and Captain Cruthers were talking in satisfied tones on the upper deck, happy in the understanding that the first part of their voyage would have fair wind.

The sea stable, the name given to the hold where the animals were kept, was ready to take horses from three o'clock in the afternoon, and shortly before that hour, Lawless came to Alan and Eve on the main deck against the bulwark.

Eve was fascinated with the scene. All around were the boisterous sounds of preparation for departure. Sailors shouted and officers called orders. Children squealed and ran about the decks, parents reprimanded. People and baggage were bustled down hatchways and along gangways. This was to be the third major voyage of her life and she felt exhilarated.

'I'll be away now, guv, and shall have Waterloo, Freedom and Milford back on board before the hour's out.'

'Yes, lad, but I'm coming with you.'

'It only needs one man, guv'nor. I will ride Waterloo and lead the others.'

'Yes, but two can keep a weather eye out better than one.'

Eve looked from one to the other. 'Now, both go, and the sooner you leave, the sooner you'll be back. I shall have everything unpacked when you return.'

Alan took Eve's hand in a brief farewell and Lawless said, ''Bye for now then, Mistress Eve,' as he turned and led the way across the deck towards the port side and the quay. He was two or three yards ahead of Alan and as he passed the wide mainmast, there was a shout from above and sailors up in the rigging yelled, 'Watch out below! Falling chain! Danger!'

Above the general hustle and din, very few people heard the shout. The heavy length of chain, which had been secured round the topmost yard near the crow's nest, had slipped from the grasp of the two men who were refastening it; it fell amidships, crashing down straight through a sail, bringing ropes with it.

Eve saw it falling and screamed in shock as she realised Lawless was directly beneath. He looked up too late to avoid it. His reflexes were excellent, and he dived to the side, but it was useless and as Alan shouted, 'Lawless!' the chain smashed into his shoulder and dragged him to the deck amid tangles of rope.

He lay inertly, face down.

They ran to him. Alan knelt and lifted him in his arms. There was blood running from a cut on his shoulder and he appeared unconscious.

'Lawless . . . Lawless, my boy.'

A second or two passed, then Lawless opened his eyes, and grimacing with pain said, 'Gawd, guv'nor, these clipper ships are dangerous!'

Alan let out a long sigh of relief.

The *Port Dennison*'s doctor, one George McManus, was called to attend, and the patient was carried below decks to the small, but well-equipped hospital.

'He's broken his shoulder-blade,' Dr McManus informed Eve and Alan a short time later, 'but I've strapped it well, and by the time this voyage is half over, he shall be as good as new.'

Eve remained to sit with Lawless who was to spend the night in the hospital bunk, and Alan left to get the horses alone. Eve lifted her hand to him. 'Let us know as soon as you are aboard again, my love, so we can cease to worry.'

He kissed her fingers. 'Of course.'

His journey was without incident and when he arrived back with Freedom, Waterloo and Milford, the *Port Dennison* rode low in the high water, for full tide and departure were less than an hour away. One at a time, he took the horses up the wide gangplank that led to the elliptical stern. The sea stable was in an aft hold. Down there, he met Mr Brown, the second mate, a capable, softly spoken man, in charge of live cargo. He marked down the three horses on his record book and enquired, 'Disembarkation port?'

'New York.'

Mr Brown pointed to Freedom and Waterloo. 'Beautiful animals, both of them,' he said appreciatively. 'Now you know the feedin' of these fine specimens of horse flesh is up to you.'

Alan nodded. 'Yes, I understand that. I ordered sufficient seed and grain this morning. I shall be back to bed them down.'

'Be here before we sail,' Brown instructed. 'I want the sea stable shipshape before we pass Farm Cove.'

As he entered the hospital, Eve stood and came to his side. He put his arm round her waist and she felt a wonderful surge of happiness. She smiled up in welcome and Lawless attempted to do the same. Alan spent a brief time with them and as it neared the hour of embarkation, he stood to leave and take care of the horses.

'In less than half an hour the ship will sail, I must feed and bed them down.'

'Wish I could help, guv,' Lawless sighed from where he lay. Then, with his good arm he gestured towards the door. 'Go on, Mistress Eve, accompany the guv. I'll be all right, and no mistake.'

Eve patted his arm. 'No, it's best I stay here. I can see you have a temperature.'

Alan touched Lawless affectionately on the arm and bent down and kissed Eve on the top of her head. Before he stepped through into the companionway, he looked back, his eyes gleaming with love for them both. 'My dear ones,' he said, 'soon the *Port Dennison* will be sailing, and that means freedom and new lives.' For a few seconds, he stood perfectly motionless looking at them, his dark figure framed by the doorway.

The sun was setting as he returned above to the aft deck. The hatch entrance was close to the bulwark of the stern and as he neared it he glanced over the side to the *Saint Louis*, the ship berthed adjacent to the *Port Dennison*, which also sailed with the evening tide.

He stood stock-still, and the blood coursed more swiftly in his veins as he recognised the man who now was striding up the single gangplank of the *Saint Louis*. Rutherford Blake was followed by David Elrington and a trooper, and below at the quayside two police constables stood on the wharf waiting.

Mind racing, Alan evaluated the situation.

He took a graphite pencil from his inside coat pocket. The only piece of paper upon him was the receipt for payment from the hotel, and on the back of this he wrote hastily.

Along past the mizzenmast, through the bodies milling on the main deck, he ran. He knew exactly where to find the man he sought, and up the companionway to the raised deck and the ship's wheel he went.

I must have time . . . I must.

There, arms raised, giving orders stood Grantley Holmes. He was surprised to see Alan, for all the passengers had been asked to remain aft and to view the departure from there, out of the way of the sailors.

'I must speak with you, Mr Holmes.'

The first mate felt the urgency in the man beside him. 'Please be quick then, sir. We prepare to depart.'

'Mr Holmes, I have no other to trust at this moment but you. I would give you long and detailed explanation if I had time, but I do not. I am not coming on the voyage.'

Mr Holmes' thick eyebrows rose in confusion.

'I ask you to give this note to . . . my wife. She is below in the hospital with my brother. But please do not give it to her until you

584

are beyond the Sydney Heads and out at sea.'

'Mr Trent, whatever is going on?'

'I wish I could tell you but I cannot, sir. The two I leave with you are more to me than life itself. Will you do as I ask? Please?'

There are moments in men's lives when they recognise that the decision they make has enormous bearing on the lives of others; Mr Holmes recognised he was in that position now. He heard himself answer, 'Yes, I will.'

'My eternal thanks to you, sir.' Alan gave him the note and shook the first mate by the hand, before he left him standing there.

To the port side he ran. Mr Brown was standing with four sailors at the ship's side in readiness to draw up the plank. His freckled brow wrinkled in amazement as Alan came past. 'Where the devil are you off to?' he demanded, his soft voice rising. 'In a few minutes we pull this up.'

'Sail without me. I am not coming . . . definitely not coming.' Then he stepped through the opening and went rapidly down the gangway to the wooden planking of the wharf.

Humanity in all its forms shuffled and moved about, shouting farewells and waving. Through the crowded quayside he strode to the base of the *Saint Louis* gangplank. Three yards away stood the police constables. At the same moment, above him on the deck of the *Saint Louis* appeared Rutherford Blake. He turned from the ship's master saying, 'I'm grateful for your co-operation, Captain. Ah yes, and may your voyage find fair winds.' Then he gestured to David Elrington to hurry. 'Come on, now to the *Port Dennison*. We might just have enough time at least to see the manifest of passengers before she sails.'

In the gathering dusk, he stepped through the ship's side and began to descend. Below him, a man stepped onto the other end of the plank and began to ascend.

Sir Rutherford looked down at the man.

The man looked up at Sir Rutherford.

For a second, it seemed as if the tumult and the excitement around them died. They both halted as the impact of recognition hit Sir Rutherford.

Then Alan turned and leaped to the wharf, running away through the noise and clamour.

'Stop him!' screamed Sir Rutherford, impelling himself forward to stumble in his haste. 'It's Alan Fletcher! Stop him!'

The two constables turned to see Alan disappearing through the throng. Along Pyrmont Wharf they ran, calling and shouting for Alan to stop. But he did not. He led them up and away from the wharfs towards the city. By the warehouses he ran and over an open field to a lane leading uphill. Very few people were here and although it was quickly darkening, his pursuers could see him clearly making for the street.

'I'll not lose you this time,' Sir Rutherford said, as he stopped and withdrew his pistol from inside his coat. His eyes narrowed in clinical appraisal of the distance between himself and his quarry.

'Don't! You might hit one of the men, sir!' David Elrington protested beside him.

'I hope not,' came the grim answer as he pulled the trigger.

The explosion sounded and Alan stumbled and fell to his knees.

The constables stopped running, and looked back in fright. But when they realised Sir Rutherford was not intending to fire again, continued the chase.

Alan rose to maintain his flight, but the wound and fall had cost him dearly and the constables were soon upon him. He knocked one to the ground and threw off the other before he vaulted a low wall at the lane end and made for the street. But the injury slowed him down badly and when the two police reached him the second time, they held him fast.

Sir Rutherford walked, pistol in hand, over the unpaved ground towards them. He did not hurry, in fact, just the opposite, he dawdled, seeming to savour the walk up to his captive as a cat might to its injured prey. He was elated! His pulse was thumping with excitement. Beads of perspiration covered his forehead and his temples. He was smiling with gratification and exhilaration.

Blood ran from the wound in Alan's thigh, down across his knee into the top of his highly polished black boot.

The expert on the bushrangers strolled up to within two feet of Alan, his eyes locked with the captive's. 'Surely, you did not expect I would let you escape this time, Alan Fletcher,' Sir Rutherford said, coming face to face with the man he had wanted more than any other in his life.

'No, I did not,' Alan answered, steadily returning his gaze.

While this exchange took place, the gangplank was being stowed aboard the *Port Dennison*, and Mr Holmes and Captain Cruthers were shouting orders to their men in the rigging. Mr Brown saw that the flags were furled, and the clipper drifted inexorably away from Pyrmont Wharf.

When Eve felt the ship drift away from the dock, she did not go above. She felt she should remain with Lawless and for some reason she did not want to witness the ship's departure.

He lay with his eyes closed and when she heard his steady breathing, she was pleased he was sleeping.

She thought many things and in the many was her life ahead with Alan. She knew she was his soul-wife and that was enough for her. What did anything else matter? Then an odd thought came to her. Perhaps John Stuart would divorce her. It was done occasionally. Some people did such things now. He might agree if she wrote from America and asked him. Surely he would be glad to be rid of her. In any case it didn't matter, she perceived things differently now and in the new land she would be Alan's wife in all that mattered.

She wondered why he did not return. It must be over half an hour since they had left the wharf.

A sailor had come in and lit the wall lamp earlier and told her that the doctor would be by shortly.

She stood and moved to the porthole. She could hear the wind but could see nothing except the blackness of the night. She shivered and, walking back to the bunk, drew a second blanket up over Lawless.

Where was Alan? Surely he would have bedded the horses down by now? Where could he be?

Suddenly it came to her. Of course. He would be entranced by being on the water again. He would be on deck, watching and enjoying the activity and thinking all the things that sailors think.

Satisfied, she sat down again.

The door opened and she turned sharply in expectation, a smile on her face. It was Dr McManus with a tray and some broth for Lawless.

'Have you seen . . . Mr Trent?'

'No, I have not, but then I have seen no one as I was in ship's medical stores until I went to the galley to get this for Mr Miller.' He put down the tray and lifted Lawless's good arm to take his pulse.

At the movement, he woke. 'Hallo, Doctor.' His eyes found Eve. 'Where's the guv'nor?'

'I don't know, dear. Will you be all right while I go above to find him?'

'Yes, you go.'

She closed the hospital door and moved swiftly along the dimly lit corridor and up a companionway to a second corridor and then to the deck. It was cold and the wind swept her hair high from her shoulders. Men were moving about and calling to each other in the vague light of the hurricane lanterns. Where was he?

It was close to eight miles by water from Pyrmont Wharf to the north and south heads at the entrance to Sydney harbour. An hour after departing the dockside, the *Port Dennison*, under full sail, headed out across the Tasman Sea.

Eve had been on all the decks, and now there was fear in her eyes as she rushed along, almost falling once or twice as the ship rolled. Perhaps he had returned to the hospital and Lawless. Yes, that would be it.

Back down the companionway she went, and there was Mr Holmes coming towards her along one of the corridors. He called to her and she halted. His pleasant face was serious, for he held the impression that he was not the bringer of good news. He was an honourable man and had not read the folded note carried in his pocket, though he had been tempted to often during the last hour.

'Mrs Trent, your husband asked me to give you this. He was particular about the time. He made it distinctly plain you were not to receive it until we were at sea.' He was holding the paper out to her.

She went cold with dread. The pulse in her throat throbbed as she took it from him. She could not speak. She made a strange sound that was meant to be 'Thank you' and turned from him.

In the cold dark corridor she dragged her eyes down to read Alan's words.

Eve,
    Rutherford Blake is upon us. There is only one hope for you both. I am returning to shore as a decoy, for I must know that you two whom I love above all else are free.
    Live in the knowledge that I love you, now and always.

                                             Alan

She stood unmoving in the passage.

Then she crumpled sideways into the bulkhead and for a long time leaned there.

She became aware of Dr McManus's voice and his bespectacled, kindly face looking at her with concern. 'Mrs Trent, Mrs Trent, are you all right? Whatever is the matter?'

Like a stranger she listened to the sound of her voice replying, 'It's . . . it's nothing I can discuss with you, Doctor. I . . . I'm sorry. Forgive me.' And she stumbled by him to the hospital door.

Lawless was sitting up. He had finished his broth. His mouth broke into a smile as she entered, but his face changed as he registered Eve's look.

'What is it, mistress? By the Lord in heaven, what is it?'

She came to him and handed him the note. She stood impotently beside the bunk, watching the colour drain out of his face as he read. He lifted his eyes from the paper and they brimmed over with tears.

'Oh, my guv'nor, my beloved guv'nor. Whatever shall we do without ye?'

They had taken Alan to Liverpool Street police barracks, less than a mile from the docks. There they disinfected and doctored his wound, fed him, and put him in a cold cell with a wall candle, a table and chair, a wooden bunk, and two blankets.

He heard a clock chime eight times somewhere in the distance. About a minute later, footsteps stopped outside his cell. The lock rattled and the heavy timber door squeaked open on its hinges.

The advisor on the bushrangers entered, carrying a hurricane lantern. He placed it on the table as two policemen peered tentatively in from the doorway.

'Come in, Wright,' Sir Rutherford said to one of them who held a notebook and pencil.

The door closed and Constable Wright stood inside near it. Sir Rutherford sat on the single chair, and Alan remained where he was, sitting on the bunk.

For perhaps thirty seconds no one spoke; the captor and the captive watched each other across the chill air of the room, each quite openly examining the other.

A self-satisfied smile sat on Sir Rutherford's mouth as he determined to break the silence. 'So, Fletcher, is there anything you wish to say?'

'No.'

'Then perhaps you will be good enough to answer my questions.'

'Perhaps.'

The captor tapped with his oval fingernail on the table, once again observing his prisoner. 'They removed my bullet from your leg, eh?'

'They did.'

Sir Rutherford gave an indulgent chuckle. 'Ah yes, you'll be able to walk to the gallows after all.'

Alan did not speak.

'How long did you reside at Treehard Hill?'

'Six years.'

'I buried your companions there you know . . . Dwyer and Cooper.'

Sir Rutherford was sure he detected his prisoner flinch. Yes, there was pain in his eyes.

'I did not know,' Alan replied slowly.

'And where is the last remaining member of your gang, Lawless Drake?'

Alan made a sound that could have been mistaken for a sigh. 'We were never a "gang", and it does not conform with my estimation of your intelligence to expect me to answer your question.'

'Then perhaps you will tell me why you were about to board the *Saint Louis* this evening?'

'I will not.'

'Ah yes, I did not really think you would cooperate, unlike your former associate, Jordan O'Day. Now, he has told me quite a lot about you.' Sir Rutherford folded his arms and leaned back in his chair. 'He won't swing, you know. Ah yes, he will turn Queen's evidence at your trial. In fact, he shall probably be allotted a portion of your reward money.'

Alan did not answer, he sat motionlessly, staring steadily at his inquisitor.

'What do you think of that, Alan Fletcher? O'Day collecting money for your head and living the high life?'

'Jordan O'Day is as nothing to me. Discussing his future will be a very one-sided conversation.'

The captor forced a smile. 'Ah yes, you are controlled, Alan Fletcher. You do not let me down. I expected as much. I am learning a great deal about you simply having this conversation, one-sided or not.'

Then, surprisingly, Alan smiled, and for some seconds the two men observed each other in silence, the only noise the scratching of Constable Wright's pencil on his notebook.

Sir Rutherford shivered and moved his eyes from Alan's face. It was damned cold in here. He noted an empty fireplace in one corner, no doubt from previous days when it had been other than a detention room. He motioned with his right hand to the constable's book. 'For the record, Alan Fletcher, I must ask you once more why you were boarding the *Saint Louis*?'

Alan did not reply.

Sir Rutherford sighed and stood up. 'I have kept her in port, you realise. She is being searched this very minute for stowaways.' Then he pointed to the door and looked to his companion. 'You may leave, Constable. I will join you outside in a moment.'

When the door closed, his eyes returned to his prisoner's face. 'This is a very delicate matter. Ah yes. It concerns . . . Mrs Wakeman. Do you know where she is?' He was watching his prisoner with all the scrutiny available to him, and he thought he noticed a change of expression come into his eyes.

'I do.' Alan answered.

Sir Rutherford's brows drew together in a frown. 'Where? Where is she?'

Alan hesitated a few seconds. 'Out of New South Wales, away from anywhere that you, or those you associate with, can do her harm.'

The police detective did not like this information. John Stuart would not like this information. He stood and walked to the cell door. There, he paused. His face was a mixture of emotions and his angular profile in shadow looked even more hawk-like than ever. He was about to leave, but he decided to ask for the information that he had been inquisitive about from the first. He turned his head back to his prisoner and they locked eyes once again. 'Why is it, in all the raids you have made, and the number in twelve years has not been inconsiderable, that your target has been the Government on all occasions except two, and those two were the most wealthy in the land?'

Alan sat staring at him, and for some seconds Sir Rutherford believed he was not going to answer.

Then he did. 'My differences have only ever been with those who exercise authority.'

The expert on the bushrangers nodded; he had always thought as much. 'I shall see you in the morning, Alan Fletcher. I hope your wound does not trouble you too much.'

He dismissed the two constables and stood outside the cell watching them depart. The satisfaction and sheer rejoicing he had experienced three hours before, when he had caught the bushranger, had waned. The interview had disturbed him, no matter how he pretended to himself it had not. He felt unhappy with the whole turn of events. Fletcher had integrity. It was confusing to compare him with other bushrangers. He was nothing like the informer, O'Day, or any of the scum he had dealt with before. Now that he had spent even this short time in his company, he admitted there was a sort of truth in the very essence of the man. He conceded that this was what he had suspected when he was at Treehard Hill; why he had felt uncomfortable there, like an intruder. Yet Fletcher was a cold-blooded murderer.

He stood in the corridor analysing his feelings. He was disconcerted and uneasy. He hated to feel this way. It was not conducive to being efficient or effective. He looked back at the door of Alan's cell and shook his head.

Down the corridor and through the iron gate he hurried. Turning left, he entered a small warm room where three constables sat at desks. A fire burnt in the grate. They all looked up at him, one was the smooth-faced Wright, who was now turning his shorthand notes into longhand.

Sir Rutherford was the talk of the barracks. His reputation, already substantial among the rank and file of the force, was now, with the capture of Alan Fletcher, indestructible. They all stood from their desks as a mark of respect.

He coughed. 'Ah yes, gentlemen. I want you to . . . I would like a fire lit in the prisoner's cell. Immediately. There is a fireplace there.' He coughed again. 'He is wounded, after all. It is a cold night. Keep it fed. You understand?'

The surprise on the three constables' faces still remained when Sir Rutherford had closed the door and was ten yards along the corridor.

He crossed the yard where a fine rain drizzled and joined David Elrington who waited for him in the superintendent's office. Twenty minutes later, they had ridden to their billets in the Police Training School, a section of the Redfern Barracks situated a little over half a mile away. Their horses were taken and they said goodnight to each other in the wide, paved quadrangle. Light rain continued falling.

'What time do you wish to see me in the morning, sir?'

'The usual, Mr Elrington. We shall meet at seven o'clock for breakfast.'

'Very good, sir,' his assistant said as he made to depart. Then he added, 'Oh, and what a great afternoon's work, sir. Congratulations!'

It seemed to David Elrington that his superior's answer lacked the enthusiasm he had expected. 'Ah yes . . . well, goodnight, Mr Elrington.'

'Goodnight, sir.'

As Sir Rutherford mounted the stone steps and opened the door that led into the building containing his quarters, a young constable came forward from where he had waited near the hall fire. He saluted. 'Constable Hubert Garner, sir. I have been assigned to you.'

Sir Rutherford nodded to the tall, neat, young man.

'What would you like to eat, sir? Cook's gone for the night but there are ham sandwiches in the kitchen.'

The preoccupied face frowned. 'What's that? Sandwiches? Yes . . . yes, Garner, anything will do.'

'And there are two men here, sir, to see you. Came some twenty minutes ago. They are waiting in the duty officer's room, sir.'

Before the expert on the bushrangers opened the door to the Duty Officer's area, he had guessed who they would be. He found John Stuart and Joe sitting by the fire waiting for him. As they stood to meet him, Joe spoke. 'Rutherford, we followed you and arrived just this evening. We stay at the Royal.'

'My friends,' he began, 'while I am happy to see you, I have mixed news for you, I fear.'

John Stuart took his hand, 'Have you found her?'

He shook his head. 'No. But I have Alan Fletcher in custody. I think we should go to my rooms and I shall tell you all I know.'

When Sir Rutherford had related the story of his long ride and the capture of Alan, he leaned back and tapped the arm of his chair restlessly. 'So, you see, I have the bushranger in my hands. And while that makes me happy, I am sorry I cannot give you the whereabouts of Mrs Wakeman. All he has told me is that she is out of New South Wales.'

John Stuart was tired; dispirited and tired. 'What does that mean?'

'I don't know. Of course, he could be lying to put me off the track. That is always possible. Because I do not see how she could be out of New South Wales. Even now I have experts searching the *St Louis*. If she is on board, we will find her.'

John Stuart looked to Joe. As always, his feelings were transparent to the older man, his misgivings and disillusion obvious. Joe's expression of concern and encouragement helped him to ask his ultimate question. 'Are we to take it, that you believe they were running away to America together? That they were . . . lovers.'

Rutherford Blake lifted his hands palm upwards to him. 'I'm sorry, my friend. From appearances, I can only assume . . .'

'Yes,' John Stuart replied. 'I . . . understand.'

When Joe and John Stuart left, it was with the understanding that if Sir Rutherford learned anything, he would send a message immediately to them and in any case, they would return to the Redfern Barracks to meet the police detective at noon tomorrow.

Finally, Sir Rutherford had eaten his sandwiches and he sat listening to the heavily falling rain. His earlier discomforting sentiments about Alan Fletcher had given way to irritation with himself. He had begun to romanticise the man. He was going soft. The man was a killer, a convict and an outlaw. He was simply a member of the upper classes degrading his birthright. What the devil was wrong? The man should not be able to affect him at all.

At half past nine, young Garner knocked gently on the door with the news that the *Saint Louis* had been searched from stem to stern, and no stowaways had been found. After the constable had gone, he stood for a long time looking out into the cold, dark, wet night.

At eleven o'clock, he went to bed and at midnight was still awake. Suddenly, his eyes opened widely into the blackness and his voice echoed around the room. 'Of course! He wanted me to chase him. It was not the *Saint Louis* at all!' He sat up and lit the candle on his bedside table.

He understood now. Alan Fletcher had lured him away from the wharf deliberately, given himself up to ensure the others would not be taken. It was the next ship that Drake and the Wakeman woman were on, the *Port Dennison*. It had sailed with the evening tide, while he had held in port the one that did not matter. Ah yes, Eve Wakeman was indeed 'out of New South Wales'. John Stuart had truly lost his wife this time. She was on the *Port Dennison* and he had been fooled by Fletcher one more time.

'Blasted bushrangers! The devil take them all!' He sighed, a long miserable sound. Still he had Fletcher, didn't he? Fletcher was the coup. The greatest coup of them all.

Sometime later, he dropped off to sleep. He awoke early and was fully dressed and had written a note to John Stuart before seven o'clock. He thought it only fair to apprise his friend of his convictions. The message informed John Stuart that it was Sir Rutherford's belief that Eve Wakeman and Lawless Drake were bound for the United States of America.

Constable Garner had just gone off to deliver it when there was an excited knock on his door. David Elrington entered.

'Sir!' he began before his superior could open his mouth. 'I have it here, here in my hands, the transcript of the Fletcher trial. Would you believe it? It was handed to me not five minutes since. Remember, we sent for it last January? It arrived aboard the HMS *Gallant* on Thursday. Inspector McClelland has had it sitting here in his office among a batch of letters for postage. He found it last night, and when he met me in the corridor just now, he went and retrieved it.'

Sir Rutherford's hand shook as he took the sealed envelope.

An hour later, he had not eaten breakfast. He sat looking out into the cobbled yard, his back ramrod stiff, his eyes glassy.

It is sometimes said that shock makes people age overnight. There is no doubt that Sir Rutherford Blake aged in the hour it took him voraciously to read the transcript of the Fletcher trial.

He had changed. Never would he be the same again. For he now knew what only Alan Fletcher knew!

His face was ashen and he was weighed down with guilt. Over and over he said to himself, 'He is innocent . . . innocent . . . Alan Fletcher is innocent.'

Having read the report of the trial, it was all apparent to him.

Abel Crenshaw perpetrated the crime to get Alan Fletcher's land.

The name of the chief witness had leaped off the pages at him. Benjamin Breely! Benjamin Breely, alias Rufus Short, alias Victor Hawke, alias Clifton Kempe. The man had been a vile murderer, though not, it was clear, when Alan Fletcher was tried. It was later. Sir Rutherford would never forget him. Hadn't he been one of the last convictions he had made before he came out to this country?

Breely, the most immoral of men, who had looked as innocent as he was guilty. He had the face of an incorruptible man and he was the devil's own vintage. He had used his looks to marry wealthy, older women and had killed them for their estates. Four women he had married and murdered between 1853 and 1861. He had died on the gibbet, brought to justice only weeks before Sir Rutherford had come out to New South Wales. His evidence in a court of law was not worth a tinker's curse.

Sir Rutherford's memory was perfect. He could recall each man he had brought to conviction and the name 'Christopher Scales', he remembered too. A thief and burglar in London, caught in fifty-seven for robbery with violence, and sentenced to ten years on the prison hulk *Redoubtable*. He had been one of the London men who had sworn they had seen Alan Fletcher commit the murder. It was ghastly! These men had been paid by Abel Crenshaw to convince the jury. And without them, the prosecution had no case, no case at all.

It made Sir Rutherford feel physically ill.

Ah yes, but none had yet been caught for unlawful acts in 1849 when Alan Fletcher was tried. They were at the beginning of their nefarious careers then. And why was the matter not re-opened when the prosecution's case had been based on the evidence of two notorious criminals? Because there had been only one man who knew about their connection with Alan Fletcher and who also would have known about their subsequent careers, and he was dead. Yes, Finnigan McGuire, who had defended Alan, had drowned off Torquay in 1854. Sir Rutherford had known of him, a clever young barrister, set to go far.

He brought his fist down heavily on the window ledge. His whole life had been dedicated to bringing criminals to justice. These last three years had been devoted to catching bushrangers, and none had he wanted more than the one half a mile away, the innocent one, who had lost his lands and been degraded into convictism. Of course he had escaped and become a bushranger! Would not Sir Rutherford have done the very same?

Alan Fletcher, who had allowed himself to be caught, so that his associates might live. Alan Fletcher who had never used violence; who had never robbed any but the Government and the acutely rich;

who had said to him last night, 'My differences have only ever been with those who exercise authority.' Of course. All clear now . . . all so sickeningly clear. He turned from the window and strode to the door.

He must go to Alan Fletcher. Tell him. Set him free.

David Elrington thought he had never seen his superior so excited. There was a tense, unnatural look about him and when he asked for his horse, he said in agitated tones, 'Bring it here to me, posthaste. I must go to the Liverpool Street barracks, immediately.'

They were standing in the quadrangle, and at that moment Constable Garner appeared and, marching formally up to them, said, 'Sir Rutherford, Inspector McClelland sends his respects and requests your company in his office. He asks if you would be good enough to see him forthwith.'

'Damn!' Sir Rutherford said frowning. Then he decided. 'Mr Elrington, you must go for Alan Fletcher. Go immediately. Bring him straight back to me here. Do not deviate. Do you understand? Hurry! It is most urgent!'

And a surprised David Elrington did as he was told.

Sir Rutherford strode across the quadrangle and up the stairs into the building that contained the offices. At the senior officer's door, he knocked and entered.

Inspector Mark McClelland's bearded face looked up from a pile of papers. 'Ah, there you are, Sir Rutherford. Good morning, I want to talk to you. Now, where do you propose to incarcerate Fletcher until his trial? The Darlinghurst gaol?'

Sir Rutherford shivered, but not from the cold of the winter's morning. He dropped into the chair opposite the police officer. 'My God, McClelland, you will find this hard to believe, but Fletcher is innocent . . . innocent of the murder charge which made him a convict in the first place.' He put the transcript of the trial on the desk as the police officer's mouth opened in amazement. 'Listen, and I will tell you what I have found out this morning.'

For a few seconds, Inspector McClelland thought it was a joke but as the explanation continued, he knew it was very serious.

'And so you see,' Sir Rutherford finished, after he had told the story, ' "the wheel has come full circle", for I, who was his enemy, must now be his champion. We must see the Inspector General, the Governor, the Premier. Set him free, no matter who is against it.'

Mark McClelland had been a policeman for thirty years. First in Bristol and the west country of England. He had come out to New South Wales in 1844, and for twenty-one years he had worked as hard as anyone to gain respect for the colonial police. He hated the way his men were often the target of lampoons, and in particular how they had been made to look foolish in the eyes of the public these last few years when bushranging had become a social menace. He had been annoyed when the Inspector General had seen fit to appoint this famous criminalist and expert detective policeman from London to advise on the problem. But McClelland was a fair man, an honest policeman and a good administrator, and had to admit that Sir Rutherford Blake had made a difference. The man had been a veritable bloodhound, tenacious and resolute. He had been instrumental in bringing in many, if not all, the notorious outlaws of the last two years, and now finally, he had caught the elusive Alan Fletcher. He was an erudite antagonist of all who broke the law, and hence, more than any man alive, if he said a man was innocent, then he was to be believed.

Mark McClelland nodded. 'You are right.'

Ten minutes later, both men waited impatiently on the small balcony outside the office building. The advisor on the bushrangers was still speaking his agitated thoughts aloud. 'I have been a criminalist studying crimes and the law for twenty years. I have been a detective policeman since the phrase was coined ten years ago, and never have I seen an innocent man sentenced, never, until now.'

Inspector McClelland shook his head. 'What is he really like?' he asked. A question from time immemorial when ordinary beings wish an insight into the extraordinary. And Sir Rutherford, in answer, sighed, and then attempted description. 'What does one say about a man like him? Dispassionate? Clever? Heroic? Noble? I suspect he is all these things. Perhaps at another time he would have been an Alexander, a Wolfe, a Nelson. There is one thing I know, he is not afraid of you or me or any man.'

The cold wind that had been blowing for the last twenty-four hours picked up some stray papers and moved them across the court in front of them, as Sir Rutherford lifted his hand with excitement. 'Here, here they come, now!'

And there, over the heads of the dozen police cadets drilling beyond the arched entrance to the yard, they saw the escort riding towards them. Two troopers in front, David Elrington riding alongside Alan Fletcher, ah yes, and it looked like two more police behind.

Followed by the police inspector, the advisor on the bushrangers jumped down the stone steps to the cobbled yard, a look of anticipation upon his grave face.

Alan had been surprised when an armed constable had unlocked the door of his cell and held it open while two more entered carrying armfuls of wood. He watched as a fire was lit in the grate.

'Orders of Sir Rutherford Blake,' the man lighting the fire explained, looking at Alan with awe.

'Thank you,' Alan said as they departed.

The heat had certainly made a difference. After it pervaded the cold dank room, his leg, that had been aching continuously, improved to where it was but a dull discomfort.

He lay back on the bunk and looked at the flickering firelight. The innumerable contingencies that had brought him to this cell . . . Rutherford Blake had proved an able adversary. A peculiar individual, arrogant, egotistical, but unquestionably clever, discerning and determined. The calibre of the man had never been in doubt, and when they had talked a short time ago, Alan had recognised his qualities. Curious that he had ordered him a fire. Curious, but surprisingly kind.

Thinking of the interview, a wan smile came to his mouth. It was a pity that he could not know Blake better; there was something about him that in other circumstances he felt he would have liked.

So, he was a prisoner again. After twelve and a half years they had him once more. Transcending everything was the fact that his two remaining loved ones were safe. That was what mattered to him; that was all that mattered now. Two lives exchanged for two lives. Danny and Sam were gone, and Eve and Lawless were free. He had given the only thing he finally had to give that would make a difference: his freedom.

He felt confidence in their resilience and courage. He closed his eyes. And there she was looking at him from inside the coach, wearing the green travelling dress, a white bow at her throat, the first time he had seen her; and there she was sitting in the bush, her head bandaged in strips of his shirt, gazing up at him with her darling brown eyes. He looked over to the corner of his cell where the fire burned brightly, warming the small space around him. He pictured her slender nakedness on the hearth rug in the fire-glow of last night. Was it only last night? He imagined the gentle mounds and curves of her body and heard the soft seductive laughter of their perfect union. He made a sad sound. 'I wish you happiness, my love,' he said aloud.

He fell asleep to the sound of falling rain hitting the windowpane outside the iron bars, and when he awoke, it was to the dull light of a cold, grey day.

They kept his fire burning. His breakfast was a small bowl of porridge, a thick slice of bacon and a slab of bread.

He thought it must have been some time between eight and nine o'clock when the door of his cell was unlocked again, and this time he saw the face of the same constable who had lit his fire the night before. Standing behind him were two armed men. The young man coughed nervously. 'Mr Fletcher. You are requested to come and bring your coat with you. You are being transferred.'

While Alan followed the constable down the hall, in his office across the yard, the superintendent signed the release form and handed it to David Elrington. Then he turned to watch through his window as the prisoner was brought from confinement down into the yard. He looked on as David Elrington joined them and they mounted up, the prisoner swinging his bandaged leg up over the horse with no show of difficulty. Then the company moved away between the buildings and was lost to his sight.

It was a short ride of some one thousand yards from the barracks to the Police Training School on the far side of Hyde Park, and as they issued into the street, Alan spoke to David Elrington who rode straight-backed beside him.

'Where do we go?'

Now, Sir Rutherford's assistant was as fascinated by the captive as everyone else, and he was glad to speak with him. 'To the other side of the park, College Street Police Training School, Sir Rutherford Blake especially requested me to bring you there immediately. No doubt, you are in for a morning's interrogation before they transfer you to Darlinghurst gaol.'

'No doubt,' Alan answered.

David Elrington would have liked to continue the conversation but, being aware of his position, he did not feel it appropriate, and in any case the prisoner looked away.

In the street, the mounted, armed entourage caused maximum interest. Alan, handcuffed and riding in the middle of four armed police, became the subject of loud speculation from the idle, the loiterers, the hawkers, and passers-by. He was certainly a striking figure with his bandaged leg and his dark clothes and knee-high, black leather boots. Even manacled, he rode easily, expertly, and the horse responded to his authority, lifting its hooves in lively fashion. He ignored the noisy observations shouted at him for his mind was not in the dusty streets of Sydney town, but far away with those he could see no more. Their faces were a jumble in his mind. Eve, his mother, Danny, Lawless, Sam, Swiftie, Womballa, and even Bluey for an instant.

And so, after all, it had come down to this day. Sunday, 8 July, 1865. Another trial?

What defence could he possibly have? Jordan would be there to give evidence against him, and all the men the Crown could muster would stand in line to convict him. Once more, he would have to listen to the slander and the lies. Once more, they would malign him and show him culpable. But this time they would not send him as a convict to a place thirteen thousand miles across the sea. This time, they would hang him. Snap his neck at the end of a rope.

Was he angry at the injustice? No. There was no rage or resentment. He had acknowledged years ago that those sentiments were useless. What had occurred could not be altered. And too, there had been joys, many joys, the love he felt for Eve surpassing them all. His beautiful soul-wife, the woman of his most wonderful imaginings. He felt the skin of her body again, smelt the dreamy, heady scent of her. The ultimate treasure was here in his mind, the memory of lying with her in the firelight. He could take that to eternity with him. His vision clouded momentarily as he stared straight ahead.

Into his mind, out of the well of his yesterdays, came the words that the soldier Parker had said to him so long ago in the convict tent when they were escaping. 'You'll hang, Fletcher . . . they'll hang you for sure in the end.'

No! It was no way for a man to die. Not hanging. He could not join Danny and Sam that way. He did not want to die at the end of a rope with the word 'criminal' his epitaph. It was the single thing that managed to evoke some bitterness; that they had condemned him a criminal when his offence had been to inherit land that his cousin coveted. Strange to think of Abel now. He had not thought of him in all these years. For a few seconds, he wondered about Long Moss House and the tenant farms. His mother's face smiled and he heard the tinkling laugh of Sophie his nurse.

Then he saw Eve again. She was on the deck of the *Port Dennison* with the wind in her curls, her hands reaching out to him across a rolling, blue sea . . .

He came out of his reverie to see that they had crossed Hyde Park and were in the precincts of the Training School. They were riding over a grass-covered yard. In front of them was a stone archway, and beyond he saw police drilling in a quadrangle.

'Enough,' he said aloud.

And David Elrington, hearing him speak, turned expectantly in the saddle towards him. The young man's face dropped as Alan's horse leaped sideways. The animal, tired of the walking pace, responded to his rider's insistence. It sprang to the side as Alan brought its head around and urged it away. The horse gathered speed, thudding through the grass.

He was fifty yards from them in the seven seconds it took the four police troopers to rally from the shock, lift their rifles, aim and fire.

Three bullets smashed into his back, the fourth went wide. The explosions drowned out the scream from Sir Rutherford who had witnessed the event as he came forward across the court.

Alan fell heavily to the ground.

'No! No! Stop!' screamed the police detective, all decorum leaving him as he ran, arms waving, through the archway towards the fallen man. 'He's innocent! Oh God, what have you done? He's innocent!'

Mark McClelland ran after him, his face full of despair.

David Elrington and the troopers were stunned. They could not believe what they saw and heard. They dismounted and stood in confusion, watching wide-eyed as Sir Rutherford ran to the bushranger and turning him over lifted him gently in his arms.

'Oh God! Forgive me! I am so sorry . . . so sorry,' Sir Rutherford said softly now to the upturned face. 'Alan Fletcher, Alan Fletcher, can you hear me? I know you are innocent.'

Alan's eyes opened and focused on the face above him.

'Oh God, man, I'm sorry. I know you are innocent. Forgive us. Please, I'm sorry . . . Oh God!'

Alan's eyes registered Sir Rutherford's. His lips parted and he said something that the police detective could not understand.

'What? Oh God, what is that you say? Please . . .'

But he did not speak again.

To Sir Rutherford it was as if time stopped. He knelt in anguish, his features ashen, gazing only at Alan's face.

Then the life-light went out of the wonderful eyes; they glazed over in death, and he quivered and lay still.

A tortured sigh broke noisily from Sir Rutherford.

Men were running from the Training School, shouting and calling out. There was din and disorder all around. But Rutherford Blake did not hear it. He was conscious of nothing but the man dead in his arms. Tenderly, he lifted the handsome face very close to his own. His lips actually touching the rigid cheek as he murmured, 'Please . . . forgive us.'

He was oblivious of the astonished stares of his assistant and his troopers; he was oblivious of the blood that seeped into his velvet jacket and stained his expensive breeches. For a very long time he continued to kneel on the wet ground, holding Alan Fletcher tightly to him.

Eve had not eaten breakfast. She could not. She was too taken over by being on the *Port Dennison* with Alan left behind in Sydney.

Some time between eight and nine o'clock she donned her warm cape and went above to make her way aft and stand alone looking back into the white, frothy wake of the clipper.

She prayed for Alan, though no longer was she sure of any efficacy in prayer. She stood with the wind blowing her curls, staring at the sea and the purple-grey line of the horizon. The ship streaked through the water carrying her ever further from the man she loved more than herself. She pictured him in the cabin doorway as she had last seen him, looking down at her the way she was to picture him for evermore.

Suddenly she froze. It was as if deep inside her something left her soul. She felt it stir and break away.

She clutched the bulwark. 'Oh no . . . no . . . no . . .'

And then she knew, as sure as if she had seen it happen. Alan was dead.

When she came along the corridor to the hospital door she stood still. She remembered his words. 'My dear ones, soon the *Port Dennison* will be sailing, and that means freedom and new lives.'

Alan, oh Alan, what is a new life without you? I am lost.

She opened the door and entered. Lawless had spent the night in hospital and now, with his shoulder firmly strapped, was dressed to leave.

She came to him and took his hand. 'We are alone, Lawless,' she said. 'There are only two of us now, just you and me.'

CHAPTER THIRTY-SIX

'Believing where we cannot prove,'
'In Memoriam A.H.H.', Prologue,
Alfred, Lord Tennyson, 1809–1892.

It was two o'clock in the afternoon of the day that Alan Fletcher left the earth, when John Stuart and Joe made their way across Hyde Park towards the Royal Hotel. The sun had come through the clouds and had turned Sydney town's weather into a crisp winter's day.

They had been with Sir Rutherford at Redfern barracks, a changed, subdued Sir Rutherford, who had told them the disturbing, unbelievable story of Alan Fletcher's innocence and his death. He had recounted how Abel Crenshaw had coveted the Fletcher lands and had arranged for Alan to be falsely charged with murder. He told them of the trial and the sentencing. Afterwards, he had looked at them with a haunted, distraught expression. 'It's been hard to tell you, John Stuart, for you of all people have been affected by your wife's association with him, but I must be the one to set things right. I shall return to England and will not rest until he is pardoned. It is my duty.'

They had not spoken since leaving Sir Rutherford, and as they came by a small stone wall where an old man and a child, wrapped well against the cold, sat feeding pigeons, John Stuart halted. Joe, at his side, stopped and turned to him.

'Old man, I feel at a loss to know what is what. I have to accept that my wife left me and somehow came to mean a lot to the bushranger; that he in turn meant a lot to her; that they planned to go to America together.' He stiffened slightly and his moody eyes rested on the child feeding the birds. 'That is the part which . . . hurts me more than I can express.'

'I know, m'boy.'

'And now, we know that he was innocent, forced into his way of life to survive. It is a great deal for any man to take in, and acknowledge.'

'It is . . . that.'

'And while my life is in tatters, I am here, and thus, I must go

603

home and take care of my responsibilities.'

'A wise decision, m'boy.'

John Stuart moved off and Joe fell in step with him again. As they left the park to cross into MacQuarie Street, John Stuart spoke once more. He did not look at Joe, his face was averted, but Joe heard him right enough.

'I don't understand any of it, and the way I feel this minute, I don't know if I ever want to. I am hurting very badly. I am angry and frustrated. All these months I have wanted to believe that everything would be all right again, and now, to think she has gone, really gone . . . there's a desolate, sickeningly empty place inside me, Joe.'

They spent a night in Bathurst on their way back to Mayfield. They arrived just before three o'clock in the afternoon and after washing off the dust of travel had taken a stroll to get some exercise after the inactivity of the coach journey.

As school was still in, there were no children waiting to see the master of Mayfield, and they walked peacefully down William Street in the cold afternoon. When they came to the corner of Rocket Street, John Stuart pointed to Mrs Ayres' Tea Room. 'Would you like a cup of tea or coffee, old man?'

'Yes, m'boy, I might at that.'

They did not remain in the little establishment long, only for enough time to have coffee and one of Mrs Ayres' famous jam rolls, and to be the centre of attention. They had departed about ten minutes when Lottie came back to the shop after running an errand for Mrs Ayres. The proprietress's pretty, elfin-like face was all agog. 'Guess who just took tea here, Lottie love.'

'Who?'

'Mr John Stuart Wakeman, that's who!'

Lottie's expression was thoughtful. 'Really now?'

'Terrible shame, isn't it?' her employer said, wrinkling up her fine nose.

'What is?' asked Lottie.

'Why, haven't you read today's *Bathurst Times*?'

Lottie shook her head.

'Well, you should. Tells all about him, poor man, says the truth's only just come out, after many months. Do you know, he's been searching the bush for his wife, and she was seen here in Bathurst only last week! Says he mounted search parties in January, February, May and June. Examined hundreds of miles of this country, back and forth like a beaver, if the truth is written. It was put abroad that

604

he was helping Sir Rutherford track bushrangers, but no. Apparently, the rumour was true that she left him on Boxing Day last. From what's been printed, he's a broken man, and him so handsome and wonderful and kind to his Mayfield folk. I think it's awfully sad.' She sighed dreamily. 'I could *never* leave him.'

Lottie did not answer, but later on her way home she bought herself a *Bathurst Times*.

Not by accident, John Stuart's and Joe's walk had taken them in the opposite direction to Bathurst park. Neither needed to acknowledge it, but there were too many memories attached to the place. So it was that after the Tea Shop, they had gone by a circuitous route to return to the Royal Hotel.

The early winter night was beginning to descend, and as they passed an 'Old Wares Shoppe' on the corner of Keppel Street opposite the gaol, they noticed a man bend inside the window and place a lantern in the display.

Joe nodded through the glass to the man. 'That's young George Bonner, the famous local cricketer. He pitched the ball one hundred and nineteen yards from a standing position here last twenty-fourth of May.'

'Looks strong enough,' commented John Stuart moving away. Then he suddenly halted. His eye had been taken by a small inlaid wooden casket with the initials 'L.B.' on the side, resting on the shelf lit by the lantern.

He stood in thought for a few seconds and then entered the door. Joe followed, and George Bonner, well aware of the identity of his customer, grinned in welcome. 'Good afternoon, Mr Wakeman, sir.'

John Stuart nodded, and pointed to the item. 'Can I look at the case?'

'Most definitely, sir, of course.' George Bonner leaned into the window and brought it out. As he did, he lifted the lid, adding, 'The top here opens, but this side drawer won't pull out, the latch be broken on the inside and I'm afraid there be no key. But then ye could have it mended, assuredly ye could.'

'Yes, it be a lovely thing to my way of thinking,' spoke up Mr Bonner's helper, a tall, bright-eyed girl who was polishing some candlesticks.

John Stuart held it in his hand and looked at it. It was some twelve inches long and perhaps ten wide. There were many such about, people kept letters and papers in them, or sometimes jewels. He had a number of them at Mayfield. Those he owned were certainly more beautiful, though this was more prepossessing than the usual, having the wooden lid inlaid with a pattern of stars. He turned it at an angle to peruse the initials L.B. carved in the front of the drawer that would not open.

Joe, stood silently watching him.

'Tell me, Mr Bonner, where did this come from?'

'Why, er . . .' he inclined his head to the girl. 'Where did this come from, Maggie?'

And Maggie, a clever child, and part-time student at All Saints' Church School, rising to the occasion, answered, 'Well, a lot of this here stuff were sold to us by the new Reverend Cornish, old stuff like, from the rectory. That there box his worship holds came direct from him.'

'I knew it, I knew it,' John Stuart said, half to himself. It was the initials that had attracted him in the first place. He felt sure the box had belonged to 'Father', as Eve had called Leslie Billings. He would buy it. He did not know why, he simply would.

Joe, who now understood that his boy wanted it, asked, 'How much is it?'

'Ninepence, sir, it be written on the bottom.'

Joe paid for it, and Maggie, winsome smile extending over her pretty mouth, saw them to the door.

Back in their rooms at the hotel, John Stuart looked at the box carefully. 'Joe, do you have your penknife on you?'

Joe laughed. 'Yes, m'boy, I do. I carry it even in a dress suit, which my wife thinks odd.'

'Good, I'd like to open this drawer.'

It was not as easy as John Stuart had imagined and after some minutes of trying, they looked at each other in defeat.

'Don't think we can do it tonight, m'boy. Best leave it and give it to a locksmith in the morning.'

'I'm not sure why I wanted to open it actually. Just a feeling. Thought there might be something in it, but in all probability it's empty.'

One last time he inserted the penknife in the lock and twisted it from side to side. He felt something give way and when he pulled it again, the drawer moved.

'Well done,' Joe said. 'Perseverance, eh?'

John Stuart nodded, pulling the drawer out further.

Lying inside were a number of folded papers and envelopes. He took an envelope. 'Ah, so it did belong to the Reverend Billings as we thought, this is addressed to him.' Then he leafed quickly through the papers. 'They mostly look like personal letters and the odd list

of church requirements, so best we just burn them in the gra—
What's this?' His eye had caught the handwriting on the top of a
sheet of paper and he could not help but notice the date and the
address. It said:

> 1st February, 1863,
> General Post Office,
> Postal Letter Box, Number 72,
> King William Street,
> Adelaide.

'But it's Eve's handwriting!' he exclaimed, mystified. 'I'd know it
anywhere.' He looked at Joe, then back down to the letter and he
could not stop himself reading it.

Dear Reverend Billings,
    Thank you for the numerous letters you have so considerately
written to me over the years.
    It seems that you and my darling sister believe that I am
unhappy with my life and would regain peace and respectability
living in Bathurst under your influence. You are both so solici-
tous and I must admit your offers at times are tempting, but you
see I am not dissatisfied with my lot and am indeed quite happy.
    Oh, I know you must regard it as shameful and unnatural to live
as I have done, but I have a new friend here now who is very
good to me, you see, and I could not leave him for anything. The
trappings of respectability – home and family and husband – have
not appealed to me for years. I do hope that does not shock you.
    I thank you once again for your charitable attention, it does
most certainly make me feel special.
    I do not need to see Eve, for whilst we are hundreds of miles
apart, twin sisters are born to a unique condition and thus I can
feel close to her without seeing her. Indeed, it is better this way,
I know.
    Unfortunately I am not an able correspondent as you doubtless
are aware by now so do please forgive my lack of discipline. I
know you are at pains to take care of my dear sister and for that
I am eternally grateful. Do be so kind as to accept that I am
competent to do the same for myself.

> I remain,
> Yours sincerely,
> Clare Herman

John Stuart was unable to speak. He did not lift his eyes from the paper, he simply stood there.

'What is it, m'boy? What the devil is wrong?'

The truth had instantaneously hit him. He was overwhelmed by the significance of the words on the paper he held. He sat down, and with a listless movement handed the letter to Joe. Then he bent forward, head down in his hands while Joe read it.

After what seemed a long time, the older man spoke. 'A twin sister . . . It was this Clare who was in Adelaide, this Clare who lived with Lake. Why didn't she tell us?'

'Why, indeed?' came John Stuart's strained voice.

Joe sighed and he too sat. As he did, his hand went out mechanically and ruffled the younger man's hair. The face beneath looked up, full of suffering, and there they remained staring at each other.

Thunder rolled in the distance and shortly afterwards the sounds of rain began on the window pane.

'I see all the mistakes I made. In truth I have seen them since the moment of her departure. I had decided all grown women were like my mother, all but Eve. I was once told not to "weave a dream" about her, but I did. I continued to tell her she was good and pure and different to other women. I, who am scornful of the Church, did my own canonising. Of course she feared to tell me of her twin, for this Clare was living the sort of life I so repeatedly told her I despised. I made it impossible for her.'

Joe's face was full of sorrow. He wanted more than anything for his boy to be happy. He shook his head. 'Don't be too harsh upon yourself. Eve was the only one in possession of the knowledge. How could you possibly understand if she did not tell you?'

'Ah, Joe, you minimise my misdeeds. I was proud . . . ah, the arrogance and self-conceit attached to pride. I was interpreter, censor, and critic.'

'Perhaps you judged her wrongly at the time, that is true, but you have tried consistently to find her to make her aware you felt differently. Her successive actions should not be passed over.'

John Stuart closed his eyes and made a gesture of confusion in the air with his hands. 'Joe, she left Mayfield thinking I . . . loathed her. She believed I thought her mean and vile.'

They were very late going to bed that night for he insisted on reciting the unhappy events of Christmas time.

When finally Joe bade him goodnight, he took John Stuart's hands in his. 'Listen to me, m'boy. I don't want you to blame yourself. The circumstances which prevailed at that time were more extensive than one man alone had the power to alter.'

In reply, John Stuart gave a weak, grateful smile. He met the older man's eyes. 'What would I do without you, Joe?'

Robert Robinson-Pike's main office was in Sydney. Four times a year he journeyed into the west to see his most important client, and he kept a small office in Bathurst, for one reason only: it was the nearest town on the telegraph line to Mayfield. And it was his most important client who came the following morning at opening time to the Bathurst branch of R. Robinson-Pike to see the man in charge, the solicitor James McIntosh.

John Stuart had lain awake thinking a long, long time before falling asleep the night before, and he had come to a decision.

Mr McIntosh was a sincere, intelligent young man, and listened gravely to all that Mr Wakeman and Mr Larmer said. Now, he made his reply.

'Well, sirs, there is such a thing in the United States of America, known as the Pinkerton National Detective Agency, run, I think, by an ex-sheriff, as they call law officers over there. They find people for a fee. Mind you, what with the recent civil war they may not be operating now. But Mr Robinson-Pike and Mr Noah, my superiors, know more about this sort of thing than I do. Would you like me to telegraph them?'

John Stuart looked to Joe. The older man shook his head. 'I don't think this can be explained in a telegraphed message, m'boy.'

John Stuart nodded and faced back to the solicitor. 'Mr Larmer is right, and this is most urgent. How would you like to leave on the noon mail coach, today? You'll be in Sydney on Saturday, which will allow Mr Robinson-Pike to have a letter written to these Pinkerton people by Monday, and it can be on the first ship leaving Sydney for America next week.'

Before Mr McIntosh could respond Joe said enthusiastically, 'Yes, m'boy, that's the answer.'

CHAPTER THIRTY-SEVEN

'But jealous souls will not be answered so;
They are not ever jealous for the cause,
But jealous for they are jealous, 'tis a monster
Begot upon itself, born on itself.'
Othello, William Shakespeare, 1564–1616.

Eve looked round at the sound of Lawless's voice.

'She's comin'! Oh, Eve, Lottie's comin'!'

He came across the few yards of grass from the back door of their small wooden house waving pages of a letter high in the air in the warm August sunlight.

Eve put down the purple honeysuckle she had been gathering from the creeper near the yew tree. 'How wonderful, Arnold. Let me see.'

It was the second letter they had received from Lottie in the thirteen months since they had left Australian shores. They had written to her immediately they had arrived here in Boston in October.

Often, it had been almost impossible for them to carry on without the strength of Alan. And there were times when both of them had thought life hardly worth living. But then they would bring out the note written on the back of the receipt from the Prince of Wales Hotel and the very sight of his handwriting would reinforce their wills.

They had been lucky, for there had been enough money left from Eve's legacy to rent this house; and a piano had been one of the items of furniture. Eve had begun to teach music as soon as she had found pupils, and Lawless had tried a few jobs before finally settling into a position that suited him perfectly; guard on the Boston Railroad Company line between Boston and Providence.

They had been very abstemious for the first few months, doing without a lot of things and scraping money together, until they knew they would soon have enough money for Lottie's passage. Lawless had made arrangements to pay her fare through the Golden Eagle Line, the very one they had come over to America upon.

As Eve took the letter from Lawless, she thought back to the first

610

letter they had received from Lottie. She reread that letter every week. Lottie had written it on the 20 February, 1866 after receiving their first letter from Boston the day before. It had told them of Alan's death in Sydney, and how Sir Rutherford Blake had nursed Alan in his arms as he died. It explained that Sir Rutherford had declared him innocent and had resigned from the police force and returned to England to fight for a posthumous pardon for Alan. Eve had cried a long time when she read that.

Then came some paragraphs about John Stuart. Eve always read these with complex emotions, the story in Lottie's unskilled hand of John Stuart's search across hundreds of miles of country for her while she lived at Treehard Hill. Lottie had enclosed a newspaper cutting with a banner announcing 'The Strange Story of the Missing Wife of Australia's Richest Man'. Her stomach had given an odd little lurch when she first read what was said to be a quote from John Stuart; 'Yes, I searched for my wife for many months, that is so. There had been an unfortunate difference between us, which was entirely my fault, and I sought to resolve it.' Fancy John Stuart saying that for all the world to read! She had felt deep sorrow at that. Sorrow that he had to expose himself that way.

She sighed as she brought her eyes down to Lottie's second letter.

Lottie wrote that she had received notification that her passage had been paid from America and she would be on a ship leaving Sydney in August.

Eve turned to Lawless. 'Oh, Arnold, that means she should be on her way now. She could be here in early December if we're lucky!'

Lawless's answer was a contented smile.

For some seconds, they stood unspeaking in the sunshine. Eve was so happy for Arnold, as she called him these days. Her 'brother', Arnold, to the folk of Boston. He and Lottie would make a fine pair. Two wonderful people united. Then she thought of Alan as she did every day. Her brief, brief, perfect life with him. A sad, thoughtful smile spread across her mouth.

'Well, Eve,' Lawless said breaking into her meditations, 'with this wonderful news, I'm off to work.'

'Yes, dear.'

'Ye know, with that new horse-car they've put on in Mount Vernon Street, I get to work ten minutes earlier. I reckon it's the horses, they're beauties. Do ye know, they say there's a man experimentin' on a car for the streets, that uses electric power. It's amazin', they won't need horses any more.'

He left in long strides across the lawn and Eve found herself thinking of the man who was experimenting on an electric streetcar.

How such a thing would intrigue John Stuart. Yes, she could visualise him now, reading all about it in one of his journals in the summer-house on a Sunday afternoon.

Her heart gave a strange little tremor as she pictured him and she sighed in remembrance and turned to gather some more honeysuckle, standing on tiptoe to reach the long trailing tendrils at the top of the vine. As she did there was an awakening cry from the bassinet that lay beside her on the grass. She bent to it. 'Oh, my little darling, you are awake.' And she lifted the baby up into her arms, kissing him. 'Uncle Arnold has just gone to work, and what do you know? Auntie Lottie is coming from Australia to live with us.'

John Stuart walked out of the new dairy and over to Diomed.

As he did the words of a song one of the dairymen was singing, floated over to him. His brows drew together in a frown.

> Alan Fletcher, Alan Fletcher,
> Lifer for a deed he hadn't done,
> Alan Fletcher, Alan Fletcher,
> Bushranger brave who never used his gun.
>
> Robbing from the Government,
> Never taking from the poor;
> Living in his hideout
> Far from the traps galore.
>
> Outlaw bold, outlaw bold,
> Died in the arms of his captor
> Outlaw bold, outlaw bold,
> History will never close his chapter.
>
> Alan Fletcher, Alan Fletcher
> Kept his face from being seen,
> Alan Fletcher, Alan Fletcher
> Pardoned by the Queen.

The Crown proclamation of Alan Fletcher's posthumous pardon had appeared in the colonial newspapers only a few weeks ago. A lot had happened in thirteen months. They had made a hero of the man here in the bush now. Songs had been made up within days of the news of the pardon and he had overheard Tommy Barnes boast more than once how he had met the man.

Rutherford had been instrumental in having the pardon granted, just as he had said he would. He had resigned his appointment with the Colonial Police Force and gone back to England and reopened the case. It was due to him that Alan Fletcher's name, rather than being infamous now, was famous throughout the land. The report in the *Sydney Morning Herald* had said the false charge of murder against Alan Fletcher had been brought about by his cousin, Abel Crenshaw, who had coveted his lands. Rutherford had got a confession from the one remaining living 'witness' from the Fletcher trial. The article stated Crenshaw had died of smallpox six years after the trial, in 1855, and the Fletcher estate had passed to Alan Fletcher's mother's cousin, a single lady from Falmouth.

It was difficult for John Stuart to think of Alan Fletcher impartially. Of course the man had been most fearfully ill-treated, and it was only proper and fitting that his name was cleared. And he realised he had been a most extraordinary and courageous man, but there were too many painful emotions connected with Alan Fletcher.

For a moment, he pictured Eve as he had first seen her coming through the park in Bathurst, wearing a light floral gown that showed the skin of her throat faintly golden in the setting sun. He made a sharp, sad sound, and mounted Diomed.

He had heard only yesterday from James McIntosh in Robert Robinson-Pike's Bathurst office that Lottie Thatcher had left the town to go abroad to America. It was the talk of the settlement, for people there did not do such adventurous things. He and Joe had discussed the news and come to the conclusion, with all the information they had about the intimacy between Eve and Mistress Thatcher, that she had gone to join Eve. He brought Diomed to a halt for a minute as he thought about it now. James McIntosh, bright young man that he was, had even gone to visit Lottie Thatcher to question her about her destination, but all she would divulge was 'America'.

He shook his head as he urged Diomed forward up the hill towards Mayfield House. He was going back home for luncheon with Daydee and would work the afternoon there, for today was her birthday, her twenty-first, and there was to be a grand celebration tonight. Last Sunday she had found him in the summerhouse and asked if it were good weather on her winter birthday, could she eat luncheon there. He had agreed. Then, she had stood up, given a mock bow and continued in a comical fashion, 'And I should like to have my birthday luncheon alone with the master of Mayfield, please, for the rest of the day I shall be surrounded.'

'If I am not busy,' he had answered.

Fortunately, this morning she had been at Mayfield House when he had come out after breakfast and she had reminded him, for he had forgotten all about it.

Joe's daughter was to gain her majority in grand style. A huge marquee had been erected on the lawns in the park, and all the Mayfield House staff were invited for refreshments and music and dancing at four o'clock. Then at eight o'clock there was to be a private party and a number of Daydee's friends from school days had been invited.

In April, Daydee and Thelma had travelled to Sydney and Daydee had been presented at the grand ball at Government House for the young debutantes of the colony. She had been the centre of attention for some of Sydney's eligible bachelors, and had written letters to John Stuart telling him all about it.

One matter that John Stuart and Joe were delighted about was Daydee's change of heart towards Roy Ford. In the last year, she had been openly friendly to him and Roy had travelled to Sydney to be Daydee's partner at her coming-out ball. In fact they had planned a surprise for her, and Roy was arriving unbeknown to Daydee for the party tonight.

John Stuart would not have ridden up from the dairy towards Mayfield House so unconcernedly had he known the real reason for Daydee's apparently altered attitude to Roy. Over the previous months, Daydee had been nice to Roy, even amicable and encouraging, for one reason only, to make John Stuart jealous; and when she had written from Sydney to him with the news of the boys who doted on her, she had prayed he would not like it.

And today was her birthday. She would be twenty-one at last! Now, finally John Stuart would take her seriously. She smiled into her mirror as Rosy brushed her hair and tied a large pink bow into it. She was having luncheon with him, just the two of them. And then tonight she would dance with him. Since *she* had gone away, life had been wonderful. But she had made a mistake in flirting with Roy; that had not worked very well, and she would never do it again. She was a woman at last. She would make John Stuart love her!

She knew all about love now. She had taken the final step in Sydney with Sir Jeffrey Hughes' son, Forrest. He was handsome and played cricket. John Stuart played cricket. Yet in going all the way with Forrest Hughes, it had not been as marvellous as she had thought it would be. She gave a giggle thinking of him, he had said he loved her and she had said it too, but she had been pretending he was John Stuart.

Lunch was a delight for Daydee. She and John Stuart alone, waited on by Baines and the servants. The hour passed far too quickly.

They left the summerhouse together and were wandering back across the lawn when in the distance through a gap in the shrubs and trees they saw an open carriage coming up the drive. Daydee recognised it as the Fords' vehicle. She started. Her mouth turned down unpleasantly as a sound of anger escaped her lips. 'But . . . *they* have not been invited. John Stuart, that is the Fords' carriage. What are they doing here?'

John Stuart acknowledged the unhappy tone and, surprised, turned to her as the vehicle continued on. 'But my dear, your father and I thought you would be pleased to have Roy here. Lately you have been so happy in his company.'

They were standing in a secluded part of the garden, beside a long, white, granite colonnade overgrown with climbing rose and jasmine vines. Even in winter, without blooms, the setting was distinctly beautiful.

Her skirt brushed the uneven granite stones as she walked a step or two away from him in what seemed to him a petulant movement. He shook his head and was about to speak severely when she turned back to face him. Her dark eyes were wide and there wrinkles of distress on her brow. Her mouth quivered nervously as her eyes filled with tears. And then, it came rushing from her at last.

'Oh John Stuart, you don't understand, do you? You never have. I only flirted with Roy to . . . to make you see me, notice me. It's you I want. I love you. I have always loved you. All my life.'

She stepped quickly towards him and as the tears brimmed from her eyes, she threw herself into his arms. 'Oh please, please love me as I love you. It's you I want, it's you.'

There was a time when John Stuart would have been appalled by this outburst. But he was more moderate in his views, more flexible in his reactions and he simply moved her tenderly from him. He looked down into the upturned, tearstained face. 'Daydee, dear Daydee. I had no idea of this. You are a child to me, don't you see? I remember your being born. I am almost old enough to be your father.'

She stood clinging with her small hands to his arms, a desperate look in her eyes. 'I have loved you all my life, what is age to me?' The tears streamed down her face. She was sobbing helplessly.

He drew her over to a stone seat in the vine-covered colonnade. He sat her down and knelt in front of her, taking her hands in his.

'Now listen to me carefully, Daydee, and attend what I say.'

She nodded through her tears.

'I cannot change how I feel about you. It is impossible. You are little Daydee to me; like a baby sister.' Then he took a deep breath and spoke his innermost thought. 'I love Eve.'

Daydee's pretty face twisted with hate. 'But you cannot love her, she is gone, never to come back! You told me yourself she was never coming back.'

'Daydee, listen. I know I said that. And undoubtedly that is so. But, my dear, I did not explain things properly, for I do love her and I always will. I simply do not talk about it.'

Daydee's look was peevish and she dropped her eyes as she said between sobs, 'But she has gone *forever*. Why cannot you love me now?'

He was quiet for a few seconds before he stood up and lifted her to her feet. He tenderly stroked her cheek, then handed her his handkerchief, saying, 'Come now, Daydee, wipe your eyes and take my arm. You must face your guests. It is your birthday. In two hours you must be in the marquee looking beautiful, and tonight you will be the belle of the ball.'

She sniffed. 'You treat me like a child.'

'No, I do not,' he answered, tucking her hand in his arm, 'for I have told you today what is in my heart.'

They walked slowly under the pergola to the open lawn and across it, through the hedges and trees, to the gravelled carriageway. They could see servants coming and going from the house to the marquee, all activity in every direction. They halted.

His look was grave and he bent towards her as he said, 'Now give me a smile and promise me that you will enjoy yourself tonight.'

She returned his look and, making an attempt at a smile, nodded.

'Good,' he replied patting her hand affectionately and raising it to his lips. Then he stepped off the lawn onto the drive and strode across to the steps. 'And we shall have the first dance together tonight,' he called back to her.

She watched him mount the steps, cross the verandah and enter the house. 'The devil take you, Eve,' she said aloud. 'You are gone and yet you haunt me. I hate you! I detest you! I loathe you!' She hurried away towards her own home.

'Happy birthday, Miss Daydee!' shouted Timothy who had been commandeered to help Mr Baines and was crossing the lawn laden with an armful of napkins. She waved peremptorily and passed on. She was running by the time she reached the gate in the hedge and hot tears were spilling from her eyes again. It wasn't fair. How could he still love *her*? Well, she wouldn't dance with that Roy Ford. Nothing in the world would induce her to. He could go to hell!

As she came in the door, her mother was coming out.

'Daydee, there you are. Did you have a nice luncheon?' Her

daughter looked at her with scorn and brushed hurriedly past.

'I'm going out for a ride and don't you dare suggest I take Leith, for I shan't.'

Just over fifteen minutes later, Daydee was in the saddle and riding hard towards Larmer's Crossing. 'He mustn't love her . . . He mustn't love her . . . He mustn't love her . . .' she repeated over and over as she took Boots from a trot to a canter along the far bank of the Lachlan to the west. She rode a mile spiritedly, aggressively.

The river path climbed here to high ground. Over the centuries, the water had eroded the earth and at times her way took her thirty and forty feet above the Lachlan. As she came near the group of men driving a herd of cattle from a river paddock to higher ground, two of them held up their hands to her and Tommy Barnes shouted for her to stop. But, Daydee ignored their signals. How dare they call and shout to her! Horrid stockmen, they probably knew it was her birthday. Taking liberties; typical of them.

She was furious with her father for inviting Roy Ford, furious with her mother. She hated Eve, and now John Stuart was treating her like a child. It was unbearable. She hated everyone, hated them all.

She urged Boots to even more speed, and was oblivious to the warnings shouted from the men who now waved excitedly at her. 'Don't stay on the river path, Miss Daydee, the ground is undermined along the high bend! There have been cave-ins! Stop, Miss Daydee! Stop!'

But on she sped, her mind full of fury, pushing Boots to even more speed, his hooves flinging up dirt as his mistress careered him along the high path above the river.

Tommy Barnes spurred his horse and rode after her, calling all the while for her to stop. His shouts died as he saw her disappear. He pulled sharply back on his reins and his horse reared as her scream echoed, high-pitched in terror. She and Boots fell, the ground beneath her giving way and crashing with her down into the river.

They lifted her as gently as they could and took her back the two miles to Larmer's Crossing, where they met Joe and Thelma coming the other way. They had been alerted of the accident by Barnes who had galloped up to tell them. The men transferred her to the cart they used to carry injured men. In this they took her little, broken body home. Dr Douglas could do nothing.

She remained unconscious until three hours later, when she opened her eyes briefly. She saw above her the strained faces of her father and mother and John Stuart; beyond them stood a clergyman. He was the new minister from Cowra and had been visiting the married workers' cottages. He was an earnest young man, Cowra was his first ministry, and he had not seen many deaths before. He thought it tragic that one so young was dying, but then it was not for him to understand the ways of the heavenly Father. He came forward as Daydee's eyes opened.

She did not look at him, her gaze was for John Stuart.

Joe spoke, 'Daydee, Daydee, love, we are all here and the Reverend Hardman is here to say a prayer for you.'

Daydee drew her eyes from John Stuart to her father. 'Am I dying, Dada?'

'Oh, Daydee . . . Daydee love . . .'

She heard the minister say, 'Dear Lord watch over Daydee Bronwyn Larmer, help her to make her peace with you and come in purity, as we all will on the Day of Judgment.'

And now she looked up at the pain-filled faces and thought of all that had happened. She stared at John Stuart and recalled her secret; the secret she had told no one. How she had found the photographic likeness of Eve and her sister Clare, and how she had burned it, so that John Stuart would never know.

Little did she realise he knew the truth now, anyway.

She lifted her tiny pale hand towards him and he took it and kissed it tenderly.

'You . . . d . . . do love me . . . don't you . . . John Stuart?'

And with tears brimming in his eyes he answered, 'Oh yes, Daydee, yes, my little one, of course I do.'

A smile, almost beatific, settled on her face. 'Good,' she answered as she closed her eyes.

An hour later she died.

One week later, John Stuart came to Thelma and Joe.

It was a bitterly cold night and they sat before the fire. Thelma was knitting a shawl and Joe was attempting to peruse plans for a modern community hall, but his mind kept wandering to his daughter's funeral.

'John Stuart,' Thelma said, as Rosy brought him in. 'What a lovely surprise.'

He sat down on the sofa opposite them. 'I have something to discuss with you, both of you.' He coughed. 'I do not want to upset you by mentioning Daydee, but her death is somehow the final, bewildering event in a series of bewildering events in our lives . . . in my life.' He looked from one to the other. 'This is hard for me to say, but I have been thinking. All my life I have been offended by what I saw as immorality. I hated my . . . mother, because of her adultery. I judged her as my father appeared to judge her. I also judged my wife, and in doing so, lost her.'

He brought his hands together, clasping them. 'I see things differently these days. Life is constant metamorphosis. Perhaps, time runs out, and then we find ourselves sorry for the past, but it's too late.'

Joe met his gaze. 'So, m'boy, what are you thinking?'

'It is thirty-five years since my mother went home to Scotland, is it not?'

The older man nodded. 'I'd say that was right, m'boy.'

'How old was she when she went away?'

Joe looked to Thelma. She thought for a second or two. 'She was a year or two younger than you, Joe. I'd say she was about twenty-eight, yes, or twenty-nine.'

'So she would be in her sixties now?'

'She would.'

John Stuart looked directly at Joe. 'I am saying all this because . . . I want to go and see my mother.'

Joe nodded. That is what he had thought, and he was taking it dispassionately enough, for that was his nature. It was Thelma's heart which pounded.

'She came from Fort William, didn't she?'

Joe nodded. 'Hard by, near Ben Nevis, wasn't it, love?' He turned to Thelma.

'Y . . . Yes, dearest, that's right. The old laird had property there.'

John Stuart leaned towards Thelma. 'Is that where she wrote from? The letters she wrote to me?'

'Why, yes, dear. From "Dunain Lodge", via Fort William, in the Highlands.'

'I see, and all we know is that she was alive and living there until I was fifteen.' He sighed and rested his chin in his hands.

Thelma made a small, uncomfortable sound in her throat and moved a touch closer to Joe. 'No, John Stuart, I know a little more than that.'

Both men looked at her.

Joe touched her hand. 'What is it, Thel? What do you know?'

She swallowed and her eyes came up directly to John Stuart's. 'Well, I wrote to her after Sir Arthur, your father, died. And she replied.'

Joe shook his head in disbelief. 'You wrote to her? Heavens, woman, when will you cease to amaze me?'

Thelma looked abashed, but in defence explained, 'I thought she should know, you see. It didn't seem right that Arthur was dead and she none the wiser. He wore her wedding bracelet on the night he passed on. I believe he wanted her to know.'

'It's all right, Thelma, dear,' John Stuart said. 'I'm glad you wrote. And she answered, you say?'

'Yes, and her letter was lovely, although I burned it.' Here she looked at Joe. 'Out of fear you would find it and carry on.'

Joe continued to shake his head.

'She said she held naught against Arthur, that he did what he had to do and that was the way of things. But the rest of the letter, while of course I can't recall the detail, was all about you, John Stuart, being the new master of Mayfield. How proud she was of you and all.'

John Stuart, to Thelma's delight, was smiling. 'What you did was right. I am so very pleased.'

'You are?' the good woman asked, emotion making the words catch in her throat.

'Indeed, I am, I only wish you had continued to correspond. At least I would know if I still had a mother.'

Thelma was now turning very pink and she was tapping her knitting needles together nervously. 'Oh? You do? Well then, I can answer that for you right enough.'

'What?' exclaimed John Stuart. 'You can?'

Joe was following the exchange with an expression of astonishment.

His wife continued, 'You see, dear, she was desperate to know about you and she *begged* me to write back, so . . .' She turned again to her husband giving a small embarrassed cough. 'You may have noticed, I've been getting a Scottish periodical each six months all these years.'

'Yes,' her husband replied, 'it's household articles and stories. Isn't that one over there?' He pointed to a small stacked pile of reading matter.

'It is, my love.' She faced back to John Stuart. 'Well now, it is inside one of those she has been sending me letters ever since your father died. And then I reply to her . . . and post it on a Bathurst visit, or when I'm in Cowra. Oh, John Stuart, she loves you so, always has. She calls me her "lifeline" – to you, she means.'

John Stuart was smiling tenderly.

'You don't hold it against me, then, for corresponding?'

'Thelly, Thelly.' He stood and, coming to her, lifted her to her feet and put his arms round her. For the first time since he was thirteen years old he actually hugged her to him.

'No . . . no, I'm not angry. I'm truly glad.'

He knew she was crying. She was pressing him close and holding onto him so tightly. He stood there with her for a long time, looking over her head at Joe, before she moved a step back to look up at

620

him. On her face a jumble of expressions fought for supremacy – love, relief, anxiety.

'Ah, Thelma, don't be sad,' he said gently. 'I am so lucky to have you, and you've had the burden of this for so long. I've been such a damn fool, an arrogant, damn fool. Please forgive me.'

'Oh no, no, no,' she said drying her eyes, 'you have not. It's me who's often wondered whether I've done right or wrong. I was simply so sorry for her, the poor thing. Take no notice of me. It's just such a release after all these years.'

She sat down and Joe spoke at last. 'You're a wonder, Thelma Larmer, that you are.'

She gave a small smile. 'There was no telling you, Joe, for you would have thought me an interfering old biddy.'

'And so you have been,' he answered. 'Though it seems just as well.' He leaned over and kissed her cheek, putting his arm proudly round her.

John Stuart sighed. 'So, my mother is still alive. Is she well?'

'Ah now, that's just it and all. It's a constant racking cough she's had in recent years. Her last letter came about a month ago. She was none too well. It was shorter than usual. Although all about you as always.'

'I would like to leave as soon as I can.'

Joe looked at Thelma, and Thelma smiled. 'Then, Joseph Reginald Larmer, you had best be arranging to leave. No doubt Mr Hennessy and Mr Watson and Mrs Smith and I shall manage without you two. Haven't we always?'

On 31 August, two weeks before they were to leave Mayfield for Sydney and the SS *Donaghadee*, John Stuart rode in from the east gate and dismounted.

Ten minutes later, he was going through the mail despatch that had arrived that morning. When he opened the letter from Robert Robinson-Pike, his hand shook a little. Enclosed was a page from the Pinkerton National Detective Agency. It was written from their head office in Chicago and dated 30 March 1866. It read:

Dear Mr Pike,

I am happy to inform you that the woman you asked us to find was located earlier this month. She lives in a rented house at number thirty-two Russell Street, Beacon Hill, Boston, Massachusetts, in the United States of America. It is a very modest dwelling, but the area is a superior one. She is known as Mrs Fletcher.

There is a man living with her, her brother, Arnold Drake.

She is in the ninth month of a pregnancy.

Thank you for the payment you made available to us through the Bank of North America.

It is always a pleasure to help people in foreign lands and if we can be of further assistance please write to us at this address.

Sincerely,
Allan Pinkerton
founder

John Stuart folded the page and put it in his pocket.

He opened no more letters. He stood and left his study and walked down the corridor. For the first time in many months, he opened the door to the bedroom he used to share with Eve and walked by the bed extending his arm to touch the drapes with his long sun-browned fingers. Over to the casement windows he passed and, opening them, moved slowly across the verandah and down the steps.

It was growing dark and there was a chill wind blowing.

He went to the trunk of the poinciana tree, and stood there, staring up; up through the naked, soulless branches into the perpetual nothingness of the bleak and pitiless sky.

And then he wept.

CHAPTER THIRTY-EIGHT

'How far that little candle throws his beams!
So shines a good deed in a naughty world.'
Merchant of Venice, William Shakespeare, 1564–1616.

Eve moved up the stairs and through the door of St Martin's Church. In her arms she carried her nine-months-old son, wrapped well against the early January winds.

Ahead of her walked Lottie and Arnold.

She followed them to the altar rail, where the Presbyterian minister waited. He had been happy to marry them. And as Arnold had said, 'A church is a church to me . . . ain't it the one, single God who is supposed to be abidin' in them all?'

St Martin's was the nearest church to Russell Street. During her pregnancy, Eve had walked here quite often and prayed alone. One day, the minister, Mr Willson, had approached her. 'I am Episcopalian really,' she had said self-consciously, and he had smiled in reply. 'That does not matter, my dear, you are very welcome here. This is God's house.' It was just the sort of thing that Father would have said and from then on she had begun to come to service here. Occasionally, Arnold had accompanied her and when Lottie had arrived, they had asked Mr Willson to marry them.

Eve moved into the pew near Mrs Willson, the minister's wife. Behind was Eve's next door neighbour, Mrs Mason, pretty, reliable, and obliging, who many times had taken care of Eve's son.

Lottie, in a lovely cream high-necked outfit with lace collar, looked back to Eve and smiled as the minister's strong, resonant voice began the marriage service.

Briefly, the winter sun broke through the clouds, and the stained-glass window behind the altar radiated a glorious light down upon the few gathered in the church. Eve sighed. Her two dear friends were being joined together, how fitting, how proper. She thought of her other friend, Thelma, so far away, and she prayed that she was well and happy.

This was the first wedding she had been to since her own, and her memory insisted on leading her through the moments when she held

John Stuart's hand at the altar in All Saints', Bathurst. How happy she had been. How excited she had been. She found herself wondering about John Stuart. It seemed he had suffered greatly since she left him. By the account in the newspaper Lottie had sent, and the stories Lottie had told since her arrival, it appeared he had followed her into Cowra on Boxing Day and searched the whole countryside back and forth for months, trying to find her. She felt guilty about all that. She really did. She had run away from him thinking he hated her, and apparently that was not so, not so at all.

Her son moved in her arms and she bent her head to kiss him. Alan Fletcher's son, the living proof of their perfect love. She saw his father in her mind's eye as she did every day. Lottie had brought the news of Alan's posthumous pardon and Eve rejoiced to know the world now recognised his innocence. As in everything else, Sir Rutherford Blake had proven tenacious in his desire to see Alan's name cleared. The proclamation had been published in the colonial newspapers just before Lottie had sailed for America. Alan's ultimate victory over meanness, hatred and injustice. Alan, oh Alan, you affected all those who ever came in contact with you.

When she lifted her gaze from her child's face, Mr Willson was saying nice things about Arnold. 'A genial man, polite, charitable, a law-abiding citizen.' Oh gracious, Arnold's shoulders lifted. Were they shaking in mirth? Arnold-Lawless, 'law-abiding'? Well, these days, yes, he was. Don't laugh, Arnold! Please don't laugh!

'I now pronounce you man and wife.'

They celebrated at the restaurant in Babette's Hotel, across the common, while Mrs Mason minded the baby. It was a cheerful occasion and sad memories only joined them once, when Lawless made his short speech after the meal.

'Today has been a mixed day for me. I am pleased and content to be married to Lottie, the woman I love. And it has been a fine thing to be able to share it with ye, Eve. But there are others I wish God had seen fit to show this day to. Swiftie, Sam and Danny, and . . . my "beloved guv'nor", most of all.' His eyes filled with tears, but he took a deep breath, swallowed quickly and finished. 'Alan once said to me, "Ye cannot live with the dead, lad. It is fine and proper to remember them with all the love ye bore them, and perhaps the places they had are never quite filled again, but life continues." ' He lifted his glass in the air and looking upwards with shining eyes said, 'Alan, we're doin' our best, as ye would have wanted.'

That night, Eve sat alone by the fire. Arnold and Lottie were spending their wedding night at Babette's. She attempted to busy herself by knitting a pair of booties but her eyes kept lifting to the window, where, in the firelight she could see snow building, little by little, against the glass on the ledge outside. Then, as the time passed, her knitting fell from her fingers and she sat staring at the fluttering flames of the fire. She thought of the wedding, and Arnold's speech.

She imagined him, faultless visions of him, striding through her mind as he had through her life. She saw him in the fire-glow on their one night of love. How sublime it had been. For a long time she sat staring, reliving the feel of his body, his arms round her, the touch of his fingers, the taste of his mouth.

Soft tears left her eyes and ran down her face as she saw him at Treehard laughing with Danny and riding through the bush on Freedom. She saw him holding Womballa's hand. She saw him jump down from Freedom's back and leap up the steps at Treehard. She saw him slap Bluey on the back. She saw him turn in the saddle to wave as he entered the Treehard tunnel. She saw him come down the gangplank of the *Port Dennison*. She saw him standing in the doorway of the ship's hospital looking down at her. She saw him smiling. She saw his incomparable eyes and then she saw him near the Mayfield coach, dressed in grey, his black boots gleaming, his sun-lightened hair long under his dark hat, his sun-browned hand raised in the air, and standing beside him . . . John Stuart.

That very same night, snow fell heavily in the west of Scotland north of Rannoch Moor when two travellers and their attendant alighted at Fort William railway station, wrapped in many layers to fight the cold. They passed out from the dim, gaslit platform into the blast of the wind from Loch Linne, and looked for a vehicle to take them the lonely miles to their destination.

There was a single dog cart parked at the side of the station and after inquiring at the inn across the street, the driver was found in the barroom.

'We wish to be taken to Dunain Lodge,' Joe said to the driver, a long individual whose legs snaked round a barstool. He sipped his stout and looked Joe up and down, and beyond him to John Stuart standing near the door. 'Weel, it be three miles, blowing snow and sleet. Cost ye a shilling a mile, not a penny less.'

It was too much, but, 'All right,' Joe agreed.

They took rooms and left Timothy with the luggage at the inn. As they crossed to the station, the driver shouted above the wind, 'And what is it that be takin' ye oop to the old laird's then?'

'We are relatives,' Joe replied.

The force of the wind did not allow conversation and it was over an hour later that the stone wall beyond which their objective lay appeared in the swirling mists ahead of them.

'Dunain Lodge,' the driver called back over his shoulder.

John Stuart had no way of letting his mother know he was coming. The miracle of the undersea telegraph cable which transmitted messages from Europe across the world had only been laid as far as Ceylon and the United States of America, and in any case it was only for world events and news, no private messages were sent. They had journeyed all the way from Sydney in the hope of finding Caroline Wakeman here.

When they reached the front of the house, a large building with Gothic shapes looming as beautification, Joe and John Stuart climbed down. Joe turned to the driver. 'We would appreciate if you would wait, we may wish to go back with you.'

'Aye. But I'll need to be cooming in out of this 'ere gale.'

'I'm sure we can arrange that.'

As they mounted the stone steps, the pale light from the windows of the house fell on them. Joe looked at John Stuart; his face was a mixture of anticipation and apprehension. 'Now, m'boy,' he said softly, 'this will be a great night, for both of you.'

John Stuart's pulse quickened. At last he was to see his mother, the woman who had given him life. All the years of rejecting her had rolled away; he was different now. He truly, deeply wanted to know her, talk to her, hold her. 'Yes. I hope so, Joe.'

Joe pulled the bell and it sounded as a distant clang to their ears. He put his arm round John Stuart, and that is how they waited until the door swung open and a lady in her middle years wearing a black dress and white apron looked out into the night. 'I canna see you,' she said. 'Please announce yearselves.'

Joe replied. 'We are here to see Mrs Wakeman, Caroline, the old laird's daughter. We have come from Australia. This gentleman is her son. May we come in?'

The woman's eyes widened and she took a step backwards from the door. She crossed herself and looked skywards. 'Oh, dear Lord Jesus in Heaven above preserve us!'

'What is that you say?' Joe stepped over the threshold, bringing John Stuart with him.

'Oh, no, no, it canna be!' she wailed, crossing herself again as she looked from Joe to John Stuart.

'Please, my good woman, what is wrong?'

'Is this m'lady's son?' She pointed to John Stuart.

It was then he spoke for the first time. 'I am her son, and I'd like to see my mother, please.'

The woman began to cry. 'Ah, sir, you may see her indeed, but she canna see you. Two mornings past she did not wake from sleeping. She lies cold now above year head, sir. It's come Friday morn, we put her in the ground.'

They remained for the funeral.

The day before they buried her, John Stuart, in company with a local guide, climbed Ben Nevis to look out over the land that had been his mother's. He could not climb to the top, for the way was blocked by snow. The sun shone briefly that day, and the temperature rose marginally. For the middle of winter, it was a kindly day; so too was the following morning, when they buried her.

All the family were there, and John Stuart met his surviving aunts and uncles, and his cousins.

How bitterly sad he was that she had died before he could see her. But life was mostly bitter for him these days. As the first sod of earth was thrown down on the ornate, walnut coffin, he murmured half aloud, 'Mother dear, in death I love you, forgive me for not loving you in life.' As he spoke, Joe's arm went round his shoulders and remained there until the cortège moved away.

They left Fort William as soon as the funeral was over, and by the time they boarded the railway carriage, snow had begun to fall again, the wind had risen, and it was extremely cold.

In London they rented a house in Curzon Street, Mayfair. On the day after their arrival, they took the letter of introduction given to them by Robert Robinson-Pike before they left Australia, and sought out Forrest Rowell Pty. Ltd. a well-known legal firm. Forrest Rowell was the brother of Robert Robinson-Pike's wife, she and her parents having emigrated to Australia fifteen years before.

Mr Rowell himself greeted them. He was a large man with a wide forehead and intelligent blue eyes. He was aware of the Wakeman name and what it meant, and in convivial manner offered them tea. After the formalities, Joe revealed the reason for their visit. 'There is a property in Somerset called Long Moss. We have no idea how big it is; all we know is that it supports some tenant farmers and we believe a single lady is the owner. She is a relative of the Fletcher family, in whose hands the estate has been for generations. We want you to purchase it for Mr Wakeman.'

Mr Rowell's eyebrows rose. 'I see. And what if the lady does not wish to sell?'

John Stuart leaned forward in his chair. 'You have my authority to make her an offer she cannot refuse.'

Mr Rowell's eyebrows rose even further. 'May I ask why we are buying it?'

John Stuart held his chin in thought for a moment before he answered, 'Mr Rowell, I hope you understand but I wish to attain it first, to know it is mine. Then I shall explain.'

If Mr Rowell deemed this eccentric behaviour, he concealed it well. He nodded sagely as Joe added, 'We would like you to make the purchase immediately. Do whatever you have to do to expedite matters.'

Three weeks later, on a wet, miserably cold February day, Mr Rowell knocked on the door in Curzon Street. Timothy let him in. He carried a large envelope which he had wrapped in leather against the rain, and when he had removed his overcoat, Timothy showed him into the parlour where a fire crackled cosily in the grate.

John Stuart and Joe entered a minute later, and Forrest Rowell came forward to them with a gratified smile on his large face. 'Congratulations, Mr Wakeman,' he said holding out his hand to shake John Stuart's. 'You are now the owner of the estate of Long Moss, eight hundred and forty acres in Somerset. Oh, and with it comes the freehold of several smaller properties in Wales.' He took the envelope from under his arm. 'It is a very profitable estate, although I must say you did not get it exactly at bargain price. Here are the deeds, sir.'

John Stuart and Joe smiled in unison, and Joe motioned their visitor to a chair and ordered coffee.

'Now, Mr Wakeman,' Mr Rowell asked, 'is there anything more I can do for you?'

John Stuart smiled but did not answer. He glanced at Joe and the older man replied. 'Yes, there is; the matter is far from ended. You come highly recommended to us by Robert Robinson-Pike whom we trust implicitly, and therefore we are prepared to put our trust in you. We live in Australia, three to four months in a ship away from these shores. It is unlikely we will ever make the long voyage to this country again.' He looked to John Stuart. 'At least, I will not. Thus, we need someone here to manage and maintain the property, in fact, properties, that Mr Wakeman has obtained.'

Forrest Rowell smiled calmly. 'We do similar things for one or two estates now.'

Timothy brought in the coffee and when he had poured it and departed, John Stuart broke the silence. 'The reason I have bought Long Moss is to hold it in trust for someone who is at present yet a baby. I want the baby to inherit Long Moss when it reaches its majority.'

'You say "it", Mr Wakeman. Do you not know the sex of the child?'

'That is correct. I do not.'

Mr Rowell looked slightly startled, and adroitly Joe continued the explanation. 'The child is in America, in Boston. As you are aware, Long Moss belonged to the Fletcher family, and as you will be handling the estate's affairs, you should be aware that Sir Graham Fletcher's son, Alan Fletcher, who was the heir, was wrongly accused of a crime and sent to Australia for life, as a convict. Hence, it ended up with the lady from whom we purchased.'

Mr Rowell said nothing but his eyebrows rose and remained high some seconds.

Joe continued impassively, 'Now, in buying the estate, we have ensured that Long Moss will return to Alan Fletcher's child, the baby in Boston.'

Mr Rowell looked at John Stuart with a mixed expression of admiration and surprise. 'That is a very commendable deed, sir. Most magnanimous. Mr Fletcher, the convict, must have been very important to you. Was he a relative, sir?'

Joe actually turned in his chair to see the younger man's eyes cloud for a moment. Joe knew the pain his boy was feeling, and he thought it was a benevolent, loving, even an indulgent act John Stuart was making towards Eve. His heart swelled with pride as he smiled with love and encouragement at the unhappy eyes opposite. A flicker of a sad smile lifted the corner of John Stuart's mouth as he took comfort from Joe and looked at the solicitor. 'Alan Fletcher's life and mine were . . .' he hesitated briefly, 'intertwined.' He hesitated again. 'It is the child's mother who is a relative of mine. I want her to be the recipient of the proceeds from the estate until the child comes of age. I desire a copy of the deeds and the documents covering the trust which I wish you to arrange for her and her child. The originals, I wish taken to her in Boston without delay. Mr Larmer and I will wait in London until the messenger returns. We do not want to tarry here longer than need be, but we realise it takes sometimes six weeks for a steamship to cross from here to Boston and back. Do you have a good man you can trust to do this?'

Mr Rowell's eyebrows rose again. Mr Wakeman wanted everything done without delay, as far as he could see. Perhaps it was a colonial trait to push forward with things so brusquely. He had to think. He took a deep breath. 'Ah, a man to sail to Boston, you ask? One I can trust, a good man. Well now, I'm not sure, but one does come to mind. He is twenty-nine, reliable, has just come out of his time, just acquired his letters. Finnigan McGuire is his name.'

John Stuart started. Joe also recognised the name, for he too had read every word of the Fletcher trial transcripts.

'Do you know him?' Mr Rowell asked.

John Stuart shook his head. 'No. But did his father have the same name? And was he a barrister-at-law?'

'Yes, that is so, a clever young man who unfortunately was drowned when Finnigan was only a child.'

John Stuart closed his eyes for a few seconds in thought as he tapped the polished oak of the armchair with his long fingers. 'Mr Rowell, this is one of those coincidences in life that we say do not happen. It is very appropriate that your young Finnigan McGuire should take the deeds of Alan Fletcher's estate to his child, for Finnigan's father defended Alan Fletcher at his trial in eighteen forty-nine.'

Mr Rowell's eyebrows rose again for an extended period this time. 'You don't say!'

'There is one more thing,' John Stuart added.

By this time, Forrest Rowell thought he was definitely ready for any peculiarity whatsoever.

'The mother of the child must never know that the benefactor is me.'

Forrest Rowell actually gulped. He had been wrong, he was not ready for this. 'But, Mr Wakeman, I don't understand.'

John Stuart sighed. It was a deeply sorrowful sound and Joe's heart gave a little lurch in sympathy as his boy continued. 'I merely want the papers handed over to the child's mother. It would be helpful if young Finnigan McGuire were to have the impression that someone here in England had arranged for the inheritance. I am very serious about this particular, very serious. I cannot emphasise too strongly that there is to be no connection with me.'

Mr Rowell was looking quite amazed as Joe completed the meeting with the words, 'Can you get Finnigan McGuire on a ship to Boston before the end of the week?'

Saturday, 22 March, was a bleak Boston day. Clouds had rolled across the sky all morning and now in the early afternoon rain was falling.

Finnigan had taken a room at the New World Hotel in Winter Place. It was his first trip out of England and he was fascinated by his American 'cousins' and their country. It was with regret that he took his room for three nights only. His return passage to Plymouth was reserved on the SS *Carmen Bonita* which was to sail at two in the afternoon on Tuesday. With the help of a uniformed personage who called himself the 'concierge' he organised to have his card sent round to 32 Russell Street, Beacon Hill. He asked for a meeting the following morning at ten o'clock.

When Lottie came in to Eve with the card, it was mid-afternoon and through the window lightning was flashing.

'Terrible afternoon and all,' she said, handing the card and the attached note to Eve.

'Who on earth is he?' Eve looked up from the card. 'I have never heard of Mr Finnigan McGuire, solicitor of Forrest Rowell Pty. Ltd, London.'

'Me neither. I wonder what he wants.'

'I have a piano lesson at half past ten tomorrow,' Eve answered, 'so he had better be quick with his business, whatever it is.'

The following day, Finnigan indeed proved to be swift in Russell Street, for Eve was so overwhelmed by the nature of his assignment, he soon took leave of her; and when little Rosy Daniels arrived for her piano lesson, she was sent home. After Finnigan had gone, Eve sat for a long time staring at the deeds to Long Moss.

When the visitor had given her the envelope and she had read the accompanying letter and realised what the contents were, she was speechless. It was like a miracle. She was to receive the proceeds from Alan's estate until her child came of age and inherited. She had kept looking from the letter up to Mr McGuire's face and back down to the letter again. Finally, she spoke. 'I cannot comprehend this. It is like something out of a dream. I am overcome. Who is responsible for this . . . magnanimous deed?'

Finnigan's long brow, so reminiscent of his father's, wrinkled in concern as he replied, 'Actually, madam, I never met your benefactor. Mr Rowell was particular that I did not have the gentleman's name. But he did mention that it was someone in England, a gentleman, important, of the upper classes, I believe. Probably titled, I would say, the respectful way he spoke of him.'

Eve's mind was in turmoil. There was only one person she could imagine it was. Yes, it had to be. A man who cared enough about the injustice done to Alan Fletcher. A man who had gone back to England and cleared Alan's name. A man of the upper classes, rich and titled, who could afford to do this. Sir Rutherford Blake. Oh, how wonderful. How could she ever express her gratitude?

When she had finally calmed her mind, she offered Finnigan some tea which he had the good sense to refuse. He could see the woman needed to be alone.

'I shall not take up any more of your time,' he said, rising to his feet.

Eve was trying to talk in a self-possessed manner, but her heart was racing. 'Yes, thank you, Mr McGuire, I would appreciate being left alone.' Then her befuddled mind realised she was not being very hospitable. 'You mentioned earlier that you are here only briefly.'

'Yes, I leave for Plymouth the day after tomorrow.'

'Would you come back to tea tomorrow? I'll be thinking clearly then, I'm sure.'

At three o'clock the next day, Eve and Finnigan took tea together. Lottie brought in the refreshments and remained to be introduced before she left them. They spoke of the journey from England and of ships and the sea. When he stood to leave, Eve handed him the letter she had written the night before to Sir Rutherford Blake. 'Please give this to your superior, Mr Rowell. I am sure he will be able to get it to its destination.'

Finnigan took it and bowed over her hand. 'Certainly, madam.'

At the front door, he hesitated. There was something he wished to tell this lady. 'Mrs Fletcher, there is a connection between myself and yourself.'

'Really?'

'Yes. Mr Rowell said that it was very fitting I be the one to carry the deeds of the Long Moss estate to you.'

'Oh, why is that?'

'He told me it was my father who defended your husband at his trial in Southampton in eighteen forty-nine. I was named after my father.'

Eve shook her head in wonder. 'That is astonishing. The son has in effect completed what his father set out to do. Yes, how appropriate.' She stood looking into the honest grey eyes and then she said something that shocked both herself and Finnigan. 'While I loved him beyond words, I was never married to Mr Fletcher.'

Finnigan was a well-bred young man, but he could not help being startled. He had been commissioned to bring the deeds of Long Moss across the Atlantic to Mrs Fletcher of 32 Russell Street, Beacon Hill, Boston. He knew the story of Alan Fletcher and the wrong done to him. This task he performed undid some of the wrong. But always he had assumed that the mother of the child had been married to the father.

'I see,' he said.

Eve held out her hand. 'Thank you, manifoldly, for the part you have played in this charitable and noble-minded deed. Thank you and good-bye.'

Finnigan took Eve's hand once more and shook it. 'All the best to you,' he said softly before he turned away.

As Eve closed the door, Lottie spoke behind her. 'Why on earth did ye tell him that?'

'I don't know. I'm mixed up, Lottie. This is a miracle. That man helped it happen. I will never see him again and I wanted to be honest with him.'

Lottie shook her head. 'Sometimes you do the oddest things, Miss Eve.' Then she sniffed. 'Who would have believed Sir Rutherford would turn up trumps? What a simply marvellous man.' She pursed her lips in memory before she added, 'And to think there was a time I was athinking him quite the reverse.'

During their stay in London, John Stuart made inquiries about Sir Rutherford. He was working for the London Police Force at Scotland Yard but spent much of his spare time interviewing prisoners who had pleaded innocent to charges of major crimes, examining their records and studying their files. He had been so affected by Alan Fletcher, he had determined never in his lifetime to let another innocent man suffer.

They were disappointed to find he was holidaying in the south of France with his wife, Coralea. Apparently, she had been someone from his past, whom he had sought out and married shortly after returning to England. He was not expected back in England until April. John Stuart was determined to remain in Great Britain until he knew the Long Moss deeds were in Eve's hands, so with luck he would yet see Sir Rutherford.

It did not take long before it was generally known in London that the wealthy John Stuart Wakeman of New South Wales was in residence and he and Joe were invited to many social functions. They refused most of them, although they did have an audience with Earl John Russell, the Prime Minister, who was eager to hear John Stuart's opinions on his dominion beyond the seas; and they took tea at Windsor, which the Prime Minister arranged, thinking it was important for his monarch to meet Australia's wealthiest citizen.

Queen Victoria was on a brief stay at Windsor. Since her widowhood six years before, she avoided London when she could and spent much of her time in her home on the Isle of Wight or at Balmoral Castle in Scotland. She was now forty-eight years old, a robust little woman with enormous presence. John Stuart had been recommended by the Prime Minister and also by Benjamin Disraeli, whom she particularly liked, and so she had seen the colonial visitor out of courtesy, but by the time he left she was quite captivated by him and had invited him back a few days later to a diplomatic dinner and given him a solid silver paperweight in the form of a miniature

Balmoral Castle. Underneath it was engraved 'Victoria Regina'.

The meeting with the Queen had taken place on a wet, cold, April day. On the way back to London, the carriage ran through numerous downpours but by the time they rolled into the west end of London the rain had ceased. John Stuart and Joe had been quiet for a time, watching the passing country through the windows of the vehicle. It was dark by the time they neared Hyde Park and Joe broke the silence.

'It is over six weeks since young Finnigan McGuire left for Boston. We should hear something any day now.'

'Yes, Joe, it should not be much longer.'

'What do you intend to do if he accomplishes his task?'

John Stuart did not reply straightaway; he sat with his head turned, looking through the window into the gloom of the overcast night.

'We will go home to Mayfield.'

Joe did not speak, he remained silently musing in the darkness until he bent forward to touch John Stuart's knee. 'M'boy, don't you want to see her?'

The coach was rolling along by the unfinished memorial being erected in memory of Albert, the Queen's late husband. There was a row of gas lamps here and the bleak illumination showed John Stuart's face. Joe continued to hold his hand on his boy's knee until at last he stopped looking through the window and brought his face round to Joe's.

Joe repeated the question. 'Don't you want to see her?'

John Stuart finally answered. His voice was controlled but there was the edge of troubled emotion in it that Joe recognised well. 'I . . . think of nothing else. But if Finnigan has done his job, then I know she will always be well looked after. I can go home to Mayfield a little more content than I left.'

'Content?' Joe sat back and folded his arms. He could no longer make out John Stuart's face in the gloom but he spoke as if he looked him in the eye. 'Would you not be even more content if you finished this whole thing properly? If you saw her one more time and made your peace with her?'

'What? Go to Boston, do you mean?'

Joe leaned forward again. 'Yes, that is what I mean. I have known you all your life and you cannot hide things from me. I'm certain you want to see her, to make your peace with her; you just have not yet admitted it. Now, Eve made choices that I do not agree with, they were mistakes, in my mind, but I know you have never stopped loving her. Didn't I ride beside you through hundreds of miles of bush trying to find her? Look, m'boy, I want what you want and I believe you want to see her; give this whole sorry business some sort of completion.'

'But, old man, if I arrive suddenly she might suspect that I am the one who has sent her the deeds.' He sighed. 'The last thing I want from her is any damned gratitude.'

'You know full well that Finnigan was told no lies but was led to believe that Eve's benefactor was a wealthy Englishman of the upper classes. We must assume that Lottie Thatcher has told Eve of Sir Rutherford's changed attitude and of his gaining of the posthumous pardon. She will not suspect it is you.' He ruffled John Stuart's hair as he often did when they were alone. 'Heck, m'boy, I'm pining to see Thel and Mayfield, pining for home; but home is thirteen thousand miles away and Boston is three.' He had said his piece and he leaned back into his seat.

A few seconds later, John Stuart called out of the window to the driver who halted the coach near Prince's Gate on the southern side of the park. 'I shall walk the remainder of the way, Joe. I'm feeling restless.'

'There's a chill wind, m'boy, and it might rain again. Are you sure you wish to walk?'

'Yes, I am,' he answered jumping down from the coach. 'Have Tim pour me a brandy to warm me on my return.'

'I will.'

The coach squeaked away and John Stuart walked into the park. There was a ghostly moon illuminating the stark limbs of the leafless trees. He pulled his overcoat more tightly round him as he trudged across the sodden earth of Rotten Row and came to a halt by the Serpentine. In the dreary light of a gas lamp, he stood staring at the floes on the surface of the water. He peered back towards Knightsbridge where in the light of another lamp a well-wrapped couple hurried along.

He turned towards Mayfair and took the path leading up by the bandstand to Park Lane. As Joe had said, Eve should have had the deeds to Long Moss weeks ago if all had gone well. Now, her life would be truly comfortable. The proceeds from the estate would see to that. There was a sickening ache in his chest as he strode along in the wind. He would always love her. He missed her every day of his life. When he had realised she carried Alan Fletcher's child, it had cut into his soul. But he had lived with that for eight months now and the pain had dulled to the extent that at times he even thought having an infant to love and cherish would be good for her. He had done his best now for her and her child. He lifted his gloved hands to his eyes. He wished by all that was sacred that the child had been his. But life was not like that. Life was 'a tale, Told by an idiot, full of sound and fury, Signifying nothing'.

Joe thought he should see her face to face. Dear Joe, who wanted only what was best for him. He was tired and wanted to go home, and yet he was willing to travel on to Boston. How lucky he was to have Joe, he was the best there was.

As he reached Park Lane and stood waiting for some carriages to pass, he thought of Mayfield. He should go home, home to Mayfield and the imperfect consolation of his beautiful rolling hills and valleys. He would find some sort of peace there. He said aloud, 'Ah, if only I could turn back time,' as he stepped into the street to hurry across Park Lane between the vehicles. The moon was watery and a fine rain was falling as he passed the paper-seller on the corner of Curzon Street but he was hardly aware of anything, for in his mind he watched a dream woman coming across the Bathurst park at twilight. When he arrived at the three stone steps that led up to his front door, he took off his glove and put his hand inside his coat and touched the thing he always carried, the olive branch hairpin she had left behind on her pillow the morning she had gone away. He took it out and raised it to his lips.

When he entered the warm, comfortable hall of the house, there stood Joe holding a brandy out towards him. 'I'm glad you're home, m'boy, I see it has begun to rain.'

He managed a meagre smile. 'Has it? Yes, I suppose it has,' he said noticing the dampness on his overcoat as Timothy removed it for him. He took the brandy and followed Joe into the parlour.

'Joe?'

'Yes?'

'I have been thinking. I have made peace with my mother, though I was thwarted in doing so while she lived. You know me well. I should see that other one whom I lost. See her, at last, and know the truth. Once Finnigan is back here, we . . . will go to Boston.'

The older man nodded. 'Then I think I'll tell Timothy to begin packing, for this envelope was here when I arrived. It's from Forrest Rowell.' He took a small dark envelope from the mantel above the fire and handed it to John Stuart.

Inside was a short note.

Inns of Court,
London.
16th April, 1867.

Dear Messrs. Wakeman and Larmer,

This is to advise you of the safe return this day to London of

Mr Finnigan McGuire. He has carried out your wishes. With your permission I shall call on you at ten o'clock tomorrow morning.

Sincerely,
Forrest Rowell.

'And another thing,' Joe said as John Stuart lifted his eyes from the note. 'A message came today to say Rutherford is back in London.'

The next morning, sharply at ten o'clock, Timothy answered the doorbell and Forrest Rowell was ushered into the sitting room where John Stuart and Joe came forward to greet him.

When the pleasantries were over, Joe spoke. 'So Mr Rowell, the deeds were safely delivered to Boston.'

'Yes, sir. Finnigan took them over to Mrs Fletcher the day after he arrived and the following day he took tea with her.'

Only Joe noticed John Stuart's almost imperceptible flinch when Forrest Rowell said 'Mrs Fletcher'.

Mr Rowell continued, 'He said the house she lives in is small and ordinary, much smaller and less grand than those around it, but it's in Beacon Hill and he tells me the area is a good place to live. He introduced himself and told her the reason for his expedition. She was astounded and could not believe it. He said he did not stay long as he felt like an intruder. "She was quite overcome" was the way he put it.'

'And did she ask who sent the deeds?' Joe prompted.

'Yes, indeed. He said he told her exactly what I had said to him, which as you both know was that the benefactor wished to remain anonymous, but that he was a wealthy gentleman here in England.'

John Stuart nodded. 'Good.'

'And I am here to tell you, the lady in question must have believed him for on his departure the next day she gave him this.' Mr Rowell withdrew a letter from inside his coat and handed it to John Stuart. It was addressed 'To Sir Rutherford Blake, per kind favour of Mr McGuire and his Associates'.

'I assume you will know what to do with it, Mr Wakeman?' asked Forrest Rowell.

John Stuart put it down on the sofa beside him. 'Yes, we shall be seeing Rutherford before we leave London. You may leave it with us.' He folded his arms before he asked, 'Did Mr McGuire say any more?'

'Yes. He said she teaches music, piano, and that she lives with a married couple. He said he saw no sign of the child, but it was

637

obvious that there was one, for there were baby's toys about.'

John Stuart nodded slowly. His face was expressionless, but his chest hurt and the awful ache was filling him. He forced himself to say, 'Anything else?'

'He said she was quite in control the second day, unlike the day before. And he told me of an odd incident when he was leaving her.'

'Oh?' Joe interjected, 'And what was that?'

'He was at the door, apparently departing. He said he informed her of what I had told him, which was that it was his own father who had defended Alan Fletcher at his trial nearly twenty years ago. Finnigan said he referred to Alan Fletcher as her husband and she answered with the words, "While I loved Alan Fletcher I was never married to him." ' Forrest Rowell waited to see what effect his words would have on his two listeners. John Stuart struggled to remain impassive but his nervous fingers rapped in telltale fashion on the edge of the armchair.

'Did you know this?' Mr Rowell asked.

'We did,' Joe replied.

John Stuart stood and walked to the fire. His back was to the legal man as he spoke. 'Mr Rowell, you will be handling the estate of Long Moss and its affairs probably for decades to come and we will remain in communication. It is time I was completely honest with you.' He turned round and a succession of expressions travelled quickly across his strong features. 'It is true that the lady who called herself Mrs Fletcher was never married to Alan Fletcher. She was . . . is . . . married to me.'

'Ah, so that's it,' the legal man said with a quite audible sigh.

When Forrest Rowell left the house in Curzon Street, he was acquainted, in essence, with the history of John Stuart and Eve. He would keep Mr Wakeman's trust, that was his duty, and part of his occupation, but he could not understand the fellow. 'You're a better man than I, John Stuart Wakeman,' he said to himself as he turned the corner into Berkeley Square. 'If my wife left me to have another man's child, I'd be damned in hell before I'd do what you have done.'

The day before they departed for Boston, John Stuart and Joe spent some pleasant hours with Sir Rutherford at his family home in Kent. It was the first day they had felt spring in the air. The sun shone and the breeze did not have the chill of a week earlier. As the carriage passed up the drive from the main road, Joe pointed to a herd of deer running in Sir Rutherford's park.

The police detective met them at the steps of his ancestral home and they hugged as old friends do. A minute later, out came Lady Coralea, a fine-looking woman with curly, auburn hair and large hazel eyes. After the introductions, she took them through the beautiful old house and out into the sunken garden where a sumptuous luncheon awaited them.

Two hours later, the three men rode along the Medway River and talked of old times. At a rustic inn, they drank a pint of ale and the locals were both flattered and awed that Sir Rutherford Blake and his 'genteel' friends from Australia had dropped by. The publican saw them to the tavern door. 'Thank ee, Sirr Rutherford, me lud. Always nice to see ee, it is, sirr.'

On the return ride, they reined in at the edge of a small forest of oaks on the top of a long, grassy ridge, looking down across the open country stretching into the distance. They dismounted and stood beneath the heavy branches covered in bursting green shoots of new life.

John Stuart walked to the bole of one of the oaks and tapped upon it with his riding crop before he looked back to Sir Rutherford. 'My friend, I have something to tell you.'

The detective policeman smiled. 'You have told me much already.'

'Yes, but this concerns Eve.'

He related the events of acquiring Long Moss and how he had constructed the trust for Eve and her son, and of Finnigan's journey to Boston to hand over a copy of the deeds of the estate. 'And so, you see, old friend, we believe Eve thinks you are the man who purchased Long Moss. I have a letter here from her which she asked McGuire to deliver to his superior and, via him, to you. Of course I have not opened it, but I suspect I know the contents.' He took it from his breast pocket where it had lain next to Eve's hairpin and gave it to him. Sir Rutherford read the letter, then he handed it to John Stuart. 'Here, my friend. She does indeed believe it is me who has endowed her so very munificently.'

John Stuart read.

32 Russell St.,
Beacon Hill,
Boston,
21st March, 1867.

Dear Sir Rutherford,

A legal gentleman, by name Mr Finnigan McGuire, has been to see me today, and now, in my hands, I hold the deeds to the estate of 'Long Moss' in Somerset, England. I cannot believe what you have done. It is so benevolent, so magnanimous, so wonderful.

For you see, Sir Rutherford, I realise the benefactor must be yourself, although I understand you wish to remain anonymous. Not only did you have Alan Fletcher posthumously pardoned (a most honourable act), but you have returned his inheritance to his son. And in doing so have generously made provision for me as well. For my son I accept your bountiful offer. It is only right that he should inherit his father's goods and lands. But I am confused by your extraordinary generosity to me. It is not proper for me to take the proceeds from the Fletcher estate. I manage to keep myself, as I have always done, and I have wonderful friends. Therefore, I must assure you, that any money I receive in beneficiary I shall place into a bank to ensure it is used only to enhance my son's life.

Sir Rutherford, we were never friends, you and I. There was always reserve between us. I misjudged you badly. Forgive me. It was more than enough that you cleared Alan Fletcher's name.

Yours sincerely,
Evelyn May

'Odd that she signed no surname,' Sir Rutherford said when John Stuart lifted his eyes.

John Stuart handed over the letter for Joe to read. 'Yes, it is.' He sighed. 'So the child is a boy.'

Rutherford took hold of John Stuart's shoulder. 'My friend, I am relieved that she thinks it more than enough to have cleared the bushranger's name, for that was the extent of my doing. You are an amazing man to do as you have done.' His eyes narrowed in habitual scrutiny as he added, 'I wonder if she will ever realise how very greatly loved she is?'

John Stuart met Sir Rutherford's eyes. He tried to smile, but failed. He shook his head as if to say it did not matter. After some seconds, he spoke. 'I have never stopped loving her. Even when I was duped into thinking her worthless, somehow I loved her through it all.' He turned quickly away and moved a few paces to look down across the Medway to the patchwork quilt of the fields beyond. The breeze had turned a little cooler and clouds now drifted across the sun. Joe had finished reading Eve's letter and moved silently across to stand beside him.

Sir Rutherford's high forehead wrinkled reflectively. He took a few steps to come up behind his guests. 'I can't allow it, you know,' he said.

'What?'

'For her to think it is me who has been so beneficent.'

John Stuart turned back to him. 'I thought as much. But even if you tell her it is not you, I must ask you never to divulge the truth. Do not write back post haste. I want to . . . go to her first, to stand and look into her eyes, one final time. I leave for Boston tomorrow. Will you do me the very great favour of giving me time to have seen her and departed before you reply to this letter?'

Sir Rutherford took up John Stuart's hand. 'You are the best of men, my good friend. I don't agree, but shall do as you request.'

CHAPTER THIRTY-NINE

'And ruin'd love, when it is built anew,
Grows fairer than at first, more strong, far greater.'
'Sonnet CXIX', William Shakespeare, 1564–1616.

May, 1867.

May in Boston is a pleasant time. The wind has lost its chill, the trees are in blossom, the flowers are budding and the days are lengthening.

A comforting breeze was blowing across the Boston Common, and the woman who walked swiftly along the gravelled path opened her cape to let it fly back as she looked up at the branches of the large beeches and elms above.

She had been to Boylston Street on the far side of the Common where she taught piano at a private home one evening a week. She was a little later than usual but she was not concerned, for Lottie was in Russell Street now to take care of things and she did not need to rely on Mrs Mason's good nature so much. It was odd really, to think that she lived here at 32 Russell Street, Boston, when in Australia she had lived at 22 Russell Street, Bathurst. For a few moments she reflected on Bathurst and Father and Mother and how serene her life had been then. She thought of the day she had burst into Father's study and met John Stuart. She shook her head gently at the memory.

The sky was beginning to darken and she accelerated as she came to the black row of pine trees that ran along the gravel path leading to the steep stone steps up to Beacon Street.

Suddenly, she heard someone call her name, 'Eve, Eve . . .'

She halted as if petrified. She knew that voice intimately; but it was impossible. Slowly, she turned as the tall figure she recognised immediately stepped out of the ebony shadows of the pine trees not six feet away. John Stuart! What was happening? He could not be here.

'Eve.'

'I don't understand. How can this be? You . . . here?'

642

He stood looking at her. The face he had longed to see . . . and his heart thumped in his chest.

John Stuart, Joe and Timothy had disembarked from the SS *Carmen Bonita* only a few hours before. They had gone immediately to the Regency Hotel in Park Square on Arlington Street across from the Public Garden and taken rooms. While Timothy unpacked, Joe went downstairs and ascertained directions for John Stuart from the clerk behind the hotel desk.

Afterwards, Joe had accompanied his boy across the road into the Public Garden. He took leave of John Stuart near an empty rose bed just inside the border hedge. He held a piece of paper up and traced over it with his finger. 'Cross the Garden and Charles Street, then diagonally over the Common into Beacon Street; then to the right until you find Joy Street, left here, then left into Myrtle Street and finally right into Russell.' John Stuart took the paper, and Joe smiled encouragingly at him. 'I shall be waiting to hear what occurs. Say what you've come to say, m'boy. And whatever happens, I am more proud of you than words can express.'

John Stuart walked slowly over the new grass and onto a gravelled path. He watched the people passing back and forth in the wan light of the evening. He crossed Charles Street and entered the Common with its native and imported trees and wide open areas for children to play. When the sky began darkening, he found himself near a row of enormous pines, evergreens, and he stood there for a moment. He was about to step back onto the path and continue up the wide, stone steps to Beacon Street, when he looked over to his left.

His pulse quickened. It was her coming across the Common, a long, pale-coloured cape flowing from her shoulders. He would know that walk anywhere. He was not prepared to see her this way. It was *déjà vu*, reminding him of that other time and place when his heart was so much younger than it was now. He was unsure what to do as he watched her coming on, closer, closer, the same swift walk. His heart was racing as she came abreast of him. And then somehow he managed to call her name and to walk out upon the path.

And now . . . she stood looking up at him with disbelief.

It was like a dream to be with her again. Greedily, his eyes examined her and he saw how she was the same and yet not the same. Her face was more angular than he remembered and her brown eyes seemed darker and enigmatic. Yet the planes of her face still held the gentility and beauty and grace he knew so well.

When he broke the silence, it was an awkward speech he made to her there in the dying day. 'Eve, I have come to see you. So much

643

has happened. I am here to . . . make peace with you, if I can. The truth is, I tried to do this before you left Australia. I wanted to, from the very moment you left Mayfield . . . left me . . . and even before that. I searched for you.' His long fingers made a hopeless gesture in the air. 'For many weary months, I searched.'

Eve was in shock. It was as if he had risen out of the ground beside her. What was he saying? He had searched for her? She knew that. She took a deep breath. She must take stock of things. Never could she have believed that John Stuart would come to Boston.

'John Stuart,' his name sounded peculiar to her ears, 'I see you here in front of me, but it is as if you are not real.'

'Oh, I am real, and I am here. I am staying in Boston only to see you . . . to tell you this.' He made another despairing gesture with his left hand, then it dropped to his side.

As they stood facing each other, the rising wind lifted Eve's cape and blew it forward to touch his trousers.

She shook her head. There was part of her that was so pleased to see him, so very pleased. 'I don't know what to say.'

'You need not say anything. I have simply come here to right things . . . if I can.'

'John Stuart,' she said his name with a sigh. 'What happened between us was not your fault alone. Truly it was not . . . I was not always honest with you. We both made mistakes.'

'Yes. I know about Clare.'

This surprised her. 'I see.'

'I was very wrong about all that . . . all that with Lake. I kept seeing you and my mother as one. I was blinded by my beliefs and I did not give you a chance. When finally, I wanted to right things between us, I came to you on Boxing Day morning . . . you were gone.'

A tingle of sorrow rose in her chest and rippled through her. Poor John Stuart. Yes, he had suffered too, and greatly, she could see. She was looking at him closely, examining him. He looked older but was just as handsome, just as imposing.

He took a deep breath. 'I believe that you must know of the posthumous pardon for . . . Mr Fletcher. Sir Rutherford Blake was instrumental in having it conferred. He was untiring in his efforts to have it granted.'

'Yes, I know about it.' She looked away up to Beacon Street where a lamp-lighter moved slowly along. It was peculiar to hear him call Alan 'Mr Fletcher'. She brought her eyes back to his. 'I now realise Sir Rutherford is a most remarkable man.'

John Stuart nodded. 'Yes, he is.'

'Lottie told me about the pardon,' she said.

'Yes, I heard Lottie Thatcher had gone abroad. I thought she must have come to you.'

She was still having difficulty believing he was here. It was weird, overwhelming. Her voice sounded odd and thin to her own ears. 'She and her husband live with me. He, too, you will remember. His name is Arnold Drake, but you would know him as Lawless Drake. He is . . . my best friend.'

Of course, her 'brother', as the Pinkerton men had called him; the last of the Fletcher band.

It was darkening around them now, but neither really noticed, they were so taken up with the presence of the other.

'How did you find me?' she asked suddenly.

He moved off the path to let two people pass by before he answered. 'There are men who do such things now . . . find people . . . for a fee.'

She thought how diligent he had been to know of such people to actually find her here, but then, he was always thorough in everything. He had always done things well.

'Eve, I know I wronged you. I am truly sorry. But I feel you . . . wronged me too. I have been wanting to know for so long. That day in Cowra? At first, I thought that you were kidnapped by Alan Fletcher. Eve, you were not, were you?'

She was looking up into his eyes, his pensive, brown eyes, in the gloom of dusk. 'No, John Stuart, I was not.'

She noticed the fleeting expression of pain that crossed his face and she found herself not wanting to hurt him, to explain how it really had been. 'John Stuart. Please do not misunderstand. I was unconscious in Cowra when Alan found me by chance . . . took care of me. In fact, wanted to bring me home to you, but I believed you and I were forever estranged. What happened was not anyone's fault . . . it just happened.'

She thought he made a bitter sound as he asked, 'Did you love him very deeply?'

Unconsciously, she half raised her hand between them as she answered, 'Yes, very deeply.'

He said nothing.

She sighed, closing her eyes. 'John Stuart, I am a mother. I have a son, Alan Fletcher's son.'

And she stared in amazement as he answered, 'Yes, I know.'

They stood, eyes locked, until he spoke again, now appearing to notice for the first time that it was almost totally dark. 'Perhaps you should be on your way home.'

She nodded. 'It does grow late.'

'This way?' He pointed up the steps.

'Yes.'

They moved off together in silence. Under the lamp on the corner of Joy Street, they both halted.

The gentle wind was still blowing. She pulled the cape around her. 'I live up here,' she said, pointing up the hill.

'Yes.' He looked keenly at her, studying her face again; the face of his sleepless nights and dream-filled imaginings. 'We have survived, Eve, you and I. I have wondered about you every day. You are happy?'

For some reason, she shivered. 'Ah, John Stuart, as happy as it is possible for me to be. I have my son; he makes me happy. Are you?'

He wanted desperately to answer, 'No, how could I be happy without you? I love you, only you can make me truly happy.' But instead, he forced his half smile to his mouth and said, 'I am happy to have seen you, cleared things between us, a little.' He looked away, pointing up the hill. 'It is dark, I will see you to your door.'

'No, John Stuart, it is not necessary. It's not far from here, thank you.'

They stood looking at one another.

'All right,' he replied reluctantly.

'Before you go,' she said, 'how is Thelma?'

'She is well. She was always your true friend.'

She nodded. 'And Joe?'

'He is here with me.'

Yes, yes, of course he would be. 'And Mayfield, how is Mayfield?'

Now he wanted to say, 'Not the same without you,' but he did not, he answered, 'As beautiful as ever.'

She thought of Mayfield then; the glorious rolling hills and valleys; the morning rays breaking through the branches of the trees of the park; the Lachlan wending its way through the orchards and the crops. John Stuart must be missing it. He loved it so. 'And how long do you remain in Boston?'

He shrugged his shoulders. 'Not long. I don't know.'

Silence fell. It was very quiet under the dim street light. No horses or carriages passed by. They both felt it, the unreality of this little slice of time as they stood regarding each other.

Suddenly, she put out her hand to him and he took it. She was very aware of his touch, the sensation of his palm on hers. 'Would you . . . care to come to tea tomorrow?'

He did not answer immediately, but continued looking intently at her until he dropped her hand and nodded. 'What time should I come?'

'I teach music in the afternoon. Would five o'clock be all right?'
He nodded. 'I'll be there.'

A smile broke across his mouth. She had always liked his smile, she saw in it what she used to believe was the benevolent essence of him. Involuntarily, she smiled back before she turned and walked away into the night.

He felt a surge of sadness. He loved her so, but she seemed so in command of herself, with the same strength of character and spirit she had always shown. She did not need him; perhaps she never had. He stood under the lamp until he could see her no more, then he crossed the street to descend into the darkened Common. He put his hand into his breast pocket and, withdrawing the olive branch hairpin, clasped it tightly as he strode on in the night.

When Eve came to the front door of her home, she hesitated on the doorstep. John Stuart was here in Boston. It was hard to believe. Such strange things were happening lately: the appearance of Mr McGuire with Sir Rutherford's wonderful gift a few months ago and now John Stuart's arrival all the way from Australia. He had tracked her down halfway round the globe to make his peace with her. 'How truly amazing he is,' she said softly, as she opened the door.

Inside, Lottie and Arnold appeared from the kitchen. 'Eve,' Lottie said, concern in her eyes. 'We were just beginning to aworry about ye. Arnold was about to come alooking.'

The expression on Eve's face was so extraordinary, they came quickly to her. 'What has happened?' Arnold asked.

She did not reply immediately. She took off her cape and put her satchel on the hall stand before she spoke. 'I'm not sure I believe it myself yet. Come into the parlour. I've something astonishing to tell you.'

John Stuart's appearance invoked so many recollections for Eve that she spent the night reliving the years gone by: her mother and the wasting disease; the death of her father on the voyage from America; her years in Sydney Town; Clare's dying of consumption; her marriage and life at Mayfield; the terrible experience with Lake and her rejection by John Stuart; her fight for life at Treehard and the days there; the deaths of Father and Mother; her loss of Alan and the struggle to go on without him, and her lonely pregnancy here in Boston, with dear Arnold. No, life had not been easy, but she was resilient and she was strong. These were the experiences of her existence, the events which had made her who she was today. She had survived. Hadn't John Stuart said something about survival tonight? 'We have survived, Eve . . . you and I.' That was true, but his life had been gentle in comparison to hers. Yet he had developed and he had changed. She had seen that tonight. He had matured; he was not the judging, censorious man she had known.

She felt a tiny sensation of guilt. To think he had come to see her at Mayfield on that fateful Boxing Day to make amends, and she had left just a few short hours before. How odd, how very chancefully odd. If she had remained merely one more day . . .

Before she went to bed, she stood holding the side of her son's cot, looking at him in the lamplight. How like Alan he was. Already he had startlingly beautiful eyes. 'You shall inherit what is yours, my darling,' she said softly. 'That is the miracle.' She left the cot and walked to the window. She looked out into the blackness and pictured Alan. My wonderful Alan, your lands will return to your son. She saw his face. How desperately she missed him. Tears rose to her eyes, as they did every night when she thought of him. Then her mind played the trick that it often did, and Alan's face changed; it was her wedding day and the coach was being held up. There, side by side, stood Alan and John Stuart.

When John Stuart came the following day, he remained an hour. It was a unique hour for both of them, filled with drifting thoughts and memories, delicate, sensitive and singular. Lottie served tea and departed quickly. Later, she confided to Eve, 'He does look so regal, doesn't he? Always was, but now he's sort of sad looking, makes him more handsome to my way of thinking.'

Eve had been particular with Lottie. Once she had served tea, she was to take the baby out for a walk. Somehow, she wanted to save John Stuart any upset that seeing her son might bring.

They had spoken of many things; of her life here in Boston and about Mayfield and all the people there she knew. She asked many questions about Thelma and Stephanie, Baines, Dr Douglas, the Hennessys, the Watsons and Mrs Smith. They were all still with John Stuart, all still at Mayfield. She felt very peculiar when he told her of Daydee's death. 'It was on her twenty-first birthday. Terrible for Joe and Thel.'

She found it hard to think of Daydee gone; all that useless energy the girl had expended in hatred of her. 'Oh, Daydee, why?' she said to herself.

They conversed not as old friends would, but not as strangers either, and when John Stuart looked at his fob watch and said, 'I've been here an hour. It's time I left,' Eve realised it had not been an awkward hour at all.

As John Stuart stood, she asked. 'How long did the ship take from Sydney?'

'What's that?'

'Your voyage here. Did you come round the Horn or the Cape Colony?'

She thought he hesitated before he answered. 'Round the Cape, yes, and then across the Atlantic. A hundred days or so.'

'It's a long voyage, isn't it?'

He nodded and, turning, walked out into the hall. He had answered her question truthfully about his route to America; he had merely omitted to say he went to Great Britain first.

She followed him as he retrieved his hat from the stand and opened the front door. He tipped his hat and walked out.

'John Stuart,' she called and he turned on the top step to face her. For a few seconds they stood gazing at each other before she said, 'I have no idea how long you are in Boston, but if you are still in town on Saturday, perhaps we could dine here together? You and Joe and me.'

'And what of Lottie and her husband?'

Eve looked inquiringly at him. 'What of them?'

'They live with you, they are your day-to-day companions. Joe and I will be happy to dine with you all on Saturday.'

It was a pleasant meal; an anomalous, unlikely group they made, but certainly an agreeable group. Lottie had worked untiringly to clean and tidy the small house and she had managed to haggle with a street vendor and purchase a fresh hen, a real treat in Russell Street. With the help of Mrs Mason she had made vegetable soup, roast hen and a lemon pie.

They had only four chairs, so Lottie sat on a kitchen stool brought into the parlour. John Stuart talked to Arnold about Boston. He was very knowledgeable about the city for someone who had just arrived. They discussed electricity and the experiments being done on electric tram-cars, while an interested Lottie listened. Joe and Eve talked of Thelma and Mayfield. When he mentioned Daydee, she could see the suffering in his face.

'I'm so sorry, Joe,' she said.

He nodded sadly. 'Yes, my little girl is gone, but at least I've still got m'boy.' He nodded in John Stuart's direction as he added, 'And he's the best there is in this world.'

Dear Joe, dear, loyal Joe.

It was close to eleven o'clock when they departed. They made their goodnights on the doorstep, and Lottie and Arnold returned into the house while Joe went ahead a few paces, leaving John Stuart alone with Eve.

As he took her hand in goodnight, he said something utterly unexpected. 'Once again, I did not see your son.'

Surprise registered in Eve's face. 'I did not think you would like to see him. Tonight he sleeps next door with our neighbour.'

'Eve,' there was disappointment in the way he said her name, 'many months ago, in your garden bower under the poinciana tree, I accepted that you and Alan Fletcher had a child.' She had no idea what he meant by that remark, but she listened as he continued, his eyes appearing almost black in the pale light from the entry hall. 'You need not hide him from me if we meet again.' He retained her hand. 'In fact, if you agree, I shall come to see him tomorrow or the next day.' He increased the pressure on her palm momentarily before he let it go and followed Joe into the night.

When she closed the door, she stood there a few moments contemplating what John Stuart had said, before she passed through to the kitchen to find Lottie and Arnold washing up.

Arnold half turned to her, 'Joe's a nice old bloke.'

'Yes. And?'

'Well, Eve, the fact is we both liked John Stuart Wakeman, didn't we, Lottie, love?'

'Yes, we did. There's no astanding on ceremony with him and nothing snobbish about him at all.'

Eve's eyes had a thoughtful, faraway expression in them as she looked from one to the other. 'No, there never was,' she answered quietly.

John Stuart did not come the next day. It was the day after, on the Monday evening, that Eve heard the knock on her front door.

Neither Lottie nor Arnold were home, and she was playing with her son on the living room floor. She answered the door holding him in her arms.

For some seconds, John Stuart stood there regarding them motionlessly. Then he smiled his crooked smile and his first words were, 'I see him at last.'

'Won't you come in?'

She was strangely disappointed when he said, 'No, I won't stay.' The child wriggled in her arms and she put him down. He took a few steps and sat on the stone entry, his head tilted, watching John Stuart.

John Stuart looked from the infant to the mother. 'I only saw his father once, but the child has his eyes.'

650

Up into Eve's head came the habitual vision of the single time John Stuart had seen Alan; in the bush on their wedding day when she had watched them both side by side. She shivered now as she had shivered then. 'Yes, he does,' she answered.

Her son had crawled to John Stuart's boot and was touching it. He bent and patted the soft, fair curls of the little one's head. Eve felt quite odd watching that.

'What have you named him?' John Stuart asked, squatting down beside him.

'Christopher.'

John Stuart looked up quickly, then after a few seconds he said in an indifferent tone, 'I think I understand. There was only one Alan Fletcher.'

'Yes.' She said it so softly he almost thought she had not spoken. He tried to smile but he could not.

Her son was now making happy noises and hitting his small hand on the shining boot in front of him. She watched as John Stuart held out a finger and Christopher took hold of it. John Stuart continued to look at her son and now his voice broke with emotion. 'Christopher is a good, strong name. You will grow up a good, strong boy.' He ruffled Christopher's hair again in a lingering movement before he stood up and tipped his hat to Eve. With a final look down at Christopher, he walked away.

John Stuart had been hurt when she said 'Yes' to his statement about Alan, she had seen that quite clearly. How hard it must have been for him to see her with her child, the child that could have been his. Her heart felt quite heavy for him.

She fell quickly to sleep that night, and dreamed of riding across Mayfield on Moonlight, but in the early hours of the morning she woke and lay for a long time looking into the darkness. Christopher was sleeping deeply in his little bed beside her. She did not know at what point she fell back to sleep, but she awoke to the most brilliant sunshine and a day of warmth and cheer.

She went to the Common with Lottie and Christopher, for she had no music classes until the afternoon. There were lots of mothers and babies and nannies all around and they were greeted by some of the women they recognised. They spread a blanket on the grass near a hedge just bursting into blossom, and Lottie tatted a lace doily while Eve read the newspaper. On and off they played with Christopher, and Lottie was giving him his morning bottle of orange juice when Eve stood up. 'If you don't mind, dear, I shall go for my walk, now. Christopher should sleep soon.'

'All right,' her friend smiled up at her.

651

Eve started off at a brisk pace. She took a walk most days, a habit she had always kept. She was soon across the Common and over in the Public Garden where she walked along until she halted to look through the trees to Arlington Street. There stood the Regency, the best hotel in Boston. The façade was very classical looking and men in uniform were darting about. She knew it was where John Stuart was staying although she had never been inside it.

She had been standing there a couple of minutes when a voice behind her said, 'Eve.'

She turned round to find John Stuart.

'My goodness, what a surprise. I have been with Lottie and Christopher, they are over in the Common.' She pointed.

He smiled his half smile, taking off his fashionable hat. 'How lovely to see you.' He was dressed in brown gaberdine and silk; she in honey-coloured muslin, and while it was only a serviceable dress, the colour picked up her creamy skin and the light sheen of her fair curls. Standing together, they looked quite exceptional and people passing by glanced at them a second time.

He motioned to a seat and they sat down.

At first they spoke of the beautiful day and the pleasant spring Boston was enjoying. He did not tell her he had just left Joe at the Seaward Line booking office where the older man was purchasing three passenger tickets for Thursday's noon sailing, destination Sydney, Australia.

After a time he crossed his legs, his brilliantly polished boot catching the sun as he half turned towards her. He was looking steadily at her and thinking how lovely she was, just as she had always been; she even made cheap muslin look like rare silk. 'It seems a long time since I was passing through Bathurst and saw you in the park that evening.'

'It does,' she replied, 'and yet it's not really. It's just that so much has happened.'

He nodded. 'Indeed it has.'

She shook her head. 'And to think you followed me home and I did not know.'

Now he turned even further towards her, his arm up on the seat back. He made a mild sound that could have been a laugh. 'Yes, what a month that was. I fell in love with you at first sight and then I had to convince you to marry me.'

'Yes, I suppose it was like that.'

He shifted and took his right knee in his hands. 'Do you recall the picnic, the day I asked you to marry me?'

She nodded. 'I do.'

'It was on the riverbank with the Reverend and his wife. He was a fine man, and she a fine woman.'

'Yes,' she replied quietly. 'I think of them every day.'

He closed his eyes briefly, leaning back a little. 'Whenever I go through Bathurst these days, I pass through swiftly, but sometimes I go to the graveyard at All Saints' and place a flower on their grave. I shall continue to do that.' He did not tell her the reason was for her.

She was moved to think he did such a thing. 'That is kind of you. After all, you are not a one for churchyards and things.'

He looked away and smiled sadly, 'No.' When he turned back to her his face was cheerful. 'Do you remember on that same picnic I asked you what you wanted more than anything in the world, and you became angry because I was amused by your serious sentiments.'

She nodded. 'I do.'

'Well, I promise I won't laugh now.'

She met his eyes. 'What do you mean?'

'I'm asking you what you want more than anything in the world now, today. And I will not laugh.'

He smiled his adorable smile and she thought how Lottie was absolutely right; he was more handsome than ever. She wondered why he would ask such a thing; it was almost impossible for her to answer him. What could she say? She wanted Alan back? Of course that was true, but that was impossible. Perhaps if he had asked her a couple of months ago, before Sir Rutherford's benevolence, she would have said the thing she wanted most was for her son to grow up with some security.

Two small children were rolling hoops nearby; one lost control and the hoop wobbled sideways towards John Stuart. He bent forward and caught it, standing to give it back to the child.

When he sat down, she answered him with the words, 'John Stuart, it's a difficult question. I am not sure. No doubt I could still answer with the same replies I gave you years ago, but now I think I want peace, happiness and peace.'

'Yes, Eve,' he said it with a sigh. 'We all want that.'

She was looking at his long, slender hands, and the oval fingernails. His hands had lost some of the heavy brown from the Australian sun but were not as pale as her own, lying in her lap.

Then, on an impulse, she decided to tell him about Sir Rutherford's philanthropy and Christopher's inheritance. It was something to do with truth and honesty and wanting to be that way with him. She took a deep breath. 'John Stuart?'

'Yes?' He turned his eyes to hers.

'I want to tell you something. If you had asked me your question some months ago, I would have answered differently. I would have wished for security for my son. But something has occurred, a sort of miracle, really. In March, a man came here from London. He was a solicitor, representing a legal firm. He gave me the deeds to the property of Long Moss in Somerset, England. Long Moss was Alan's ancestral home. Christopher is now the legal heir. You see, Sir Rutherford Blake has purchased the property and is holding it in trust for him until he comes of age. There are funds that will arrive regularly and my son will never want.' She sat looking at him. 'I will be grateful to that man as long as I live. He has done so much. It is just too wonderful.'

He faced away from her so she would not see his eyes. Forcing delight into his tone, he remarked, 'Eve, I am so very pleased to hear that. That's marvellous. So you too, are provided for?'

'Yes, there is money for me, but I shall keep it for Christopher. I can manage to take care of myself.'

He thought how indomitable her spirit was, one of the things he had always loved, respected. He loved her so very deeply. He was troubled though, for the reason he had bought Long Moss had been to take care of her as well as to give the child his rightful inheritance. He was unsure how to say it, but say it he must. 'It is not my business, but if there has been money provided for you, then I think you should use it.'

'I see it as my son's,' she replied.

He thought of her small rented house and tiny parlour with the threadbare chairs and forced himself to sound matter-of-fact. 'No doubt Rutherford did also, but perhaps he believed that if the mother was well provided for, then the son would naturally be.'

'Yes, perhaps,' was her answer.

He did not dare continue with this subject, so he finished with the words, 'Nevertheless, you will know best.' His eyes followed two elderly women passing by as he spoke again. 'Eve, now I want you to know something.'

'Yes?'

He made an attempt at a smile. 'I must tell you this.' He looked up at the treetops and then back at her. 'When I knew you were actually with Alan Fletcher, that you were not coming back home, I was hurt, jealous, angry, bitter, disillusioned. When I found out you had his child, something in my heart died. But, for some long time now, I have realised that Alan Fletcher was no ordinary man, and those sentiments no longer exist in me. And you, my dear, are an extraordinary woman. Now that I have seen you, and Christopher, to put it simply . . . I am pleased that I made the journey to Boston, to have been with you again and to know you are with good friends who care.' He stood up and taking up her right hand bent over it and brought it to his lips.

The whole of her attention was on him. She did not see the gardens or the children playing or the people walking; she saw only his face and lips on her hand. A peculiar thought filled her mind. She was still married to John Stuart; this was her legal husband kissing her hand.

When he straightened up, he said, 'Would it be possible to call on you again?'

'Certainly, of course.' She wondered when he was leaving, but somehow she did not want to ask. She did not want to remind him of leaving.

'Are you in tomorrow?'

'No, I teach at private homes until close to five o'clock.'

'Then I might come the day after tomorrow, on Thursday afternoon?'

'Any time Thursday afternoon, I give no lessons then.'

For a few moments he stayed staring down at her, his gaze lingering on her, taking in every detail. He knew he would not see her Thursday, and he was sorry for the subterfuge, but he did not want to tell her he was leaving that day; he could not bear to say goodbye. It was best for her to believe he was remaining and for him simply to slip away. His pulse quickened as he acknowledged this would be the last time he looked on her face, then he nodded goodbye and turned from her.

She watched him as he walked through the trees, his long stride moving him swiftly out of sight, and she acknowledged that she was already looking forward to Thursday when she would see him again. Suddenly, she remembered Lottie and Christopher and she left the seat at a run.

When John Stuart entered their rooms at the Regency, Joe stood from his chair by the window. 'M'boy, I was surprised to find you not here.'

'Yes, of all things I ran into Eve.' But that was all the information he gave.

Joe took an envelope from his breast pocket. 'I have the tickets, we sail noon, Thursday.'

Later, after a meal in the hotel's dining room, Joe said goodnight and went early to bed. He lay there thinking, looking at the evening sky, still faintly light through the window. It would be wonderful to be home at Mayfield again. How badly he had missed it and his darling Thelma. There had been times while they had been here in Boston when he had thought a miracle might happen, that somehow

Eve would come home with them, but that was just an old man's dream. He had even fancied that John Stuart might adopt Eve's son and that they could get a pardon for Lawless Drake. The other night, he had actually dreamed about arriving at Mayfield. Eve and John Stuart, at last, home together. The whole of Mayfield had echoed with the roar of hundreds of delighted cheers; the master and mistress united again. Ah, what a grand dream that had been. He rolled over and closed his eyes.

At the same time, a little more than half a mile away in Russell Street, Eve sat on the tiny back porch looking at the waning light in the evening sky. Little Christopher was asleep and Lottie and Arnold were next door with Mrs Mason. They had asked her to come with them, but she had preferred to be alone.

The perfume of an early blooming honeysuckle vine hung in the air, evocatively reminding her of the diverse bush smells on Mayfield. She thought of the miles of gum trees and scrub, of the valleys and hills and remembered the day she fell from Moonlight. She recalled the wonderful, fearful excitement she had felt when she realised who had found her.

She stood up and went to the porch railing. She grasped it tightly, seeing that other small verandah at Treehard Hill and thinking of how often she had held the railing there. She heard the words Alan said to her on the rug in front of the glowing fire on their one consummate night; 'Eve, I want you always to be happy, remember that.' And my darling Alan, while I have loved your son and been strong and faced the world without you, I have not been happy. Forgive me, for I know you want me to be happy. I love you, Alan, as I always will love you, but you have gone from this earth. My darling one, what we had together was too exquisite to last. Nothing that sublime can continue in this human world, I understand that now. I have wept for you until I feel I have no more tears. I have mourned your death in some way, every single day and thus I have not let your spirit rest, and have kept you in troubled unsleep. That was so very wrong of me. At last I realise I must leave you in tranquillity. I am here, I must live with those who are here and I must let you go. It is time. I must release your soul and let you be happy too. She put up her hands to the sky, arms extended, palms open. 'Goodbye, my darling, Alan Fletcher.' Suddenly, a raincloud seemed to come quickly from nowhere. Sombre and mysterious, it hung low in the sky, and then drops were falling heavily on the palms of her hands; clean, pristine drops of water from the heavens, from the place beyond human comprehension; and quite surely she knew he had heard her.

* * *

The following afternoon, little Jimmy Gibson was not well; when Eve arrived at his home, a maid informed her there would be no music lesson. Jimmy would have been her last pupil, so Eve went home, walking the mile and a half to Russell Street.

There was a laneway between Irving Street and Russell and she took it to Mrs Mason's side gate and through her back yard to the gate in the adjoining fence of number thirty-two. She was mounting the few steps to her porch when she heard voices in the tiny side garden. Peering through the trees and vines, she saw Lottie, and close by Christopher wandering around investigating.

But they were not alone. To her surprise, she saw John Stuart. What was he doing here? It was Wednesday, and he was not coming to see her until tomorrow afternoon.

Something stopped her from going down to join them and, full of curiosity, she leaned forward intently as he spoke with Lottie who smiled and nodded. Then he walked over to Christopher. Her heart rate accelerated as John Stuart bent down and picked up her child in his arms. He spoke and Christopher clapped his hands with pleasure and they both laughed. To Eve, standing there watching, unknown to any of them, it seemed unreal. For the next seconds, her awareness was heightened, as if she saw her son and John Stuart magnified, their faces side by side. Her son hugged him and laughed and 'talked'. She stared enthralled as John Stuart kissed him on his cheek. Then he held the merry boy out at arm's length, to dangle laughing in the air, before putting him down. He spoke again to Lottie, knelt back upon the ground to ruffle Christopher's curls, stood, and walked away.

Once she was sure he was gone, she rushed down the steps and round to Lottie.

'My gracious, Eve. I was not expecting ye yet.'

'What did John Stuart want?'

'Oh, he just came to say he would not be able to avisit with ye tomorrow. He had some sort of an arrangement with ye, but he cannot keep it. Said something important was astopping him.'

'Did he say when he would come?'

'No, but no doubt he'll be amaking another time with ye.'

On and off for hours Eve continued to see the vision of John Stuart with her son in his arms.

Later, when Eve wished Lottie good-night, her friend said, 'It was nice to see John Stuart today. He was so lovely with Christopher, kissed him, he did. Oh, and when he was aspeaking of ye, he called ye Evvy. Was that his pet name for ye, like it was with the Reverend?'

Eve did not know why, but she trembled. 'Once or twice he called me that . . . once or twice.'

She did not sleep well that night, she tossed and turned and kept waking and looking at the blackness. It was close to dawn when at last she fell into a deep sleep. She woke to Lottie's voice. 'Eve, Eve, you've overslept, young Dorothy Dence will be here within half an hour.'

She went through the music lesson in a distracted fashion, and during the one that followed her concentration lapsed continually until halfway through she came to a decision and sent the child home.

Lottie looked up from her sewing in amazement when Eve came bursting into the parlour. 'Lottie, I am going to the Regency, I must see John Stuart. You and Christopher will be all right, won't you?'

Lottie recovered quickly and nodded, smiling at her charge. 'We will, won't we, my honey?'

Eve did not know why she was doing this. All she knew was that something was amiss, that she felt very uneasy, and that she must see John Stuart.

She grabbed her bonnet and cape from the hook in the front hall and hurried through the house to the back door and down the steps of the porch. She went through Mrs Mason's back yard and was soon out in the lane and hurrying into Irving Street. The fastest way to the Regency Hotel was to weave through a number of back streets and lanes down the hill.

By the time she entered Arlington Street, she was moving very briskly. As she neared the hotel, a hansom cab pulled away from the front door and went at an easy pace in the opposite direction. She was soon inside where huge chandeliers hung in the foyer and grand staircases went up to right and left. There was the hustle and bustle of guests, and uniformed pageboys and porters wandered about.

At the rosewood reception desk, a clerk looked over his eyeglasses at her. 'Madam?'

'I have come to see Mr John Stuart Wakeman.'

'He's gone, madam.'

'Gone? Gone where?'

'Left the hotel, departed, madam.'

'But he can't have.'

The clerk's colleague standing beside him looked up from the guest book. 'Yes, he's only just gone actually, saw him get in a hansom just now, although his valet went hours ago with most of his luggage.'

Eve must have looked so distraught that the clerk with the eyeglasses inquired, 'You're not a Mrs Fletcher, by any chance, are you, madam?'

'Yes, I am.'

'Oh, then he left a letter for you.' He turned back to a pile of papers and found what he looked for. 'Here it is.'

Eve felt sick, her head was aching. 'Thank you.' No, he could not have gone, not without saying goodbye. She did not want him to go. She walked away from the desk, ripping the letter open in her haste. Now she realised why he had come to Russell Street yesterday. Oh God, he came to say goodbye to Christopher, that is why he kissed him . . .

She read what he had written through the tears that filled her eyes.

Dearest Eve,

I cannot bear to face you and say goodbye. You see, my dear, dear one, I have always loved you, from the moment I saw you in the Bathurst park and I shall continue to love you, until the last breath departs from my body.

I wish you the peace and happiness you said you wanted more than anything in the world when we spoke in the Public Garden yesterday. If I could have told you what I wanted, I would have said, 'You' but that was not to be.

I will treasure the moments we have had together in the short time I spent in Boston. To see you again and be near you again was more than all the world's treasure to me, and that will sustain me all the days of my life. I have one beautiful, bitter-sweet picture in my mind, and I shall keep it as the years pass by. It is you and your son together at the door of your home.

Goodbye, Evvy,

John Stuart.

Oh no! It could not be. The words were like stab wounds in her heart. She had loved only four men in her life. Three were gone from this earth; John Stuart was the lone, remaining one. He must not leave her. Not now.

She ran out the hotel door calling to the pageboys and porters, 'Tell me, please, which way did Mr Wakeman's cab go? Where was he going? Please help me.'

One of the youths spoke up. 'That's it there, lady.' He pointed through the trees. 'It's just turned the corner of the Public Garden. Driver's got a red hat on.'

'But where is he going? Please, do you know where he's going?'

'To Commercial Wharf, he sails on the noon tide.'

Noon? Oh no! There was no time. She must stop him, but how? There were no hansoms anywhere.

Abruptly, she started running, her mind distracted. Don't go, John Stuart, please. I cannot lose you, not now, not when I know you love me so much.

She avoided the vehicles in Arlington Street and seconds later was in the Public Garden running by children and nannies and people who looked up in amazement to see her speeding by. She ran, her heart pounding, her mind reeling from thought to thought. A red hat, the driver of the hansom wore a red hat . . . Now she was crossing Charles Street, darting in and out of horses and carriages and carts and people; now she was in the Common.

John Stuart was heading to Commercial Wharf; that meant he would continue on past the deer park and round the Common into Tremont Street. She must stop him, reach him, tell him how she felt. A red hat, where was the red hat? She was impelling herself on, dodging people and garden beds and bushes and trees. No, don't leave me, not you too. John Stuart, wait!

Keep running, Eve, keep running. She felt the ties of her bonnet slacken then come undone and fly back over her shoulder while she tried to hold it on. She was really racing now, moving faster, faster. She could hold the bonnet no longer and she let go to feel it dangle briefly behind her before it was gone. She heard someone call out but she did not stop. Then her cape, too, became loose and began to slip from her shoulders. It was slowing her down when suddenly it caught in some bushes and ripped from her shoulders, but still she did not stop, she was glad it was gone.

She was along the Tremont side of the Common now, her eyes reaching, straining, alert and searching. Cabs going to Commercial Wharf took Bromfield Street. Was that a hansom turning right up there ahead?

A number of carts and street vendors plied their trades along here and a few shouted at the woman racing by, eyes frantic, head bonnetless. Running, running, like a person possessed. Her heart pounded, her pulse raced, her eyes searched the street. On she went until, at last, she was at the corner of Bromfield Street, her breath coming in short gasps, and there at the bottom of the road, just turning left, she saw it, a hansom and a scarlet spot up on top. She screamed out, 'Stop! Stop!' But it disappeared.

The perspiration stood in beads on her temples and her brow; there was a pain in her throat, her chest hurt and her shoes had come loose. In a swift decision, and to the amazement of a group of elderly women, she threw off her shoes, setting off again, willing herself to continue, to run like she had never run before.

Looking like a fleeing gypsy girl, barefoot, capeless, bonnetless, she sped on. At the bottom of the street she turned to continue the chase but her heart sank. The hansom with the crimson spot perched on top was accelerating, gaining speed. It was hopeless. Her eyes grew wide with dismay. She had lost him.

She halted there on the corner, her gaze never leaving the bright speck as it got further and further away, more indistinct, taking away the only man on earth she wanted.

Her throat hurt, her head hurt, her feet hurt, her heart hurt. She stood, eyes fixed on the remote vehicle. Her chest heaved and she panted from the continued effort. Then the words came out from the core of her, from the innermost sanctuary of her psyche; the truth, the clear admission, the fact: 'I still love you,' she said aloud, and as if the acknowledgement gave her the miracle of renewed strength, she began to run again, even though she knew it was useless and the speck of red was getting ever further away. Smaller, remoter, the redness faded away.

People halted and pointed at her, shouted and laughed, but she did not see them; she saw nothing but the point of scarlet disappearing through her tears. She was gasping, her breath coming in short painful bursts, but still she forced herself forward, running, running, her mind obsessively set on continuing onwards.

And then a miracle happened.

The dot of crimson was not getting smaller any more. It remained the same size. It was stationary. Oh Lord, it was stationary!

On she flew towards it. She did not feel the pain in her feet and chest, her whole consciousness was centred on the hansom. Then she heard drums and music, and still the red spot did not move. It got bigger, more and more clear. Now it became a hat, on a head, on top of the one-horse cab. The music became louder and she saw there was some sort of parade which had held up the vehicles. A band of men were walking and playing in the intersecting street in front of the hansom where it stood waiting in the line of vehicles and horses.

Oh God, thank you, thank you.

Closer she came, closer, closer, the sound of music louder in her ears, past the lined-up carriages and carts and horsemen. She could see the driver distinctly now, sitting jauntily up on top of the small carriage, and there strapped securely behind him was the small chest in which John Stuart always carried his personal papers. She was only yards away, so near now that she could read his name on the side, John Stuart Wakeman, and underneath were two stamps. In big blue letters, one read: SYDNEY–SOUTHAMPTON and below it the other in yellow said: SOUTHAMPTON–BOSTON.

Then she understood! Penetrating her mind, the realisation burst upon her, the impact of the words ramming into her head like a physical blow and bringing her to a standstill two yards from the back of the hansom. It was clear at last. John Stuart had been in England! He had been in England! It was not Sir Rutherford who had bought Long Moss. It was John Stuart. The wonderful, modest, decent, good man, the essential John Stuart, the one she had never stopped loving. He had done it to take care of her and her son.

She stumbled to the side of the cab as the driver gaped down in shock at the barefooted, fierce-eyed lady.

Her heart expanded with joy and gratitude as she lifted her hand, damp from the continued, massive exertion, to take hold of the side of the vehicle as the two men inside saw her and reacted with sudden, startled movement.

'Eve!'

Her eyes shone, her face gleamed as her arms reached out to John Stuart and she uttered the words, 'Please, don't leave without us.'

She saw the change explode inside him. It was as if a flame of rapture ignited in his eyes. The troubled lines left his forehead and his cheeks, smoothing his face in a flood of love and happiness.

Suddenly, he was on the cobbled street with her, lifting her into his arms, holding her as if never to put her down. She felt his kisses in her hair, on her eyes, her cheeks, her lips, felt his arms entwined around her.

This was peace, this was happiness. She could feel it in the very vibrations of his body, a promise of lasting, eternal trust.

She lifted her mouth from his to look through her blissful tears into the face of her husband. There was truth and understanding filling the air around them; no mistrust or fears, nothing unrevealed or secret.

From her heart came the words, 'Take me home to Mayfield.'

PATRICIA SHAW
RIVER OF THE SUN

When Perfection Middleton catches the eye of Darcy
Buchanan, all hell breaks loose. Joint heir to the vast estate
of Caravale in North Queensland, he's a catch all right, and
far too good for a housemaid whose parents came over on a
convict ship. That's what his family thinks, anyway, and his
brother Ben dreams up an ingenious plan to prevent the
marriage. It's a plan that goes tragically wrong...

Lew Cavour is very taken with Perfy, too, but he gets
caught up in the gold rush and the race to stake a claim on
the river of gold, as does Ben Buchanan, who sees it as the
only way he can buy out Perfy's share of Caravale. But their
journey to the river of gold is dogged by disease, madness
and murder.

Diamond, an aborigine girl, has a profound effect on all
their lives. Brought up by a kindly German widow, she feels
she is at odds with both worlds: too intelligent to be content
as the menial slave to which her colour condemns her; too
sophisticated to return to her tribe.

Patricia Shaw's magnificent new saga celebrates the
pioneering spirit of the men and women whose courage and
ambition laid the foundations of modern Australia.

Don't miss Patricia Shaw's previous Australian saga
Valley of Lagoons also available from Headline.

FICTION/SAGA   0 7472 3658 5

A selection of bestsellers from Headline

FICTION

STUDPOKER	John Francome	£4.99 ☐
DANGEROUS LADY	Martina Cole	£4.99 ☐
TIME OFF FROM GOOD BEHAVIOUR	Susan Sussman	£4.99 ☐
THE KEY TO MIDNIGHT	Dean Koontz	£4.99 ☐
LEGAL TENDER	Richard Smitten	£5.99 ☐
BLESSINGS AND SORROWS	Christine Thomas	£4.99 ☐
VAGABONDS	Josephine Cox	£4.99 ☐
DAUGHTER OF TINTAGEL	Fay Sampson	£5.99 ☐
HAPPY ENDINGS	Sally Quinn	£5.99 ☐
BLOOD GAMES	Richard Laymon	£4.99 ☐
EXCEPTIONAL CLEARANCE	William J Caunitz	£4.99 ☐
QUILLER BAMBOO	Adam Hall	£4.99 ☐

NON-FICTION

RICHARD BRANSON: The Inside Story	Mick Brown	£6.99 ☐
PLAYFAIR FOOTBALL ANNUAL 1992-93	Jack Rollin	£3.99 ☐
DEBRETT'S ETIQUETTE & MODERN MANNERS	Elsie Burch Donald	£7.99 ☐
PLAYFIELD NON-LEAGUE FOOTBALL ANNUAL 1992-93	Bruce Smith	£3.99 ☐

SCIENCE FICTION AND FANTASY

THE CINEVERSE CYCLE OMNIBUS	Craig Shaw Gardner	£5.99 ☐
BURYING THE SHADOW	Storm Constantine	£4.99 ☐
THE LOST PRINCE	Bridget Wood	£5.99 ☐
KING OF THE DEAD	R A MacAvoy	£4.50 ☐
THE ULTIMATE WEREWOLF	Byron Preiss	£4.99 ☐

All Headline books are available at your local bookshop or newsagent, or can be ordered direct from the publisher. Just tick the titles you want and fill in the form below. Prices and availability subject to change without notice.

Headline Book Publishing PLC, Cash Sales Department, PO Box 11, Falmouth, Cornwall, TR10 9EN, England.

Please enclose a cheque or postal order to the value of the cover price and allow the following for postage and packing:
UK & BFPO: £1.00 for the first book, 50p for the second book and 30p for each additional book ordered up to a maximum charge of £3.00.
OVERSEAS & EIRE: £2.00 for the first book, £1.00 for the second book and 50p for each additional book.

Name ....

Address ....

....